The
AVAILABLE
PRESS/PEN
Short Story
Collection

Cover design by Bill Toth, based on the
Available Press logotype created by
Donald E. Munson

Book design by Iris Bass

The AVAILABLE PRESS/PEN Short Story Collection

From the PEN Syndicated Fiction Project,
a cooperative venture of the PEN American Center
and the National Endowment for the Arts Literature Program

INTRODUCTION BY
ANNE TYLER

**AVAILABLE
PRESS**

BALLANTINE BOOKS · NEW YORK

CONTENTS

PREFACE

The PEN Syndicated Fiction Project was established as a joint venture with the National Endowment for the Arts in 1982 to spearhead the return of quality short fiction to American newspapers. Since then, a small renaissance has occurred in this art form for American readers and writers alike. We no longer need to talk nostalgically of a time when fiction in newspapers reached thousands of eager readers each month.

The basic idea in this project has its roots in American literary tradition beginning with Edgar Allan Poe's stories in the *New York Sun*. By the 1880s, newspapers were syndicating short stories by the likes of Bret Harte and Henry James. In the early and mid-1900s, the tradition flourished with writers such as O. Henry, Mark Twain, Stephen Crane, F. Scott Fitzgerald and John Steinbeck.

In recent years, however, short fiction faced a steady decline as production costs escalated. Before the PEN Syndicated Fiction Project began, papers with an interest in publishing good fiction, especially smaller papers, were discouraged from doing so because of the lack of staff to screen stories. Also, funds were necessary for an endeavor that did not produce income while it used potential advertising space.

Generous grants from the National Endowment for the Arts, private foundations, and corporations have changed the picture and helped bring about the return of the short story. The project is administered by the PEN American Center, one of eighty centers that comprise International PEN, the only world association of literary writers. The Fiction Project is a non-profit, non-commercial venture that has returned hundreds of thousands of dollars to support the writing community in prizes and syndication fees. Profits from the sale of this book will contribute directly to the continuation of this program.

The PEN Syndicated Fiction Project may not yet have become the Pulitzer Prize for the short story, but it has acquired a significant reputation in a very short time. Each year nearly a hundred talented writers, both established authors and talented newcomers, receive national recognition when they win the competitions. Each month writers have the potential of reaching millions of readers with their work in major American newspapers. This volume adds an exciting new dimension to the project and will help maintain a vital service to the American reading public.

INTRODUCTION

When I was a child I used to have a friend with a huge collection of paper dolls cut from Sears, Roebuck catalogs. She kept them in a cigar box—smiling women with 1940s shoulderpads and rolled hairdos, girls in short dresses, handsome men, and improbably neat little boys. But what I remember most clearly is not the dolls themselves but a fascinating conceit their owner employed whenever she brought them to my house to play. Turning her back to me, she would open the box and at the same time, ventriloquist-style, she would utter a whole torrent of sounds. "BURBLE-burble-burble!" she would cry, and "Tee-hee! Chatter-chatter!" For a moment you could imagine it was the dolls themselves you were hearing—their pent-up voices, released at last, swarming out of the box the instant the lid was raised.

I thought of that cigar box while I was helping to choose the entries for the *PEN Syndicated Fiction Project*. My share of the stories arrived in large packages—intimidatingly large packages. So instead of sitting down to read the topmost story first, I began by flipping through the pages of one entire package just to see how difficult this job was going to be.

BURBLE-burble-burble! Tee-hee!

All those voices, all those characters. And nearly every one of them spiky and demanding and alive.

It was going to be very difficult indeed.

But fun: no doubt of that. There were Hungarians and Chinese and American Indians. There were city dwellers, country folk, and people of no fixed address. There were ghosts and water monsters. There were convicts, itinerant baseball players, ambassadors and pipeworkers, housekeepers and cropdusters, and college professors.

There were family members galore in every possible configuration: mothers, fathers, stepmothers, stepfathers, crotchety grandfathers, fading grandmothers, newborn babies and young children and children fully grown, and runaway nephews, wistful wives, kind maiden aunts, difficult or eccentric husbands. And these people were fighting and making up, joking, falling in love, working and playing and sickening and dying.

Has anybody thought to be amazed at what's going on here?

It is astonishing that there are so many skilled and gifted writers at work in just this one country, in just this one period of time.

Take the case at hand: All of the nearly two hundred stories from which I made my selections were readable and interesting, and at least half were of top quality. From this half I was forced to discard some fifty pieces solely because they didn't fit the purposes of this particular project. That is, they were unsuitably long, or inappropriate for the intended audience. But that left almost another fifty— and bear in mind that I was only one of the judges. Elsewhere, the other judges were unearthing the same kinds of treasure.

And when I had finished choosing, and packed up the stories and sent them off, it was something like sending off a crowd of houseguests. Whew! you say. You wipe your brow. You go back inside your house to sink into a chair, try to recover from the chaos. And then all at once you're surprised to find you miss it—all that color and vitality, that dazzling wealth of voices.

Anne Tyler

"IT GOT SMASHED"

by Raymond H. Abbott

The Indians carefully looked over the young stranger—the priest they knew well enough by now. But several must have thought it a bit unusual, though, for a Jesuit priest to be going around with a Mormon Elder, for everyone on the reservation knew the Catholics and the Mormons were enemies, since the latter had arrived on the reservation five years earlier and immediately tried to convert long-standing Roman Catholic families to Mormonism.

The priest—Father Keegan was his name—watched with an amused expression as the Indians studied the stranger. He thought, they really must be puzzled as to what he was doing with a Mormon. No one asked, however. The priest was perhaps in his early fifties, thick built, and what hair he had left now, remnants of a once thick head of hair, was on the side of his head near his ears and it was completely white. Little specks of dandruff clung to the hair, eventually landing on his shoulder. The dandruff was very noticeable against the black of his suit, a suit shiny with wear. He didn't seem to notice, however, or if he did he stopped caring about how he looked a long time before. There were other things too about his appearance that said he cared less now, less than he once had. His weight for one thing. He was rapidly putting on pounds, and he slouched as if he were depressed, which he was, but it wasn't something he admitted to even to himself.

And there had been a time, and it wasn't so long before either, that he cared very much about how he looked, as much as a man might be permitted within the confines of being a Jesuit priest on a rural Indian reservation in South Dakota. After all, he like his fellow priests had taken a vow of poverty when he became a Jesuit Father and came to this reservation many years before.

Just how many years had it been now on this reservation? he thought. Twelve, or was it fourteen? Sometimes he couldn't recall, and there had been other assignments before this one.

The man with Father Keegan was not a Mormon, however. By South Dakota standards he was an easterner. He came from somewhere near Columbus, Ohio, and was on the reservation that week for his first time. He had been there for what seemed to him like the three hottest days he had ever spent anywhere. The temperature so far had been near a hundred degrees every day. Later he was to observe that a Dakota winter—especially when a northwester blew in with the heavy snows—was like nothing he had ever known in Ohio, or even Boston, where he was born and spent ten years before his family moved on to Ohio. He wore a suit and tie and was beginning to feel somewhat silly and damn hot dressed in this way. But he felt he had to do this, for he remembered the words of the tribal Chairman, a man by the name of Amos Featherman, who had said to him and others upon their arrival that he wanted the professional people working for the tribe, and he would be working for the tribe, to look the part—to look like the professionals they were— and that meant wearing ties and jackets at all times. It was Featherman's opinion that appearances and especially the way a man dressed was an example to the Indian people. A goal they might work toward themselves, he said in his little homily that first day they were on the reservation. To John Magley—that was the young man's name—what Featherman said didn't make a hell of a lot of sense. He couldn't see that anyone in this little village of Cut Meat afforded him more respect because of any suit and tie he wore. If anything, he thought they looked at him as if to say, "What a God damn fool that white guy is to wear such uncomfortable clothing on a hot day." Yet he was new to the reservation and didn't wish to violate the instructions of the powerful tribal Chairman, Featherman.

The priest didn't understand either why the young man wore a suit on these hot days. He thought it must simply be a habit, a habit he would soon get out of along with a few others as well, he would guess if he were a guessing man, and he was. Father Keegan was now pointing to land across from where they stood on the steps of the post office in Cut Meat village. It was barren sun-baked land, where only a water windmill stood. The windmill spun rather wildly in the strong wind. Several head of cattle were clustered around the large metal tub that served as a trough. Dust devils scurried across the plowed stretches of a section of land where someone had planned to plant something and never got around to do it. Much of the topsoil had already blown away.

"That's all tribal land," he said with no particular enthusiasm, almost as if he might be pointing at the surface of the moon instead of reservation land. "And we can build the houses there. In a cluster if enough people want to live that way. But these people out here have strange ideas sometimes. They may not go for the cluster idea right away. A lot of people don't like their neighbors and would welcome a chance to move off by themselves. We'll have a time convincing them there is an advantage in living in a cluster— things like sewerage and streetlights and paved streets and a central water system. I guess you can't blame them really—there is so much trouble in these towns on the weekend or whenever a few people have some money for a little booze. Then all kinds of fighting and commotion breaks out; you'll see quick enough."

Father Keegan was talking about a housing project that after years and years of planning—many surveys and countless trips to Washington, D.C., to see the bureaucrats and much, much more—was finally going to happen on this reservation. The funding had already been approved and the young man, John Magley, next to him was the architect who was to design two different houses. Both were supposed to be simple but well-made houses, and for the next year and a half or two years Magley would be returning to the reservation to oversee the construction of the housing units. It was an important project to the young man. Important to his career as an architect and important on a personal level. He very much wished to help poor, downtrodden Indians.

As the priest and the young man stood talking and pointing at the land across the gravel road a squat Indian woman approached. She was of an age difficult to determine—although she had to be beyond thirty and probably older than that. She certainly looked every bit of thirty-five or even forty. She came up to the priest and stood in front of him. She said nothing, waiting until she saw he was done talking with the other white man, the Mormon—that's who she thought John Magley was. It didn't seem at all incongruous to her that the Jesuit priest was with a Mormon. All she saw was his suit and tie, and only Mormons wore those, even on the warmest days.

Father Keegan saw her right away, however, but he continued talking, not paying her any attention at first. Then he spoke to her as if he had seen her for the first time. He spoke in Lakota, giving her a warm greeting, one he had used in a similar situation at least a hundred, no a thousand times before, he thought. He still hadn't got over how indifferent some Indians could be to his efforts to speak their language, especially the women, he had found. They would usually nod or grunt as they might to any white man who spoke to them. There was no acknowledgment that he could determine anyway that even hinted he was somehow different because he spoke their language a little, something most white people were unwilling to try to do.

This day she nodded and sort of smiled, he thought, and answered him in English, using short, clipped sentences to convey what was on her mind. She began to enumerate a few of her recent problems—how difficult life had been for her. Father Keegan knew immediately what this was to lead to—it meant she wanted to borrow two or three dollars until the sudden crisis in her life passed. He had heard it all enough times before to know the signs, but even after a dozen years the use of the word *borrow* still troubled him. He was sure it had to mean something else to Indians, something different at least from what it meant to the white man, because he couldn't remember—with one or two glaring exceptions—when an Indian had ever "borrowed" two dollars and come back with the intention of repaying him.

As he listened to her story he thought that if he gave every person who approached him for money what they asked for he would be without any money at all for anything, so he had learned to anticipate these requests and at times was capable of maneuvering around in such a way as to keep the request from being made. But he seldom did this and when he did it was because he knew the person asking would spend the money on liquor and it wasn't his place to support the liquor industry, and with the requests for cash assistance growing by the month, indeed by the day, he had to be careful, and that meant being selective. He was good at it, although being cunning wasn't something he enjoyed doing.

For some reason he remembered this woman, although she wasn't from his parish. Her name was Gail Yellow Hawk, and he was sure he had seen her a month or two before at the tribal office building or the public health hospital. She had then been late in pregnancy. Now quite obviously she was not pregnant. He wondered what might have happened, for he hadn't heard of her being at the public health hospital to have her baby. It was not so uncommon for women to have their children at home, especially those who lived in remote distant villages, but somehow he didn't think this had happened with Gail.

After a couple of minutes of meaningless chatter he asked what was on his mind. "What happened to your baby, Gail? Did you have it at home?" He almost said again but he remembered in time that it was Eileen Two Hawk, not Gail Yellow Hawk, who had had a baby at home last year.

"No, Father," she replied, offering no additional explanation. But he was used to this kind of reply and he also was not timid about getting what he wanted in information, especially if someone was about to borrow money from him.

"So what happened?" he asked. "Where's the baby?"

"It was born in the Valentine Hospital. I was shopping that day when the time came," she said.

"Is it still in the hospital in Valentine?" Valentine, Nebraska, was off the reservation by about sixty miles to the south. It was one of the shopping centers for reservation Indians. It was also a favorite drinking spot for locals.

"No, Father, it died."

John Magley was watching all of this very carefully, as if in what went on between her and the priest there might be something he could learn about Sioux Indians. These native people so far were very much a mystery to him. And he wasn't at all sure he would enjoy working on a reservation for two long years with a people who were at times so difficult to understand, and for him to make himself understood to. He had already discovered that when he was talking about one subject, the Indian he spoke to as often as not had not made the transition from the subject that had ended five minutes before. It was frustrating for him, and it was driving him nuts the way everything he said was taken so damn literally.

But when the woman had said her baby died Magley couldn't see any expression of grief on her face, and that puzzled him. She had just said the baby died like she might have said she was going to the market for a loaf of bread.

What an awful thing to have happened, he thought, although he didn't know the circumstances. Still, he knew how he would have felt or, worse yet, how his wife would feel if they lost one of their sons shortly after birth as obviously this woman had.

The priest did not follow through in his questioning and so John Magley did.

"Well, what happened? I mean, how did the baby die?" he asked. He was nervous—this was one of his first conversations with a back-country Indian. So far he had dealt almost entirely with tribal leaders, and many of those seemed to him like white people. Businessmen with a tan, he had heard someone describe them once.

His voice broke a little with emotion as he asked his question, and the voice held all the kindness and sympathy one could bring forth for a near stranger who had recently faced tragedy. But he wasn't prepared for her reply. Then nobody could have been, he thought later, except maybe for the priest. He might have seen the answer coming. And for that reason didn't go on with the questioning.

The woman looked at him, rather sternly he thought, because he was interfering in a way with what she had set out to do that afternoon, and that was to borrow three dollars from the Jesuit priest, Father Keegan. She very much needed three dollars this day. Maybe she felt obligated, but for whatever reasons she answered him again in her abbreviated way of speaking, saying rather matter-of-factly, Magley thought, "It got smashed." That's all she said as she turned back to the priest and asked him for the money she needed.

Magley said nothing, but suddenly he felt keenly aware of the other Indians standing nearby, although it was unlikely they were paying much attention to what the white men and this woman were saying. And why he should care what they thought of him didn't make sense to him either, but he did. It was, after all, a reasonable question to ask considering what had already been said. But he did feel stupid and a bit depressed. And for a moment he wished he weren't standing in this depressing Indian village in South Dakota and was someplace else, like in his air-conditioned office in downtown Columbus.

Father Keegan finally handed the woman one dollar and she walked off toward the shanties behind the post office and country store, and they walked silently toward the car and got in and drove away over the dusty gravel road toward the junction of Route 18, which led into Mission Town twenty miles on down the road. The dust hung heavy behind the car as it moved toward the crossroads. The outline of the village was obscured by the dust.

The priest's eyes twinkled; his depression had lifted somewhat. He had enjoyed watching the exchange between Gail Yellow Hawk and John Magley. He had some difficulty in keeping from laughing, but after a few miles of silence Magley loosened his necktie, looked over to the priest, who was driving, and smiled and said, "Just like that she tells me, 'It got smashed'—that's all, and then she asks you for three dollars. My God!"

The two men then laughed so hard, the priest had to stop the car for fear he would run them off the highway and into a ditch or into an approaching vehicle.

THE BILL COLLECTORS

by Robert Abel

—for H.B.S.

Morrison had taken up a kind of crab-wise walk, his legs making the motions of the hindquarters of a dog that knows he is in dangerous territory, in order to get the jump on any of his creditors. He had had close calls twice yesterday, and discovered that the minimum safe distance (MSD) between himself and a bill collector was that which allowed him to bound up the stairs (key at the ready), unlock, open, shut, and relock the door. Of course, once secure in his own home, the collector peering in the windows, the telephone would start to ring. Perhaps the telephone had been ringing all along, but an event at such a remove from Morrison's own experience allowed him to be philosophical: If no one heard the telephone ringing in the wilderness, could it really be said to be making any sound?

Neither was Morrison so young anymore that making these sudden sprints, through traffic and across the town square, or down the alley behind the bank and the stationery store, did not leave him panting, weak, sometimes headachy. Experience had taught him, however, that taking his car anywhere was a foolish tactic: it was too easily recognized and sabotaged, and once even Larry Fairn had lain on the floor in the back and nailed Morrison as he slid into the driver's seat to start the engine. His car was also, potentially at least, though of course Morrison did not really own it, not yet, and was a dangerous number of payments behind, collateral. The car was locked in the garage, taken out only rarely, and then only in the dark of night, and being kept ready for the Big and Final Getaway Morrison knew he would have to resort to if his last few schemes fell through.

Morrison was on his way now to Elmira Overstreet's. Elmira was on the verge of being convinced to invest a few hundred dollars in

Morrison's latest (so far) paper enterprise, a sort of X-rated carwash and drive-in where adults could purchase pornography and erotic paraphernalia from the privacy of their own automobiles—something on the order of a utilitarian burlesque show, maybe even topless, if he could just pull the the right strings down at City Hall. Elmira was aware of the general drive-in concept but oblivious to the specifics, and Morrison had carefully hedged his bets with her, indicating that "questions of atmosphere and the like" should be left to him. It was a touch-and-go situation so far. Maybe she would deliver and maybe she wouldn't.

Ahead of him on the sidewalk old Mrs. Greene appeared like a soft mountain, as usual, in a plain black dress and a black, straw pillbox hat. Her eyes were lost in friendly folds of puffy skin, and today she was clouting a pink and white soft drink cup down the sidewalk with her cane. She had been, after all, a long-time resident in town, and no doubt resented the strewing of litter by passers-by, tourists, and others with no respect. It might be that, Morrison thought, or it might be she felt like clouting anything at all, a kind of sublimated protest against the fate of growing old. Frustration. Morrison understood such a feeling all too well. By God, if he had a cane, he would undoubtedly wallop something too, a passing dog, say, or he would dent the forehead of the first bill collector to stand in his path. Mrs. Greene looked up from her hockey game with such a smile that Morrison was utterly disarmed. Obviously she had mistaken him for someone else or believed a good smile was the best possible defense against attack. Morrison passed on; he swung his head from side to side, the better to catch glimpses of any pursuers in the periphery of his vision.

It was an idiot way to go through life, Morrison observed, dodging bill collectors and hustling middle-aged women. A young, bearded man looked up from his book as Morrison clipped by the porch where he read, then returned to his pages. He hears me and looks up, Morrison thought, to make sure it isn't some monster approaching, or some friend, anything recognizable, and, being neither, is ignored—I'm ignored. Just a vague buzz on the brain surface, and gone. That's what we are, what I am. Not true, Morrison reminded himself: he was all too recognizable on a certain stratum of life. In fact, he might have been making some sort of (at least local) history after all, might have become an image not too easily rubbed out. He was into local history (he winced again) to the tune of almost thirty thou. It was one way to make your mark.

As if to confirm these ruminations, a specifically identifiable silhouette appeared on the periphery of Morrison's perceptions, not even the whole silhouette, but enough of the sloped shoulders and the curl of the natty hat brim slipping along behind the bushes to be recognizable as Rudy Klein, angry former partner in a land-fill deal. Amazing to Morrison: the simple slope of the hat above the gorgeous, sun-shot green of the hedge could both conjure up an entire sad, guilt-ridden history, and set him running, low and crablike, the hackles on the back of his neck raised in fear. Klein was a long-time pursuer, and shrewd enough now to predict some of Morrison's turns, favorite getaway gambits, and hiding places. Damn! The cellar doors behind Larson's were freshly padlocked; Morrison ripped past the toolshed and ducked between the rows of tomato plants before peering over the alley hedges. Klein could be any-where at this moment but ah! (great relief) only came trudging into Larson's backyard, fists clenched at his sides, surveying. Morrison, keeping to the narrow grass lining of the gravel road, crabbed Cossack-style down the alley, then vaulted a dense clump of laurel and resumed his rapid walk toward Elmira's. He took pains to cross lots and drift behind houses at every intersection, lest Klein, intimately familiar with the loan-dodger mentality, surprise him as he came around a corner with a high hedge. Morrison was panting now, and sweating to the extent he was afraid he'd offend the rather delicate sensibilities of his intended victim.

"You poor man!" Elmira exclaimed as Morrison stood wavering at her back door, face running rivulets.

"I've just been attacked," Morrison lied, and once safely seated in the cool, shadowy, clean white-enamel kitchen, went on to say: "The town's getting too big for the streets to be safe anymore."

Elmira readily agreed. Since her husband's death, she rarely went anywhere, unless accompanied by relatives, who visited irregularly and who, Morrison knew, lavished only what attentions they thought necessary to get themselves into the widow's will. In the freshly painted white garage, a two-year-old Buick languished, dusty of hood, so rarely driven as to be in mint condition. Morrison coveted the car. In a quiet way he coveted Elmira, too, though he reasoned through his attraction as being anything but lustful (normally, Mor-rison was too harassed by survival demands to think about sex) and more likely born of a revenge wish on her former husband, a man who had never taken Morrison seriously enough to remember his name.

Probably the most secure woman in town, Elmira was neverthe-less convinced the streets were lined with muggers. Therefore, the dodgy precautions she observed Morrison to make when approach-ing her house seemed only natural and right. It made good com-mon sense to her that he would arrive by diving over a hedge and crawling up to her back steps. She believed, from hours of television-watching and newspaper-reading, that respectability of any kind, even in a town as small and middle-class as her own, was beleagured at every turn by mobs comprised in equal measure of the truly unfortunate and the wastrel, or revolutionary. Blinds closed to the quiet dapple on her own lawn, her world became the world of the media, and was therefore ablaze and rumbling with violence and corruption. Morrison was, too, all the more heroic for braving this chaos beyond the outer walls and managing what success he could in these bitter realities of life. As Morrison himself had plotted it, this was the best possible interpretation Elmira could have of his hustling. On the other extreme, she could have recognized him for the jinx and bounder he was, but this possibility Morrison refused to entertain. He had to have some faith in something, if only in his ability to pass (if only momentarily) himself off on the best possible terms. The true test, of course, was whether or not Elmira would write him a check. Beside this, every other consideration of Morrison's life had decidedly paled.

Elmira gave Morrison a glass of iced tea and sat down across the table from him. Like everything else in the kitchen, the table was enamel-white, and where objects and arms touched its surface there were the partial beginnings of an upside-down world, blurred but still recognizable. Morrison could see his own face as a kind of anonymous pink blob below him. He ached for some kind of definition.

Elmira's voice had an edge of despair, and might have been described as tobacco-thick, except that she didn't smoke. Morrison noticed, with a little gasp for the decay of his own physique, that the muscles along Elmira's arm were soft to the point of quivering, very pale, though gently freckled. It was more pleasant to look at her seemingly solid, heart-shaped face, with only a few lines around the eyes and mouth, altogether an illusion of greater youthfulness than the rest of her body conveyed. She lamented in educated, baroque phrases his near slaughter on the sidewalks of town and condemned the local police force for "barbarian neglect," whatever that meant. Morrison encouraged her to talk, because it helped him remember how her mind worked, and therefore what moves he could make to accomplish his exploitations. He still did not feel on safe ground with her; she came up frequently with surprises.

"I talked to my cousin Wilbur about our drive-in," Elmira said.

The phrase did not entirely register for a moment, and when it did, Morrison's heart sank. *You promised not to talk,* he wanted to shout. "Wilbur Cosgrove?"

"Yes. He's very discreet and I didn't think you'd mind. I felt I needed advice badly."

Morrison sipped his tea: an ice cube bumped into his front teeth. "He's doing pretty well for himself, isn't he?" Driving range and dry-cleaning store and, so the grapevine went, plans for some automatic carwashes. Morrison hated Wilbur Cosgrove's success, because it was based on an absolute failure of the imagination.

"He's doing swell," Elmira said, "and he thinks a drive-in's a good idea, *if*"—she wagged her finger at Morrison—"*if* the location is—what's the word he used?—prime. He said he doesn't understand your mumbo-jumbo about zoning laws. You weren't planning to sell any liquor, were you?"

"No, no," Morrison began, his words falling into a pit, "it's just that prime lots are too expensive."

"Wilbur says they pay for themselves faster than the others because you do so much more business, so in the long run they're actually cheaper."

"I understand that," Morrison said. "But, as I've indicated, my share in the enterprise can only be minimal until, uh, my broker makes his move."

"Wilbur says he doesn't understand that, either. He says you can buy and sell America with a phone call."

"Of course he's exaggerating."

"Of course," Elmira said. She leaned back in her chair and looked sadly at Morrison.

He couldn't meet her gaze. "Well," he managed. "Well, you seem to be having second thoughts."

"I'm afraid I am." She folded her hands a little too primly and lacked only horn-rims at the end of her nose to look like the perfect spinster prude. It was the expression of an attitude that Morrison could never bear.

"What I really wanted to do," Morrison said, "was to open the world's first porno drive-in."

"What?"

"A porno drive-in. I was going to call it *Tit for Tat,* or . . ."

"Never mind, please," Elmira said. "I might have known there was some reason for your being so vague."

"It's still a good idea."

"It's terrible."

"About the same as driving ranges and automatic carwashes."

"You don't have to be any more insulting, do you? I'm sorry Wilbur understood you so well. Otherwise I'd have been quite happily convinced to go along with you."

"I suppose I should leave," Morrison said, "though, frankly, I'd hate it to be on such a crummy note. You see, I'm a bit desperate lately, since . . ."

"Go away, please," Elmira said. "I mean at once."

"Elmira," Morrison said, "we're both adults, and you needn't pretend to be all that shocked. For that matter, you could still *loan* me the money and . . ."

"I wouldn't. Not for any such thing."

"Why not?"

"Why should I? It's my money. It doesn't have to be used for things I disapprove of."

"You disapprove of helping me out, then?"

"Dan Morrison," Elmira interrupted, "I don't owe you a thing. You're treating me as if I had some kind of obligation to you, which is *not true*."

"Don't you *feel* it to be true?" This line had worked before, he knew.

"No! Why should I?"

"I need help, and you could give it."

"You need help, but I don't think it's money you need."

"Look, Elmira," Morrison said. "Can't you see I'm begging? I'm asking you to do me favor, one human being to another. It's not exactly easy for me."

"But it's easy to refuse, Dan," Elmira said. "I wish you'd just go."

"How about a pizza place, then? I know a guy who might have a line on a franchise."

"Just go."

"A bowling alley?"

"Another minute, and I'll call the police."

Outside, Morrison slunk away along the high redwood fence that separated the lawns of Elmira and her neighbors from the Fiedler estate, with its glowing, yellow-brick mansion and its asphalt driveway strewn with colorful sports cars. Apparently some sort of celebration was going on there, under a yellow and white striped tent, in the kind of silence that only the very rich can bring to significant and otherwise merry occasions. Morrison had once shined Mr. Fiedler's shoes, and the old bastard was still alive and still rich, and probably in all that time had never stooped to polish his own footwear or, for that matter, to mount his own golfballs.

Such idle thinking led Morrison into the trap of momentarily dropping his guard, and when he turned his eyes away from the elegant tippling beyond the fence discovered Rudy Klein and two other bill collectors bearing down on him from different directions. Like foxhounds, they began to bay as soon as he moved, as soon as he hauled himself over the fence and thereafter chugged through the forest of tuxedoes and down a lane of parked sports cars and back into the real world of the rest of town, through sandboxes and across ditches, past garbage cans, under clotheslines, over manhole covers. . . .

Somehow Klein and the others persevered longer than usual, and when Morrison had finally eluded them, as always, his sides heaved with fatigue. He was tired of it all. Elmira had turned him down. The porno drive-in was still a great idea, and so, with beef prices so high, was cattle-rustling. There were lots of ways to make money, and all he needed was a little stake to get himself started. With that, he could pay off his debts in no time. Mrs. A————on Pearl Street and Mrs. M————on Langdon Lane had both answered his ad in the paper, just as Elmira had, and he therefore had doors he could get his foot in. If his creditors would just lie back, he had prospects, even great ones.

Suddenly Morrison sat indiscreetly down, not far from a large bush and quite near the sidewalk. He was an easy target here. On this spot, even old Ranshelm could lay hands on him, Ranshelm-the-patient, who had waited a year before he finally closed the doors of his grocery to Morrison forever. The telephone company manager might find him here, or Sterne and Vetcher Collection agents, or R. Gordon Thistlewaite, bank president and mortgager of houses. On this spot his creditors could easily find and surround him, and, once in their hands, he would have to stand and watch as they dismantled his house and his life and his prospects and his *credit.* . . .

Still, Morrison did not move. He couldn't, his legs ached so. He lay down with his hands folded behind his head and there rested, oddly at peace.

A young woman walked by, beautifully made, her shoulders bare to the sunshine and her hips covered by a brief and bell-shaped denim skirt. Morrison would have hired her for the drive-in or the carwash.

"Come on, come on now, boy," the woman said, looking at Morrison, smiling, slapping her thigh.

Morrison sat up. *Who?* he wondered. *Me?*

"Come on. Come on."

A dog scampered from the bushes, pink tongue flopping, skirted Morrison with a brief sniff at his buttocks, and cruised behind the woman's perfect legs.

No, not me, Morrison thought. *Not this time.*

YOU ARE WHAT YOU OWN: A NOTEBOOK

by Alice Adams

I can't leave because of all the priceless and cumbersome antique furniture that my manic mother had flown out from St. Louis—at what cost! My inheritance: it weighs me down as heavily as my feet, a part of me. Like my husband, who is also heavy, to whom I am connected, whom I cannot leave. Where do I end? and he begin? In this crazy hot California weather we both are sticky. We are stuck.

Our house is perfectly box-shaped, the way a child would draw a house. "A real *house* house," we said, laughing at our first sight of it; we were trying to convince ourselves that we took it because it is so amusing, not because it is the only one near the university, Stanford, that we can afford. An expensive box, it costs exactly half of Carl's instructor's salary. Half the floor is living room, one-fourth kitchen, one-eighth each bathroom and bedroom. It makes a certain sense, if you think about it.

It is hard to walk through the living room, though, without bumping into something: small French tables, English desk, baroque Spanish sofa. My legs are regularly bruised. I think my mother would be surprised to see where the precious furniture has landed, crowded into a redwood box. But now she is depressed (lithium does not work with her) and she is not mailing any more furniture, or traveling. She does not believe in sending money.

An interesting thing about the walnut desk and the rosewood table is that they both have broken left feet. I should have called Air Express, or someone, but I wasn't sure who, and I didn't like to complain. Mrs. Nelson, our neighbor, sighs whenever she comes over from across the street to look at the furniture, which is as often as I don't see her first and hide in bed. "Such lovely pieces," she sighs. "We've got to find a really good workman to repair them." If

I told her that we couldn't afford a really good workman she would not believe me. People with lovely furniture also have money, Mrs. Nelson believes.

So many of the people in my life seem to be oversized. Mrs. Nelson is one of them. An enormous pale woman with pale large blue eyes and a tight white mouth, she stands in the doorway, filling it, her heavy arms hanging across her chest, nothing about her moving but her eyes; her gaze moves ponderously all over the room, from one broken leg to another, all over the dust, and settling at last on me. The weight of her eyes is suffocating. I become hotter and thinner and messier than I am.

"A really good workman," she says. "You can't just let nice things fall apart."

I can't?

At another time when she was manic, my mother sent me a lot of clothes, and they are what I wear, worn-out C. Klein shirts and jeans, old sweaters and skirts (A. Klein, B. Blass). My yellow hair tight in a bun. Skinny and tense, with huge, needful eyes. A group of artists lives in a big old shabby house down the block: Artists are what I believe they are, Mrs. Nelson says, sniffling, "Gays," but to her that might mean the same. "Gay artists" surely has an attractive sound, to me. In any case, they all wear beautiful bright loose clothes. I am in love, in a way, with all of them; I would like to move over there and be friends. I want to say to them, "Look, these clothes aren't really me. I ruined my only Levis in too much Clorox. I will loosen my hair and become plump and peaceful. You'll see, if you let me move in."

When Carl is at home he is often asleep; he falls asleep anywhere, easily and deeply asleep. His mouth goes slack, sometimes saliva seeps out, slowly, down his blond, stubbled chin. Once I watched a tiny ant march heroically across Carl's face, over the wide pale planes, the thick bridge of his nose, and Carl never blinked. We have a lot of ants, especially when I leave the dishes in the sink for a couple of days, which I have recently begun to do. (Why? am I fond of ants?) Ants crawl all over the greasy, encrusted Havilland and Spode, and the milk-fogged glasses that Mrs. Nelson refers to as my "crystal." At least that stuff sometimes breaks, whereas the furniture will surely outlast me.

I could break it?

Awake, Carl talks a lot, in his high, tight voice. And he does not say the things that you would expect of a sleepy fat blond man. He sounds like one of the other things that he is: a graduate student in psychology, with a strong side interest in computers. He believes that he is parodying the person that he is. When I give too many clothes (all my old Norells) to the Goodwill he says, "If only you were an anal retentive like me," thinking that he is making a joke.

Carl complains, as I do, about the bulkiness of our furniture, the space it takes up, but I notice that he always mentions it, somehow, to friends who have failed to remark on it. "A ridiculous piece of ostentation, isn't it?" he will say, not hearing the pride in his own voice. "Helen's mother shipped it out from St. Louis, in one of her manic phases. She's quite immune to lithium, poor lady."

But one Saturday he spent the whole day waxing and polishing all the surfaces of wood. He is incredibly thorough: for hours his fingers probed and massaged the planes and high ornamental carvings.

How could I have married a man who looks like my mother? How not have noticed? Although my mother's family was all of English stock, as she puts it (thank God for my Welsh father, although he died so young that I barely knew him), and Carl's people are all German. Farmers, from the Sacramento Valley. I thought my mother would be mad (a German peasant, from a farm) but she likes Carl. "He doesn't seem in the least Germanic, not that they aren't a marvelous people. He's a brilliant boy. I'm sure he'll be a distinguished professor someday, or perhaps some fantastic computer career." And Carl asks her about the hallmarks on old silver, and I wonder if I am alive.

I devise stratagems to keep Carl from touching me, which sometimes he still wants to do. Unoriginally I pretend to be asleep, or at dinner I will begin to describe a headache or a cramp. Or sometimes I just let him. God knows it doesn't take long.

Carl ordered some silver polish from Macy's (fourteen dollars!), silver polish that an ad in the *Chronicle* said was wonderful. It came: a whitish liquid with a ghastly, sickish smell. Carl spent a perfect Saturday (for him) polishing all the silver and feeling sick.

When and why did I stop doing all the things that once absorbed my days? The washing polishing waxing of our things. When Carl said I was obsessional? No, not then. When I couldn't stand his tours of inspection? Perhaps. When I noticed that he often repolished what I had done—so unnecessary, I was an expert silver-polisher in my time. Is this my sneaky way of becoming "liberated"? (I know that I am still a long way off.)

*   *   *

Mrs. Nelson is obsessed with the "gay artists" down the street. (So am I, but in a different way.) There are two girls and three boys in that house, and Mrs. Nelson knows for a fact that there are only two bedrooms. So? The only time she got her face in the front door, collecting for the Red Cross (they all hooted, "We gave at the office"; not very funny, she thought), she distinctly did not see a couch where a person could sleep. So? I tell her that I don't know. I find the conversation embarrassing, and I do not mention the possibility of a rolled-up sleeping bag somewhere. Nor do I mention the nature of my own obsession with them: how do they get by with no jobs, and where (and *how*) did they leave whatever they used to own?

This insane climate has finally made me sick—physically, that is. In the midst of a February heat wave, some dark, cold wrapping rains came down upon us, rattling the windowpanes of our box house and the palm leaves outside, and I caught a terrible cold with pleurisy and a cough, so that it seemed silly to get out of bed. Carl said he thought it was an extension of my depression (I am depressed? I thought my mother was); he said to stay in bed, and went whistling into the kitchen to clear up dinner dishes and make breakfast.

Carl is delighted that I am sick; he is in love with all my symptoms. What does this mean? he wants me to die? No. He wants to be free to do everything that he thinks that I should do, and that he should not want to do, but he does? Yes.

I think I married Carl because he said that I should. I have always been quite docile, until I stopped washing dishes on time and polishing things—but perhaps that was further compliance? it was what Carl wanted me to do all along?

He brings in a tray. "Now, how's that for a pretty little omelette?"
Then, as suddenly as I became sick, I am well, and the rain is over and it is spring and I am in love with everyone I see: the beautiful garbage collectors and the butcher and especially the extra boy in the house down the street, who must sleep in his sleeping bag on the living room floor. He has long pale red hair—he is beautiful! One Saturday while Carl is polishing the silver I brush down my hair and go for a walk and there he is, the red-haired boy, saying hi, so warmly! I walk on, after saying hi also, but I feel that now we are friends. I give him a name: John, and from then on we have long conversations in my mind.

On another day I see a girl coming out of their yard, a girl with long dark hair, and we too say hi to each other, and I think of her too as a friend, from then on. Her name is Meg, in my mind, and we too talk.

Looming Mrs. Nelson caught me napping. "My, your things look so *nice* since you took to working on them," and her pale eyes glitter as though they too were polished. I do not tell her that it is Carl who does all that; it seems a shameful secret.

I point out to Carl that we would have more money if I got a job. He tells me that there are almost no jobs for anyone these days.

That is true, but it is also true that he does not want me to work.

For his computer course, Carl is working on a paper. The title seems most ominous to me; it is called "The Manipulation of Data." Manipulation? *Really?* He reads paragraphs to me aloud, usually when I am reading something else. I think that Carl would like us to be more nearly interchangeable with each other, but he is becoming more and more unreal to me. I regard him from my distance, and it seems odd that we know each other, unspeakably odd that we have married.

In a charitable way I try to think of a girl who would be good for Carl, and I imagine a young girl, probably a junior in college, who is also studying psychology and computers. They could do everything together, read and cook and eat and polish everything in the house, all day long, on Saturdays.

My mother is right; Carl will be a distinguished professor. But I am surely undistinguished, as a wife.

The spring is real, though, wild and insistent: yards full of flowing acacia, fields of blossoms, and wild mustard as bright as sunshine, and light soft winds.

Mrs. Nelson sighs because there are only three stemmed wineglasses left, and it occurs to me how little I know about her life: who and what was Mr. Nelson, and was she sad when he died? But it seems too late to ask.

I tell John and Meg (in my mind) that I think perhaps Carl and I bring out each other's worst qualities, and they agree (such wise gay artists!). I try to tell Carl that, but he says I am simply depressed. I am not depressed, really.

Watching the flowers grow, I go for many walks, smelling, breathing air. One day when I come home and find Carl asleep on the sofa, quite suddenly I am mortally stricken with pity for him, so fat and unhappy and unloved, and in that illuminated instant of real pain I understand that he is boring because I cannot listen to him. And if I can't love him and listen, at least I could leave? I rush into the bathroom, crying, but he doesn't wake.

In my head John and Meg both say, "You could probably get *something* in the city. Or at least you'd be up there."

"But what about all the furniture?" I ask them.

"That's easy," they say.

Dear Carl, I think we have been making each other very unhappy and that we should not do that anymore, and so I am going up to San Francisco to look for a job. I took five hundred dollars from our joint account but I will pay back half of it when I get a job. Please keep all the furniture and things because I really don't want them anymore, but don't tell Mother, in case you write to her. Love (really), Helen. P.S. I think it would be nice if you gave Mrs. Nelson a silver tray or a coffee pot or something.

A MIGHTY FORTRESS

by Colleen Anderson

Claudia and her mother are at it again. When her brother, Eric, ventures into the kitchen, as if into a battle zone, Claudia hardly notices him. He's a quiet kid, anyway; he pours his Rice Krispies into a bowl and pads to the kitchen table in his bedroom slippers. He doesn't even slurp.

"I can't help it. I just don't believe it!" Claudia's voice is modulating from a whine to a whimper.

"You don't have to understand to believe. I don't understand it either, but I accept God's word. You've got to have faith."

"But I don't! Can't you see that's what I'm talking about? I don't believe it—I don't think I believe it. And as long as there's any doubt in my mind, I can't do it."

They are arguing about Claudia's first communion in the Lutheran church, Missouri Synod, which is supposed to take place in a week. Claudia has decided that she can't risk taking the sacrament, because she may be damned eternally for not believing the wafers are actually the body of Christ. Her mother is having a fit, because she has invited thirty-seven people to a party after the church service, including Claudia's godparents, who have bought an expensive gift. And now she supposes Claudia expects her to call them all up and say, sorry, the party's off, my daughter has decided to go to hell instead. Well, Claudia can just call them herself. There's the phone, right on the wall.

"All you care about is your stupid party! You don't care about me at all!" Now Claudia stomps through the hallway and slams her door with such force that the eyelet ruffle on her bedspread sways. She can hear her mother furiously washing dishes, making louder-than-necessary clanking sounds with the pans. She hears her father come in.

"Nothing much in the mail this morning," her father says. "I saw Fred Mueller at the post office." She hears the sound of his keys on the table.

"I have to go to Linwood to check a transmitter this morning," her father says. "Want to go along for the ride, Eric?"

Then Claudia's mother's voice: "Why don't you take Claudia?" She lowers the volume, but Claudia, straining at the wall to hear, can make out the words. "The way she's moping around here, it's driving me crazy. I've had it right up to here!" Claudia can imagine her mother drawing her hand across her forehead in a motion like a salute. Perhaps a fleck of soap will stick to her hair. Then she will dry her hands on her apron, looking worried.

"Still thinks she's going to the devil, then?" Claudia's father sounds less than terrified.

"I don't know what she thinks! She thinks she can run every-body's life, like nobody else in this household matters!" Claudia hears the sound of her mother opening the drawer below the oven, where the pots and pans are kept.

"She says she doesn't want a party." Her mother's voice is a grunt—she must be bending over to put away the big frying pan now.

There is the sound of her father's keycase snapping and unsnap-ping. "Well, Judy," he says, but he doesn't continue.

"Well, Judy, my foot!" her mother's voice explodes. "You talk so high and mighty, but you haven't done a thing to help me get ready. Martha's bringing a whole set of china and silverware for eight. Carrie's baking a cake, and Lucille is going to help her decorate it, just like a bakery, with little roses." Her mother is crying now.

"Eric," her father's voice booms, "put on your sneakers and tell your sister she's coming with us."

"And turn off the TV," her mother wails.

It is a short drive to Linwood, about fifteen minutes across flat, scrubby land gridded at one-mile intervals by straight roads. Seven Mile Road. Eight Mile Road. Here and there the line of the horizon is interrupted by a clump of trees. Most of the trees are beginning to show their leaves, small and tender and shiny; the yellow-green willows, though, have been out for more than a week.

"Are you going to climb a tower?" Eric asks his father.

"I don't know. Have to take a look inside before I figure out what I'm going to do."

"How come the weeping willows come out before the other trees?" Eric asks. Claudia appreciates Eric's questions; he probably doesn't really want to know the answers, but he's the sort of person who tries to make the situation better. Claudia, sitting beside her father in the front seat, has been staring out the side window for the whole time, refusing to look at either of them, much less talk.

"Here we are," her father says. The car swings from asphalt onto a narrow gravel road. Ahead of them is the tower, moored in concrete and tethered on four sides by steel cables. It looks just like all the other towers Claudia's father has climbed to install radios or repair them. Sometimes he makes color slides, from different angles, of his installations, as Claudia's mother calls them. The slides always end up in a tray with pictures of family birthday parties or groups of relatives standing around a Christmas tree, and when they flash on the screen Claudia's mother says, "Oh, there's another one of Eddie's installations. I don't know how that got in here," as if there were something nasty about the image. All the pictures look alike to Claudia; there is always a lot of sky, sliced into geometric pieces by the criss-crossing lines of the tower. Some of the pictures show a small, low building like the one they are approaching now.

Her father gets out of the car, and Claudia calls out, "Dad? Can we listen to the radio?"

"Just a minute, I need to get inside the building."

"Can I go in?" Eric asks.

"No, it's too dangerous. High voltage—see that sign there?" He points to an orange sign on the chain link fence that surrounds the building and the base of the tower. He unlocks a lock at the gate and another one at the door of the building and goes inside. After a few minutes he comes out again. He tosses the keys into Claudia's lap. "I guess I've got to go up," he says. "Don't run the battery down, now."

"I won't." She turns the key in the ignition until the generator light glows on the dashboard. She switches on the radio and changes the station from her father's favorite, easy listening, to WTAC, rock 'n' roll. She slides down in the front seat until her knees are jammed up against the glove compartment, both hands resting on her belly, and watches her father start up the tower.

He climbs deliberately, pulling himself from one crossbar to another; not slowly, exactly, but with a solemn rhythm that tranquilizes Claudia to watch it. She leans her head back and watches her father grow smaller and smaller. She wonders what he is thinking right now. Once, when she asked him that, he laughed.

"What? What do I think about? Oh, you mean about climbing. Well, I don't know—I mean, it never bothered me. All of my brothers were like that, too. Never bothered any of us. Chuck and I used to eat our lunch up there sometimes."

Claudia tries to imagine eating lunch up in the air like that. She can't. There's a tower out in back of their house, smaller than this one, for her father's ham radio transmitter, and she tries to climb it sometimes. She tries not to think about what she's thinking, like her father; but at a certain point, roughly the height of the roof of the house, she is incapable of moving her feet any farther, and her eyes stray to the ground, although everyone knows looking down only makes it worse.

The disc jockey on the radio is talking about a local dance place. "You make the scene at the Foxy Lady," he is saying, "because we are going to be there, with your favorite music. And we are going to party."

"Why don't you want a party?" Eric asks Claudia.

"Who said I didn't?"

"Mom said you didn't want a party. I heard her."

Claudia makes a sound with her tongue and sighs a long sigh. "You wouldn't understand."

"Yes, I would."

"No you wouldn't. Believe me, Eric,"

"Are you going to hell?" Eric says after a time.

"Maybe. If Mom has her way." She turns the radio louder. The Beach Boys sing a song. She snaps her fingers with the rhythm.

"It's eleven thirty-eight," the disc jockey says, "and I'll be with you till noon." He plays another song. There is a crackle of static; it hurts her ears. Claudia turns the volume down slightly.

"She's such a hypocrite," Claudia says.

"Who?"

"Mom. She makes a big show out of being a good Christian, and really all she cares about is what other people think of her."

"But why can't you just have the party?"

Claudia turns around so that she can fix Eric with an expression of exasperation. "Because Holy Communion is a sacrament."

"So?"

"So you don't fool around with sacraments."

"Fool around?"

"I mean, we can joke about a lot of things in the church, and there's nothing wrong with it. Like, remember the time Mom was visiting Grandma, and she took the checkbook with her, and Dad put an IOU in the collection plate?"

"Yeah! Boy, did that make Mom mad! Remember when Carla's little sister was just learning how to talk, and she sang 'Itsy-Bitsy Teeny-Weeny Yellow Polka-Dot Bikini' real loud when everyone else was singing 'A Mighty Fortress Is Our God'? I saw Pastor Meyer smile, even."

"Right." He was a smart kid, too. "But when it comes to sacraments, you have to quit fooling around. Because they're holy and they have special powers, and . . . it's sort of like playing with a gun. It could backfire."

The radio crackles again. "It's hot in here," Eric says, and rolls down a back window. The wind is blowing hard outside. It whips up the dirt around the base of the tower. Claudia leans back. There's her father, up at the top, and he doesn't even look like a person, up so high—he looks like a little insect or something.

"Why would you want to fool around with a sacrament?" Eric asks.

"It's not that I want to fool around. The thing is, I'm just not sure," Claudia says. "I want to believe that the little wafer is really Christ's body, and the wine is really his blood, but . . . I don't know."

"Look at the wind blowing," Eric says.

"And the catechism says that if you take the sacrament without really believing, you take it to your damnation. Eric, are you listening at all?"

The radio crackles loudly. "What's wrong with this stupid thing?" Claudia says. She switches channels, and the static erupts again. Off to the east, over the bay, lightning flickers like a snake's tongue. This time, after the static crackle on the radio, there is a dull roll of thunder outside the car.

She looks for her father. Yes, he is coming down, in the same measured, solemn way he ascended. He has a long way to go.

The sky is changing fast. The storm is coming in off the bay; the clouds are low, purple, black. Claudia opens the car door, and the wind slams it shut again, violently.

"I wish Dad would hurry up," Eric says.

Big, angry drops hit the windshield. Then the water comes in sheets. Eric climbs into the front seat beside Claudia, and she puts her arm around him. On the other side of the windshield, her father's form is a wavering shape in the rain, advancing toward them steadily, with great dignity.

Lightning stabs the earth again, and the thunder is with it. Eric's face is bright with terror. He digs his fingernails into Claudia's arm. Her father is very close to them now. He comes on slowly.

There is a flash, and an awful crack, and someone screams—she can't tell if it's Eric's voice or her own.

And then her father is there, opening the car door and bringing with him a smell, a strong and sharp odor like metal. And there they are, all three of them in the front seat, and her father's wet arm is over their shoulders. Claudia starts crying now, but softly. "I was scared," she sobs.

"I was scared, too," her father says. "I haven't been scared like that too many times."

They sit there, all together, for what seems like a long time. The storm moves off. Her father locks up the little building, locks the gate. Then he takes them to McDonald's, and when Eric asks for a vanilla shake and fries, he doesn't even argue.

Claudia takes her first holy communion right on schedule. The white dress she wears is a little too tight; kneeling to receive the wafer and the tiny glass of wine, she wonders if the fabric on either side of the back zipper is pulled out by the tightness. Her hair has been styled by a beautician and is as stiff as frozen grass. The wafer tastes like a kind of candy she sometimes buys at the corner store— the only difference is that this wafer doesn't conceal a number of small candy balls. It sticks to the roof of her mouth the same way, though. The wine is sour. When she turns and walks down the center aisle of the church, she feels only slightly sick to her stomach. Her mother is beaming.

The party is afterward, at their house. Everybody comes, even Grandma, and the cake is indeed just like a bakery cake. Claudia eats four pieces of it, and the roses from the top of someone else's piece.

It might be the cake that is keeping her awake now, after everyone else has gone to sleep. She sits up in her bed, staring out the window into the backyard, where her father's ham radio tower stands like a stalk beside the house. The moon is bright and seems to have a kind face.

Claudia knows many facts about the moon and the solar system. She knows that the earth spins around its own center, around the sun, and in other, larger orbits. She accepts this, but she has never before felt the earth move.

Now, with an almost perceptible lurch, it does. The earth, and on it Claudia's house, with Claudia sitting up in the back bedroom, hurtles through clear black space, compelled and controlled by invisible forces, prevented from careening off into cold nothingness by no more than some fragile, coincidental relationships with a million, or billion, other flying objects.

STEPMOTHER

by Carol Ascher

Louise pulled a cigarette from her smooth leather purse as she and her stepdaughter inched their way out of the theater toward the crowded lobby.

"Shall we go for coffee or soda?" she asked, touching the soft skin of Ricky's arm.

Going for something to eat had become part of their theater afternoons together. For almost a year, Ricky had come in alone on the bus—a big step, at first, for a sheltered twelve-year-old girl—and the two had spent their Saturday afternoons together. When Louise and Ricky sat next to each other in the red velvet seats of a theater, they created a protected space where fondness reigned. Louise felt her mouth go dry at the thought of giving up these afternoons.

"You know where I'd like to go?" Ricky asked as she flung her arms into her woolen coat. "To the Stage Delicatessen, where we got those huge turkey sandwiches and saw Kris Kristoffersen. Remember?"

Louise smiled. "We could do that. But I'd sort of like to go someplace where I could have a drink. I think I know a restaurant you'll really love!"

Louise opened her arm so that Ricky could put hers through it, but Ricky tucked her hand in the silky lining of her stepmother's coat pocket and grinned up at her as she squeezed up against the fur like a cat.

All this they had together, thought Louise as she led Ricky in and out among the shoppers to 57th Street and the Russian Tea Room. The question was, could they keep it up without Donald—the husband-father who connected them?

Louise had been nearly twenty-nine—a journalist who was doing well because she had given everything to her career—when she had met and rapidly married the elusive Donald. Then, what she had seen was that he would give her the time and space to continue her work. Now she looked back on five hard years of quenching Donald's first wife's anger, of finding a way to be with Ricky that everyone could tolerate, of holding Donald to her and to her home. She had had to step so carefully; and always, she had felt her hands were tied.

Louise inhaled her cigarette, drawing in the smoke to stop the dark thoughts. Ricky was wearing the camel's-hair coat she and Donald had given her for Christmas. The girl's black curly hair shone like an eclipsed sun above the collar. Ricky had a face like a Mediterranean Lolita. And just these last months, little mounds had appeared like soft marshmallows through her sweaters. Soon she would begin to go out with boys. From Louise's own selfish viewpoint, Ricky's had been a short childhood.

Everything seemed to fall through Louise's bound hands. Donald, whom she still loved with a swell of pain, when had he walked out with his suitcase? Was it two weeks or three weeks already? Somewhere another woman believed that she could hold him; but she too would become confused between an arm extended in love and in grasping, until Donald would once more be on his way.

"Did you like the play?" Ricky was asking in her sweet bouncy voice.

Louise felt Ricky's question like an offering. I don't know. I used to like it a great deal," she said, collecting herself. "I used to think *A Doll's House* was one of the great plays. I used to love Nora's final speech when she's leaving Torvald."

Every woman dreamed of being Nora, Louise thought, a delicate flower breaking out at last from the protective love of her husband into full womanly independence. Yet it rarely happened that way. Instead, Donald had left Ricky's mother (a strong and resourceful woman like herself), just as he had now left her for another woman who would probably have much to give.

"Listen," she said, putting her arm around Ricky and giving her a squeeze, "that play is from a time when it seemed that if women could just leave men they could be whole beings. I guess it's still true." After all, she had come to understand Donald, see his grave inadequacies, without being able to leave him. "Only maybe the men get to it first." She gave a hard laugh. "I don't know; it all seems much more complicated.

"Torvald wasn't such a great husband. I didn't like him," Ricky said decisively.

"No, he's not very likeable in the end." Louise squeezed again, as if protecting Ricky from a strong wind.

They had reached the Russian Tea Room, with its darkened windows and thick, discreet door. Louise steered Ricky through the gilded entrance, and they gave their coats to the woman in the hat check booth. An elderly waiter in a red jacket led them to a table for two along one of the mirrored walls. The Edwardian lamps and heavy silver gave the room an Old World opulence and made it seem as if they were royalty or actors on an elegant stage. Ricky blew out her cheeks and opened her black eyes wide. Louise winked.

"Do you come here a lot?" Ricky fingered the pink damask tablecloth.

"Not a lot, but sometimes. Sometimes I come here for business lunches." Louise remembered how, as a dazzled teenager, she had first gazed at the Stork Club with the same wondrous eyes. The Club no longer existed; she didn't know when it had come down.

"It's really elegant! I bet famous people come here," Ricky said, always on the lookout.

Louise smiled. "Maybe we'll even see some."

When the waiter came, Louise ordered a double scotch and a bowl of borscht. "Why don't you try a Russian crepe?" she suggested.

"What's that?" Ricky wrinkled her nose.

"A pancake filled with sour cream and caviar."

"Will I like it?"

"I think so. Try it. You can order something else later, if you don't."

"Okay."

Louise felt her mind pulling away again. How was she to bring up the subject? Should she just start talking? Why couldn't Donald have done this all before leaving town? When the scotch arrived, she gulped it down. The heat burned her throat and stomach like a shock, and for a moment her mind clouded.

Ricky had started to chatter about *The Treasure of the Sierra Madre*, which she had seen on late-night television. She was a movie fan, and sometimes stayed up till all hours by herself. "You can ask me what year it was made," she said.

"What year?" asked Louise.

"Nineteen forty-eight." Ricky beamed. "Ask me other Bogart movies. Also who starred in them."

Louise complied, but her mind wandered. How had Ricky gotten this exaggerated energy for competence, so like Donald's. It was strange how a man could leave his family for all but rare Sunday visits, and still pieces of his personality would stay with them.

The crepe came. Ricky puffed out her cheeks at the delicate

pancake, with its white cream floating outward and tiny black fish eggs like blackbirds sailing over a cloud.

"We had caviar once at home, and I didn't like it," Ricky admitted. "But I think this is going to be more like a blintz."

How did one say it? How did one discuss it with a twelve-year-old? Your father and I . . . What was the end of the sentence? What questions and answers followed? For a moment she felt almost grateful to Donald for having forced the situation. Yet why should his daughter go through this a second time?

"Is it good?" she asked, seeing Ricky's confused face.

"I think so. I can't tell yet."

"Do you want to taste my borscht?"

"In a minute." Ricky spread her pink napkin neatly on her lap.

Louise's own mother had warned her against Donald. She had said that a man running from a marriage would leave her as he had left his wife. She still had her mother to tell about Donald.

Louise smiled at Ricky spooning the thick cream. "Well, I guess the caviar's okay."

At home, what she had feared was crying like a victim as she told the girl or, as bad, showing the anger she felt toward Donald. But now the tears she felt behind her heavy eyelids were for Ricky. A woman at work had once said how her child had kept her going in the first months after her husband had left. A mother could touch the skin of her child for hope when her courage faltered. Yet Ricky had come with, and might well leave with, the father.

Ricky was looking up at her with a serious expression. "I forgot. I wanted to ask you something."

Louise tensed. Could the girl have figured out what was happening? What traces might Donald have carelessly left?

"I've been thinking about my name. Do you think I should call myself by my real name?"

Louise's diaphragm relaxed, and the breath she took was almost painful. "You mean Rebecca?"

"Mommy doesn't like the name, because she says Daddy made her name me after his mother. But I think I should use my real name. What do you think? Is it a good name?"

"I like the name. Rebecca." Louise rolled out the letters slowly, aware that she was entering a web of parental bitterness. "I think Rebecca is a good name." She sipped the watery end of her scotch. "But then, fashions in names change, so it's hard to say what kind of name you'll want when you're in high school or college."

"Ricky." The girl wrinkled her nose, and the dark of her nostrils twitched like a filly's. "It just sounds too boyish."

"It's getting pretty hard for you to seem boyish these days," Louise teased.

"Well, I think I might start using Rebecca. Daddy will be pleased, won't he?"

"Probably." Louise smiled, and her lips seemed cracked and dry.

While Ricky went to the bathroom, Louise paid the check. They had finished eating without her being able to say anything. Perhaps out on the street, she thought, with the noise of cars and the rush of people. Here everything seemed too solemn.

Outside, the streetlights had come on. The greenish color of the early-evening sky sent a rush of romantic pleasure through Louise. She would be all right on her own: she'd make plans and meet new people. And she would find a way to keep Ricky in her life.

"Let's walk back to the bus depot," she said, taking Ricky's arm.

They strolled along Broadway, slowing down in front of the stores that sold cheap costume jewelry, theater makeup, and exotic undergarments. Louise remembered Ricky had once asked her if she would ever buy the brassieres with holes for the nipples. Feeling relaxed, Louise had confided, "No, but sometimes I'd like to," and they both had giggled. A little further south were the shops selling exaggerated platform shoes, and then on 47th Street, the big Castro convertible sofa store, with its couches like giant colorful snakes filling the show windows.

"Listen," said Louise with a sudden burst of courage. "Your father and I aren't going to live with each other anymore."

She felt Ricky's body slow down deep inside, as if the machinery had hit a chink and were coming to a slow stop. There must be another sentence she ought to add, something to smooth it out and make it less abrupt.

"What I mean is, he and I probably aren't going to be married any longer. I think your father feels he's been married basically all his adult life, since he was very young. You know, he married your mother and then right away he married me." How reasonable it sounded; of course he would want to leave.

"You mean, you're going to get a divorce."

Louise searched for a cigarette in her leather purse. She lit one and drew in a long breath. "Yes, probably, but not right away. What we're going to do now is live separately. He'll probably be able to tell you more when you see each other, but I wanted to tell you myself." Perhaps it wasn't her right to tell Ricky, but Donald had left town without telling his daughter—the one piece of his behavior that could infuriate her whenever she recalled it. With his busy schedule, his traveling, and his reluctance to confront difficult matters, Louise knew it would be months before he told his daughter.

He would even be pleased that she had said something, relieved him of that awful first sentence she herself had found so hard. "I don't know; maybe he should have told you first."

"No, that's good," Ricky answered distractedly. She was working out something in her mind. Finally she said, "Does that mean you won't be my stepmother anymore?"

"Did you think of me as your stepmother?" Louise answered, grateful. She had always been afraid that with Ricky's mother taking care of the child, "stepmother" gave her more legitimacy than she was allowed.

"Sort of. A little bit. I sometimes told the kids at school I had a mother and a stepmother."

They walked awhile in silence. Louise was trying to figure out how to say that she still wanted to be Ricky's . . . But that was the problem; there would no longer be a word. Without the connection of kinship, a relationship between a grown woman and a little girl sounded pathetic and almost perverse. It made her seem too needy, like the lonely old people who had "little brothers" or played foster parents on the weekend.

"I guess we could still go to plays," she heard Ricky say. "I mean, you usually get the tickets free anyway."

That was it, how simple! "I'd take you even if I have to pay for the tickets." Louise laughed with relief.

"It's just that my mother's going to think it's really weird."

Louise felt stung. "You mean, us going to the theater together?"

"No, I mean Daddy breaking up with you."

She laughed. "I guess she'll think it serves me right."

"She didn't think Daddy should marry someone else right away."

So many complications for a girl to figure out, Louise thought. She couldn't imagine working out all these angles when she was twelve. But then, even suburban girls like Ricky were more sophisticated nowadays. "Your mom was probably right," she said, offering a gesture of reconciliation toward the woman who had been such a constant shadow.

They had walked up 41st Street to avoid the wild hustle of the movies and arcades on 42nd. Now the Port Authority Bus Terminal faced them squarely, its purple brick shining new and elegant from the street lamps. Inside, the Sunday-night crowd was like a waterfall flowing in from one door and pouring out toward the multitude of bus outlets.

"Can I have some candy for the way home?" Ricky asked.

They stopped at a newsstand, and Louise glanced at the headlines while Ricky picked up a bag of red-hots.

It was easy not to say anything as they moved rapidly along with the crowd through the vast depot. Louise felt the numbness of someone walking mechanically toward a fate long ago sealed.

At stall number 237, the red and tan New Jersey bus prepared to leave. Ricky stood on her toes to give a quick kiss.

Louise put her arms around the girl and held her with unexpected desperation. "Go! I love you," she said, her voice breaking.

GETTING INTO THE GARBAGE

by Jane Barnes

Until things had been settled with her husband, Alice had sworn she would not communicate with her lover, but still the foolish sweetness rose in her heart and she had to put it down to ease the pressure. "Honey," Alice wrote on the yellow legal foolscap, "say hi to your car for me. Every time I see a '69 Chevy, my heart goes pit-a-pat."

Then Alice returned to the lecture she was writing, "Seismic Tremors in the Old Regime in Russia in 1902." She was describing the life of Prince Ourusoff, a kind of noble Bronson Alcott who had tried to convert his immense farm into a collective and his canning factory into a phalanx of the sort Fournier had tried to establish at New Hope, Indiana. Despite Ourusoff's goodwill and his earnestness, his modern notions could not save him from woes as old as man himself. Alice portrayed him reading philosophic tracts aloud to his extended family of twelve at breakfast; she told about his wife's berry-picking party and the pie that resulted, his opportunistic business manager and the ruin of the wheat crop by rain.

"I saw Woody Allen in New York," Alice wrote on the foolscap again. "He was eating lunch in a restaurant, and I'm sure he wanted you to know he's thinking about using your life story as the basis for his next film. I'm thinking of you too, dear," she scribbled, and the real seriousness of this admission, the sinking of her heart that accompanied it, stopped her pen in its tracks.

She looked over at the basset whose name people often confused with hers. Olive, the dog, was stretched out asleep in the sun, her pretty face almost hidden under one long, seductive tan ear. Through the window above Olive, Alice looked at the view of the green pines covering the opposite banks of the Hudson. She might have been looking out the window of her family's house in Isleboro, Maine, but she was in their Riverdale palazzo, waiting for her daily appointment with Donald. A half mile to the south, New York City's vicious reach ended in a handful of dilapidated high-rises, overhead rails, a few dirty markets and dangerous bars. Then suddenly a lush belt of trees sprang up, protecting the wealthy suburb that had been simple farming country when Alice's grandfather had bought his land there sixty years before. He had built Nonesuch, a mansion in the mock-Tudor style, and when he died her father, a Wall Street lawyer, had moved his family out of the city. Now he and his wife had retired to Isleboro to raise mussels, leaving the Riverdale house available for any of the six children who might need or want to live there. As it happened, Alice and Donald, both professors at the University of Rochester, the first husband-and-wife team to get tenure together, had taken sabbaticals to nurse their marriage through a critical illness. After twelve years and two sons, they were desperate for a home away from home.

They were both historians; they both cared for tradition, though Donald, an American historian, cared for a somewhat different one than she did. This difference, like all their differences, had for a long while seemed complementary within their tacit understanding that they were both smart. He was just a little smarter. They were both sexy, flirtatious, and attractive. He was just a little more so. They were both oldnew people. He was just the greater master of maneuvering in an amoral society without losing his essential self. Alice was a perfect wife by being the lesser man until, as if a little masculinity was a contradiction, necessarily containing the challenge to wear all the pants or none at all, Alice fell in love.

She melted, became dreamy and preoccupied, was wreathed in smiles, though as easily touched to tears, and, in the process of finding herself as a woman, extended her male prerogatives to include the double standard. Though they both had been flirtatious, neither of them had ever strayed in the flesh. Now she began an affair when Donald was still chaste. At first, it seemed so natural, so easy, so like swimming, there seemed no danger in it. Then her love for the graduate student made her conscious of what had been missing in their marriage. She needed somehow to bring this joy to Donald's attention, if only to unburden herself of having something that was precious and desirable and that until it was equally distributed would keep them lopsided and lurching. Even if she was absolutely wrong to succumb to the young man's kisses, and unforgivable for trying to talk to Donald about her happiness, she still felt that she had earned some right to her mistake. She had for so long been like Donald that it seemed only fair that he be a little like her for a while.

Donald turned to stone and, when they were together, managed, by a powerful assertion of will, to block conversation from getting beyond the initial stages of her saying anything resembling a reference to her feelings, let alone mention of her new relationship. At first, she thought the difficulty arose from the moral questionableness of her position; before she could speak to Donald about the love lost between them, she should leave the affair. But if that's what he wanted, then, she gradually felt, that's what he could ask for. The point was he would neither ask nor explore, not even the slightest bit. She was willing to lower the pressure, to take up an easier, smaller piece, but he would not give her the time of day on a part any more than the whole. So she went back to wanting to talk about it all. Until she met Donald's furious resistance, the joy had seemed completely innocent, and it had been completely natural to go to bed. True, it was one step beyond anything either of them had done before, but all their words and all their deeds, if carried to their natural conclusions, would take them to a sophisticated place where they agreed that nothing was stopping anyone from doing anything.

She felt the least he could do if, after all, he did have morals, was to state them; if he had feelings, he should state those. But Donald was not available for comment on anything. He was a big man, broad-shouldered and fit, with a wonderful head of chestnut hair and a face that was dear to her from years of intimate familiarity. By subtly swelling in size, either by holding his breath or sulking or both, he became absolutely forbidding to her, seeming with silent laser beams to be cutting off her sentences in mid-expression. Sometimes, if she pushed beyond the difficulty of saying, "My feelings are troubling me," he could stop her by putting his mighty hands on the arms of his chair and squeezing them until he had pressed down to the very bones beneath the padding. Once at dinner, after their two sons had gone upstairs to do their homework, she cried, "Donald, we have got to talk," and he picked up a cheap glass goblet and hurled it against the wall, smashing the thick stem and bowl to smithereens.

He had reached her. She was terrified. She broke off the affair because she could not support the contradictory worlds. Yet no matter how she picked at her joy or analyzed it or mocked it, the memory remained. It was a fact on earth, in her, and nothing could keep her from knowing that she had felt it. Then a terrible thing began to happen. The indestructible reality of her joy made her question the marriage. Why was Donald so threatened? Why did he *hate* this joy so much? What in their marriage made this joy the worst insult she could deliver? Was it the joylessness of their manly fellowship, remembering, of course, that she was the little man and he the big one? Was his greatness dependent on the absence of this joy? Then she became truly terrified and fell into a silence even deeper than Donald's.

He did not understand that she now felt they had never been happy because when she did experience happiness he denied absolutely that happiness was something they could share. Donald thought she regretted her intemperance, and moved back toward her, taking up where they left off, as if nothing had happened. He became talkative, and he urged her to be the same, only a little less so. He talked about every woman he met in terms of how much she aroused him, though he also liked to speculate on his effect on her. He invited Alice to join him in these speculations on the unspoken condition that she not mention any experience of her own. She felt what he was doing had a certain fairness in it, yet it was still misguided. He wanted to regale her with lists of empty conquests, but he never spoke of having any feeling for these women.

One day she burst into tears and said, "Love . . ."

"What about it?" he asked in a voice that might have been neutral except that he flattened his hands with silent violence on either side of his dinner mat.

Alice began to suffer nervous symptoms such as dizziness, seeing funny, and hearing voices. She met her lover again, and seeing him restored her sanity while they were together. But then the prohibition against her feelings at home made her crazier. She had to go to bed every few weeks with what she called "flu" and her doctor called "depression." One winter day, when she was incapable of getting out of bed on a Saturday morning, when the boys were destroying the downstairs in their roughhousing, Donald found her and said, "You've got to stop lying to me. I have to know what's wrong."

"I can't talk to you."

"That's it. We're going to a marriage counselor," he said. "But we're not doing it here, where every second person we know sees someone we bump into at cocktails Saturday night."

That was when they decided to spend their sabbatical year in the Riverdale house. New York City offered plenty in the way of historical research materials, as well as therapists otherwise unbeknownst to them. The boys could go to Riverdale Country Day School, from which she herself had graduated. Olive could roam the meadows between the suburban mansions instead of having to depend on leashed walks whenever Alice or Donald had free time. They would retreat from the scene of Alice's crime and work on their work, as well as their marriage. For a moment, once the terms of the cease-fire were set, they could be relaxed and frank. Alice admitted she was still infatuated; Donald asked her to agree not to communicate with her lover. She did. Then what they said in their openness hardened them in their shells. The truce became a freeze. They were immobilized, on hold, waiting for the moment when there would be an outside referee to witness and maintain the purity of their different points of view.

Finding a therapist presented no problem except the one from which they had tried to flee. Her parents knew the name of a woman in New York whom everybody went to, and Donald and Alice gave in on the theory that there wasn't time to keep moving until they found the perfect community of strangers.

At the first appointment, Donald entered the ring with a small library of their publications. When asked to describe his position vis-à-vis the distress in which they found themselves as a couple, he delivered a short introductory speech on the need for Mrs. Edelheim to know their professional accomplishments, three-to-one for him in the realm of books, though Alice had many articles and was extremely popular as a teacher. After describing the unusual tenure decision that had promoted both partners in the marriage, Donald explained with some pride how there was now talk of merging their jobs into one appointment, a project Donald felt would represent true progressive change in the institutional structure of the university.

"And you?" Mrs. Edelheim asked, turning to Alice. "How would you describe your problem as a couple?"

Donald's statement had, by its competitiveness, perfectly demonstrated the problem Alice felt she was up against. Still, she did not want to seem to take her own side in her opening statement. Without referring to anything he said in particular, she plunged into abstraction that was nonetheless a specific ideological critique of what he'd said, aimed to appeal to the other woman's intuitive understanding.

"Love," Alice said, "love and consciousness. While we at every moment have formalized our liberal values and become more and more visible for our mutual accomplishments, stars of greater and greater magnitude, I feel less and less that the truth is admissible between us. As our life becomes more visibly fused and apparently consecrated to equality, I miss the love of man and wife. . . ."

"This is her German-in-translation mode," Donald said, sitting forward defensively when love was mentioned. "Under all those words is a very simple attack on me."

"Ah," said Mrs. Edelheim, lighting up as if they had played into her hands in spite of their individual attempts to strike her as a unique case. "Blaming. The first principle of this counseling is no more blaming. Part of what I will try to help you do is detach from the other, to see your own part in your problems instead of focusing on what you think is being done to you."

While this provoked movement on the surface, talk about their individual pasts before the marriage, the prohibition against blame stifled real revelation about their feelings toward each other in the present. It took the therapist several weeks to realize that her clients, both master conversationalists with her, were still incapable of talking to each other. When this dawned on Mrs. Edelheim, she smiled and lit up again, saying, "I am going to give you some homework. From now on, I want you to set aside an hour a day during which you will sit down and talk to each other."

This hung over them like a prison sentence as they drove out of the city, where the sun had already set, to Riverdale, which was drenched in the rich, melancholy light of late October. The emerald green lawn was streaked with brilliant streamers of red and yellow leaves. The banks of pines across the river seemed Nordic, as if Nonesuch were actually Ourusoff's estate outside of Moscow and the blue heavens were Russian. Donald got out of the car, sighing and saying he felt the sky and view had never seemed so American, suggesting so many untapped resources just at a time when he felt personally spent.

The boys called to him from an upstairs window, urging him to come quick, as an important football coach was being interviewed about the game on Saturday. Olive wanted Alice to go somewhere, but when she tried to get the dog to come down the steep back slope, Olive refused to risk the incline on her short, unsteady legs. Alice backed down, clapping and urging Olive to "Come on, Olive, come on. You can make it. Let's run away and be free. Let's run away to Stalinsville." But the basset only wagged her tail with greater and greater intensity; finally her whole white and tan rump was swinging back and forth like a willow branch while she barked, at first rather companionably, as if she were saying, "Come on. I don't want to go. *You* come back." Then her barking grew crosser until she really sounded furious with Alice for trying to persuade her to do something unsafe and treacherous.

Alice gave in and walked back up to where the basset was waiting, though now Olive was so stirred up she had grown confused and thought it was time to eat. She began to bob and prance as she did when it was lunchtime, and Alice relented. She took Olive to the kitchen for a few hard milkbones. When they got there, Alice found that Olive had already helped herself to some chicken bones, which she had strewn all over the floor with the rest of the trash in the plastic container by the stove.

"Olive," Alice said. "You dog, you. What is this?"

Olive, however, kept smiling brightly, refusing to acknowledge the mess she had made, continuing with supreme good humor to encourage Alice to indulge her. And feeling, after all, that Olive's hedonistic view, so friendly and tolerant, was approximately how she felt about things herself, Alice also pretended not to see the trash on the floor—lest Olive think she wouldn't punish her if she knew about her crime—and gave the dog some bones on the back porch. Alice went back in and cleaned up the garbage, her love rising in her heart in silly little sentences that she finally relieved by going to her study and scribbling on the scrap of paper, "Do you love me still? Be frank. No, be yourself, but tell me true if thou a true lover be. . . ."

Then she had emptied the naturally upbubbling pool for that day and could go to her next appointment with Donald without a sense that she was hiding anything. Insofar as she could show herself to him, she was as transparent as she could be. They sat in overstuffed chairs on either side of the fireplace in the little downstairs sitting room, where her parents always went for coffee after dinner. Donald and Alice looked like civilized people in their L. L. Bean shirts and turtlenecks, their khaki and twill pants, and their his-and-her boots for a weekend in the country. But no matter which direction they tried to steer the conversation, immense barriers rose up like obstructions in an uncleared jungle.

He started after her affair, but she would not let him treat it like a pure injury to him. She tried to place it in the context of their history, but Donald would not let her relate her wrong to his virtue. Every stab at talk ended in crossed swords and heightened tension as their fury mounted and their self-control redoubled. When through clenched teeth she said, "This is degenerating into blame," he replied, "Yes, and it's your fault."

That ended that day's exchange, but when they met again the next, they took up their mute, stifled rage where they had left it. Their opening exchange was so constipated that they had already shut off all avenues to exploration within minutes, and simultaneously, in their proud mutual refusal to be the first to break, they had raised the level of suppressed anger to the point where Donald was hardly breathing and Alice was nearly breathless. "Oh darling," she wrote later on the scrap of paper, "how, fainting with pleasure,

I have dreamt of falling into your arms one last time before I faced all this; how sometimes when we are face-to-face here, on the verge of murder, I swoon with some combination of immense fear and great desire, falling down in terror and waking up in your arms." When she finished, the foolscap was full and she crumpled it up and threw it away; then, just to be completely safe, she emptied her wastepaper basket into the big trash in the kitchen and pushed her stuff to the bottom of the general garbage.

At the marriage counselor's, Donald and Alice interrupted each other to complain of how the other had made it impossible, in Donald's case, for him to say how her affair had hurt him or, in Alice's case, for her to say how no amount of imitating him had ever satisfied him long enough for him to recognize her existence.

"Ah," said Mrs. Edelheim, "now you must go home and say these things to each other."

But the powerful emotions were silenced in the absence of the third person. As Donald and Alice joined the whizzing homebound traffic on the West Side Highway, the intense expressiveness they had displayed moments before was gone. A fiery sun was setting to the west over the industrial ruins of New Jersey, and to Alice it seemed as though they were internalizing the furnace, taking nature and harboring it unhealthily so that their complexions were lit with yellow from within. Soon their only choice would be to die in suicide from swallowing the poison or to launch it murderously at each other. Either way, it had begun to look as if there were going to be no survivors.

When they got home, they fell away from the car, stumbling in opposite directions—she to the lawn and the view of Russia, he to the house and his sons. Alice stood on the brow of the hill, gazing at her fantasy of the past, some tender, coherent period of history in which she would have found a place more easily. The green pines darkened as she stood there, spreading mysteriously until the river and the far bank seemed all part of the same forest. She thought no more of her lover. Therapy had been successful in making her see escape was hopeless. She could not get around her marriage; she had to go through it. Now Alice drank from the oncoming night and tried to refresh her exhaustion by breathing the dark in and out. Then her eldest son called softly from the terrace, mixing a conspiratorial tone with a warning one, "You'd better come in, Mom."

At last she heard the roaring. She was set for any emergency, for a runaway beast or an insane invader, but as she came through the French doors into the dining room, it took some adjusting to realize only the inevitable was happening. Donald was bellowing and destroying the kitchen. China was crashing, glass was shattering, the wooden cabinets were splintering. Before she realized how terrified she was, Alice stepped to the kitchen door and looked in. Amid Donald's destruction, Olive stood over the ragged hole in a big black garbage bag that had been sitting on the floor, tied and ready to go out. Between friendly but baffled glances at Donald as he beat on the counters with his fists and sent a toaster flying, Olive gobbled at the remains of last night's hamburger in coffee grinds. This was one opportunity she was not going to miss, not even for World War III.

Donald saw Alice and he stopped to look at her, drunk with anger, his hair plastered down on the wrong side. " 'Honey,' " he snarled. " 'Say hi to your car. . . .' 'How, fainting with pleasure, I have dreamt of falling into your arms. . . .' You bitch, you stupid, lying bitch."

Before she consciously understood, she knew what had happened, saw him coming and her own death rising up in front of her like a soldier falling in the first row of infantry. Alice stepped into the space left by her death, bathed now in freedom, cleansed at last of her putrid timidity, her stinking pride, her rotten fear, no longer caring what happened to her, said, "Don't be silly. I never sent it."

"You loved another person," Donald spat out, his chops trembling and his lips a full, violent, meaty purple.

"That's right," she seethed. "I've loved someone else. I could probably love a thousand other people. Give me time. . . ."

"You jerk. Rules, society, the containment of ego . . ."

"I want to love, Donald. If you won't let me love you, let me love someone else. . . ."

"Don't say it. Obey, society, me . . ."

"You selfish fool," she cried with relish.

"You whore, you pathetic whore . . ."

They opened their mouths and the infection poured out: his hatred for her immorality, her attack on his heartlessness. They screamed and screamed. Their children cowered, giggling with hysterical fear upstairs. It did not take Donald and Alice long to unload the viciousness of years. Only an hour passed before they were reduced to the inarticulate howling of animals, but then at last they recovered the common sense that nature endows creatures with in the wild. Under his "society" was his bullying, and under her "love" was hers, and when they had beaten on each other with their arguments and she was revealed as women had been to begin with, defenseless and promiscuous, and he was revealed as men had been, menacing and promiscuous, then she rolled over and showed her throat as wolves do when they surrender in a fight. He responded with civility, restraining himself from using his greater physical strength and triumphant advantage to tear her jugular out of her neck. Within days, they were living separately; within weeks, they had initiated divorce proceedings, but it would be years until they recovered, rearmed and remarried.

BIG FISH, LITTLE FISH

by T. Alan Broughton

"Eat, Albert, eat," Mrs. Lindstrom said.

Albert lowered his eyes. He had been watching the thin lips and oval panes of glass her eyes pressed against. Now he stared blankly at his fork and the macaroni on his plate—chopped slugs blotched with drops of melted cheese. She wanted him to stab the dead things with his fork. But he was not hungry.

"My birthday?" He moved his eyes across the tabletop to her hands tightly folded as if in prayer.

"Tomorrow. Hurry."

"Cake?"

"Yes."

"And candles?"

"Yes, yes."

"How many?"

The hands jerked open, pressed their palms together, and then fingers began flailing against one another.

"Thirty-two, thirty-two. If you don't eat we shall be late, and you know how Dr. Gorson does not like to wait."

Albert closed his eyes, the better to open them with a snap as though his eyelids were jaws. The macaroni was still there. He hated macaroni.

"Not hungry," he moaned.

"Nonsense. You shall not be allowed to watch *Mister Ed* tonight if you don't eat. Tildie fixed your lunch early just so we could go on time. Wasn't that nice of Tildie? Mustn't disappoint her."

Poor Tildie. He was bad. The fork was so far away from his hand.

"Tildie is nice."

"Albert. Please."

"Mac'roni not nice."

He could tell by the way the table trembled briefly that she had stood. His milk quivered in its glass. It would be awful not to see *Mister Ed*.

"Feed me." He looked up.

She leaned close over the table, lips so straightened that her flesh had been melted together. The eyes blinked, and then he saw the fork rise below him, carrying a white load.

"I am angry with you, and we shall have some punishment for this. You are much too big a boy to act in this way."

He did not take his eyes off her the whole time. She frowned with the concentration of her work, and he listened to the sound of his chewing. He tried to ignore the taste and told himself it was cake, the kind he liked best—white with orange frosting, sugary flowers, and words spread across it. Candles to blow. When she was through she brushed his mouth vigorously with a napkin and gave him his glass of milk.

"Drink up, and swish it around. We haven't time to brush."

He did what she said, but rinsed too vigorously and choked.

"Oh, you exasperate me." She wiped his mouth again.

She walked fast down the hall, and because he kept pausing to look at the rooms they passed, he finally had to lope to catch up with her. Donny was in the book room, but he was not doing what he should. He had piled a whole shelf of books on the floor and was starting on another. Donny knew that was no way to treat them. Books were not for making towers, because they fell over and got dirty on the floor.

When they reached the coat room, he pointed back up the hall.

"What is it?"

"Donny, he . . ."

But she was holding out a coat and he tried to concentrate. She held it by the shoulders, facing him. It was inside out to him, armholes spread and gaping. He closed his eyes, could not remember how it was done, and, stretching out his arms, impaled the two holes on them as he leapt forward.

She shook the coat so his arms waggled helplessly. "No, no, no. You know better. Turn around."

He disengaged himself, turned his back to her, and flung back his arms like a swimmer about to leap to the gun. Wrong, he was always wrong. Far down the hall a bell was ringing.

"Lunch?" But her hand was firmly on his elbow. She turned him to the front door, and, taking his hand, she led him out onto the porch and down the stairs to the waiting car.

He liked cars. He smiled at her when she sat on the back seat with him and closed the door. They began to move.

"Cars are good," he said.

For the first time that morning he saw her smile. So it was all right. He could not remember what had been wrong anymore, but now it was fixed. He laughed and let his hands rise to clap in front of his face a few times, a sound he liked and had discovered could be made in a variety of ways if the fingers were open or closed. He stamped once with his foot. She put a hand on his shoulder, still smiling, shook her head, and said, "Not too much excitement." He laced his fingers together on his lap.

"Oh, Albert." She put a hand on top of his. "What are we going to do? You were naughty not to eat your lunch when I asked, and I shall be most disappointed if we have to learn about coats all over again."

Albert was about to start crying, but a truck passed close by his window and he turned to watch its giant wheels. Then he did what he always liked to do best in a car. He stared at the back of the driver's head so that he could see not only it rising in the middle of his sight like a balloon but also all the scenery coming up and over and around them. Everything moved except the head, and he was a huge effortlessly swimming fish, like the big shark they had watched on TV—a long white muscle with teeth that twisted and lunged without sound.

"Good," he said. "Good."

A woman was behind the desk in a vaguely familiar office. Mrs. Lindstrom sat him in a smooth black leather chair and went to talk to the lady who made the phone ring all the time so she could play with it. Albert sat very still, trying to keep his head from lolling and wavering. When he stretched out his feet to cross them, he noticed the big brown leather shoes with little holes in them that he was allowed to wear only on special occasions. They were very shiny, and he uncrossed his feet for fear that rubbing them together might make marks. He did not care for the smell in the room. It began to make him very uneasy. Something like this had happened before and it had not been pleasant. Was he being punished?

But Mrs. Lindstrom was talking very happily with the other lady, and he did not hear his name mentioned. They did not even look at him. Albert scanned the top of the bookshelf. A set of huge teeth but no face. Just teeth spread for a bite, white surfaces polished and wet, the red gums naked. Albert tried to believe it was smiling, but it was not. It was simply hungry, gaping, advancing on a squat lamp at the other end of the shelf. He turned to the women, but they did not notice. That they were not afraid reassured him. He looked back. The teeth had not moved. Albert smiled. It was a trick of some sort.

Something was moving on the table near his elbow, and, slowly revolving on the chair, he found a small square tank full of water. The more he looked at it, the more he saw. Wavy, long plants stretched up from the bottom with fur like a cat's tail. Bubbles were rising in one corner to the top, where they made a blister of water. Even a small house with an open door and two windows crouched among the weeds. And fish were swimming slowly in and out among the plants. One passed through a window and threaded its way out the door. Albert was delighted. Fish. Fish.

He started to clap his hands but decided not to. He wanted to see this by himself. His fish. He would watch them and then try to sneak them home. Mrs. Lindstrom had her back to him. What a thing this would be to have in his room or show to Donny. Then, when he was punished, he would not care at all. He would take them out and watch them swim.

Again the narrow fish went through the house, passing partway out the door to peer with eyes bulbed and fins twitching slightly. Albert shook his head disapprovingly. Not right to go in the window. He would teach them to go in the door only and use the windows for looking out. He tried to count them all, but they kept moving in dizzy patterns and he ran out of fingers. Some of them were too small and one had almost no body but was a great flutter of silky tails and fins. They moved their mouths constantly, eating the water. Albert wondered why they were so thirsty.

Almost before he could focus on it, a large black fish darted out of the green tangles to seize a small red-eyed fish and disappear. Albert leaned forward, nose against the glass. Where had it gone? What was it doing there? He had to warn the other fish. He tapped once with his finger on the glass, afraid to break it. His eyes watered and blinked from staring.

Once more, just as he focused again, the black fin slipped back into the weeds, and he was certain he had heard a noise, something like a very distant cry of a bird. There were fewer fish. He started to stand, and then hung there, paralyzed.

The fish slipped out of the weeds. Its scales caught light and made dark glints like mica. The eyes, distended, and broad, under-slung jaw kept snapping open and then gradually closing in a sleepy motion. The thin fish approached, the black one tensed, and before Albert could move, it had slid forward, taken the slim one halfway in its mouth, paused for a moment with its eyes drooping, and then sucked in the tail. Tiny bubbles rose from the fish's mouth and it grinned.

"Fish, fish," Albert called excitedly to Mrs. Lindstrom at his side. "Fish." He opened his mouth wide.

Mrs. Lindstrom smiled. "Yes, Albert. Fish. Had you forgotten Dr. Gorson had fish? Aren't they nice?"

"No, no. Fish eating, fish eating."

Mrs. Lindstrom nodded at the other woman. "We had fish for dinner last night. Disturbs him. Albert, he's a very tender one. Here's Dr. Gorson."

Albert turned to the new figure, an oval face with gray moustache. Beyond him a white chair gaped with gleaming chrome. He forgot completely about the fish.

"No," he said emphatically.

"Are you going to behave?" Mrs. Lindstrom clutched him firmly by the shoulder.

"No," he whined. He knew where he was now. They had come before, and steel things were put into his mouth that made him hurt, and that was even the same man. He was certain Mrs. Lindstrom had promised they would not come back. "Please."

She shook her head. The thin lips disappeared again, the eyes plumped firmly up against their glass. He whimpered as Dr. Gorson tilted back the chair, tried not to look at the bright round glass over his head. The whole room wavered with light, and people bubbled up around him. Mrs. Lindstrom left and said she would wait for him in the other room. Only himself and Dr. Gorson now.

"Well, well, Albert." The moustache and its beaked nose floated over him for a moment. "We won't hurt you. Open up, my man, and let's have a look."

Albert leaned his head back, opened his mouth a little, a little more, then so wide that it closed his eyes. His arms tightened against his sides, merged and folded into the flesh, and black scales grew like cool slate down his back. He was terribly, terribly hungry, a dark and reaching hole that only his mouth could provide for and every one of its teeth ached to rip and tear.

He closed his mouth as hard as he could and opened his eyes wide. Dr. Gorson's face floated over him, the flesh bright red, mouth open in a prolonged howl. He was showing his own teeth to Albert, and even though Albert's head shook from side to side now as the thing in his mouth moved, he could see all the pretty metal. A nurse came, and Mrs. Lindstrom, their faces bobbing around Dr. Gorson's, which had started now to turn very pale, and they were all talking at once, their hands pulling at his mouth. Albert started growling. He wanted to say "Leggo, leggo," but then he would have to let the thing out of his mouth, and it was his. He was Barracuda, Mrs. Oliphant's dog. If you gave him a sock he would hold one end in his teeth and you could grab the other and tug him around the room, but he would not let go, a deep growling coming out of his chest. "Rrrrr," Albert said, and now Dr. Gorson was moaning.

Someone was tickling him and that was the end of it. Hands were all over his ribs. He slapped at air helplessly, his eyes closed, watering happy tears, and his mouth sprang open. The chair was tipped so far back that he could not get up and away from all the fingers, but it did not matter, because suddenly they had stopped.

"Get up, Albert. Get up this minute." That was Mrs. Lindstrom.

He opened his eyes and sat up so abruptly that he cracked his forehead against the nurse's, and she staggered back toward the window. Everything was in a horrible mess. Little steely things were scattered all over, the tiny fountain had come unhooked and was sending a limp jet onto the floor. Dr. Gorson was hunched in the corner, sitting on his heels, hand held in his crotch, and face, almost black now, fixed in a toothy grimace.

"Fish eating, fish eating." Albert grinned. "Dog play. I'm Bardecooda. Woof."

Everything happened very fast. Mrs. Lindstrom stood him up, the coat was heaved onto him, the scarf wound so tightly he hacked out a cough, and he was led out as if he had told Mrs. Lindstrom he had to wee-wee. Which he decided was true, but she was not listening. As they passed the fish tank he tried to warn everyone in the room about the black fish, but they only gaped at him. In the elevator he could not help it. He whimpered as the warm stream ran down his leg. Mrs. Lindstrom was staring too sternly ahead to notice, staring so hard she made the doors sigh open with her eyes. He stepped over the puddle, into the afternoon.

They sat next to each other in the back of the car. He snuck a glance at her from time to time, but she too was watching the driver's head. Again, her lips had gone. He began to smell himself, knew it would be better to tell.

"Albert wee-wee," he murmured.

Her face turned sharply to him. She blinked.

"Albert sorry."

The hand in her lap fluttered up. To hit him? It had before. He did not cringe, though. Suddenly the lips were moving. She was not speaking. They trembled together like tiny minnows. Then her eyes were making water for them.

The voice said, "Oh Lord, Lord, when will you end all this, when will it all be over?"

Albert saw she had lost her breath. He did not know who this person Lord was, but he was very sorry the man had made Mrs. Lindstrom so unhappy, and so he put his arms out and to his surprise she held him very close, his face against her neck, where he could hear something far inside beating to get out.

GOING HOME

by Joseph Bruchac

"Look, Tommy, down there in the valley. Look at all those little houses. Look at how they are all like little boxes, those houses in that little town of theirs. They always like to build in the valleys, those white people." The new Ford van rolled along the thruway as Jake Marsh pointed with one long brown finger out the window, the Indian accent coming out from between lips held carefully unmoving. The half smile of Trickster was on his face, a can of ginger ale in his other hand.

Behind the wheel, Tom Hill shook his head and laughed silently. "Yes," Tom said. "Yes."

"Oooh, Tommy, maybe there is a college in that town. Yes, there is a college there. Maybe it is the college where Sonny is going to school. We are always sending money to him at school. He has been in college for a long time now."

"Twelve years," Tom said, coughing.

"He always writes to us for money. He is a good boy. He is doing well in the college. Someday we will go and see him. All of us will go and see him. If he ever tells us where the college is."

"All of us," Tom said. "All hundred and twenty of us."

"Yes, Tommy, we will go for his graduation ceremony and have a giveaway. We will give away many blankets. Then he will come home. They say at the agency they have a good job for him. Janitor. That will be a good job for an Indian boy with a college degree. It will have vacation time with pay."

"Retirement benefits," Tom said, keeping his face straight.

"Tommy, you know he has a girl at the college. But he won't tell us about her. I think maybe she is white."

"She is white."

"But Sonny will not have any children by her. He is going to come back home and marry Dolores Antelope. She comes from a good family, even if they are a little stupid. Yes, when he comes home he will marry Dolores. She has been waiting for him."

"Only twenty years now," Tom said. Then he started laughing.

Jake laughed, too. They laughed at the person Jake had been for a while, that gentle, bemused tone in the voice, that simple way of saying and seeing that—even as they came close to mocking it—was laughing with them, laughing at them. Jake drained the can of ginger ale and began striking his palm against the dashboard, beating out the rhythm of a forty-niner.

> Someday we will be together
> till eternity, ah whey ya hi ya hi . . .

He sang it in a low voice at first, his voice rising higher with each repetition. Tom strained his own vocal cords to stay with the song until both men were singing in voices thin and quavering as the last note of a coyote's call. The song ended and they listened for a while to the silence. Tom's throat felt tight and good.

Jake began striking his palm against the dashboard again, trying to find another beat. "Funny," he said, "when I used to drink I could remember a thousand songs. Now it's hard to remember one." He crushed the ginger ale can in his hand and dropped it into the plastic litter bag hanging from the knob of the glove compartment.

The hills were rolling down to the river near the road. On top of some of them single pine trees stood. They looked like men with arms held out from their sides, waiting for something. Tom thought that for a moment, then shook his head. *No, not men, trees. The trees look like trees.* It had been a long time since he had seen them this way.

"When I was at Fort Grant," he said. Then he stopped. He had to let the words come together in the right way. Jake sat, waiting for him. Five miles passed. Then a red-tailed hawk glided over the road, angling toward the south. "There weren't a lot of Indians there," Tom said. "Most of them were Pimas or Papagoes. In for stealing something while they were drunk, most of them. One or two were in for murder. The murderers are the ones you can trust. The ones who forge checks are the worst. You can't trust them. But the murderers, you could always trust them. You could understand them. One of them was a guy from Oklahoma. His name was Harold Buffalo. Comanche. His uncle is that painter. I had met his sister in Tulsa once."

"Her name Mary?" Jake said.

"Yes, with a little boy. About six years old now."

"She's on the East Coast, too. She's up working for *Notes*."

"Ah-hah," Tom said. He shifted his hands on the wheel and pointed with his lips at the sign that read REST AREA. Jake shook his head and they passed the turnoff without slowing down. "There wasn't anything for us in that prison," Tom said. "It was so far out in the desert it cost wives and girl friends more than thirty dollars just to come and visit. It was called a rehabilitation center. A training center. For rehabilitation they would have us dig holes and then fill them up again. And for training they had us build walls. Long stone walls. They looked like the Great Wall of China, except they were only about three feet high, the walls we built. They had us build them at the base and up the side of the mountain that rose behind the prison. That mountain was beautiful. It was the best thing there. You could feel its breath blowing over the camp. But there was nothing for us inside Fort Grant, especially for the Indians. So we asked to be allowed to have a sweat lodge. There were sweat lodges in the other prisons, but none at Fort Grant, even though we had more than twenty Indians and we all knew we needed it. Damn."

"Right rear tire," Jake said.

Tom pulled the van over to the side of the road. The flat tire went *wha-that wha-that* on the pavement and then growled into the gravel. Both men got out and stretched. They walked up the side of the grassy bank and sat down. It was a crisp day in early September. The air was sweet to breathe as the taste of well water. Jake leaned on one elbow to look closely at a small plant.

"It says I should pick it," he said.

"Your uncle was the medicine man," Tom said. He looked at the plant. They were both smiling, but Jake pulled the small plant up and wrapped it in his handkerchief, leaving a little tobacco on the ground where a few grains of gravel had come up with the roots. They walked back to the van and began to change the tire. They worked with the slow ease of men who had spent years doing that sort of thing. When they were done, they spat, wiped their hands on the seats of their jeans, and got back in.

Jake sat behind the wheel. He started the engine. "What did you do next?" he said. He slipped the van into gear.

"First we did it their way. We went to the prison chaplain and asked him to be our sponsor. There was only one chaplain for all faiths—Methodist, Baptist, Catholic, Jewish, Mormon, even the Black Muslims. He was a Catholic priest from Boston, Father Malley. So thin we used to say he was scared to cross his legs for fear he'd cut his knees. Father Malley said it was not possible. That was when

Harold Buffalo spoke up. 'Sir,' he said, 'there is going to be a sweat lodge here. When something like that is going to happen you can't stop it.' "

"Did they interpret that as a threat?"

"They interpreted that as a threat." Tom smiled and looked out the window. "Ten miles," he said, reading the sign. "First they thought of transferring him out. Then they thought maybe that was what he wanted them to do. He'd asked to be transferred from Fort Grant twice before and been refused. Finally they decided to restrict his privileges and not let him take rec with everyone else. Harold didn't mind, though. He started running by himself every day. First he ran a mile every day. Then he ran two miles. By the time they decided it hadn't been a threat and let him back into population, he was running ten miles a day. He had been a Green Beret and knew a lot about survival in the desert. Maybe that was why they'd been worried about him. Everybody in Arizona remembered the Fox."

"I heard about the Fox in Nevada," Jake said. "Another Green Beret."

"He escaped from Florence. He was in for killing four men, two of them police. He knew they'd never give up on trying to catch him, but he didn't even try to get to Mexico. He just stayed out in the desert near the prison. Nights he'd sneak into the camps of the men hunting him and steal food. He even climbed back over the wall into the prison and left his calling card for them, right where the captain would step in it the next morning. It took them a long time to catch the Fox, but they say they finally did. Trapped him in a box canyon and shot him to pieces. But none of the prisoners ever saw his body. Some say he just stayed out there or finally did make it to Mexico. So they kept a close eye on Harold because they remembered the Fox. But all he did was just run, further and faster every day, around and around inside the fence." Tom pulled out a pack of Camels and shook two cigarettes loose. Jake took one, then lit both with his lighter. The smell of the tobacco was strong. Blue smoke filled the inside of the van. Jake jerked his head to the right and Tom nodded. They pulled off onto the exit.

A state police car was parked near the toll booths. Tom opened the glove compartment and slid the automatic pistol out without looking at it, his eyes held straight ahead. He put the gun between his legs and covered it with his red handkerchief. They stopped at the toll booth.

Jake smiled at the fortyish woman with dark hair in the booth. She looked as if her feet hurt, but she smiled back.

"Hi, chief," she said.

"Indians get to use this road free, don't they?" Jake said.

"You tell that to the people at the other end when you got on?" she said. She showed her teeth in a wide smile. "That's a nice ring you got there. Make it yourself?"

"They didn't give me any ticket and I did make the ring. You like it?"

"I like turquoise. Blue is a good color." She waved them on. "Have a nice day."

They turned onto the four-lane that led into the city.

"I think," Tom said, "the state cop in that car wasn't really sleeping. I think he was watching which way we were going."

"They aren't stupid these days," Jake said. "I'm sure he saw us take eighty-one south, right?"

"Right. No one is following us, though."

Jake looked into the rearview mirror. He swung the blue van to the left, crossed over the divider in the center of the road with a bump, swerved, and steered back into the northbound lane. He took the next exit. It led to the smaller road, which bypassed the city. "Unless they already got a chopper watching us, we're okay for a while," he said.

"What happened next," Tom said, "was that one morning Harold Buffalo was just gone. They found his pillows stuffed under his blankets. Even the bloodhounds couldn't pick up his scent. They looked everywhere for him and couldn't find him. He was gone that day and all that night. But the next morning when we looked up to the top of the peak above the prison, just at dawn, we saw the light of the fire and the smoke rising. It took them most of the morning to get up there. They found him sitting in front of the fire, just where he sat to pray and greet the dawn. 'It's a good day,' he said. Then he said, 'There is going to be a sweat lodge at Fort Grant.' " Tom leaned out the window and looked up, then back. "All clear," he said. He took two more cigarettes from his pack, lit both, and handed one to Jake.

"*Niaweh,*" Jake said.

"Everybody had seen that fire of Harold's. By now reporters had come from Tucson and they'd seen the smoke, too. So the guards hardly beat Harold up at all before they brought him back down and took him to the warden. When he got to the warden's office, Harold told the Man he knew how to get out anytime he wanted to. He could get out without anyone seeing him. He could teach other people how to do it, too. In fact, there were already nineteen others who knew how to do it. That was what he told the warden. Then he told him they needed a sweat lodge. Three days later, we had our first sweat at Fort Grant."

They were on a little highway on the other side of the city now. They turned onto an even smaller, winding road, which led down through the hills. On all sides the vegetation was thick. A rabbit ran in front of them and Jake slowed the blue van down. A raccoon walked across their path. To their right a roadside dump sprawled. Car bodies and garbage were piled by the roadside.

"Indian recycling station," Tom said. He took the crushed ginger ale can from the litter bag and tossed it out. It spun through the air and bounced off the cracked enamel side of an old G.E. refrigerator.

"If I was a state cop," Jake said, "I would set up a nice little roadblock at the edge of the reservation. Maybe around the next corner where this runs back into the state road." He pulled the blue van off the road and put on the emergency brake.

Tom took the duffel bag out of the back of the van and slung it over his shoulder. "Well, they won't have to look far to find this." He patted the blue van. "So long, Big Blue," he said.

"They're going to catch us," Jake said. He had picked up a long stick from the roadside. He was whittling at it carefully with the big knife he had taken from the sheath at his side. The turquoise ring glinted with sunlight as his hand moved with small quick strokes and the keen edge shaved off curls of wood.

"Not before we get to the mountaintop," Tom said. It was impossible to see his eyes behind the dark glasses, but Jake knew they were black and hard and laughing.

"Yes," Jake said. "It is good to go home." Together they walked into the trees.

AT HOME

by Frederick Busch

Northern Connecticut was heavy around us on a humid Sunday night, and while the children slept inside, Lee and I sat on our porch steps, looking across the road at our nearest neighbor's house as his lights, going out, left us alone in the world.

"Don't worry," Lee said, leaning against me. Her bare arm felt cooler than the night, and she smelled of Johnson's baby powder and Italian wine. "Don't worry," that's when I understood how worried I was.

The man who lives across the road from us has lived a disappointed life—a bad first marriage that lasted into his middle age, a second marriage that bred shouting and deep silences, a couple of sons he loves but toward whom he often is cruel, a manager's job in a small factory from which he was fired, an antique shop in his garage that hasn't made him much of a living, and cancer. Last year, physicians at the medical center told him he had five days in which to order his affairs. The cancer was between the heart and lungs, they said, with ganglia that reached to the kidney, the liver, the spleen.

As disappointing and ordinary as his life always seemed to me, it was valuable to him, and too complex for easy winding-up. He chose chemotherapy. A year and some months later, as hairless and as soft as an infant, lined and gaunt and yellow-white, he still is alive. He gains weight, prowls his little shop, bellows at his boys, and is, according to his doctors, probably going to live.

It seems necessary to me that I appropriate something of my neighbor's miracle, and I don't know how. I don't like him very much, and I refuse to fake affection because of his remission or rebirth. Nor do I wish to offer homilies to anyone on his account;

and even if I did, I wouldn't know what lesson to say he has taught me. His is a wonderful will, but possibly not always for his children and wife. His is a great good luck, but certainly not for me. So I think of him, stay out of his way—like most survivors he needs always to talk: about weight loss, diet, drugs, and pain—and I behave like a man who has found a handsome rickety chair in a little shop of antiques: I have no place to put it, and it never can hold my weight, but I insist upon taking it home with me, and moving it from room to room.

Years ago, when I was a junior editor in Greenwich, working on a controlled-circulation magazine that featured stories about business management, Lee and I took a long weekend for a visit with my parents in Millbrook. Lee was exhausted at the end of a year among fourth-graders. I was exhausted because I didn't know how to edit a business magazine but had, for months, been telling myself and my employers that I did. We drove in silence, the top of our Corvair down, our eyes watering because of the gasoline wind. And the silence was on account of not only fatigue but anticipation.

A year before, when I had taken Lee to meet my parents, my mother, after a long and difficult dinner, had said, "I've always hoped that my son would want to marry a woman from Africa." Lee, from Gary, Indiana, had shrugged her apologies for color and continent, and I had spoken desperately of Jomo Kenyatta and racial politics, and the evening had moved glacially toward bedtime—my mother sitting at the round claw-legged Victorian table, and my father, already feeble, in the rocker near the cold Franklin stove. On the drive home, Lee had said pushing a peanut with her nose through broken glass would be preferable to another weekend like that one.

But we had gone to Millbrook often enough afterward, for my father's heart was deteriorating. "It doesn't beat," he'd told me once. "The pacemaker ticks it for me. Here." And he had taken my hand by the wrist and had pushed it against the soft square shape inside his shirt. And each time I saw him again, I would think of the permanent softness in the wall of his chest, and of a little battery that, if I pressed my head near his heart, might hum a terrible small tune.

So we drove once more to Millbrook, and we sat around the dark circular table at which I had eaten boyhood dinners in Manhattan and Long Island, and which I had seen moved upstate while all Syosset had seemed to watch it float on the back of one of the seven Santini brothers toward the truck where my mother waited to see it safely stowed. We sat, with drinks from six to seven, with dinner from seven-thirty to nine. We sat as my mother told us about the handymen she was required by my father's weakness to engage—to clean the chimney, to fasten ice-melting cables over the side door, to attach new roofing, to scythe and mow their dozen acres, to remove the storm windows and put up the screens and paint the garage, and otherwise manage for them as my father couldn't. My father joked at first about his lack of energy, and then he swallowed some pills, and then he slowly moved to the rocker near the Franklin stove, where he squinted until my mother told him he must sleep.

Lee walked with him to his bedroom in the farthest downstairs wing, the room he had used as a weekend office before he was forced to retire. My mother had been waiting. Her face, which looked smoother and younger than a sixty-two-year-old's, clenched around the mouth, and she looked seventy. "Well," she said, as if it were the final word of an elaborate proof or undeniable argument.

"Dad seems pretty good," I said.

"Oh, *he's* fine, as fine as he can be. He's sick, but he's fine. He saves his energy; I'll say that for him."

I rose to clear the table, and I kept moving. I scrubbed the old table with a damp rag. I washed the dishes, although my mother told me to use the dishwasher; I swept the kitchen floor. My mother sat close to the edge of the table, her hand propping up her chin, her eyes bright and angry, her mouth pinched shut.

"There," I said.

She said, "There," to tell me that she'd understood my flight and was not charmed by boyishness.

"I'm sorry," I said, sitting again, across the table from her. "That you feel so trapped, I mean."

"Trapped is trapped," she said. "You don't desert somebody."

"After thirty-five years."

"Or thirty," she said, naming my age.

"You do get out, don't you?"

"I take walks. I run errands. I go to meetings of the Audubon Society if they're not too far away. Dad mustn't be alone too long. In case something happens."

I fled again, for coffee and an ashtray. When I was seated, I said, "You remember the time when I was in high school, or junior high; I don't remember which. You flew off to a convention someplace in the West? You were gone for a week or more, and when you were coming back, Dad made me dress up and drive with him to the airport to meet you—it was a surprise. He was very nervous. I don't remember ever seeing him that nervous again. And when you got off the plane and saw us, a kid in his sport jacket and Dad in his seersucker Saturday-at-the-office suit—he was even carrying flowers."

"Dad never understood I want *wild* flowers. You find them on long walks in the woods."

"And you started to cry."

"Because I saw how sad he was. How *baffled*."

"And you were trapped. Even before you got home. You almost left him, didn't you?"

"I almost didn't come back from Oregon."

"And Dad knew that?"

"He knew. Most of the time he just pretended that he didn't. He never *understood*, but he always knew."

"And now the kid's gone, and Dad's sick, and you feel that you have to stay here all the time."

Her eyes were wet by then, and I looked away, then went away. When I returned with more coffee for me and a cup for her, she was drying her eyes, and I was telling myself to remember for a long time that I hadn't been able to walk around the table and hug her, then.

"I take walks," she said in a shaky voice. "I run errands in the car. I get Dad his newspaper first thing in the morning because he doesn't know how to start the day without his *New York Times.* You know how I am about flowers. Years ago, for Valentine's Day, he gave me a very handsome, expensive crystal bud vase. For flowers you buy in a store. I threw it into the fireplace as hard as I could, and it broke. He's been afraid ever since to give me anything on Valentine's Day, so he finally learned. But this year, I gave him a present. It was a coffee mug. You know how he loves his morning coffee. It had red hearts all over it. And you know—he drinks his coffee from it every morning. He's such a sentimentalist."

Her eyes were tearing again. I was held to my place at the round gleaming table. I noticed that I was rubbing my stocking feet against the toes of the claw legs underneath. "I cut a heart-shape out of the front page of the *Times,*" she said. "I put it in the coffee mug when I gave it to him. And do you know—he keeps it in his bureau drawer? He's such a fool not to understand it!"

I could only nod. I could say only, as if it were twenty years before, "What, Mom?"

"What I was *tell*ing him. That he loved only *The New York Times.* What else could it mean? What would you think if Lee gave that to you?"

LIFE AT THE EQUATOR; OR, A METAPHYSICAL EXPOSITION OF THE CONCEPT OF LOVE

by Kelly Cherry

"Time is therefore a purely subjective condition of our
(human) intuition (which is always sensible, that is, so
far as we are affected by objects), and in itself, apart
from the subject, is nothing."
—Kant, *Critique of Pure Reason*

I

Arriving at the equator, he set up a beach umbrella and a folding
chair and arranged himself in the folding chair in such a way that
the umbrella shaded his face from the sun. The book that he placed
open upon his lap and proceeded to begin to read was about love.
He had a certain interest in love. He had never himself been in
love, but he thought he might be someday, and he wanted to be
prepared for the eventuality of that experience.

As the day wore on, it grew hotter. The sun beat down on the
beach umbrella; the sand at his feet shone like glass. He was wearing sandals, white trousers, a white linen jacket, and a white shirt
with a very pale yellow pinstripe. The shirt was open at his throat.
He had not brought sunglasses.

Every day he arrived at his place at the equator, setting up his
beach umbrella and his folding chair and taking out his book in this
way. It was his habit. As dusk encroached and the many hidden
birds and insects that live along the equator grew more vocal under

cover of night, he folded his folding chair and the beach umbrella and closed his book and returned to his hotel, which was a mere fifty yards from the equator.

II

Life at the equator varies at different places along the equator; however, at any given point along the equator, the sun rises at the same time every day.

One day shortly after the sun in this particular place on the equator had arisen, and shortly after the young man had arranged his chair, his umbrella, and his book and had begun to read about love, a young woman appeared. Her hair in all that bright light seemed startlingly dark, almost obscenely dark.

The young man at the equator watched the young woman settle herself at the equator.

The young woman, wearing a black bikini that set off her already accomplished tan, lay down upon a large yellow beach towel, caressed her bared skin with oiled palms, and, placing sunglasses over her eyes, fell, apparently, asleep.

Soon the young man realized that he was no longer reading his book about love. He was instead watching the young woman at the equator sun herself.

What country was this in? When did these two meet? But these are irrelevant questions.

The next day very much the same sequence of steps took place. Once again, the young man discovered himself unable to concentrate closely upon his book, although he did make some minor progress. The young woman spent most of the morning lying on her stomach with the bra of her bikini unhooked, her back to the sun and to the young man.

On the third day, the young man approached the young woman, asked her if she would care to dine, and, happily learning that she would, folded his chair, his umbrella, closed his book, helped her with her beach towel and her bra and her sunglasses and her suntan oil, and escorted her to the dining room of the hotel some fifty yards from the equator.

III

The book about love which the young man was reading is titled *Life at the Equator*. In it, this passage may be found:

People think love is an emotion. They think that love is something they can feel, or that it is something someone may someday feel for them. Love is not an emotion. Love is a condition for the possibility of perception, as space and time, but preeminently time, are such conditions. That is to say, just as space and time are pure intuitions of the human mind, so love is a pure intuition of the human mind, *a priori* to any perception that the mind may seize or receive.

Let us say even that the mind is located, is "geometrically" fixed, by a hypothetical outsider's constructing a triangle whose points are *S* for space, *T* for time, and *L* for love. Should any of these points, *S,T,* or *L,* be absent, triangulation will of course fail, and the mind in question will remain outside the realm of the wholly perceivable, nor will it be able wholly to perceive the world beyond itself; in other words, it will be something less than *really apparent* and *apprehending*.

Lacking the location in space, time, and love that would make it accessible to the perception of other minds, lacking the conditions by which fully to perceive the reality of other minds, it nevertheless may *be* real, to a degree if not to the highest possible degree, and consequently capable of affecting the world beyond itself.

We may further designate the hypothetical outsider *G* (for God).

IV

At night, long breezes trail through the room, rustling, an anxious, silken sound that makes the young man dream of women in ball gowns waltzing on waxed floors above deep dungeons in large houses. Memory is a flower that blooms at night. A young woman and a young man will lie on sweat-dampened sheets, shower and dry themselves with a yellow towel while a monkey chirrs in a cage in the hotel's lobby and small equatorial fish swim in an aquarium in their room. Clouds will rush by the opened shutters, threatening rain that will not come. In the morning, the sun will rise precisely at the hour and minute at which it arose this morning. The young woman will sun herself on the equator in her black bikini, her long black hair pinned above her nape, her eyes hidden behind black sunglasses. A young man dressed in a white linen suit and a white shirt with a pale yellow pinstripe will seat himself in a folding chair beneath a folding umbrella and begin to read about love.

BEFORE THE FIRING SQUAD

by John Chioles

The sound at first was a low moan, and you knew the momentum would build as soon as the hand-cranked siren, managed by teen-aged boys, would pick up speed. No matter where I was, my knees turned to jelly, my pulse quickened, instinctively I would look up the hill to the bell tower of the church feeling betrayed that I could not be up there; at least there, watching the crank turn, the sound didn't frighten me. But the watch at the bell tower was for the older boys. You had to be at least twelve. From atop, where the giant bell hung, the boys kept a lookout for movement of vehicles; on a clear day they could see seven kilometers in the distance, beyond the bend.

Their convoys came from the main road. The moment they turned the bend that brings you full face with the town, their approach would echo against the side of the mountain. A hollow reverberation. The siren had by then stopped, to be replaced now by the rumbling of their trucks and heavy artillery. A moan of a different kind. The boys would run from the bell tower down the narrow streets to their homes. In no time, the dissonance of the enemy, something as ugly, efficient, and foreign to these parts as the unclean death they brought, appeared and disappeared, taking away the sun, leaving behind clouds of dust. They rarely stopped. But if they did, it could only bring down the reign of terror on all our heads. Mostly, though, they rode through on their way to Mani, where they would embark on ships bound for North Africa. To that end, they would ride roughshod over the Arkadian mountains. What interested them most was to make sure they passed through the towns and hamlets without incident or delay, ready to crush any attempt at interference.

Their garrison of twelve soldiers stationed in the town wore mustard-colored uniforms, not the sinister black kind worn by the ones in the convoys. These soldiers seemed very young and curiously happy. Everyone said they spoke a softer kind of German, without the harsh sounds of those northern peoples; most of them knew ancient Greek even, and liked the lilting songs of Homer. Their weapons were limited and not always in evidence. The whole town was ready to swear that these youths had never fought even a skirmish, let alone been in a war. My father used to call them Hitler's boy-soldiers, sent to promote a peaceful occupation, playing on the conscience of the partisans, counting on their decency. And, a curious thing, these young soldiers were never ambushed; none of them died in the everyday activity along these mountains, the daily sabotaging of the main artery, the only asphalt road leading down to the sea. While killing was the order of the day during that spring—ten townspeople executed for the death of one dark-uniformed German—these twelve had become practically the mascots of the town.

"I don't want you talking to this Fritz so much," Father said one day. "Everybody treats him like one of us. It isn't right." All the nice Germans we called Fritz and all the mean ones Ludwig; except that Fritz was really the name of my friend.

"He's harmless," I said. "And sometimes he brings his ration of chocolate and biscuits to share."

"He's the enemy," Father retorted the way he did when he would have no more discussion.

But the siren prevented any further talk. They came late in the afternoon of that day. My father was caught unawares. One convoy had already passed earlier, and he had run to the mountain and back again. They rarely had more than one a day. His reflexes were so swift that he practically knocked me over when he jumped to his feet.

"Put your warm sweater on and let's go." He had never taken me with him before. Women and children never ran to the mountain. The siren was for the men, whether they were part of the road sabotage teams or not. My father often stayed in the mountains for days; we never knew what he did there. "Hurry, we have no time. We'll take the back way so Fritz will not spot us. Your mother will know I've taken you with me."

The small garrison, our German mascots, lived across the street from us. They had requisitioned the best two-storied house, using the ground floor as offices and the second floor as living quarters. They were fully aware of the siren, but they pretended it came from the partisan stronghold in the mountain. Some said they even welcomed it; it gave them time to put on battle outfits, grab their guns, and move, a fierce-looking patrol, along the road. They never asked about the men of each household; their frequent absences from home they were content to believe had to do with working in the fields and vineyards. So Fritz had never asked about my father. Much like any of my friends, he was shy in his presence and avoided passing by whenever it was obvious Father was at home. Often he would come over to show us photos of his parents and his sisters, tell my mother how homesick he was, express joy or sadness whenever he would receive mail from home. And always my mother would find something to give him by way of comfort, a bunch of grapes or chestnuts or a few raisins. But whenever Father was at home it was understood he would never come over. He seemed no more than a boy and was treated much like the rest of us.

"Run faster! They're getting greedy today, and they could be mean." As we ran through brush foliage I would scrape my legs and thought how nice it will be when I get to wear long trousers in another year or so.

"When we get on top I'll pick some wild tea leaves and camomile buds for Mother. We don't have to come right back, do we?"

"We'll stay as long as we have to. Till they're gone." My father's furrowed brow told me this was not a usual run. The enemy was changing its routine; that meant everything would become unpredictable.

"Whoever is not alert, and doesn't expect the worst, will never know the unexpected when it comes his way," my father was saying to his friends when we reached the thick forest of pines. Below us, like ants in the distance, carefully covered heavy artillery rolled along the asphalt road. The atmosphere was highly charged. An unusually large number of people had taken to the mountain. The mood had changed as the sun went away and a cold mid-afternoon chill set in. All the world turned dark green and it smelled of rain, even the canvas covering the moving guns and trucks below took on the color of running oil in the absence of the sun.

"It's best to do nothing for a couple of days. They'll have patrols everywhere," one of the older men was saying to Father.

"We could've blown the far bridge yesterday. We should have been warned about this."

"Maybe this is only the beginning of moving out their heavy stuff. It's up to us."

My presence in this adult conversation went unnoticed. Yet I knew I should not be hearing what was being said. So I slipped away quietly. Nearby, some goats beat their grazing rhythm on the bushes; they made the acanthus bob up and down. I had no time to wonder why the goats seemed so nervous. Just then I stepped on a dried branch which flew up at me, my feet got tangled, and I came tumbling a good ten meters down the slope. Though I was stunned, I felt hardly any pain. But the fear was real, for I heard the pounding of a machine-gun and felt the whistle of bullets flying above my head. I stayed down, hardly breathing. The machine-gun, rattling but unable to pin down movement in the vast forest, moved on along a horizontal line, then stopped.

As the moan of the convoy became more distant, I felt my father's hand lifting me up. I was more ashamed than hurting. Not until I stood upright did I see the blood running down my leg and a whole patch of skin from my knee hanging upside down.

"It's nothing," my father said, and quickly used his handkerchief to patch it up.

"It doesn't hurt any," I said.

"It will. Why did you come this far? Didn't we say we never come into full view of the road?"

"I fell down."

"You'll be all right. I'm going to have to send you home with your cousins. Your mother should take care of that knee."

I said nothing but followed sheepishly the downward path, my father's handkerchief tied behind my left knee. He had made the knot too tight and I felt a numbing pain but did not let on to my older cousins. Father had whispered something to them, that they should take care of me, I guessed, so I did not want to show I needed looking after.

At home there was commotion; our window was open. Mother had been putting my baby sister to sleep; she had lit the oil lamp. Across the way, the German soldiers were playing phonograph records, their usual sad music. (Only, Fritz had told me many times that their music was not at all funereal as the townspeople thought—it was happy and exultant, he'd say; still, it sounded sad to me.) Nobody got wind that I limped into the house at dusk. Stealth was always my strong point.

When Mother saw me, there was an uproar and a lot to answer for. I explained quickly, and, seeing that my wound was still bleeding, she softened her tone as to the mystery of my whereabouts all afternoon.

"Here, sit down. Let's have a look."

I clenched my teeth while she cleaned the whole knee with a sponge. It stung good and sharp now.

"You must be starved, too. Fritz has brought you a surprise. Uncover that bowl on the table. It's all for you."

A bowl of food, rice with bits of chicken, cubed chunks of meat in a thick white soup. Never had I eaten anything so tasty before. It came from a fancy tin that my friend received on special occasions. If each of us had to cherish one memory of food that would make our taste buds water, Fritz's bowl of chicken with rice on that evening would be mine. I felt no pain from the leg while I ate to my heart's content, nor did I notice that he had come to the window, looking in, and already my mother had silently shown him my knee. In no time, he returned with a first-aid kit and set about to dress the wound. He spoke admonishingly to me in German, but also found the right phrases in Greek to let me know he was unhappy with me.

"Children don't become partisans, you know." But his smile gave him away. He only meant I should be careful. Then he became serious again. Whenever he looked serious his eyebrows went from the straw color of his hair to a darker shade and he looked older. Even his eyes did not keep their blue but went dark like the sea.

It seemed a cloud hung over the fate of the twelve German soldiers of our town. They would be transferred soon. They might be taken to the front lines. Everything was becoming very unpredictable, he was telling my mother. I had never seen Fritz so sad before. He hung his head low as he pulled out of his trouser pocket a letter he had just received from his mother. She lived, he told us, in a big city in his country that was being bombed constantly now, and they had even less to eat than we did.

"I do not know if I will see them again."

"You will, you will. All this will soon be over and you'll get to go home. You'll see," my mother consoled as best she could.

The next morning the news was out. The whole town became concerned. If they left, would they be replaced by the black-uniformed ones? What would be in store for us? The neighborhood around us began to treat them like departing friends; they offered them sweets, dried fruits and nuts, and whatever parting hospitality they could. In their turn, the boy-soldiers responded with moist eyes, uncertain, and very scared of the weeks ahead. My mother always said, remembering those last few hours, not one of them looked a day over sixteen.

An old philosopher who dwelled along the dusty plains of Asia Minor once said there will come a Great Year whose summer will be a World Conflagration. That's just what happened to us that summer. On the very day they came to collect their soldiers and depart for good, they also set fire to nearly every house in the town.

Activity along the mountains had been fierce lately. The far bridge had been blown up; so had the narrow pass beyond. The siren howled urgently at full speed on that day. When they turned the bend they began to slow down, rolling into town at a snail's pace to cover for their foot soldiers, who darted off the road, torches in hand, setting fire to every house, every barn, every haystack in sight. That way they took a long time to get to us who lived near the square; but we had seen the smoke and the flames and we knew what was in store for us.

My mother refused to run away, hoping, with children in hand, she might at least save the house. But as the confusion around us got worse, the shooting in all directions, the trails of smoke, the terror-filled sounds of homes bursting open under the flame—no one could possibly be reasoned with, no one caught up in such careening panic. Every black Ludwig looked like a madman in passionate play with fire. During these terrible moments Fritz was nowhere to be seen.

We stood at the door of our house and watched the commotion all around us, until a burst from an automatic hit near our feet and we were routed and shown the way to the open space in the middle of the square. While she held the baby and I held on to her sleeve, my mother shuffled us to the gathering place. We never looked behind. But we knew. All around the square the trucks were moving slowly, never at rest, making a terrible din, which drowned out the cries of the dozen or so women and children huddled in the middle. We were shoved against them, and for the first time I saw a number of our town mascots, the boy-soldiers, armed to the teeth, some guarding us, some being given stern orders by an officer, while others were already jumping onto the moving trucks with all their gear.

The officer pointed in our direction and began to scream an order to his subordinates. Three of them rushed over to our group and kneaded us all into a straight line. I saw to my horror that Fritz was one of them. His eyes were dark and furious, hardly anyone recognized him; his whole body and movements had taken on a different shape. I felt a crushing disappointment. He looked old now like the others.

Their mission accomplished, the three ran back to the officer. He gave them what seemed final instructions and climbed into the cab of his moving truck. The three raced to set up just ahead of us a machine-gun with tripod at the front of the barrel. One of them brought the ammunition, and I saw Fritz reach into the box and bring out a magazine, which he loaded onto the gun. Just then, whistles began blowing, those piercing kind they use at train platforms to signal an imminent departure. They didn't want to remain sitting targets for the partisans, so they had to make haste.

Suddenly the motors got louder; speed was only seconds away. Fritz, now arguing with the other two soldiers, appeared even more fierce. They were pushing to get behind the machine-gun, but he seemed to win out. While they rushed to jump on the trucks, he fell on his belly and hugged the gun, groping for the trigger. We were all frozen with fear. I searched for his eyes in utter disbelief. Time fled and backtracked toward me again. I was aware only that the trucks were moving faster, that Fritz was frozen in his place, his right hand now on the ground, too far from the latch of the trigger. Then in a flash he jumped up, lifted the gun from its tripod, and let it sing half across the sky, while in the same motion he chased the last truck, leaping headfirst into it. His torso, writhing wildly to get his weight into the truck, was the last thing I saw of Fritz, who had in those last dancerlike movements transformed his body once more into the boy that he really was, waving good-bye at us with his legs.

LIGHT SLEEPER

by Charles H. Clifton

Serious. That is the advantage my wife, Sylvia, has over me. She is always serious, like the night, when everything casts long shadows. My advantage, in turn, is that I am playful. This is also a disadvantage. The mother of my wife's best friend, Gloria, calls my wife "Saliva." It's a joke that Gloria and her mother have together. The two of them sit in Gloria's mother's tiny kitchen and titter about my wife's first name over herbal tea—cinnamon, rosemary, camomile, all names as beautiful to me as the name of my wife, Sylvia. Gloria is homely but intelligent. Why is it that the word *saliva* sometimes pops into my head and I can do nothing to prevent it?

Sylvia. Sylvia. Saliva. Of course Gloria and her mother are only joking, being playful. It's a little secret. When Sylvia is at her most sociable and cheerful, she is liable to start talking about Gloria, how she accepts the burden of her mother so resolutely, how her mother accepts the burden of her arthritis with such stoical equanimity, and the echoes of laughter from the tidy kitchen make me morose. At the end of the day I am all played out. When my head hits the pillow I fall instantly into a deep sleep beyond dreams that is like death's other face. Sometimes just before I drop off I hear laughter. Once Sylvia, seized by the irrational as she so often is during the long night, even held a mirror to my lips. Sylvia is a light sleeper.

There is a stone statue in our little village park called "Light Sleeper." It was sculpted by a young man who went off to graduate school to study art and who now works in Chicago. For a long time he was thought to be feckless, but now he is quite respectable. The statue is of a recumbent, featureless young man whose head once rested on a stone pillow long since broken off by vandals so that now the boy's head rests at a forty-five-degree angle in midair, giving the blank eyes a look of furtive anguish. The reason I am talking to you now is that my head has not yet hit the pillow; it has only begun its slow decline. When it completes its fall, I will be plumbing the uncanny depths like a benthic creature in its cave unable to speak a word of the secrets it knows so well.

I used to have conversations with my son at bedtime during which we would remember the first and last things we had said. Schoolbus to the moon, dime to diamond, angle to angel: We would retrace our steps over the geography of language as one place led oddly to another. The things we thought of were amazing to us, how one word caught another. When his teacher asked the class what they had eaten for supper the previous night, he said, "Owl meat."

Thud. It was just a little noise, from upstairs.

"Someone is in the house," said Sylvia, lifted from the bed like a marionette on strings.

"It's just the cat knocking over the guitar," I said, for I had heard a ghostly chord, a thrum after the thud. Once, we slept in the back bedroom of the beachhouse at Laguna Beach loaned to us by Gloria's mother, who thought we needed a vacation. It was during the Laguna Beach Living Masterpieces festival, where people get themselves up like famous works of art. Then, after posing, the famous works of art walk away. That time it was I who woke up in the middle of the night to see a shadow moving purposively toward the bed. For a moment I thought it was Gloria, naked underneath her quilted housecoat. Then I realized it must be a stranger, a burglar; just pretend to sleep and let him steal awhile and leave. But what if he had a knife or tire jack? I didn't want to be murdered in my pajamas, not the red striped ones. So I sat bolt upright and said in a big important voice, "Good morning." Of course it was my son, lost on his way to the bathroom. Though Sylvia is a light sleeper, she never woke up. That's the story of how I saved us from the burglar.

Ring.

Sylvia answers the phone. It's getting to be morning now and my head has not yet hit the pillow, though it's declining fast.

"It's Gloria. She wants us to come for dinner."

"Tell her I want owl meat."

"Silly. We'll be delighted. . . ."

I'd like to stay awake to watch Sylvia get dressed. She is already glowing with the astral colors of early morning. She has a certain aroma, like a fingerprint, her own bouquet, flowers, red firecracker salvia, night-blooming cereus.

THE SEAMSTRESS

by Wanda Coleman

Mama comes home tired from the sweatshop. She is so tired her body stoops—the weight of slaving on the double-needle power sewing machine from seven-thirty in the morning till four-twenty in the afternooon. So tired she can barely push open the door. So tired we are silenced by the impact of it on her face.

Mama comes home to the imperfect dinner almost ruined by the eleven-year-old anxious to please. To the petulant ten-year-old eager to play outside. To the five-year-old banging on his red fire engine. To the three-year-old crying for lack of attention.

Mama comes home to us so tired she must lie down awhile before she does anything.

So tired, baby, I could cry.

She goes into her room and collapses into the bed. I watch from the hallway. She cries for a few minutes—a soft plaintive whine. I go and set the table and serve the meal. I fix her a plate and take it to her on a tray. She is too tired to come to the table. *So tired, baby, I could die.*

We eat and my older brother and I do the dishes. Papa has not come home. He calls. I take the phone to her. Her side of the conversation is full of pain, anxiousness, and despair. So tired she sounds.

But it's the beginning of the school term. And we need clothes for school. We need. And I watch her rise.

"You know, it was hard today. The white man boss don't want to pay me what I make. I work fast. Faster than the other girls. They get jealous of me. They try and slow me down. My floor lady is an evil witch. She won't give me the good bundles. And she lets some girls take work home to make extra money. But not me.

"I don't care. I'm so fast I do it all right there. And those Mexican girls—they make me so angry. They all the time afraid. Won't speak up for their rights. Take anything they'll give 'em. Even work for less money, which weakens all our purses. We say, 'Hey—don't be afraid.' I don't understand them Mexican girls."

She fills my ears with her days when she comes home from work. I am the one she talks to. There is no one there to listen but me. Sometimes Papa is gone three or four days without word. And my brothers—little boys too impatient for such stuff as a woman's day is made of. And her few friends—she talks to them by phone now and then. She's too proud to tell them how hard it is for us. And since the hard times, few friends come by.

She goes into the bathroom, washes her face in cold water, and dries her eyes. She goes into the front room and sits at the coffee table and slowly, carefully, counts out the tickets that will determine her day's wage. I help her make the tally by reading off the numbers aloud. Her eyes are too tired to see them even with glasses. She marks them down on a sheet of paper and adds them up. Satisfied, she gathers them up and binds them with a rubber band.

I bring her fresh water from the kitchen. She drinks it in long slow swallows and then gets up slowly and goes over to her single-needle power machine, sits and picks up the pieces that will become my new dress. Within the hour I will try it on. She will pin up the hem and then sit in front of the television and stitch it in. And tomorrow the girls at school will again envy the one who always has new clothes.

But now I watch her back curve to the machine. She threads it with quick, dark cedar hands. She switches on the lights and the motor rumbles to life and then roars. Zip zip zip—the dress takes shape.

And this tired. I wonder as I watch her. What must it be like? And what makes her battle it so hard and never give in?

THE HIRED GIRL

by Sheila Cudahy

That summer the gypsy moths attacked the woods behind our house. In the morning I could see them from my bedroom window, disgusting wormy things swinging among the branches on the long sticky threads they spun from their insides and at night even though I pulled the pillow over my head I could hear the strange noise they made, a sound like raindrops falling from leaf to leaf after the rain has stopped. "They're crapping, that's what they're doing," my brother Edmund said, but I knew the trees were being eaten alive. By October the maples and oaks had turned into skeletons. Only a big clump of overgrown bayberry bushes at the edge of the woods still had their leaves. My father told me to stop worrying about the trees. Nature would take care of them. At the end of a three-year cycle the gypsy moths would die, actually explode from a virus.

"Nature's super-disgusting," I said, but both my brothers enjoyed the idea of masses of self-destructing bugs popping like bubble gum in the woods.

Edmund and Willie and I quarreled a lot all that summer. Somehow we always felt angry and the minute our father left for the farm supply warehouse in town we'd gang up viciously two against one. The boys would torment me for being a girl. Other times one of them would team up with me. If the odd one happened to be Willie, it wasn't much of a battle, because he's the youngest and kind of small for his age. By the end of a hot afternoon the three of us would be kicking and pummeling whoever happened to be within reach. Then someone would shout "I'll get you next time," and, too exhausted to fight, we'd each go off alone, bruised and aching to let the anger build to a new pitch.

This was the stage we'd reached one dusty October afternoon.

Willie was in the woods behind the bayberry bushes, hiding from Edmund, who was lying flat on his belly in the tall grass near the house. I could see both of them from my bedroom window, where I sat sulking and listening to the gypsy moths. Willie had a Canada goose in his arms. Every fall a flock of wild geese stop to rest and feed in our pond. After a few days they leave. Willie was struggling hard to hug the bird against his chest. He lifted one hand to pat it on the head. The goose honked, flapped, paddled the air, and finally twisted its neck and bit him, first on one cheek and then on the other, right on the bone below the eye. Willie let out a yelp. That's when Edmund, who'd been crawling toward the bushes, pulled the trigger. The goose broke free and tumbled down the hill to its mate in the pond. Willie crumpled and disappeared behind the bushes. I heard the front door open and our father call, "I'm home." Martha, that dumb hired girl who was supposed to keep an eye on us, was waiting for him and primping in front of the hall mirror. That's all she ever did—wiggle and primp—and every afternoon when he came into the house she'd pounce on him like a puppy, but this time, hearing the shot, she ran into my room, which is just off the front hall, and began screaming for him. I knew he'd come rushing to her, so I jumped on my bed and closed my eyes tight so as not to see him getting upset and Martha in her red dress wriggling around him.

As his heavy footsteps crossed the room Martha bawled, "Edmund's killed William."

My father dashed out and by the time I got to the window he was climbing through the bayberry bushes. Martha, still bawling, stood next to me and watched.

"You dumb stupid disgusting-as-a-gypsy-moth girl," I snarled. "We've had lots like you in this house, only prettier than you, and they've all gone."

It was true that since our mother's death there had been—not exactly lots—but quite a few Marthas, but none had been as pretty or as young as this one. None had stayed as long.

I must have shocked her, because she stopped crying and stared at me with her stupid blue eyes. Then my father's shouting for her to call Dr. Mason sent her to the kitchen phone.

Lying on the porch sofa, Willie looked like a small dead clown, his face chalky except for a red spot on each cheek.

"Cold water and a washcloth, Martha," my father bellowed although she was standing in front of me right next to him.

Edmund had disappeared into the toolshed and before Martha returned—the dummy brought a plastic pail with a dishrag floating in it—Dr. Mason had finished poking Willie in the ribs and was pulling back an eyelid the way they do in the movies to show you that the person is dead. Willie squirmed, sat up, and said his head hurt. Dr. Mason told him that he had hit it on a rock when the goose had knocked the wind out of him.

"Powerful birds, Canadas," the doctor said, "and beautiful, but they are wild birds. They don't want you to pet them."

Willie blinked and lay down again.

While my father was walking Dr. Mason to his car, Martha tried to dab Willie's cheeks with the wet rag but he knocked it out of her hand and Edmund came squealing out of the toolshed and onto the porch.

"Dumb Martha's got blood all over her dress," he chanted, dancing around her.

She looked down at her skirt where the water had turned the red to an even brighter crimson. Then she called us a lot of bad names, said that because we were so wicked God had taken our mother away and this time He'd punish us but good. The thought of God reaching down like King Kong and plucking up our mother stunned us, and when we didn't answer back Martha went into the house and slammed the door to her room.

Our father got supper out of the freezer: pizza with sausage and chocolate swirl ice cream. We ate on the porch so Willie could stay quiet, but our father didn't seem to be hungry and when I asked if I could have his ice cream he just nodded without looking at me. After we had finished eating he told us there would be no school the next day and perhaps for several days because of a teachers' strike. We would be left on our own until he could find someone to take care of us and the house. He wanted us to help one another instead of fighting all the time.

The next morning it rained, which seemed to silence the gypsy moths. We couldn't think of anything to do in the house, so we went outdoors and walked down toward the pond, where the wild geese were floating silently. As we approached they roared out of the water, a great thundercloud of dark wings in the wet air. Edmund was in front of Willie and me and he was first to see it lying at the edge of the pond, its long neck stretched out toward the water. Willie began to cry and I did too when I saw the bullet wound.

We dug a hole behind the bayberry bushes. Before we closed the grave Edmund ran to the toolshed and I guess to prove to Willie how sorry he was he came back and put the twenty-two down next to the Canada.

"Wild geese have only one mate forever an' ever," Willie sobbed as Edmund and I shoveled dirt into the hole. "They're monogagus."

We knew what he meant and when we got back to the empty house we each went to our own room and closed the door.

THE SOCK

by Lydia Davis

My husband is married to a different woman now, taller than I am, about six feet tall, very thin, and of course he looks shorter than he used to and his head looks a little smaller. She's not really what I had in mind for him. I had thought of someone shy and friendly and a little dumpy—wide hips, sandals. But who am I to choose?

They came out here last summer for a few weeks to see my son, who is his and mine. There were some touchy moments, but there were also some good times, though of course even the good times were a little uneasy. The two of them seemed to expect a lot of accomodation from me, maybe because she was sick—in pain and sulky, with circles under her eyes. They would walk up slowly from the beach to my house and shower there and later walk away clean in the evening with my son between them, hand in hand. I gave a party and they sailed in and impressed my friends and danced with each other and stayed till the end. I made them a picnic once. They used my phone and other things in my house. I went out of my way for them, mostly because of our boy. I thought we should all get along for his sake. By the end of their visit I was tired.

The night before they went, we had a plan to eat out in a Vietnamese restaurant with his mother. His mother was flying in from another city, and then the three of them were going off together the next day, to the Midwest. His wife's parents were giving them a big wedding party so that all the people she had grown up with, the tall blond farmers and their families, could meet him.

When I went downtown that night to where they were staying, I took what they had left in my house that I had found so far: a book, next to the closet door, and somewhere else a sock of his. I drove up to the building and I saw my husband out on the sidewalk flagging me down. He wanted to talk to me before I went inside. He told me his mother was in bad shape and couldn't stay with them, and he asked me if I would please take her home with me later. Without thinking, I said I would. I was forgetting the way she would look at the inside of my house and how I would clean the worst of it while she watched.

In the lobby, they were sitting across from each other in two armchairs, these two tall and handsome women, one very dark, one very fair, both wearing heavy lipstick, different shades, both frail, I thought later, in different ways, both in need of a lot of attention from a man. The reason they were sitting here was that his mother was afraid to go upstairs. It didn't bother her to fly in an airplane, but she couldn't go up more than one story in an apartment building. It was worse now than it had been. In the old days she could be on the eighth floor if she had to, as long as the windows were tightly shut.

Before we went out to dinner my husband took the book up to the apartment, but he had stuck the sock into his back pocket without thinking when I gave it to him out on the street and it stayed there during the meal in the restaurant, where his mother sat in her black clothes at the end of the table opposite an empty chair, sometimes playing with my son, with his cars, and sometimes asking my husband and then me and then his wife questions about the peppercorns and other strong spices that might be in her food. Then after we all left the restaurant and were standing in the parking lot he pulled the sock out of his pocket and looked at it, wondering how it had got there.

It was a small thing, but later I couldn't forget the sock, because here was this one sock in his back pocket in a strange neighborhood way out in the eastern part of the city in a Vietnamese ghetto, by the massage parlors, and none of us really knew this city but we were all here together and it was odd, because I still felt as though he and I were partners, we had been partners a long time, and I couldn't help thinking of all the other socks of his I had picked up, stiff with his sweat and threadbare on the sole, in all our life together from place to place, and then of his feet in those socks, how the skin shone through at the ball of the foot and the heel where the weave was worn down; how he would lie reading on his back on the bed with his feet crossed at the ankles so that his toes pointed at different corners of the room; how he would then turn on his side with his feet together like two halves of a fruit; how, still reading, he would reach down and pull off his socks and drop them in little balls on the floor and reach down again and pick at his toes while he read, and sometimes he shared with me what he was reading and thinking about and sometimes he didn't know whether I was there in the room or somewhere else.

I couldn't forget it later, even though after they were gone I found a few other things they had left, or rather his wife had left them in the pocket of a jacket of mine—a red comb, a red lipstick, and a bottle of pills. For a while these things sat around in a little group of three on one counter of the kitchen and then another, while I thought I'd send them to her, because I thought maybe the medicine was important but I kept forgetting to ask, until finally I put them away in a drawer to give her when they came out again, because by then it wasn't going to be long, and it made me tired just to think of it.

THE HERMIT JOURNALS IX

by Jack Driscoll

IX

While you're in the blind, motionless, huddled low in the branches, listening for twig-snap or leaf-rustle, lots of memories lope through your mind. Surrounded by popples, the leaves yellow-green, brilliant against the flat rust of oaks, I'm thinking again about Johnny, how, as soon as I got my driver's license, he would send me out alone with the wrecker on road calls. Not accidents up on the highway, but out in the country to start a stalled car or tow it back to the station. Sometimes he let me use the wrecker to go bow hunting after work.

One Sunday, early November, I'm on my way out to the Karlin Hills, but first I have to swing across Bush Road to jump-start Blossom and Earl Wyatt's old Cadillac again, dull, flake-metal blue, 1962. I'm wearing my camouflage jumpsuit, camouflage gloves, and bandanna tied Gypsy-style around my head. I don't like hunting with hats, the brims always interfering with the clean draw of the bow. And my face is streaked black to break the glare. It's a long driveway, rutted, bumpy, and I'm in third gear going too fast, swerving, holding tight to the wheel, the tow-bar chains and crowbar and empty beer cans bouncing and clanking in the back. From a distance Blossom, walking from the house, looks like a young girl, hair red and cropped short, and she's wearing loose jeans, faded, a pair of new tennis shoes. But close up, when I step down out of the truck, her face quivers as if darkness is pushing out, cold from under her thin white skin.

Earl is inside. I can see right through the house, through the two picture windows, and Earl between them, a shadow, the lake calm behind him, and across the water, the hills. Blossom smiles, slides behind the steering wheel, says nothing while I lift both hoods and attach the jumper cables. I nod and she turns the key, the battery so dead even the juice from the wrecker won't turn her engine over. There's a light north wind and somewhere, coming down on the lake, geese honking. I wedge a block of wood on the wrecker's accelerator to beef up the charge, jiggle the cables, and wait. Surprising me from behind, Earl whispers, "There's a battery in the garage." Whispers it not because there's one there, not because it could ever start the car. He says it in desperation, like it's the only conversation possible, like he's rehearsed that one sentence all day. I turn around as if he's called to me from a long distance or from a dream. A watch cap is pulled low over his forehead, and he says it again, moving closer. His mouth stays open as if he can't breathe through his nose, as if he's going to be sick, these words shifting some old illness inside his belly. I turn away, a little nervous, and when I brush some maple leaves from the dented hollow between the hood and fender, Earl circles to the other side of the car, raises one knotted hand, almost blue, and tries, with all seventy-six years of concentration, head tilted, to lift a single leaf, tries to will it between his twisted fingers. But the leaves, bright red, seem locked in the metal, locked beneath a thin film of ice. Blossom stares through the windshield. Low in her seat, hand still on the key, she waits, patient, the tinted glass darkening her brown eyes.

There is a set of antlers mounted above the garage door. Earl does not remember the antlers are there, and he has turned away from me now that Blossom, without instruction, turns the ignition and the Cadillac purrs, despite the squirrel's nest over the carburetor, the dirty oil, the miles worn deep into the bald tires. Pressing open the electric window, she calls to Earl, who's pointing down the driveway, the white tails of three deer disappearing into the silent woods.

SURVEYORS

by John Dufresne

There were six rows of twelve tomato plants each. Each plant was pruned to a single stem and tied with ribbons of plaid flannel to sturdy five-foot-tall hickory stakes. Training the vines made the weeding and the liming easier, he said. It exposed the fruit to more sunlight, which produced a richer color and a sweeter taste. Glossy, elliptical Earlianas bunched in clusters on tender-vined plants. He also grew Burbanks with thick, solid skins and juicy flesh. These were his favorites. The huge Bonny Bests were brilliantly red, flattened and globular in shape, and often swelled in size to six inches across. He gave these away like trophies to his friends. The littered, overweeded lot next to his apartment building had become my grandfather's tomato garden. And every July evening in 1953, the year of the polio epidemic, he and I would finish supper and sit out on the grass beside the cinder driveway and watch the garden.

He was a housepainter and a difficult man at times. Whenever he wore one of his two suits he drank too much. Every time he drank too much, he took off his leather belt and strapped somebody. One night after returning from a nephew's wedding in Lowell, he locked his wife and children out of the house, fired four .22-caliber bullets into the walnut body of a console radio, and hid all of the food from the icebox under his bed. That was before I arrived for the summer, and before the garden was planted.

I carried his green glass bottle of warm Tadcaster ale like a chalice to our grass seats. He wore a beige straw hat with a narrow downturned brim and a seersucker band. He surveyed the garden, his green eyes inspecting each plant in turn. He stood up, picked his teeth with the edge of a matchbook, took off the hat, and fanned his face. His thin chestnut hair was even then graying at the temples. The pleated brown-flannel trousers were zipped but un-buttoned and were held up by olive Y-back suspenders that followed the white paths of his T-shirt straps over his large shoulders. I see the ones, he said, and flopped away in his cordovan slip-ons to gather our dessert.

My tomato smelled of linseed oil from the touch of his short thick fingers. He drew a yellow shaker, shaped like a tiny ear of corn, from his pocket, took his first taste of tomato, and sprinkled salt into the bite. He told me the Depression story. He had lost his home, a seven-room cottage that he had built himself with the weekend help of six of his fifteen brothers. The red house sat on a shaded avenue away from the factories. It had a backyard large enough for two pear trees, a rhododendron bush, and a small vegetable garden. He wiped his stiff-bristled mustache with a hand-kerchief and then erased a thin pink river meandering down my wrist. That's why, he said, he hadn't deposited one dime in a bank for twenty-three years. That's why his savings were stashed like memories where no one else can find them—locked in steel boxes and hidden in the secret cavities of floors and walls and ceilings.

The fussy old French priests in this parish are as crooked as ward bosses, he said. Every one of them. Joe McCarthy is the only politi-cian in this country who cares about poor people, he said. We're going to make him president. We had watched Ted Williams play baseball for the first time that summer on my grandfather's new twenty-one-inch Motorola television. My grandfather was captivated by the enormous beauty of Mr. Williams's perfect act of defiance, that intelligent disregard for the world, its probabilities, and its physics. That swing, he said, it's so sudden and thunderous. That thunder is art. Mr. Williams wins even when he strikes out because of the impertinence of his challenge. Mr. Williams knows that he will line a double into the gap next time.

No, those aren't telescopes, he said. They're transits. The men are surveyors. They've come back. I returned with another bottle of ale and saw him talking with a young man in a Sanforized green jumpsuit. The man wore a Yankee baseball cap on the back of his head so that the bill pointed skyward. He stood near the edge of the garden between rows of Burbanks and held a striped range pole with his right hand. When he blushed at something my grandfather said, he looked like another tomato plant. They're going to build a house, my grandfather said. They start tomorrow. But it's our garden, I said. But it's not our land, he said.

In the morning he dressed for work in his white bib overalls, white shirt, and white Pratt & Lambert painter's hat, and sat quietly at the kitchen table, drinking coffee. He heard the horn and walked outside and told his friend Studley to go on without him; he would catch a bus to work later. He carried a galvanized tub to the garden and began a final harvest. By the time the flatbed truck delivered the bulldozer and its driver to the lot, he had filled and unloaded the tub three times. He gave me a grocery bag from Candella's market and told me to fill it with tomatoes and give them to the driver. We have enough tomatoes. I refused. He's going to kill our plants, I said. The man is doing his job, he said.

We took our grass seats and watched the bulldozer rip the land and crush the plants into the rocky soil until there was nothing left to look at.

SHORTCUTS

by Richard Elman

This woman is walking down the street with a man who is not even her boyfriend. They have a relationship because it is early morning.

Like they have with so many others.

Very much later that same morning they stop at the subway entrance to say good-bye. It's often like that when the two of them get together after a night spent at his place, or at hers.

He will soon ask if they can make another date.

She always does whenever he seems uncertain if they have really had one.

Of course they will agree on another time and place.

Because they always do.

From two blocks away another man drags his feet walking his dog. He had had no relationship with this man or woman, or with any others for quite some time. Just because they were once all close friends is, presently, not of very much interest to anybody.

The woman goes her way; the man his. The former friend of both and neither stops at a neighborhood store to purchase a new pair of jeans.

The dog squats in the street, after circling his tail three times.

Another man comes down the street with another woman.

It seems to be getting later.

In a little while it will no longer be early morning. The man who has gone his own way calls his only real friend and gets a busy signal.

Home again, the woman feeds a quick breakfast to her child and goes off to see her doctor.

The dog is back inside the house of the man with the new pair of jeans who has gone off to work.

The happy couple say good-bye and go their separate ways.

When they leave each other they do not, I think, say to themselves I am happy. They just are. That, too, can happen sometimes for a little while.

At his nearby office, the doctor, and dog owner, in his new pair of jeans, among other things, prepares to receive his first patient of the day. She is a woman who has just fed breakfast to her child.

It so happens he is only a Ph. D., and she has come to tell him about the date she thought she had last night.

He advises her not to make another with the same person unless they are both in a better mood.

It's Arty's birthday. He was nine. The children who are his best friends are going off to see a movie. Arty's idea is it should have a murder in it someplace. His mother has annotated New York to pick out just the right sort of a film, and to get the times of showings clearer in her mind.

Later she will shop for paper plates, candles, and bunting. For the party Arty did not wish to have.

There will be no cake today ordered three days in advance with Happy Birthday Arty in buttercream script.

The *New York Times* has not been delivered.

There's still an energy crisis.

The cleaning man has failed to arrive, again.

In a little while people will be expecting more than they should, such as free doctors.

Potential murder victims are warned not to watch certain children's programs on TV.

The Chinese Delegation to the United Nations thinks of moving from its motel into more elaborate quarters. Such as any ordinary Upper East Side apartment building as they do in Paris in the building where Ernest Hemingway used to live with his wife and child.

They could call a broker who has just sold a hundred-year-old firehouse to a religious sect.

He just might be the wrong person, as he is an Israeli, and does work for the City of New York only between elections.

If you call the Arab he will tell you there will have to be an auction, provided they can find a suitable property.

Meantime, as they are located very close to the former Lincoln Center, all the interested parties in the deal are advised to enjoy the cocktail lounge, Mandarin cuisine, and, of course, the heated in-door pool at the motel.

A rabbi from Columbus, Ohio, writes about the marital problems of physicians in a psychiatric journal.

He does not seem to be recommending tranquilizers, though many such advertisements of formerly unhappy couples are inter-spersed.

The man without the dog remains idle throughout most of the rest of the day.

The rabbi points out to his chagrin, for example, that most medical students spend more time with their cadavers than they do with classmates of the opposite sex.

He does not elaborate on classmates of the same sex getting together once in a while. Just to talk . . .

The woman who once fed her child breakfast before going off to a doctor's appointment has just left the doctor a second time. She suffers from the medical management of obesity and thinks about getting herself a dog.

The children assemble to see their murder movie.

The happy couple call each other. They are both feeling a bit down, and wish to confirm the date they made earlier on the street.

There is a crossed wire somewhere. Due to the recent overload on underground cable in the neighborhood, somebody is overheard speaking rapidly in Chinese.

"I'm glad I had children."
"I've never been really sorry myself."
"They are really just little people."
"They demand to be treated fairly."
"Like hospital workers?"
"More like little people."
"I see. . . ."
"No you don't. Have you talked to your child recently?" asks the only real friend in the world when his friend finally gets him off the phone.

He says, "You macho son of a bitch, I'm not gonna cut my throat for you. You have far too many light romances with women in which I do not even wish to compete."

"As I am not a Christian," his only real friend replies, "I won't apologize to you for that."

His only real friend interjects, "It was climbing Mount Marcy last summer that really did it. Not that upper New York State isn't beautiful. May I be the first to admit it . . . I love New York. . . ."

"It's a shame we don't get there very often. . . ."

"I feel like giving you a big hug, friend."

When left to himself the dog of the man is restless. He chews empty book bags, and the gluey bindings of fine editions. Stuffing gets all over everything.

Especially the red carpet.

The man and his dog are once again walking down the street together. With them are some strangers, two or three paces adjacent.

He is really the non-dog-owner type, which means he just walks this otherwise well-behaved animal once in a while, though they are both far from perfect at it. Essentially heeling.

The man thinks about getting his very own dog.

And he thinks of all the friendships he still does not have.

Lately, he has been told, people are getting fonder of him.

In the early evening of the same day the man without the dog gets together with the doctor's patient who has just fed her child dinner after learning she might, in fact, be pregnant.

The male part of the happy couple breaks a date with a woman who has not yet been mentioned in this account by anybody.

She was recently a very successful real estate broker from the suburbs of Philadelphia who, in the last minute or so, called the doctor to make a date with him to have an affair, if not more so.

The female happy partner also has a date, with the basic non-dog-owner.

He should be called Senator. This or that. Because he is almost trained.

Fatty has been fed and taken out again.

Senator, at present, rests on all four of his haunches in the living room, which also has a red carpet, the darker spots being where Fatty once or twice peed during his training.

All the children from the birthday party will be sleeping together again tonight so there will be no nightmares.

The other animals in the house have become increasingly territorial.

A cocktail party, for her new book, at five in the afternoon, at the home of her mother, is being given, by the prominent Fem poet who calls herself Mom woman after her cycles and is often taken seriously in the better journals.

It should be very well attended.

Even her husband, the Chinese doctor, will be there. He never goes swimming.

The man without the dog comes, as he has also been invited, though, not having RSVP'd, he can't stay very long after closing time.

Besides, he has a date with somebody's patient in real estate and is thinking about tax shelters.

In between feeding her child supper and a midnight snack, his date tells him for the first time ever she was also a doctor. Because she has given up practicing they make love, and fall asleep.

Later they wake and have a late snack, and more so.

She tells him she is also an expert in astronomy.

"I can't take any chances. With my eyes. I mean, they mean an awful lot to me."

"I understand."

"You do?"

"I do."

He is so pleased he tells her his greatest fantasy is to write a book about dogs because he knows so little about them he might learn something for once in his life.

"Do you feel that way about everything you don't know?" she asks, in his arms.

"Everything I don't know well . . ."

The first wave of divorces ended quite some time ago. Now some of the same people are getting divorced another time, and some are dying of heart attacks and strokes, mostly the men. Chinese do not seem to get as many of these as the rest of us. Perhaps because they swim in their motel pool.

The doctor wakes up every morning wondering when he will die of a heart attack or divorce, though he continues to walk his dog etc.

"There's a part of my life I have to reserve as private," he tells his wife, and patients, after they have made love or taken tea together.

His wife is seeing a handsome Chinese attached to the Chinese equivalent of the KGB.

She needed somebody in her life after breaking up with that biographer who always wrote about dead people.

"It's morbid being a biographer," she told her husband at supper one night.

"Go to see somebody with whom you can talk," he said. "Talk to somebody else. A professional."

"And you?" she asked.

"I wouldn't like it," he said. "But I wouldn't like talking Chinese. . . ."

"They all speak English," she explained. "He does, anyway."

"The way they swim," her husband said.

On the whole they are really very happy together because they communicate so well.

Their friends all say, "Look at them."

In a big city like New York it's nice having friends who will say that about you.

THE IMMACULATE CONCEPTION OF CARSON DUPRE

by Louise Erdrich

Carson was named after Johnny Carson. That much he knew. Things he did not know were whether his conception had been planned, if Flobert was his real father, if it had hurt Otalie very much to give birth to him, and why he was the only child. He had not wondered about these things until he left Havana, North Dakota, for the university where young men occasionally discussed their origins. In Havana nobody asked their parents much of a personal nature.

Otalie Dupre was nearly seventy years old. Flo was slighty older. How had Carson managed to slip beneath the wire?

"Was I adopted?" he asked the backs of their heads. "Or did you really ..." Even then he could not bring himself to utter the possibility. "... were you watching *The Late Show* when it happened? Did you notice what was going on?"

This was cruel, but they wouldn't hear him. The car traveled in a loud rush of air and in the front seat the radio was blaring.

" 'Silent night, holy night.' "

Otalie turned the dial. She and Flobert were big healthy pink people with dimples and two chins, while Carson was fragile and intensely pale with staring brown eyes. He didn't even seem left over from the stuff that made Otalie and Flo. He was different altogether. That was why he sometimes thought he might have been dropped off on their doorstep, hidden in their Quonset hut, shoved into their big rural route mailbox.

He closed his eyes and leaned back into the warm plush.

"I don't know why I bothered to come home," he said. "You're not even going to pretend to listen."

"No," said Otalie, "the stores were closed."

The radio gave a strange shrill chuckle.

"Gift items," Flobert said.

Carson was dressed in shabby secondhand woolens. His coat sported the moth-eaten pile collar of the college intellectual. Otalie had sewed a complete college wardrobe for him the summer before he matriculated, but in the second week of classes Carson had carried his suitcase into the local Salvation Army store and asked to exchange the bright patterned checked and striped garments for a more suitable wardrobe. He was now elegantly drab.

"Bringing you an inspirational message," the radio said.

Otalie turned up the volume. A man's deep voice filled the car.

"The Christmas heart is the most beautiful heart that ever beat . . . perhaps it is better this way. Those who mean so much to us . . . let's push up the shades of their window so light may fall into the sick world of the healing medicine of love. Let us light all the candles so the glow may light up the world for others. And make this a permanent thing. Let's do it. And Merry Christmas to your Christmas heart."

"Amen," said Otalie.

"I'd like to shoot that radio," said Carson. He was filling with rage.

A woman's voice came on.

"We have other outstanding specials! Take for instance the console with Mediterranean styling and remote control so you can sit there in your easy chair and never move."

"I wouldn't mind remote control," Flobert said.

"You are on remote control," said Carson. The weight of their stupidity was overwhelming him. He was losing control. "Oh God, oh God," he groaned, "why did I ever come back?"

"You sleeping back there, Carson?" Flobert shouted. "You're sure quiet."

"I'd like to shoot your damn radio," Carson said.

It began to snow in large, lazy wet flakes that stuck to the windshield and hood. The sky turned dark gray and puffy. An odd green light came from behind the clouds. The flakes condensed, fell faster, and wisps of snow began to slither across the highway.

"A white Christmas," said Otalie in her loudest voice.

"Hazardous driving conditions," said the radio. "High winds and heavy snowfall can be expected throughout the tristate area."

In the back seat, Carson made himself drift off over his book, so he didn't know it when Flobert made the wrong turn and lost the road. He woke to the first argument he'd ever heard between his parents. He listened with intense interest, not to what they said but to the undercurrent of strain in their voices.

"We should have hit Hennessey by now," Flobert said.

"We did."

"Well, where the hell was it? I never seen it."

"Overpass."

"You mean to say they remodeled this road again?"

"No, they never remodeled it. That long curve was always an overpass."

"It wasn't. Next chance I'm gonna turn around."

"No you don't."

But Flo had already slammed on the brakes as Otalie said this, not because he'd found a place to turn but because, Carson saw, lifting his head, they were completely enveloped in whiteness. Then they were sliding and then, suddenly, they were falling for a long minute. They landed still moving, fishtailed, and then they fell again. The car smacked into something and stopped.

Carson had flown, light as a bird, into the front seat between his parents. Everything was perfectly still for a moment. Then the radio went on.

"It's cheaper, I'll grant you that," the voice said.

"Turn that thing off!" Flobert reached for the dial. It was jammed on, however, and only spluttered cheerfully and jabbered louder when he tried to disconnect the wires beneath the dash.

"Oh, Flobert, leave it on," said Otalie. "It's connected to the heater. Let's see where we are."

Flobert worked his way out of the driver's door and disappeared. After a few moments he opened the door and got back inside.

"We fell into one of those deep storm ditches, Otalie. Even if I had a bucket of sand, besides my shovel, we couldn't get it out of here. Our best hope is to put a flag up on our antenna, and maybe one out by the road. Then there's nothing to do but wait it out."

"You have some red flags in the trunk, Flo?"

But he didn't, and Carson's suitcase held only simple grays and browns.

"What did you do with the clothes I made you? *You threw them out?*"

Carson thought that Otalie seemed more shocked and frightened by this than at their plight or the dropping temperature. But then, of course, it meant she would have to give up her brilliantly colored coat. She took it off. Then she and Carson put on everything that they could find. Otalie tied Carson's shirts and slacks around her legs and wrapped herself in another blanket they kept in back. Flo got back into the car and lit a candle out of the emergency kit. He stuck this in a pie tin and gave it to Carson, still between them, to hold. The aluminum pie tin was supposed to catch and reflect the heat from the candle. Flobert turned the heater on for a few minutes and warmed up their feet. It was getting colder. As soon as the heater went off, Carson felt the coldness seeping up through the rubber mats and metal floor, flowing into his legs like a weak electric current.

Carson drew his feet up under his coat and crouched between his parents. The three leaned together, a bit self-consciously at first. Flobert made a little joke about conserving warmth. After a while, though, they hugged out of real need because Flobert didn't dare turn the engine on too long. They were low on gas. He could hardly afford to recharge the battery that the radio was wearing down

Flobert managed to turn the volume low but still it blabbed constantly, giving them useless warnings about the storm system, playing "Have a Holly Jolly Christmas" and "O Little Town of Bethlehem." The candle flickered in the pie tin, and Carson felt the warmth of it ebb and flow in his lap. Vaguely, he considered something he'd never known before—he could get so cold that he could feel warmth itself moving in molecules. His parents were no longer people to him but parcels of heat-generating flesh. Once, when they kissed over his head, he felt a small burst of warmth from their touching lips. For the first time he reacted to their touching not with disgust but with outright pleasure, and wished they would kiss again.

As the hours went on with no change except to become darker and colder, the three went deep into themselves. Flobert and Otalie hunched into their clothing and seemed to sleep. Carson stayed awake with the last candle in the pie tin, watching it burn lower. The radio was still on. At one point the man's voice came back on the air.

"The Christmas heart. It defies contradiction in the human world. It is a guiding thought and magnet of peace that supports us through each day. We must never let it down, for it will renew us with its endless consolation. Let it be yours from this moment on. Let's make it part of us. And Merry Christmas to your Christmas heart."

The candle burned completely down to a pool of wax on the tin and warmth began to flood quickly away. Carson knew that the mindless voice would go on until it ate up the battery and the heater and the gas and they were dead. He fell asleep with the pie tin on his legs. Much later, he woke to silence. The radio had gone out, and with it the battery. Flobert tried to turn the engine over, but all he got was a sluggish whirr.

*   *   *

He believed, at first, when his parents bent over him, that they were going to keep him warm in the human cave of their bodies. He thought they truly were going to give him life this time, that he was going to be conceived again and born of them as he never had before. Then later, when he grew cold, he knew the opposite was happening. They bent over him the way they would huddle over a small flame, to absorb what warmth they could. Helplessly, they were taking back the life they had given him. He knew, but by then it was too late. He felt them growing heavy, bearing down on him with their cold, unconscious bodies, while he contracted around the bit of warmth he had left. That grew smaller. Then he was shrinking into the dark, trying to capture and nurture that little flame before it vanished.

He put his mind to the point of light and pursued it, reaching deeper and deeper until he thought he had it. He stretched and brought it toward him, huffed until the light widened, grew, and still kept widening.

When the light flared he thought that he had never seen anything so beautiful. The light gripped him with wonder. He breathed it still brighter, determined to use his last breath on it. Breathing, breathing, he used everything he was as fuel and kept burning, so that the last thing he knew of himself was when he caught into a great surge of forgiving radiance that flowed out of him and wrapped his parents over and over in its raveling fire.

CHRISTMAS IN A VERY SMALL PLACE

by Robert L. Flynn

When Newly looked at his watch it wasn't the time he was looking at, or the date. They were of no importance. He was looking at his watch, the new Seiko he had bought only a week ago in the Freedom Hill PX. Already it was grimy and he was worried that staying wet for a year would ruin it. He noticed the date only by accident. December 25. He looked for someone to tell. Ortega seemed to be asleep. "It's Christmas," he said to the old papasan, who sat in another corner, slowly adding rice straw to a small fire. The papasan smiled and nodded.

Since the Marines had come to the ville the Viet Cong had not come to take rice and young men, but they shot at the Marines in the ville, dropped mortars on it, and set booby traps along the trails. Since the Marines had come to the ville, the families had been safer, and the threat of violence had been greater. The papasan knew these things the way he knew the monsoon and the mosquitoes, the dry season and the dust. They came when they wished and they were to be endured until they passed. He did not know why the American was excited. He nodded as he always did and smiled for the Americans.

Not satisfied, Newly looked at Ortega again. The squad had moved three times during the night, in and around the ville. Because they had no barbed wire and no bunkers and their only support was the artillery at the combat base five miles away, frequent movement was their only security. That and the almost animal awareness some of them had. Ortega had the long, lithe body and the senses of a coyote. He could go to sleep anywhere and be instantly awake.

Newly brushed his hand against the straw side of the hootch and Ortega's eyes opened. "Know what day it is?" Newly asked.

Ortega looked at the months and days he had crossed off the calendar he kept on his helmet. "Twenty-fifth. I'm short as peace," he said. "Fourteen days to go."

"It's Christmas day."

Ortega shrugged. "Ain't but two days that matter. The day you go on R and R and the day you go home."

Deflated, Newly picked up his rifle and stepped outside into the early-morning mist. Mother was conferring with the Popular Forces honcho. Mother, who was built like a dark street corner, big, black, and intimidating, was a twenty-one-year-old high school dropout Marine corporal who was responsible for the security of the bridge and the road that connected the ville to the market and the Marines to the combat base, five miles and a lifetime away.

Mother was also responsible for the safety of the families in the ville and for training the Popular Forces to defend it. Mother, who had never been anything but unnecessary back in the world, was on his second tour in the ville. He was wearing sandals with his trouser legs rolled up. He had shrapnel wounds in both legs that would not heal because he could not keep them dry.

When Mother and the PF honcho finished talking, Newly said, "It's Christmas day."

"Damn," Mother said. "That means we won't get a replacement corpsman today." The doc had been wounded the day before in a fight in the cemetery. "They won't send a replacement out here on Christmas. He's in Danang right now, his feet dry, eating turkey."

"Won't we get turkey?" Newly asked.

"Man, what are you talking? Turkey is for pogues in Danang. We'll get turkey when they put it in C-rations. On Thanksgiving we got hamburger patties. On the corps's birthday we got ice cream. Last Christmas we got roast beef. If we're lucky, that's what we'll get today."

"Merry Christmas to you too," Newly said. He was not going to let anyone spoil his Christmas. He went to a hootch and looked in. Dig was sitting on the damp floor cleaning his machine-gun. "Hey, Dig, it's Christmas Day."

"It don't mean nothing," Dig said.

"It means there's a truce, don't it?"

"It ain't real," Dig said. "We lost Bear and Lower Alabam the last time we had a truce."

Mother loomed in the doorway of the hootch, holding the radio. "Old man says we only got to pull one patrol today because it's

Christmas. Plus an alley cat tonight. I need the machine-gun, Dig, and I want you on the radio, Newly Arrived. I want you to get to know every face and hootch in this ville. It's the only way you'll ever know when something's wrong. Let's go because the jeep driver is bringing roast beef and stewed tomatoes for Christmas dinner, and toys for us to give to the kids."

"It ain't real," Dig said. On an earlier tour Dig had been the only survivor of a platoon ambushed in the Quesons. The experience left him with definite opinions about what was real. "I'm walking but I'm dead," he said. The Marines had sent him back to the world but the world did not conform to his expectations of reality. "You can't do nothing to me but bury me," he said to parents, peers, and protestors who tried to change, honor, or chastise him. "So dig." After three months he asked for Vietnam.

When they stepped outside the hootch, Ortega joined them. "You don't have to go," Mother said. "You're short."

"It's as safe on patrol as it is here," Ortega said. "And it's the only way I got to make the days go faster. Thirteen days and a wake-up."

"It don't mean nothing," Dig said. "You think you're going back to the world but it ain't real."

Ignoring him, Ortega took the point. Ortega had the best nose in the squad, only Mother knew the ville better. They slipped along the muddy footpath between the hootches. Mother stopped to bow and speak to the PFs and the peasants, looking into each hootch.

They walked past the garden where the Marines raised carrots, cabbage, and beans. Groups in the States sent seeds and the Marines gave the seeds and produce from the garden to the Vietnamese to encourage them to diversify their crops and improve their diets. The only barbed wire in the ville protected the garden from water buffalo and the swaybacked pigs.

The footpath led beside a grove of areca trees, across a ravine, to an intersection of three other trails. While Newly and Dig stood watch, Ortega and Mother checked the trails for recent traffic. Finding nothing suspicious, the patrol followed a trail across a stream, along the cemetery, through a bamboo thicket, and along the edge of the ville.

Scarred banana trees and bunkers were all that remained of three hootches that had been destroyed in a firefight between the PFs and Viet Cong. Every hootch had a bunker for the family to hide during the fights and when the Viet Cong dropped mortars on the ville.

"Someone's in this bunker," Ortega said. He stood beside the bunker with a grenade, ready to roll it inside.

"Lai dai," Mother called. Come out. *"Didi."* Get away. No one came out. "Toss it," he said to Ortega.

"Sounds like someone crying," Ortega said.

"I ain't sticking my head in there," Mother said. "And we ain't leaving until we know."

Ortega thought it over. Fourteen days. "I'm too short," he said. "*Lai dai,*" he called, sticking his finger through the ring on the grenade pin. Still he waited.

"They can't do nothing to me but dig my grave," Dig said. He slowly crawled into the narrow opening holding a cigarette lighter in his hand. When he was halfway in he wriggled out again. "Girl," he said. "Not from this ville. Having a baby. No weapon." He picked up the machine-gun and waited for Ortega to move out.

Ortega took the lighter and looked inside. "She's having trouble," he said.

"She's Viet Cong or she wouldn't be here," Dig said.

"We don't have a corpsman," Mother said.

"It don't mean nothing," Dig said. "What's one more kid in a place like this?"

Ortega looked at Mother. Mother, too, had been one more kid. "Newly, call the squad and tell them exactly where we are and tell them to stand by. Then get first squad's corpsman on the radio and stay close enough I can touch you. Ortega, get over there where you can cover the trail and the ville. Dig, I want the machine-gun covering the trail and the paddy ."

When Ortega and Dig were in position, Mother turned to Newly. "What did the corpsman say?"

"He said as much as possible leave it up to her. Try to keep her calm. And keep everything clean."

"Clean? There ain't nothing here that's clean. Give me your battle dressing. Get Dig's and Ortega's. I'll wrap the baby in that."

Mother crawled into the bunker. It was damp and close with animal smells. Flicking the lighter, he looked at the girl. She looked like a frightened child, her teeth and eyes big, and she made moans and whimpers and little animal sounds.

"There ain't nobody to help but me," he said, reaching out his hand. Her eyes rolled watching his hand, but her head did not move. He laid his hand gently on her forehead and she seemed to shrink under it. Not knowing what else to do he began to sing the first song he could think of. "Hey Jude, don't be afraid, take a sad song and make it better . . ." He could feel her begin to relax. When she closed her eyes he moved his hand, but she caught it and squeezed it in her own.

After a while he crawled outside. "Give me a cigarette," he said. "Tell the corpsman she lost her water. Where's the squad?"

"The squad changed their pos. They're at the pagoda."

"Tell them not to come past the ditch. What are you doing?"

Newly had taken out a lighter and was running it over the blade of his ka-bar. "Corpsman told me to heat a knife," he said. "Don't touch nothing with it." He handed it to Mother and Mother crawled back inside.

Newly smoked another cigarette, occasionally shrugging when Dig or Ortega looked at him. "He's not breathing," Mother yelled. "Tell the corpsman he's not breathing."

"Mouth-to-mouth," Newly called. "Doc says give him mouth-to-mouth."

The next time he emerged, Mother was holding a red, raw, wrinkled thing. "I got me a boy," he said.

"Its eyes ain't even open," Newly said.

"You can't take it with you," Ortega said, appearing beside them. "If you leave it here, it ain't got a prayer."

"I thought you was keeping watch," Mother said.

"If there was anybody out there, they would have already hit us," Ortega said.

"It ain't even got its eyes open," Newly said.

"If I was born in this country, I wouldn't never open my eyes," Ortega said.

"This ain't no real country," Dig said. "Ain't nothing here but hunger and hatred."

"He's alive, ain't he?" Mother said.

"It don't mean nothing. We might as well dig his grave right now," Dig said.

"I breathed life in this kid. Don't tell me it don't mean nothing."

"He may be breathing but he's dead. He ain't never gonna know anything but death and hunger."

"He can choose," Mother said. "As long as he's got breath he can choose. If you want to be dead, you can be dead. He's alive."

"It ain't real," Dig said. "Ain't nothing real in this country except dying."

"You ain't walking dead, you're alive and crawling," Mother said. "You're afraid to live because you're afraid to die. Well, this kid's alive. They can kill him but they can't say he didn't live."

"It's the lieutenant," Newly said, holding up the radio headset. "He's sending the jeep with toys for the kids. He wants us to teach them to play touch football."

"It ain't real," Dig said.

"Maybe it ain't real, but it matters," Mother said. "And don't never tell me again it don't matter. I breathed life in this kid, and that matters. Now give him back to his mama," he said, placing the wet, wriggling thing in Dig's hands.

Dig held the baby before him, as cautiously as if it were a booby trap. The baby wrinkled its face and began to make little sucking sounds. "This ain't no good place to be born," Dig said. "This ain't no good time. There ain't a whole lot out here but grief. And mama." Slowly he sank to his knees before the bunker.

RITA LAFFERTY'S LUCKY SUMMER

by Elaine Ford

The summer I was sixteen I had my first real job, selling pastries in Jojo's Bakery on Broadway, near Sullivan Square. Over the machine that dispensed tickets was a hand-lettered sign: TAKE A NUMBER. Like my aunt Grace saying, "Take a card, take a card," when she was going to do a trick or tell my fortune. Maybe the ticket machine was a lucky-number machine, I liked to think. When I called out "Seventeen" or "Fifty-three" to the customers waiting their turn to be served, I half expected one of them to wave her ticket and shout "Bingo!" Nobody ever did, though. They'd be trying to shush their yammering kid or figuring out whether one pineapple cake could be sliced thin enough to feed eleven people.

It was hard work. On your feet all day and no goofing off; whenever the stream of customers thinned out, Jojo would always find something for you to do in back, washing cookie trays or making up boxes. What I really wanted to do was work the pastry tube, but no chance of that.

Rita Lafferty, who worked at Jojo's with me, fell in love that summer. Rita was thirty, though she didn't look it. Her teeth were as buck as though she'd spent her childhood opening tonic bottles with them. She lived with her mother over on Fosket Street. Mrs. Lafferty was forever calling up the bakery, trying to talk Rita into leaving early so she could run some errand for her. She'd even have made up the excuse that Rita was supposed to tell Jojo. Poor Rita didn't know whether to be afraid more of her mother or of getting fired.

The best thing about Rita was her hair. It was reddish brown and so heavy and dense that even the awful hairnets we had to wear couldn't squash it. Once she made me examine the roots to prove to me that the color came from God. Not that I'd suspected otherwise.

Rita's boyfriend was a motorman on the Orange Line; he spent his working hours riding from Oak Grove to Forest Hills and back. They'd met in the Star Market, when he dropped a can of cream-style corn on her toe. He was a bachelor who lived alone in Magoun Square and cooked for himself. His name was Frank Hodges.

Rita limped around for a few days, smiling goofily whenever anyone asked how she'd hurt her foot. And then, the day Frank's gift arrived at the bakery, she began to confide in me.

He'd sent it to apologize—possibly to head off a suit, though I didn't suggest that to Rita—a large ceramic donkey with a clump of geraniums in each raffia saddle basket. "Isn't it cunning?" she said. And how had Frank guessed that geraniums were practically her favorite flower?

"Maybe he thought they'd match your hair," I offered. The donkey had a somewhat toothy expression, but I didn't mention that to Rita either.

"My hair's not *that* kind of red. Still, to men red is red."

"That's what I mean," I agreed, from my own extensive knowledge of men.

"He asked me out," Rita went on, "when I called to thank him."

"How did you know his number?"

She looked only a little sheepish. "I looked it up in the phone book. Well, I *had* to thank him, didn't I?"

They went to the movies that weekend, and the next weekend, on Sunday afternoon, to Fenway Park to jeer at Don Zimmer. Finally, Frank came around to the bakery. He turned out to be a better-looking man than you'd imagine Rita could catch, even with her great hair. Not tall, but plenty of muscles and so tan you'd have thought he spent every day stretched out on Revere Beach instead of inside a subway car. Maybe not quite as old as Rita, but it was hard to tell for sure.

"He seems nice," I told her later as we were bringing out trays of cream puffs. Rita only smiled. When she kept her mouth shut, she was surprisingly pretty. Especially after Frank came into her life. I began to notice things. She had nice breasts—we'd strip out of our nylon uniforms at the end of the day, the two of us crowded into the tiny john in back—and she had kind of a sexy smell about her, too. Not that she was *sleeping* with Frank, I was sure, but her excitement was there in her delicate sweat and in the new way she moved her body. She even talked back to Mrs. Lafferty once or twice when the old witch called demanding to know how soon she'd be home.

Now I began to wonder why no man had noticed Rita before, why she had seemed so obviously virginal and fated to remain that way. Of course, there was the buck teeth. And she did tend to giggle, particularly in a crisis, and she fell all over herself agreeing with you, no matter what outrageous thing you'd said. Still, look outside the plate glass window onto Broadway: women walking by who are unmistakably married—someone once made love to them and planted babies in them—and how that all happened is a mystery. Arms puckered with fat now, gold teeth and false gold hair, voices like fishwives.

Frank started picking Rita up after work. He drove a yellow Corvette, only slightly dented. The car worried me a little, because I calculated what it must cost to keep up the payments and wondered whether there'd be enough left over to support a wife, let alone babies and a mother-in-law. They'd gone to Virgie's, she'd tell me the next morning, or to Davis Square for a pizza.

"How come Frank is always available to pick you up?" I asked her. "Whether you work till four-thirty or seven-thirty, he always manages to be here."

"He arranges his schedule around mine," she said, gazing at the birthday cake display. For some reason the glass on that particular case makes a good mirror.

"How can he do that?"

She smiled, tucking a few wisps of hair into her hairnet and letting the elastic snap. "He has a lot of seniority. He gets first crack at the work sheet."

Well, I believed it if she did.

And then all at once it struck me that she *was* sleeping with him, after all. There were no more reports of what movie they'd seen, or what they'd had to eat at Virgie's. If I asked her, she'd say, "Oh, I forget." Rita was a terrible liar, no inventiveness, no acting ability. I imagined them in Frank's steamy apartment, making love to the rattle of traffic in Magoun Square, and I feared for her soul.

Then Rita showed me the ring, her engagement ring. Frank had bought it downtown on Washington Street and made a very good bargain, she told me. Diamond solitaire, one-quarter carat, platinum setting. They planned an October wedding, she said shyly.

I was happy for her. At least, I hoped, Mrs. Lafferty would have to start hewing and drawing for herself once in a while.

The Saturday after Rita confided to me her wedding plans, Frank failed to pick her up. Ordinarily I would have left her waiting in front of Jojo's without giving it a thought, but that day she had the curse. Rita was afflicted with theatrical, extravagant menstrual flows, during which her body seemed bent on flushing out her entire blood supply. Since she looked a little shaky, I lingered with her, watching for that sleek yellow vehicle to come zipping along from Magoun Square.

No Corvette. Rita twisted the engagement ring around her finger. A fidgety rain began to fall. It got to be seven-forty, then ten of.

"What do you think I should do?" she asked me finally.

At that moment I spotted the number 89 bus moving slowly in the traffic, heading west out of Sullivan Square. I grabbed her arm and pulled her across Broadway to the bus stop in front of the firehouse. "We'll go over to Frank's place and see what's up. Maybe he's sick," I said.

"Shouldn't we call first?"

I gave her an exasperated look. If she'd been in his bed every night for a month, did she have to call first before visiting him? "There won't be another bus for forty minutes," I said.

His apartment was a third-floor walk-up over a sub shop. We rang his bell, and when there was no answer I pushed the street door open and we went upstairs, past bicycles and strollers on the landings.

"Which door is Frank's?" I asked her.

She pointed it out, knowing she was compromised but seeing no alternative. I guess she was grateful to have me take charge.

I knocked. We could hear staticky music from inside, but nobody came to the door. "Well, now what?"

Without saying anything she dug around in her handbag and came up with the key.

For a bachelor Frank was neat as a pin; I'll have to give him that. Everything was in place: plastic tablecloth on the table, sofa cover free of wrinkles.

As in a trance, Rita walked into the bedroom, and I came behind her. Frank was lying on the bed, out cold. The radio signal had shifted since he'd tuned it in. An empty bottle sat on the bed table next to the radio.

"He drinks," she breathed.

"Let's go, Rita."

"No, you go. I'll stay with him."

"Come on, Rita." I pulled at her arm.

"No, it's all right," she said. I saw the buck teeth when she spoke. She didn't giggle, even though it was a crisis, and she settled down to watch over him.

I think they got married, though I'm not sure. After I quit working at Jojo's to go back to school I never heard from Rita, and I never ran into her on the street. Probably she and Frank moved to Stoneham or Billerica, the better to escape Mrs. Lafferty.

WHEN THE RABBIT
FALLS OUT OF THE BOX

by Carol Frost

Out the window of my office at Hartwick College I see my twelve-year-old son in his red and blue jacket, and I say to my student. Archer, "There's my son." The conference is about over, and it's a way, I suppose, of letting her know that.

"Where?" she asks.

"See, down there, in the jacket," I say. Soon she gets up and leaves, smiling in an especially friendly way, and I wonder if she's surprised that I have such a big son.

Daniel waves to me when I stand at the window, then comes on up. He has on his blue trousers that I don't like, and they are very dirty. I've decided earlier in the day that when he and I drove over to Cooperstown to visit his friend Josh we'd go out to dinner at a nice place. Annoyed, I say to him, "Why did you wear those pants? What were you doing today? Let me see your hands."

He holds his palms up and shrugs, then looks at his pants. I point to the smudges on his jacket and after a minute tell him I have one more conference. He asks me if he can get something to drink—he's thirsty; he hasn't had lunch.

"Drink some water," I say, but relent and hand him fifty cents.

I have the last conference, which is quick, and when I usher my student to the door, there's Dan, looking at the essays pinned to my bulletin board. When I bring student papers home, he often asks to read them and wants to know the grades I give. He and I go out to the car and drive the twenty miles to Basset Hospital in Cooperstown.

Joshua is very sick, although we expect to see him better when we get there, imagining that the doctors were right the day before— that he has microplastic pneumonia and that the antibiotics will work. He has gotten a little better in the hospital, and now, we think,

108 //

he'll be nearer to being all well. He can eat a little now, or could eat yesterday a little bit. And the day before.

But when we get to his room his mother, Janet, is on the phone, and Joshua looks pretty grim and gray. It's clear he isn't as well as we'd hoped.

"Hi, Joshua," I say, and he doesn't reply and doesn't look at Dan.

Janet says to the person on the phone, "We don't know what's wrong, but this is Columbia University teaching hospital, and it's a fine hospital. No, he doesn't have to come to New York."

She's very happy to see us and takes out a cellophane bag of dried pears to offer to Daniel. Dan declines. The two boys sit down to play a board game called Sorry. As soon as Dan has had a chance to look at the rules for the game, the doctors come in—two teams of doctors. Two doctors for arthritis and a third doctor, who belongs to the team for childhood diseases. They begin to examine Joshua. All three of them look at his joints. They prod his stomach and chest. When Josh lies down he coughs, and he needs to lie down for the doctors to look at his knees, but he sits up to stop coughing and the doctors ask him to lie back down. Every time Josh coughs he's in pain. His liver and spleen are sore, Janet tells me, and the pain shows less as a mask than as a dimming of his eyes. None of the doctors looks squarely at Josh's face.

One of them says, "What's the name of your dog?"

"I don't . . ." Josh starts.

But the doctor answers his own question, "Ralph. Oh, that's a nice name. Ralph."

Two of the doctors leave. The one left says that there's no clear picture of what's wrong with Josh, that the lungs are involved and the joints are involved, that the tests show a great deal of fluid on the knees, and that the fluid has a lot of white blood cells in it but no crystals. They'll give Josh another liver scan in the morning.

The boys settle down to play again, and the nurse comes in with Josh's tray and with food for the old man who's in the bed next to the door. The hospital is filled up and the pediatric center is filled half with children and half with older patients. The curtain was drawn for Joshua while the doctors were examining him. All the time the doctors were with Josh, Daniel stood uncomfortably against the wall, watching. At one point I had the feeling Josh might be embarrassed with so many of us in the room with him, and I moved closer to the window. I could see Dan's reflection on the glass and, eerily, behind him a spring shower of snow. Every time Josh coughed and winced, Dan's shoulders moved a little on the wall, and he clenched his hands. Now the man gives the curtain a weak push from his bed, and Janet sweeps it open for him. She turns back to Josh to take the lid off his dinner plate.

Seeing the mound of spaghetti, she says enthusiastically, "Who ordered this? You or your father?"

Josh looks a little disgusted and mutters something about why anyone would want to cut up spaghetti, but he takes the fork Janet offers him. While he's chewing, he grins at Dan.

The woman who's sitting in the chair across the room from the old man and watching both of them eat speaks to Janet and me: "Having a friend here—that makes him want to eat."

The man nods toward Dan. "Yup, he's the best medicine."

It's hard to tell if the man and woman are married. She looks much younger. His face is deadpan and gray. A tube for oxygen is taped to his nose.

When the nurse comes in to give him an intravenous antibiotic, the woman leans forward and says in a soothing voice, "The soup is good. Isn't it, Henry?"

When Josh is done and the tray is put on the sill, the boys begin again to play Sorry. Janet and I go downstairs to the cafeteria for a cup of tea. When I stop by the cashier, Janet reaches in front of me with her dollar bill, and I let her pay for both of us. We sit down to talk about Josh's illness. The doctors think raw goat's milk may have given him tuberculosis or an odd strain of pneumonia goats sometimes carry. The lab has tested the blood and saliva of the Woolfs' goats and found no such diseases, but the doctors think the test results are inconclusive. Or else it could have come from the carcass of an animal. In the farmland where we both live—in the Otsdawa River valley across from each other, so from Dan's room on the upper story I can see their house next to a linear grove of white pine and locust—in that valley roaming dogs, domestic and wild, run the deer down. I've seen how Platt the farmer on lower Green Street leaves carcasses of felled deer and an occasional disease-ridden cow lying in his field. The doctors have said those carcasses also carry tuberculosis and other bacteria and viruses that somehow may have gotten into Josh. But they aren't sure.

When Janet is speaking she watches me with the animation and care of those willing to change the topic of conversation at the slightest indication of boredom. Her face is freckled, the corners of her eyes criss-crossed with lines, and I realize this is the first time I have looked closely at her, really the first time we have spoken, aside from the friendly greetings of two mothers whose sons are good friends. I spoke once with her husband, David, a gruff-seeming, short, and heavily bearded man. He was delivering a birthday present from Josh to Dan, and we stood in the driveway, as

near as he would come to the house, while he explained the seriousness of Josh's illness. This was when I learned that Josh was in the
hospital and that his parents were dangerously close to despair.

"Let's give them a little more time together," Janet says, looking
at her watch.

"Good idea," I say.

Janet Woolf is a writer, and she and I talk a little about the
impulse to narrative. She tells me about a famous storyteller who
lives in the Adirondacks near Glens Falls—Sarah. Janet went to visit
Sarah, knocking on the door and introducing herself. Sarah and
Janet hugged. Sarah is blind now. An accident. And Janet walks
into her house and offers to take her shopping or to do anything
with her that she, perhaps, hasn't done in a while. Sarah says she
would like to go out to lunch, so they get into Janet's car and begin
to drive to the restaurant Sarah wants to go to. But Janet can't find
it because the blind woman's directions seem incomprehensible.
And finally, after fifteen minutes of being lost, Janet, though she
hasn't wanted to stop and ask for directions and possibly hurt
Sarah's feelings, does. When they arrive, they discover the restaurant is closed for the season. They end up eating at a diner, and
Sarah enjoys it very much. When they get back to Sarah's house,
they sit on the sofa in the living room and Sarah tells stories, not
Scottish or French stories, but stories from her life. How when her
father came home drunk at night she had to get out of bed and
hide. And how the family would sit around the potbellied stove in
winters and listen to the grandmother tell stories. Sarah must have
found some beauty in those stories and held on to it all the years of
her childhood. When she became an adult she became a storyteller,
too. They each tell a folklore story and sing. Sarah's not happy with
her voice any longer, almost as if, Janet thought, she felt her new
blindness affected her ears, too.

"That was the only note of self-pity I heard all afternoon," Janet
says, nodding solemnly.

I nod too, imagining that Janet is speaking for herself, and
Joshua, and David, as well as for the lonely blind woman in the
mountains.

When we get back upstairs Dan and Josh are sitting in different
seats, Dan across the room from Josh, and at first it looks as if Josh
has gotten too tired to play or talk anymore, and Dan is giving him
some distance. Instead, they're playing another game.

"Pot roast, Mom. I told him pot roast," Dan says. "I was supposed
to think of something that might be in a kitchen, and I thought of
pot roast for him to guess."

"Did Josh get it?" I ask.

"Of course," comes Dan's reply.

Now I see that the flushed look on Josh's face is triumph, and that Dan's face is also flushed.

Then it's time to leave. The boys' good-byes are nearly inaudible. As we drive toward home I tell Dan that if he washes his hands and face and rolls up his sleeves, we can go to dinner at the Farmhouse restaurant. Just as we near town I tell him we can go to a Pizza Hut or anyplace he wants, but he says the Farmhouse is nice.

As soon as we sit down, an elderly man in tails and a top hat comes in. In couplets of a sort he describes a magic act where he has a hollow rectangle and a hollow cylinder. He puts the cylinder into the rectangle, turns the rectangle four times around, speaks his own equation for magic, and pulls a stuffed rabbit out of the cylinder.

Everyone at the table where he's performing looks at the stuffed toy strangely, and he says, "So you think Irmagold isn't a real bunny? Then I'll put her back in the cylinder."

He throws the bunny into the cylinder, switches the rectangle around a couple of times, and pulls out a live one.

He repeats some other lines of magic, puts the bunny into a small box, spins it, and the bunny disappears. His blue eyes are nearly dancing, but as he turns away from this last trick, the bottom of the box falls apart, and the rabbit flops onto the floor. The praise and laughter stop.

The old magician crumples for a moment, but seems to catch himself and stands back up tall. When he gets everything put away he turns around and makes a small, stiff bow and says, "Thank you."

Everyone claps a little too politely. Daniel wears the same clipped expression he had when the doctors were examining Josh, as if he disapproves of the audience's reaction but is himself more embarrassed for the old man than he'd like to be.

When the waitress comes over to take our order, I ask her about the magician. "Oh, that's Mr. Barnett, who drives the fiacre in the parking lot," she says. "One day a few weeks ago he came into the restaurant and pulled a live rabbit out of his hat, and the people who own the restaurant, Loretta and Jim, asked him to keep it up."

Dan orders lasagna, and a salad comes with it. With the new retainer in his mouth he can't chew the lettuce because, he tells me, it's too flat. Then he takes the retainer out with a hand motion that resembles suppressing a yawn. He puts it on the table discreetly and turns a saucer over it, looking at me, checking with me the whole time. I order veal. Then while we're waiting for our dinners, Dan tells me about the act he's preparing for his class at school. He calls it Largo, after a song in his trumpet book. He's memorized from a tape recording of a BBC program a comic routine told in a laconic voice about what it was like in the old days when the Cockney speaker was a boy. He explains that he's written all of it down and marked the Cockney inflections and accents with mispellings:

> *I'll never forget the 'irst dai at Bitmere and me faddah werked a seventy-two 'our shift and then he walked 'ome foty-three mile thrru snow in 'is bare feet, 'oodled inside 'is clothes made arten old sacks . . .*

The narrative is filled with a crude pathos and violence which the speaker is innocent of, and as Dan recites, his eyes twinkle. When he's through he says he wants to have his trumpet teacher play "Largo" softly behind him when he performs for his class. He hums the first plaintive notes for me, and I am surprised by his sense of irony, which I'd thought children didn't understand.

We finish our meal. Daniel pops the retainer back into his mouth and wipes the back of his hand across his lips. It has gotten dark now.

Halfway out the door of the restaurant, Dan says, "Oh, my knees! My liver!" And I reprimand him for trying to be funny about being ill.

Out of the blue he says, "The only thing I don't like about Dad is that he blames me for things I don't do. He starts in on me and says I've done something, and he even knows I didn't do it. But he gets mad. I don't know why."

I say nothing, try to look like nothing, so he won't always depend on me for an answer. My sympathies are all on the side of his childish protest but somehow, I think, he knows one's sympathies are insufficient. As I turn away, I see the fiacre man petting his horse in the snowy light of a lamp in the parking lot. Dan sees him too. I take his hand, nearly as big as mine, firmly but gently, and we walk to the car.

"Good night!" Dan says out loud.

Then to me, "You know, he's not a bad magician."

A GOOD MAN TO KNOW

by Barry Gifford

I was seven years old in June of 1954 when my dad and I drove from Miami to New Orleans to visit his friend Albert Thibodeaux. It was a cloudy, humid morning when we rolled into town in my dad's powder blue Cadillac. The river smell mixed with malt from the Jax brewery and the smoke from my dad's chain of Lucky Strikes to give the air an odor of toasted heat. We parked the car by Jackson Square and walked over a block to Tujague's bar to meet Albert. "It feels like it's going to rain," I said to Dad. "It always feels like this in New Orleans," he said.

Albert Thibodeaux was a gambler. In the evenings he presided over cockfights and pit bull matches across the river in Gretna or Algiers, but during the day he hung out at Tujague's on Decatur Street with the railroad men and phony artists from the Quarter. He and my dad knew each other from the old days in Cuba, which I knew nothing about except that they'd both lived at the Nacional in Havana.

According to Nanny, my mother's mother, my dad didn't even speak to me until I was five years old. He apparently didn't consider a child capable of understanding him or a friendship worth cultivating until that age and he may have been correct in his judgment. I certainly never felt deprived as a result of this policy. If my grandmother hadn't told me about it, I would never have known the difference.

My dad never really told me about what he did or had done before I was old enough to go around with him. I picked up information as I went, listening to guys like Albert and some of my dad's other friends, like Willie Nero in Chicago and Dummy Fish in New York. We supposedly lived in Chicago, but my dad had places in

Miami, New York, and Acapulco. We traveled, mostly without my mother, who stayed at the house in Chicago and went to church a lot. Once I asked my dad if we were any particular religion and he said, "Your mother's a Catholic."

Albert was a short, fat man with a handlebar mustache. He looked like a Maxwell Street organ grinder without the organ or the monkey. He and my dad drank Irish whisky from ten in the morning until lunchtime, which was around one-thirty, when they sent me down to Johnny's on St. Louis Street for muffaletas. I brought back three of them, but Albert and Dad didn't eat theirs. They just talked and once in a while Albert went into the back to make a phone call. They got along just fine and about every hour or so Albert would ask if I wanted something, like a Barg's or a Delaware Punch, and Dad would rub my shoulder and say to Albert, "He's a real piece of meat, this boy." Then Albert would grin so that his mustache covered the front of his nose and say, "He is, Rudy. You won't want to worry about him."

When Dad and I were in New York, one night I heard him talking in a loud voice to Dummy Fish in the lobby of the Waldorf. I was sitting in a big leather chair between a sand-filled ashtray and a potted palm and Dad came over and told me that Dummy would take me upstairs to our room. I should go to sleep, he said; he'd be back late. In the elevator I looked at Dummy and saw that he was sweating. It was December but water ran down from his temples to his chin. "Does my dad have a job?" I asked Dummy. "Sure he does," he said. "Of course. Your dad has to work, just like everybody else." "What is it?" I asked. Dummy wiped the sweat from his face with a white and blue checkered handkerchief. "He talks to people," Dummy told me. "Your dad is a great talker."

Dad and Albert talked right past lunchtime and I must have fallen asleep on the bar, because when I woke up it was dark out and I was in the back seat of the car. We were driving across the Huey P. Long Bridge and a freight train was running along the tracks over our heads. "How about some Italian oysters, son?" my dad asked. "We'll stop up here in Houma and get some cold beer and dinner." We were cruising in the passing lane in the powder blue Caddy over the big dark-brown river. Through the bridge railings I watched the barge lights twinkle as they inched ahead through the water.

"Albert says good-bye, son," my dad said. "He likes you. Albert's a businessman, the best kind." Dad lit a fresh Lucky from an old one and threw the butt out the window. "He's a good man to know. Remember that."

HARDWARE

by Lester Goldberg

The football spiraled into the sky. I cut right, leaped and grabbed it, tucked it in, ran a few steps, then turned toward my father and lobbed the ball back. Cut right, cut left: he threw pass after pass. As the sun dropped behind the factory roof and the Pyrene Fire Extinguisher sign glowed red, we knew my mother could see it from our apartment and it was time to head for home. On the way, walking a few feet apart, I still had to be alert—my father might pop the football at me underhanded. He told me about his dream backfield: Marshall Goldberg, Pittsburgh Panthers, halfback; Sid Luckman, Chicago Bears, quarterback; Paul Robeson, Rutgers, fullback. Two Jews and a Negro.

After dinner, my father, moving a purple grape and two green ones around the kitchen table, tried out the backfield on my grandfather Gershon.

"I don't know Goldberg and what's-his-name," my grandfather said, "but Robeson, he's the top choice."

"Why Robeson and not the others, Gus?" I said.

My father picked up the purple grape. "A fighter for human rights," he said, flipping the grape in the air, head cocked back, mouth open, but it hit his chin and dropped to the floor.

"A Jewish *neshuma*," my grandfather said. "He's good for the Jews."

At that time, Grandpa added to his income from the hardware-junk business by taking on small plumbing jobs. He'd hang up a sign—OUT TO LUNCH—orange letters on black—and off we'd go in his old Ford pickup.

He drove with both hands on the wheel, hunched over it. Sitting next to him on the torn seat, I ran my hand into the space between the backrest and seat and scooped up a few coins. "Keep them," he said when I started to place them on the dashboard. I think he started planting these coins for me to find when I was very little. And he just kept it up. I slipped the coins into my shirt pocket.

"Gus, why don't you change the sign to CLOSED FOR THE DAY. You never get back to reopen."

He pushed the directional signal forward and as we started around the corner into Avon Avenue, a few black faces here, he pushed it back again. He'd never let the signal assert itself, return automatically. "I don't like to close, ever."

Grandpa pulled up in front of Rothstein's luncheonette. "Get us two coffees and the *Ledger*." He handed me a dollar. I hopped out and was back in a jiffy. "They don't serve coffee anymore." I put the paper down between us. "A colored guy in the store. Rothstein's gone. It looked like a bookie joint."

He eased the clutch and shifted into first. "I can live without coffee and Irving Rothstein was no angel."

No mansions on Avon. Salamis used to hang in the delis, skins shining as if polished with wax. Pigs knuckles and ham hocks were starting to appear in the butcher-shop windows. The kosher signs faded.

I grabbed the pipestand and threader off the truck, put them under one arm, and pulled out a piece of inch-and-a-half and a piece of two-inch galvanized. Tried to cradle them under the other arm, to avoid another trip to the cellar, when Grandpa shouldered me aside. "Always in a hurry," and he grabbed the two pieces from me. I followed him up the stoop of the building into the vestibule. "Go upstairs," and he tapped each of the eight mailboxes. "Knock and tell them the plumber's here—they should draw water. Then meet me in the cellar." Three bells were ripped out, wires hanging and two mailbox covers missing.

I edged down the cellar stairs, a dim bulb at the bottom, and picked my way around broken baby carriages, torn-open valises, tripped on a tricycle. At the far end of the cellar near the water heater, Grandpa's drop light shone like a beacon. He grunted with each pull on the wrench. "This one's a real *schlechter*," he said, mopping his forehead. "You forgot the pipe cutter and oil." I hated to leave but off I went, up the stairs, back to the truck. Then we worked together: old pipe disconnected, new piece cut to size, thread both ends, and with two couplings we were ready to put it into place.

A voice from the stairs. "You the Jew-bird who owns this shithouse? Why don't you fix it up?"

I turned, still holding my end of the pipe, blinked under the spotlight. A dark face leaned over the cellar stair railing; the body and legs invisible in the shadows. "Shiiiiiiiit, man. Think we gonna pay good money for cold water."

"Shah, mister, shah," my grandfather said. "I'm the Jewish plumber who's fixing the boiler so you get hot water. I'm a working man—just like you." He didn't look at the man. "Raise the pipe, just a little, sonny." Waved his wrench in the air. Then clamped it on the coupling and started to draw it tight.

I was glad to get out of there. We passed a storefront synagogue, blue Star of David on yellow over the door; a sign flapping above the transom: MT. BETHEL BAPTIST CHURCH. Grandpa said if he only could learn how to do a good sweat joint, he could handle copper tubing in addition to galvanized and find plenty more plumbing work.

I ran all the way home the day I made the varsity, ran upstairs, burst through the door, grabbed my mother, swung her around, and yelled so the whole world could hear. "I'm first string. I beat out the Eyetie, that big blob of spaghetti. I'm first-string left tackle."

My mother shook herself loose. "I brought you up right. If your father heard that word . . ."

Just then my dad stepped out of the bathroom, holding the paper in his hand. "In our house," he said, waving his *National Guardian* in the air, "there are no Eyeties, bowties, dagos, wops, or niggers—just humans." My skinny father still had that rueful smile on his face. The *Newark News* photo caught that smile a few years back. Caption underneath read: LOCAL RED TAKES THE FIFTH AMENDMENT. He smiled before you started talking to him and, whatever I said, just kept smiling. Eyes always crinkled. I looked for a tear, a break in the smile. Never.

"I meant, Dad, I beat out a fine young American of Italian descent. You'll come to the game next week, won't you? Against Barringer."

"Maybe, if I'm in town." That long sentence had exhausted him. Laid off from the furniture factory, and when he's not working, he's always tired.

The only game anyone came to watch that senior year, and only Grandpa came, was against South Side. I smashed through, tackling runners all over the field. No one could get past me. My friends in the stands screamed: Go-go-Buster-go. Eat 'em up alive, Buster baby! My best game. We only lost by 38 to 6.

*   *   *

At Rutgers there were lots of good football players and I took an awful razzing because I came from Weequahic High and my old team hadn't won a game from '55 to '59. Later, when the blacks came along and joined the squad, we started to win a few. The freshman coach said I was strong enough but I ran out of steam. I should work on running, do lots of wind sprints.

The record player was on full blast and Paul Robeson's deep rich voice filled the kitchen:

> He don't plant taters
> he don't plant cotton
> and those that plants them
> are soon forgotten . . .

Still in striped pajamas, Dad's head was buried in the help wanted ads. Mom had found a job in the payroll department of Continental Can. Without looking up, he pushed the sports section across the table. I sat, leafed the paper for Rutgers sports. Then Dad joined Robeson, his tenor under Robeson's bass. "Old man river, he just keeps rolling along."

He looked up, someplace over my head. "When I'm not working, I feel okay only on Saturday."

"Want some more coffee?" I got up and filled my cup and added more to his.

"I'll dig up a job. Get your education. You know I only want the best for you."

"Sure, I know that."

"You know, I love you more than . . ."

"Sure, Dad." He's not smiling this time, looking square into my eyes.

"Would you want me to warm your underwear on the radiator, like my father did for me?"

"What for?"

"How do you know?"

"Know what?"

"That I love you. As much as your mother or anyone."

"I see you check the gas jets at night, make sure they're turned off."

"Joker." He leaned over and clapped me on the shoulder; he who rarely touched. "My father did that, too."

Robeson's booming "Tsene tsene" now. No trace of a black or Jewish accent.

"He was an all-American football player at Rutgers," my father said. "Did you know that?"

"I'm not all-American, Dad. I may not even make the team."

The phone rang from the living room. I jumped up. "Pop the toaster down," my father said.

I hit the toaster on my way out and picked up the phone. "Turn down the record player," I yelled through the doorway. "I can't hear."

"It's Grossman from next door," I heard. "Come right down. Your grandpa's hurt."

"What's wrong!"

"Robbers, robbers, but he's not too bad—stop talking and come quick."

In three leaps I sprang into the kitchen. "Gus was mugged, Dad!" I stuck out my hand. "The car keys—give me the keys."

"Car's on the fritz," he said. "Wait! I'll get dressed." He headed for the bedroom. "On the fritz, I told you. Don't you ever listen?" I couldn't wait, ran downstairs to the corner, and sprinted for the red light that was holding a cab. Hammered on the window, jumped in. "Quick, please, Bergen Street. My grandpa's hurt." The cabbie gave his cap a tug and the cab leaped from the curb, throwing me back against the seat. "Haas Hardware, near Renner, hurry!" Down Bergen Street, weaving in and out of traffic, and I glanced at the cabbie's permit—Glucksman, a Jew, I'm sure. An ambulance came flying out of a side street, siren clanging, and the cab slid into its wake and followed, until the ambulance peeled off toward Beth Israel Hospital. We pulled up behind a police car in front of the store.

Six, seven people stood in front of the smashed plate glass window. I reached for my wallet, didn't have it. "I forgot my money," I told the cabbie. "I'll get some in the store and come right out."

I shouldered past a man blocking the doorway. Grandpa sat on a chair next to the cash register. Grossman from the stationery store stood behind him, his hands on Grandpa's shoulders. The cash register was open and I looked in to grab some bills—empty. Just loose change.

Two men in white coats were talking to a young policeman whose foot rested on Grandpa's large balance scale. A sergeant was squatting in front of Grandpa and looking up into his face.

"What did they look like?" the sergeant said. "As tall as him?" He stuck his thumb at me.

Grandpa shook his head from side to side.

"His size?" and he pointed to the young cop. "Just nod your head."

Grandpa dropped his head on his chest, then raised his eyes to mine, mouthed some words but no sound came out.

"There were two of them, right?" A nod. The sergeant scratched in his black book. He straightened up from his squatting position. "Colored?" No answer.

"White men?" Grandpa closed his eyes.

"Were they negroes? Nothing to be afraid of." A small head shake.

"Why'd they break your window?"

One of the ambulance attendants unrolled a stretcher onto the floor. The other tapped the sergeant on the arm. "We gotta take him away, Sarge. Can't you question him later?"

As I pushed my way through the growing crowd outside, the baker at the corner grabbed my arm. "Those *schvartze* bestids. Give Gus a regards from me." I shook him off and put one foot on the rear step of the ambulance when I felt a hand grabbing my back pocket. I swiveled around, right hand balled into a fist, and tripped on the step. Sat down hard on the ambulance floor. "It's a little nothing," the cabbie said. "My address is in your back pocket. Just send me the money when you have it."

"Don't worry," I yelled as the attendant slammed the door. "Drop dead," under my breath.

"You owe it. Mail it like he asked." As I turned, the ambulance started and my head bumped the roof. Grandpa threw off the blanket and tried to sit up.

I squeezed in next to him on the side bench and pressed him back gently with my open palm. "Easy now, Gus, just rest back."

His color was better. His Adam's apple popped in and out. "Let me talk!"

"Don't strain—"

He grabbed my fingers, squeezed. "Don't interrupt!" A deep breath. "Two of them come in, not bad dressed, like workmen, and ask for a saw. I give them a cheap saw and the bigger one says, give us a better one. What kind, I ask. A good sharp one, he says. So, just a minute, I say. I see he knows something and I sell a couple pounds nails to another feller who walked in and go to get the saw. A Diston, I get him. So the smaller, lighter-colored one says, need a two-inch gate valve—you got one? Ah, hah! Small plumbing contractors I figure, nice fellas—why not. I should have known then. Would a carpenter need a two-inch gate valve? I call myself a half-ass plumber. Do I use a saw?"

"It's possible, Gus."

He sat up. His forehead was scraped raw and swelling. A blue bruise on his left cheekbone. "Not on your life! I go to the back storeroom where I keep the bigger valves in a box—not much call for them—they follow me—knock me down from behind, choke me, kick me . . ."

"Sons-a-bitches! Cowards! If I were only there . . ."

"Bigshot. They'd hit you with a hammer."

"And you never said a bad word against negroes all your life."

"Bums, robbers. It's nothing to do with color. Why don't they study, learn . . ."

The ambulance stopped at the emergency entrance, turned down the ramp.

"Why'd they break your front window? What do you care. You're insured."

"For this, I'm not insured. I smashed it with a hammer."

An attendant opened the rear door. I held Grandpa's arm. The attendant unrolled the stretcher and Grandpa didn't protest when they eased him onto it.

I rested my hand on his shoulder and walked alongside. "Why, Gus, why'd you break it?"

"I was ashamed."

"Why? For whom? What in the hell for?"

"For me, because I couldn't do nothing. For them. Who knows?"

I stayed with him in the emergency room, surrounded by blacks— cut and bruised and sick, until my mother and father arrived. Then Gus insisted that my father and I leave and check the store. So back to the store we went and I helped my father nail a plywood frame across the smashed window.

They held Grandpa at Beth Israel for a few days because he complained of dizzy spells. At the end of two weeks he was back in the store. At least that's what my mother said, but I bicycled over three times and each time I found a sign up, a new one I'd never seen before: CLOSED FOR THE DAY.

One Saturday, no football practice, so I decided to work out in Weequahic Park. In shorts and sweatshirt I ran down Runyon Street toward the synagogue where I used to get a quarter from the old *shamus* for turning on the lights on Friday. He was convinced that a kid with dirty-blond hair, who never came to temple even on holidays when you could get free cake and soda, must be a Gentile. Right on time, whitey, he used to call me when I arrived at dusk, dirty and tired from an afternoon of sandlot football. I jogged past the iron gate that enclosed the temple courtyard, sidestepped two old men, and stopped short—when I spied Gus, in a long coat, standing at the door of the temple. I grabbed the black iron bars, stared at him. He looked around, didn't see me through the bars; he looked around again like he was getting ready to go into a girlie strip show on Market Street, then ducked inside.

I continued toward the park and started running along the path that circled the lake. A nippy morning and no one except a dog walker on the grass, collar turned up against the wind.

I ran, took my position, charged from a crouch, ran, and stopped again. Around the end of the lake, even quieter here as an early-morning train pulled by, chugging along toward Penn Station. I heard running steps behind me, lengthened my stride, racing the unknown runner when I was hit in mid-back, thrown off stride, went flying down a slope, tripped, and fell to one knee. I jumped up and ahead of me, a tall lean negro kid in a track suit loping along the path. Hit me with his shoulder! No reason for it! I started after him, not sure what I'd do. Didn't want a punching match but can't let him escape unpunished. I began to stretch out; he ran deliberately, tiring maybe, because I was catching up and getting ready to charge down on him and smash him with my shoulder as I ran by. Leaner than me and taller. If he wasn't in track clothes, I wouldn't tangle with him—who can tell what he might be carrying in a pocket, but he was as naked as I was, long black legs flashing. An uphill slog now, the lake glistened, a woods to my right, great spot for an ambush—gaining on him, ten yards away, now five, when with a burst of speed, he opened ten yards between us, then twenty, and I tried to gear up but couldn't make it, and finally drew up panting, kicked a stone in front of me—and he disappeared around a turn in the path. He never looked back.

I couldn't wait to see my grandfather that afternoon. It was quiet in the store and I offered to clean out the cellar. So down I went, the steps very steep, felt the morning's running in my thighs. I sorted the odd lengths of pipe, threw scraps of iron into bushel baskets, and then started rearranging the stoves. I placed the small potbellied ones in one row, some square Thatcher stoves in another row, left space between the aisles, jockied two black kitchen stoves against a rear wall, ballbusters those two, and now I was really sweating. Grandpa had a reputation for buying and selling old coal and wood stoves and homeowners would drive in from the suburbs and buy a stove for a country house or hunting shack. I heard him on the staircase.

"What did you do?" was his greeting. "Cleanup—all right, but you messed up the works." While I stood by speechless he began picking up stoves in his two arms and hauling them back to their original positions. "Come upstairs," he said with a hand on my biceps, "before you make more trouble."

"Just a minute." I shook him off. "Gus, were you ever afraid?"

He scratched his head, hair thick and black.

"When those negroes mugged you?"

"Of those hoodlums? No. We had some fine Jewish gangsters on Ferry Street in the old days. They'd collect protection from the pushcarts. From the pickle man, the banana king."

"I saw you go into the synagogue today, Gus."

"Very nice. My daughter sent you to spy on me."

"You know she wouldn't. Why'd you go in? You never do."

"I was looking around. Is there a law against it?"

"Did you find anything, Grandpa?"

"They had a good *chazan* from New York. He sang nice. No, there's nothing there. I don't agree everything with your father, you know that, but one thing I do agree: religion is the opium of the people. Come." He took my hand. "I hear the bell ringing—a customer." He led me up the stairs.

Just one week later, a young, light-skinned black walked in and Grandpa picked up a box of locks lying next to the cash register and emptied them onto the kid's head. Cut him up badly. When the cops came, the kid denied saying it's a holdup as Grandpa claimed.

The boy had a wooden toilet paper holder clenched in one hand and swore that was all he came in for: another holder and two mousetraps. Grandpa didn't carry either item. The boy looked fifteen or sixteen but turned out to be only thirteen.

My dad almost seemed to enjoy the ruckus. He got the lawyer who represented him when he was called before the House Un-American Activities Committee. The black kid's family settled for medical expenses and $250.

Gershon Haas, my grandfather, closed the store shortly afterward and put a FOR SALE sign in the window. He listed the place with a broker on Lyons Avenue but no one wanted it.

We carry the smell of the wet hemp runners, the locker room, the swimming pool; the chlorine carries it along with us from the old Jewish Y in Newark to Rutgers gymnasium in New Brunswick, to the new Y on Green Lane in Union. Jewish dank. Worse than Jewish angst because this has a smell that is unmistakable; can't be spirited away by psychiatrists, rabbis, or exorcists. It stays on, lives with me forever.

WHAT LANGUAGE DOES GOD SPEAK?

by Bernice Grohskopf

I watched my mother spread the clean white linen towel, starched and ironed to an enamel shine, over Ellen's dressing table, smoothing the cloth with both hands before she set on it two silver candlesticks. A monogram at one end of the towel, embroidered in swirly letters, caught my eye. I was just learning my letters. AFL it read, the *F* larger than the letters on either side.

"What is the *L* for?" I asked.

"Loesser. My name before I married your daddy."

"But why is that at the end? *F,* for Feingold, should be at the end."

"No, this way it's fancier." She lowered the shades, glanced over at the bed, then put her finger to her lips to silence me.

Ellen lay quietly in her bed, the covers neatly pulled to her chest; her arms in a long-sleeved nightgown were outside the covers and in her hands she held her beads with the crucifix. Without her usual rosy flush, without her silver-rimmed glasses, lids closed over her bright gray eyes, her lips softly murmuring her rosary, I wasn't sure it was my Ellen who, I assumed, lived with us for my sake, as my personal friend, although she was actually our housekeeper. I stepped closer. Her steel-colored hair fell back from her forehead. My Ellen never looked like that, so white, so sad. Again my mother put her finger over her lips and led me out of the room.

"Why does she look like that?"

"She's sick."

"Will she get better?"

"I think so."

"Is the doctor coming?"

"Soon."

"Is that why you put your fancy guest towel on her dressing table?"

"No. That's for when the priest comes."

"What's he going to do?"

"Pray."

"Pray?"

"Yes. Pray to ask God to make her better."

"How will he do that?"

"I don't know how he does it. Maybe like the rabbi when he prays."

"What will the priest say?"

"I'm not sure. Something in Latin. Like when we say the *Shema*."

The *Shema* was my nightly prayer. Instead of "Now I lay me down to sleep . . ." I said to my mother each night, "*Shema Yisrael Adonai eloheinu Adonai echud,*" always followed by the English, "Hear, O Israel, the Lord our God, the Lord is one." It meant little to me, but it was the token effort on the part of my parents to help me remember my religion. Other than that nightly ritual, and the annual seder at my grandmother's, I knew little about my own faith. My parents told me I was too young for Sunday school, but Ellen went regularly to early Mass and, on occasion, let me come along with her. In the big church, I felt small, but comforted, my eyes drooping, my body lulled by the sounds of the bells, the droning voices. Dimly, I was aware of Ellen kneeling and bobbing up, kneeling again, crossing herself, muttering things I couldn't understand. I loved the music of the deep male voice, hollow, as though coming from some distant sphere.

"Will the priest say the *Shema*?" I asked.

"No. He says another prayer."

"Why?"

"He doesn't know Hebrew. He speaks Latin."

"Will God understand him in Latin?"

"Of course."

"Will He make her better?"

"I think so."

I was allowed to open the door for the priest, who startled me, because, dressed in his black suit and black hat, he looked just like the drawing of the naughty man in one of my picture books. He wore a white collar, however, and when he took off his black hat as we stood in the small entryway together, I looked at his gray hair, his round, flushed, kind face, his gray eyes behind silver-rimmed glasses, wondering if he might be Ellen's brother. But I didn't ask, since he understood only Latin.

His expression was gentle as he bent down, smiling into my eyes, and shook my hand. To my surprise, in English he asked my name. I told him.

"That's a lovely name. I'm Father O'Hare."

"Are you Ellen's father?"

His laugh, rough-edged with phlegm, exploded, bouncing off the walls of the tiny hallway where we stood. I felt my face grow warm, my eyes smart, a reaction that occurred whenever a grown-up laughed at something I said.

I trailed behind as my mother led him to Ellen's room, saying in her grand voice, "She'll be so happy to see you, Father."

Father? *My* mother called him Father.

While he was in Ellen's bedroom, I found many reasons for walking up and down the hallway to pass Ellen's door, slightly ajar, so that I could hear the murmurings of the priest and glimpse the lighted candles, stately and elegant on the white linen cloth. Those flickering flames in the shade-darkened room, the glow of the white linen, and his low voice asking God to make my Ellen better, revealed to me a glimpse of something that I didn't understand, but that looked, in my childish imagination, like a vision of peace and perfection.

How beautiful and silent the candlelight.

Was it making my Ellen better?

When the doctor came, the door to Ellen's room was kept tightly closed, my mother in the room with them, and when they emerged, they were talking seriously. Soon after that, Ellen was taken to the hospital.

Hospital I understood, even operation, for one of the other children in nursery school had just had her tonsils removed.

"Will they take out her tonsils?"

"It's like that," my mother told me. "Something hurts her on her insides, and the doctor wants to make it better."

"Will he take out her insides?"

My mother's eyes closed, a trick I had already learned occurred whenever she invented a tale. "Just the appendix," she murmured.

"In her tummy, like Betsy Bernstein's mommy?"

"Yes."

How could my mother have explained to me what a hysterectomy was?

Ellen's absence, while it was a trial for my mother, who worked and disliked staying home, was a time of total desolation for me. No Ellen to play with me while I had my bath, no Ellen to tell me stories of Mr. Hucklebee, no Ellen who scolded my koala bear when he didn't tidy the room, glancing at me as she did so, her eyes merry with our secret, that her words were meant for me, no Ellen to make French toast for me in the morning or to lure me into eating things I disliked, with stories and imaginative names: a "chrysanthemum egg" was a hard-boiled egg grated to a fluffy burst of yellow and white over creamed spinach; a "speckled luluberger" was chopped vegetables held together with mashed potato and egg. I loved to count the many colors, but Ellen always managed to find one I'd not spotted.

"Take a look at that yellow," she'd say.

"What's that one?"

"Yellow squash."

"I see some purple, Ellen."

She'd lean close, examining it, her face serious. "Looks as though a scrap of your mom's new blouse got in there." She'd wink as she watched me take another bite.

While she was in the hospital, every night after I was in bed, after my mother and father had kissed me, as soon as they had turned out the light, I took from under my pillow a strand of plastic beads that I had won at a birthday party, multi-colored beads, strung with tiny gold-centered balls between each. I held them, as I'd seen Ellen hold her beads, in both hands, moving my lips as Ellen did, wondering what I was supposed to say. I'd try, "Please God, make her better," which didn't seem a long enough or impressive enough sentence for God to hear. He'd probably prefer Latin, which I didn't know, but perhaps He'd listen to Hebrew. It was worth a try, and so, moving my beads between my fingers as I'd seen Ellen do, I said, "*Shema Yisrael Adonai eloheinu Adonai echud*," repeating it fervently. If I could have done so without causing more anger from my mother than I felt I could handle, I would have placed a shining white guest towel on my bureau and lighted candles to be sure He heard me. But I hoped that even without these magic additions, and even though I did not know the Latin words, God would understand what I was saying.

Ellen came home from the hospital looking almost as she'd always looked, with her pink cheeks and her gleaming silver-rimmed glasses on her smiling eyes. Was it the beads? Perhaps, after all, God did know Hebrew.

We resumed our life together. When I came home from nursery school, I "helped" her clean and cook. As in the past, we played school, and tea party, and Go Fish; we sewed clothes for my dolls and had early dinner together in the kitchen as she talked and joked me into finishing what was on my plate. We also started going to confession together.

Ellen would change from her gray and white everyday uniform into a dress, always the same long-sleeved dark blue with matching blue buttons down the front, and her blue church shoes. She'd sit patiently at her dressing table to let me comb her hair before she put on her blue felt church hat, a close-fitting inverted felt bowl, pleated into slanting folds across the front. I liked to watch the expression on her face when she put that hat on, smiling at herself in the mirror as she set it, just the way she liked it, straight across her forehead. Then, hand in hand, we walked six blocks to the Church of the Little Flower of Jesus, a secret vault of miracles and mystery, far more impressive to me on weekdays, when the pews were nearly empty, and candles burned, silent and faithful, holding the prayers and sorrows of those who'd placed them there. Each time we stepped into that cool, dark silence, the afternoon light shining through the stained glass windows high above the dim interior, I felt indescribable wonders, as though I would find there all the answers to my four years of questions, solutions to the puzzles of the grown-up world would be revealed to me.

The very first time we went, I saw Ellen remove her glove to dip her hand in what looked like a marble bowl. I couldn't reach it.

"Can I have some?"

"It's not to drink," she whispered, repressing a smile.

"What is it?"

"Holy water," and, smiling, she touched the wet tips of her fingers to mine. Then, facing the altar, she dipped a brief kneel as she crossed herself. I wobbled as I tried to do the same dip and cross, but I saw her clap her hand over her mouth to smother her laughter. My face grew warm. "You needn't do that," she whispered to me, patting my shoulder, still struggling to control her laughter.

Before Ellen went into the confessional, I was assigned the task of holding her pocketbook, an honor I considered sacred. Always, as she handed me her bag, she did so solemnly, gently impressing upon me the full responsibility of my assignment. It was a square box-bag, much like a mini–cosmetic case, covered in blue leather, and I remember thinking that perhaps someone seeing me holding that important grown-up handbag might mistake me for a grown-up. Ellen would settle me in one of the wooden seats, my legs sticking straight out, the pocketbook in my lap, and whisper, "Now, hold on to that, and try to sit quietly. If you're very good, you'll see Jesus, right up there."

I sat in the faint, dusky light and the silence, watching, not certain what sort of person I was to look for, wondering if he'd be naked as I'd seen him in pictures, wondering what to say to him if he did show up, and, in a way, hoping that he wouldn't notice me, because he, no doubt, spoke only Latin. I suppose the wait must have tired me, because one day Ellen's pocketbook, which I usually clutched tightly with both hands, slipped off my lap onto the wooden floor, setting up an astonishing clatter in that great hollow place. I felt tears flood my eyes, but from someplace I heard muffled laughter that sounded like Ellen's.

I suppose the job of housemaid in a large household became too much for Ellen, because when I was about ten years old, she went out of my life, back to Albany, her hometown, to take a job as cook at St. Mary's Rectory. Letters were exchanged at first, as well as snapshots, until, with time, we lost touch except for the annual Christmas card.

But Ellen did not go out of my life. Not entirely. When I was in my late teens, I found myself drawn to Catholicism. I studied, prayed, read, talked with the patient priest who tried to help me work through my questions and doubts, until eventually, confused and conflicted, I made peace in the best way possible with my divided spirit, convinced that God, whatever His persuasion, whatever His language, would see me as I was, a stray who had wandered from one fold to another, feeling I belonged to both, and to neither, and that if I couldn't find Him, He would find me.

My mind lingered on Ellen and the mystery of her profound goodness. I recalled that I'd never heard her speak of her family, or anyone in her life. Who had loved her? Whom had she loved? There must have been a time when her love was given to someone close—a mother, or father, or lover. But I never heard her speak of them. Nor did I ever hear her express anger or impatience or bitterness; she held life and love sacred, without passion or aspiration, without irritable reaching after facts, or unattainable goals.

I realized that those years of my childhood with her are filled with memories sweeter to me than to her, for while she enriched my life with humor and love, her life was one of daily menial chores and duties, a lonely time that was, no doubt, made more tolerable by her faith and, I hope with all my heart, by my devotion to her. Perhaps she was content simply to give, in a large abstract way, the saintlike embrace of all through her selfless love, a spiritual donation, an impersonal benediction to bless and nourish and enlarge the spirit of others.

A PUBLIC DENIAL

by Allan Gurganus

Despite persistent rumors to the contrary, my grandfather did not die driving a Toyota across his pond. As I will demonstrate, this is a bald mistruth. Admittedly, he had become somewhat senile or eccentric in recent years. In view of the attempted firing of the courthouse cannon last July, it would be foolish to state otherwise. But certain exaggerations now in circulation are unfair to his family's memory of him and must be corrected.

While bizarre, many of the stories about his attempts to secure the local Toyota dealership are true. Just after Corona wagons were introduced in this country, he bought one for use on his farms. For reasons none of us will ever know, he began to take an interest, a very active interest, in the well-being of the Toyota company. He decided at age seventy-one to become the local dealer for the car, but because of his advanced years and idiosyncracies, the franchise was withheld. He bought three more Toyotas, either to endear himself to the home office or maybe out of pure enthusiasm. These, Corona convertibles, he gave to grandchildren. (One is still in the author's possession and running like a top.) But not even his extra purchases brought so much as a discount from the mother office.

At this point in Grandfather's quest for the franchise, he staged the much-discussed "pond drive." Having read in the owner's manual that the Toyota is more perfectly watertight than almost any other car, he decided to personally demonstrate and document this fact, thus winning the long-sought-after approval of Toyota International. To his farm near Little Easonburg, he summoned six tenant farmers and one twelve-year-old grandson. They were stationed at five-feet intervals along a pond bank, each man equipped with a loaded camera borrowed or bought for the occasion. The pond itself is a small one, dug for irrigation purposes in 1959. My grandfather, a conservationist long before it was fashionable, had at one time stocked the pond with bass, which shiftless tenant farmers are said to have fished out and eaten before any achieved maturity.

His theory was that the rotating rear tires would propel the car through the water. He evidently drove it slowly down the east bank, honking the horn: a prearranged signal to "aim all cameras." Eased into the water, the car actually floated, moving slowly to the center of the pond. Once there, it veered toward shore, the speedometer registering 110 mph while the vehicle advanced at only about 3 mph through the water. Some moisture did seep in, but hardly enough to sink the car, as many have falsely reported. The experiment, in short, was an overwhelming success. When the Toyota containing my grandfather finally scrambled up the opposite bank, the six tenant farmers and one grandson, the writer's first cousin, are said to have let out a spontaneous cheer.

It was immediately afterward, while taking the car for a quick land drive—toward the nearest public telephone some two miles away—that the fatal accident occurred. Maneuvering the curve along Bank Road, he evidently lost control of the car. It crashed over a low bridge and into a farm pond much deeper than his own. He had lowered the car's windows, to dry what little water had originally seeped in. With all the windows open, his Corona did not float long this time. He went down with it.

I have given all these specifics to point out that the pond in which he drowned was more than a mile and a half from the original site of his *successful* experiment. This, I hope, will put an end to rumors that his death was somehow foolhardy. Though the "pond drive" photographs proved inconclusive (exhaust fumes, of the sky, etc.), we still have the witnesses' spoken accounts. In short, the man died having proved something, which is more than we can say for most of us. Toyota International, hearing of his death, sent our family a letter signed by a vice president of that company. It expressed gratitude for Grandfather's "pioneering consumer spirit," and went on to say, "We could certainly use more customers with his brand of courage and devotion." This, I hope, will finally quiet local cynics and permit his widow and his bereaved children and grandchildren to live normal lives again.

SATURDAY MORNING AT AUTOPSY

by Richard Harteis

I

They sat in the lobby of the medical examiner's building, eating cherry danish, drinking coffee from the corner deli.

"You want some, Prudence?" Robert asked, handing the cup to his classmate. "You look a little lived-in this morning."

"Oh, Robert, I couldn't." She laughed. "I was partying at my cousin's till two this morning. I don't know if I'm gonna make it. Look what my mother made me bring, just in case." She took from her purse a lace handkerchief that had been doused with toilet water. The lobby filled with Jungle Passion.

"Whew. That stuff could raise the dead," Barry said. He held his nose. "You'd better not pull it out when we start carving."

They had nervously avoided talking about the morning's autopsy. They could sense each other's moods almost the way husbands and wives can read each other after years of marriage. But of course it would be Barry who would raise the subject. When they were learning to draw blood or to feed a stomach tube down each other's noses, Barry always volunteered to be the first guinea pig. When a teacher accused the class of cheating, Barry stood up to him with such insults that the entire class nearly failed the course. His classmates saw in him the courage and stupidity of a boy who tortures a wounded animal with a stick to see if it is alive or dead.

A lot of the city students wore old army jackets, but in Barry's case the jacket and insignias were legitimate. Unlike most veterans, he was filled with stories of Viet Nam and all he'd seen there. Once he'd buried an enemy's head he had found along a trail when he hadn't even been ordered to. It was true how Asian whores concealed razor blades to slice up amorous G.I.'s. He never pretended to be a hero, but insisted on his experience the way other students might invoke wealth or athletic ability to achieve social standing. Barry would float through the student union as though he were greeting a press conference. He wore a gold chain and a Star of David that he'd bought on R and R in Hong Kong. Robert had caught him once in front of the men's room mirror arranging it in a mat of chest hair.

Robert discounted him as an "airhead" but was annoyed by the fact that Barry's tuition was paid for by Barry's wife and the G.I. Bill, while Robert had to work long hours at the admissions office to earn his. He didn't mind Barry's "cool" at exam time or the way he could talk teachers into raising his grades. But it bothered Robert that most of the women in the class couldn't see through his performance.

"I've heard a lot about you," Barry said when they first met. "Sometime you'll have to tell me your side of it."

"I understand you've been making Asia safe for democracy," Robert said.

They hadn't squared off yet, but the friends who formed cliques about each of them knew it was just a matter of time. One sensed the possibility of it when they shared a room as sharply as the smell of carbolic acid announcing the morning's autopsy every time a technician opened the door to the laboratory basement.

"You'll be okay, Prudence," Robert said.

"I'll catch you if you pass out, Prue," Barry said.

II

It seemed semesters ago that they had all done the cat and the baby pig. It hadn't been easy that summer to forget the beach and go every day to a drawer reeking of formaldehyde to pull out Tom once again. It would require months of practice before they could take a scalpel to human flesh. They were still awkward at the job, but eventually everything got seen that needed to be seen: the nerves, the vessels, the tiny ducts connecting gray organs. At first they went in like a bulldozer and often mashed what they were looking for. Gradually they had improved their technique.

"You wanna pass this course, you have to work delicate, nice," the lab instructor would say.

They had to be reminded again the first day they got their box of human bones, a terrible jigsaw puzzle asking to be assembled and memorized.

"Knock it off, Barry," the same instructor had warned after Barry had decked the skeleton in lab coat and stuck a lighted cigarette in the skull's teeth. "Somebody was walking around in those bones not too long ago, somebody like *you*. They aren't plastic, for Christ's sake," He was half a head taller than Barry, and almost a skeleton himself. "Let's have a little respect, huh?"

Before they began the autopsy, Dr. Kim led them on a little tour, like making hospital rounds for the dead. They followed one another in single file down a spiral staircase to the basement. The smell of chemicals and putrefaction brought out a sort of animal anxiety in the white-coated students. They knew they shouldn't be there, the way horses go wide-eyed at a slaughterhouse.

"Robert," Prudence whispered, "look over there. Is he . . . ?"

"He ain't napping, Prudence," Barry said.

An old man lay naked on a stretcher, parked at random in a corner. His face was blue, his nakedness embarrassing. His toe was tagged, as in a second-rate detective film. It was not the fact of the corpse but the casual way it had simply been left sitting around that bothered Robert. He wanted to cover the body with a sheet. They'd been trained never to leave a post-op patient unattended. Here the bodies didn't require that attention. The battle was lost. But it seemed like breaking the rules.

Barry walked over to inspect the body. He pressed his index finger on the bloated belly, engrossed.

"I want to show you some interesting cases before we begin," Dr. Kim said. "Follow me, please."

He began pulling out shelves. Some came headfirst, others sideways on slabs opening like bureau drawers. He described each case, giving the essential details for them to note. In one drawer they found a slim Puerto Rican man whose body was intact except for deep purple rope marks on his neck.

"The poor kid," Gayle said almost to herself. "I wonder what made him do it."

The boy could have been any brave punk standing on Flatbush Avenue on a Saturday night, but now he was frozen forever in his private desperation. His mustache was only beginning to grow. The face was puffy as though he'd been crying.

"Maybe they raised the ceiling on his rent," Barry said. He made a gesture pantomiming the noose, tongue hanging from the corner of his mouth. Robert saw a look of irritation and slight disgust on the instructor's face.

"We're here to study pathology, Mr. Schneider. If you can't behave appropriately, I'm going to have to ask you to leave."

Barry smiled repentently. "Sure, Dr. Kim. Uh, sorry."

They continued the inspection. Robert was beginning to dread each new horror. One body had sunken burn patches on the chest where a hospital staff had tried to shock the heart back into action. One had two empty holes where machines had for a time sustained life. Several corpses were wasted away to practically nothing from cancer. A woman lay with her throat slit like a melon; a male rape victim had been castrated.

"This is a nine-year-old female," Dr. Kim said. He pulled a plastic sack out from the shelf with Barry's help.

"Remember, you are bound by law to report every suspected child abuse case. X-rays done on this child revealed many old fractures, which could have easily been picked up by an emergency room physician with a high index of suspicion. No one caught the pattern before she was finally tortured to death."

There were no recognizable features; the body lay like a pile of charred leaves that had been left in the rain. The stench was nearly visible. To lift the sack back onto the shelf, Barry and Dr. Kim had to make a kind of hammock with their arms. The body filled the sack like liquid.

"Dr. Kim, I don't feel so good," Prudence said. "Could I be excused?"

"Very well. Why don't we all take a little break and meet next door in fifteen minutes."

Prudence went to the rest room. Robert, Gayle, and Barry sat in the lobby and smoked.

"I don't know how Kim takes it," Robert said. "Can you imagine doing that every day of your life? I wonder what his dreams must be like."

"Probably sleeps like a baby," Barry said. "He's a scientist. He's got to be objective about it."

"Yeah, but that little girl."

The odor clung to his clothes the way the smell of butter soured his mustache after eating corn on the cob.

"It's all the same when you're dead. I found that out in 'Nam." He shredded his cigarette.

"You think you're pretty damn tough, don't you?" Robert said. "Think you have it all figured out."

"Tough enough to take care of your ass, if you want to check it out."

Robert felt an urge to hit Barry. But the grotesqueries of the morning had left him disgusted and slightly anesthetized. He sat on the green plastic bench, preoccupied with the abused child.

Barry was tough. Robert wouldn't have voluntarily gotten that close to the rotting corpse, though he always managed to do what was required. But Barry hadn't been told to handle the terrible sloshing bag. Something needed doing and Barry had instinctively lent a hand. Robert was angry at his jealousy as well as Barry's insult. He sat like a student who'd just failed an important exam.

Barry stood up lazily when Prudence returned to the lobby.

"Oh, Barry," she said, "I don't think I can go back down there."

"Sure you can, Prue. I'll just light you a little joint here and you'll think it's all a Hollywood movie. Gayle, get your big butt over here. We're gonna get Prudence a little wacko to help her through the day."

Gayle remained seated and spoke across the room.

"Barry, you're crazy. I swear to God."

"I just want to say a prayer for those poor souls and go home," Prudence said. "It's so awful."

"Well, they're out of their misery now," Barry said. "Unless you believe in the great toke in the sky." He inhaled deeply from the marijuana.

"I'm a good Catholic girl from Brooklyn," Prudence said. "What do you expect?" Her faint blush was bluish in the fluorescent light. "What about you, Robert? Do you think there's an afterlife?"

"Well, I don't think we go on the way we are now," he said. He was aware of Barry's attention. Was it mocking? "I mean, I think personality dies with the brain that formed it, but our essence goes on. It's like the Zen thing where we die and don't die at the same time, you know?"

"Yeah, well, the dead part we're sure of," Barry said. Those bodies down there aren't coming back anytime soon. Ain't that right, Gayle honey?" He put his arm around her considerable waist.

Gayle had a reputation for being a straight shooter, and her size gave her an added authority. She had perfect skin, golden curls, blue eyes, and was very fat. She had come home one night from serving drinks in a Fort Worth bar and found her child had eaten a box of mothballs while the old man was out on the town. She took the child to the emergency room, then went home and nearly beat her husband to death. Two weeks later she arrived in New York with baby, her pick-up truck, seven hundred dollars, and some used furniture. The class took turns baby-sitting and never revealed her latest address to the state agencies or creditors.

"I think heaven or hell exist only for the living, right here in this world," she said. She spoke slowly, as if she knew what she meant but had never tried to word it. "I'd like to think there's something beyond. But I've got my hands too full to give it much time right now. You can always hope, I guess. Hope there's someone out there minding the store."

"Don't eat any flies, man," Barry said to Robert when they were called back downstairs to their work. Robert thought of Gayle's notion of hell. Hell was here and now, with devil-technicians busy in the basement.

III

For months they had been trained to minister to the wounded. They learned how to change a dressing quite gingerly, careful not to pull tissue from a surgical scar. They cleaned a burn or maneuvered a broken bone with great tenderness to avoid causing pain. Now they walked into a room of failures. Here the movements were abrupt; the bodies were handled roughly, quickly. With live patients you were always touching to reassure, to examine, to comfort. But here the physician touched only when necessary, would step back quickly from the body as soon as the job was done.

Dr. Kim had a surprise for them. All morning the radio had broadcast the news of a gangland-style assassination in Brooklyn that threatened to produce a new war of revenge. He stood at the foot of two tables on which the victims lay.

"In forensic medicine we must never assume anything," he said. "You must be extremely thorough and collect proper samples when you suspect something. Your responsibility to the victim of a crime is very great." He moved to the side of the table. "And I would ask you to please respect medical confidentiality while the police continue their investigation. Because of the importance of this case, my assistant and I will perform the autopsy today."

The two young men lay on the table as though in sleep. The paper had said they were twins, age 24, but the boy in the fetal position seemed a little younger. His brother lay on his back as though he'd found a private beach and gone skinny-dipping. Their bodies were well-developed, the dark hair and features consistent with Italian origins. They could have been Roman sculptures stuck away in some dusty corner of the Vatican. They were so pale, the dark brows and lashes gave them almost a feminine quality in sleep.

The assistant Dr. Kim introduced wore a T-shirt that fit his muscled torso snugly under a loose green bib apron. His wholesome face might easily illustrate a box of cornflakes except that it was expressionless. He wore plastic gloves.

The assistant turned the first body on its side. Gravity had pooled the dead boy's blood, and from heel to buttocks to shoulders the corpse was deep purple-black, as though he had gone to sleep in a vat of wine.

What Dr. Kim's assistant did next might not have bothered Robert as much if the assistant had been ugly or deformed. But watching this clean-cut young man work on the other with the stamina of a deer hunter, without the drapes of a surgical table, without the precision of a surgeon, would keep Robert from sleep for many nights to come.

The technician made several deep slashes at the base of the neck, grabbed the scalp firmly and in a quick up-and-over movement pulled the boy's face off as though it were a rubber mask.

"Oh, my God," Gayle whispered.

He took an electric saw and quickly cut a cap from the skull. Bone dust filled the air, producing an odor that made Robert sick to his soul. The assistant separated the dura mater from the skull, with great sucking, ripping sounds. He cut it at the base and handed the brain to Dr. Kim. This took four minutes.

With careful probing, Dr. Kim found the two bullets, the angle of entry proving that the projectiles could not have shattered the thin bones over the orbit of the eye. He dissected the brain, demonstrating to them certain areas that had only been difficult color illustrations in an anatomy text until then.

Now he opened the chest cage with metal clippers and evacuated the organs. The boy's heart had been just singed by a bullet, the four chambers untouched. The ripe scrotum was turned inside out, the intercostal muscles and ribs lay exposed like a side of beef, the assistant ladled black blood from the caverns he was creating.

Robert knew he was wrong in his thinking. The boy was dead. A clean and efficient analysis must be done. But the damage they were wracking on the corpse seemed worse to him than what the assassins had done.

Throughout the ordeal Barry's wisecracking had continued. The snide remarks on top of everything else made his face numb. He felt he might scream the way one feels a sneeze coming on.

He knew what he knew. They had been tied at the feet and wrists and gagged with newspapers. One brother had a bowel movement when he witnessed his brother being shot in the back of the head. He would be shot there too later, but he had suffocated screaming. Robert imagined the execution, incredulous, until Barry brought him out of his daydream.

He was bent over the first corpse, his long pageboy falling into the yawning chest cavity. He cocked his head. "Hey, Prudence, His Master's Voice."

"You son of a bitch, Barry," Gayle said. She came at him with a fist ready. Robert grabbed her and was almost unable to hold her.

She was not grandstanding. She knocked him up against the bodies and he felt his seat grow wet with blood and gore.

With her assault Barry pulled his head out of the chest cavity quickly, catching his gold chain on the dead boy's sternum. The gold Star of David dropped into the body with a plunking sound.

"That's enough, that's enough," Dr. Kim shouted.

"I'm sorry, Dr. Kim," she started. "I . . ."

"That's enough. And you, Barry. You think this all a laughing matter? I've had about all I can stand from you. Leave this room. And when you go upstairs I want you to talk to the old couple in the lobby. They are the grandparents of these victims. They wish to know how their grandsons died, and since you are so unaffected by all this, I'd like you to explain it to them."

"But Dr. Kim . . ."

"Don't argue with me. If you want to remain in this course, you go upstairs and talk with them right now."

"Do you believe he's actually doing it?" Prudence asked Robert as Barry left.

"Why not. That bastard's all heart," he said.

IV

Dr. Kim finished dictating his report and left the assistant to sew up the remains.

They moved on. With the final corpses their horror had diminished somewhat. Reluctantly they took diseased organs in hand to get a sense of their texture, listened to details, stuck to their work. The last case was that of a woman with terminal cancer who had committed suicide by barbiturates. Dr. Kim said he would have to continue to work, but perhaps they'd seen enough for one day. He asked them to return the following Saturday. They thanked him for his time and wandered out of the room. They gathered their books and knapsacks in silence.

It had turned black out. Third Avenue was freezing cold and dirty. They stood at the subway entrance, unwilling to leave one another. Their stillness was odd in the flow of people always rushing to get somewhere on a Saturday night in New York.

"Look," Gayle said finally. "I've got a poet friend over on Twenty-third. She's always got some brandy around. You want to go get drunk?"

"Why not?" Prudence said.

"Sure," Robert said. "Let me just hit the loo."

Barry stood over a basin, washing his face.

"Well, if it isn't Brooklyn's finest stand-up comedian."

"Yeah," Barry said. He didn't raise his head.

"Did you leave 'em rolling in the aisle?"

"No."

"I can't believe it. You mean . . . ?"

"Look, Robert, will you just forget it, huh?" Barry looked at him. He had been crying.

"Well, what happened, Barry?"

"It was Mrs. DiMarco. I went to grade school with her grandsons, Anthony and Gabe. They used to live in my old neighborhood."

"You mean you knew who they were when we . . . ?"

"No, no. I didn't recognize them then. I mean when we were in there I was getting sicker and sicker, you know. It just seemed so unfair to slaughter them like that, you know. When he ripped the face off Tony I thought I was gonna scream, but you know me, I sort of joke around when I'm nervous, you know . . ."

"Yeah, I know."

"Then I saw Mrs. DiMarco and it all hit me. Tony and Gabe. And we were down there ripping them apart. She stared and wouldn't speak to me. I felt like such a ghoul. Man, I feel so goddam dirty. I just want to go home and lay down beside my wife and hold her, you know?" Tears rolled down into his mustache.

Robert felt exhausted suddenly. The grotesque morning came over him once again like the quiet and disbelief after an airplane crash. And he couldn't bear the sadness of the victim in front of him now. He put his arm around Barry's shoulder and sat holding him a little while.

"Yeah, I know what you mean, Barry. But it could happen to anyone. You just didn't recognize who they really were. That's all. It could happen to anyone."

They went up with Gayle for poetry and brandy. There would be other, more difficult days. Now they sat quietly in the small apartment, grateful for the poet who wouldn't stop reading, for the end of this day, for one another.

MISSING KIN

by Shelby Hearon

"Old people expect to be called early in the morning," my mother says on the phone.

My mother is talking about Joe Don's grandmother, who has disappeared. It is her birthday, and we have sent her a dozen red roses and a Western Union Candygram, which we hope is a Whitman's Sampler. But she is not at home, and, by long distance, we have to make the decision whether to spend our Saturday being worried that she has fallen and broken a hip, or whether to get back to our own lives.

"She expected to be called in the morning," my mother says.

My mother is picturing someone frail, someone who lives a solitary life with no family or friends. Who woke up on her birthday and wanted the phone to ring. What my mother is not acknowledging is that Joe Don's grandmother is just her age, has dyed blond hair, wears long red fingernails, and smokes four packs of cigarettes a day.

"Old people are like that, Flower," Mother says.

Is she thinking, I wonder, of some elderly woman in her past? It is doubtful. Her own mother died at thirty-four, her grandmother at twenty-nine. The women in her family came and went in relation either to small pelvises and large babies or to the high blood pressure that comes from handsome husbands and separate bedrooms. More likely she is imagining herself in some future time down the road at a stage called Old: waking before the sun, having her cup of coffee, watching the clock, and waiting for her daughters to call. She is feeling future anger that it has become noon and later, and no one of us has got around to remembering her day.

The fact is that they—we, the daughters—would be doing what

Joe Don and I were doing this morning while letting the long-stemmed roses and Candygram carry the message to his grandmother: making love, listening to old Sons of the Pioneers records, eating.

Eating. We make fun of couples who make a production out of it. Gourmet couples who spend Saturdays doing quiches and ceviche and their own special eggs (not Benedict or Sardou, but eggs Charles or eggs Betty.) We think it an affectation peculiar to couples like us, who cohabit late, after those early marriages and diapered babies; who get together as productive consenting adults, and, then, well, what do you do when there are not children clamoring for an excursion or common sessions over maintenance and upkeep? You cook, and we do it, too. Even as we acknowledge its origins.

This morning, because it was my turn, I made French pancakes with powdered sugar, sausages and broiled fresh pears and bananas, and we ate in bed, on the love-rumpled dark blue sheets.

"You should have waked her," my mother continues, "with 'Happy Birthday.' You know there are services that call old people who live alone every day, check to make sure they are all right. I always thought that would be a nice thing, when the time came, a nice cheery voice saying, 'Good morning, Nan, and how are you?'"

"She's probably gone out for cigarettes," I tell her.

"Can she drive?" Amazement in her voice.

"Mother, she's seventy-four."

"Oh, I thought . . . his grandmother . . ."

We have been through this generational puzzle before. How is my mother the age of his grandmother? Is she, Mother, old enough to be a grown man's grandmother? I remind her that his grandmother was fourteen when she had his mother. Her mind jams at that. In some way it connects up to the women in her family who married late, had a child late, died from it or shut their doors. The fact of someone her generation beginning it all at fourteen and living sixty more years in the bargain sets uneasily. She hasn't got over the guilt of her own survival—of making three daughters and sleeping with my father to the end, and thus becoming the first woman in her family ever to bury a husband. To do such tricks as if it were nothing; well, it makes her nervous.

Joe Don thinks we borrow trouble. His grandmother, he conveys, can take care of herself.

I am remembering the afternoon my mother, in her distress at finding herself in a public place, husbandless, lost her keys in a department store, somewhere between Gloves and Better Dresses. Breaking into her house while waiting for a locksmith to arrive on a football Saturday afternoon, we crashed over her stand of African violets, deep purple from their daily feeding with cold coffee.

Those were the days of early marriages, when Saturdays were for helping the helpless—when there was a dollar seventy-five left to your name, and a young sullen cousin with red Janis Joplin hair appeared on your doorstep, and you got a can of tomato juice and some gelatin and everything in the refrigerator became an aspic.

"Mother says we should have called her earlier," I report.

"Your mother can't go to the store alone."

"She keeps up with things; she's current."

"She's afraid of the dark."

We don't quite fight. We can't. We have made a choice for the present, people like us, and are careful not to tatter it with bits from the past.

Toward the end of the day Joe Don gives in and deals with his missing kin. The time has been lost to fretting. Anyway, the pancake plates are still on the bed, the blue sheets half on the floor. Outside it is getting dark, the sort of early-evening twilight in which the mockingbirds make their last pass at stalking cats, and the dry hot air carries the smell of drooping flowers.

"Could you call a neighbor to check on her?"

"They're all Mexican." Which means, of course, that his grandmother does not acknowledge them.

She lives in an old part of Houston on the fringes of downtown in a neighborhood that is turning from rundown and tri-ethnic to one that is fashionable to buy into and restore. It is hanging on the cusp of turning from one to the other and so even walking around past the old elementary school and the small wood-framed hamburger stand feels unreal. It is no longer a place where people live; it is now a real estate value. An Episcopal church has bought a whole block in order to minister to the heart of the area—and for capital gains. People like us, who take turns cooking for each other on weekends, who are well out of those early marriages and have been through upward mobility and come out the other side, are buying into his grandmother's neighborhood.

If something happened to her, we could live in the very house where Joe Don was born and raised and it would be a good investment. The thought depresses him; there is no way now that moving back would be going home.

I have the address book out, making a list of friends to ask, those who are sharing eggs Helene with one another, when she calls.

She explains she went out shopping and has bought herself a

brand-new pantsuit. "Red as a fire engine. I look like a million dollars. I thought, why not, it's my birthday. It was half price."

The roses and candy, which was Russell Stover, ended up next door. She thinks the Mexican woman who brought them over has sampled the candy. "There's a piece missing from the bottom layer; she thinks I didn't notice."

My mother is relieved to hear that we've located the missing grandmother. It sits better for everyone to be where she should on a Saturday night. She has to get off the phone to watch the news— the Middle East has taken a lot of her best hours lately. Her mind is always engaged with what's going on; she's a young woman still, and active.

"You should have called her first thing this morning," she concludes. "Then you'd have known."

I hang up, looking down the road to some future time. I am unable to locate a red pantsuit; I lose my car keys somewhere in Better Dresses.

"I should call her once in a while," I conclude, feeling close to my mother. "Just to say good morning."

Joe Don remembers it is his time to cook. "How about green enchiladas," he says.

TO THE GATE

by Ursula Hegi

Afternoons she leaves the house that's gray with the smell of her father's dying and heads for the racetrack, letting the colors, the sounds, stab at her: the green of the track, the blue of the hot sky, the red of the flowers.

Shouts: "Come on! Come on . . ." "Get it up! Get it up. . . ."

Jockeys—sexless and raised above flashes of trembling horseflesh. Cheers. Disappointment. A flurry of tickets on the ground. The rush to the windows to cash in on winners.

She's dizzy from the sun, the noise: yet she keeps walking. Smells of buttered popcorn. Spilled soda. Hot dogs and ice cream. Young men in red T-shirts: *Saratoga*. Their arms brown, smooth with sweat. She drifts through the grounds, wishing she could feel something. Arms and T-shirts. Red. She brushes her bare arm against that of a man passing her. No sudden twinge. Like touching a wall. Others. Her flesh against theirs. Skin. Young skin like hers. Nothing.

Nights she lies on the cot outside her father's open door, her head beyond the frame so she won't see his face, only his hands on the white blanket, veined and large, too large for his shrunken body. Spots of light brown on his crinkled skin. The gray smell of his cancer has permeated the walls. His breath is shallow. So faint it could stop any moment. And though she can't see his face, it is with her as she lies on the cot, stiffly. His shriveled lips partly open. A pattern of veins on his yellow skull. Like those pictures of emaciated beggars in religious books. This is my father, Elise tells herself, eyes burning, dry. *This is my father who is dying.* Yet she feels nothing.

*   *   *

Mornings, after the nurse arrives, she gets up from the cot. Moves into her room across the hall. Closes the door. Sleeps without dreams. Wakes in the early afternoon to his dying smell, surrounded by things he built for her: the bookshelves, her desk, the window seat. On the wall his charcoal sketch of the farm in Vermont where he grew up, a white cape dwarfed by the weathered timbers of the barn.

When she tries to remember what it felt like to love him, she can't. It's as though she were tilted back to the first six years of her life, when she felt like a fraud each time her parents told her they loved her. She wasn't sure what it meant—this thing they called love. Whenever she replied, *I love you too,* she was afraid they'd find out and send her away. When, finally, she began to link her feelings to the word *love,* she felt relieved, grateful.

Lying in her room, weighted by the heat of the August afternoon, she finds it impossible to imagine herself returning to law school. Finds it impossible to imagine anything beyond this summer.

Men in red T-shirts. She walks into their way. Collides with them. Wants the shock of another body against hers. Wants to suck up the energy of the races, the colors, the sounds. Perhaps this is what it's like to be dead—to feel nothing. Yet she felt when her mother died five years ago: rage, grief, guilt.

The sun burns her bare legs and midriff. She wears her briefest shorts, a blue halter. Sandals. Her hair twisted up to keep her neck free. The grass shimmers under the heat. Shouts. Laughter. Children running. The smell of steamed hot dogs. She eats to service her body. Drinks orange soda that tastes flat. Welcomes the pain in her tooth as she chews the ice. Stares into the sun until everything swims yellow.

When he opens his eyes, they're milky. Clouded. He doesn't recognize her and whimpers when she sets the straw against his lips. Lifting his neck with one hand, she flinches at the touch of his papery skin against her palm. His head lolls back—a limp puppet. His hands move across the blanket as if searching for something.

Last fall, when he pruned the apple trees behind the house, his hands were steady. His hair thick and white. He wore a red chamois shirt that smelled of clean sweat and pipe tobacco. She can't connect that man to him whose face is a nest of bones against the white pillow.

The bar is half dark, filled with people though it's only late afternoon. She finds a stool by the bar, orders beer, wanting the bitter taste in her mouth. A man asks her to dance, and she presses against him on the crowded floor, swaying with the music, trying to drown within the noise, the bodies. He brings her tighter against him, runs his hands down her back, her buttocks. Slides them up along the sides of her body to her breasts. She lets him. They dance, his breath heavy, and she wills herself to feel lust: yet her feet move automatically, and she knows it wouldn't make any difference if she went to bed with him.

The nurse has prepared a light dinner for her: a salad with pale strips of turkey and cheese spread over the top like a wilting flower.

"You don't need to sleep in the hallway, Elise. Your room's close enough."

"I might not hear him."

The nurse is a kind woman, a thin woman with strong hands who likes to earn overtime. "Stay as long as you want to," she encourages Elise every afternoon. And she advises her, "Hang around the fifty-dollar window. That's where the pros bet. I always do before I take my money to the two-dollar window."

But now she walks from the house, and Elise watches her through the kitchen window, the white of her uniform, of her shoes and stockings, until she gets into her car, a bright red Toyota. Upstairs, in the silence, *he* is waiting for her to watch him die. Her legs feel heavy as she walks up the steps and stands in the open door of his room. His nose juts from his sunken features: yet his chest still rises with each breath. Nothing has changed. His hairless skull yellow in the dim light. His hands like broken birds on the white blanket.

Lying on the cot, she tries to replay the colors of the track, the sounds, the body of the man in the bar. Yet everything has faded, has become gray as though it had happened inside this house. Her father's breath is faint, so faint that sometimes she thinks it has stopped. But, straining for it, she hears it again. It's almost dawn when a familiar voice startles her.

"Three feet to the west . . ." *His* voice. Strong. "From this point two hundred thirty feet straight to the gate post."

Somewhere, within his decades of memories, her father is walking the property line of the farm in Vermont. She remembers the gate post. Weathered. Smooth. There was no gate, but at the other end of the post stood a picket fence. As a child she spent summers on the farm. Until her grandparents died and it was sold.

"And from the gate post twenty-eight rods up the hill to the granite marker."

She pictures him in heavy boots, counting his steps as he walks uphill through a low stand of pines in the frosty morning air, measuring the land he knows so well. His voice is steady, that of a man who knows his territory, who takes pride in the land he returned to every summer with his children. Perhaps he helped his father clear it with his hands, muscles swelling on his arms as he lifted cut lengths of timber.

"From the granite marker south . . ." His voice rises. ". . . to the brook."

The brook where she piled rocks into a dam, sectioned off a small basin to sail the boats he made for her from twigs and leaves. She couldn't see the house from the brook. Only meadows. Clumps of grass to her ankles. Her heart beating, she waits for her father's voice to take her down the wide dirt road through the orchard, past the shed with the cider press.

She finds herself standing by his bed, leaning over him, wanting to keep him connected to his memories. Her memories. "The orchard. We're walking through the orchard. . . ."

But his voice has stopped. His eyes are closed, and his breath catches each time he exhales. Yet only moments ago he was free, striding the boundaries of his parents' land, deciding his own direction.

Lifting his head, she carefully supports it with one hand while raising his pillow. Now his breath comes easier. The blanket above his chest rises. Falls. Rises. A blue vein pulses in his temple.

Her throat aching, she whispers, "The cider press. Remember the smell of the apples?"

His lips move.

She draws closer.

"Three feet to the west . . ." He has returned to where he started out. "From this point two hundred thirty feet straight to—" He moans. His fingers pluck the blanket.

She lays her right hand over his frail fingers. They tremble. Then yield to her touch and rest. His skin is warm. Dry. "To the gate post," she urges him on.

"To the gate post. And from the gate post twenty-eight rods up the hill . . ." Her father's voice swells. Fills the room. ". . . to the granite marker. From the granite marker south . . . to the brook . . ."

THE RAILROAD FEAST

by Steve Heller

"Act of charity," Father Jaworski demanded.

On the other side of the big oak desk the boy stared down at the floor of the rectory and squirmed his toes inside his shoes.

"Act of charity," Father Jaworski, whose broad face was round and white as an onion, repeated.

The boy bit his lip. He should have learned this one by now. He should have learned them all; the Father had reviewed the whole list with him once. Now they were starting over with the A's.

"Charles Francis?"

And it came to him. "An act of charity," he began in the slow, serious voice the Father liked, "is an act of the will." He paused until Father Jaworski nodded, his fat white neck bulging over the front of his collar. "An act of the will by . . . by which we show our love of God above all things." He looked up hopefully.

"Because?"

"Because he is infinitely good." That was right; he knew it. He bounced once on the balls of his feet.

Father Jaworski's voice changed key. "And why are acts of charity especially important *now*?"

The boy frowned; this wasn't in the book. He stared out the window of the rectory at the pigeons lining the red tile roof of the Church of the Sacred Heart. "Because of the Depression," he said suddenly.

Father Jaworski smiled briefly. "Act of contrition."

The boy beamed; this was an easy one. "An act of the will by which we express sorrow for having offended God."

"And?"

"And declare our hatred for our sins and promise to sin no

more." He paused, wondering if reciting the definitions of the holy terms from the catechism was an act of contrition or just punishment. Father Jaworski had made him start memorizing them last month as penance for stealing a bottle of wine from the sacristy. The sin was venial, not mortal, the Father explained, but it was serious all the same. Still, reciting the definitions didn't seem like very strong punishment—the priest would have made him learn them all sooner or later anyway.

Father Jaworski stood up behind the big oak desk. "Very good. We'll stop here for today. Tomorrow we'll review the list again and begin your instructions for assisting the Mass. Three o'clock."

The boy nodded and waited for the Father to reach for the papers on his desk, which meant it was time to go.

Father Jaworski started to reach, then looked up again. "Tell your parents Charles Francis Kellerman will soon make a fine altar boy."

The boy smiled as much as he dared and held his breath to keep his chest from swelling out. A moment later Father Jaworski reached for the papers.

On the way home he met Eddie Magril outside the Summit Theater.

"Hey, schnoz, what's the hurry?"

Charles felt his face turn blood red. He hated to be teased about his nose. "I got to get home."

Eddie Magril screwed up his face and kicked an empty beer bottle into the gutter. "Yanny got a nickel off his old man and bought a ticket. He's gonna sneak me in the side door—wanna come? It's a cowboy movie."

Charles looked at the poster beneath the marquee: A man in a white hat shooting a rifle at an Indian. Charles frowned and chewed his lip as he looked at the red fire shooting out of the rifle barrel. "I guess not. I gotta go home and eat."

Eddie Magril spit on the sidewalk. "Sure. 'Fraid to smell the popcorn, banana-nose?"

Charles made a fist and Eddie backed away.

"Okay, okay. Catch you later," Eddie said, and hurried off into the alley beside the theater.

Charles glanced again at the poster before walking on. He could smell the popcorn from here—the fresh corny scent drifting out through the big double glass doors—and the hot butter and salt too. He sighed and turned away and ran down Summit Street toward home.

In the kitchen Mother was frying fish. She wore a big gray apron that stretched all the way to her ankles. "Go get Dottie, then wash your hands," she said, even before he could tell her about what Father Jaworski had said.

"Hold up—he's got to go get some coal first." It was his father's stern voice, coming through the screen door from the back porch, where he always sat in the evening drinking Muehlebach beer from a copper stein. He'd been working steady at the brewery for nearly six months now, since Prohibition ended.

Charles inhaled deeply through his nose. Catfish. Probably Uncle Ludwig or Ernie Simmons had caught some extra down on the Kaw.

Mother braced her fists on her hips. "Does he have to go all the way down to the railyards right this minute? Can't he go after dinner? We're almost ready to eat."

"No."

Charles's shoulders sagged as he felt his empty stomach twist. The voice from the back porch never changed its mind. He picked up the dusty coal sack next to the stove.

"I'll put dinner in the oven till you get back," Mother promised, and gave him a dime for the coal.

He nodded and started to retrace his steps toward the front door when the voice from the back porch stopped him.

"Charles!"

He stopped within earshot, though there was really no point; he knew what the voice was going to say. "Yes, Father?"

"Stay away from the trainmen."

He sighed. "Okay."

In a few minutes he made his way to the wooden railing where Fairmont Street dead-ended at the edge of Mulligan's Bluff overlooking the point where the Kaw River joined the Missouri. From this spot he could have looked back to the east and seen the red tile roof of the Church of the Sacred Heart in the middle of the city. Instead, he looked down, where the tracks of the Kansas City Railyards spread out in a familiar pattern between the bluff and the river. From here the trains in the railyard looked tiny, like the toy trains in Meyerson's Five and Dime. For a moment he imagined himself reaching a giant hand down from the top of the bluff to guide a long Burlington freight train to the coal pits.

It took a quarter of an hour to descend the main path down the bluff. At the bottom he stepped gingerly over the loose gravel beside the rails, stopping occasionally to adjust the piece of cardboard in his shoe. He carried the empty gunnysack over his shoulder, black coal dust staining his shirt underneath. His eyes opened wide, watching the huge gray engines belch black smoke as they chugged along the switching tracks. The heat rising from the yard made the more distant trains shimmer as they passed under the 23rd Street Bridge, where the Kansas & Berger Streetcar, small and serene, glided by overhead. He imagined himself controlling it all, guiding the long trains through the haze with his own hands.

Guiding them, until he heard the familiar whistle of Engine 909, chugging into the yard with a train of A&P icebox cars. Now the pattern of the yard, so clear from the top of the bluff, fell apart. He felt himself shrinking smaller and smaller as the big locomotive approached, clouds of white iron-smelling steam hissing from the pistons. Screeching and puffing, the train stopped by the coal pit. Above the steam he recognized the engineer who had once let him blow the whistle—a giant of a man in gray overalls and a blue Burlington cap.

"Hey, bub!" the engineer shouted from the cab. "What do you say? Hungry today?"

Charles felt his stomach twist again as he shrank away, hearing another voice that seemed to come from deep inside the boiler of Engine 909: *Stay away from the trainmen.*

But before he could get away the engineer climbed down and took his hand. "This way, bub." He resisted, but the engineer was too big, too strong, pulling him past the icebox cars to the red caboose at the end of the train.

"What you got there, Homer?" a short red-faced man standing on the rear platform of the caboose asked. "Looks like a trash-eatin' hobo to me."

"Could be," the engineer said, lifting Charles up to the platform. "But look at that honker on him—could be a Jewboy in disguise."

Charles turned and tried to hide his nose.

"Jewboy?" The red-faced man stared down at Charles, who wanted to say no, but could make no sound come out of his mouth. "Why, Jewboys know better than to show their little kike faces around here." The red-faced man lifted Charles's chin and stared into his eyes. "Mmmm. Way we can tell for sure. Jewboys always squirm a little at our table—we'll see."

Feeling confused, dazzled, Charles watched the red door of the caboose open into a dark room containing a table piled high with food—more food than he had ever seen, ever imagined. Slices of ham and beef and salami and other kinds of meat he didn't recognize; a block of Swiss cheese and cheddar; whole loaves of black bread and white, with butter, oranges, and fresh milk. He felt himself grow faint.

"Who's this one?" Two dark men with black beards and blue

Burlington caps leaned forward on wooden crates marked A&P DAIRY FRESH TO YOU. *Stay away from the trainmen.*

"Could be a Jewboy."

The bearded men looked at each other and nodded. The red-faced man closed the curtains and flipped on the electric light.

Charles looked at the food again—fresh pink meat and white milk—feeling empty and itchy inside as the first bearded man reached under his seat and set a small black crock in the middle of the table.

"Hungry now, bub?" the engineer asked, and pushed away all the meat except the plate of ham. "You are? Well, this could be your lucky day."

Eager, frightened, he felt their eyes watching as one of the bearded men pushed the crock slowly toward him and opened the lid. The stench bit him in the face like a club. He jerked his head back to get a breath, thinking of the day his father made him crawl under the house to look for the dead rat.

"Yessir, this could be your lucky day," the engineer continued. "Mmmm! Don't that smell fine! Tastes as good as it smells, too." He took a knife and sliced off a piece of black bread. "Now the nice thing about Limburger is its texture." He dipped the knife into the crock and spread a yellowish glob over the bread. "Just like fresh, warm butter. Course, no sandwich is complete without a nice big slice of *ham,* right, bub? You can eat *ham* now, can't you, son?"

The faces in the car were dark and silent as the engineer carefully laid the ham on top and handed the sandwich to Charles. Sweating, he held his breath and pretended the yellow smear underneath was butter. The odor penetrated his nostrils as he took the first bite, making his eyes tear. He ate quickly, trying not to taste the fumes in his mouth.

"Don't act like no Jewboy to me," the red-faced man said. Then the other voices, warm and congratulating—

"A sight, that one!"

"Your lucky day, bub."

"Lucky is right."

"You never had it so lucky!"

They piled the food in front of him—breads and meats and cheeses. His taste quickly returned as he bit into spicy-hot smoked salami and sweet apple pie. Amazed and unbelieving, he ate.

"Like a blowfly on a shit pile." They laughed.

"Like a Chinaman climbing Rice Mountain."

He ate until he could eat no more, held back by the strange new *full* feeling. Then he sat, too weak and stuffed to move, and listened to the men in blue caps tell stories of the railroad. Their words were strange—payloads and trunklines and cities with faraway names: Black Hawk, Chi-town, Onalaska, Maiden Rock. And through each city roared great engines with names stranger still: Mikado, Zephyr, Silver Streak. Closing his eyes, he tried to imagine the sight.

Then everyone was saying good-bye.

"Have to open up a dining car for this one!"

"Next time bring your appetite!"

"Mum's the word on where you got all this stuff, Lucky," the engineer whispered in the doorway, and handed him the gunnysack—filled not with coal but with bread and meat and cheese wrapped up in newspaper. "Remember, mum's the word."

Elated, he ran all the way across the loading yards to the bluff. Then climbed, proud, up the trail the longer, secret way—where there would be no tough kids to steal his prize—through the bramble bushes and pawpaw trees, across the neighbors' backyards and into his own. He saw his father still rocking on the dark porch, sipping beer from his copper stein.

Charles slowed to a walk and gripped the sack tightly. As he approached, his father rocked forward in the light. In the twilight his father's eyes looked grim and piercing, like a hawk's.

"Well, what?" the stern voice asked.

"I got this." He handed over the sack, studying his father's expression, the hawk face leaning further into the light as he emptied the contents of the sack into his lap. The grim expression did not change as he unwrapped first the meat, then the cheese, sniffing both.

Your lucky day. Eyes on his father, he waited, out of breath, remembering the two other times he had brought things home without telling his father. The time he borrowed Eddie Magril's Red Rider wagon and hauled home the big catfish he'd caught in a muddy tide pool by the Kaw River—the surprise and delight in his father's eyes when he saw the huge black fish, head and tail hanging over each end of the wagon. *Rose, Rose,* Father had called to Mother. They built a bonfire in the middle of Fairmont and shared catfish steaks with the rest of the neighborhood. *My boy caught this,* he remembered Father saying to Uncle Ludwig. And the other time, only a month ago—the swift anger in Father's eyes when he found the bottle of sacramental wine from Sacred Heart Church hidden under the house. *Religious boy* was all Father said as he unstrapped his belt. Mother was at the A&P. An hour later, after confession, Father Jaworski took him into the rectory and asked him to remove his blood-stained shirt. *Your father did this because he loves you,* the priest explained as he put iodine on the welts—and handed him the catechism with the list of holy terms to learn.

"Where'd you get this?"

The accusing tone of Father's voice brought back the engineer's warning: *Mum's the word, Lucky.*

"Well?"

"Down at the loading yards . . . It was given to me."

Father raised his eyebrows.

Charles swallowed. "It was an act of charity."

Father frowned and shook his head. "This is no charity. The trainmen are thieves—they steal from the boxcars." He rewrapped the cheese and meat. "You take all this food to Father Jaworski and tell him where you got it." He paused for emphasis. "And *never* go near the trainmen again."

Charles looked down at his feet. "Yessir."

The sack hung heavy over his shoulder as he started off for the rectory. Behind him faded the squeaking sound of Father rocking on the dark porch.

He took the long way, along the edge of the bluff. The last rays of the sunset were fading into gray, but he paused at the lookout, seeing again the pattern of the loading yards below—hundreds of boxcars dividing into long rows as they disappeared beneath the 23rd Street Bridge. He listened for the familiar whistle of Engine 909, speeding away toward cities with faraway names. . . .

As he looked and listened, he felt a hand, large and invisible, reach up to him from the railyards. He felt its fingers close around him, gripping him in a huge fist, and begin to pull him over the edge of the bluff—down, down, to the railroad yards where Engine 909 was pulling out, heading across the river.

He shut his eyes, grabbed the railing, and hung on with all his strength. Moments passed. Then the grip of the invisible hand began to loosen, the clutching fingers to slip away. When the feeling had passed, he took a deep breath, turned away from the scene below, and opened his eyes. He did not look back, but hurried on toward the rectory, toward his punishment.

UNSOLVED MYSTERIES: A TALE

by Joanna Wojewski Higgins

Unsolved mysteries are as unsatisfying as a single glass of water when one is very thirsty. What happened then? How can that be? one wants to know at the end of such a story. But the storyteller can only admit, with a shrug of the shoulders, It's not known. Both listener and storyteller may be disappointed then, even a little ashamed.

Once deer hunters—all farmers—found a black leather trunk under an ancient cedar deep in a woods some miles from the village of Metz. The soil is swampy in that region, and the trunk would have soon rotted, leaving its contents to sink into the earth or else molder and shred like autumn leaves. But before that could happen, hunters chanced upon the trunk and called to one another until five men stood in a semi-circle around the oblong shape appearing like a deep shadow. Finally one man, a man named Koszak, stooped down and pried a large stone from the earth. Then, clutching the stone, he stepped forward and gave the lock one crack with the stone, then another, and still another until sweat made his forehead gleam and the lock fell open, dangling by one curved piece of metal. The men were silent. Who could tell what such a gloomy box might hold? Koszak dropped the stone, set his gun aside, and with both hands lifted the top of the trunk, throwing it back as far as it would go. Then he made the Sign of the Cross. The others leaned their guns against trees and moved closer to see.

The trunk contained a fortune in silver coin and bills. Koszak himself counted the money, but then—somehow—he disappeared with the trunk, leaving family, friends, and his farm. He was never seen near Metz or Posen again.

How did he manage to get the trunk away from the others? It's not known.

How much money was there? No one knows.

How did it happen that a trunk was left in the woods, far from any road? Who can say?

And no one saw or heard from him again? No, never.

And when he finished counting, he just disappeared? He disappeared.

And no one knows where. Oh, there is always someone who claims to know something. There was a man, for example, who settled in a certain village. No one knew where he came from, but it was said he'd murdered someone somewhere and then had run away. This fellow settled in the village and operated a drugstore and grocery. One son became a county official. One daughter became a nurse and later married well. The family was considered one of the best in the county.

What happened to them? Nothing. They grew old and died.

And the story of the murder? It remains a mystery. Like this story about Antoni and Alexsandra Urblanski who came to America from Poland in the early days of this century.

Antoni and Alexsandra were homesteaders who'd bought at nominal fee a tract of land near Metz. You couldn't call it a farm, for it was all woods—white pine, hemlock, some hardwood. They cut a few trees and threw together a cabin that was little more than a shed. They had left better in Poland, but this was America, where, God willing, all things were possible and where life would show itself to be better. Antoni—still young and very strong—hired himself out on timber crews, and Alexsandra scratched the earth around the cabin and planted a few potatoes, a few beans, and several tomatoes from seeds she'd brought from home, smuggled in her corset. Soon they were able to buy a few chickens and a goat. When they earned a little money—he with his timber work, she with her fancy sewing—they would clear their own land and begin to farm properly. And then—God being good and merciful—they would send for their children, Walery and Józefa, who were living with Olicia and Konstanty, Alexsandra's sister and brother-in-law.

Antoni and Alexsandra wrote letters, asking about Walery and Józefa, about their father, Wroblewski, about Olicia and Konstanty and Michal, their son, and about all the family. They asked about crops and weather and sickness and the new parish priest. They wrote about the timbering, the garden, and about prospects for good farming in America. But they didn't mention the little hole in the earth under the floorboards and the washstand where they planted a silver coin each month. Who could tell who might read the letter? Letters were lost, sometimes stolen from the money they might contain. Soon, maybe in two years, maybe a bit longer, there would be enough to purchase two ship tickets for Walery and Józefa. But the tickets must be cabin-class and not steerage, for Antoni and Alexsandra had learned what was best. Cabin passengers need not pass through the Isle of Tears; neither would the children of Antoni and Alexsandra.

The Isle of Tears? *Tranen Insel, Isola delle Lacrime,* oh, a hundred names for the same thing. Americans called it Ellis Island.

From the steerage deck, Antoni and Alexsandra had watched a boat flying the American flag drift up close to their ship in the harbor. Uniformed officials had come aboard, and then all second-class passengers were called into a saloon. There, Antoni had learned, a doctor glanced at one's eyes, while an official asked a simple question or two. The first-class passengers were not required to go to the saloon or anywhere else to be officially permitted to enter America. Instead, the officials merely looked over a certain list of names and then—all done. "You see how simple it is in America!" Antoni had told Alexsandra. But that was before they'd been taken to the Isle of Tears.

When their ship arrived at a pier in the Hudson River, Antoni and Alexsandra were herded off with the other steerage passengers, and while the cabin passengers went into sheds of the shipping company and then out into the city, Antoni and Alexsandra and the others were ordered into ferries and barges and taken to the Isle of Tears. Then there were hours of delay in the hot and overcrowded Registry Hall that could hold, they say, as many as five thousand people. Narrow passageways marked by metal railings divided the big hall, and one went along these passages from inspection to inspection. Sometimes, for no reason anyone could see, an inspector would make a certain chalk mark on the back of one's old coat. An *H,* for example, or an *L,* or even an *X.* "But what does it mean?" Alexsandra whispered, nearly frightened out of her wits. For those with chalk marks on their coats were shunted off into a wire mesh pen and held there. Antoni, who did not know what it meant, told his wife that those who were so marked must have done something wrong, something that offended the authorities. Antoni would later find out that the humpbacked woman who limped was marked and taken from the line because she was lame. That is how it was. If you limped as you made your way along the iron rails, or if you blinked too much, or if you breathed too heavily or looked stupid, then off, off with you into the pen. There, other inspectors would look more closely at you, and then you might be sent to the hospital. More likely back to Europe.

When Antoni learned from an old woman that her child, a boy of ten years of age, had been sent back to Europe alone, he made a vow that he would work day and night so that their children would not have to pass through the Isle of Tears—where anything could happen—before entering America. Nothing will happen to them, he told Alexsandra. The children would step off the ship at the pier where he, Antoni, and she, Alexsandra, would be waiting.

So Antoni and Alexsandra had to save money for cabin-class tickets and also for train tickets to New York City—an immense journey, it seemed to them—and return tickets for all four of them. How would they do it? they asked each other. They worried as much about the money as about the difficult arrangements and the long journey in an unfamiliar country, where English words still ran together too quickly, like rapid water.

"Never mind," Antoni would tell Alexsandra on summer twilights as they watched the sun color the western sky with purple and red streaks long after ten in the evening. "Somehow we will manage. This is America."

Sometimes, not too often, they would talk of home—of a favorite cow, of the church at Plonka, just being built when they left, of Alexsandra's great-aunt who, at one hundred years of age, threaded her own needles and knelt on bare floorboards when she prayed. Sometimes they said nothing at all, content to know the little hoard of silver was growing in the earth, like a seed that would soon sprout.

Finally the day arrived. Letters with money had been sent, and letters had been awaited and received. Directions, admonitions, and prayers filled sheets of paper sent either way across the Atlantic and halfway across America and Europe. Walery and Józefa, now ten and eight years old, would travel with their Uncle Konstanty, who would see them to their cabin on the ship. Then Antoni and Alexsandra would meet the children in New York, at pier such and such, on a particular day in July.

Antoni and Alexsandra planned their voyage so that they would arrive in New York a day ahead of time. They would find lodging near the station, then go to the pier early the next morning. There they would await the ship's afternoon arrival.

And so they boarded the Detroit and Mackinaw passenger train at the Metz stop—little more than a siding—and began the journey that would once again take them through villages and towns strung along Lake Huron. They were to change trains in Detroit, Cleveland, and Rochester. Alexsandra and Antoni wore their best clothes—Alexsandra a suit of light mauve material and a pale yellow straw hat, Antoni a brown jacket and trousers and a black hat. They looked prosperous and very American. Alexsandra had packed a basket of food sufficient for a week. It was their only luggage, and she never allowed it out of her sight. Throughout the long trip, she clutched her husband's rough hand. Despite the July heat, her own hands felt frozen and lifeless.

On the way to Detroit Antoni ignored the rolling green hills and the brilliant blue lake and instead studied the packet of train schedules he held in his lap. His forehead broke out in an icy sweat in Detroit, where they had to leave their train and find another in a cavernous station that echoed with clanging and shouts and filled their heads with fumes.

"You see," he said after they'd boarded the Cleveland train, "how simple things are in America?"

Three years earlier, in 1901, they had made the journey from New York to Michigan, but it had been much different then. They were traveling with others in a group. Dazed, they had taken in little until the train had left them at Metz, their new home. Only then had they begun to wake up and study the land carefully. So New York appeared like a vision—huge and bewildering and larger than anything they'd ever seen. Alexsandra grew faint at the doorway of the train, but Antoni was there at the bottom of the step to help her. Even the conductor rushed over.

"God is with us," Alexsandra whispered when she could speak. "We are here."

The next morning they found the right pier with the help of strangers and began their vigil. Their eyes were dark-rimmed with lack of sleep, for they hadn't been able to find suitable lodging and had sat all night, leaning against each other on the wooden benches at the station. Exhausted but unable to rest, Alexsandra paced a short distance in either direction from the bench in the waiting room of the shipping company. She tried to see out of clouded windows. Sometimes she called out the name of a ship.

At last the right ship arrived, much later than scheduled. The waiting room was crowded with eager relatives, pushing forward and speaking in German and Polish, some in English, others in Russian. Alexsandra and Antoni, too, pushed forward, trying to see. Antoni held the basket tightly. Soon there was an awful milling— cries and shouts and tears and people throwing bags and boxes to the floor and embracing. But where were Walery and Józefa? The hall began to empty, and no children had appeared, holding each other's hand as they had been instructed to do. Did the clerk in the ticket office know? Antoni pulled Alexsandra through groups of people and asked at the barred window. But he couldn't understand the clerk's words, nor could the clerk understand his. Then the clerk spoke a few rushing words and pointed toward a tall man in uniform. Antoni and Alexsandra shrank away, then rushed like panic-stricken beasts to the doorway leading to the ship. There, men kept them from going farther.

Alexsandra began to sob and shout in Polish. Antoni tried to comfort her and at the same time explain their situation to the men. But the men couldn't understand! It was all a bad dream: Antoni shouting the simple English he knew, and the men shaking their heads. Finally one of the men seemed to understand. He left the doorway and returned minutes later with a message. "The ship is empty. There's no one left. Perhaps a mistake? Perhaps another ship?"

"What another!" Antoni shouted, enraged. "This ship! This ship!" He tried to fight his way by them. Without meaning to, they knocked him to the floor. Food spilled from the basket.

When Antoni stood, it was as if he'd lost all his strength. His arms hung at his sides and tears ran unchecked, wetting his face. Alexsandra grew pale but did not faint. Her face smooth as stone, she gathered the food—jams and cakes and fruits—and led Antoni to an office where she explained in halting English and fluent Polish.

But record-keeping was poor in those days, and the office had no mention of a Walery and Józefa Urblanski on its manifest. The clerk, another one, let Alexsandra read the lists for herself. Then Antoni mutely handed over his sister-in-law's letter that gave all the directions. Yes, this ship. Yes, this day. Cabin-class. Second cabin! Yes, yes! Not steerage. But the clerk, who could speak and read Polish, simply shook his head after reading through the letter twice. "I'm sorry," he said. "There's no record of any children by those names. I don't know what happened."

From the Barge Office landing slip they watched the arrival of ferries and barges coming from the Isle of Tears. Again there were shouts and tears and laughter. Many threw away stinking old coats and put on new American jackets. Antoni suddenly wondered if the children had somehow been taken to the Isle of Tears after all. Perhaps they had been transferred, by accident, to a ferry or barge and taken there. So Antoni and Alexsandra procured passes and ferried to the island and there watched from behind a wire mesh fence as men, women, and children, coming from a dark corridor, blinked their eyes in the fierce sunlight, then excitedly boarded waiting ferries. Thousands of people would pass through the Isle of Tears on that summer day, but as for the children of Antoni and Alexsandra, they were nowhere to be found.

Antoni and Alexsandra waited in the dusty hall of the shipping company for several days, dozing from time to time on the bench, waking to eat the last of their provisions and watch with dismay the joyful pandemonium of another arrival. Finally Antoni and Alexsandra took the train back, retracing their long journey and hardly caring if they made the right connections or not. Their food was gone and they ate nothing. Sometime after their arrival at Metz, they received a letter from Konstanty and Olicia saying that the children had been safely dispatched as directed and that, God willing, they hoped all were safely united by the time the letter reached America.

What happened to the children? The mystery has never been solved. Such things happened in those days. Perhaps even today. Who was there to help? Who could find two children who spoke no English?

But something must have happened, you think. Someone must know. Oh, yes, something happened. Perhaps they arrived and, missing their parents in the confusion, found themselves in the great city. Or perhaps they were transported to the Isle of Tears and then, for some reason, sent back to Hamburg. Perhaps a woman found them crying in some corner and took them both by the hand—a woman who might have lost her own children or who'd had none. Perhaps they died and were taken, like angels, into Heaven.

Antoni and Alexsandra had no other children in the new world, but their dream of a great farm became a reality. The disastrous fire of 1908 cleared their land of timber, and two of Antoni's brothers came from Poland to help dig out stumps, plow, and plant wheat, rye, and potatoes. In return, Antoni gave them small pieces of land and helped build their cabins. Soon there were wives and children, and the children grew to help work the farm. All prospered. The children—Antoni and Alexsandra's nieces and nephews—referred to them as Uncle Tony and Aunt Sandra. It was the American way. Several of those children later changed their name to Urblan and forgot their Polish. But Alexsandra? She would not speak English and would have refused American citizenship had not Antoni begged her to change her mind.

Antoni and Alexsandra wrote numerous letters—to officials in New York City, to the shipping company, to Konstanty and Olicia. One can imagine such letters, sent out like prayers. One can also imagine Antoni and Alexsandra many years later, sitting in a cut hayfield at sunset—Antoni saying quietly in Polish, "But you know, anything at all can happen in America. Anything is yet possible," and Alexsandra, drawing a severed stalk of timothy from the clump near her hand, saying nothing as she watches the western sky burn red from top to bottom.

A CZECH POLICE STORY: THE CASE OF THE RESTROOM CONSPIRACY

by Jiri Hochman

For breakfast Major Adolf Ztopor had sour milk. It had never agreed with him, but his wife declared:

"The milk turned sour."

Why the regimental surgeon had forbidden him to drink tea, coffee, cocoa, and even all alcoholic beverages, Major Ztopor had never fully understood. He had no professional presuppositions. However, the reasons must have been serious, since the regimental surgeon told him at that time:

"Dear comrade, your liver, kidneys, stomach, gallbladder, and even large intestine have gone to the dogs. Since you are a non-smoker anyway, all I can do for you now is to put you on a milk diet."

Therefore, when his wife told him that the milk had turned sour, Major Ztopor had merely looked at his watch to see whether he could make it in time to the milk bar around the corner to have some regular milk. However, it was already too late for that. He had to make do, therefore, with sour milk in order to have something in his stomach, because his duty was strenuous and sometimes even long. Moreover, it required also a clear mind and, of course, circumspection and vigilance. Still, he drank that sour milk distrustfully. It had never agreed with him, and as far as he could remember, he had really never drunk it before on an empty stomach. It was a careless action on his part, and since it was Tuesday, it was, frankly speaking, a dangerous experiment.

For every Tuesday morning the Supreme Governing Body sat in session, and Major Ztopor had to accompany there the Comrade entrusted to his personal protection. It seemed to him that this time the trip lasted an eternity. That damned sour milk appeared to have just flashed through his entrails, in order to raise regular hell in their lowest tract. Nevertheless, with his face contracted by convulsive pain, he managed to accompany his Comrade to the place of destination, handed him his briefcase, and happily observed how the big padded door closed behind him.

And now he was sitting here, in a diminutive room, sizewise appropriate to its purpose, and he was sitting here during the past half hour already for the third time, so mercilessly did that kefir chase him! However, luckily it had all passed without the worst consequences, the iron will of the Major had won over nature. Now, as he was getting up and pulling up his suspenders, the pain and urge had already passed, and Major Ztopor almost felt like singing. At that moment, however, his eyes rested on the left-hand wall, where in printed letters, skillfully executed, even professionally drawn, in dark red on a yellow latex base, close above the tiles in the lower part of the room, could be read all too clearly:

COMRADE . . . . . IS AN ASS.

There could be no doubt about the fact that the inscription had been executed professionally, and who could judge that better than Adolf Ztopor himself, by profession originally, oh God, how long ago that was, varnisher and sign painter?

He was not mistaken; he even put on his glasses for the purpose of counting once more those dots—there really were exactly five of them—and outside sat Colonel Babor, who was in charge of this place and who had let him in only because he knew him, trusting that he would do no harm here, and that he, Ztopor, had been chased here merely by an uncontrollable urge that would not have allowed further transportation of at least one hundred and fifty yards to an ordinary men's room, assigned to them, since this one here was an exceptional men's room, destined exclusively for members of the Supreme Governing Body, one of the best-guarded toilets in the world, where professional staff checked even the water for flushing, even the toilet paper delivered here, and frisked the cleaning woman every time she entered, although she had been checked and screened officially already twelve times. And outside in the hall sat a continuous guard at the service desk with a telephone and records book, a guard that never slackened and that changed four times a day, a guard of high standing, where the lowest-ranking officer was just now Colonel Babor, since the section assigned to the care of the physical gratifications of the members of the Supreme Governing Body were exclusively generals.

Poor Ztopor, who was still staring fixedly at the inscription, did not have much imagination due to his specialized intelligence, and, therefore, it did not occur to him what an interesting example of dialectics he was being offered here, since the same inscription, even without dots, he would find without surprise in the toilets of the whole republic, whereas here he was justifiedly shaken by it, although it was merely dotted. Instead, he was thinking feverishly whether he would be given a chance to prove with the aid of forensic specialists what a devastating effect sour milk had on his organism on an empty stomach, because above all he would have to prove w h y he had entered this place to start with, besides which, of course, also, Colonel Babor would have to explain somehow why he had let him in. But how relieved can a man feel if they tell him that he won't be executed alone but in pairs?

Colonel Babor in the meanwhile was sitting tranquilly at his service desk, and a gentle old man's smile played on his withered face. For a very long time he had not kicked class enemies in the teeth, because years had passed, times had changed, Babor's temples had turned white, his veins had hardened, and fatigue blunted his former untiring vigilance. Instead of harboring now a healthy suspicion with regard to possible intrigues on the part of Ztopor in the toilets reserved exclusively for the Supreme Governing Body, he remembered with sclerotic foolishness how once, in his youth, ah yes, it was at the boy scout jamboree, he himself could not make it in time, although he had already taken hold of the doorknob. And now he felt frankly a scoutlike satisfaction at the fact that he had done a good deed when he had let in Major Ztopor, not less than three times in a row, seeing his vain battle with his urge written mercilessly all over his face, as well as the limits of the distance to the men's room for staff.

In the meanwhile the desperate Major Ztopor, trying not to believe his own eyes, went so far as to feel with his fingers that utterly incredibly blasphemous inscription in this almost sacred place, in order to estimate its approximate age, but immediately he realized that in doing so he had aggravated his situation, why, he might have even sealed his own fate entirely, for thus not only was he leaving here behind proof of his criminal act which he had not really committed, but in addition his fingerprints on it, which, of course, he would not be able to deny.

The inscription was dry and didn't stick; however, it was not necessary to explain anything about dactyloscopy to Major Ztopor. Completely broken, he still managed to smell it, and barely uttered:

"It's xylol-based paint."

Yes, that made it even worse, he continued to speculate, because an oil-based paint would need at least two days to dry so thoroughly, a synthetic paint at least a day, only a xylol-based paint dries so fast, I am caught, no one else around here could be more suspect than myself, at the time of crisis I also vacillated, once I even refrained from voting and, what's more, maybe nobody has been here yet today! The leading Comrades, of course, cannot even be suspected; besides, there are six toilets here, twelve users, and provided that they had been here already, they had evidently used those on the outside, why did I, fool that I am, have to go to the last one?

But hadn't he chosen the one farthest from the door on purpose, shuffling his way across painfully, precisely, in order not to be in the way if one of the Leading Comrades were to rush in here in great necessity, one of those solely authorized to use these exceptional facilities in which he, Ztopor, was lingering, in fact, illegally? Where would this lead to, after all, he reasoned, if everyone were to take care of his needs where he felt like it, without regard to which facility was assigned to him officially for that purpose?

But even this politically mature and simultaneously spontaneous thought didn't bring Major Ztopor any peace. It was clear to him that it was too late for regret. Here not even paint thinner 1009 would help him, since with it he would only smear everything all over the wall, and that could be even more suspicious, because then they would have to come inevitably to the conclusion that he hadn't put there only those five dots (which, of course, was entirely sufficient), but that he had written it down in its entirety, word for word and letter for letter, documentary evidence for criminal proceedings possibly according to all the paragraphs for the protection of the socialist system, and that under aggravating circumstances, since also the special character of this place would have to play a role, because writing such things precisely here was qualitatively worse than treason in the service of a foreign power. Yes, in this inscription, at which he was gazing, his true character was revealed; he had been hiding it deceptively for nearly thirty years, while shamelessly taking advantage of the benefits of the people's rule in order to show finally his true attitude, which, as could be clearly seen on this wall, was hostile.

Major Adolf Ztopor was completely overcome by these considerations. Not even trying to put on his coat properly, he staggered out with the strap of his shoulder holster loosened, took a few feeble steps past the unsuspecting Babor in the direction of the building's exit, and collapsed without uttering a sound.

While the unfortunate man was driven away by an ambulance, the proceedings of the Supreme Governing Body continued without interruption. Important state affairs can't be delayed by trivial individual tragedies. Colonel Babor took the initiative in arranging for another officer to be on duty in lieu of the fallen Major Ztopor, and quiet reigned once more in the hall.

At 10:37 a member of the Supreme Governing Body entrusted with questions of heavy machinery and culture made use of the special WC; however, he visited the first little room next to the entrance and, having remained there not quite six minutes, returned spryly, why, almost happily, to the meeting hall. As the session continued, others also kept arriving, and Colonel Babor faithfully wrote down their names into his book of visitors, as well as the time of their arrival and departure.

Some came quickly and left slowly, some sauntered on their way there and back, and, as Colonel Babor noticed, one who was in charge of labor unions ran both ways—most likely they were just debating wages. Two came together, prudently discussing something on the way, but Colonel Babor overheard only one of the comrades saying:

"That, my dear fellow, I hope we won't live to see."

Then they disappeared inside, but they returned separately, one presently after three minutes, the other only after fifteen minutes. But Colonel Babor was not surprised, he already knew his clients.

Also the Supreme Comrade came twice to relieve himself, and each time Babor heard him singing to himself. Both tunes were folksongs, which made Babor come to the conclusion that the political situation appeared to be favorable. He looked at his watch: less than an hour was left of today's duty. At 2:55 P.M. Major General Cibulka would arrive to take his place. He would hand over to him the area of concern, together they would convince themselves that everything was in order, and Babor would go home. The burden of heavy responsibility would slip off his tired shoulders at least until morning. . . .

Thus reasoned Colonel Babor and remembered at that moment with pity poor Major Ztopor, who this morning had fallen on the cold marble floor before his very eyes in the course of performing his difficult duty. Babor had been informed already that the Major had had a heart attack. We sure don't have it easy, the Colonel thought to himself, and got up. His watch showed already 2:40 P.M. He would make the rounds of the object entrusted to his care to make sure that there was no flaw in it, and then he would merely wait until the manly step of his successor resounded in the hall. The records book is already open, prepared for official entries, also all writing material and stamps are at hand, well then, old boy, said Colonel Babor to himself, let's go and have a look in there!

He took hold of the doorknob and entered the men's room, put on the overhead light, and circumspectly examined the small passageway. Everything was shining clean, including the doors of the individual cabinets provided for reasons of order with the roman numerals I through VI. Colonel Babor opened the window and checked the iron bars to make sure they were intact. He passed his key over them, and his experienced ear took note of a purely harmonious, ringing sound with which he was intimately familiar. He closed the window, returned to the first cubicle, and opened it. The door, opening left and inwards, covered one wall; however, in this cubicle it did not matter. The inscription was only in the one next to the window.

He then proceeded rapidly from one to the next, until he reached the last one, which that day, by coincidence, had not been used by anyone except Major Ztopor. Here, also, the open door mercifully covered the treacherous inscription. It nearly came to pass that Babor left even this place with a feeling of duty done, and very likely it would have come to the same even during the common inspection with General Cibulka a little later, since in this area inscriptions were not the object of concentrated vigilance. Here no one expected them, and as far as memory could reach, none had ever been found here, not even during the time of crisis! An expert would easily infer from the above how significantly this facility differed from the nationwide average of these utilitarian establishments. . . .

Babor was about to leave when it occurred to him that, as he was here anyway, he could just as well quickly take care of his own needs before going home. Colonels of the secret police are also just human beings, why, even generals . . . At that moment he couldn't yet suspect in what far-reaching a manner he was entering history as a very special deus ex machina by this humble decision of his, predestined obviously by unknown powers to a saving intervention at the twelfth hour.

Concentrating still on the pleasure from the relief he was going to permit himself, he entered once more and closed the door destined for the protection of the privacy of much more prominent dignitaries than himself. At that moment, however, he, too, found himself face to face with that terrible inscription, even faster than the unfortunate Ztopor, who had been in a greater hurry. He did not need glasses; he wasn't nearsighted. The thoughts of physical relief left him, however, immediately. For a moment he remained as if frozen to the spot.

In contrast to Major Ztopor, Colonel Babor was older, more experienced, politically more mature, and had stronger nerves. He no longer thought of the unhappy Ztopor at all. Other combinations flashed through his mind, combinations of a higher type, more complex and audacious. At their end, then, a conclusion of logical concreteness: in this inscription, in an area accessible only to the Supreme Governing Body, Colonel Babor could see one thing only: a silent preparation for a coup d'état. Because, if from the viewpoint of some member of the Supreme Governing Body (and who else could have written it here?) Comrade. . . . . is an ass, and he who wrote it dared to publish this here, things must have gone very far. Who knows whether behind the padded door of the meeting hall another tragic vote hadn't taken place already. . . .

What could be the result of such a vote? thought Colonel Babor rapidly, while his fatigue disappeared on the spot. It could, of course, result in favor of the Supreme Comrade, but it could also come out against him even if he had been singing here frivolously to himself before. The outcome could also remain undecided. However, in any case, the responsibility could later fall only on the one to whom had been entrusted the guarding of this place, which had been treacherously misused for intrigues. Conclusion: Colonel Babor said to himself in the accustomed style of official announcements. The conclusion is that I have to do something about it.

And Colonel Babor acted quickly, because he didn't have much time left. He, too, rapidly excluded the technical possibility of removing the inscription completely. There remained one possibility only: to fill in the missing word; however, to do so in a politically innocuous and civically responsible manner. In the drawer of the service desk there was fortunately a big red-tipped pen, which facilitated this operation. Then it all was merely the work of a moment.

When Major General Cibulka came marching down the hall at the stroke of 2:55, he found Babor quietly standing at attention.

"Is anything the matter?" asked the General, since this was clearly apparent from the Colonel's attitude.

Without replying, the Colonel led him inside, into cubicle number VI, where the overwhelmed General read on the latex-painted wall:

"Comrade Babor is an ass."

It seemed to the General that he saw in the eyes of his old comrade-in-arms tears of genuine grief.

"Ungratefulness rules the world," said the General, in order to comfort Babor. "That's how they repay us after so many years of devoted service. What for, Comrades, what for?"

His broken voice reverberated sorrowfully through the men's room of the Supreme Governing Body, but no one answered him. They walked out; there was no sense in remaining there any longer. Besides, the facility was rather small for two.

When they parted, they shook hands with an expression of touching understanding. Major General Cibulka added, to complete the thought:

"Tomorrow it can easily happen that they will write there that I am an ass."

Colonel Babor said nothing; he just rapidly counted in his mind the number of letters in the General's last name.

He went home with a feeling of great self-sacrifice.

The coup d'état did not really take place.

SOCIAL SECURITY

by Norah Holmgren

My mother and I were sitting in the Social Security office. It was on the eighteenth floor of an old building in the heart of the city, but I could still hear the swish swish of cars passing on the freeway below. If I stood up I could see them—long ribbons of them.

I don't live in the city anymore. The sight of ten thousand cars a day began to get me down. Where I live now, out in the country, I can distinguish each of my neighbors' cars by sound alone. In the evening when I come home from work the children can hear me coming closer and closer. In the morning when I hear the rattles and explosions of the Ford truck next door, I know it's time to get up.

My mother had asked me to come with her to Social Security. She wanted me to speak for her and hear for her. She speaks English perfectly and her hearing is unimpaired. She simply can't believe what is being said. If I came with her, she said, we could talk things over later and try to make sense of them. It would be too late then, but it's better to try to understand anyway, isn't it?

In the waiting room we were among the Mexican families, the slim, young Chinese girls, the Filipino men, the gray old German men, and the old Swedish ladies like my mother who had been cooks and maids and seamstresses and bakery clerks. The music of these languages rose and fell. The clerks had to shout over the din. When it got too noisy an armed guard would parade by us once or twice. We all had something in common: we were waiting for our names to be called.

The procedure was this: when we entered, a woman at the door questioned us about our business. If she couldn't turn us away, she gave us a number from 1 to 50. When that number was called, we turned it in and got a number from 51 to 99. When that number was called, our name was entered on a list. When our name was called, we could be shown in. We were told to expect to wait two or three hours for these transitions.

We sat side by side, not talking, observing the people in the room as they observed us.

When my mother's name was called, we stood up and were shown through a doorway into a vast room with rows and rows of desks. Our clerk beckoned to us. He was young, freckled, and dressed in a short-sleeved white shirt open at the neck and chest to reveal a spotless white undershirt. We sat down. I was going to do all the talking.

"I'm Mr. Sisk," he said.

"Ssss?" said my mother.

"Sisk."

"Yes," she said.

His last customer was still hanging around though he had clearly been dismissed. He was a good-looking, tall old man who was standing very straight. He ignored us. It was Mr. Sisk he wanted.

"Why can't you be reasonable?" he said. "I'm an alcoholic. You know me. I never should have told you I haven't been drinking lately. It makes no difference at all. You know that."

"No, that's what I don't know," said Mr. Sisk.

We watched unashamed.

"You don't want to know."

"You aren't drinking now. Maybe you don't need a treatment program."

"I can't hang on much longer without help."

"The rules are clear. The key words are *currently* and *presently* and *at this time.*"

"Bend the rules a little. If I take a drink I'll be gone for months. Lost, lost, lost."

"Don't ask me to bend the rules."

My mother stood up. "The rules must be stupid and cruel," she shouted.

"Who are they for?"

Mr. Sisk looked at her. He didn't speak, but his eyes were blinking rapidly.

He stood up and led the man away.

"I couldn't help it," my mother said. "Do you think it will ruin our chances?"

"I don't think we have any chances to be ruined."

Mr. Sisk returned. He had buttoned up his shirt and put his

jacket on. My mother handed him the letter she had gotten from Social Security. He looked it over and said, "What's the problem?"

I said, "What does it mean?"

"It means we paid her too much money and now we have to get it back. We are going to suspend her payments until the money is made up. It will take nine months."

"Is there no alternative?" I said. "It isn't her fault you gave her too much money."

Mr. Sisk drew himself up in his chair. "We don't use the word *fault* here. She can fill out a hardship report, stating that she cannot live without her Social Security allowance." He found the form in his desk and handed it to me. I looked it over. Declare all your valuables. Declare all current sources of income. Declare possible sources of income. State names and addresses of family members. An inquisition.

My mother had a few old valuables. Her husband, my stepfather, had a pension. They could live without her money. It was just that she thought of her Social Security check as her own money, money she had earned by forty years of labor, money she could spend on herself with a clear conscience, not that she ever did spend much money on herself.

I said to her, "We don't want to fill out this form. All of this is none of their business. It seems that they have the right to withhold your money unless you tell them how much your wedding ring is worth and everything else."

Mr. Sisk addressed my mother in a very loud voice. "Are you willing to fill out this form?"

"I'm not deaf," she shouted at him.

He shuffled his paper. There was a commotion at the next desk. A red-headed clerk was yelling at an old woman in black. "Come back when you're sober."

"I'm not drunk. I've just had a little drink," she said.

"Sit down, then," the clerk screamed.

"Something about this place makes you want to yell," my mother said.

"It's because they think we're all deaf."

"I get so mad," my mother said. "Sure that woman had a little drink. Sometimes you get so mad, sometimes you get so fed up, you just take a drink."

We got up to leave. "If you get a check from us by mistake, be sure to send it to me," said Mr. Sisk.

"You're going to make more mistakes? What's wrong with you people?" my mother said.

I took her out to lunch. I tried to minimize the loss of her money.

She said, "Stop trying to cheer me up. You're making me feel terrible." We sat in silence then.

After a while she started to talk. "I've worked and worked," she said. I sat very still. I hoped she would tell me story. She rarely spoke about her early life. I knew only the generalities: Dad was good, Mother was a martyr, times were hard, you wouldn't believe it.

"When I was eleven—that was during the war—not much food then, the whole family got the flu at one time. There were seven of us children. Dad and I were the only ones who didn't get sick. Oh, how we worked. We cooked, we cleaned, we did the chores. I was so tired at night, I fell asleep in my clothes. My youngest brother died of pneumonia and was buried before the doctor got to us. My mother cried for months and months about that. It was just me and my dad doing all the work. We made soup, we dug potatoes, we fed the chickens. Oh, how we worked."

I waited but she didn't go on.

"What made you think of that story?"

"Mr. Sisk. I'd like to show him what work is."

We got up to leave. "I'm lonely," my mother said. "I'd like to go see Alice. Will you drive me over?"

Alice was a friend of hers I didn't care for. "I'll drive you, I'll wait for you, but I don't want to come in and visit."

"I don't want you to. I want to talk about places you've never been, times before you were born. You'd just be in the way."

After I'd dropped her off, I went into a little park near Alice's house and sat down with a book. There were an unexpected number of people in the park. A large table stood under the trees with paper cups full of water on it. People were watching the path expectantly. Soon tired men and women came running into the park. As each one crossed a chalk line, the bystanders would applaud and cheer. Friends would come forward to hug the runners. The event repeated itself over and over. The applause and cheers didn't diminish; they increased.

My mother soon came limping up the path. Runners passed her on either side. She paid no attention to them. I wanted to stand and applaud her, whose every race had been run without applause, but she would have been angry.

"Why are you smiling?" she said. "Are you laughing at me?"

"No, I'm appreciating you."

"Alice didn't remember the flu of 1917, but she was glad to see me."

Later that evening when I was back in the country and the children were in bed, I wrote a little note to myself. I planned to read it every now and then. It said: "Develop a terrifying persona for when you are old and at the mercy of systems. Save your money so you can always be independent. Never look as though you could be hard of hearing."

This morning when I was cleaning out my desk, I found it. I laughed first, then I called my mother to say hello.

POWER FAILURE

by Bette Howland

I was sleeping on the couch under a pile of blankets and coats and
the fire scratched in the grate. The power was out, had been for the
past twenty-four hours—one of those freak spring storms that knock
down trees and lines. The world was a snow-swamp; the Everglades
turned white. Limbs bent low under loads of snow like lush tropical
vegetation. Everything bowed down in silence.

The only other soul I'd seen all day was the caretaker who looks
after that big summer place across the way, the one that belonged to
Colonel Somebody-or-Other. The heirs are in court, squabbling
over the estate—who gets what and which was promised when (so
the story goes)—and in the meantime the house just sits there,
jigsaw gingerbread, flagpole, widow's walk, getting picked clean by
vandals. They would have made off with the squatting cannon by
now, only it's up to its neck in concrete.

The old man seems to have all this on his mind.

He comes by nearly every day. I hear a car door slam, I look up,
there he is—hefty lumberjacket, hunter's cap, struggling out of his
low-slung yellow hatchback. A Japanese make, which I mention
because there are so many in this neck of the woods; the local
dealer must be one helluva salesman. The energetic little cars go
charging up and down this patriotic landscape, almost a part of it,
like red brick and bow windows, the bumpy blue pyramids of the
mountains, the white birches. (You think other trees are white too,
until you see birches again.)

So here he comes. Collar up, earflaps down, hair gleaming on his
thick, cracked neck, pipe extending the angle and purpose of a
stubborn Yankee jaw. He swings his game leg like a gate—creaking

on its hinges. He's been nailing up boards, rigging wires and alarms, and he looks to be spoiling for a fight:

Next time those wise guys show up, they'll get the surprise of their life.

I think he'll be sorry if there is no next time: now he's ready.

Today the house was safe, buried under a ton or two of savage bright stuff. You could scarcely look at the snow for the weight of the sun on it. He shoved his hands into the pockets over his stomach. His eyes had a nippy glitter; his breath stiffened and staggered. A bluejay was flitting about, the colors of the wintry day. Black/white/blue. Trees/snow/sky. Spreading its wings, it became a miniature landscape, something painted on a fan.

I read by the fire in earmuffs and mittens. (You'd be surprised how hard it is to turn pages with mittens on.) When it got dark—whenever that was, the clock had stopped—I cooked supper over the flames. Burned the potatoes black. Blew ashes into the coffee. I was good and mad at myself, too lazy to take the trouble to do things right. Just because the situation was temporary. Some excuse. What isn't temporary—if you really want to get technical? Is that any way to live?

And how long have I been meaning to buy a kerosene lamp, in case of emergency, and replace the dead batteries in my portable radio?

By the time I went to bed I had fed the fire just about every scrap of paper in the house. And if there's one thing there's plenty of around here, it's scrap paper. All the same, the last I saw—turning my back to the fire, pulling the covers over my shoulder—the last I saw, in the red flickering glow—was one scrap overlooked. Stuck to the bottom of the wastebasket. A letter from my mother, the envelope raggedly ripped.

Even in my sleep I knew this must be the reason for my dream.

Now, please. Don't get me wrong. I don't want to bore anybody. I get discouraged myself, when people start talking about *dreams*. Especially in stories. Because what's to keep them from telling lies? Making it all up? Are there any rules? Besides, everyone knows that *dreams* aren't just *dreams*. I get the sneaking feeling that someone is trying to tell me Something—with a capital *S*. I don't know about you, but that makes me nervous.

All right then. I apologize. But what can I do? Am I trying to put one over on you? This isn't a story, and I was dreaming. And I'd just like to see if I can get things straight.

In the dream my sons seem to be infants again, just learning to walk—chunky wobbly legs, trembling hands, eyes somber with excitement. Their two heads—one light, one dark—are at the same level. My daughter seems older (though that can't be right, can it?)—the size, the special gravity, of a child of three. Her legs are narrow and bare; her short skirts lift and stick out in front and show the puckered trim of her bloomers. (Her brows pucker too.) What's odd is her hair: dark and smooth, heavy-hanging, as if water-weighted, and so long it surrounds her like a cloak. She is mantled in hair, hooded mail. Some children are born that way, right from the beginning, come into the world wrapped in the mysteries of their own personalities. You can see that my daughter is one of these.

I know what's going on; I recognize this dream. I've had it so many times before—though never in my sleep. My heart glares with gladness; as dazzling, as hard to bear, as the sun on the snow. This is it; I'm getting my wish. My children are small again. We have it all to do over.

I can't tell you if I read my mother's letter or not; ripped open doesn't mean anything. I might have been looking to see what was inside. In the last year or so, she has taken to sending me checks. "Go buy yourself something." "How's the money holding out?" This is something new. Maybe I cash them, maybe I tear them up; no rhyme nor reason. It all depends.

I see I have just confessed—and put it in writing—that I am the sort of person who opens a mother's letters in case there might be money in them. So now you know. Why stand on ceremony? And I'm not the only one; it's not just me. Lots of friends tell me they can't read letters they get from their mothers either. This condition must be very widespread. There's safety in numbers.

But is there truth?

What good is it? What's the use? Why open up a letter and read it, when you know darn well, beforehand, what it's going to say? What has been written, preordained, from time immemorial? The standard formula. A little disappointment, a little resentment, a little guilt. Here we have a stock situation, the old antagonism: Mothers & Daughters. You've heard this song before.

My friends must feel the same way I do when I see that familiar handwriting on an envelope, the wavy postmark, the cancelled stamp. About the way it feels to see my name on a bill:

REMIT IMMEDIATELY OR ACTION WILL BE TAKEN.

And after all, she is presenting the Bill. It's that Time. Payment is due, overdue, past past due. She means to Collect. Only—only—it has been established by now that I am never going to come up with her currency. And she won't accept mine.

So how can I pay up? How to find the wherewithal?

Like they say, the letter killeth.

You know how it is when you try to recover a dream.

A tug on the line. A quiver, a gleam. You grab hold, try to hang on. It struggles and squirms. Maybe you hook it, bring it to light. Maybe it sinks into the depths.

Gone for good. Splash! Just like that.

Well, that's how it is in my dream, only the other way around. I know I'm dreaming, and I'm trying to recall real life—my own life—the wide-awake past. Only the same thing happens. It slips from my grasp. I reach for the past—and it isn't there.

I should have known. This dream was too good to last. My sons I can picture as infants. That means the past is there—somewhere. I could lay my hands on it if I wanted to. But my daughter! Looking closer, I can see that she isn't really a child at all. She is only reduced in size, in scale: a miniature. Except for her hair. It must be every bit that long and straight now. I don't recall girls having hair like that, either, when I was her age; so lithe, so shiny, like an animal coat. Her eyes have the same liquid gloss. Shouldn't have let the folded socks and starched skirts fool me. Leotards and jeans would be more like it. And fragile-boned, tough-soled bare feet.

Something tells me I am seeing my daughter in my dream just exactly as she has always been: a grave little image, a stand-in for her grown-up self.

Well, who got her ready for school, then? Who brushed her hair, who tied her shoelaces, who buttoned her blouse down the back if I didn't? Who kissed her scrapes and bruises? Who painted orange stuff on her cuts and stuck the thermometer under her tongue? (Don't tell me she never hurt herself?) Who read her good-night stories and tucked in the covers and told her things a mother tells a daughter? Someone must have. Who else could it have been—if it wasn't me?

The brightness fades; a cold white light creeps through me. Blank and numb as my memory. No fair! No fair! This isn't what I bargained for, not what I meant. It's not my wish. I said I wanted to live the past over again. I never said I wanted to lose it.

What made me say *handwriting*?

My mother prints, loose block letters. This is likewise something new. Maybe it's hard for her to write? She has a touch of arthritis in her wrist; it could be acting up. (I ought to know; I have it too. I'm feeling it right now.) Maybe she thinks it's hard for me to read? Her letters could be addressed to a child. It's like opening a telegram. And she writes, more and more, a telegraphic style:

> Got to go. Big shindig tonite. Milt Ross. Remember him? Birthday. 65th! Going to be "roast." Can't think of darn thing. Except. Daughter's wedding. Milt took movie pictures. Shot up 3 reels. Guess what? Cap on Lens whole time. Was his face red. She got herself very nice boy. Love, Mom.

Wait a minute. Just a minute. Whoa. Hold on. So she calls herself Mom? Since when? How long has this been going on? As far as I know, no one ever calls her Mom. I call her *Mother*. And get introduced to her acquaintances—as I have been all my life long—as "my daw-ter." No name. Strictly generic.

"*Moth-er*," I say. "Is that nice? Is it polite? How are your friends supposed to know what to say to me? Hi, You There? Hello, What's-Your-Name?"

"So what?" Hiking up the arcs of two plucked pincered eyebrows, the style of her youth. Movie vamps with platinum hair and bow lips and icy teeth. (Her own features have the amplitude, the dignity, of a high Plains Indian.) "What makes you think they'd remember your name if I told them?"

So she thinks of herself as Mom. She wants to be Mom. That's news to me. What do you make of it? What's in a Mom?

And just where does she write these letters? Anyhow? Since there's no place in the whole darn house where a person can sit down, in a comfortable chair, under a decent lamp, to read or write. That's what comes of moving to a retirement village in Florida, where the skies are as blue as the ocean and the clouds are as white as golf balls. (Except in the morning—bashful plumy pink, flocks of flamingos.)

Guess that leaves the kitchen table.

My mother doesn't drink herself, but she likes to keep a little something on hand, just to show how broad-minded she can be. Pours me a stiff glass and eyes me—stiffly—while I get it all down, every last drop. It's no use telling her I don't drink; even if it were true, she'd never believe me. She knows better. I'm divorced.

I hate to be blunt. But. When can I ever quit worrying about you?

What is her currency? A life she can approve of—what else? What does any mother want? Why can't I be like her friends' children, acquiring things, habits for a lifetime? (*Got herself very nice boy.*) Instead, she has been ashamed of me, blamed me. She believed that the fact that I wanted and needed her help and affection was proof positive that I deserved none of it. And to tell the truth, I believed it too.

Go explain to your mother that there has been a breakdown—a blackout—in what is called "personal relations" (in case she didn't know) and that when that happens, when circuits short, fuses blow, institutions fail—you're on your own. You take your chances. You need a lot of luck, or a lot of character.

And I only said that, about the character. Thought I'd throw it in. How would I know?

P.S. Say. Just wondering. Ever get that check I sent?

The caretaker told me they were fixing to get the power back on during the night, and I figured I'd be the first to know. This cottage has oil heat, but an electric switch kicks it on; and I do mean kicks. I'm listening for it in my sleep. Snow is skidding off all those pitched roofs and pointy firs—plopping and dumping down clods and clumps, blow by blow. Heavy as mud or sand or wet concrete. There are too many covers; the fire is low, flames nibbling at logs with sharp rodent teeth. That is what's real. And I want to wake up, throw off the weight of this dream, the covers, the burdened branches.

I know it's a dream—only a dream.

Winter dusk. A pearly slush packs the skylight. Wet galoshes lean outside doors. I smell dinners getting cooked, fat spits and spats in frying pans. The hallway of a rundown apartment building. I'm looking for someone behind one of these doors.

But who? Where? Won't anyone answer my knock? Why do the hallways keep changing? Different buildings, streets? How come room after room is empty, and not just empty—deserted? People pack their bags, they move on, they leave no forwarding addresses. Nothing but the waterlogged wallpaper they have been hating all these years. Windowshades fly up with a clatter—flap like tongues.

Frozen snow glazes the glass.

I've found the past; I'm in it. This is it—all there is of it. Not even a memory. Nothing to revise. The children were small; money was scarce; I got sick. My daughter went to live with strangers. That's why the missing memory, the missing years. It wasn't me; it was someone else all along.

How could I have let this happen to us? Didn't I know better? Didn't I mean better? But it's too late now. I can't get out of it, can't change anything. My daughter and I have no history, only the History of Mothers & Daughters. I know exactly how she is going to feel toward me. I have forfeited my one and only chance.

* * *

I didn't tell you what it felt like when I saw my mother's letter.

It felt as if they'd got the juice back on—thrown the switch. A jolt, a shock. It went right through me. Just for a second, but the force surprised me, so strong, I didn't know what to call it. And what difference does it make? Call it anything you want. It's all the same power—it all comes from the same place. So that's the way we're wired up.

I didn't know there was that much left, in our connection.

Mother, Mother. Why can't you be one way or another? So I could feel one way or the other? Why have we wasted our time like this? Why couldn't we have called it something else?

What good are checks and letters now?

Somewhere the object of my ambivalence is sitting at a kitchen table, ball-point pen in hand, gazing out at newly planted palms—all in a row, swaying like grass-skirted utility poles. Her face carved teak from the Florida sun, her glasses sidling down her nose, her eyes in their lustrous depths as large and lurking as goldfish. You know that look of trusting expectation old people have.

Old? Did someone say old? My mother?

The frames are mother-of-pearl, white and luminous as her hair.

What is my currency? That is the question. And how long since I have offered any? What am I waiting for? A more favorable rate of exchange? Or maybe I hope to wake up one fine day and find that things have changed, overnight; all of a sudden it's *easy*?

But it's no good just saying something. The trick is to feel it.

I wake, frozen stiff. The windows are streaked in leaky gray light; someone just kicked over a bucket of water. The room is cold, the clock still stopped, the fire out: powder and ashes. Cold sweat clings to me—a sheet wrung from the wash. It takes me a minute or two to understand that it's all right. I'm awake. It was nothing, only a dream. No one is going to feel that way toward me. It's not exactly a relief. Because who was she? Who is she? And what do I do now?

I never had a daughter.

THE CONTRACT

by Harvey Jacobs

Martin Harlen, a young man who believed in responsibility, took on the job of going through his aunt's papers and possessions a few weeks after she died. Annie Harlen Fine had lived for eighty-five years, sixty of them in the same Brooklyn flat. The family had tried to pry her loose from the "old neighborhood," which was turning into a slum, but the old lady would not budge.

Everyone assumed her decision to remain was sentimental. She had come to the little court off Flatbush Avenue as a bride, lived there through her marriage and raised two children in those rooms. The slow inventory of Aunt Annie's accumulations now made Martin Harlen think it was not so much sentimentality as gravity.

As he sorted through ancient documents, saved advertisements for products long since gone from the market, as he moved past heavy upholstered furniture, as he explored closets filled with dresses, coats, shoes, bags, as he brewed coffee in a kitchen loaded with pots, pans, dishes, cups, plates, utensils, an incredible collection of drinking glasses decorated with pictures of Shirley Temple, Snow White and the Seven Dwarfs, glasses that once held cottage cheese, memorial candles, Lord knows what, as he sorted mustard jars, horseradish bottles, tubby ketchup bottles, slender wine bottles, aristocratic seltzer bottles that perched like birds on high shelves, as he fumbled through drawers holding receipts, rubber bands, balls of foil, single stockings, hairpins, curlers, paper clips, clothespins, bottle caps, souvenir spoons from the 1939 World's Fair ... the combined weight of Annie Fine's personal property added to enormous tonnage.

How could she move? It would have taken a caravan. Where could she move? To Radio City Music Hall? He had already filled ten cartons from the A&P with his aunt's leftovers and marked them for the Salvation Army. And there was hardly a dent in the mysterious glut.

When Martin Harlen volunteered to dismantle his aunt's apartment (Annie's son lived in Phoenix, her daughter in Santa Barbara, and neither could spare the time nor cared for the fate of the objects that remained after rings, watches, bonds, and the will had been removed from the safety deposit), he never expected such trouble. Still, someone had to do it. The apartment had to be vacated by the end of the month.

The work was slow and tedious. It was the fault of the *things* themselves. It was somehow necessary to stop and muse over the tiniest objects. Martin Harlen decided that possessions are transformed at the moment of their owner's death. Bits of ghost enter unlikely containers like empty jewelry boxes covered in plush, compacts, lamps, ashtrays, even rusty Flit guns and cans that held mothballs. *Why did she keep it?*

Martin Harlen loved his aunt. She was a tough lady, like a military jeep rolling from place to place on thick tires. She was the only one in the family who would tell him about the past. She admitted that her father went senile. She called her brother, Sol, a miser. She was glad when her children married and moved out of town. So if Aunt Annie's ghost had fractured and fragmented into a pile of junk, her nephew was determined to give the pile its due. He saw that as the fair price for the stories, the holiday meals, the brutal advice about the "world," the tours through albums of brown photographs.

When the bell rang, Martin Harlen thought it was another furniture dealer. He had suffered through three so far. They came in shabby clothes to look like poor men, they sniffed around the bed, the dresser, the end tables, the sofa, isolated mounds of towels and linen, scatter rugs, they browsed the kitchen, they sighed, wheezed, moaned, suffered, then quoted a ridiculous price for "the whole shebang." They told Martin Harlen *he* should pay *them* for the carting. Their names and offers were jotted down on a pad. Part of the responsibility was to get the best price he could for his aunt's heritage. That was not just because a dollar is a dollar. Annie Harlen Fine was a hard bargainer. Since it was to be that her *things* would go to strangers, dispersed to flea markets and second-hand shops, then price had to do with pride. She deserved a good deal.

What the Salvation Army didn't get would be converted to cash and the cash would be used carefully for necessities and pleasures. The guilty son and daughter said the whole ball of wax should go to some charity. Martin Harlen argued for keeping a share. Aunt Annie was a practical woman. Some to charity, then, and some to divvy up. It had to do with Annie's fresh ghost and what would bring peace.

The intercom to the downstairs door was broken. Martin Harlen could hear only a crackled voice in response to his yells. But he buzzed the visitor. It could be a furniture dealer or a thug with a hammer or a dragon. Life in the city demands chances. Besides, the greatest favor would be an arsonist in a mask. No such luck.

A knock, a tap, a clearing of the throat, was heard at the apartment door. A small, rotund, puffing man wearing a heavy overcoat and a Russian hat of Persian lamb (Aunt Annie had a stole like that) stood in the doorway holding a wooden box with a black handle.

"They said snow," he said. "It is cold. I should wear a scarf and gloves but I lose them. Like umbrellas."

"This is the Fine apartment," Martin said.

"I know. I read the obituary. I'm sorry. My condolences. Can I come inside?"

"Come in."

"I can't believe she passed. That was some lady. How are you related?"

"My aunt. Actually, my great-aunt."

"I met her children years ago. They didn't look like you. Maybe around the eyes. My name is Jack Pinsky. Pleased to make your acquaintance. Better on a happier occasion."

Martin Harlen introduced himself and shook a thin hand. Jack Pinsky slowly took off his coat and hat and laid them over a chair. He carried his wooden box with him to the sofa and placed it between his feet.

"I'm sitting without an invitation. You wouldn't believe it, but I am a seventy-seven-year-old man."

Jack Pinsky looked a hundred. His face was a pale triangle blotched in red and blue from the weather. His lips were lavender, like Aunt Annie's drapes.

"So you knew my aunt?"

"Knew her? From a girl. At least, a very young woman. Beautiful woman. I once offered her plenty just to take off her clothes and let me gaze. She wouldn't do it."

"Excuse me, but are you talking about Mrs. Fine?"

"Fine is right. Delicious. What a face. What a body. So what are you doing here? Are you the executor of her estate?"

"Is that any of your concern, Mr. Pinsky?"

"I asked in a nice way. It is my business. My name don't ring any bells?"

"I'm afraid not."

"Then you didn't find the contract yet? It wasn't in her vault? I would think she'd keep it in the vault."

"I'm not aware of any contract. Look, I don't know what you're after, but . . ."

"But? But it is your responsibility to find the contract. That upon the death of the principal the contract should be returned to Jack Pinsky. It's in the contract. I need something hot to drink. You got coffee?"

"I'll make some instant. Mr. Pinsky, you're going to have to explain yourself. And I'm telling you, I am aware of scavengers who follow the death notices and show up with false claims, if you know what I'm getting at."

"Scavengers? Soap in your mouth. I can't believe she didn't mention the contract. Did she die sudden? Unexpected?"

"She died suddenly, yes."

"Ah. Ah. That explains that. You mind if I go in the bedroom?"

"Yes, I mind."

"Hey, I have been in there plenty of times. I'll prove it. There is a bed with posts. There is a window with a curtain of hand-embroidered angels holding harps. There is wallpaper with a scene from France of sheep with a lady and plenty flowers. Next to the bed, two tables with curvy legs. And across from the bed is a fantastic painting in a gold frame of a sunset over the Brooklyn Bridge. And in the lower righthand corner of that painting is the signature in gray of one Jack Pinsky. No saucer. No spoon. No napkin. Just in a cup is sufficient. Did I convince you?"

"I'll make the coffee."

While Jack Pinsky sipped hot coffee, Martin Harlen verified the signature.

"So?"

"You're that Jack Pinsky?"

"You want credentials? What do you want? Diners Club? Social Security? Medicare? What? Jack Pinsky in the lower righthand corner near the organ grinder with the ape written like it was in cement on the sidewalk. Right or wrong?"

"I saw it."

"You know when I painted that picture for Annie? Guess. The month she moved in here. I was still a kid in high school. Her friend, Hannah, knew my mother, may she rest in peace. Annie Fine needed a picture, so they sent me over with a picture and she bought it. My first sale. Three dollars. 'Sunset on the Brooklyn Bridge.' Painted from life. I don't begrudge Mrs. Fine the three dollars. Not the lousy price. The contract."

"What contract?"

"She made me sign a piece of paper. What did I know? I was a kid. I would have signed anyhow for that girl. She was very gorgeous."

"You told me."

"Terms and conditions. What did I know about terms and conditions? I signed. You're interested in the terms and conditions? The terms and conditions were that whenever your aunt changed her drapes or bedspread or the walls she could call Jack Pinsky to run over and fix the painting to match her new colors. And for nothing. No pay except the cost of the oil paint. Can you imagine? You know how many times that woman called me? In 1930 she got pink crazy. All pink in there. In 1939 she bought all new. God knows where she got the money. In the middle of World War Two she changed again. Beige. I hated it. During Truman, yellow. Eisenhower, she went green. During Nixon, blue with purple. Six times she called me. Change. Fix. The sun. The sky. The water. The bridge. The ape's jacket. She yelled at me. She cursed me. I came. And between you and me, I gave up art during Franklin D. Roosevelt's second term. But I came. I fixed. I honored the contract, which was probably illegal, since I was eighteen when I signed it. But I am an honorable man, maybe the last. Jack Pinsky signs his name, he means it. He changes. He fixes."

"I almost sold that painting to a dealer this afternoon."

"For how much?"

"It's hard to say. It was part of a parcel that included lamps, a gown, ornaments."

"You didn't sell. Something in you, a little voice, said don't sell."

"Exactly right."

"You got an eye. Like your aunt. Congratulations."

In the bedroom, Jack Pinsky ran fingers over the surface of "Sunset on the Brooklyn Bridge."

"It seems to have held up well, considering," said Martin Harlen.

"Considering the abuse. See here? In the original the bridge was more black. The sky was before a storm. Now it looks like a gypsy birthday cake. The damn wallpaper with the French sheep. Fix, change. But I did it. I am a successful man. Textiles. Flocking. I could buy and sell the whole Fine Family ten times. But I came. I remember when her husband died. Her children moved. I got the whole story. She stood over my shoulder telling me colors. Please, get me my box."

Martin Harlen brought in the box from the living room and watched Jack Pinsky open it to remove a smock and a small palette.

"What are you doing, Mr. Pinsky?"

"Terms and conditions. Upon the death of Mrs. Fine the artist shall have the right to fix back his painting titled 'Sunset on the

Brooklyn Bridge' to its first combination of colors. Furthermore, the artist should get back the contract to rip up once and for all. I made her put that in the document, because while I was a kid I was smart. A term and condition was she could sell the painting with me to fix it. I knew she would never sell. I let her have that if when she died I would get back my rights. She died. Who can believe it? Rest in peace for a thousand years. But I'm not taking chances. I don't want any claims on me or my painting. I don't want any calls. That contract must be found and destroyed by me personally, and I will not leave until I have it in my hand."

"Be realistic, Mr. Pinsky. Look around you. I'm sure your contract is somewhere in those mounds, but how long will it take to find? If I find it."

"The stipulation is clear. In the event . . ."

"Calm yourself. I'll go through everything. I'm not promising to spend my life here, but if I find the contract, I personally will send it to you or burn it or whatever you want."

"Not enough. I'm getting back what I gave away and I am entitled."

"I agree to allow you to fix the painting."

"Restore. Not fix."

"In fact, Mr. Pinsky, I insist that you take the painting as a gift."

"Are you crazy? That painting is worth plenty today. I'm not interested in robbing the dead. Now, let me go to work. I would appreciate more coffee, not so dark. But let me work."

Martin Harlen put more water in his aunt's kettle and set it to boil. He went to the living room, where he had stacked a random ton of papers gathered from around the apartment. At the top of the pile was a *Daily News* with a headline about Eleanor Roosevelt feeding hot dogs to the King and Queen of England. Under the paper was a letter, under the letter an ad for Fairy soap, under that a lease, under the lease a song sheet, under that a recipe for honeyed sweet potatoes.

He heard Jack Pinsky humming from the bedroom. An old sunset would throw shadows on a still-young bridge. Under the recipe was some fabric, maybe cut from the bottom of somebody's pants. Under the fabric, a chart of stars, under the chart a map of New Jersey.

"Are you looking? Is there coffee?" said Jack Pinsky. "You think there was something between me and Annie? Your uncle was no Cary Grant. You want to ask me questions?"

Under the map of New Jersey was a collection of coupons and under the coupons a *Reader's Digest* contest letter with gold seals, more letters and a photograph of Annie Harlen Fine eating a jelly apple on a boardwalk. Martin Harlen sat on the floor near the papers. He examined a toaster lying there, a big Emerson radio, some books and a white plaster head of Mozart.

"When I rang downstairs you shouldn't have let me in without knowing who was coming up. That's the most dangerous thing," said Jack Pinsky. "You know, I'm surprised she didn't keep the contract in her vault. She must have had a vault."

"She trusted people," said Martin Harlen.

"A big mistake," said Jack Pinsky.

SUNDAY IN THE PARK

by Bel Kaufman

It was still warm in the late-afternoon sun, and the city noises came muffled through the trees in the park. She put her book down on the bench, removed her sunglasses, and sighed contentedly. Morton was reading the *Times Magazine* section, one arm flung around her shoulder; their three-year-old son, Larry, was playing in the sandbox; a faint breeze fanned her hair softly against her cheek. It was five-thirty of a Sunday afternoon, and the small playground, tucked away in a corner of the park, was all but deserted. The swings and seesaws stood motionless and abandoned, the slides were empty, and only in the sandbox two little boys squatted diligently side by side. *How good this is,* she thought, and almost smiled at her sense of well-being. They must go out in the sun more often; Morton was so city-pale, cooped up all week inside the gray factorylike university. She squeezed his arm affectionately and glanced at Larry, delighting in the pointed little face frowning in concentration over the tunnel he was digging. The other boy suddenly stood up and with a quick, deliberate swing of his chubby arm threw a spadeful of sand at Larry. It just missed his head. Larry continued digging; the boy remained standing, shovel raised, stolid and impassive.

"No, no, little boy." She shook her finger at him, her eyes searching for the child's mother or nurse. "We mustn't throw sand. It may get in someone's eyes and hurt. We must play nicely in the nice sandbox." The boy looked at her in unblinking expectancy. He was about Larry's age but perhaps ten pounds heavier, a husky little boy with none of Larry's quickness and sensitivity in his face. Where was his mother? The only other people left in the playground were two women and a little girl on roller skates leaving now through the gate, and a man on a bench a few feet away. He was a big man, and he seemed to be taking up the whole bench as he held the Sunday comics close to his face. She supposed he was the child's father. He did not look up from his comics, but spat once deftly out of the corner of his mouth. She turned her eyes away.

At that moment, as swiftly as before, the fat little boy threw another spadeful of sand at Larry. This time some of it landed on his hair and forehead. Larry looked up at his mother, his mouth tentative; her expression would tell him whether to cry or not.

Her first instinct was to rush to her son, brush the sand out of his hair, and punish the other child, but she controlled it. She always said that she wanted Larry to learn to fight his own battles.

"Don't *do* that, little boy," she said sharply, leaning forward on the bench. "You mustn't throw sand!"

The man on the bench moved his mouth as if to spit again, but instead he spoke. He did not look at her, but at the boy only.

"You go right ahead, Joe," he said loudly. "Throw all you want. This here is a *public* sandbox."

She felt a sudden weakness in her knees as she glanced at Morton. He had become aware of what was happening. He put his *Times* down carefully on his lap and turned his fine, lean face toward the man, smiling the shy, apologetic smile he might have offered a student in pointing out an error in his thinking. When he spoke to the man, it was with his usual reasonableness.

"You're quite right," he said pleasantly, "but just because this is a public place . . ."

The man lowered his funnies and looked at Morton. He looked at him from head to foot, slowly and deliberately. "Yeah?" His insolent voice was edged with menace. "My kid's got just as good right here as yours, and if he feels like throwing sand, he'll throw it, and if you don't like it, you can take your kid the hell out of here."

The children were listening, their eyes and mouths wide open, their spades forgotten in small fists. She noticed the muscle in Morton's jaw tighten. He was rarely angry; he seldom lost his temper. She was suffused with a tenderness for her husband and an impotent rage against the man for involving him in a situation so alien and so distasteful to him.

"Now, just a minute," Morton said courteously, "you must realize . . ."

"Aw, shut up," said the man.

Her heart began to pound. Morton half rose; the *Times* slid to the ground. Slowly the other man stood up. He took a couple of steps toward Morton, then stopped. He flexed his great arms, waiting. She pressed her trembling knees together. Would there be violence, fighting? How dreadful, how incredible . . . She must do something, stop them, call for help. She wanted to put her hand on her husband's sleeve, to pull him down, but for some reason she didn't.

Morton adjusted his glasses. He was very pale. "This is ridiculous," he said unevenly. "I must ask you . . ."

"Oh, yeah?" said the man. He stood with his legs spread apart, rocking a little, looking at Morton with utter scorn. "You and who else?"

For a moment the two men looked at each other nakedly. Then Morton turned his back on the man and said quietly, "Come on, let's get out of here." He walked awkwardly, almost limping with self-consciousness, to the sandbox. He stooped and lifted Larry and his shovel out.

At once Larry came to life; his face lost its rapt expression and he began to kick and cry. "I don't *want* to go home, I want to play better, I don't *want* any supper, I don't *like* supper. . . ." It became a chant as they walked, pulling their child between them, his feet dragging on the ground. In order to get to the exit gate they had to pass the bench where the man sat sprawling again. She was careful not to look at him. With all the dignity she could summon, she pulled Larry's sandy, perspiring little hand, while Morton pulled the other. Slowly and with head high she walked with her husband and child out of the playground.

Her first feeling was one of relief that a fight had been avoided, that no one was hurt. Yet beneath it there was a layer of something else, something heavy and inescapable. She sensed that it was more than just an unpleasant incident, more than defeat of reason by force. She felt dimly it had something to do with her and Morton, something acutely personal, familiar and important.

Suddenly Morton spoke. "It wouldn't have proved anything."

"What?" she asked.

"A fight. It wouldn't have proved anything beyond the fact that he's bigger than I am."

"Of course," she said.

"The only possible outcome," he continued reasonably, "would have been—what? My glasses broken, perhaps a tooth or two replaced, a couple of days' work missed—and for what? For justice? For truth?"

"Of course," she repeated. She quickened her step. She wanted only to get home and to busy herself with her familiar tasks; perhaps then the feeling, glued like heavy plaster on her heart, would be gone. *Of all the stupid, despicable bullies,* she thought, pulling harder on Larry's hand. The child was still crying. Always before she had felt a tender pity for his defenseless little body, the frail arms, the narrow shoulders with sharp, winglike shoulder blades, the thin and unsure legs, but now her mouth tightened in resentment.

"Stop crying," she said sharply. "I'm ashamed of you!" She felt as if all three of them were tracking mud along the street. The child cried louder.

If there had been an issue involved, she thought, *if there had been something to fight for . . . But what else could he possibly have done? Allow himself to be beaten? Attempt to educate the man? Call a policeman? "Officer, there's a man in the park who won't stop his child from throwing sand on mine. . . ."* The whole thing was as silly as that, and not worth thinking about.

"Can't you keep him quiet, for Pete's sake?" Morton asked irritably.

"What do you suppose I've been trying to do?" she said.

Larry pulled back, dragging his feet.

"If you can't discipline this child, I will," Morton snapped, making a move toward the boy.

But her voice stopped him. She was shocked to hear it, thin and cold and penetrating with contempt. "Indeed?" she heard herself say. "You and who else?"

CAMBODIAN DIARY, 1979: THE SECOND DEATH

by Edmund Keeley

January 21. Phnom Penh has fallen again. It seems it takes the loss of our city to still another enemy to make me open this notebook after so many months of telling myself that any writing outside my class roll book and my ledger of accounts would simply be a self-indulgent way of escaping from the reality of life on this border. Now I begin to feel something near the opposite: to write here, even if it proves to be for my eyes alone, may be the only way I have of grasping that reality and holding on to it before it too becomes part of the life we have lost. News came to our camp two weeks ago over Thai radio that the Vietnamese had entered Phnom Penh, what was left of it, and now new refugees from Cambodia have crossed the border to our camp with more details about what has taken place in this latest violent shuffle of political absurdities inside our vanishing homeland.

The Vietnamese have apparently set up a new People's Revolutionary Council in what they still call "democratic Kampuchea," this council to rule our country on terms acceptable to Hanoi. The Khmer Rouge command and most others belonging to their administration have fled once again toward the jungle forests and the mountains. They tell those they encounter in their flight that they will struggle on relentlessly wherever they can until our capital city is liberated again, the city they themselves emptied overnight except for a few hungry dogs and maniacal snipers when I last saw it four years ago. Our Prince Sihanouk is back in China now asking the world to ignore the puppet government of the invading Vietnamese and to recognize the fleeing Khmer Rouge instead, the very regime that was responsible for killing his own sons and then for turning him into a bourgeois husband under house arrest for three years.

They say that he weeps for his sons at the same time that he pleads the Khmer Rouge case.

This, my dear Tan Yong, is the latest turn in our country's fate. I address you as I come back to this notebook because you more than any of the others who have found refuge outside Thailand would want to know what is now happening on the other side of the border beyond our camp, and you would also be the first to appreciate the ironies of it. For my part I will feel more at ease recording these latest political idiocies and their cruel consequences if I can imagine a familiar and sympathetic audience listening to me, especially since it still seems wise for me to write in the English language you and I would turn to in our moments of secret dialogue after we came to trust each other in those early days here.

I don't really expect you will ever read this. It is now over a year since you left us for America, and still no word from you. I don't mean that to sound like a complaint. As you well know, I am not the kind of woman to exploit sentiments of trust for some emotional advantage. I don't know what part of my very mixed Sino-Khmer blood makes that impossible, perhaps a legacy from my Scottish grandmother, who apparently governed my father's childhood in Hong Kong with quiet Anglo-Saxon terror. Or perhaps the sternly moral English nanny he later imposed on me. In any case, I'm sure you've done what you could to help those of us here who put our best hope in you. That is what makes me feel we are not likely to see each other again. Your pride would not allow you to get in touch with me unless you had something useful to offer, and that means the obstacles have proven too complicated. We are well aware that the quota of those found acceptable for immigration to America is becoming ridiculously small compared with the number of those here who are hungry to go, and it seems to most of us who came across the border as long ago as you and I did that our time has now run out.

I myself am no longer hungry to go to a third country. If it weren't for Thirith, thoughts of America or France would no longer clutter my mind. My work is here. But she is still so young, not yet twenty; she deserves another chance to live some kind of normal life. And though I inherited her from the rain on the highway outside Battambang, she is now my daughter as much as any I might bear, and I worry about her as much. Not possessively. Her future obviously has to be free of my need, and I have to survive without the hope her youth carries. I'm not afraid of that. If I learned one thing in making my way with Thirith through the forests and the mountains that now face us here, it is the simple virtue of stretching what little one has to the limit while looking no farther ahead than where it seems one can safely place the left foot after the right without stepping on a mine or on somebody else's shattered corpse—that is, except when it might shield one against a possible hidden danger underneath.

And another thing I learned was to look with deep suspicion on whatever abstractions might come into my head to give me a sensation of hope. In the jungle west of Battambang one doesn't find political or philosophical refuges to help the mind survive the damp nights, no erotic retreats, no easy place for ideological excursions, no comforting images of America or France. There are only the trees with no name and the sharp bamboo and the bushes covered with thorns, the poisonous plants, the treacherous open grassland. There are the snakes and the malarial mosquitoes that turn out to be nothing beside the imaginary wild animals, the tigers and panthers and bears that they say actually live there but that never quite show themselves. And there is the unseen enemy who has stretched wire between two stakes with grenades at either end and buried boards holding spikes that can penetrate rubber, leather, anything one has left to wear on the feet. And of course the waiting patrols, heard and unheard.

Still, even when you are frightened so that the perspiration pours down your face at the coldest moments and every new noise seems to signal an ambush that could leave you dismembered but still alive to crawl, like the half-bloated bodies with bones exposed that one sometimes came across in clearings near a pond or waterhole—even at the very worst times, I found no room for mystery. There was only thought for the next meal of young leaves and the next sip of your own urine if the waterholes proved to be dry again.

I remember one time—did I ever tell you about this?—when Thirith and I came to a sudden clearing in the trees that may have been manmade but looked more like a natural defect in the forest, very frightening as one moved across it because the brush and grass were taller than what the eye was used to and the pattern of sounds different, so that every hidden thing one stumbled into seemed at first a part of something unburied and the whole place an unmarked graveyard. I was leading Thirith as usual, keeping just enough ahead of her to create a kind of path and to anticipate any trouble if I had time and luck enough, and about halfway across the clearing I lost her. I turned to find that she'd vanished out of sight behind me as though she'd fallen into an open pit. I went back and finally spotted her off to one side, squatting on her haunches behind a bush, her eyes wide, fierce with terror, her lips in motion but not shaping anything I could understand around the same low moan her real mother used to make in her madness when talking to the spirits that haunted her during our nights on the highway. I didn't give Thirith any argument. With one hand I held her shoulder and with the other I struck her face as hard as I could, then struck it again, almost knocking her over. When I raised my hand again, she screamed at me in rage, but that ended the moaning. And I never had to hit her again, because that pause in our journey to the border apparently ended all conversation with the unknown.

I'm sure you know what I'm talking about. You had your own jungle to get through south of ours and at a time when crossing the border to our camp was dangerous beyond anything Thirith and I had to face. If you came out more of a believer in the unknown than I can be, I think we still share the same unsentimental knowledge of this particular godless reality that appears to have chosen our country for a playground, entering from more directions since we lost our neutrality than even the godlessness of politics can justify. At least I hope that is one thing you and I still share, because I need to assume it now.

February 11. The new refugees have begun to arrive at our camp in large numbers, several hundred this past week. Some are Khmer Rouge fleeing the Vietnamese, but most are ordinary Khmers fleeing the Khmer Rouge, who have begun to gather up what civilians they can in their retreat and are driving them off to the mountains to make guerrillas out of them. A new mass migration is under way in "democratic Kampuchea," with the Vietnamese invaders urging the Khmer citizens they find herded in work camps to return to their former villages for the winter harvest, and the Khmer Rouge trying to intercept the returning villagers before they make their way back to whatever homes they still have left. The invading enemy plays the liberator and the retreating defender plays the enslaving enemy—a familiar game that is of course not a game at all. The very young and the very old again have to fend mostly for themselves, because those with any strength and cunning seem determined to use this latest disruption to make their way across the border. As of course you and I would have done.

The stories they bring with them are also familiar—the forced labor, the ideological ruthlessness, the ever-present spying, the sudden disappearances at night—though it seems the threatened Pol Pot government grew increasingly paranoid in recent months and the killing became capricious beyond what even you and I knew. The invading forces have apparently uncovered new mass graves full of blindfolded skulls and wired wristbones, and also new evidence of school buildings used for reeducation by torture, all of this now rich food for Vietnamese propaganda. And there are the usual accounts of betrayal and revenge and separation. I don't have to tell you these stories. Still, though one hears yet another version of personal loss and family death from each of those arriving, the familiarity doesn't change the fascination we give them, the attention to some new detail of horror, some new confession of a child sacrificed because it began crying too loudly at a dangerous moment or of a wife left behind because she was too pregnant to go on walking fast enough. And we continue our almost ritual participation in everybody else's sorrow by recounting our own again, as though the only communal faith we have left in this green refuge is our shared knowledge of cruelty and our shared guilt in having successfully escaped it, at least for the time being.

The dark side of this faith is suspicion of one's new neighbor. Most of us who have become firmly settled in here do what we can to take in the new arrivals and make them at home, but some of us have begun to see them as a threat. There are rumors that the Thais will not allow more refugees to enter if this latest exodus keeps bringing them into the country at the current pace, that they will try to force those entering back across the border, just as one hears some of those arriving by boat have been forced back to sea. And since they can't possibly keep everyone out who is determined to cross over, the talk is that they may eventually have to come into the overcrowded camps and remove the new refugees. If that happens, who will be chosen to distinguish the old from the new—that is, if anyone still cares to make the distinction by then? So some here have begun to speak of the new arrivals as possible Vietnamese spies, or Khmer Rouge agents pretending to be guerrillas, or collaborators with one or another former enemy, the old system of defense through accusation that I thought I'd left behind with the one-armed Khmer Rouge leader who bullied us into creating a village out of the forest west of Battambang. But of course there are all kinds among us now, and this undercurrent of insinuation not only has changed the mood in our camp but may signal a true danger to us from our hosts after so many months of almost boring—what is the phrase the Americans would use?—domestic tranquility.

I try to keep all this at a distance by occupying myself with more teaching, not only the larger classes in English and French that I've accepted, but now informal history as well—modern history, unrevised. I can see you smile at this, take it for my last stand at the ramparts of our dying civilization. And there may be something in that. But to the extent that I can understand my own motives, I think it is a thing less pretentious. I simply want a few of those who go out of here to another country to have some notion of what their own country was in this century, the good that was brought into it from foreign places and the evil that came along at the same time, how it was corrupted by the war and how its treasures were damaged and sometimes annihilated before many here were old enough to know them. And I'm not referring only to things like Angkor Wat and the other monuments that have suffered but to the Khmer tradition of living that my mother grew up with and my sister and her children and that I myself used to be so ready to disparage.

If all this strikes you as hopeless nostalgia, let me offer another excuse: I want to keep the history of our generation fresh in my mind so that I don't let myself slip—it is so comfortable sometimes, so entertaining—into easy cynicism. I want the hatred this history generates, the anger that comes with its harsh ironies and absurdities, to keep my own sense of location from dying while I'm still capable of passion.

Outside the classroom I occupy myself, no doubt too much, with trying to keep Thirith out of trouble. And by that I don't mean keeping her a virgin—I long ago gave that up as a futile and meaningless business. She is, after all, close to twenty years old now, and though younger than that in some respects, her body is as ripe as one could hope for in someone brought up on what she had to eat while she was still growing. I mean trying to keep her from getting so caught up in the—how shall I put it?—fecund aura of this place that she gets pregnant and then has to marry somebody who complicates her chances of leaving Thailand when her luck begins to work for her again. Before you left, breeding children had perhaps not yet become the leading business of our camp and its best recreation. Now it is more prosperous than our handicrafts, our weaving and sewing and carpentry, our gardening and trinket-making. And the native instruments and dancing we sometimes provide for entertainment can't compete for musical exercise with what goes on behind our thin partitions anytime there is enough darkness to suggest privacy.

This must surely influence Thirith. Lately she spends less time on her language studies and less time on her vegetable garden—last year's great obsession—and more and more time where I can't find her. I'm certain she has a lover. And I'm certain she will do everything she can to keep him hidden from me. Again you may smile. What else would a daughter—especially a daughter found on the highway—do with a substitute mother like me? And why shouldn't God's lucky children be fruitful and multiply? That's fine for you to say from the security of your brightly lighted New York, or wherever you are in America. But what about those of us who have nothing but the future of our young—even if adopted young—to give us an image of possibilities? The trouble is, if Thirith does finally come to me to reveal what you may think she shouldn't, I'm afraid I will have made myself unacceptable as a person to offer her healthy advice. I now have a lover too.

March 4. The past few weeks have been unsettling. We had "important" visitors from the Thai government recently, and you know what that means: they come to a place like this only on the dark days, when they sense trouble or hope to cause it, never when the sun is strong on our planting and the air mildly perfumed. The problem seems to be gold. One wouldn't think that refugees who arrive the way these are dressed would create a problem of gold, but hiding gold and jewels from the Khmer Rouge—hiding them sometimes very uncomfortably, as I'm sure you know—has apparently continued to be a means of private resistance in the years since you and I escaped. Anyway, those arriving these days have come out with enough gold to establish a black market with Thai traders all along the border, from Aranyaprathet south to Trat, it seems. The refugees are of course hungry for the simple things that they've been denied during the past four years, things that now strike me as so ordinary that I have to recognize how spoiled we've become: needles, soap, candles, nails, matches, sugar, salt, hats for their heads and sandals for their feet, and maybe a necklace of flowers to celebrate their successful conspiracy with benevolent spirits.

The Thai traders are taking in refugee gold in such quantities and spending it so freely in Bangkok that it appears the government has become concerned enough to investigate not only the camps near the border but much of forest in between them. One rumor is that they merely want to collect their share of the gold. Another is that they want to eliminate not just the black market but all traffic across the border by planting new mines and heavier patrols. And the worst rumor of all is that the true purpose of their activity in our area is to establish routes that will supply the retreating Khmer Rouge wherever they settle in near the border. This would make them agents of the Chinese on behalf of Khmer Rouge guerrillas, but of course for the patriotic motive of defending Thailand against possible aggression by the Russia-supported Vietnamese. And we Cambodians without a country or an ideology would end up trapped between one enemy and another. As usual.

I may soon learn from an authoritative source about what the Thai government is really up to. I told you I had a lover. I didn't say more not because I was being coy but because I didn't know exactly what tone to take in telling you about him. That disturbed me then and it still does now. Tone was never an issue between you and me when we were together. In serious matters we were simply candid—at least I always was with you, and I'm prepared to believe you were with me until you candidly tell me otherwise. And beyond our personal feelings for each other, we managed to hold an objectivity about the situation around us, see it for what it was and talk about it truthfully, never allowing personal feeling to jeopardize the work we did together organizing the classes in the camp. I think we were also very careful about the boundaries of our intimacy—and I don't mean to put aside our one tender excursion into more dangerous regions under my persuasion. That you followed me then was as important to me as your not pressing for more in the days thereafter, when we both knew you would be leaving and when I think we both became especially sensitive to the damage that might come from letting our friendship take that route again in our last days together. And strangely, I remained celibate for many months after you left, feeding myself off other resources, some of which— perhaps the more selfless kind—you were responsible for discovering in me and nurturing.

Is that why our friendship has remained strong enough—in my mind, anyway—to make you my necessary audience here? And if so, why is there a problem of tone? Because for all this candid accounting on my part, I still have a sense that talk of a new lover is bound to make you uncomfortable, maybe a little jealous (is that bold of me?), maybe a little suspicious of where my thoughts seem to be directed these days, so that no tone would be quite right. Especially so when I tell you that he is not a Khmer but a foreigner. Anyway, since I can't speak to you directly, I'll simply have to let questions of tone answer themselves. The facts are these: he is a large Dutchman, reasonably handsome—blond, square-jawed, thick brows and lips—reasonably intelligent, evidently in love with me. He works for one of the international relief agencies under the United Nations, a new one that has come into our area since you left it. His headquarters are in Bangkok, but he travels to the camps once or twice a week—and that is about as much of him as I need. We are discreet. I would never let his—shall I call it his courting? —compromise me with my students here, and I don't mean only the children but the older ones too. He has a small covered truck—the foreigners here say "van"—that he uses for his rounds, and this is our pleasure boat, carrying us as far as we need to go to be safely private.

I won't deny that I delight in him most of the time—he is considerably younger than I am, and his body is still untrained yet wonderfully receptive, wonderfully malleable. But there are times when he is quite boring. Especially when he proposes sociological theories—German and French theories on the whole—about how refugees are best handled in an area of conflict between Marxism and capitalism. I have to shut him up then and not let his babble ruin my taste for his ripeness (which in this climate sometimes makes him sweat too much). In his defense I have to say that at least his theories have brought him out here to the front line. And the way things have begun to move along the border, that may soon demand more courage than even he expected to need. In any case, he says that his work in Bangkok brings him into contact on occasion with certain government sources that may prove useful in determining just what is going on.

Oh yes, by the way, his name is Maarten. He calls me Sameth as you did, because I haven't yet told him my real name nor much else about my past. And we also talk English when together, because his French is insufferable.

March 18. It has been only a month or so since the new refugees began to cross into our region in large numbers, yet what we see in them has already begun to change. They now arrive more exhausted, thinner, less animated. That may be because they have come from greater distances and have been on the road longer, but it isn't only a physical thing. The mind too seems to have changed. The substance of the stories they tell about what they've been through remains what it has been all along—the mass killing under the Khmer Rouge, the cells for torture, the leg-irons, the clubbings, the endless work, the hunger—but it comes out of them with less passion, almost indifference. It's as though the horror of it all became so routine at some point, so ordinary, that those who had to watch it day after day where they were living and then take to the highways again finally came to look on their own past as they might someone else's drawn-out death by sickness or, worse, as the slow imposition of fate.

This lack of passion they show, this acceptance or fatalism or whatever it is, now strikes me as appalling in its way as the stories they tell. Maybe it's a process by which the mind protects itself against indelible wounding, but I don't care what it is. I can't bear to see this happening, people treated as these have been now losing too much of their anger, their hatred of what has happened, their unforgiving recollection. The inhumanity of others now eats away at their own humanity, the tortured gradually become as callous, it seems, as the torturer. And if it goes on, that is how the Khmer Rouge will finally win. Memory will eventually die, and blame along with it, fate will become the evil that replaces the one these people have known, and before long, time will have purified the enemy of their crimes so that a new round can begin again. As it has so often in our century.

I work to keep memory alive wherever I have influence, but the effort is hopeless sometimes. In my French class for the youngest earlier this week I got myself so wrought up trying to find a way of explaining Sihanouk and his talent for accommodation that I apparently frightened some in the front row and suddenly two little girls began to weep. It occurred to me finally that those who came out of "democratic Kampuchea" at the age of five or six have no clear idea who Sihanouk is, and since very little in the past four years has educated them about him, he is a name with no specific shape. I must have portrayed him in a way that made him seem the kind of evil spirit who goes after children when they haven't behaved properly. I ended up trying to sweeten my language so as to calm the front row, but it was too late. In that class Sihanouk is now a forbidden subject. And in the classes for adults, I find that history in the abstract is the easiest way to bring a dull mist into the eyes of my listeners in the back rows of our YWCA school. They all have their own version of history, their own personal demons, and what memory remains seems to be confined to the lost family and the lost village that for most now begin to fade into a private mythology that has little to do with the country's fate and the old stories of political disaster that brought us where we are. Instead of inspiring my fellow refugees to remember with emotion as I talk about their common past, I seem to bring myself under suspicion for talking too little about the sister I lost and not at all about the village I never had—at least not until the Khmer Rouge invented one for me.

I became so depressed after the Sihanouk episode this week that when Maarten came to visit he felt he had to take me away from here not to make love to me but to have a serious conversation. We went on a long excursion yesterday, through the plain of rice fields west of Aranyaprathet and then south to the mountains called the Khao Soi Dao Tai. I'd never been half that far. We left the highway and walked toward the base of the mountain range, and this was exhilarating even though it was hot. We ended up in a place that was very green, a table of grass between rocks where we could look up at the mountains, and we spread ourselves on a blanket under a coconut palm.

Maarten hardly said a word on our way there, I think hoping to calm me down by leaving me to myself, and when we were fully rested and the sun was getting low, he still kept to his side of the blanket. He said that he had been worried about me for some weeks, actually from the time Phnom Penh fell again, worried at first because that news seemed to put me at a distance from him in that I hadn't wanted to talk about it with him very much even though it was clearly on my mind (what would he say if he knew that is when I started to write in this notebook for your eyes alone?). But eventually he found his worry becoming less personal; he began to sense what he called "a deep melancholy" in me that didn't have to do with him or even so much with myself but with the way of the world around me. I almost laughed when he said that, but I managed to hold myself back because I knew he wouldn't understand my amusement (he doesn't have your keenly sharpened sense of irony, nor your talent for appreciating understatement). He went on to say that he didn't want to pry into why things had suddenly turned so sour for me, and though he knew it didn't have to do specifically with the camp, where my work still appeared to keep me fully occupied and generally content, he wondered if it might not be good for me to get away from the camp for a while and move with him to Bangkok.

I was tempted then to reach over and take his hand and say: "Sweet young fellow, how is it possible that the milk of human kindness hasn't curdled behind those pink cheeks of yours even after what little you've seen of the way of our world since you've been on this border?"—but I was too shy or despairing or self-protective. What I said was that I felt grateful for his worry; it showed that he was sensitive to my nature and cared for me, all of which was very touching, but I couldn't possibly leave my work at the camp and my responsibility for Thirith and just pack a suitcase to go off with him to Bangkok. He answered that he meant for Thirith to come with us, that he had in mind finding work for me that would be just as important as what I was doing in the camp at Aranyaprathet. I pressed him on that point, really out of curiosity more than anything else, and he said he saw no reason why, in view of my knowledge of languages and my Anglo-French education and my general experience (that made him lower his heavy-browed eyes), I wouldn't qualify for a position with one of the international refugee relief agencies, perhaps even his own.

So there is it, dear Tan Yong. I was made an offer that would have seemed two months ago as the next best thing to immigration to another country or repatriation to the old Cambodia, and all I could do was shake my head and touch the man's hand gently to thank him for what I couldn't possibly accept. And of course that made him suddenly as depressed as I must have appeared to him in recent days. I tried to bring him back the one way that had always worked with us, but it was no good. I'd managed to lead him into the circle of my own hopelessness, and there wasn't anything so obvious that would ease him out. We drove back to the camp in silence, and now I'm not even sure I'm going to see him again.

He has forced me to think about my situation, though. I now see that the camp has become my excuse for not looking closely into myself. I hide in my work, concern myself with what others don't see out there, so as to avoid what I can't bear to see under my own roof—that is, I keep from facing my own situation at the same time that I complain about how insensitive others are to the larger view. I turned forty this month. That is a fact that I haven't confronted. My childbearing years will soon be gone. And even if Thirith were not almost twenty and so ready to fly off on her own, I'm not really her mother. Do you understand where that leaves me? I'm certain you do understand, but what good is it to me when you aren't here to tell me if I'm being foolish not to grasp Maarten's offer while there's still some warmth left in both of us?

April 1. I'm going to Bangkok, it seems. Anyway for a week. Maarten convinced me that I owe him at least one trip there, for my sake first of all but also for his, because he apparently feels that our life together has become too much a matter of brief exercise in green places with too little shared experience of ordinary daily living, meaning his ordinary daily living. I don't know whether this domestic impulse of his emerges from naiveté or strategy—some deeper plot to get me to settle down with him in Bangkok. In any case, I think I'm old enough to resist whatever subtleties he may have in mind, and the truth is, I'm willing to believe a few days away from this camp will not only do me good but will prove a relief for my students as well. So he comes on Friday in his white van to carry me off to the city of new cement towers and new gold, and if it were not for my worrying about Thirith, I would begin to let myself enjoy some of the same nervous excitement that I knew as a schoolgirl waiting for my first trip from Phnom Penh to Paris—which perhaps shows what has happened to my psyche after almost four years of confined simplicity.

Getting permission from our leaders here for a week of leave required much persuasion on my part, first because they tried to tell me that the Thai authorities are becoming difficult not only about the new arrivals who are officially designated "illegal aliens" but about those of us who settled in long ago as displaced persons with recognized refugee status. I wasn't convinced by this line of argument, since, displaced as I still may be, I would be under at least unofficial United Nations protection, one step closer to the lowest form of actual citizenship.

But their stronger argument was that I would be abandoning my classes, going off when I was really indispensable, etc., a thing that should have flattered me, I suppose, but that actually brought me close to tears. It is the first time in recent months that I was made to feel trapped in this place, not only condemned to the daily routine by my own need and what I sense to be the need of my students—which of course includes Thirith—but trapped by those in charge of our life here. It brought out the old impulse to escape, to head for the sea, for open country, anywhere to break out of intolerable boundaries, that which once took me to France so easily when I was still a girl and divided me from my family when I got back and finally saved me from the Khmer Rouge. Only now there is no open place nearby, and the more distant regions one might think of going to—were there a choice— sometimes seem even more threatening than where one has again entered the circle. Anyway, I won my case in the end by offering to solicit larger provisions for our camp with any of the relief people that Maarten may introduce me to during our week of free domesticity.

Getting permission from Thirith proved simple by comparison— too simple, I'm afraid. At first she didn't say anything when I told her about Maarten's plan, just stared at the ground. I thought that was her shy way of responding to the news that Maarten and I had an intimate relationship and that he and I would be living to- gether under the same roof for a week. But when I tried gently to explain the full character of the relationship, she looked up to say "You don't have to tell me about it, Sameth. I understand." She said it so dryly that it was clear to me she'd known about our meetings all along. And her saying it that way didn't leave me much room to tell her that she had no reason to see Maarten as a threat either to her or to me, if that's what was on her mind.

But what truly unsettled me was how readily she accepted the idea of my going to Bangkok and being away from the camp for a week. "Why shouldn't you stay that long?" she said. "If it's me you're worried about, please don't be. I can take care of myself perfectly well." Again her tone made me feel that she was saying less than she could. I was very tempted to ask her if she was so easy about my going to Bangkok because she had a lover of her own and would be just as happy to have me out of the way for a while, but instead I tried to be light about it, less direct. "You don't seem at all sad about getting rid of me for a week," I said. "Am I that much in your hair?" Thirith looked at the ground again. "Why should I be sad? I'm envious. I would give anything to go to Bangkok for a week. Or longer." "Would you?" I said, smiling. "I hear it's now more than half a modern city and full of danger for young people. Especially for young women. They sometimes kidnap them and put them to work doing unimaginable things." Thirith shrugged, a new gesture someone has taught her. "What do I care about danger? There's no danger for me anymore. Not since I died the first time four years ago."

One could of course take that kind of remark for late adolescent cynicism or mock Buddhist fatalism or what have you, but I've seen that attitude too often in this camp and among some who are older and more mature than Thirith. There are those who carry a seemingly endless burden of depression, as though a tap in the brain opened at some point on the road here to leak a steady dull fluid that causes lethargy and indifference as consistently as the juices that stir appetite. And then there are those who seem ready to risk anything because they feel they have risked everything already, so they begin with insolence toward anybody in authority, including those who may want to help them, and sometimes they go so far as to run off through the forest and cross the minefields along the border just for a show of reckless will.

Thirith now seems to be moving from the one state to the other. My worry for months after we came here was her almost unbreakable silence. Now she talks, but what she sometimes says makes me wonder if soon she won't be quite beyond anything I can do to help her. And that puts the pressure of time on my hope to get her out of Thailand and away to a place that will turn her sudden new energy and lack of care into something healthier than this camp or even Bangkok will ever allow. That is, dear Tan Yong, if it isn't already too late. I'm obsessed now with the thought that it may be, and that brings a fear as cold as any I knew in the jungle. Too late for both her and me, not to mention our country.

STONEBOAT

by William Kittredge

The Mexican steers were every color, a few mottled white, and one, who was to seem a leader as the summer passed, a jug-bellied near-dwarf, was black with a splotched white star over his forehead. The rest were shades of red and orange and blue, even reptilian green, the colors lying like rock moss over their tight, short-haired hides.

Back from the railroad cars, four men and a boy stood near the unloading chute. There was just the sound of those animals rustling and banging inside the cattle cars. Twelve hundred and seventy-four came down the chute from the creaking and dung-heavy Northern Pacific railroad cars that morning in the late spring of 1945, lean and quick animals with horns like opalescent hooks. They had been gathered off the deserts of northern Sonora almost three months before and had waited nine weeks in Alamosa, New Mexico, because of the wartime shortage of railroad cars, before being shipped north to Oregon.

Sonora lay just south of Arizona on the boy's creased, heavy-paper *National Geographic* map of Central America, an area colored pale yellow and almost empty. Damon Booth, his uncle, who owned the steers, had told him yellow was a good color for that desert country. In the streets of Hermisillo the smell of orange blossoms had been thick and heavy according to Damon, almost yellowish at twilight, mixed with odors of urine and cooking spices, and warm while children played between the thick-walled adobe houses in near darkness.

Damon was standing on the elevated walkway beside the chute, shaking his head. "Horned dogs," he said. Heads tipped high, a few steers were trotting nervously in the corrals, sniffing at the morning air as if they really were some sort of carnivore. The boy wondered what they could be smelling, if the air here was different from on the Mexican desert, maybe brighter and fresher: water, he thought, the wettest place they ever smelled. Then his Uncle Damon, only twenty-eight that year although he seemed older than the boy could ever imagine being, rubbed the back of his hand across the side of his mouth to scrub away the tobacco juice and began jabbing at the animals passing down the chute with the butt end of a two-by-four pried from the mounded dry manure alongside the crowding pen. He cursed as one of the animals kicked back, splattering him with yellowish scour droppings tromped off the sand-covered floor of the railroad car, and gestured for the boy to help.

The rusting black steam engine, in service after thirty or maybe fifty years of use only because the newer engines were hauling materials and troops to the Pacific war against the Japanese, jerked and clattered the cars as each was moved forward to be emptied, and finally all the steers had come down, turning their heads so the curving horns wouldn't catch in the sides of the narrow ramp. They had been cropped in the cars over a week and unloaded only once, in Sacramento, for water and now they were dry and hungry, milling the corrals at a steady churning trot, seeking the gate. The dust was white and flourlike in the sunlight, rising straight in the morning sky.

Damon always said they were lucky that morning. The steers were used to traveling for their water and could smell it for miles. At the Booth place, one unpainted shiplap building far out in the Klamath marsh, on an alkali knoll beside a round horse corral with timbered mountains blue in the distance. Damon would be squatting on salt grass, fondling his second or third bottle of beer and peeling the label with his thumbnail while behind his voice lay the buzzing midday silence of a few flies moving. Beyond the pole corral and the well house, where snow-cold artesian water seeped over the moss-covered casing, a few summer mallards would circle down to the sod-banked fishing stream where the cattle watered.

Damon would tell how those steers lined down that narrow roadway through the timber at a hard run, the leaders having smelled water and traveling fast as a man on horseback, filling the track, and leaving the riders to charge through the thickets of jackpine alongside or follow behind, bringing the stragglers. "All that damned burnt-out summer," Damon said.

The war ended that year, spoiling the boy's winter game of maps and strategy and ending his uncle's purgatory of staying home from the killing, and the summer was dry as the worst drouth years of the early thirties, when the channel of the creek was empty across the swamp except for the deep holes where the frogs survived. The peat ground cracked into gaping rifts sometimes a hundred yards in length and wider than a ridden horse could leap. The old Indian who helped them unload the steers, Hazzard Beal, claimed the cracks led to the underworld and had opened many times in the past. According to the Klamaths and the Modocs, he said, laughing as he talked, as if disguising the dark seriousness of what he was saying, or maybe, as Damon claimed, covering up for his own lying, the cracks were the cause and not what came of the drouth. The old man claimed the cracks were always there, just waiting to be opened by spirits on bad years when the world was evil; the spirits coming out to cause burnt grass and no water birds in the fall. The Indians stayed away from the swamp on drouth years according to Hazzard. The boy imagined the swamp abandoned and sunbaked, prowled only by the vengeful and unhappy spirits of the dead and, knowing it was silly, imagined his dead grandfather haunting the world into this war.

It had been an afternoon in late fall and his mother had not let him look when the men brought his grandfather's body to the two-story white-painted house, his grandfather's house surrounded by yellow-barked pines far up the swamp where Blueback Creek came out of the timber. The house was sold now, and the boy lived winters in Eugene, over west of the Cascades in the rainy Willamette Valley, alone in a yellow house with his mother, who taught English at University High School. He thought maybe it would have been better if he had looked the day his grandfather died of what was called an accident with a rifle, because now his father had been killed by the Japanese during the invasion of Tarawa, and he dreamed of his father coming home, woke remembering the dark, tanned man walking toward him through a blur or dream. Maybe if he had seen the old man dead he would be able to imagine his father dead instead of just gone.

"No accident about it," Damon had said, talking about the grandfather's death. "Just killed himself." The boy was unable to see any way in which being dead would be something you wanted. Yet his father had gone to the war when he could have stayed home with a rancher's deferment. It was almost as if he had wanted to be dead. His mother still locked herself in her room, crying before she walked down the hill from the yellow house to church in Eugene.

"Their war," Damon said. It has been evening, the cooling air carrying the slight odor of manure from the corral, and his uncle finished rolling a cigarette and snapped a kitchen match over a thumbnail and then wandered to the well house and came back with a dripping cold beer. Beyond the open swamp, the skyline of the

Cascades was black. "The idea is not to be a fool who can't live," Damon said. The boy sat looking across to the dark timberline and listening to his uncle clank the iron stove lid as he laid the fire for morning.

The train had jerked and creaked away, flowering steam and frightening the steers into a run at the corral fences. The men sat their horses in the shade of straggling jackpines alongside the road heading slightly downhill toward the marsh, the horses sweeping their tails at the flies. "They're going to scatter," Damon said. "Clear as anything . . . all to hell."

The road was not fenced, and on either side stretched miles of open Forest Service and Klamath Reservation timber. If the herd broke, there would be little chance of rounding them up except a few at a time, over the summer. The jackpine grew in impassable thickets, the open spaces overgrown with brush and scattered with rotting logs, aftermath of a fire that had burned off the flat fifty years before.

The boy had ridden the brush behind his uncle, holding his breath while they plunged through whipping branches. Damon had stayed away from the war and yet always went full out in the timber. It was a thing the boy thought about in the night as he remembered clutching at the saddle horn and waiting for his horse to catch its forefeet and slowly cartwheel forward. He rode with his feet out of the stirrups, letting them clatter and beat on his shins, ready to cast off when the animal went down, ashamed because Damon knew he was frightened. "My log-jumping horse," he would say, grinning at the boy and saddling his long-legged gray gelding before sunrise, teasing the boy, because they were going to spend the day riding the timber.

The old man, Hazzard Beal, sat in front of Damon, grinning from under his black hat. Half his front teeth were missing and his smile lopped to the left, but he wasn't foolish at all. Over seventy years he had come to own nearly six hundred good Hereford cows and the land to run them on. During the Depression he had traded cattle for land, the virtually unsalable increase from his herd for more acres, managing to live almost without money, eating venison and vegetables from the careful garden out behind the log house where he lived with his enormously fat, silent wife. During the drouth of the thirties, Hazzard pumped water every day in summer with a pitcher pump from a hand-dug well on the edge of the timber, carrying the water in buckets on a pole across his back to irrigate his garden when the ditch from the creek stopped flowing and the swamp dried up and cracked. Hazzard cocked his head to one side. "Be noon pretty quick," he said.

"You going to help?" Damon asked, nearly shouting. The boy had caught himself doing the same, shouting at the old man, and stopped in the middle of what he was saying, because Hazzard would be grinning, indicating not only that he could hear perfectly but that he had heard the same things from many boys and that the boy would know better after a while.

"Not much of a horse I rode this morning." Hazzard just kept on grinning, not bothering to excuse himself for having ridden the wrong horse from his herd of nearly fifty.

"Boy tells me they're going to head straight out," Damon said.

"Them boys don't know nothing," Hazzard said, grinning sideways. "But that's all right."

By the time the gates were tied open the herd was shouldering and jarring the posts, and then they were ahead in the road, trampling a ground-shaking run toward the swamp. The boy rode with the old Indian, following behind in the clouding pumice dust, their horses moving in a long hard-jarring run. He could see only the rumps of the stragglers, hear the drumming sound of their running and occasionally a shout. He kicked his old horse through an opening into the timber and just tried to stay horseback, hanging on and ducking the whipping, stiff branches and clamping his knees tight to avoid having them jammed against the black-barked jackpines. Dust hung between the trees and he could hear the hammering of the steers running and ahead the brush thickened and then they were through and abruptly he saw the open meadows of the marsh. They were almost to the fence.

And then the horse went down, cutting in soft footing around a burn-blackened Ponderosa stump, and it was not like the boy had imagined at all. His leg was trapped between the rib cage of the horse and the soft pumice, and he was twisting in the saddle, trying to get away from the floundering animal, but the horse was rising, forelegs first, and everything changed. For the first time the boy was not frightened. The slow event seemed something that could bring no harm, and the boy forgot his fear and joyously kicked the horse into another run in which they escaped the final thicket of jackpine and turned onto the slick grass of the meadow to confront the fence.

The steers were charging through the gate, soundless and dustless on the sod. He was alone. He had ridden the timber, and fallen, and was all right. Just that little distance away, the steers, and beyond them, no one. Watching the steers passing into the meadow, he looked back and could see the glacial summer snow atop the peaks of the Cascades.

Posts on both sides of the gate went down, creaking, and then crushed outward by the packed and charging bodies. A few animals floundered into the tangled wire while others were slowing and fanning out toward the creek, the steers breaking from the wire streaked with cuts, and then the last of the herd was at the gate and the boy began to feel the scratches on his face and the aching of his knees. The black near-dwarf was yards behind the others and followed by the dusty figure of Hazzard Beal. The other men were coming from the timber. "We was lucky as hell," Damon said when they were grouped before the ruined gate. The steers were far across the meadow, almost to the creek.

Hazzard Beal laughed. "That boy was right," he said. Then Damon told the boy to guard the gate and the men trotted off, not toward the places they lived, but following the steers. The boy knew his uncle would ride through the animals while he had some help, making sure none were badly cut-up in the wire. Then he would return with posts and tools to fix the gate.

Shadows from the timber reached across the flat like fingers, and Damon was coming with his team, the man and animals at first far away as the steers, who were trotting the fence lines in bands. Damon was standing on the stoneboat, a low sled with runners of skinned and waterlogged jackpine. The lunch was canned Spam, a red and white box of soda crackers and a half case of Acme beer, bottles damp from the cold water overflowing an artesian well.

"I guess you earned a beer," Damon said. "You done the best you done so far." He twisted open the Spam and cut slices with his knife while the boy sipped cold, bitter beer. Damon talked while they ate, of how the steers were settling, if they would settle, and then they began replacing the broken posts, digging in the soft, damp soil, dropping the new posts into fresh holes and tamping around them with shovel handles. The boy was sweating and had not even finished the first set of brace holes when Damon was done straightening the wire. The man handed him another beer and took the shovel. Raw blisters glistened on the boy's palms while he drank that beer and then another. His head swimming, he helped set the final posts and restretch the wire. The steers were lining toward them across the half-shadowed meadow. "Full of water and looking for Mexico," Damon said as they watched the animals coming through the shadow edge between sunlight and evening. "Going to be at it all summer."

Riding home on the stoneboat, leading his old horse, the boy imagined the steers wrecked in California, scattered through fields and fencerows like bits of colored cloth, searching for Mexico, and he remembered his room in Eugene with the maps and pins and ribbons on the walls, marking the progress of troops through France and Germany to the Rhine and beyond, his pictures of the Pacific war, sand, broken-topped palms, bodies rising and falling in shallow tides, maybe somewhere in sun-warmed water the bone remnants of his father being absorbed into coral. Shadow covered all the marsh.

The boy crawled forward on the stoneboat and opened a beer and handed up the bottle and the man smiled after sipping at it and handed it back. The sun was down, leaving the mountains perfect and black against the red sky. Beyond was noontime over some island. The steers were searching the fence line along the timber, refusing to settle. The sled was nearing the cabin, and by the time the horses were rolling in the corral dust, the air was growing cold. The boy dreamed of Hermisillo and the odor of spices, urine, blossoming orange trees—a city he could only imagine—fell in love, grew old, stayed home.

"THE WAY I'D TELL ABOUT MY BROTHER AND THE TOWN WHERE I WAS BORN"

by Diane Lefer

In the center of town, of the town where I was born, we had two monuments: a statue of Benito Juárez and a rusted, broken-down Cadillac. That's the car that Epifanio Rodríguez drove up to the municipal president's office one day in 1946. That was before the road was put in. He wrecked up that car something bad, but that just shows how much money he had, money to burn and throw away, money he made up in the United States while the gringos were off at war and needed us to work their farms.

Epifanio Rodríguez stayed in town about a month and told everyone about Wyoming. Then he headed north again. I wasn't born yet then, but back home in San Pedro, people still tell all of Don Epifanio's stories.

He saw snow, and he saw machines that milked cows. He saw that gringos take baths even when they're hot and sweaty from work. They don't believe the way we do that water will do you harm right after you've worked up a sweat.

He said in the North even the farmers were rich and dressed in suits. He said one rich rancher took all the men home to dinner and they were served on the best china. He said the rancher's wife cooked and the daughters served, and after dinner the rancher took out a guitar. "You must miss your country very much," he said, and then he sang "Las Mañanitas" and cried. Epifanio Rodríguez had lots of stories.

That time that Epifanio Rodríguez came to town, the buses didn't even go as far as San Pedro then. And when his new car wouldn't start up anymore, he left it and had to leave on foot, just a poor Zapotec Indian like the rest of us. I don't know if he walked all the way back to the United States, or if he got a bus when he reached the road. I don't know where the road started in those days.

I don't think Don Epifanio ever came back, but he sent money every year so we could have fireworks for the day of our patron saint. San Pedro was our patron saint, and that's why our town was called San Pedro. It's six years now since I left home, but I can picture it all more clearly than some people who still live right there right now: the way they used to set up the castle there in the plaza, higher than the tower of the church, with its rockets and shooting lights. I remember the noise and the smoke. When I was a little girl, it always made me think of war—of the gringos going off to war so that Don Epifanio could work on their farms—and then there were the stars falling all around the rusted wreck of Don Epifanio's American car.

When I was a child, even when we were all very young, just as far back as I ran remember, I remember my brother Nacho saying, "I'm going to go north. I'm going to go." By then, we had buses, and sometimes a teacher came through. People talked about cities and towns and modern things. It was interesting, but I never thought about leaving the place where I was born. It was just Nacho, just my brother Nacho—and there were nine of us, but he was the only one who used to say he was going to go. He said it every time he saw that car; he said it every day; and each morning, we'd wake up and Nacho would still be there.

Every morning when I got up, my mother would already be kneading the corn flour dough. By the fire, on her knees, she'd make the tortillas and put them to cook on the *comal*. And every morning, my father and my brothers ate first. My brothers were always hungry, but my father never ate much in those days. When he was drinking, he didn't need food. My sisters would go to get water and they'd carry the babies around while I'd hurry back and forth with tortillas and coffee and beans for the men. The hot food burned my hands, because I was just a small girl, but my mother could reach right into the fire and it didn't bother her at all.

Nacho's hands were as hard as my mother's, and he could reach into fire, too. But he complained that hot coffee burned his tongue, and he wouldn't drink it till it cooled. When the other men headed off for the fields, Nacho would stay behind, still swirling his coffee around in his cup and saying *Gracias, chaparra* when I brought him more beans. He always called me *chaparra*—shorty—and he always ate more than anyone else. My sisters would watch Nacho eat, and they'd wonder how much would be left for them. And every morning after Nacho left for the fields, I'd serve the girls and they'd say

Gracias, chaparra, imitating my brother in the most ugly voices you could hear.

And that's the way it was every morning. But one day when I was twelve years old, I got up and Nacho was gone.

To be very honest, I didn't miss Nacho at first. I had never really known that I loved him. We were all very jealous of one another at home: there were too many of us and never enough of anything to go around. And our parents were very ignorant. It wasn't their fault. What did they know about modern ideas? No one had ever told them that when a new baby is born you have to tell the other children you still love them. My parents worked hard and made sacrifices for us; they didn't have time to talk about love.

Anyway, with Nacho gone, there was a little more to eat and a little more room in the house, and so no one was too sad that he had gone. Except for my mother. I think she must have missed him. In fact, I'm sure she did. She cried a little every day and said, "He said he was going to go and he did. He said it and he did it." But I got up every morning as usual and hardly gave Nacho a thought.

But after a while, once Nacho was gone, I started to realize he was the only one of my brothers and sisters who'd ever cared about me, who'd ever played with me, listened to me, brought me ribbons from town. No one called me *chaparra* anymore once Nacho was gone, and after he'd been gone awhile, I missed him very much. After all, it's right to miss your brother.

One day we got a letter. A teacher who'd stayed in San Pedro once had taught me some things, so my father gave me the letter to read out loud. It was from Nacho, and he was living in Tijuana, on the border. He was looking for work, and he wanted us to know he was well.

"He said it and he did it," said my mother.

I wrote to Nacho right away and told him we were all well and were happy to know he was well and living at the border and looking for work. I think my parents were proud of the letter that I wrote, and my father bought the stamp. After that, I waited every day for another letter from my brother. I didn't want to go to the market or work in the fields then. I wanted to be home at every minute, waiting for Nacho's letter to come. My mother thought about him, too. In those days, sometimes she would stop what she was doing and suddenly start to pray. Then, though she didn't say anything about Nacho, I knew he was in her heart. She never noticed me then and I could stop my work and daydream and she wouldn't even see. I remember in those days I always wanted to be left alone. I didn't like being bothered then. There were so many people living in our house, but the one brother I loved was very far away.

So I waited for another letter from Nacho, but it never came. I waited to see if my letter would be returned, but it never came back, so he must have received it, I thought. I decided that when I was old enough I would go to Tijuana and find Nacho. I started saving money just the way Nacho must have done.

I did it differently, though. I never told anyone I planned to go. I never said anything about the North. I could imagine my mother crying; I could imagine what it would be like after I left. I could hear her crying and saying, "He said it and he did it. But *she* never said a word." I was the first girl born in the family, so I know my mother loved me very much.

When I was almost thirteen, my parents said it was time for me to marry. What I really wanted was to go to school, but there was no school in San Pedro then. So I said I would rather work. Hilaria Chávez bought a knitting machine about that time and I got work with her making sweaters. I told her my parents didn't let me buy ribbons or underthings, so she lied to them and told them she was only paying me so much, but really she paid me more. I gave them so much and I kept the rest. I didn't spend it on ribbons. When I find my brother, I thought, that's when I'll want ribbons in my hair.

No one ever suspected. Because after all, I had never wanted to leave the place where I was born. But Nacho was so far away, and I was afraid he might be sick or hurt or alone.

I left San Pedro on the bus one morning. We hadn't heard from Nacho in two years then. Maybe he was living in the North, driving around in a Cadillac, I thought, but maybe he was sick. Maybe he hadn't found work. Maybe he was in jail.

I got to Tijuana, but I didn't find him there. Then I knew he must have made it across the border, to the North, and that I would have to follow. First I found work there, but only during the day. I didn't have the right papers to stay in the North overnight. Each morning when I walked across the bridge I thought of my mother. I was grateful to her for teaching me to work hard and never grumble. That's why I always found work and why the ladies in the North liked me so much. One of the ladies wanted me to live in her house and work for her and no one else. She got me the papers so I could live in the United States and I moved to her big house, thinking of my brother.

It was a lonely house with no neighbors nearby, but I didn't mind. When I've worked here awhile and saved my money, I'll go find my brother, I thought.

All day long I ironed and cooked and cleaned with no one to talk to but the television set. I knew three languages then—not only Spanish, but the Zapotec of San Pedro and the English I learned from the TV. Sometimes I thought it was strange, to speak three languages and have no one to talk to. Back home in San Pedro, I never talked very much, but once I left home there were many things I thought about and wanted to say.

Once a week the gardener would come. He was very lonely, too, because his wife and children were still in Mexico and didn't have papers to join him. Every month he sent them most of his pay, but he hadn't seen them in more than a year. He worried about his family the way that I worried about Nacho, and once a week, how we used to talk! How we would relieve ourselves then!

Now that's the story the way I'd want to tell it, not the way all these welfare people want—asking me how my baby was born.

In San Pedro, the women don't even know when they are going to have a baby. They say, "Oh, my head hurts, call the *curandera*," and they go inside, and the next thing you know, there's a baby in the room. Of course, once a woman's already been a mother, she must know the symptoms. She knows, but it's a secret she keeps. We don't talk about those things, and with the wide skirts, you really can't tell. Maybe when a woman is going to have a baby, she tells her husband. Probably she does, but who knows?

One day you don't know anything, and all of a sudden there's another baby in the house. And the babies of San Pedro, the babies of the town where I was born, they come out so very small. They come out like monsters sometimes, with two heads and with their guts hanging outside their skin. I think it's because the women work so hard. They get up long before the sun to kneel on the cold ground and make tortillas. It's because a woman carries so many burdens, I think. That's a woman's life. It's because the women don't get much to eat. First they feed their husbands and then their children and then sometimes there's nothing left. *Women suffer,* my mother used to say. That's why children love their mothers, for suffering for them, just like Jesus Christ. My mother worked and put her hands in fire. *Women suffer,* she'd say, and she'd shrug as if it didn't bother her at all. And when I asked her, *For what? Suffer for what?* sometimes she told me I was selfish, but most of the time she'd just shrug.

In San Pedro, the burros have an easier life than the women. It takes money to keep a burro; anyone can have a wife.

When I was fifteen, my parents decided to marry me to Arnulfo Díaz. That's when I took my money I'd saved from the knitting machine and went to find my brother.

I was very ignorant when I left home. When I was a girl, my mother never told me anything about babies. Now I suppose I could say to her, "One day I had a headache and I went to lie down and suddenly there was a baby in the room." But it wouldn't work. She'd still know the truth, and she'd still be ashamed. She may never have told me where babies come from, but of course she knows. She never told me about kisses, either, or how good it feels to hold a man. Back in San Pedro, we didn't talk about those things.

In the North, it's different. In the North, you're supposed to tell everything, especially if you're on welfare. What did you come here for? Who got you pregnant? Ask *him* for money, they say. Why are you bothering *us*?

That's not the way people talk to you at home. And sex and money—that's not what people talk about.

When the lady I worked for saw I was going to have a baby, she bought me a bus ticket to send me home. But I couldn't go back to San Pedro. Not with a baby. Anyway, if I had to take the bus through Mexico, who knows? I might meet the wife of my baby's father, and who knows what she might do? So I changed my ticket at the station and kept on going north. I work hard and never grumble. I was sure I'd find a job.

On the bus, I thought of my mother and how my disgrace would make her suffer, and I knew I could never face her again. And after I thought of my mother, I thought of Nacho. Maybe something happened to him in the North, too, I thought, something that made him ashamed, and that's why he didn't write to us again. And as soon as I thought that, I realized we were two of a kind, my brother Nacho and me. And I knew that no one else had ever understood me.

Now if I could tell my story the way I'd like to, this is what I'd say:

Some people talk about searching for a better life, about the chances you take when you look for a better way to live. In the North, some people talk about searching for themselves. But to talk about all that is very complicated. Welfare doesn't want to hear all that from a simple person like me. It's easier just to say that I'm looking for my brother, my brother Nacho, who said he'd go. He said it and then he did it. He left when I was twelve.

Sometimes I have a sort of dream, something I like to think about. That instead of all these bad questions, all the things they want to know, I'm going to go into Welfare someday and they're just going to say, "Roselia, okay, tell me your story. Don't tell me who you've slept with and where you've spent your check. Just tell me about San Pedro, the town where you were born."

THE SUMMER FAMILY

by Sarah Litsey

They came east from California. It was well that summer would cushion them before the Atlantic turned gray and loud-mouthed and snow drove down from Nova Scotia and Boston. They came with five children—her three, his two—in the large black Buick station wagon, looking for a new home, a fresh start, a different ocean.

They were seven strangers, to one another and to themselves, even Ann and Jarvis, the parents, even though they were married. At night, with their bodies locked in love, these two were stronger than strangeness, and yet the strangeness was still there. It settled with them into the house when they found it.

A high, old-fashioned house, it was girdled with porches, supported by scrollwork posts and adorned with gewgaws. They painted it yellow, having brought with them from California the thought of sun. The gewgaws and posts were white and the wide-awake windows looked over the roofs of the small beach cottages to the open water.

"Why did we buy a house like this?" Ann asked one night as they lay in bed, the children all asleep.

"Because you have a Puritan soul." On one elbow, Jarvis smiled down at her. "My beautiful odalisque."

A moon just past its full silvered the roofs of the summer cottages and lay across the shining floor and across their bed. The silent house beat with the pulse of five other lives.

"I'll bet your grandmother had a house like this one."

"She did," said Ann, "out in Kansas. On Sundays in summer, she made peach ice cream on the back porch and let me lick the dasher. It tasted so much better than in a dish."

"How did you get all the way to California?"

Her finger traced the firm thin line of his lips as if they were something she had just discovered. "Looking for you," she said.

"I love you, Ann."

"I love you. But darling, have we . . . ?" Her hand roved over his face.

"Have we what?"

". . . harmed our children?"

"Ann, don't!"

"They rattle around this house like strangers."

"They *are* strangers. So are we sometimes." He smiled. "Only not now."

"I love you so . . . but did we have the right . . . I mean, to uproot them? Sigmund worries me most; he's only six. A tight little box with the lid on."

"Look, darling, kids adjust. By the end of the summer, you'll see."

"It's not that easy."

"I'm not saying it's easy; just true."

He lay back with his face in the pale cloud of her hair.

They slept.

On the long drive across the country, packed in with all the luggage, the children had time to harden their separate egos. Ann's three were Bruce and Dotto and little Sigmund; for that pregnancy, she had been in analysis. Maisie and Lance belonged to Jarvis.

Ann said once, "They look like a chess set, don't they? The light and the dark."

Jarvis laughed at her. "So do we."

His black hair was flecked with gray and his lean face still was shadowed by an earlier marriage. Ann was lifting that shadow while stubbornly, desperately, the four oldest defended themselves against what had overtaken them. Only Sigmund did not. He felt light and unattached, like the tumbleweed that blew endlessly past them through Arizona and Texas.

The pain in Sigmund was nothing new. As the car rolled on over the long gray highway, he took it into himself and cuddled it, as he would a puppy. It was part of him, like the brown house that had been their home, the worn rug in the living room and the mango tree in the backyard, and his father with sad, blurred eyes and the big mustache that kept leaking the smell of whiskey night and day.

"Siggy," he said, "I'm no good, Siggy."

That was when Sigmund had started to hurt inside, but he knew that his father loved him and nothing then was strange. Even his mother's tears, he had always known and felt safe with. But riding across the country, he stared out at the flat, uninterrupted land and wondered who he was now, stared at the dark head there beside his mother. Maybe his father no longer loved him, Siggy. He hadn't come around to the brown house to say good-bye. The silent boy beside him belonged to that other stranger in the front seat.

Shoved in beside Sigmund, Lance, eight, since this mix-up had discovered that, after all, he was not a princeling. His mother had played him up against his father. Maisie, older, had observed the charade with hot black eyes. Lance was so convinced of his eminence that even a few encounters to the contrary had not pierced his ego. Now his mother was somewhere far behind him in a haze of happenings he could not fathom. All he could piece together was the fact that she did not want him anymore; she was going to marry another man.

This knowledge left him at the edge of a precipice over which he was constantly falling as the car plunged east. It seemed that at fifteen Maisie understood. That last day, waiting for Jarvis and the station wagon, marooned among their luggage, Lance had slithered his hand down the brocade velvet love seat. "Why aren't we taking all this?" he asked.

"Because our mother is taking everything." There were chips of ice in his sister's voice, but her black eyes were hot with anger. "Let her have them," she added, "and good riddance. We've got Daddy."

After that, Maisie did not speak again, not once on the long trip, as if she had said it all. In the station wagon, she sat behind her father. She had seen him suffer, and that was over. Her furious loyalty was small and hard, like a buckshot lodged in her stomach, where it shifted when nudged by her jealousy of Ann. "I'm a displaced person," Maisie said to herself as they spun along between buttes and canyons. She turned Donald's high school ring on her index finger. It was much too large. She had wound it with string on the inside to make it smaller. "Like this makes us engaged maybe," Donald said in his escalating voice. "When you come back to Palo Alto, we can get married, maybe?"

"Maybe," said Maisie.

Now the string was dirty and she could no longer see Donald's face. The harder she tried, the more it blurred, then evaporated, like other mirages above the hot red desert.

Dotto was twelve, with a pug nose, was perpetually sunburned and had chewed-off hair. She'd spent most of those years in an earnest attempt to be a boy and now was disgruntled to find that she was not one. Her undeniable girlhood was as new and strange as these people jammed in around her in the car. They were *not* her father, her brother, her sister. Okay, she must share her mother with them, but share herself she would not. Seated by Bruce on the back back seat with a foot locker ramming into her, over the drag of endless miles, she watched the black silk curtain of Maisie's hair lift and turn, lift and turn. Once a strand of it trailed across Bruce's nose and he swatted it. Maisie did not know.

At every chance when they stopped, she would glare at Maisie, who was everything Dotto was now doomed to be. Maisie's firm high breasts under the light blue tank top seemed to lead her around as if nobody'd had them before. Dotto groaned and tried to pin her shoulders together in front.

Bruce, too, had watched Maisie's hair doing its fan dance in the air from the open window. He was sixteen. Its undeniable loveliness, the small pink ear that occasionally winked out, twisted the knife in his guts another turn. He hated her for something she could not help: that she was not Sandra. That last night, as they lay together in the little cove where they swam, it seemed to Bruce that his life began and ended. He was as unprepared for the glory of it as he was for the wrench of leaving her. He was a man now; they could not take him off. It simply couldn't happen to him. And yet it happened. With each speeding mile, he felt himself being drawn away from Sandra, and the pain of it was hot and hateful all through his body. The distance drew tighter and tighter, like an elastic band that in time must snap. When it did, what would he do? What *could* he do? God, yes, his mother deserved a new deal; it wasn't that. He wondered what Dotto thought about it, humped there beside him, her white canvas sailor hat on the back of her head, her pug nose peeling. And poor little Sigmund. At the end, he was the only one left who loved their father.

With a continent behind them, they assembled their rootless pieces in the yellow house. Ann was a tall, handsome woman with pale hair coiled in a low knot on her neck. By day, she moved in an honest, orderly way through the sprawling house, between the children, who drifted like shadows and spoke only when spoken to. At night, her hair came down in a torrent and flowed between her face and Jarvis's face. As they lay together, the strangeness crept off into corners of the room, which had too little furniture. Throughout the house, there was too much space around them all, an emptiness that in usual families has grown its own safety of give and take.

There was not much money, no rugs or curtains yet. "Come winter, we'll get them," Ann said. Still, the windows let in great swaths of watery sunlight, and the beach was only a block away. Soon the children had turned a healthy tan and there was a pleasant gritty scruff to the floors. But at meals they ate mostly in silence, each child regarding his or her plate as if detecting poison, while across the big round table, Ann and Jarvis talked of the day that had parted them. Afterward, in the kitchen, each one, from Bruce to Siggy, performed a portion of the cleaning up without the gift of speech.

Ann bought an old-fashioned hammock for the porch, with a little bolster and fringe, and Jarvis hung it where it would catch the breeze. "Maybe the children will like it," she said, her blue eyes begging him.

"Maybe" was all he could manage, but he smiled his love.

The children never went near it, any more than they ever went near one another.

But one day Bruce came down in his swim trunks, heading for the beach. For weeks Sandra had not written, and under the shag of blond hair, a permanent scowl was sunburned across his forehead. He was just about to jump off the porch when the hammock moved. He stopped to glance at the loathsome thing his mother had bought to bait them. There was a body in the hammock. Another look, and the body was Maisie. Her long black hair fell over the side and melted into the fringe and her eyes had a sleepy look but they were open. They were looking straight into his own eyes, and Bruce suddenly felt that he had two heads and both of them were spinning.

"Hi," he said.

"Hi," said Maisie.

They were silent, staring. The hammock hung very still.

Then Bruce cleared the rosa ragosa in one leap. He ran all the way to the beach, plunged into the water, and started to swim to Long Island, but changed his mind.

Still Lance was arrogant. His mother had cut the princely clothes to fit him and he could not shed them, though he was learning to shed her. The velvet love seat and all those fancy trappings were a mess compared with the yellow house, where you could do what you pleased. Even Maisie had shut up after saying, "*Don't* put your feet *there!*" People still turned to look at him. . . . "What a handsome child!" And he was a carbon copy of his father, which turned a special nerve in Ann, since she could not reach him. He was never rude, but he sat, walked, stood, as if facing an invisible firing squad. His dark, solemn eyes were capable of looking down on someone much taller. One pleasant summer day, this didn't work.

"Hi, snot," said a voice behind him as Lance made his way past the cottages. Joey was one of the cottage kids, of which there were many.

Lance walked on. A beach towel adorned with bright red whales swung casually behind him, but not for long. It was suddenly waving in front of him as Joey danced and jeered, a crusty little tough about Lance's size, with squinty, insolent eyes.

Lance stood quietly erect. "I don't know you. Give me my towel."

"You don't know me, huh? I been watchin' you. So maybe this ain't your towel."

A few others had gathered around them from the beach, skinflints in dinky swim trunks. "He don't know me!" Joey informed them with a sneer.

A few of them grinned uneasily.

Lance gave them his superior eye to no effect. Then something wonderful happened. The deadness was gone; his mother was gone, with all her stupid slogans. The precipice over which he had dangled for six long weeks was filling with anger like a rising torrent. It flowed hot in his arms and legs and made them tingle. It rose in his throat; it beat in his ears. He could hardly wait.

Joey spun clear around and sat down on his bump in the sandy road before he knew what had hit him. Lance took up the towel, shook it clean and walked on.

"Hey, boy!" The others ran after him. "You wanna come and play water tag?"

"Sure," said Lance.

And he did, for hours.

When he got home, hot, tired, and happy, he found Bruce on the front steps dangling a can of Coke between his knees. Lance ran up beside him and punched him in the shoulder.

"Hey, what the . . . ?" Then Bruce grinned, because Lance was grinning, the first time his face had cracked open since they came.

"Any more Coke?" asked Lance.

"Plenty. Get me one, too."

As they sat on the steps together, drinking, the hot day began to sizzle down in the water that turned a darker blue. A breeze sprang up, stroking their naked shoulders. Maisie came to the door and looked out at them, side by side, and walked quietly away.

As darkness seeped up the lawn, Lance said, "Know something? I knocked a guy down this afternoon."

Bruce smiled. "It's about time."

August. A haze on the water. Bare feet running the rooms, slithering on the stairs. Little drifts of sand in the corners. In the airy rooms, space was beginning to fill with voices and with the needs of others. Ann smiled in her sleep and Jarvis, waking to see this in the moonlight of another month, thought—my wife, our children—and slipped into a deeper peace than he had ever known.

Then one evening, as some were drying dishes, some setting the table for breakfast, Bruce's big, bronze hand that had outgrown him his sixteenth summer, brushed lightly against Maisie's as she dried a cup with the blue and white dishcloth. She looked up; he looked down. The Delft clock on the mantel ticked very loud, yet no one noticed. Quietly, as if she were in church, Maisie set down the cup and walked out, with Bruce close behind her.

"So what's with them?" asked Dotto.

"They'll be back," said Ann.

Dotto stared into the abandoned cup, as if from it some mystery might be resolved. Meanwhile, at the corner of the garage, where a moonvine trailed large white blossoms in the darkness, a new world had been discovered.

After that evening, Dotto no longer glared at Maisie but shrewdly followed her every move. She felt rather than saw that the older girl had attained an invisible beauty that had something to do with Bruce, and that was a puzzle for you. During the summer she had turned thirteen and dimly understood that something like that might happen to her someday. Boys weren't all that bad, after all.

But Sigmund still floated free like a tumbleweed. At night in his little room on the third floor—the room he wanted—he lay awake and thought about his father. The sad eyes, the sad mustache, the stench of his breath when they hugged. Why couldn't he forget them? Some nights he would go to the window and look far, far out on the dark water as if he might see his father rowing toward him in a little boat all the way from California, or maybe walking the bright path that the moon laid down. Then he would go back to bed and curl himself tight around the hurt he could not name.

Over Labor Day weekend, Sigmund fell in the yard and cut his knee on a stone. It hurt, but he did not cry. He walked off behind the moonvine, where no one could see, sat down in the grass, and stared at it. It was like a mouth, a wide red mouth in his own skin, and he drew up his knee and kissed it. Somehow there was comfort in the warm, salty taste of blood, like his mother's tears in the brown house when she held him, saying, "Your father, Siggy . . . your father . . ."

All the shaken pieces that rattled around inside him began to reshape and settle where they belonged. That was when he noticed the small blue flower right by his foot. It was just a weed, but he leaned close and counted the petals: five . . . frail and perfect. Sudden joy that he had not harmed it brought tears to his eyes. Hot and good, they streamed down his face till he could no longer see the tiny flower, but he saw something else as plain as day. The new cut on his knee and the old hurt he had carried so long were alike, and they both would heal.

That night as they lay in bed, the house dark and safe around them, Jarvis found her hand.

"What did I tell you about this summer?"

"I know," Ann said. "Even Sigmund."

"Is the cut on his knee going to be all right?"

"Of course. For some reason, he's very proud of it."

THE PRECISION OF MOMENTS

by Richard Lyons

Saul, at the time just six, asked me one of life's big questions:
"Dad, what's streaking?"

We sat at the kitchen table, looking out at the wet winter day. We could count the hours left to his semi-annual visit. Time seemed to ooze and burst after a good close week. In a matter of hours it would be over.

"Dad . . ."

"I heard you."

We'd used up all the possibilities of things to do. The movies, the sketch pads, checkers, TV. There was a look in his face, clear, simple curiosity. He'd asked me a serious question. He deserved a thoughtful answer. A serious answer. I wanted to *say something.* He sat patiently for another ten seconds.

"I know it has to do with being naked. But I don't get it."

I might have begun with swallowing goldfish. Then gone on to marathon dancing, flagpole sitting, young men with striped scarves jamming themselves into telephone booths. He was good about listening to extended explanations. He once asked me how a car worked. I told him, simply as possible, and after I'd finished, his gaze upon me was one of utter restraint and patronization. The thing about him is that he asks questions for the sake of asking; he doesn't much care about the answers. Yet if I don't answer, he nags as though I've done him an injustice.

"It's just a crazy stunt making the rounds these days. What you call a fad."

"They run naked?"

"Yes."

"And everyone can see them?"

"That's why they run," I said.

Such cleverness put lines in his forehead. The charm of his face when he frowned—the struggle for comprehension, the simple deep eyes, blue and direct, round and innocent.

"It's a grown-up thing?"

Ah, Saul, what could I tell you? I hope you'll know someday that I wanted everything I ever said to be worth hearing, things you could credit—as though they were promises that were kept, disappointments that were avoided. I wanted everything I said to be reliable. What more could I offer than a solid, dependable sense of character.

"Yes," I said, "but that doesn't mean it's not childish."

"I still don't get it."

"I know, I know. I haven't told you anything."

"Did I do something wrong?"

We put in an hour playing music, drinking hot chocolate. He asked if we could make cookies.

"Do you really want to make cookies?"

He shook his head. He picked up a magazine; he stared at the clock. He sat in the living room with the magazine over his lap. For a minute he was absorbed. A minute later he let the magazine slip to the floor. He asked me:

"What time do we leave tomorrow?"

"Early. The plane leaves at eight."

"Sometime I'll come and stay. How would that be?"

"Saul, that would be the best."

He wrapped his arms around me. I pressed my hand across his narrow back. The bones of his little body were like the struts of a model plane, humming and whirring.

"Dad," he said, "you wouldn't go streaking with me, would you?"

He held my hand. One of us led the other to the couch. We sat and let the question stir around in my head. I considered the immensities possible between fathers and sons. Issues of life and death and money: family separations, distance, education, and how old you have to be before you can stay out all night. But this? Fathers and sons go fishing and camping together; they go to ballgames and work together. They even go to bars together. Millions of words have been written, even preached, on the mystique of fathers and sons. His fingers pinched my thumb. An expression of demand and patience.

"If you really want to go streaking, I'll go with you."

A simple thing—I said it and he took me up on it at once.

"Should we do it now?" he asked.

"We could wait until it got dark."

"Does it count in the dark?"

We talked it through. Every second that passed, every word we spoke, was a gram of lead accumulating in my feet. But I had said it—I'd go with him.

"All right," I said, "here's the plan."

He listened like a player in a huddle.

"We'll go out the back door. We'll run to the left around the garage, along the side of the house, then around the front of the house and when we get to the lilac bush, we'll run back."

He nodded. He grabbed his belt.

"We have to be careful," I said.

"We might be seen by the neighbors."

I saw the neighbors, the faces of people, faces with eyes. "That's true, Saul, and," I said, "it's slippery after all the rain."

"You'll be right next to me."

"You can bet on that."

"Let's get undressed," he said.

Were we really going to do it? Was I really going to take off my clothing and run around my own house with my own son? His shoes were off; his pants were down around his ankles.

"Come on, Dad."

Come on, Dad, said my son Saul, come on, take off your clothes! Here we were in the kitchen. What had happened to the day? I unbuttoned my shirt. I counted my years, each day lived through with clothing over my body. I'd seen college students run naked past the courthouse, passersby gaping, police chasing. I heard the solid dependability in my voice when I'd said:

If you really want to go streaking, I'll go with you.

The words had become vivid lights in his eyes. He was ready. How could I turn back from that?

Saul was naked, his trim little body declining in a V from his shoulders to his waist, smooth as marble. I touched his shoulder. He pushed my hand aside. This was no time for affection; it was time to get down to business. All right, I thought, all right. How long could it take? Less than a minute, a quick dash around the house and we'd be back inside. We'd clear the door, draw it shut tight. We'd throw our arms around each other and laugh our hearts out. All right, then, off with everything.

We stood at the storm door, almost touching. The inner door was dark at my side. We stared through the glass into the backyard. The hedge, the hillock overgrown with blackberries. Above was the street of a hundred neighbors. To the left was a street of a hundred neighbors. How many hundred more in the front? Still, only a minute and we'd be back, we would have done it. We'd stand under the shower, relishing the dissolution of chill, the rush of hot water. We'd hand the soap back and forth. I'd dry him with a fresh towel. We'd go out for pizza. We'd walk down the street like conquerors, I knew, and beam in each other's light.

My hand pushed the storm door open.

"Now?" he asked.

The clarity of the day, of the image of Saul and me standing naked before the world, was lashed by all the restraints by which history defined me.

"Saul . . ."

"Dad!"

"I can't. I just can't. Maybe I can explain it someday. . . ."

He backed in. I let the storm door close. I closed the inner door. We put on our clothing in the gray afternoon light.

Not a word on the subject has since passed between us.

THE AVIARIAN

by Patricia McConnel

The very day that Winifred Oglethorpe turned sixty-two, she quit her job at Van Klamp's Bake Shop and went downtown to the Social Security office to have her pension turned on. Her next stop was Millie's Madcap Fashions for Mature Ladies, where she bought an orange and magenta flowered muumuu, and from there she went to Union Station, bought a book of crossword puzzles, and boarded the 3:08 train for Miami. She took with her only those worldly possessions that would fit in one navy surplus footlocker and two cardboard boxes. On her lap, so as not to crush it, she carried the starched Dutch-girl cap she had worn while selling tea cakes for twenty-five years.

In Miami she found a hotel catering to thrift-minded people and used it for her temporary headquarters while she looked for a permanent home. The other senior residents of the hotel were unanimous in the opinion that a retired lady of limited means could do no better than to buy a trailer, as trailer park rentals were cheap if you went out of the tourist zone. They sent her to North Miami to Helen's Hibiscus Heaven Trailer Home, which catered to senior citizens.

The Hibiscus Heaven had just the thing, a lovely little trailer only recently vacated by a lady gone on to a more idyllic retirement, as the manager put it. There had been no heirs, and the manager explained that she was willing to pass her little windfall along to Mrs. Oglethorpe for practically nothing, which in this case amounted to five-hundred dollars. The trailer was very tiny, and its plywood walls were warped and cracked from too many years' exposure to Florida sun and rain, but the price was right, and it sat under a magnificent magnolia tree.

The first thing Winifred Oglethorpe did was to paint the trailer lavender inside and out, and the second thing she did was to set about indulging her life-long interest in birds. She built a birdbath under the magnolia tree and concealed herself behind some hibiscus with *The Bird Lover's Guide to Tropical Birds*.

The days passed pleasantly, and the little birds that frequented Mrs. Oglethorpe's birdbath grew fat on the tidbits the benevolent lady put out for them. Only one thing marred the perfection of Mrs. Oglethorpe's bird Eden—the catbirds picked on the smaller birds mercilessly, driving them away from the birdbath and hogging the choicest bits of bird feed. But lack of resourcefulness had never been one of Winifred Oglethorpe's failings, and so she fashioned a slingshot from a forked branch and a strip from an old inner tube and soon became a remarkably good shot. Mrs. Oglethorpe killed catbirds with the vengeance of a knight slaying dragons.

So that is how it happened that Mrs. Oglethorpe was hiding in a clump of hibiscus when Mr. Pippin moved into Trailer No. 82. (There were vacancies in the rented trailers at Hibiscus Heaven only when someone died, usually, but Miss Tillie Wheelright, the former occupant of Trailer No. 82, had been forcibly ejected by the management for the questionable way in which she supplemented her retirement pension.)

From her vantage point in the hibiscus, Mrs. Oglethorpe discreetly took inventory of Mr. Pippin's belongings as he moved them in. She noted that he had a good many books and surmised that he was a man of culture. He had very few clothes, some cooking utensils, and nine parakeets. In fact, Mr. Pippin rather resembled a tiny gray bird himself, for he was a small-boned man, thin and frail-looking. Mrs. Oglethorpe reflected that any man who owned nine parakeets must have a sensitive nature, and she determined to know him.

Mrs. Oglethorpe emerged from the hibiscus and went over to introduce herself. She offered to help get Mr. Pippin settled and went home for cleaning supplies without giving him a chance to make a polite refusal. When she returned, she set about scouring the stove, which was crusted with burnt-on pizza sauce, and then she cleaned the tiny icebox, which reeked of sardines, beer, and papaya, all in various stages of decay. While she worked she filled Mr. Pippin in on the biographies and characterologies of the residents of the trailer park, with some editorial comments on who was worth cultivating and who was not.

Mr. Pippin did not seem to resent the intrusion but twittered to and fro, fussing with his parakeets and accomplishing very little. Mrs. Oglethorpe, for one thing, being slightly plump, completely blocked the passage between the rear of the trailer and the door, and Mr. Pippin did not want to try to squeeze past, for fear of being misunderstood. He was confined, therefore, to putting things away in his sleeping area.

In the course of her cleaning, Mrs. Oglethorpe inquired where Mr. Pippin intended to keep his parakeets. "I'll let them have the run of the trailer as soon as they are used to being here," he replied. "The screened porch area is almost like being outdoors. That's the reason I rented this particular trailer; I want my birds to be comfortable and happy. They should like it here, don't you think?"

Mrs. Oglethorpe agreed.

It was the beginning of a cordial, pleasant relationship. Mrs. Oglethorpe went every day to cook and clean, although Mr. Pippin had never asked her to. On the other hand, he never objected when she did. Once in a while he felt that perhaps he might enjoy puttering for himself, but then he couldn't quite bring himself to reject Mrs. Oglethorpe's kindness. It seemed an ungrateful thing to do. If occasionally he protested mildly at some extravagant generosity, Mrs. Oglethorpe looked so injured that he quickly retracted his protest. He had a vague feeling that to reject her kindness was to risk losing her friendship, and he was, after all, a lonely man.

Mrs. Oglethorpe, on the other hand, ecstatically welcomed the opportunity to look after someone. She had survived three husbands, each of them sickly, and she had dedicatedly nursed each one of them right up till his dying moment. It had been a long time now since she had had someone to take care of.

And so the terms were set. When Mrs. Oglethorpe was in the trailer, Mr. Pippin sat perched on the edge of his chair in the porch and watched her with beady bright eyes.

The parakeets soon had their run of the trailer and they seemed to enjoy the porch, as Mr. Pippin had predicted. On the eighth day, however, there was an unfortunate accident. Mrs. Oglethorpe was taking a cup of sassafras tea to Mr. Pippin in the porch, when one of the parakeets tried to dart through the screen door that separated the trailer from the porch. The door, alas, had a strong spring that snapped the door quickly back into place, and the parakeet was not fast enough.

Mrs. Oglethorpe was most upset, of course, but Mr. Pippin was philosophical. "He took a gamble and he lost, my dear. He shouldn't have been so daring. Freddie was always given to sudden decisions and impulsive actions. You must not blame yourself."

Mrs. Oglethorpe, who was one of those wonderful people who are always able to take charge in a tragedy, regained her composure, and they had a little burial ceremony by the birdbath that very afternoon. It was marred somewhat, however, by the fact that Mr. Pippin collapsed right in the middle of Mrs. Oglethorpe's eulogy. Mrs. Oglethorpe, who was also very good at emergencies, managed to drag him to his bed and called the doctor.

Mr. Pippin seemed unable to speak or move, but the doctor from County Welfare could find nothing wrong with him. He asked Mrs. Oglethorpe if she knew of any extreme stress situation in Mr. Pippin's life that could cause great feelings of anxiety and helplessness. Mrs. Oglethorpe replied, "Why, no, Mr. Pippin hasn't a care in the world. I spend every day with him, and he seems as free as a bird."

The doctor said that unless Mr. Pippin could arrange home nursing care for himself, he would have to be moved to the county hospital. Mrs. Oglethorpe, who had not left her friend's side since the collapse except to call the doctor, of course declared that she herself would care for him.

Seeing a look of distress in her mute friend's eyes, she assured him, "It's no trouble, Mr. Pippin. I'll move a cot into the porch so I can hear you in the night. I'm lonely, you know, and it will give me something to do."

Mr. Pippin's little beaklike nose quivered with emotion. Mrs. Oglethorpe was happy to have saved her friend from the county hospital, for he certainly couldn't afford home nursing on his pension. That very night she began to sleep—fully clothed, of course—on the porch, and although she spilled over both sides of the cot, she did not complain. The next morning she fashioned a perch for the birds over Mr. Pippin's bed and conscientiously cleaned the bird droppings from the coverlet as fast as they fell.

Mrs. Oglethorpe lavished attention on her charge, and he lacked nothing in care or entertainment. In a few days he had recovered enough to speak, although weakly, and he suggested that people might be gossiping about her living in the trailer with him, even though he was partially paralyzed, and that to satisfy propriety perhaps she should go home at night.

But Mrs. Oglethorpe declared that if anybody cared to peek, they could see her sleeping fully clothed on the porch at night, and that furthermore she wouldn't think of leaving him alone in his condition, even if she were to lose her reputation. So the subject was closed.

In the course of her daily cleaning, Mrs. Oglethorpe noticed that spiders had taken up residence in all the nooks and corners of the porch, and, horrified by the idea of their crawling over her at night, she sprayed the porch generously with her Flit gun. Within an hour five parakeets lay dead on the grass rug. Mrs. Oglethorpe, hysterical with grief, slammed the screen door on a sixth as she ran in to tell the horrible news to Mr. Pippin, and slammed the door again on a seventh when she returned to the porch to gather up the bodies.

Mr. Pippin had a new seizure immediately and completely lost what little mobility and speech he had regained.

There was now only one parakeet left, and this one showed a distinct reluctance to return to the porch. Mrs. Oglethorpe was distraught with grief about what happened, of course, but she realized that her first concern was for Mr. Pippin and that no matter how bad she felt, she must keep up a cheerful countenance for his sake.

It seemed to Mr. Pippin that she was decidedly *too* cheerful, and he began to repeat in his head, "Go home, Winifred, go home," until it became a chant that he hoped would magic her away. But Winifred stuck to her duties, and Mr. Pippin resigned himself. "I'm ungrateful," he thought. "After all, she is devoting her life to me."

That evening Mrs. Oglethorpe was boiling a pot of soup on the stove when she noticed a fly buzzing around the sink. A fastidious woman, Mrs. Oglethorpe gave chase with a fly swatter, but the fly was agile and quick-witted, and Mrs. Oglethorpe's attempts to flatten him grew more and more energetic. Finally the fly lit on the kitchen table, and at the exact moment that Mrs. Oglethorpe let go with a stupendous swat, the one remaining parakeet flew in her path on its way to a favorite perch on top of the sugar bowl. The bird might have survived had Mrs. Oglethorpe not batted him straight into the soup.

This was too much for poor Mrs. Oglethorpe. She couldn't bring herself to tell Mr. Pippin what had happened. She was staring numbly at the soup when the idea came to her. Quickly she turned off the fire under the pot, fished the bird out with a spoon, and wrapped it in a newspaper. She put on her hat and took her purse down from a hook by the door.

"Mr. Pippin, I have an errand to do," she sang. "I'll be back in a very short while."

Mrs. Oglethorpe hummed happily to herself as she hurried to the bus stop, pausing only long enough to deposit the last parakeet in the trash barrel (a funeral for every bird seemed impractical at this point). She was possessed by inspiration for a surprise that would surely cheer up Mr. Pippin and make everything all right again.

By the time she got back from Woolworth's, her excitement was uncontainable. "Mr. Pippin, Mr. Pippin," she cried as she struggled through the door with her cumbersome load. "I have a surprise for you!"

She hurried into the trailer and laid her gift on the coverlet. Mr. Pippin stared at the nine lively parakeets in the cage, then his eyes began to move from bird to bird, as if he were counting them. He looked at Winifred's face with disbelief, then he counted the birds again. His eyes widened as he understood that the last of his pets must be gone and that Winifred was starting over. Then his eyes glassed over and he was very still.

"He is overcome," thought Winifred happily. "Mr. Pippin, how do you like your new birds?"

Mr. Pippin did not make any sign. He did not even blink his eyes. He was so still that finally Mrs. Oglethorpe knew something must be wrong. She put her hand in front of his mouth and felt no breath, then she looked for a pulse and found none. She sighed and looked sadly at her friend. "Ah me," she sighed, remembering her three dead husbands, "I suppose it was inevitable."

Then she looked at the birds twittering busily in the cage—her wasted gift. After a moment she smiled and leaned over so that her nose pressed through the bars of the cage. "Don't worry, little fellows," she chirped, "you can come and live with *me*!"

THE FAT WOMAN

by Cynthia Macdonald

The fat woman finally found her ideal job. She was able to put behind her the years as a *Daily News* photographer, a job that had become progressively more difficult as her bulk increased. No more wedging herself through subway turnstiles to catch a shot of a man, leg similarly wedged between car and platform. No more moving through the Armory Antique Show aware that a sudden turn to snap a Louis XV Coromandel Commode de Nuit might dislodge a whole shelf of the china made especially for tea magnate Thomas Lipton's yacht.

When she suggested to her long-time friend Millicent Taxall Tawny, who'd just replaced Crow Randall as editor-in-chief at *New York* magazine, that she, Florence Scribner, be made restaurant reviewer, Millicent said, "Do you really want the job? And wouldn't you be a bit recognizable?" Florence answered yes to the first question and yes to the second, "But let's face it. I may be more conspicuous than Craig Claiborne or Mimi Sheraton, but I'm not more recognizable. You know as well as I do that any restaurant worth its salt knows what all the important reviewers look like. I've even seen a picture of Sheraton behind the maître d's stand at Mi Chiamano's." Millicent agreed that she had too and gave Florence the job.

Paradise. To make the obsession of your life your job. Florence went to at least one restaurant a day, often two when she was working theme pieces. Ideas for these came to her in bed as she drifted off between eating and sleeping:

Moveable Feasts: The Staten Island Ferry, the Gourmet Greyhound, the Queen Elizabeth II.

New York's Melting Pot: White, Black, and Chocolate: the Best Truffles.

She was successful and enormously happy. Anticipation and satiation, those delicious twins, always at her fingertips. When, occasionally, someone asked, "But don't you miss your photography? I've never forgotten your shot of the woman breaking the fireman's net and being caught by you inches above the pavement," she'd answer, "No. I don't miss it at all. My Weegee phase lasted for years. But enough is enough."

The combination of her more sedentary job and its particular pleasures caused rapid growth in Florence's person. Soon she could go to restaurants only with booths or banquettes. And while doing her piece on chocolate chip cookies, when she couldn't get into the ridiculously narrow space between counter and wall at David's, home of the best, with its chunks of Swiss chocolate and cookies crisp with butter, she had to hire an assistant for part-time purchasing duty.

At lunch one day at one of her favorites, La Plage du Neige, she finished her fresh Strasbourg Pâté en Croute de Feuilletons Noisette, her Bisque Homard, her palate-clearing Sorbet d'Ananas, and was allowing herself a moment's salivation before beginning her Caneton au Poivres Verts when she realized that the lower part of her face felt peculiar. She addressed herself to discovering what the problem was but could not until she lifted the first bite of moist duck with its crisp, golden covering studded with green dots of pepper: she could not find her mouth. Or rather, she knew its location but it seemed to have disappeared into her cheeks. She poked with her fork for the aperture and then, feeling the duck smearing its greasy juice on her upper dewlaps, removed it from the fork. Fearful that bare tines might pierce her skin, she took up a spoon to continue probing. Finally the skin parted and she succeeded in getting the bowl of the spoon in, but the difficulty she had in pulling it out again made her realize that she must conclude her lunch unsatiated.

When she signaled the waiter to request the bill, she found she could no longer speak clearly, but managed to grunt and gesture.

"Is the Caneton not to Madame's satisfaction?" She indicated it was; at least she hoped that is what she had indicated. But the waiter hurried off to summon the maître d', who, after inquiring about the Caneton and hearing the parts of speech that escaped through the place of her mouth, accompanied by her gestures of yes and no, asked if she would like him to summon a doctor. Florence had begun to wonder if she'd had a stroke and considered saying yes. But she shook her head no and indicated she would rise.

Tugged to her feet like a great ship by the waiter and maître d', she sailed slowly out. As she waited for the doorman to hail a cab, she was cheered by her mobility, relieved that her capacity to move normally demonstrated that she could not have had a stroke.

In her apartment, Florence undressed, put on her sleeping muu-muu, and lay down, exhausted, to rest. When she woke, it was dark out and the clock read 1:20. "I must have been more affected than I thought. And no wonder. Perhaps I'd better call Dr. Meyerson. Yes. . . . No. First, I must have something. I had hardly any lunch and no dinner. No wonder I feel so empty."

She started to rise, to go to the kitchen, but could not. Her arms moved but her body wouldn't. She struggled to push herself up, to haul herself up, pulling at the headboard. She worked to slide herself up and off, grasping the mattress, pulling and pushing. Nothing. It was as if her body were encased in lead. "Lead. Like a coffin. Are coffins still made of lead?" She thought of her shot of Frank Costello's body in the funeral parlor, his mother weeping into the lilies, and shuddered. "I must calm myself. Florence, calm down. Think about getting help. Not coffins." She couldn't reach. And would she be able to talk clearly enough if she could slowly move toward that side of the bed? "And how will I have strength if I cannot eat?"

She spoke aloud to see if she could speak; she couldn't tell. She'd thought in the restaurant that enough words were coming through to make her decisions clear, but . . . She imagined her speech moving into the dark air of the room like bubbles out of the tiny pipe of her mouth, bubbles like those conveying the characters' thought in comic strips. Bubble: "Help, get me out of here." Little Lulu.

She woke, feeling weaker. Light through the Levelor blinds striped the walls into zebra, no, convict stripes. Seven A.M. She tried to move toward the phone, pushing and pulling at the mattress. Nothing. And saw herself arriving at an apartment very much like her own. Smaller. West Side instead of East. But not too different. The cop at the door had known her. "Morning, Miss Scribby." She'd walked through the apartment, heading for the bathroom. The call had come in that a woman had been found dead in the tub. Too fat to get out of it. Florence had had to get the cop and plant him in front of the tub to cover the actual nudity. Though it was clear enough the body was nude in the picture, one fat-festooned bare leg still against the tile wall in a parody of bubble-bath girlie shots. The policeman had served the bubble function. Bubbles. Her comic strip bubbles.

Would she have to lie there until she thinned enough to move and talk? She could feel hunger. Scratching. Long fingernails. Starvation.

"Ridiculous. I'll be found before I starve. Dorothy will call tomorrow. Millicent on Monday to discuss the "Suburban Bets and Bests" piece. Surely I can say something into the phone—if I talk slowly and distinctly. People can talk through pursed lips." She ran her hands over her face. Yes, her cheeks felt pursed. "And when I don't answer, they'll realize something is wrong." "Suburban Bets and Bests." "They won't. Dorothy knew I was going to Connecticut. No one will call until Monday, and then they'll think I'm out. But surely by Tuesday. Maybe not." Her heart fluttered. Or was it her stomach? She forced herself into calmness, the old *Daily News* emergency stance.

Light projected through the side of the blind onto the opposite wall. A slide show. A range of mountains. Snow-covered. Light shimmering off them. One taller than the others. Mont Blanc. Her mouth, inside the purse, watered. Mont Blanc. How beautifully they did it at Voisin. The marrons mated to a mound of whipped cream and cognac, the base of perfect meringue, the drifts of whipped-cream snow.

The mountain range was turning pink. She looked at the clock. 8:27. She knew she had not been awake that long. My God, could she have slept through the day? The dwindling light told her she must have. The mountains were gone; the room was getting dark. What day was it? "Don't be ridiculous. If your mouth closed up at Friday lunch . . ." She envisioned her face with the skin stretched smooth over her mouth, covering it like the skin on a baby's soft spot. "If it closed at Friday lunch, this is Saturday. Saturday evening."

> Today is Saturday,
> Today is Saturday,
> Saturday baked beans
> Friday fish
> Thursday noodles

She could hear herself singing along with Uncle Don. Her beloved Uncle Don. She'd heard the famous program but she'd been too young to understand what he'd said. He'd just disappeared from one day to the next. Monday had been spinach. What had Tuesday been? Full of grace? Fair of face?

*   *   *

Florence, the fat woman, breathed deeply, trying to summon her inventive powers from the old days, when she'd dealt with emergencies every hour, snapping them, flashing them. "If I could rock the bed back and forth enough to make it collapse, it would make a terrific crash. I wonder if I'd be badly injured. I wonder if the Daleys have gone to the country or if they're home. And if they'd understand the crash was not a piece of furniture falling over."

In 8F, the Daleys woke and listened to the regular creaking and thumping overhead. "Do you," Harry Daley said to his wife, "do you think . . . no. Do you think Miss Scribner could have a lover?"

SHRIMP WIGGLE

by Ruth MacDougall

The night before they were to move to Ninfield, John had died of a heart attack. In the ensuing chaos, Louise had somehow remembered to call the moving company, whose dispatcher was surprisingly solicitous, assuring her, "We can store everything, ma'am, or reschedule."

"No," she'd said, deciding only as he suggested these solutions, "I'll move on schedule."

That had been last May, and now it was nearly the end of December, with the house finally in such order she had even been able to find the box of Christmas decorations for the tree she'd made herself put up, telling herself it was excellent therapy for somebody living alone. Just one of her sons and his family were able to come for Christmas dinner.

"Face it, Mom," Bill explained. "You're off the beaten path now. But that's what you and Dad wanted."

So they had. To retire to Ninfield had been their goal ever since they had first seen this village on the lake ten years ago, driving up from their home in the suburbs of Boston to spend their vacation in the White Mountains of New Hampshire instead of, as usual, at the ocean. The village had been bypassed by the highway, so they might never have laid eyes on it at all had not John run out of cigarettes, necessitating a search for a grocery store.

A village of white houses overlooking a blue lake, shaded by cool green trees. There were large, fanciful summer cottages with gingerbread gables. There were smaller cottages, both old-fashioned and new, and year-round homes, trim, plain. The village store sold rat-trap cheese, the likes of which she and John hadn't tasted for years; they had a picnic of this and common crackers down on the public wharf, sitting like children, their feet dangling over the water, and the resolve came to them with as gentle an ease as an approaching white sailboat came to rest at the wharf.

"Winterize," John had said, using a word new to her then. "Someday we'll buy a cottage here and winterize it."

A year ago, with John's retirement only a few days away, they had at last decided upon this house and she had begun to learn what "winterizing" really meant. Long-distance phone calls between their Massachusetts home and the New Hampshire contractor; insulation; storm windows and doors; a hot-air furnace; a grim battle to make the fragile old cottage sturdy enough to withstand the wind off the lake that lay at its doorstep.

Despite these efforts, however, there still remained a faint aura of wet beach towels and bathing suits, tracked-in sand, barbecued hamburgers, frivolous summer. And for this Louise was thankful, especially now as she discovered all the other aspects of being "winterized" here, alone.

The cottage had windows on both sides of the door, so therefore it had a face, with the snow that overhung its low roof giving it a forbidding frown. The steep driveway froze into snow ruts as tyrannical as trolley tracks. John had bought an elegant Norwegian woodstove, intending to heat the house entirely with wood, talking enthusiastically about chopping and splitting in the invigorating country air. Remembering this, she had consulted Mr. Wilmot, the owner of the village store, and then ordered three cords of wood from a nearby lumber company, but she asked for it split. The pink-salmon color of freshly split wood delighted her when the load was delivered, though after stacking the first cord she began to think that a thermostat was a far more beautiful sight. John had said the furnace would be for emergency use only, yet now as the winter progressed she turned it on often, feeling unfaithful.

But she *was* being faithful, staying here. How she wanted to sell the place and flee! How she yearned to return to Cheltenham, where she and John had lived all their married life, where Bill and his family now lived. She hadn't gone home since John's funeral, fearing she wouldn't be able to force herself to go back to the isolation of Ninfield. After Bill's Christmas visit, images came thick and fast of a cozy apartment in Cheltenham, near but also tactfully distant from Bill and Sally's house. The grandchildren were too grown to need baby-sitting anymore, yet she could make herself useful in so many other ways, such as—what?

Well, she could do some of the special cooking for Bill and Sally's parties, offering all the knowledge and skill she'd acquired during the years of her own parties, in particular the annual New Year's

Eve party she and John had been famous for, with its shrimp wiggle finale.

At this thought, she realized two things: that she dreaded this New Year's Eve, two days away, more than any other holiday so far, and that she was talking to herself as she switched TV channels around and around from soap operas to game shows to soap operas again.

When she'd first moved here, grief had kept her from accepting— or even paying any attention to—an invitation to a garden club meeting, and afterward everyone had left her alone, apparently respecting her privacy, her widowhood. She snapped off the TV. Two days. Time enough to get ready for a simple party, though not for the elaborate parties of the past. The main problem was names, for the people to invite were the single women she'd met in the village store, presumably widows like herself, but she'd only discussed the weather with them, without introductions.

Hoping Mr. Wilmot wouldn't be busy, Louise hastily drove to the store, a notepad in her pocketbook. Before another customer arrived, she got from him all the names she wanted and much more information than she'd dared hope for.

"Who's the nice woman who drives the red Jeep?"

"That's Betty Patterson. Did you hear about the chimney fire out at her place the other day?"

"And the pleasant woman with the English sheepdog?"

"That's Helen Howe. I guess you know how she likes everything English; she even gave a party a year or so ago for that royal wedding. Up at the crack of dawn to watch it on TV, with champagne."

"You don't sell shrimp, do you?"

"Better try the supermarkets in Gilead, or the fish market there."

Daunted, she drove home. A champagne breakfast party! She and John had never given such a party. If they'd lived here then, would they have been invited? Her voice tremulous with nervousness, she phoned her way down her guest list, telling each woman, "It's an impromptu New Year's Eve party. I'd be so happy if you could come." As she'd suspected, not everyone had a gala evening planned; out of the six women she called, four accepted, sounding taken aback, Helen Howe among them.

Louise launched into housecleaning, and the next day she drove to Gilead and bought all the party supplies, including cocktail napkins, eschewing the type that proclaimed "Gin Makes Me Sin" and choosing chickadees instead. No party hats, however, for John had always forbidden them because he felt like a fool in one. Driving home between snowbanks cleaved by the highway, she allowed herself to think if not of Cheltenham then of Florida, where so many of their friends had moved.

However well-prepared she was, the first doorbell ring on the night of a party always stabbed her with panic. The cottage had no doorbell, and now she learned that even the knocker wasn't necessary, because the sound of cars coming down the driveway loudly crunching frozen snow was signal enough that her guests were arriving. Heart thudding, fiercely regretting the whole idea, she rushed to the door and found in the light from the outside lamp that snow had begun drifting down, covering the drab snowbanks in her dooryard where hilarity was abounding as three cars and one Jeep maneuvered for parking space, instructions shouted out open car windows.

"Hello there," called Gertrude Cram, turning off her headlights. "What a lovely snowfall. It makes things clean again."

"Nonsense," said Esther Hartwell, who owned an antique shop up on the highway, "it'll be just enough to be messy."

Betty Patterson hopped down from her Jeep, laughing. "You two! Esther, your cup is half empty, while Gertrude's is half full. On tonight of all nights you should think like Gertrude, shouldn't she, Mrs. Glidden—may I call you Louise?"

Louise was remembering how John used to direct such party traffic. "Oh, please do, and I was so sorry to hear about your chimney fire. Do come in."

"Isn't this lovely," Helen Howe said. "Everyone always thinks everyone else has something planned on New Year's Eve."

Parkas removed, boots, woolen scarves, Louise's guests revealed themselves dolled up for her festivities, and she was relieved that her lace blouse and long plaid hostess skirt hadn't proved too dressy. They were all admiring the cottage now, exclaiming over everything, the wallpaper and curtains, the Christmas tree, the steeple clock John used to make a ceremony of winding in Cheltenham each evening, the buffet of hors d'oeuvres arranged on the harvest table at the end of the living room. Nibblies now, Louise thought, taking orders for drinks, shrimp wiggle after midnight, as always. Lifting the lid of the ice bucket, she remembered how efficiently John had played bartender, and the longing for him that swept over her was so deep, she feared she would drown.

Then she looked at these women settling into her armchairs and sofa, exchanging news. All of a sudden their sheer courage struck her. What a *luxury* husbands were!

"Never in all my born days have I ever won anything, but sure enough, that was my stub, and I had won a laundry basket at the hardware store's Christmas bonanza!"

"Not really!"

"Yes, indeed, and it isn't a plastic one; it's a nice wicker one that makes hanging up my clothes a very elegant chore. My old one was all in splinters."

"The younger generation. Just before I left I called my grandson to wish him a happy new year and he told me he was spending tomorrow baby-sitting his ex-wife's new baby."

"No!"

"Doesn't that beat the band."

"He told me it's so that she and her new husband and the older children—my grandson's children, my great-grandchildren!—can go skiing, because they can't afford such outings often. Well, he was always my husband's favorite grandchild, but I wonder what Harry would say about this. Delicious pâté, Louise. And such a handsome woodstove. Where do you buy your wood?"

After a discussion of prices and quality of cordwood and an account of Betty Patterson's chimney fire, the conversation meandered on through Ninfield gossip, all references explained to Louise, into reminiscences about the suburban homes they'd moved here from. Just as it dawned on Louise that she could start telling her guests a little about John and Cheltenham, midnight was announced by the steeple clock's chimes, glasses were raised in toasts, and it was time to get the patty shells ready for the oven, to light the chafing dish on the buffet table and create the shrimp wiggle.

"It's a combination of family recipes," she explained as the women gathered around, "a shrimp Newburg recipe from my side of the family and the shrimp wiggle that my husband loved from his side. So there are peas in it as well as sherry, and—"

FALL OF SANTA CLAUS

by Michael Patrick Malone

How often does something like this come along? Once? Twice during a reporter's career in the suburbs? This story could have been my ticket to a job with a Chicago daily. It could have gotten me out of the dead-end weekly rag known as the *Elk Creek Beacon.*

I've covered some strange stories before. The suburbs aren't as safe and sane as they'd like you to believe, not by a long shot. There was the couple who lived in a house knee-deep in garbage, hadn't thrown out a thing in years, walked their two Irish setters in the guest room. The mailman noticed the smell finally and told the police. It took the garbage men three days and six trucks to clear the place out. And the wife was a nurse. Sure, I've covered a few strange stories.

But not like this one. I was right there, camera in hand, tape recorder not more than fifty feet away, in the glove compartment of my car. I took photos until I ran out of film and then took down the names of some of the witnesses. I got most of them on tape that afternoon or the next day and had the story ready to run on Wednesday.

Did it ever run? No, it never ran. They just didn't want to admit it happened, but I know it happened. Here are the pictures. This. And this. You can see why they couldn't use this picture, I don't even remember taking it. I got him about ten feet before he landed; I was shooting at one-thousandth of a second. You can actually see his face, and it looks like he's smiling.

And I have this tape. It starts just about three minutes after it happened and runs for about five minutes. I couldn't get anyone to talk to me at the time, and after the cops arrived they pushed me back and got rid of the crowd. But listen to this part, here, it's coming up.

Hear?

Hear that? That's a mother telling her kid over and over again, "No, he's not the *real* Santa Claus."

This next one is a tape of the first witness I talked to. Let me see, yeah, this one: Vicky Smith, housewife, age 33.

"That's me there. God, I look a mess. Those slacks."

(I showed her a photo of the crowd, with her and the kids up front.)

"I took the kids there. You know kids—they hear about something at school and the next thing you know you've got a station wagon full of them going off to see the damnedest things. We got to the shopping center a little early so I could pick up a few things at the Ben Franklin—a few picture frames and a lampshade. The kids were snooping around the flatbed truck they had out in the parking lot, sneaking past the wooden horses to run up and touch the white cross painted on the parking lot.

"See that bag in the photograph? That's my lampshade.

"You know how kids are. They want to get as close as they can to the action. Go to a movie? First row. Go to see the porpoises at the zoo and it's no fun unless you sit so close you get soaked to the skin every time they jump through the hoop. That's why we're in the picture. I remember thinking that it takes a real sick person to take a picture at a time like that. But now that you tell me that you're a newspaper reporter, I guess that's all right. You're supposed to be sort of rude; that's your job.

"But I really don't remember much of what happened, and I told you already that I won't let you talk to the kids. I thought I would have all kinds of trouble with them, but after the first few hours the questions stopped and we haven't talked about it anymore. I remember that man, the one from the kiddie show—Uncle Jerry. He was telling some jokes, tripping over his shoes and giving away balloon animals. He was trying to build up the excitement, I guess. He started singing, but the kids weren't listening.

"They were just staring up into the gray sky."

Let me switch tapes. I've got the pilot and Uncle Jerry on the next tape. Did you hear that part about the Ben Franklin? Well, this whole thing happened at the Elk Creek Plaza, the pride of Elk Creek—twenty storefronts anchored by a Jewel Food store and a Ben Franklin. A stinking little shopping strip.

Actually Elk Creek's a stinking little town. No elks. No creeks. The town fathers were going to buy some elks once and put them in a compound by the railroad tracks, but they bought a machine that chops branches into little bits and spits them into the back of a truck instead. Here it is now; just rewind a little more. Okay, here's the pilot.

"Strap in. I must have told him three times to strap in. The last time as we were making a wind test and getting down a landmark to measure the jump spot. He said that he didn't want to wrinkle the uniform. He was very careful about that. He got out some glue and really plastered down the mustache and beard because he didn't want the wind to rip it off on the way down. He said he didn't want to disappoint the kids when he landed. He leaned out of the plane and even stepped out onto the wing once as we passed over the parking lot and waved to the crowd. It was almost like back in the barnstorming days—he was playing wing-walker.

"We agreed that we'd make one more pass, get a little more altitude, then circle and come back for the jump. He was crouching by the door, checking his reference points. When we got over the target, he turned toward me, gave me a little salute, and stepped out of the plane like someone walking out their front door.

"I never saw anything like it.

"That sounds stupid, I guess."

Let me stop it here and hit the fast forward. The pilot gets a little technical from this point on and becomes real concerned about the FAA and losing his license. What we want is Uncle Jerry. You have to get a load of Uncle Jerry. Here it is; it's starting now.

"Listen, you don't make payments on a camper like this off the salary you get from a local kids' show. These public appearances, they're the real difference; they pay for the little extras. And my public appearance schedule could go right down the toilet with this disaster. Word gets around about Santa taking a dive on me and all of a sudden I'm bad luck, you know?

"I had my hat down over my eyes, walking around on the stage like I couldn't see, waving one leg over the edge, pretending to almost fall off the stage. The kids go nuts over stuff like that; they were eating it up. I got the cue from the stagehand. They had some sort of radio hook-up with the plane and they cued me that the plane would make one more pass and then he'd jump.

"So, I push the hat back on my head and say that now it's time for Santa to come to Elk Creek. But he won't come unless we give him a big Uncle Jerry cheer. So I get the kids screaming 'Come down, Santa, Come down, Santa.' We were all watching the plane and then we saw him, leaning out, waving.

"I started singing *Santa Claus Is Coming to Town*, totally ad lib, you know, totally unrehearsed. I just prayed that I would remember enough of the words not to tip the kids off that I hadn't rehearsed. I figure I'll have time to get through the first verse and maybe vamp a little until the guy lands, when land he does, six bars into the song, just as I'm telling the kids not to pout.

"The first thing I think is, well, that's show business. I've been around. I've worked with high-wire acts and daredevils, demolition derbies and all the rest. I worked with some weird novelty acts—one guy wore roller skates and had himself towed by a car until he got up to about fifty miles an hour, then he'd crash through a flaming barricade. Two shows a night. Twenty-five bucks a show. Accidents happen, especially if you're not working with a professional novelty act.

"Then I see that it was no accident. The guy jumped without a parachute.

"Jesus Christ, talk about not being professional."

Now, this is the last tape. I could have gotten more interviews, I could have gone a lot deeper, but I figured, what the hell, Herb's never going to print any of it anyway. No one wants to think about why the kid took the dive; no one wants to know why. That's what he told me when I floated the idea of an in-depth follow-up to the suicide. First he says, "What suicide?" Then he says why don't I think about the family, why don't I think about the good of Elk Creek, why don't I think about what dragging all this up could do to his race for village trustee in March? Why do I always think of myself? he asked. Why do I always just think about my career?

He actually called it a career. Then Herb says that he's going to make me the assistant news editor. Another line on the résumé, he says.

Anyway, this is the last tape; this is the kid's mother. The old man wouldn't talk. He just sat at the kitchen table and glared. As soon as I turned on the tape recorder he pushed his chair back from the table and went down to the basement. It was after this tape that I gave up on the story.

"What did they teach him in the army, that's what I'd like to know. When they were trying to sign him up they gave him all these brochures showing all these young boys working with computers and such. He was working at the drugstore, the same job he had all through high school. He showed us the pictures of the young men sitting in front of computers and radar and it looked a lot more promising than the drugstore.

"Most of his friends were gone. Some were in college; some had already joined the service or were drafted. Some, like Teddy Jenkins, just took off for California for no good reason at all. It seemed that Marty was the only one left from high school who wasn't *somewhere,* doing *something.* College didn't appeal to him; he got mostly C's in high school and for a while I tried to talk him into starting out at the junior college, but he said he could learn more in the 'real world' than he could in college. Like Marty knew what the 'real world' was. He lived in Elk Creek ever since he was five; that's when we moved out here from the city. He went to school and worked in the drugstore. The real world.

"His father encouraged him. He'll deny it now, but it's true. He wanted to be able to answer when people asked, 'So, how's Marty doing?' He wanted to be able to say, 'He's in the army working on computers.' Later he started answering, 'He's in 'Nam.' His father started calling it 'Nam after Marty enlisted.

"I don't know what happened over there and I don't want to know. We never talked about it. Everyone knew the war was over when Marty was sent over there; everyone knew that we lost, even back then. But they sent him anyway and they taught him how to jump out of airplanes.

"When he got out he came back home and nothing had changed. He was back in the same boat again. Most of those friends he had, they either stayed away or came back so changed you'd hardly know them on the street. Marty, he came back just the same, like nothing had happened, like the four years had never happened.

"There were no jobs for people who could jump out of airplanes, though. He liked jumping out of airplanes and he used to hang around the little airport by the Cal-Sag Canal. I guess they had a little business out there, teaching people how to fly planes and how to jump out of them. Marty used to get some free jumps and he liked that.

"That's how he found out about the Santa Claus thing. He came home real excited about it. All week he could talk about nothing else. I thought it would do him a world of good, bring him out of the doldrums.

"I saw him roll his chute in the backyard that morning. I took a picture of him with his costume on, holding his parachute. The drugstore will have the roll developed by Monday, they said.

"The police came around asking us a million questions and they wanted to look through Marty's room. I didn't want them to, what's the use, but Marty's father told them not to mind me and showed them upstairs. I listened from the bathroom. They were looking for a note, or a diary. Something to make it easier on the coroner's grand jury. I knew they wouldn't find anything.

"They came back downstairs to the kitchen and asked a million more questions. They got no answers. I told them over and over again, we never talked about it."

That's it. That's as far as it went. I haven't thought about it in ages, really, but knew I kept the tapes. You don't just throw things like that away. I guess it's just a question of laziness, or boredom, or plain not wanting to know the truth. But you have to admit, there's a story there somewhere.

SAVE THE DAY, ANGEL BOY

by Laura Marello

Angelino wheels into the gas station in his '56 Chevy pickup; stopping, parking, and jumping out in one motion. He goes immediately to the pumps; Nello, the head mechanic, goes into the shop. Nello has to finish a brake job before noon on his '51 Belair Power Glide.

Angelino is the boss. Of course Angelino doesn't realize they're overbooked; Nello would like to make the boss money but he schedules too heavily. He's the boss though, Nello thinks, pulling his baseball cap down over his head and wiping his hands before he works the hydraulic lift. Nobody knows what the boss is up to.

Angelino helps Ronny undo an impossibly rusted gas cap, thinking, "I always save the day around here." He laughs and breaks out into a popular song that he used to dance to on the Esplanade in Viareggio. This reminds him that today he has to call his mamma and go to the County Building to pick up his permit to construct his home on the vineyard.

If he's still homesick after thirty years, maybe he should go back home to Italy, taking his American wife and two American teenage sons with him. But no, he thinks, they don't want to move.

A young girl in a new Renault Le Car asks Angelino where he's from, remarking that he has an accent. "Do I?" he grins, wiping off her side mirror with a flourish. "Thank you a very lot. I Italian."

"But you have red hair!" she insists.

"Do I?" he says, and pinches her cheek. They love that.

Gloria jumps out of her Fiat, screaming, "I don't want all this flirting. I just want gas!" and heads for the unleaded tank. She is late to the university. Angelino collects the money from the girl in the Le Car and runs to the unleaded pump before Gloria can put her hands around the spout.

"Morning, Gloria honey, pull the hood?" Gloria sighs, goes back to the car, reaches through the window, pulling the hood release.

In the shop Nello is trying to overhaul the brakes on the Belair Power Glide but he is constantly interrupted by the ringing phone. "Is Angelino there?" "Angelino said I could drop by for some transmission fluid." "Angelino said if I came in before ten someone would check my coolant." "The red-haired guy said I can leave my car for two hours and get the battery recharged. The red-haired guy's the boss? Really?"

Angelino has left to go to the County Building to get his permit to build on the vineyard. Ronny is working the pumps alone now and the lady in the purple Rambler is tugging on his sleeve. "I'm a widow; could you check my tires? Oh thank you so much. And if you could just blot up the suds from the squeegie. You see, it's the original paint job. I have cataracts and have to go to the doctor in Oakland, so I had to come this morning. You're so busy. They want to take them out. Two of them."

In the shop Nello finishes the Belair Power Glide and washes his hands before he goes home for lunch. Ronny puts out the TEMPORARILY OUT OF GAS sign because he has to lube and service John Rapalli's pickup before one. As Nello washes his hands he complains to Ronny that things were fine when Angelino was on vacation in Italy. The boss means well but he's too soft with the clients and schedules too much work. Ronny smiles and drives Rapalli's truck onto the lift. Nello leaves for lunch, shaking his head. Nobody knows what the boss does, even the wife doesn't know what he's up to.

Ronny hoses off Rapalli's truck before he raises it on the lift. Rapalli owns the sprout farms up the coast; his trucks are always covered with mud. As a joke one day John offered Ronny a job. Ronny *thinks* that was a joke. He tried to say, "Buon giorno, come sta?" But Rapalli said, "What? You're going to the beach?"

At the County Building Angelino is still waiting for his name to be called. Finally he is summoned to the counter and the receptionist tells him about the permit. "Because of Proposition M all permits for this year have been rescinded. Since you declined your permit last April, you're not eligible again until the first of next year," she says, "unless Proposition M is declared unconstitutional, in which case there would be thirty more permits issued July first. You want to build low-cost housing?"

Angelino explains that he turned down his permit because his loan hadn't cleared, and he couldn't see the loan sitting in the bank getting five percent interest when inflation was at eight percent. "I'm a self-made man," he says, "I jumped ship with fifty dollars. I thought this was a free country. If I wait till next year to build, the costs will go up so much I'll have to borrow twice as much."

The receptionist tells him she can't understand much of what he's saying because his accent is so thick, but if he doesn't like it here, he can go back to his own country. "Furthermore, what I did understand was impertinent," she says.

He says this is his own country. He walks off swearing, *"Basta! Fongula!"*

"Mamma mia, pasta! Pasta!" she yells after him.

Angelino drives back to the shop; Gloria is bringing her Fiat back so he can clean the carburetor. He would like to start Gloria out— she's just turned eighteen—but it would cause talk. He means well by it; he's watched her grow up. He remembers what it was like when he got started and wants it to be like that for her. He can do whatever he pleases if he wants to. And he can make a decision just like that.

When Angelino arrives Nello tells him that the Power Glide is ready and Ronny yells out that Rapalli's pickup is just now done. Nello insists that the Oldsmobile is due at two, Marielli's Pinto is in for service, Stephano's Pontiac has a rumbling noise, and that the wife has called twice. Angelino tells Nello to take Gloria home.

Ronny calls Angelino inside because he can't get the thermostat housing off the Oldsmobile. He says he drove the Pontiac but couldn't locate the rumble. Angelino sends him out to sell gas, pries the thermostat housing off with a screwdriver, replaces the thermostat. He drives the Pontiac around the block. There are rocks in the left rear hub cap. "I always save the day around here," he thinks.

When Angelino comes back the wife is waiting for him. She says that he always takes long lunches when Gloria is in for repairs; someone slept in her bed last weekend when she was away and Nello was obviously trying to cover up for him. Angelino tries to pacify her. He tells her he doesn't know what she's talking about. He tells her he didn't get the building permit, that they might not get it until January.

At seven Nello puts on his jacket, picks up his coffee thermos, and motions to leave, saying that he gets paid for only eight hours, that he does the best he can, that he said when he started he couldn't work on foreign cars, and that if Angelino wouldn't schedule so heavy, he'd be able to make some money for him. But he's the boss, he's the boss.

Ronny closes up the pumps, reads the meters, empties the trash cans, and flattens out the paper towels so that Nello can reuse them when he does grease jobs. Rapalli arrives with fresh sprouts in exchange for his pickup, Ronny delivers the Belair, Pontiac, and Oldsmobile. The Fiat and Pinto will have to wait until tomorrow. Ronny locks up.

Wrapping up work orders and counting the money, Angelino decides it is too late to call his mamma. He heads for the vineyard, thinking that maybe he should get out of the gas station business, specialize in something, radiators or carburetors. Maybe he should buy a boat and sail it to Italy. Maybe he should start Gloria out anyway.

He arrives at the vineyard, parks under the tree, and decides that he'll sleep all night there, in the back of the truck, under the stars. He doesn't have to go home. He doesn't have to do anything he doesn't want to. And when he makes a decision, he makes it just like that. Boom. And he always saves the day around here.

MARCH OF DIMES

by Michael Martone

As we walk to the next house, I tell my son to hold up. The back of his coat is folded up from sitting. It looks like a little tail. Beneath his coat I can see where his white shirt has come untucked. It glows raggedly against the seat of his pants. "Stand up straight." He does. He's all bundled up. His arms, in the quilted sleeves, seem to float at his sides. His hood is up and cinched around his face, glowing like his shirt. His face is pale and smooth in the light, so that you want to touch it. In the corners of his mouth, I know there are those little smile lines made by the Dixie cup of grape Kool-aid at the last house. "Wipe your mouth." I put the envelope and clipboard down on the ground by his feet as I kneel in front of him. Reaching around behind, I work my thumbs into the back of his elastic breeches, tucking as I go, then a quick zip around each half of the trunk of his body like the cartoon of ski tracks around a tree. "There." I yank down at the hem of his coat with both hands. The hood tightens around his head. He hops a little after each yank as if he were a compressed spring released. His arms seem connected to his body only by the sleeves of his coat. I tuck some hair back up inside his hood and touch his face.

I pick up my things and stand up. We start walking again to the next house. There are not many lights on in the houses on the block. All downstairs. The blue light of TVs or fish tanks. Cars pass rarely on the cross street up ahead. I can hear the corduroy switch of his trousers as he walks next to me. My husband thinks I bring our son along as some type of illustration. An example of good health. A general reminder. The moon is full and in the trees. I exaggerate the swinging of my arms so I can feel the coins slide back and forth in the envelope. Some stick in the tight corners. I can feel the face of one through the paper. My writing on the envelope is distorted by the coins beneath the surface. I can rub the pencil back and forth using the long part of the lead and make the face appear.

The next house has an enclosed porch. I can hear the slap of his oxfords on the cement walk. The jingle of coins. I never know what to do when I come to a house with an enclosed porch. I've done both. I've stood outside the porch door and pounded, hoping they would hear me through both doors. I've pounded so hard the screens rattled. And I have crept into the porch with its shadows of summer furniture or old sofas, the bikes and rag rugs, and tapped on the inside door. When I first hear the conversation stop or when they are just silent differently, I know they have heard something. And then I tap again until I feel their footsteps coming to the door through my own feet. I try to be but never am ready for when the door swings open and I am discovered in the half light. I find myself in some half room of their house. "The Mother's March," I say.

This house has a doorbell outside, and my son wants to ring it. The doorbell is lit, a little dime-size moon. I lift him up, and when he pokes the button, the light goes off. In the house, we hear the bells, three of them, the silence, and then someone coming. The doorbell light pulses on again after he lets up. "Pick up the paper so you can hand it to the lady." The porch light comes on. The inside door opens, then the storm, and then a Mrs. James Payne pads across the porch. We can see her through the porch storm. She still can't see us because the glass of the storm reflects the light inside back toward her. The overlapping louvers on the storm slowly open as she cranks them. We are watching her be cautious.

"Who's there?"

"The Mother's March," I say.

"Come in. Come in."

In a way, my husband is right. My son sits in another chair, holding a glass of something else, which he supports with both hands. He never takes the glass from his lips. Tips it a bit now and then. He swings his legs, looks around the room over the rim of the glass. The woman whose house we are in is reading through the brochures, tsking over the children with braces. Those children have brilliant smiles. She steals a glance at my son, who has focused his attention on an array of porcelain thimbles next to him on the table. I know it is a matter of touching and not touching. The newspaper, still folded, is beneath his swinging feet. She is going to get her purse, more soda.

I am unspooling that endless twine from the two red paper

buttons on the back of the envelope. I have been opening and closing the envelope flap all night, and each time I do, I wrap the string around in a different pattern. This is my first winter collecting for the March of Dimes. I am halfway through the names and addresses. My map is spotty with at-homes and aways. Many people still talk about Roosevelt. It is an older neighborhood. Few children. These women make me lonely with their grown-up children framed on the coffee table. My husband is only half right. "Don't touch," I tell my son.

I wish I was able to repeat the things my son says in the way he says them. But I can never find the words. Precious, you know, cute. But anytime mothers repeat the words of their children, it never sounds quite right. It is always the parent talking. Still, children mimic their mothers and dads, I know. That is what makes them cute. Or maybe it is both ways. In any case, my husband is right about some of the uses for children. My son keeps me company between the houses even though we are silent. "Let Mommy talk," I say to him as he pushes passed the neighbor holding the screen door open. He finds his own chair. Let Mommy talk, indeed. See how the words change when we use them.

It is eight o'clock, and even though we are not tired, we turn for home. The pamphlet that comes with the soliciting kit suggests this. We are walking again. He hasn't asked me to carry him. In this neighborhood the streetlights are the old candy-cane type, globes suspended over the street, the top hemisphere blackened still from the war. He wants to know about polio. I am a mother with no fears now. The vaccine's already found. My baby is already born and walking. Perfect. All his toes and fingers. He started talking early. Perfect. I am collecting for this, for him. For the time when I didn't know yet. It should be more than that. I tell him about polio and the summers his grandmother wouldn't let me swim. How, when I was his age, I was never allowed to be cold. I think quickly to ask if he is cold now. He isn't. As he switches and slaps in the dark next to me, he chants *polio* again and again. It will be his word for a while, repeating it when he is thinking as he did with the word *sum*.

When we get home, my husband is mixing blood in the kitchen. He is a safety director for the local phone company. He investigates accidents when company cars or trucks are involved and writes up the police reports in passive voice. On the dashboards of the mangled vehicles, he has already stuck decals about backing and looking both ways. He lectures on artificial respiration, electrocution, and shock to linemen and switchmen. The blood is for some first-aid simulation he does. In the trunk of his car, there is a kit filled with realistic rubber casts of burns, first to third degree, and fractures, simple, compound, and complex. He fills a special bladder with the blood. He wears it strapped beneath a beat-up shirt. Hoses are taped to his body and along his arm. He squeezes a rubber ball from an atomizer to pump the blood to a severed artery at his wrist or knee. I have seen him die a couple of times when rookie framemen applied the wrong kind of direct pressure or put the tourniquet below the wound. In times of emergencies people just yell, "Don't move him. Don't move him." He bleeds to death.

He is sprinkling an old shirt with blood, using the 7-Up bottle and the plastic spray spigot I use to dampen clothes I'm ironing.

"How did it go?" he asks, gore to the elbows.

Odd. He is the type who gets queasy at things like that, leaves the room when I do my nails because of the ether smell, turns off hospital shows. He lets me dig for splinters, pop blisters. At the doctor's, he faints when his reflexes are tested. He stumbles out of the office, sicker than ever before. As I fill the prescription he sits on the little couch with his head between his knees. He cannot stomach listening to people tell of their operations or having their hands closed in doors or even losing toenails. At night in bed, he will toss for hours, cannot sleep if he hears his own heart beating in his ears.

"I was the one they watched in driver's education class when they showed the films," he told me. I think it is the words that bother him most of all. Laceration for cut. The slow accumulation of the sounds.

His hands are red and he squeezes me on both my arms with the inside of his.

"What did the little one bring in?" he asks.

"He's counting it now," I tell him. "We're halfway through. We'll go out again tomorrow."

He turns back to an old bowling shirt, TONY on the pocket. "Like an organ grinder's monkey."

I'm used to it. You get used to it.

I tip my finger in his blood, touch him lightly on the forehead, square on his football scar.

"Hey," he says. He can't do anything about it now. His arms raised at the elbows. He looks like a surgeon with gloves on.

Our son has been counting and stacking the coins. He gets to keep all the pennies. He stores his pennies in an Old Grand-dad bottle his father says he came out of.

"How did we do?" I ask him.

I think he thinks it is somewhat like Hallowe'en but grown-up, without the candy, and he seems to arrange the coins like candy about him except there is less of it. He freezes most of the candy bars he gets for trick-or-treating and eats the chocolate coins wrapped in gold foil right away. He tells me $27.20. He has 36 pennies for his bottle.

"Aren't you tired?" I ask him. I'm tired. Without my glasses, the stacks of coins seem to be sprouting from the carpet, silver stocks. It has been a sheepish March. Nice during the day, chilly at night. It is supposed to snow a bit tomorrow. He has gone to get the plastic sherbet tub we keep the money in. I can hear him making faces at his father's mess and then giggles and splashes. Of course, he will come out and try and touch me with sticky hands. I am already halfway up the stairs when he reaches the bottom, hands out and clawing. Maybe when he grows up he won't be like his father that way. Used to it. He took his boosters okay as long as I was there and squirted the neighborhood kids with the syringe the doctor gave him. His father could not look at the TB test on his son's arm and made him wear long sleeves in early fall. Maybe blood will never be real to him.

"Come here, you monster." I drag him by the elbows into the bathroom and wash it off into the sink. I strip him to his underwear. He is brushing his teeth, back and forth, not up and down. As he stands there, using every muscle he has in his body to keep his head perfectly still while his hand saws away, I notice the button of his vaccine. It seems to be the head of the pin holding his arm on. Still, in relief, pinker than his skin, still round. The center of a black-eyed Susan. I remember when the scab fell off. We were so careful not to touch it before it did.

He pees for a long time because of all the soda and Kool-aid. As he does he whispers something to himself.

Tucked in bed, he tells me the name of each face on the coins, wonders why Lincoln is facing the wrong way and Roosevelt's neck is too short. He says he likes going into other people's houses and can't wait until we go out again tomorrow.

"I couldn't do it without you. You're a good helper." I catch myself from going on in this way, talking like other mothers talk. *Mommy's little helper.* Why do I want to talk this way? "I'll see you tomorrow. We'll go out again."

Downstairs, my husband is done with blood and washed his hands. He has forgotten where I've touched him. I can still see the edges of the print beneath the fringe of hair. He is at work now, diagramming accidents on graph paper with colored pencils. Sometimes he scoots tokens from board games across the grid to give him a better feel for what happened. He goes over and over the accident, concludes, finally, it was following distance or overdriving headlights.

"You have to get the big picture," he tells me. "Drive defensively. Leave yourself an out." He says these things over and over. When he drives in his own car, he mutters at other drivers, becomes furious at old women in crosswalks. I watch him from my side of the seat as he thinks about his job while our son complains from the back about the radio station's doctor's-office music. I say nothing, find my right foot pressing the floor, try not to move so he won't say, "What you jumping for? We're okay. We're okay."

My son's miscounted. $28.35. I throw in my husband's loose change. I feel in the reports. The poster child is thanking me. It looks as if she has climbed the long ladder of printed lines that scale the left margin of the page—staff, directors, honorary chairmen—to her perch in the upper corner. Roosevelt looks at her across the top of the page, through *Liberty*, chin up, hair cut, without his glasses too. The date on the coin is the date of my son's birth. I dump the coins into the sherbet tub. They arrange themselves the way coins do, scalloped or scaled, deepening in sound as they deepen in the tub. The poster child has braces and metal crutches, the tops of which are strapped to her forearms. She leans out from the paper. What would she say? I draw a cartoon balloon coming from her mouth. *Polio. Polio.* Not, *Won't you help me? Sometimes, I am weary of courage.* But a child would not talk that way.

My husband heads by me, up to bed. He runs his fingers across my shoulder as he goes.

"I'll be right there." I plan my route for the next night, sharing the streets with paperboys collecting, girl scouts and cookies, cars driving down the side streets with their brights on. People can't guess who is at their doors.

I look in at my son's room. I wait in the doorway until my eyes adjust. The moon is high now and in the window. The linoleum has an egg-speckled pattern on dark brown. We ironed it to the floor ourselves. I can hear only one-half of his breathing—breathing in—so it sounds as if he is making a higher-pitched sound each time he does. I see his head on its side, a shoulder and arm emerging. He looks like my coin rubbings, soft and out of focus. The light picks up something on his finger. A Band-Aid? I go over and kneel down beside him. It is a porcelain thimble. Bathroom-sink white. There is a bundle of violets painted on the collar. The little pock marks of the tip have their own shadows, each a phase of the moon in the moonlight.

I ease it off his finger and put it on mine. I don't like the way it feels. Touching but not touching. The way being touched someplace is never the same as touching the place yourself. But touching the head of the thimble itself, its curve, its roughness, is pleasing. It almost feels grainy, as if instead of scoops there are spheres dotting the tip. What would it feel like if I didn't know what it was? Its opposite? The ridges of a finger?

I slip it back on one of his fingers. A different finger. Will that make him think in the morning? Wonder how it got there. His fingers walk. His thimble goes from house to house.

I am about to wake my husband and tell him, but I don't. I don't know what I would tell him. We all have our own lives in this house, and these two do not meet here. He is dreaming of game-board tokens making wrong turns, graphs of fatalities. Accidents. He wasn't drunk that night. I wasn't drunk that night. The only difference was our son. He took.

My husband's back is toward me. He has slept through the noise of his heart. I can barely see his vaccine, dimpled in his arm. A cirque but eroding. A print. A daylight moon. I touch it as I fit in behind him.

About the time I became pregnant, we took the oral vaccine in the national program at the junior high. It was a Sunday, and the halls were filled with well-dressed neighbors lined against the lockers leading toward the girl's gym. We would take a couple of steps, then stop. He would fiddle with the nearest locker. I read the brochures, sometimes reading parts aloud to him. The hall was close and warm. The ceiling was low. "No shots," I told him, "just sugar."

Down the ramp and into the gym. We stopped to sign our names. The hallway opened up to two stories. The sun slanted through windows with metal screens to protect them from the balls. It gave the sunshine in the gym a mottled look. The floor was linoleum. The boys' gym was wood. A doctor and several nurses handed out the sugar cubes. The way they were bricked together made them look like a junior high school project on the walls of Troy.

"Do you have some water?" my husband asked.

"You don't swallow it. Suck on it. It's just sugar."

"I'd like some water," he said.

"In the hall. Outside."

The sugar tasted sweet, of course. My teeth rang when I bit into the cube. My mouth was sticky. My husband could barely get his down. We were out by the line again, by a drinking fountain much too low for him.

"Oh, c'mon. It's not that bad," I said.

"Yeah?" he said.

"Like a Life Saver "

"I just don't like sweet things. Okay? Okay?"

People in line looked at us. Crouching, he drank with his eyes open, his face as white as the fountain. We sat on the steps outside for a long while.

Sweet thing, I am used to it. I have lived with it long enough.

There is only a powder of snow. We are marching through the neighborhood. It seems that everyone is expecting something. The porch lights are all on. This is what charity should be. Door-to-door. Face-to-face. I do not like the loose change in checkout lanes with the plastic hour glasses or the cardboard sheets with penny-loafer slots and fading football players. I'm a mother, too, not a movie star. This is my son.

The moon is full again but starting to melt. Its light looks good on the snow, white with streaks of yellow from the porches. He reads the house numbers and tries to guess the next one. Our envelope is heavy. The coins knife back and forth.

At a corner, before we cross, I ask him about the thimble. I smile to myself as his eyes widen. I know they widen even though I cannot see them. What can he say? Has he even been able to explain it to himself? He says nothing, repeats something to himself. I suggest we return it to the lady, and he agrees. Tomorrow. Yes, tomorrow. He needs it one more night. He can show it to me, now, himself.

On the bank of our yard, the one my husband hates to mow in the summer, we make very poor snow angels. The money jingles as I make the wings. There isn't enough snow here. We lie back down. The bank is steep. We are not far from standing, more like leaning backward. We blow our breath away into the night. I tell him the moon is dime-size, no bigger. And he doesn't believe me. It is hanging there at least half-dollar-size. It is the moon after all. I sit up and unravel the flap of my envelope, reach in, and feel for a dime. I find one. I tell him to hold it at arm's length and close one eye. "Put it over the moon." And he does.

Tomorrow, we will go out again, collecting.

FISH WALTZ

by Jessica Maxwell

The opah didn't fit in the bucket. It was round as the moon. It looked like the moon. The moon with big orange lips glued to it. The moon bent in half and thrown away.

"What is it?" the girl asked the fisherman.

"Opah. Tropical fish. Never seen 'em this far north before. Got a real warm current runnin' out there, that's why."

The girl ran a dry finger across the fish's cold mauve skin. There were no scales.

"Can you eat it?"

"Not much meat on 'em. Mostly fat. Gotta dig it out from here," the fisherman said, knocking on the hard, round breastbone.

Sadness ran a damp finger across the girl's warm brown skin. She had never felt sorry for a fish before. She loved the ocean and all the things in it, but fish were so cold-blooded, it didn't seem to matter much whether they were dead or alive. She liked them both ways. And, besides, when they were dead she could play with them. She loved to play with them. It was so rare to be able to hold a wild thing in your hand.

She could push back the lips of the sheepshead and show their sheepy teeth and make them look like they were growling at the customers. She could put a piece of French bread in the claw of a boiled crab and label the display "crust station."

The lobsters, however, were very much alive. Unlike fish, they moved slowly, and if she moved slowly, too, they were easy to catch. The hard part was holding on to them. Not because of their claws. These were Pacific Coast lobsters and they didn't have any. But because they bucked like little horses, and the girl would have to turn her hands into rodeo cowboys and dig her fingers into their flanks and ride them until they tired. It was a fierce and muscular contest and sometimes they got away. But the deck was stacked. The animals couldn't win. If they didn't die in somebody's stew pot, they would eventually die in the tank.

"You should never have allowed yourselves to be caught," she would tell them more than once, one of the big ones had crept over and run its long antennae gently across her knuckles. It was a wonderful, wet, wiggly world, this fish market. Far more interesting— and safer—than the one outside.

"Mybabyleftmean'shedidn'tsaywhybutIdon'tcare!"

Oh, God, it's Rockstar, the girl thought.

"Gimme one combo, heavy on the crab, and some dimes for this quarter. I got-to-got-to-got-to make a phone call, baby. Oooooo! I feel good."

Though he was a young man, his hands shook violently. He wore no shirt and he dragged a happy puppy on a rope behind him. He wore red sunglasses, a blue headband, and white stuff collected in the corners of his mouth when he talked.

"I need more sauce, Sugar tits."

The girl shuddered. He always said that. His hands shook so badly, he always spilled half his cocktail sauce on the sidewalk and he always asked for more like that. She hated it. But it didn't do any good to get mad at him. Rockstar's mind was all speakers, no receivers.

"Mybabyleftmean'shedidn'tsaywhybutIdon'tcare . . . 'bye, baby."

"What's wrong with that guy, anyway?" the girl said.

"Drugs," said the fisherman. He threw the last halibut on the scale. "Okay, seventy-eight on the butts, forty on the sole. Yeah, he shoulda stuck to beer."

The girl looked at the moon fish. She looked at its bright vermilion fins and its delicate tail. She looked at its big kiss of a mouth and its elegant skin and the silver crab of sorrow clawed at her heart again.

"What about the opah?"

"Aw, tell Vanessa to pay me what she wants for it. I'll be in tomorrow. An' tell her to smoke it; the fat keeps it tender."

It was six o'clock. It was already dark. The girl wiped her hands on her red apron, grabbed the locks, and went around to the front of the market to close up. Her boots sang a rubber song to the sea as she walked.

The three front shutters rolled down like eyelids. She locked them, one by one, at their bases, with three clean clicks. Three metallic finger-snaps banishing the failure of the late twentieth-century from her senses for the rest of the night. This was the part she liked best. The market was hers.

She could hear the dock drunks arguing about money. She could hear the mineral voices of their strange young women. The men called them cows. They laughed at their shrill theatrics. But the women stayed. Sooner or later, the liquor lost its fire and the men needed something more substantial to warm them. Little loves were born that way, and sometimes little marriages. This is what the women hoped for. It was all they could hope for. And the girl considered it merely the lower register of the voice of men and women all over America. They were all singing the same song, and the theme wasn't love; it was need. Personally, she would rather play with the fish.

She tuned the radio to the only classical station in town. She threw buckets of water on the cement floor and chased all the debris of the day down the drain. She scoured the white plastic cutting board until it shined like marble and she laid her knives down beside it with great precision. Then she took a mackerel and, holding it with both hands, she offered it up to the Goddess of Fluorescent Lights.

"You should never have allowed yourself to be caught," she said to the fish, "but since you were, we will honor your death with ceremonies proper to your natural godhead."

Chopin oozed from the radio. Blood oozed from the fish. Dark blood. Quiet blood. The color of heart tissue and dried roses and a young girl's first spot of womanhood. The sight of it both calmed her and quickened her pulse. It took her to places in the female psyche where few men have ever traveled. She was so deep in her marine meditation that she didn't hear Patrick's offer.

"I said, would you like some nice ice?"

The girl looked up. The clean British edge of Patrick's voice always startled her. It seemed to come from a much younger man, not this sad, tired sixty-year-old who drank too much and had heart trouble.

Patrick had taken it upon himself to fetch the ice for the girl every evening. Even though she lugged swordfish bellies and shark carcasses around all day long, even though she smelled like a sushi bar, Patrick insisted on this one patronage.

"I can't bear to see a woman lift more than I can," he'd say.

The truth was he didn't understand women at all these days.

"They've all gone mad," he'd tell his friends. "Driving trucks and climbing telephone poles and running marathons until they have no hips or breasts left. They're not feminists; they're masculists! Why the blazes do they want to be like us? We're a bloody mess!"

He looked at the girl. She especially perplexed him. She was such a tender one. They all were, but she didn't even bother to put up a front. She didn't stomp around or talk in a too-loud voice or laugh too hard. She didn't even like beer. And several times when she was busy with customers he'd come in just to watch her hands move. They flew around like little pink birds and when they wrapped fish they reminded him of his own English mother wrapping Christmas presents.

Patrick was about to violate his habitual adherence to protocol and ask the girl why in the world she was working in this pile of eel poop when he saw the moonfish.

"What the devil is that?" he said instead.

The girl followed his eyes, and tears suddenly swelled in hers.

"It's a dead opah," she said.

"That's what we said when my father died: dead ol' Pa."

"Oh, Patrick, that's not funny. Look at this fish. It's beautiful. It should be alive. I don't care about halibut and stupid old sole. They're ugly and they smell. They deserve to be eaten. But this fish is a work of art. Look at it! It should be cherished and protected. Oh, Patrick, why is everything so mixed up? Why can't things just be what they're supposed to be?"

Patrick looked at the girl. "My sentiments exactly, my dear," he said. "Care to dance?"

The Viennese waltz had just stepped daintily from the radio, and Patrick swooped the girl up in his arms, fish scales, rubber boots, and all.

"Now, that's more like it. We danced like this when I was a captain in the British Army. Stiff upper lip and a quivering lower one. Except, of course, I would be in full dress uniform and you would be in a regal ball gown."

The girl laughed an uncomfortable laugh.

"And I suppose you'd tell me all your war stories," she said.

"Yes, indeed. This scar here: Tel Aviv in '48. I was in the King David Hotel when it blew up. Just a bit of shrapnel, my dear. Everyone needs iron."

Something was happening to the girl. Something was pulling at her. Something deep and internal. It hung inside her, old and brittle, like the shell of something else. It ached. It hung and it ached. It tightened her throat and closed the space between her shoulder blades. It pulled down through her chest and coiled its tail in her viscera. It was a hollow thing, and she could breathe into it and when she did it began to move. It shocked her to feel how much of her body it occupied.

"Patrick," she said. "I think I'm haunted."

"Of course you are," he said. "You all are. You are haunted by your own womanhood, or lack of it, I dare say."

"What do you mean?"

"I mean that you and your generation, in a commendable attempt to right the wrongs of the male ego, have somehow managed to worship it. You don't understand your own feminine power anymore. It's a pity," Patrick said, and lowered the girl in a daring dip, which automatically threw the girl's head back. She closed her eyes. When she opened them again she was staring directly at the moonfish and she saw that it was glowing.

"Patrick!" she gasped, and snapped her head back up, only to be confronted with a chestful of medals.

Patrick was transformed. Gone was the golf sweater. Gone were the old trousers. Gone was the rumpled English riding cap and the sensible Hush Puppies. In their place was a fitted jacket with gold buttons and epaulets, fine woolen slacks with a ribbon stripe down their side, a smart captain's hat and shoes as black and glossy as cannons.

Patrick's elegance was matched only by the girl's. Her gown was a miracle of mauve and silver beadwork, and one deep vermilion lily sprung full-bloom from her waist.

The girl looked around the tiny room. The tank, the display case, the walk-in cooler, had all retreated into a powdery haze. The radio had become a platform for an orchestra of bright orange lobsters playing instruments she had never seen before. Their antennae swayed in time to their watery music.

Mackerel and albacore twirled in the air. Crabs with castanet claws clacked out a waltzing rhythm. And squid pumped themselves around the room in wide, graceful arcs.

Patrick looked at the girl. Her cheeks were like apricots. Her hair had braided itself up into a wonderful sculpture that showed off the sweet shape of her face. But there were still clouds in her eyes. An emotion. Something between sorrow and distrust.

"Romance is lost on your generation, isn't it, my dear," Patrick thought. "Why, in my day, a woman was courted. Calling cards. Roses. Dances like this one. Well, not quite like this one," he added as a company of pink shrimp sailed backward under his nose. "Your generation's idea of courtship is a drink before bed," he continued. "Bloody shame, too. None of you know what you're missing."

The girl narrowed her eyes.

"I'll tell you one thing we're missing," she thought back. "We're missing having men tell us what to do, and personally, I don't miss it."

"No," Patrick replied silently. "But you *are* missing the point, which is that you are a woman. Of course you should do exactly what you want to do. You have fine minds, many of you. But the point is that you should do it as a woman, not some ridiculous caricature of a man.

"You simply don't understand that the very style you love to imitate is the result of thousands of years of cultural repression. It's bad enough that since women had the babies, men had to hunt woolly mammoths."

Patrick shuddered.

"Gives me the woollies just to think about it. We *had* to be focused and unemotional to survive. If we hadn't been, you wouldn't have survived either. Then, for those of us unlucky enough to descend from the northern tribes—Anglo-Saxons, Germans, Scandinavians— why, we had to add on layers of sub-zero weather, which doesn't exactly make for warm personalities. And which is why I started hitting the anti-freeze at an early age. The tension is terrible. Makes men emotional cripples, and that is a very serious weakness. Oh, we have feelings all right. We just don't know what to do with them. You women are so free to feel. It keeps you honest, and there's great power in that. So, you see, it is we who should be imitating you, and not the other way 'round. It is absurd that you confuse feigned self-sufficiency with power. It is absurd that you're all running around trying to grow a hard shell over all your lovely feelings so you can be like Robert Rumford or something."

"Robert Redford," the girl mentally corrected him.

"Yes, well, you cannot *be* him, no matter how hard you try. And you should not *want* to be him."

"Why not?" the girl's eyes replied.

"Because it is a crime against nature! You are, by nature, soft. He is, by nature, hard. Your hips, by nature, are wide, so you can give birth, so you can give life. His hips, by nature are narrow, so he can chase after wild animals and protect you. You are lunar, you change with the phases of the moon. He is solar; his energy is constant."

"Patrick, you're a helpless romantic."

"Romance has everything to do with this. What happens to romance when we don't need each other anymore? Where does romance go when everybody's so damn self-sufficient they don't know how to share their lives with someone? Men and women are built to take care of one another. See this? This is my door-opening muscle. I was built to open doors for you. And look at your breasts," he thought, glancing at the brown skin rising like planets above her beaded bodice. "Your breasts are made to swell with milk. Your nature is to nurture. My nature is to protect. Now, what's so bloody terrible about that? What's so terrible is that everyone's pretending they can take care of themselves, so you're not taking care of each other. How can I take care of you if you won't let me? How can you take care of me if you refuse? It takes two to tango, as you can readily see, and if you refuse to dance, the music stops, which is precisely what's happened to your whole wretched generation. So go on! Drive your bloody pickups and fight for your bloody promotions, but remember, you are still a woman, and your men and your children are dying for your care. We've learned our lessons. You've taught us well. We will not tyrannize you anymore. You have effectively altered the path of history, but you cannot alter the wisdom of nature. You can be whoever you care to be, but please, dear woman, come home."

The waltz ended. The rosy mist lifted. And somewhere up the coast a foghorn sounded. Medals vanished, petticoats disappeared, and the glow of the moonfish was lost to the flicker of fluorescent lights.

The girl blinked. Patrick was looking at her with eyes like oceans. She looked at him with eyes like moons.

"Might I walk you to your coach, m'lady?" Patrick said.

The girl grew very still. Her face, which had looked so new, was now glorious and full. She smiled.

"Why, yes," she said. "Yes, thank you. I think I'd like that very much."

Patrick followed the girl out into the salty night, and as she turned to lock the door she took one last look at the moonfish and she was sure she saw it wink a silvery lid quickly over an opal eye.

THE LAST OF THE RAIN

by Bill Meissner

He is driving up Oak Street into the low sun at eight A.M. in his 1948 Plymouth, and from her garden she is the only one who watches him leave; the other neighbor women are busy hanging out pure white linens on the wash lines near their gardens. She thinks she hears the fear, like a distant noise, beginning again. But the man must have a job, she thinks, the same way the white shirts on the cord must have the wind to fill them, to balloon them out until they are dry.

Now she moves from room to room, opening windows. The dry drafts buff at her from all sides, and she begins to feel as if half of her mind is being softly pushed out of her ears by the breeze, her thoughts seeping into the air like loose strings of clouds. Yes, the children are her very own. This is what we must do, she thinks as she looks out at the garden where she spends hours weeding each day; the wife must do the best she can with the house and the three children. But there were just some times when she didn't know. If one of the children got sick or cut a knee, she couldn't decide what to do—she was afraid she would lose sight of the other two. And the baby always has his mouth slightly open; once a fly flew in, and then back out, just like that.

In a few days he will be back, she thinks, back from the roads and the selling of feeds to farmers and businessmen, back from the elevators filled with grain and corn, the bits of gold. For a moment she remembers that one time Father returned after two weeks, and he hardly knew his own children, the way he closed and locked the bathroom door.

She listens to the radio. In a few days he will call from Davenport or Iowa City or wherever he is, and he will tell her exactly when he will be home, and she will tell him about the baby being sick again and ask him what should she do. "He'll be fine in a day or so," he will answer. The Iowa dust will rise from the fields and twine around the telephone lines as they talk, their voices spurting back and forth between distant plastic. The distance is not really that far, she will think.

Then when she hangs up, she will remember the time she said: "Don't ever leave again," when she knew all along that he must be behind his steering wheel again in the morning and all the way to Cedar Rapids by nightfall. "All right, I'll see what I can do," he answered as he reached for the hat rack, then slipped off his charcoal coat and handed it to her.

On that night it was as though the house were full again, she thought as she read the *Ladies' Home Journal* in her bed; it was as though the bushel basket brimmed with shining red tomatoes. And she reached for the light—"her lamp," he had called it once. Her lamp ever since they began sleeping separately two years ago. But this time when she turned it off, she felt as though she were glowing in the dark—her whole skin a faint silvery yellow, like a luminous cloud. She wondered if he could almost see her from his room through the wood slats and the plaster, as if he were awake and not breathing so regularly, a wheeze in and out like the sound of the deep gusts of wind filling up the laundry on the line.

He could not have understood her fear. Whenever he left, it was a kind of noise somewhere inside her, like the hum of a thin metal wire pulled too tight. It rattled the bed, the whole room, and sometimes spread to the kitchen and even knocked the water glass off the table before he had come home—the glass she had swept from the tile floor into the dustpan and not mentioned. It even echoed and played faintly in her head as she fell asleep, like a train whistle that stretches thin but never quite disappears into the dark distance of the flatlands.

That next morning it was newspapers: the hush of the sports page in his hands, the headlines of *The Freedom* stamped in thick ink, the corner of the advertisement page soaking up brown coffee as if it were dying of thirst. And the two oldest sucking on orange slices and the baby spilling and sloshing tomato juice all over his high-chair tray. This was the way the morning began to inflate after he left: larger, larger, until it floated, a balloon bobbing tautly against the plaster ceiling.

But all that was weeks ago, and this morning she is trying to make things different. The oldest has her grapefruit section caught down her blouse, and the baby has his fingers stuck until they're blue inside the milk glass, and the middle one has dropped his jelly spoon and is watching it fall the amazing distance from the table-cloth to the floor. But the mother turns her chair toward the window and begins to imagine fleecy white clouds in the sky—any clouds will do—beyond the thick fading draperies. She hears their mouths behind her like dark-red balloons and she waits. She waits.

But this is the way all life must be; there would be no life without all this, she thinks as she washes the clothes, hangs them out, and lets them dry in the wind and then takes them back to the basement and washes them again in her Maytag. Before it breaks down or wears out, she has to use it, to make it work for her over and over. The children trace circles in the dirt of the backyard with sticks from the oak tree, and then they run circles faster and faster. Then the baby falls and cries loud at the blood on his elbow until the mother's legs come gasping toward him.

By three in the afternoon, the mother just sits on a blanket in the grass of the yard, staring at the blue, blue sky and the garden, wondering if he will return tonight. She notices the crows that land on the wires each afternoon and stay there until six o'clock or seven, crows that will stick to the dusk like pieces of flat, black paper.

Later, when the children are asleep, she still feels it. It feels like the time he rented the flat for a month in Mason City, only stronger. The fear, the wire, the noise. This time it is as though he will never return, not ever. The noise is making so much racket now in her head that it is like the air-raid siren on top of City Hall; it is dissolving her brains into something white, something lighter than air. She walks slowly across the hall with the lights out and wants to tell the children she is sorry there will be a hollow spot inside each of them, like the wind-filled arm of a shirt. She wants to tell them Daddy is gone forever, but something strong as clothesline wraps her fingers into a fist.

She hears the front door click. He walks through the hall and stands there, half in blackness, half in the glow of lamplight and she flows down the stairway toward him, closer toward him. He is back, back for a while, and she knows he will be there, asleep in the darkness of the next room, for one more night.

TOUGHING IT OUT

by Stephen Minot

The first week wasn't as bad as he had expected. He began each morning just as he always had—shaving carefully, dressing meticulously, appearing for breakfast on time at 7:15, kissing his wife, Martha, and his daughter, Kim, and reading the front page of the paper while eating. If he allowed any variation in the familiar pattern, it was to be just a bit more considerate—telling Martha how good the eggs were one morning, asking Kim how her homework went the next. These were a calculated part of the plan too. Little shows of affection were not entirely out of character for him, and they would help hide the fact that his stomach was tight as a clenched fist.

Kim's departure for school was generally less hectic than most fifteen-year-old girls he had heard about. She almost always had her books and papers ready. She never forgot to kiss her parents good-bye just as the school bus rounded the corner. But this was not really surprising. Manley Thompson had spent much of his adult life as a cost systems manager, and order was important to him. He had married late and with prudence, making sure that the woman with whom he would share his life would share his values as well. Martha was tall, serene, and self-contained. So it was natural that their one child should be quieter and more sensible than the average teenager. He didn't have to worry about them.

Here it was Friday, the end of the first week, and everything had gone exactly as he had planned. Perhaps he shouldn't have worried so. But then, he had never faced anything quite like this.

Ten minutes after Kim had left on the school bus, Manley was on the road, taking the old, familiar route just as he had every morning that week—through the suburban Oakdale area in which they lived, down Washington Avenue, with its auto agencies and muffler shops, and finally to the business district. It was all unchanged, of course, the same as it had been for years; but at the same time it was strangely unfamiliar. It was like seeing a movie in which they had used his town for a set. Here was the very area in which he had lived and worked for twenty years, yet he seemed to be looking at it for the first time.

It unnerved him a bit, this strange sense of numbed suspension. It was as if all his emotions had been shut down. Could he have caught some kind of virus in addition to everything else?

He swerved suddenly, making a quick left turn without signaling. A truck blasted its horn. A stupid error. It was not like him to daydream while driving. Not like him at all. Amazing, the force of habit. Well, now he had a new habit to learn. As he headed for the west end of town, he realized that he would have to tighten up a bit, keep his mind on his business.

In fifteen minutes he was at a branch library he had found at the other end of town. It was too small to be used by anyone he knew. Often he was the only patron there. When there were others, they were seedy, unshaven types—retirees or even bums. How could anyone let himself get like that?

He slipped into his familiar seat, his back to the reference desk, and began studying the paper. The library subscribed to three, two of them from larger cities. It took him most of the morning to cover them carefully. The afternoons he reserved for *Time* and *Newsweek*.

"Can I help you with anything?"

Manley jumped. Until that day, neither of the librarians had said a word to him. He had assumed that they never would. Having to deal with them was not a part of his plan.

There were two of them, a woman who seemed to know what she was doing and an older man who was either new or stupid. The man often had to ask her where to file this or that. How did someone like that hang on to his job? And how come he was the one offering assistance? As if he could help anyone with anything.

"Just doing a little research," Manley said. He wasn't going to be lumped with those unshaven bums. But perhaps the librarian had noticed that Manley hadn't asked for a single book. Just the papers and the magazines. What kind of research did that look like? "Research," he repeated, struggling for some plausible way to finish the sentence, "on the employment situation. How it differs in these three cities."

"Sounds interesting," the man said. "If I can be of any help . . ."

Manley nodded and pretended to study the news item in front of him—something about a pedestrian who had been hit by a truck on East End Avenue. Had the librarian noticed? He would see at once that the article had nothing whatever to do with employment. Perhaps he would put all the pieces together, realize that Manley had been fired, that he would never find another position at his age, that he was nothing but a bum in disguise. What a story that would make! The man would blab it all over town. Manley stared at the photo of the accident victim. He was bleeding from the temple.

When the weekend came, Manley realized he would have to do something extra to assure his wife and daughter that their lives were in perfect order. Although he had no appetite, he invited them both to go out to dinner. He chose a little steak house they used for each birthday and anniversary. The girls, as he called them, were surprised—not knowing that he was celebrating, in a sense, his first week of endurance. But they were delighted. "You're loosening up in your old age," Martha said, smiling. He forced himself to smile back, rigid as a poker.

At the restaurant he did his best to keep the conversation humming right along. It helped to have read three newspapers a day for a week. He figured that world, national, and local events for each of five days should take him right through to dessert. But when Martha started looking at him oddly, he switched tactics and asked Kim to tell him about each of her courses. "I really want to know," he said, trying hard to make his voice sound perfectly sincere.

As she told him, course by course, he found himself recalling the little office in which he had spent so many years. No, he did not love it. But what had that space become without him? They had talked about reducing personnel, about eliminating his position and even his title. Perhaps they had taken the very room as well. His associates would walk down the hall and find the door missing. Just a blank wall. Would they even notice?

Kim had just stopped talking, so he said, "And what about the math class?"

She looked at him with amused astonishment. "I just this minute got through telling you about that."

The second week didn't go as well. He had planned to go on long walks to get in shape and to read the novels he had never had time for at college. But somehow this drab little branch library was draining all his energy. He couldn't even focus his mind enough to read fiction. Here he was, ten years from retirement, and feeling like an old man already!

To make matters worse, the nosy librarian would not leave him alone. Manley was tempted to be rude, but that was not his nature. Besides, wouldn't he get thrown out if they caught on? So he compounded his lie about the research project. He began looking up back copies of the papers, pretending to be interested in which occupations were hardest hit in the recessions of previous years. He even got back to the big Depression of the '30s. What an appalling catastrophe that was! He'd been born in the middle of it, but what does a kid know about those things?

Reading about that period reminded him of his parents. Somehow they had hung on to their corner grocery store through those terrible times, and only years later did he learn what a struggle it had been for them just to pay the rent. Not once in all that time did they share their troubles with their only son. They didn't even ask him to help out around the store. He always tried to admire them, telling Martha how courageous they had been. But privately he felt some kind of resentment he didn't understand.

As the weeks passed, the nosy librarian turned out to be not such a bad sort. His name was Max and his interest was genuine. Actually, he wasn't even a librarian. He'd been a machinist for thirty years and had been permanently laid off. "I never finished school as a kid because of the Depression, so volunteering here gives me something of what I missed."

"Volunteering?"

"Well, they've got a budget problem like everybody else."

Without quite planning to, they began to develop a research project that interested them both. There were some occupations in the area that had been hard hit with every recession, and then there were others that seemed impervious. Little was being done to re-train those in vulnerable areas. Max felt there was a newspaper or magazine article here, and his enthusiasm was infectious. Manley began to look forward to his work at the library. Occasionally, he almost slipped and revealed everything to Martha and Kim. He reminded himself that he must tighten up and watch his step. He had no right to get careless with their happiness.

In three weeks he and Max were well into the article. Max managed to dig up figures from his union hall records, and Manley applied his statistical abilities to the data they were gathering. When Friday came, they had a rough draft typed. He decided to invite "the girls" out to dinner again. It was an odd sensation, having something to celebrate and yet not being able to mention it. But he couldn't share the news about the report without revealing the rest, so this would have to do.

They were well into the meal and chatting almost as if everything were normal, when he heard a familiar voice:

"Well, Manley, how goes it?"

There was Max. And a woman. His wife? What on earth was he doing on this side of town?

"Well, what a surprise." Surprise? It was a disaster. Stumbling like a kid, he made introductions as best he could. The woman's name turned out to be Francine and was indeed Max's wife. She was outgoing, almost hearty. So much the worse.

"So I finally get to meet the fellow writer," she said. And to Martha, "They've really got something good going."

"All I hear is how busy he's been."

"Busy? That library hasn't been so well used since they built it."

"The company library," Manley said in a low voice to Martha, but not low enough.

"Company?" Max asked. "What company?"

Manley closed his eyes and ran his hand across his brow. It was damp with sweat. He wanted to smash Max against the wall and his wife, too, but Manley hadn't hit anyone since playing football in high school.

"Could you excuse us?" Martha said. "We're having a kind of family conference here. You know how it is. How about coming back to the house for coffee when you're through?" Before Manley could think of how to object, Martha had given them directions.

As soon as Max and Francine had left the table, Manley started to get up, muttering something about the men's room. He had some notion of telling Max that . . . what? That Kim was seriously ill and they really shouldn't have guests to the house, but that Martha didn't know and . . . It was all hopelessly out of hand.

But Martha put out her hand and stopped him. "Wait just a minute," she said, smiling. What could he do but sit down again? "You were going to tell us tonight, weren't you? Kim and I figured you were going to do it tonight."

"Do what?"

"It's really great," Kim said. "What you're doing with Max. But we wanted to hear all about it from you."

He looked from one to the other. "Max called on a Saturday," Martha said. "Three weeks ago. You weren't home. He wanted to give you a message about some more data he'd found. He so admires you. Did you know that? Well, we got to talking and, well, it all came out."

"About the job? Everything?"

"But you were going to tell us tonight, weren't you?"

He nodded tentatively. Then shook his head. "No, I wasn't. I wasn't ever going to tell you."

"Why on earth not?"

"Because . . ." Good God, did he have to say it out loud? Yes, he had to. "Because I was scared."

He reached out and held the hand of each of them. The faces of these two women, these two marvelous women, turned liquid in his vision, swimming, but what strength there was in their grasp!

COLD SOUP

by Dorothy Monet

Funny, almost every one of my really close friends—women, that is—has at one time or another tried to commit suicide. When they talk about it, they're almost apologetic. About having blown it, I mean. They insist on the sheer fortuitousness of events that robbed them of that shining hour, that moment of furious lucidity. One thing about these resurrected women—there's always a man that's buried along the way. I know all about it, though trying to kill myself is something I've never done. What I *did* try to do is not as easy to talk about. Especially when your family is Sicilian.

It seems a hundred years ago. I was only in my twenties. We were still in Vietnam hunting down the Viet Cong. At home we were hunting down soup. One thousand, one hundred ninety-six cans of it. I personally knew about one.

I had discovered it in my refrigerator right after the very first cases of botulism were reported in the papers and traced to a shipment of Bon Vivant vichyssoise. It looked innocent enough. Not even remotely convex. But when I checked the serial numbers on it against the ones that were published as identifying the contaminated lot, I knew I'd hit the jackpot. It was the only lottery I'd ever won.

The last I ever saw of it, it was bobbing up and down, Bon Vivant amid the flotsam that floats along the river bank, trailing a ghostly condom alongside. I thought to put a rock in it so as to sink it right away. But didn't. I tossed the lid in after it and watched it sparkle and spin as it cut the water, razor-sharp, like it comes off my electric can opener. Those days, I always had a Nikon around my neck, so I took a parting shot of it. It's the print that got a *Camera News* award and started me off to fame and glory. I submitted it untitled, but they called it "American Gothic." Hardly original, but not uninteresting, considering. . . . But I'd better get on with my story.

From the river I walked west toward Madison Avenue where I worked as a photographer's assistant. On a Saturday in summer there'd be nobody using the darkroom and I remember the Nikon socking against me as I walked, faster and faster, spurred by an urgency to hide in the dark of that red-eyed sanctuary.

A sky like a grimy plastic dropcloth shrouded the city, and I hoped it would split and let the dirty rain rain down. A splash of singles at Second and Third gave way to a storm of provincials charging at Bloomingdale's, but west of Lexington and into the Sixties there was virtually no one on foot. Weekends in summer, people with money and/or each other, didn't hang around in that murderous haze. Grimly united, they took to the thruways and left the Big Apple to singular persons like me.

Farleigh would normally be on the turnpike by now. Hell-bent for Southport, Connecticut. For seven years I'd spent my summers in Manhattan so Farleigh could use the excuse of his publishing house to come in on Tuesdays and stay on through Friday before rushing home to his Sparkman and Stephens fifty-foot sloop and his wife and his kids in Connecticut.

The boat was a beauty. Farleigh said it was yare. I can only vouch for its beauty. Farleigh was always bringing me color transparencies of it to develop for him. And some of the children. And one of his wife, whose name was Hallie and who looked like a horse. But a good one. The kind that wins at the races. She demonstrated her teeth and her sun-struck mane whipped across her face in the salty wind. Her turtleneck sweater was most likely red instead of sick pink. Farleigh's color transparencies were always overexposed. She was narrow in the beam and fashionably flat-chested with interminable legs that ended in long, narrow sneakers. Correction: tennis shoes. On me they'd be sneakers. It wasn't the only difference between us. For example, I worked for a living. For another, I've got breasts as big as Sophia Loren's in *The Gold of Naples*. Big enough breasts for the biggest baby there ever was—Farleigh Garrison Goodenow.

Well, that's what she looked like, Farleigh's rich wife. I used to say *wealthy*, but Farleigh said practically no one had wealth anymore; better say *moneyed* or *rich*. Farleigh's rich wife, then, whose name was Hallie, just sat on her poop deck the livelong day with her hair on the wind and the boom right behind her and the light from my bed lamp shining through her teeth and her tumult of hair and her absence of breasts. And I'd just lie there staring, hallucinating the boom suddenly swinging and bashing her head in and I'd fancy how Farleigh would plunge into mourning and how I wouldn't let him near me till the *shivah* was over and he faced up to how badly the children needed a mother: me.

Then *I love you*, I'd whisper to transparent Amanda, *I love you, Farleigh, Jr.*, I'd say. *Do you think you could learn to love me like a mother though my real name's Valentina Campanella and I'm lucky they even taught me to swim?* And then I'd say *merde* and turn on the television and close ranks with Ida Lupino.

Sometimes, when everyone else had left the studio, I'd put Farleigh's color transparencies in the projector and blow them up till I was reduced to absolutely nothing. If I had an analyst, I know what he'd have asked me. He'd have asked me if I didn't see what a superego-constricted moral masochist I was. But I didn't need an analyst, because I had Farleigh's analyst, who asked him if he didn't see what a superego-constricted moral masochist I was.

Farleigh's analyst, Dr. Aschenlocher, saw only patients who were healthy and wealthy. Aschenlocher was consummately wise. Here is a doggy bag Farleigh brought home to me of some of the wise things he said: That though I was a superego-constructed moral masochist, I had a hard core of health in me, hidden resources and untapped creativity. That I was still very young and already orgasmic and no one need lose any sleep over me. Whereas, Farleigh's wife, Hallie, had only been sheltered and overprotected, which anyone could see was much more traumatic than just being hit in the head with your high-school diploma and told to bring home the prosciutto.

Moreover, that for Farleigh to leave Hallie in the middle of her menopause might precipitate a complete disintegration of her ego boundaries (he might just give a thought to *Medea*), that the children needed a father now more than ever as they teetered on the brink of pre-pubescence, to say nothing of Farleigh's publishing house, of which Farleigh's father-in-law was still the biggest stockholder.

Besides, said Dr. Aschenlocher, compared to what Farleigh gave to me, he gave poor Mrs. Goodenow virtually *niente*. Need I be reminded that it was with me only that Farleigh's trick manhood neither faltered nor flagged nor collapsed in a heap at the thorny gates of perdition.

"Jesus, Val! Do you know what a tribute that is, coming from Aschenlocher?"

So that's what I had. Farleigh's boat and Farleigh's wife and Farleigh's untraumatized children. All in lousy Kodacolor. And Aschenlocher's tribute. Farleigh had me. He had had me first when I was barely twenty, unwrapped and unpunctured and saving it all for a big Italian wedding. We first met at a shoot for a big ad campaign to launch his paperback division. It was practically porn and all of us underlings were having some trouble playing it cool. The first thing that struck me was how much he looked like Governor Rockefeller. The next thing that struck me was that with three top-flight models lying about with nothing on but each other, Mr. Goodenow was looking at nobody but me.

For seven years thereafter, then, since I was barely twenty, life had had a kind of bruised insistence, a battered harmony, with Farleigh stopping long enough to bring me news and booze and pre-pub books, to eat my sixty-minute gourmet dinners and fill me full enough of Aschenlocher's tribute to last me till a subsequent apparition.

Till a morning in June, when Farleigh rolled off me, reached for his glasses, and said in his favorite, forthright manner that I wouldn't be seeing him in quite a while.

"What's happened? Where are you going?"

"Abroad. The Continent, most likely. I've got to think things over."

"Take me with you. Can't you get me an assignment?"

"Look, Val. It's you I want to get away from. I just don't think when I'm with you."

"What do you do, then? Salivate on cue?" I asked him. But not out loud. You didn't make cracks like that with Farleigh. He had no sense of humor. He was Episcopalian.

"Listen, Val," he said like Gary Cooper getting set to shoot his wounded horse. "It's something I've got to prove to myself. I know it seems cruel, but Aschenlocher says I've got to prove I can make it without you."

I was beginning to bleed. "With Hallie, you mean?"

"I mean on my own."

"What the hell is that supposed to mean?" I screeched. "Whacking off?" When I really hurt bad, I revert to the Bronx.

Farleigh winced. Farleigh never talked dirty once he had his glasses on. "I mean, with someone else," he said.

"Like who?"

"Like *whom.* Oh, just someone else. Anyone."

"Is that what Aschenlocher thinks? That you're ready to be weaned? Off the breast and back to the bottle, right? *Chivas Regal!* Isn't that about all you had going between you, you two? Hah! Second honeymoon! Man, that's a howl!"

"I don't see anything strange about that," he said, buttoning down his shirt. "Why *shouldn't* a man be able to make it with his wife?"

"How the hell should I know why he shouldn't! Ask Aschenlocher why! You haven't made it with her in years, that's why. Not in years before I met you, neither!"

"Either."

"Maybe it's because she's got no . . . Look, you're the one that said she was flat-chested."

"Sexual functioning should not depend upon things like that, Val. You know it shouldn't. I should come to you with successes. Not with failure. Besides, what if she had?"

"What if she had what? Now what are you talking about?"

"My wife. Suppose she had everything. Breasts, hips . . . all the rest of it. Suppose she was every bit as feminine as you?"

"Jesus Christ, Farleigh! What if my uncle were my aunt! This is the nuttiest conversation I ever heard! What are you suffering from? Prosperity? It's not your fault you make it fine with me in bed. Besides, it's not the only thing we've got between us. Boy, when I met you, you were really out of it. You didn't even know what books your company was publishing. You remember you told Tom Wolfe how much you loved *Look Homeward, Angel*? And you thought *The Village Voice* was a Catholic newspaper?"

I broke down and cried. When he finished tying his shoelaces, he sighed and pulled me to him. What I really wanted was my mother. According to my mother, married women are *a priori* madonnas. Unmarried women are whores.

"Listen, Val," said Farleigh tenderly, "give me some time. I've got to make some decisions. For both of us, don't you see? We can't go on like this forever. It isn't fair. Especially to you. You'd make a wonderful mother, Val. You deserve to have a baby."

Lunging at a tarnished ray of that eternal-springing hope, I pressed his head between my celebrated breasts.

"Farleigh, listen to me. . . ."

He shuddered and held me so tight I crumpled and stared at the place on top of his head where the scalp glistened pink through a carefully lacquered, gossamer veil of hair. I kissed it better. I loved him. I never doubted that I loved him.

"Farleigh, listen. . . ."

He nodded, busy with the tiny buttons at the back of my nightdress.

"Do what you want," I told him. "Go where you want. But promise me one thing. Will you, Farleigh?"

He grunted, intent upon the available topography. I lifted his chin in my hand and looked him square in the eye.

"If you won't take me with you, promise you won't take Hallie."

"I promise," he said, and took off his glasses.

*   *   *

At first, I crowded the days, took on more work, marched on the Pentagon and to Shakespeare-in-the-Park. I hooked into N.O.W. and rapped with the best of them. But inside myself I was directed only toward Farleigh's first letter, Farleigh's first call. I'd never been allowed to write *him*, of course. It was imprudent, he'd said. O'Malley, his secretary, was in the habit of opening everything. He had inherited her from Hallie's father. She wouldn't take kindly to his doing Hallie in.

"Besides, she's Catholic," he said.

"I'm Catholic."

"That's different."

He had promised he'd write from the first place he stopped at. He had said it distinctly. Paris, most likely. For what he had in mind, I figured, France seemed a nice old-fashioned place to go. I remembered my old shell-shocked grandpa marching about the house in his World War I helmet singing a song about the girls over there.

I had never had trouble being alone before. After photographing beautiful people all through the day, it was good to get home to my scruffy, anonymous cats. I read a lot and listened a lot to WNCN. I tapped my resources and dipped into my reserves. But more and more I had to face that what had sustained me was that focus, that marker, that place in the week when Farleigh would come, which was what the rest of the days were really about.

Now life came to seem like a long, aimless walk in Manhattan. Infinitely perpendicular. Leading nowhere but to the rivers. No respite. No square or piazza. Nor illusion, at least, of punctuation and purpose. As the days added on, and I finally despaired of his calling, I got so I couldn't leave my bed till the mailman had come. I would wait for the clatter of the letter boxes and keys and at last the slamming of the outside door. Then, reckless, I'd fly in what little I had on to ransack my box for an airmail letter that never came.

Weeks passed, and to add to my torment—if not to allay it—I began to fix on the real possibility that something had happened. A fine rain in Normandy. A slippery road. Farleigh forlorn at the wheel of an unfamiliar car. A furious Frenchwoman chain-smoking beside him, a sulking, sarcastic, contemptuous shrew he hadn't been able to function for. A screeching of brakes. A head-on collision. Farleigh lies dying and whispering my name as to the rain-washed evening sky his manhood, triumphant, endlessly mounts!

It wasn't the only death I worked out for him. Some were brave and some ignominious as my flagging spirit moved me. The humiliating truth was that if something had really happened, I'd be the last to know of it. In Farleigh's curriculum vitae there was sure as hell no mention of me. Nor in his passport. Nor in his card of identity. In case of emergency, it didn't say to notify Valentina Campanella, from whom he had taken maidenhood and prime.

On Sundays, I didn't have to wait for the mailman to come but just trotted down and gathered up the increasingly buxom *New York Times* delivered at my door. I remember the front page on that Sunday. There was a picture of Henry Kissinger cozying up to Chou En Lai. And a feature story about the notorious Bon Vivant soup.

Grim Detective Case: Search for Vichyssoise Intensifies was the headline. Or words to that effect. It went on to say that the search for the lethal botulin-contaminated cans of Bon Vivant vichyssoise soup was still in progress. They described the gruesome death of one of the early victims. They were trying to round up hundreds of cans from the contaminated lot before they might kill others.

I read the story with a proprietary interest because of the one I had in my refrigerator. I had decided to keep it as a ghoulish sort of pop-art loving cup. As I said, it was the only lottery I'd ever won. But all at once I bolted out of bed, sending cats and Kleenex and newspaper flying. Dear God! Could I have given him that soup that day? That awful last day he had stayed for lunch? God knows, *I* wouldn't have felt like eating anything and I was out of my mind enough not to know what the hell I was doing! Steady now, I told myself on the flight into the kitchen; it sure as hell would have been in the news. Of course, the Bon Vivant vichyssoise was still in the refrigerator, lurking perniciously behind a shrunken head of lettuce. I hauled it forth and set it on a bookshelf, where I could keep an eye on it from bed.

But that *something* had actually happened to Farleigh; a stroke, a prostatectomy—whatever, I was less and less in doubt. But who could I go to? Who would tell me? I would have braved O'Malley then and there, but it was Sunday. Anyway, from what Farleigh had said about her, she'd be sure to take the Fifth. Friends that Farleigh and I had in common were, to tell the truth, all mine. The rest of his friends were Hallie's. He said they never left Connecticut.

"You'd have to extradite them," he had added. "I doubt they'd even drink your water."

Emboldened by the sheer unlikelihood of Aschenlocher's being in the city, I dialed his number. August is when all the shrinks disappear, leaving their patients to bartenders and other qualified people. But we were well into September.

"Aschenlocher speaking."

Panic.

"Hallo. Hallo."

"Oh, gee . . . I'm sorry. . . ."

"Yehz. . . ."

"It's Val, Dr. Aschenlocher."

Silence.

"Val Compton?"

Silence.

"Valentina? Valentina Campanella?"

Silence.

"Mr. Goodenow's friend?"

"Yehz. . . ."

"Look, I'm desperate. I'm worried. I haven't had a word from him. . . ."

"My deah yonk voman, do you really eggspect me to give out invormation aboud fon of my patientz?"

"But I . . . But it's me!"

"See heah, I voodn't dizcuss my patientz vid the F.B.I.!"

"Up yours!" I told him after I hung up.

Having whetted my appetite for sheer disaster, I plowed giddily on and dialed a number that I'd never dialed before. A woman answered.

"Mrs. Goodenow?" I asked her.

"Yoost a minute, please. She's yoost comin' up the driveway."

Christ! United Nations Day. My feet went cold as ice as I envisioned her springing lithely up the mossy steps on her long white tennis shoes.

"Happy Goodenow, here. Who's calling?"

It all blew out from her farthermost teeth in a born-rich Katharine Hepburn sort of way that made me feel like Anna Magnani on a stolen bicycle.

"It's . . . Miss Magnani. From the office," I told her. "I've got a contract here that's got to be sent to Mr. Goodenow immediately . . . and the office is closed and I haven't got an address for him. In Europe, I mean."

"Yes, I see, but why in the world are you calling me?"

"Well, it's an emergency. I thought you might just tell me where—"

"But see here," she interrupted, "you aren't reaching his residence, you know. You're reaching Mrs. Hallie Goodenow, Mr. Goodenow's *former* wife. And this is *certainly* no longer his number. I think it's high time you people get that straight."

I went all damp and light-headed, reeling from what she was making inescapably clear. I clutched the slippery receiver, too paralyzed to speak.

"Hello, hello!" she was calling, "Are you there? I really didn't mean to snap at you."

"I'm sorry," I managed. "I'm really sorry. . . ."

"Oh, there's really no harm done," she said, mistaking my chagrin for solicitude. "No harm at all. It's time I got used to it!" And she let fly a burst of rich and hearty laughter. "As a matter of fact, it doesn't bother me at all. We're really all the best of friends! Wait! I think I can tell you *exactly* where they are. The children got a cable only yesterday. It's got to be here, someplace . . . let's see . . . don't go away. God! Isn't it just like Farleigh to be working on his honeymoon! Oh, here it is. Let's see. . . ."

She seemed to be reading the message more or less to herself. Or was it the trip-hammer in my gut that was drowning her out? She surfaced.

"I wouldn't send him anything now. The way it looks, they'll be back in the States in a day or two."

Two days I dug in the fetid dark of my too long unmade bed. Like a fetus aborting, I curled in upon myself, sucking the unsustaining air, suffering sweat and vertigo and cramp. Quickened with hate, I lay. All through the day, the night, dreaming and malign. On the third day, he telephoned. From Kennedy, he said.

"Christ, I missed you . . . it drives me crazy just to listen to your voice . . . let me come up for an hour or so before I head home. . . . I'm picking up the Bentley at Haug's. It'll take them almost that long to get it ready. . . . Oh, just a little something, maybe. Sure, cold soup might just hit the spot."

By the time he arrived the vichyssoise was cold as death. I livened it up with a good dose of curry and sprinkled it with chives. In my grimy little garden I set it down before him in his very own grandmother's Staffordshire bowl.

"Yum! Chicken curry! But baby, where is yours?"

"I've eaten. I'd eaten when you called."

"Aah, sweetie! All this trouble just for me!" he purred, fondling the nearest part of me.

"Eat!" I commanded, and watched in an exultation of vengeance till he'd slurped down the very last drop from his spoon.

It was after I'd bolted and locked the door behind him that I was suddenly struck with the unthinkable. Nothing, simply nothing at all, might very possibly happen! What if only a minuscule number of cans in the whole goddam lot were actually lethal! Faced with the underside of overkill, I desperately thumbed through the Yellow Pages and found the number for the place where they serviced his Bentley.

"Did you say, *Mr.*? *Mrs.* Goodenow is here," the Haug man said. "Oh, wait a minute. Here he is. He just came in."

"For me? Hello. Who is this?"

"You know damned well who it is. I've got something to tell you."

"Not now, O'Malley. Hold it for me."

"Not anymore I don't. You listen! It wasn't chicken curry."

"What? What the hell are you talking about?" *Sotto voce.*

"The soup. It was vichyssoise. Vintage. All the right numbers on it. Remember?"

Heavy breathing.

"Are you flatulent? Can you swallow? Have your eyes begun to cross?"

"Hold on, this isn't funny."

"Funny! Why should it be funny? It's not a valentine, you bastard. It's a wedding present. A Sicilian wedding present!" And I slammed down the phone.

Well, that's how it was with me that many years ago. It doesn't even rile me anymore to think that he's alive and well in Southport, Connecticut. At least as alive as anyone else who lives there.

ABSENCES

by Kent S. Nelson

You forget what it's like to walk across traffic, and you don't remember the color of the curtains in the living room, if there were curtains, or the sound of a soft voice. You can't go to the refrigerator for a beer or turn up the heat or put on Cannonball or telephone a woman you liked in the bar. The trees have no bottoms, and you can't take a crap behind a solid door. You get used to those things, adjust to them, stop thinking. But the worst is something you can never quite handle. When one thing gets out of place, when something starts to slide and the tension stretches the air, there's nothing you can do but sit tight and wait.

It's nearly free time, seven-thirty, but something hurts. Across the tier and down the rows there's an undercurrent, a strain that is like the clouds' tightening on this hot summer evening. Arrangements are usually made in advance, but this time there was no warning. If there is heat, for instance, everyone hides his weapon in a shop or in the hollow pipe of the bed leg or behind an air duct. Or if a screw is nailed bringing in porno, you can live for a while until someone else fills the gap in the market. But pills are something different. They give you the pills to calm you down, a steady flow from the hospital, or maybe from a screw if you want something heavier, or from another inmate who has a connection. It's all known, a part of the *plan*, just like putting scabs on the block or sending a pixie to appease a troublemaker who wants meat.

But when they cut the power without warning . . . look out.

Whitcomb stands across from me, sixty feet away. My cell matches his, and I can see into his life the way he can see into mine. Whitcomb's life is not fun to watch. He has the same desk, the same bed, same coverless john. He's smart but a loner, doing time for kicking his wife to death in a drunken stupor. He didn't mean to, but he was crazy. Is crazy. He fidgets, screams, sometimes has visions. Last year he threw a homemade cocktail in the dining room with the vague notion of getting out. The screws were the first to run because they're targets, and the alarm went off. A couple of scores were evened: Danny Pina was stabbed with the shard of a plastic plate, and Booker Conrad, who on the outside raped an eleven-year-old girl, got slugged senseless, but nothing really happened. In all the running and yelling, Whitcomb just stood there, and he ended up with nine months in the Plant. That was when they started him on pills.

James C. Enoch is making out fine, reading a sci-fi thriller. He's below Whitcomb on the next tier, a little left. Maybe he had advance word and he bought a stash. There are preferences. So maybe he will sell to Whitcomb and Whitcomb will be all right. Maybe not.

Nothing means anything to me. I'm the nonobserver. All the rules. Do what they say. No ripples. I've done three years of a five-to-seven cheap shot, so I get along. When something happens I turn my back so no one catches me looking. I haven't seen anything. If someone asks a favor, fine. I kept the peek for Bellinger in the cell beside me because he has a lot of friends. And he paid me plenty to stand on the rail and watch for screws and listen to the moans. Lovers and ex-lovers. It didn't affect me one way or the other when Garland short-circuited Bellinger's cell door and torched him.

I don't like it when the routine gets broken. The screws are holding us longer than usual for free time, and I'm ready to go paint. Education, reading for the blind, Christian Action—all for parole, chess and TV, painting and woodworking. Stay busy. Whitcomb paces around. I can see he needs it.

On the left side of me, opposite where Bellinger was, Iron Balls is talking to himself loud and clear about nothing. I don't listen to the nonsense anymore, don't even hear it. He's like a radio announcer in the background. The story is that six years ago he tried to go out in a heavy fog and got to the top of the wall. He had sneaked across twenty yards of asphalt, hooked the top of the wall and scaled twenty feet, and was just straddling the electric wire when a tower guard threw the switch. Iron Balls: the juice scorched his scrotum and threw him over for a few seconds of freedom.

Someone yells "open the fucking doors!" and a chant starts up. The noise of voices and the clattering of cans on bars rises until the block is bedlam, and a screw gets on the loudspeaker and cools it off with the threat of no free time at all.

Why does the warden cut off the pills? It doesn't matter to me.

I've stayed away from whatever might make me vulnerable, whatever might give me more time. Maybe he wants to show a state senator that the department needs more money. Or the screws once in a while want some action, a chance to break heads. Or the sadistic side: to make some of us suffer, to make deals, to show power, to harass. Maybe it's a way of beating the natural cycle and get the upper side of violence, so that after the storm, things will be calmer.

The doors slide open electronically. There's a shout about nothing, almost a furor, and everyone goes out. I get to the bottom of the stairs and wait in line for my pass. Whitcomb is behind me, a slight man with a shy smile, dark red hair, a young-looking thirty. If you saw him in a park, you'd never think he was capable of killing his wife. He looks at me, and I read his question, so I turn away.

"Henschel," he says, calling me.

I nod and say hello. Sometimes he goes with me to art; before the pills he went to basketball. Once in a while he tries chapel. Nothing helps him, and he never sticks with anything long enough to get good. Tonight he says he's going to the hospital.

"I need help," he says.

"I haven't got a button or a dime," I tell him. I try to take any hint of sympathy from my voice.

Along the line there is con talk: cheers teers meers beers. The screw, Dolan, looks up and pretends to understand. Someone wants coffee, is all.

Booker Conrad walks by on his way to play checkers, and Whitcomb grabs him. He hangs on close, terrorizing Conrad, and asking him for a hit.

"Cut it," Dolan shouts.

But Whitcomb holds on, and the two men dance like exhausted fighters.

"He doesn't have anything," I tell Whitcomb.

Whitcomb stares at me and lets go.

Dolan gets up and measures Whitcomb, but I stand between them. Other men pressure Dolan to get the line moving.

Whitcomb takes my interference as a sign of aid and leans closer. "Listen, down in avocation you'll see Muhammad."

"He's in woodworking," I say. "If he goes."

"So it's across the hall. You can get over there."

We move up and Dolan has my pass ready. He gives it to me, and I pass the desk. But he stops Whitcomb.

"Not tonight, hot stuff," Dolan needles lightly. "You stay in the block where we can watch you."

I don't even turn to see Whitcomb's face, and I blot out the argument and Whitcomb's pleading voice. I walk up the immaculate corridor, take a right, and descend the steps to the cellar.

What a studio for painting! A low ceiling, ducts and pipes, a couple of sixty-watt light bulbs. An afterthought of a riot. Tonight is particularly stifling—airless and hot. But I can live through anything. If I were serious about my work, it might be different; I might complain. But I don't pretend to have talent. My sense of proportion is awkward and my eye for colors has become exaggerated. My reds are too bright, blues too brilliant. At first I came here to get away, but I've grown to like the rumbling of the heating ducts, the clicking of expanding metal, the shaking of the gym floor overhead as the men run their half-court game. I have given up painting for design, simple arrangements which can be measured with a compass, a protractor, and a straightedge.

Fair. No one said anything about fair. I get left alone while Whitcomb gets hassled. Fresno Gagliardi gets raped because he doesn't know enough to cover his every move. Iron Balls belongs on the Ranch, not here. You have to deal with things as they are.

I give my pass to the screw in the hall, get out my apron, pencils, and set up the drawing board. Like anything, the more I practice, the more complex things become. I silk-screened for a while, but when material got expensive, I slid back to something easier.

Muhammad saunters past in the hall, smiling. He's fine, high, a friendly john with the pity of a cobra. Seeing him suddenly makes me uneasy, as if it's not safe to be in the cellar on a night like this. I think of Whitcomb and James C. Enoch, but it's none of my business.

For twenty minutes I hold on to this feeling. The room seems to grow hotter, and I sense those clouds, which I cannot see, moving slowly toward me. I can't think. The design I've started, a hexagon repeated three times with varying shades of red, suddenly means nothing to me.

Finally I get up and put things away. I cash my pass, claiming I don't feel well, and head back to the block.

At first glance, everything seems calm. The games of dominoes and betting are under way; Ordway and Julio Cruz are playing chess. The television is blaring, and several men lounge upon metal folding chairs, staring at Suzanne Sommers in a garish comedy. No one laughs.

"You back?" Dolan asks.

"Where's Whitcomb?"

Dolan points toward the corner where Whitcomb is walking away from James C. Enoch. For a moment I am relieved, and I hesitate, giving Dolan a chance to chat.

"You know something, Henschel?"

I crack a smile. "Never."

"You're a smart one, ain't you?"

I nod. "Very smart," I tell him. "But not tonight. I have a headache."

I start toward the stairs and Whitcomb sees me and comes over. "You see Muhammad?" he asks almost without breath, as though he has been running.

I shake my head. His eyes are pinwheels, screaming at me. "What about James C.?"

"He says no."

"No?"

"He has it but won't sell."

I do not ask the reason. Either he has customers he's promised, or he's waiting for men like Whitcomb to get desperate so he can raise the price. But I'm not the one in trouble, so why do I feel anything? Whitcomb is not worth the worry.

Yet I feel that edge, just for a moment, long enough for me to recognize that it's the same helplessness I felt on the outside: that something ought to be done, something had to be done, that I was watching myself waste away like a piece of sand sculpture in rain.

But the feeling does not last. "I'm sorry," I tell Whitcomb.

Whitcomb turns away abruptly, and I climb the stairs and walk along the tier railing toward my cell. Iron Balls sits with his head in his hands, still gabbling to himself, clutching his hair as if to pull it out. He looks up at me as I pass.

The cell is open, but I pause at the rail and gaze over the block. James C. Enoch is kibitzing for Julio Cruz at the chess game near the wall, and Ordway complains. Cruz moves. There is some joke.

This clean place, safe from the outside, is taut, as if this one moment were suspended from a weak thread. I feel each second is about to happen, that time is freezing slowly, and I am trapped beneath the ice.

Whitcomb moves nonchalantly toward the chess game, another figure in blue denim, wiry, red hair against gray wall. A few others may have followed Whitcomb, too, but if they have they are not watching him now. Dolan is talking idly with another screw. I know I should do something, yell, but I can't. I should look away, so as not to be a witness, but instead I hold tight to the rail and lean forward. Whitcomb nears the game and takes a piece of pipe from under his shirt. With only a slight hesitation to make certain of his grip, he raises the pipe over his head and takes two long strides. Enoch turns, but too late, and Whitcomb smashes the pipe into the side of Enoch's head.

Enoch crashes through the chess game and pieces go flying. Cruz topples over backward from his chair; Ordway jumps away. James C. Enoch raises himself on his hands and knees, his face already bloody, too bright, and he crawls unsteadily for a few feet as though searching for something on the floor. No one looks at him or tries to help. Whitcomb moves forward and begins to scratch through Enoch's pockets.

Then all at once there is running and screaming. Two men grab Dolan while others wedge the desk into the door so the door cannot be closed from Control. The other screw runs into the hall, and the siren goes off. Dolan tries to get away, but someone hits him with a metal folding chair. The next block erupts, too.

In this frenzy Enoch has collapsed on the floor. Whitcomb stands a few feet away against the gray wall, calmer now, knowing he will be okay.

I turn and go into my cell. From beneath the mattress I take out a file I have shaved into a knife in case I have an enemy I do not know about.

Tomorrow pills will be available again at the hospital. Maybe there will be a day's lock-up to cool things off, but the routine will start up smoothly in a couple of days. I take a deep breath and sit down on my bed and wait.

PRO WARS

by Jay Neugeboren

The reporters waited in the lobby of the hospital, listening to the Yankee game. The day was broiling and most of them had their jackets and ties off. There were only a half-dozen of them—including three who had flown up specifically for the news conference—but in another three weeks, when the baseball season moved into the homestretch and the football exhibitions were in full swing, there would be more. They sipped cold drinks and smoked and talked shop—about what had happened, about what it meant for the team's chances.

"Still," one of them said, "he made good copy. You've got to admit that."

"More trouble than he was worth, Frank. You ask me, Ralph is getting off easy, getting rid of the kid this way. He was trouble from the word go. Hell, Ralph's lucky the kid never busted *him* up!"

Then they talked about the kid, about how he had been an all-American three years running—probably the best linebacker to come out of the Big Ten in a decade. They recounted the familiar anecdotes—how he had been kicked off the team just before the Rose Bowl for slugging the coach; how he had held out for the biggest bonus ever paid to a rookie defensive player; how he had reported to camp late; how he had refused to attend game movies, to tape his ankles, to follow the team's conditioning program.

"I asked him about that," Frank said, "and you know what his answer was? He said, 'You tell the coach I been getting in shape my own way ever since I put on cleats and that if he don't think that's good enough I'll take on any guy on the team who thinks he's in better shape.'" The reporter laughed. "He nearly did it, too—took 'em all on, I mean. How many guys he fight with, Mel?"

"Who knows?" Ralph always hushed it up quick—but I'd say six or seven at least." Mel winked. "And that doesn't count reporters." The men laughed. "I wrote up once about how they couldn't find a football helmet his size in camp and the next day he comes up to me with the column in his hand, asks me what I meant. He would have blasted me good if some of the other boys didn't grab him around." Mel blew air through his lips and tapped his cigar on an ashtray. "I'll tell you, though, he's got as much raw power as any man in the league right now. I don't care who you name—Brown, Marchetti, Ditka—" He stopped. "Who knows? Maybe Mike taught him a lesson this time. Maybe if he sits out a season he'll grow up a little. But I doubt it."

When they were let into the hospital room a few minutes later, the kid was in bed, grinning. Ralph Neelson, the team's general manager, nodded toward the doctor. The doctor looked at his clipboard and spoke: "Yes," he said. "Thank you, Ralph. This is what I can tell you. The patient sustained a severe varus injury of the knee, resulting in a complete tear of the fibula collateral ligament, an avulsion of the iliotibial tract, and a severe contusion and stretching of the common peroneal nerve with probable permanent damage."

The doctor looked up. The reporters laughed. "C'mon, Doc—in English—"

The doctor smiled. "The patient has what we call a dropped foot—actually his knee, which was struck on the inside—that's the only way this kind of injury could occur. His knee will be fine, but due to the stretching of the nerve, he won't ever be able to lift his ankle."

"For how long?"

The doctor wet his lips and looked toward the bed, where the kid sat, suntanned and huge under the white sheets, staring at the reporters. "For good," the doctor said. The reporters stirred. They looked at the kid's face for some show of emotion. The kid stared back at them, showing nothing. "The operation was successful, as these things go, and we'll take the cast off in about three months, then fit the leg with a brace that will enable it to be used quite normally—as well as you and I use ours—but as for his ever playing football again, I'd say it's out of the question."

"That's tough, kid," one of the reporters said. "Real tough."

"Yeah," the kid said, and turned his head sideways and spat.

"How do you think this affects your chances this year, Ralph? You were counting on him, weren't you?"

The general manager leaned back against the railing of the bed. "We thought he would help us, sure—we won't deny that," he said.

"But we still have Mike, remember. We felt the kid would have given us a lot of depth at linebacker. As you know, we went all-out to get him away from the other league. You tell the fans that. We gave the kid a bonus in excess of two hundred grand, and we're not sorry, even though things have turned out the way they have. We'd do it again, too, because our only aim is to bring the best football we can to the people who back us. Got that?" He paused and wiped perspiration from his forehead. The room was quiet. "As for the coming season, like I said before, we still have Mike here, who's been on the all-pro team seven of the last eight seasons, remember. And I'll tell you something else—I don't care what you've been writing—Mike was going to be our middle linebacker opening day against the Bears. The kid hadn't taken his place. Not yet. What we were really planning to do," he went on, moving forward a step, "—no reason not to tell you this now—was to switch the kid to an outside linebacker position, where his speed would have done us more good. We lose a little bit without the kid—depth mostly—but, remember this, we're essentially the same team that went to the playoffs last year and we've shelled out a lot of hard cash for a lot of young blood besides the kid here. You tell the fans we're confident we'll make it again." He glanced quickly toward the kid, then smiled. "Now, how about a few pictures—maybe bring the nurse in, you know—"

"You don't get off so easy, Ralph," Frank said, tapping his pad with the rubber end of his pencil.

"How's that?"

"What's the lowdown on how the kid got busted up? Most of us heard something about a fight between him and Mike. Everybody knows it's been brewing since the first day the kid hit camp. Any comment?"

Ralph turned to the bed. The kid shifted, throwing off the sheet and revealing the new white plaster cast that encased his leg from knee to foot. He scratched himself just above the knee, where the cast began. "Glad you asked that," Ralph said. "I really am, guys. We want the fans to get this straight. But maybe the kid here is the best one to tell you about it—"

"Yeah," the kid said. He bit off the end of a cigar, lit it and drew in until the tip glowed. He puffed smoke toward the ceiling, then spoke quickly, evenly. "There wasn't any fight, okay? Yeah. Me and Mike were just horsing around, letting off a little steam. We stopped by this bar, see, so Mike could call home to his wife and kids and then we had a couple beers and got to horsing around. That's all."

"What kind of horsing around?"

The kid looked straight at the reporter. "Mike here was like a father to me, see? All through training camp he took me under his wing, see? Sure. He was the best friend I had on the team, always willing to help a youngster like me learn the tricks of the trade. Taught me more than all the coaches I ever had, high school or college." He blew a smoke ring toward the ceiling. "So, like I say, we were in this bar and we got to talking about plays and we pushed a few tables aside so he could show me how to make this move for piling up an off-tackle slant, and while we were horsing around I slipped in some stuff somebody must of spilled. Okay?"

"That's the story, guys," Ralph said, moving toward the reporters. "Now, how about some pictures of the kid and Mike shaking hands? . . ."

When the reporters had asked a few more questions, and taken some pictures, they left. Mike stayed behind.

"I wanted to tell you I'm real sorry about how things turned out," he said.

"Sure." The kid laughed. "How much is Ralph giving you to be sorry?"

"Nothing. He didn't even know I was coming here. I did it on my own."

"Bull."

"You don't have to believe me."

The kid looked away, across the hospital room to the trees outside the window. "That was a lot of crap Ralph gave out about me moving to outside linebacker. You know that, don't you?"

"Maybe."

"Sure. You're over the hill, buddy. Like I said when I got to camp the first day, they should of called it the old-age home." He laughed at his own words, pleased. The nurse entered and said the kid should be resting. She asked Mike to leave. Mike stopped by the bed. His skin was tanned a deep brown and the leatherlike folds of his neck bulged from the white collar of his dress shirt. He looked very unnatural in suit and tie. "The nurse said you can go. What are you waiting for?"

"Thanks for not saying anything," Mike said.

"About what?"

"You know." He paused. "Or did Ralph pay you off for that too?"

"That's my business."

"You're real tough, aren't you? Still."

"I'll get along."

"With the brace?"

"With the brace or without it." He laughed. "Listen—I'll tell you something. I got no regrets, me. No grudges. The way my lawyer worked out that bonus, I'm set up for the rest of my life—go back home and open up a bowling alley or maybe a big bar and restaurant, be able to get all the tail I want, see?"

"Sure."

"You think I loved the game? Shit, you got to be crazy to love this game. But I did okay. Now I can take my bag of money and get out of here. Yeah. I'll see you on TV, Mike—"

"And wish you were playing?"

"Nah." He sat up. "You don't believe me, do you? I swear to God I ain't gonna miss it. With all that money? I'd have to be nuts! You go bust your chops every week—and for what? Fifteen, twenty grand a year? Hell, I made more already than you'll make if you play another five years, and I ain't even played in a regular game once. I played it smart." He chewed on the inside of his mouth, and nodded. "Yeah. I could of had a bonus to play baseball, too, you know that? But I figured with the NFL and the AFL fighting each other now, you got to take advantage. I'm telling you, the way I got the contract worked out, I'm set for life." He looked up. Mike didn't say anything. "Another year or two they'll get smart, start some kind of draft together the way baseball did, so they don't have to shell out so much. You'll see. But me, I was born at the right time, I guess. You didn't have it so good when you come into the league, did you?"

"No."

"Tell me something, Mike—I mean, what do you got to lose? I heard they were gonna trade you 'cause of me."

"Maybe."

"C'mon, tell me—what's the difference now? I did you a favor, didn't I—keeping that stuff out of the papers." He shook his head. "You better watch yourself, an old man like you going after stuff like that. Jailbait. You gonna do it, see, you got to keep quiet about it—not get into fights with guys—" The kid watched Mike open and close his fists. "No hard feelings. I mean, I didn't own or anything— still, you want the truth, she wasn't worth it. A real two-bit bitch, you know what I mean? Small-town trash." He smiled slowly. "What made a guy like you do it? You really go for that young stuff, or did—?"

"They were thinking of trading me," Mike said. "We need a good flanker back—and you had the goods."

The kid sat back, then grinned and cracked his fist into the palm of his hand sharply. "I knew it," he said. "I knew it. Like they say in the papers, I'm a real hungry ballplayer, right?"

"You're not hungry," Mike said. "You're mean." He said it flatly. "You mean to be mean."

The kid laughed. "Maybe," he said. He stretched his arms sideways, as if yawning, and looked out of the window. "Beautiful day, huh? Weather sure has been nice. Jesus, I'd love to be down at the beach today. I'll tell you something, though—it worked out okay, you know what I mean?"

"No."

"I mean I got what I want and you got what you want. You got to stay with the team. I mean, an old-timer like you having to switch teams at your age—move your family to some new city—it ain't easy. I really feel for you."

"I didn't do it on purpose, that's all," Mike said. "I wanted you to know."

"Jesus!" the kid said. "I know that—what you think I been saying? We had a good fight, you and me, and I got a little careless. Must of been standing flatfooted with the leg flexed for that to have happened—too many beers—but what's the difference? Sure. I got what I want and you got what you want. You don't got to worry, though. You still hit hard."

"Still, I want you to know it wasn't on purpose. I didn't mean to do this to you."

"Sure—hell, rather have it happen this way than get carried off the field with the whole stadium clapping their asses off. You watch out on those cold days this year, Mike. Your bones, they're not so young no more. Those cold days, you can crack anything."

The nurse came into the room again. "I got to be going," Mike said. "I'll give your regards to the guys—"

"Sure," the kid said, then laughed. "You do that." The nurse smiled at the two of them. "I got a pretty good deal here, huh? Hey, nurse—c'mere a minute—"

The nurse approached the bed. When she was almost there the kid raised himself onto his elbows, then suddenly, with a swiftness that made Mike blink, he darted sideways, snatched the nurse around the waist, and pulled her to him. She struggled to get away, appealing to Mike, asking him to help. Mike hesitated at the door. "Ah, don't listen to her," the kid said. "She loves it, don't you, babe?" He held her to him fiercely, and laughed, the cigar stuck in the corner of his mouth. "Don't you?" She blushed and pushed at the kid, but not, Mike could tell, as hard as she might have. Mike opened the door. "Have a good season," the kid called. "Yeah. And don't get hurt now, you hear me?"

MEMORY LOSS

by Charlotte Painter

I was stepping out of some too-tight slacks, surrounded by merciless images of myself in the fitting-room wall mirrors, when a young woman came in and said, "Ms. Harris, how nice to see you."

I didn't recognize her. I said, "Hi there," a shade too brightly.

She piled some things on the bench next to me, placed a few dresses on a hook above. An attendant was hanging garments on a moving conveyance for return to the outside racks. Otherwise, we had the huge dressing room to ourselves.

The merest glimmer of memory stirred, not strong enough to light up her name. Tall and slender, an animated face, high-heeled sandals. Who *is* she? I wondered. A friend of my son's? A former student? She was chattering, anticipating responses. "I love Loehmann's, don't you?"

I looked in the mirror. Only at Loehmann's could I see myself so clearly, in this open try-on room, where all four mirrored walls pressed at me with evidence of lumps and bulges, my belly spilling over, my legs nubbed with veins down to my nylon ankle stockings, a dumpy, middle-aged bargain hunter. I did not love Loehmann's.

The price tag of the slacks I was taking off snagged my ankle stockings and I staggered getting free.

"I come here once a week," the girl was saying, "to see what new designer seconds have come in. I haven't seen you in *ages*." The attendant took the slacks from me and hung them on her return rack.

"I know," I acknowledged. This was just one of many recent lapses—a faintly familiar face, an exchange of pleasantries, while I teetered over a chasm of memory loss. "How have you been?" I asked.

"Wonderful." The mirror drew her eyes. She smoothed an eyebrow with her forefinger, then gazed at my image in the mirror. "You're looking great."

I realized I was hiding behind a garment I had taken from its hanger. "I've got to lose ten pounds. My figure's a disgrace."

She clapped herself on the behind. "Look at this fat fanny." She slipped a yellow skirt over her head.

"You look much thinner," I guessed. Always a welcome compliment.

I would have asked her name but on an earlier occasion I did ask and made matters worse. A young woman I couldn't place had stopped me on the street. "Jane," she said. "I'm Jane." I widened my eyes at the sidewalk, where her name froze like a carving on soft cement. I said, "Oh, Jane, I feel so stupid," and waved myself away. Another time I was leaving a movie with my teenage son and his girl friend, before the second feature, a Marx Brothers movie. A young woman waiting in line grabbed my hand, reached out and startlingly kissed my cheek. "Marian, it's been so *long*." Too long. I smiled and wrung her hand, grateful for the darkness outside the theater. This young woman had come out into the night alone to see *Duck Soup*. Who would do that? An irretrievable film buff? Someone suicidally depressed? Fortunately, my son and his girl friend had walked ahead and I could wave myself away with: "Imagine bumping into you at the movies."

And now this—caught in ankle cheaters. All three encounters with women, young women. Did that mean something? Maybe I had reached an age when all young women look alike the way old ladies used to.

The girl was admiring herself in the skirt, a yellow print that she zipped up to her narrow waist. Underneath she had on a navy blue leotard she had worn into the store under jeans. This skirt would help her image-change, she said; she thought she'd buy it. "You remember my *classic* Radcliffe clothes. Style was anathema to me."

A graduate student then? Or a transfer? How long ago in Radcliffe? I reflected that if I waited, said nothing, she might fully reveal herself. As she turned to see how the skirt flared, her movement stirred in the mirrors around the room. She was engaging, really, had such a candid face.

She asked, "I've improved a bit, though, don't you think?" She leaned toward the mirror as if for an answer.

"Of course," I assured her. It was safe enough. She was twenty-five or -six, the age when young women always improve. But who *was* she?

"I'm doing a lot of pictures nowadays. Have a tech job in the photography lab. Just a few hours a week. I get to use the dark-room in my spare time."

Photography. Something was trying to melt out of my frozen memory cells. I pulled on another pair of slacks. These had an elastic waistband and might not bind so badly in the waist. Would anything but a robe ever be comfortable again?

"And then on weekends I have a waitress job that pays a lot in tips. At Pier 14. Very expensive." All right, I thought, she'd have to have been an English major. Some of the best waitresses in the city had been English majors.

"I get over to your building now and then," she said, "because—oh, you probably know him—" and she named a man, a T.A. in the department. She said, "We live together now. He's my new honey."

Suddenly the girl's story broke loose, turning my mind into a hive.

She was Natalie Bunsen. She had come west four years ago after painful experiences in Boston. She had told me everything, had written it for me when she was my student. As a teenager she had a breakdown. This came about after her mother's second marriage, to a man of wealth who tried to seduce Natalie. She hadn't used that old-fashioned term, though. She said he tried to get her to make it with him and when she refused he raped her repeatedly. Finally she told her mother what was going on; her mother's response was to commit Natalie to a private sanitorium and take a trip to Europe with the man. Over the next two years the sanitorium gave Natalie a series of shock treatments. Other women inmates comforted her, she said, kept her alive. She came out of the experience a lesbian and moved to the Coast. When she took my comp course, her hair was cropped straight and she must have weighed thirty pounds more.

Natalie pulled on another garment, a print dress with tiny blue flowers and tinier buttons. Not at all a dress she would have worn before. "It's a Cacharel," she said. "My mother used to buy things like this for me. Maybe I can come 'round to this sort of thing again."

A few other customers had come into the dressing room. Reflections of women stirred in the mirrors, undressing, pulling garments over their heads, setting them aside, murmuring to one another.

"How do I look in this? Is it too frilly?" A dark, saturnine woman about my age, who also wore ankle cheaters, had turned to us. "I had a color-style analysis, and they told me to wear pink ruffles." She tugged at a polyester knit with a pink ruff around the neck. I felt helpless. "I'm no judge," I said. But Natalie moved toward her, straightened the jacket. "No," she said, "the fabric's wrong. But they're right about the ruffles." I was touched by this charity. The woman snatched the dress off. "Thank heaven you're here. I'll be right back," she said, zipping up her own dress.

"Do you know her?" I asked.

"Not that I know of." Natalie laughed.

Her lively eyes turned reflective. She said, "I read that book you gave me so many times. Countless times."

What book? I betrayed my confusion. Natalie said, "Oh, I imagine you've forgotten. You can't remember every book you give a student, I'm sure. But it was so important to me. *The Yellow Wallpaper*."

Then I remembered the rest of Natalie's story. She came to visit me in my office. She couldn't do the assignment, she said, which was to write of a childhood experience. The class was all women, quite by chance, and so I had assigned only women's essays and stories. A warm generosity pervaded the group, and many of the women became good friends. "I love this class," said Natalie. "I want to do this paper in the worst way." But her childhood was a blank. She felt disconnected from her past as a result of her treatment at the hospital. I suggested ways she might get at the problem. As we talked, Natalie leafed through a copy of *The Yellow Wallpaper* by Charlotte Perkins Gilman which lay on my desk. It was an extra copy and so I told her to take it, to keep it.

She came back to the office a few days later and said that reading the story of another woman's dissociation had helped her accept what she'd been through. She began to remember things, to piece together her past. The rest of the term she wrote of the hospital experiences.

We had a party at the end of the term, where she told me of a plan. She wanted to take pictures of all the women who had helped her. She would make a personal narrative book, with a picture to accompany stories of women she wanted to acknowledge. "Women taught me to live again," she said. She even had a publisher for it, a women's press. I'd like to take your picture for it," she said. "Your giving me *The Yellow Wallpaper*—I never realized before how a book can change a life."

I had stalled. I didn't want Natalie to take my picture for a reason I don't like to admit. I was afraid I might be the only straight woman in the book. It was one thing to accept the sexual preferences of others but something else to be pegged mistakenly, I told myself. Like getting credit for Greek when my elective was romance languages.

Natalie apparently understood my evasion and didn't call about the picture. She didn't come to see me either. We hadn't met again until today, when she had transformed herself into this attractive young woman who lived with a man she called her "new honey."

She sat down on the bench with her back to the mirror, looking up at me with a soft earnestness. "I had forgotten everything, remember? Until you helped me."

I felt a rush of emotion, stammered a denial. "You did it yourself, you know." My own memory failure seemed so trivial compared to what Natalie had been through. Yet it wasn't trivial; to forget was terrible. I tried to think of my lapses as absurdities. I had never told anyone of them. I glimpsed myself now, all lumps and veins and nylon ankle stockings. Maybe Natalie would like my picture like this—"Forgetful Lady."

As if reading my mind, she said, "You told me that everybody tends to backslide into forgetfulness."

"I did?"

"Knowledge is a spiral, and sometimes it turns, eclipses, and when it spirals back around we have to relearn on a deeper level what we knew before. I'm *quoting* you."

I glimpsed my face in the mirror; it was flushed, blotched. Sweat had broken out on my nose.

Images of other women in their underthings moved in the mirror. None of the women in the dressing room had figures like Natalie's, I realized. Some were scrawny, most were at least as lumpy as I. They wore bras that did not uplift, stockings that left red bands at their thighs or waists, shoes that pinched. The woman nearest us had taken off some high-heeled boots; the great toe folded over her others, permanently displaced by tight shoes. These women had riffled through the racks outside, had come into this mutual space with the fruits of their efforts and were trying on something that might enhance their lives, help them to beauty, grace. They spoke to one another, asking opinions about garments. They offered reassurance, solicitude, encouragement.

Suddenly I sat beside Natalie on the bench, groping for Kleenex. To my disgust, I was about to cry. Natalie knelt down as if in supplication, speaking softly, elatedly. "You're going through menopause, aren't you? I hope you're not embarrassed. I mean this is one of the real things women go through, after all. I'll be there before I know it, and can't help wondering what it's like."

I had to laugh. "Don't be in a hurry."

"What I'm trying to say is, *only* women can know anything about a hot flash, for instance. I mean *really*."

I blew my nose. I myself called those surges in temperature that burned up my interest in life simply "flashes." The "hot" part seemed an ultimate humiliation, an aspersion on failed sexuality. Maybe I was also trying to endow the flash with mysticism—a flash, a charge of insight, a revelation. But if it was that, I somehow kept missing the point. Or ducking it. *Duck Soup*. Now I had the name of the young woman going into the movie. Eleanor Barrett, a music student, Nate Barrett's daughter. She was writing a paper about the piano of Chico Marx.

I laughed. Suddenly I was telling Natalie all about it, that I had forgotten not only giving her the book but had at first forgotten who she was, had trouble remembering everything these days, would get into my car and forget where I was going, go to the store and not know what I meant to buy, start a lecture and after a few remarks have to stop to recall the subject. And Natalie was writing down the name of a wiz of an older woman doctor who had been through it all and was saying, "I mean I always think of what you said—you have to try everything, even if it's hard to keep challenging yourself. *You* said that to me."

I shook my head. "I don't remember." Natalie laughed.

As we were getting ready to leave, Natalie said, "I had a lovely dream after that course. I had to go back to the psych ward because they had only let me out on leave. And when I got there, the place was gone. It didn't even exist anymore."

Our gazes crossed and rested on each other's image. "Thank you, Natalie," I said.

The dark woman came back with more ruffles. "What about this one?" she asked Natalie. It was a blouse of the same colors, black and pink, but the fabric was silk.

"Much better," said Natalie. "Let's see how it looks on you."

The woman dived into it. As her head came through the neck opening, she said, "I know one woman who had a color-style analysis, and she's seeing altogether different people now. The right combination can change your life."

"You better believe it," said Natalie.

A HAPPY WOMAN

by Molly Peacock

I am a happy woman. Let me tell you about me. Something happened in my life to make me happy. It happened when I was a child. Have you heard about out-of-body experiences? I don't think they are so unusual. It means only that you separate your mind from your body. I think we all do that. Haven't you heard people say all your life, "Try to take your mind off your troubles"?

When I was about ten, I used to like to ride my bike. I felt free with the wind all around me. One time after dinner I rolled to a stop at a stop sign a few blocks away from my house. It was summer and there was no school, so I was on my way to what was left of a farmer's woods at the edge of the surburban development my family lived in. The sun was setting. Time had slowed down, down, down, until it seemed as though I were in the middle of one of those silences that would fall between my parents and me whenever I asked a question. It seemed I was waiting interminably for a station wagon to crawl across the intersection of Ogden and Floradale roads. I was so impatient!

I could hardly contain myself, so I began to roll my eyes in their sockets, leaning my spine against my bicycle seat. I looked up and saw the sun setting. It was then that I saw heaven. The sun was a magenta ball disappearing behind a bank of clouds. A peninsula of clouds broke off from the main bank to become an island, completely hiding the sun. The island of clouds was a streaky magenta, like watered silk. I saw that it had trees, a lake, and celestial rocks. I saw that it was just waiting to be inhabited. It seemed I climbed higher and higher toward it in my mind, though I was still standing with my bike at the stop sign. Far below me the station wagon inched across the intersection. The clouds had begun to move, or the sun behind had begun to move, for the magenta had become purple, regal, and the cloud had cleared a field through its trees. It was waiting to receive God. Soon the purple clouds were edged with gold by the moving sun and then, as I watched, rays of gold emanated from beneath the clearing in the clouds, rays that must have come from beneath the fingernails of God. Tendons of light raked across the sky, just as a godlike claw must have raked the earth to form the Finger Lakes I lived on then, and now live on.

I had seen heaven and I knew it for sure. The clouds were too big, wild, and unmoving to be only water and air clouds. I believed in science and God and I knew that God had allowed the barometric conditions conducive to the revelation of heaven to occur. The television stations might even interrupt their regular programming to announce it.

If I went home, it might even be on the news. And I could show both my parents if I hurried home, and I knew I had to hurry because God would not reveal his home forever. What surprised me as I pedaled back up Floradale looking frequently over my shoulder and up at the sky was that the heaven I saw did not move, did not move at all, and was with me just as the star of Bethlehem was with the shepherds who found Christ. I was happy. This is what, as a child, made me happy.

It is not what makes me happy as a woman. What makes a child's happiness will never make an adult's, no matter how childish the adult is. I tipped my bicycle over in the driveway but did not bang it against the concrete. I came into the house quickly and silently, for there were no lights on in the house, although our car was in the garage. The sun was setting in earnest now, in its last leap toward the horizon. My heaven had changed radically, but there were strong, clear remnants of the rays of God's fingers in the sky. It was dusk and all the other houses had lights on except ours. So even though I was breathless, I was quiet because clearly something was wrong. I closed the screen door softly and crossed into the living room where I saw what was wrong immediately. I also saw that it was ordinary.

My father lay on the couch, passed out and snoring. The television was on with the sound turned imperceptibly low. His arm hung off the couch and his head lolled. He was drunk. I stood in front of him, trying to catch my breath. I had seen heaven and I was sure he would want to know. His stomach inflated, then deflated, with his moist, mucusy breathing. I turned toward the TV and saw that it was tuned to a regularly scheduled situation comedy. I waited for the small white letters that announced special news items to move across the screen, but they did not. My father was unconscious and heaven was not being announced.

I walked through the living room, through the darkened hall, and into the kitchen, which was also dark. I was looking for my mother, to tell her I had seen heaven. I heard, from outside, the scrape of a metal lawn chair across cement. When I went to the back screen door I saw my mother, illumined by her cigarette, staring into the blackened yard. The sun had set and God had withdrawn his revelation. A deep disappointment settled into me as the night air from the lake settled into the house. I stared at my mother's back in the metal chair and stared at the nearly immobile features of her stiff face. She held her head at an angle. Her profile lit up when she dragged on her cigarette. Although she was preoccupied, she was awake. I might have been able to stage a bold enough introduction to what I saw so she would not just nod or send me on an errand—more than likely to fetch my younger sister from the elementary school playground nearby—but I might not.

Instead of trying, I walked back to the murmuring television set and my motionless father. I waited for a while, but I must have missed the announcement of the discovery of heaven. I was swelling with my news and about to burst. I had to tell someone, yet I did not try again to wake my father or interrupt the vigil of my mother. My sister was both absent and too young. The news of heaven was dilating my veins as if I were a maple tree in a cold month, engorging with sap. As the sap runs to the branch tips, so I let the vision rush to my head. It swelled my head and became a form of conceit. Although I stood in the living room, I *saw* the house with my father and my mother from *above*, as if the roof were removed, though of course it was not, and I stood next to my father, who surprised me by waking up. It was my chance, but I did not take it. I did not say, "I saw heaven!" Instead I went to my room.

Keeping a secret does not mean a secret happiness. I was not happy then, for I was lonely. But my loneliness as a child became my happiness as a woman, and this is how it occurred. Years later my father died from a stroke and diabetes. My mother removed herself to the mountains where she herself had grown up. She now lives her life in a remote house without a telephone. My sister is interred in her fourth alcoholic treatment center. I alone still live in the Finger Lakes. I am director of financial aid at a large university. I live with my husband, Eduardo Bonmartini, an engineer whom I met when he pinched me as I bent to retrieve a package in the lobby of a bank in Neuchatel, Switzerland. My sister, who was drying out at the time of our wedding, did not bother to send regrets, but my mother sent a note that she hoped I would understand how it was, that her social security check was small and fuel was high, and that she could not afford to come down off her mountain for my wedding. Besides, I was nearly thirty-eight years old. I just had time to send her a check, but I did not because I could not afford the despair I would have felt had she found another reason not to come.

I told Eduardo in a hotel room on Lake Neuchatel that I saw heaven. He was not the first person I told. Many of my friends know that I thought I saw heaven, and when I was younger I always told, ceremoniously, each of my lovers. Recently I told a woman I think might become my friend. Each time in my life that I have told someone, I have shed a little of my loneliness. As I grew older and told more people, I accrued happiness as a sort of interest on the capital of my loneliness.

When grammar school opened again after that summer, they took us downtown to visit a grand ornate bank as part of our weekly savings program. Because I was bored during the tour, I craned my neck all the way back to look straight into the bank's gilt dome. It was a little like looking into heaven, only almost reversed, the way looking into a glass paperweight to watch the snow come down is almost the reverse of looking into a real storm. The gold dome didn't really look like heaven; it only reminded me of it. But from then on I liked the gilded, cathedrallike interiors of old banks, and I still choose them for my business when I can.

Little bitty versions of the overwhelming almost always make me grin, for instance, a one-inch-square map of the world in a doll-house. When I clattered across the floor of the bank in Neuchatel, then stood in line to wait to cash my check, leaning back out of boredom to inspect the gold dome, I grinned so wide, I started to laugh. That made me a little unbalanced and I dropped my package, because the dome is not only gold leaf but contains little raised clouds in bas relief, just like a caricature of my heaven. When I bent over to retrieve my package and Eduardo pinched me, I swore at him in English with a wicked grin on my face.

Eduardo also loved the bank, for different reasons. He was the engineer who planned the conversion of the bank's garden cloister into more offices. I waited to tell Eduardo the story of my heaven until the middle of a blue, blue afternoon. My hotel windows were open to the lake and we lay in bed talking. Eduardo was restless and almost homeless because he had left Lake Como for Neuchatel and now his part of the construction job was ending. It was time for me to go back to the States, to school and my job. I lay there watching his chest glide up and down with intake and exhalation. My head was at the edge of the bed and I looked, upside down, out the window at the lake, which seemed to become the sky, the sky looking like water swelling up from underground. I told him, hanging half upside down off the bed, that I thought he ought to try the lakes on my side of the world. I said this very fast and, almost as a cover, told him then how I thought I saw heaven from my bicycle. I told him what it looked like after God's fingers had clawed the sky, how I did not tell my parents, how I have told so many other people, and how he would not be the last, though I loved him, because I planned to go on telling and telling for the rest of my life. Then I told him about banks and why I smiled when I swore at him when we met under the gold dome.

Not too long ago I was sick with a low-grade fever. I left my office in turmoil, stayed in bed, and became depressed. That night Eduardo came home late from a demolition job, got in bed with all of his clothes on, took my head in his hands, and said, "Let me tell you a story." He rocked me from side to side and told me the story of how I saw heaven. He said "Floradale Avenue" and "fingernails of God." Then I trailed downstairs after him and watched TV next to him, happy that I still lived in these lakes and that my mother was far away on her mountain and my sister was far away in her treatment center and my father was long gone. For it is not, after all, the ones I have told about my vision, but those I would not tell who began my happiness.

Somehow, then, in the dimness of that dim suburban house I knew, though I was ten years old and couldn't, couldn't have known to any depth, not to waste what was left of the godly elation on those lost, impassive undergods, my parents. And so I let my mind rise up and over my body to look down on the emptiness, which gradually in my life I have filled. It was that decision that made me happy now—or, as happy as I can be, having somehow swallowed that emptiness.

What if you had been different? I say to myself. What if you had slammed the door and rushed to your father and screamed, "I'll show you heaven!" What if you had said, "Mom! Have you been watching the sky?"

Oh, I don't know how I could have. He was passed out on the couch night after night, and she sat on the porch in summer and in a wing chair in winter, smoking and staring. And I was so impatient! But keeping that secret meant I took a parcel of their emptiness inside me. And it is still there, wrapped in the happiness I made by saying over and over again what I saw. I had to have something to wrap my happiness around, something to which it would adhere . . . though the way I did it meant that the parcel of emptiness would have to stay put there. But now, I must tell you, I think the parcel has become very small.

THIS IS MY VOICE

by Jonathan Penner

Before I speak, can I say one thing? This has all been very upsetting. But I know you've got a job to do, and I know you're extremely intelligent people, and whatever punishment you decide I deserve is fine.

I guess it all began in August, when I first came here. Professor Delavette was still on Martha's Vineyard then. Her boarder got pneumonia and had to be hospitalized. His name was funny, something Saint something.

A saver, this guy was. I found drawers of empty Yoplait containers. He'd wash out the Nine Lives cans after he fed Professor Delavette's cat.

George St. George.

So I was looking for a place to get some writing done before the fall semester began, and the secretary had the keys to Professor Delavette's. St. George had developed something with his liver. He went home to Baltimore, I believe it was.

The secretary phones Professor Delavette and tells her a very large, very young man is available. Extremely, she says, looking up at me. I'm standing there in front of her desk, keeping my arms behind me, because all I did in high school was lift weights. And then I talked, and Professor Delavette said it was fine, so I stayed in her guest house and took care of things.

I have to tell you, and I know Dean Beechel has a meeting. This will be quick. I just have to tell you that Professor Delavette was the main reason I came here in the first place. I consider her one of our finest living writers. You know how informal she is, and the other students call her Gina and so forth, but for me it was thrilling just to cut her grass. Her power mower broke down, so I used a hand one.

Once I turned over a wheelbarrow behind the tool shed, and underneath was a footprint in the hardened mud, and every day for the rest of August I came back and looked at it and wondered if it was hers.

I need to explain about me and writing. Too many ideas is what my trouble is. Even for the first word! And the crazy thing, what's so frustrating, is I feel like I already *know* the stories. Is that possible? I could swear they exist, I already know them, somewhere in here, or in here. Writing them down should be so easy, like unwrapping presents, and I'm so amazed when I never can.

Of course I signed up for her workshop. And that's really where I should have begun—I shouldn't have told you about St. George, and the cat, and the secretary. That was a terrible beginning. I signed up for her workshop, and next thing everyone else in the class is handing in stories. She'd get them duplicated and we'd all discuss them.

And what do I know, I'm the last person who should criticize. But I always felt terrible, reading those stories. The characters in them were always learning something important about life—they never just wasted their time, not a minute.

It was enough to make any actual human being feel poor. Is that good writing?

But I couldn't write any stories at all. After three weeks, I showed her a paragraph. Professor Delavette read it fast. Then she gave me a funny look, and sat down and read it slowly, with her finger moving down the margin and stopping sometimes to rub the paper in little circles. Then she hands it back and tells me, "I'm impressed. You have a voice."

Why did she have to say that? I sat and stared at that paragraph. It was something about the vacation I subbed at the post office. It was about carrying mail. It was idiotic, the things I remembered, like my shadow humping over the lawn, and songs I'd hear in my head all day, and places on the route where I could, you know, relieve myself. I tried reading it aloud, alone in my room, and I had to stop in the middle of the first sentence. I think it was right then that I started getting angry at Professor Delavette. When she told me I had a voice. Because it stank, and I'd written it the only way I could.

Whatever punishment you gentlemen decide is okay with me. I'm grateful to you and Professor Delavette for not telling the police. But what I want to emphasize is this. All this time, I was taking care of her place, and all through the semester I tried to do my best.

I swept her steps. I washed her windows inside and out. I kept her grass cut and raked out her hedges. Somehow she got her power mower going again, this old beast of a reel-type. It'd run awhile and stop. I'd pull the cord until my muscles felt like balloons, and take off my shirt and keep yanking, sometimes jerking the whole machine off the ground, until my right hand was cramped into a ball. Then I'd go up to the house, and Professor Delavette would come out and remove the air filter, or clean the plug, or just whack the carburetor, and it would run awhile again. She told me she couldn't afford a new one. Maybe that was my fault, because she'd said I didn't have to pay any rent for the guest house, except the value of my labor.

I guess it actually began when this young kid arrived, the Maharish. His friends call him that now. I don't want to get him mixed up in this. He's from my hometown; I used to baby-sit him and his sister. He quit high school and came to find me at the university, and I was amazed how he's changed. He brought a calendar with scenes of his guru doing yoga between vases of flowers. When I used to take him and his sister to play on the swings, he was a regular kid with a regular name.

Now he wants to be an artist, but he doesn't know how to paint. He doesn't have any paints. He said the first step was getting himself in tune. That's why he came to me, because he thought I was a writer and I'd inspire him. He's been sleeping on my floor in his dhoti. Like a loincloth?

I was afraid to tell Professor Delavette, but I made him phone his parents. He won't eat meat, and I've been trying to get some protein into him. But all he does is read all day, and meditate, and do his tantrum.

Tantrum. You sit a certain way and breathe a certain way.

Well, he saw I wasn't doing any writing, and he gave me some stuff to read. Stories from the Orient. The people in them learned wisdom from locusts and fish.

Next he brought out a magazine, *Ursa Major*. Fantasy. I love that stuff, but it was trash. I assume you gentlemen have all been shown one of those stories, the one where the couple become the slaves of their dog. At the time I just passed over it.

With the Maharish there, things got harder. He never left the room, and I didn't know what to do with him. By this time I'd dropped all my classes except Professor Delavette's, and I'd spend hours every day, sitting with cotton in my ears, staring at my typewriter, until it made me sweat just to roll in a piece of paper, with the Maharish doing his tantrum on the floor behind me. Even with the cotton, I thought I could hear the rhythm of his breathing.

No matter how I tried, I couldn't write a story, and sometimes I felt like I'd kill Professor Delavette, or else the Maharish. The only other thing in the world I could imagine doing was delivering mail again. So I went down to the post office and applied, but I'd gotten a bad report the time I worked for them as a sub.

The postmaster told me forget it. "Trouble with you," he said, "you got an attitude." He looked me up and down, and just from his body type, which was pitiful, I knew what was coming. "Like most jocks," he says, and starts shaking his head. "You think you can get through life on muscles."

No matter how you dress, if you lift too many years, they know. They know from your neck.

In October, there were leaves to rake, and you've heard about the fire. Professor Delavette came out with the garden hose. Then in November a pipe burst in the guest house bathroom. The Maharish discovered it, because he slept on the floor. The next thing I knew he was standing in the middle of my bed, dripping on me.

I pulled on some pants and went outside to shut off the main. Then I looked for a mop, but all there was was a handle with an empty clamp. Professor Delavette came out and said her water had gone off, and for some reason I felt shy, even though I had my pants on. I leaned around the guest house door and told her the story.

"I've seen a naked man before," she says.

I'm sorry. I shouldn't have told you that.

I finished getting dressed and she gave me her car keys, and I went to the hardware store for a mop. They had mops. They had mops of every kind and size and shape. It was just the same as writing a story. Then I saw a replacement head and I was happy, and I bought it. But when I got it home, I couldn't get it into the clamp on Professor Delavette's old handle. It was too big.

We were on the porch of the guest house, and she stood there watching me. I went and got a hammer. I thought maybe I could just modify the clamp a little. Professor Delavette didn't say anything. She just looked at me so—seriously, or something—that I felt like I'd explode. I was kind of trying to hammer the clamp on my lap, and I could see she was afraid I'd hurt myself, but that she knew I'd be hurt more if she even opened her mouth. Then I did mash myself, a good one on the index finger. "My God," she says, and throws away the hammer. I'm squeezing the finger. "Let me see that," she says, pulling at my wrist.

Just then the Maharish comes out of the guest house. He stands there in the doorway in that loincloth of his, blinking at the daylight. "Something's happened," he tells me. "I'm in tune. I can feel it."

Well, Professor Delavette just looks at him, this practically naked little kid. He smiles at her. "Shanty, shanty, shanty," he says, kind of blessing her with his hand. She nods at him, and says "Shanty, shanty," herself. Then she says she'll go call the plumber.

I knew what she was thinking, and I followed her up to her door. "He's just this kid," I tell her.

"He's lovely," she says. "Whatever helps. All I want from you is a story."

"I'm having trouble."

"You've got a voice," she says. "Use it." It was a command, like from a queen.

I should have told you that first, because this is when the bad part really began. The Maharish painted all day, except he didn't use paints. He couldn't afford them. He used food. Peanut butter, ketchup, mayonnaise. He used toothpaste and mud. He finger-painted. All this time I was trying to write. Then he said that since I'd helped him, now he was going to help me.

And that's when he came up with the idea for me to hand in that *Ursa Major* story. The one where the couple become the slaves of their dog. Just to get me started, just to get me going. I stood up and I felt like strangling him.

I sat down and tried again to write, and my ideas were like bugs around a streetlamp—all the people I could write about, everything I could make them say and do. And that's when I knew, I really understood for the first time, that there was no way in the world I could write a story.

"Let's see that magazine," I said.

And you know the rest. I stole it.

I was scared to death Professor Delavette would catch me, so you've seen the changes I made. It didn't need to be a couple that got enslaved, so I made it a guy. Instead of a dog, I made it a hobo woman that he befriends. She doesn't exactly enslave him—in fact he makes her hit the road, at the end—but she does, in a way. I thought I better slide in some things, about the job he works at, cleaning up alcoholics—that's where he meets this hobo woman— and about this old Thunderbird his girl friend is after him to buy. It's more confusing than in *Ursa Major*. At least there the story was clear. And in *Ursa Major* they had good writing, all soft and bouncy. Anyone would know I couldn't write that well—the sentences made me think of actual pillows—so I had the guy tell it the way I would, if it were me. If I were him. I titled it "His Master's Voice."

When I finished, my shirt was sticking to me. I didn't know if I could hand that story in. But it was that or give Professor Delavette nothing at all. I knew I couldn't put it in her hands, so I left it in her mailbox at school.

It was about two weeks after the pipe broke, and we were having Indian summer. The grass needed one more mowing. I started at the back and was working my way forward toward the house, when I saw Professor Delavette coming toward me across the lawn. Right away I was sure she had me. Something was in her hand, and I guessed what it was.

I shut off the lawnmower, and you know how quiet that makes it. She just stood there. There were *tears* in her eyes, and I didn't know exactly what or how, but I knew right then that something terrible was going to happen.

"This is beautiful," she said. "This is wonderful."

She held it out to me and I took it. I just looked at the first page. She'd filled the margins with notes. *Rings true,* and *Captures it,* and *Good!* and *Yes!* all over the place.

I handed it back. "It's garbage," I said. "It isn't even mine." And I told her how I'd gotten the story from that trashy little magazine. But she just kept standing there, smiling and shaking her head.

"This is *yours*," she says. *"This is your voice."*

Then she must have seen that I was starting to feel pretty bad, because she reached out and touched my arm, and said, "We'll talk about it later. Come up to the house when you're done." She gave the lawnmower a kick. Then she walked away with that awful story in her hand.

Well, I pulled the cord and it started right up. Exercise helps. You go to the weight room all in knots, and come out after your shower all peaceful. I pushed that lawnmower back and forth faster than most people jog.

But it didn't help, not this time. I went roaring past the guest house, where the Maharish was out in front on a blanket, trying for a tan in his loincloth. It was probably the last afternoon of the year that would be warm enough. The guy had inner peace, you've got to give him that. He'd given up his tantrum, and had just told me that morning he didn't need to paint anymore, either. He thought he was about ready to go home to his parents.

He waved his hand at me to slow down, but I couldn't. And the faster I went the worse I felt. And I'm ashamed to admit it, but you know what bothered me? She had no idea who I was. If she really liked me or my writing at all, she should have known that wasn't my work. And you know what else? Not the fact I plagiarized the story, though I'm ashamed of that too. It was the fact that she let herself be fooled. The more I thought about that, the longer I mowed, the more I lost all my respect for Professor Delavette, like I was cutting it down one row at a time.

By the time I finished the lawn it was all gone, and that's the only way I can explain what happened. I was right outside her living room. I shut off the lawnmower, and I knew I would never push that thing again. I felt like throwing it away. I lifted it by the handles, and I never felt so strong in my life.

I began to turn, stepping backward in a circle, leaning against the weight. It's all in the forearms. I got it a few inches off the ground, then higher. I leaned back and got it knee-high, thigh-high, until I could get my legs and shoulders into it, and the lawnmower and I were just whirling each other around, and then I gave it everything I had. It just cleared the sill of her big living room window and went crashing through.

You could hear the thump and clank as it hit the carpet, and the glass tinkling like wind chimes. Then an upstairs window opened, and Professor Delavette leaned her head out.

"What in the world," she says, "was that?"

I tell her, "That was my voice. *That* was my voice."

Well, I know Dean Beechel has to go. I guess all you gentlemen do. I guess I'll be getting a letter after you've decided.

I just wanted you to understand what happened. Naturally, I feel different now. In the last week I've read Professor Delavette's books again, and I can't be angry at her—only grateful. She truly is one of the finest writers alive.

And I realize that's the problem right there. For her, writing is just so easy, it doesn't take any effort at all. She can sit down and write a story anytime she wants to. So how can she understand the fact that I can't?

I know you gentlemen will be writing an official report. I hope you'll say I tried my best. Please put that in my permanent file. But say it was like trying to burn an ice cube.

Say it was like trying to teach a hippo to dance.

Or a sewer to sing.

Then if anybody—some future employer—if anyone ever wants to know about me, they'll simply look it up—I waive my right to privacy—and they'll know. Or the government. They can just read your report, and they'll know the truth. Teachers, in case I ever come back to school—they can look too. I waive my right to privacy—do I have a right to privacy? I don't care who sees it, even Professor Delavette herself, in case someday she needs to put me in a story, and she's trying to get my voice, but all she remembers is a broken window, and the smell of grass coming up her stairs.

FOOTFALLS

by Catherine Petroski

Winston Wise regards himself, shaving. He puts down the razor, turns off the water. God, he says, what a handsome dog. He guesses it is so. That is what everyone says, has said as long as he can remember. He wonders will it never cease, even when he's old and gray and feeble. Possibly not. Will it ever do him any good? Will it ever mean anything?

Winston regards his handsome life, his considerable, measurable, verifiable accomplishment: D.D.S. private practice, phenomenal gross, and he's only thirty-two. Porsche 935, BMW 530i. A sound system no one can believe in an apartment everyone would give his eye teeth to have. Hartmann luggage, Club Med—for a while; now windjammers and Land's End. What the hell. Perennial tan. Fantastic health. His own curls in his own hair, his own beautiful straight white teeth.

Winston brushes his hair quickly, smiles at himself, and gets into his running clothes. Once everything would have been by Adidas, but now he is comfortable with a mongrel ensemble. He will probably do the five-mile loop this morning. He'll see how the first three go, then decide. No. He tells himself that is no way for a serious runner to think. He tells himself one commits oneself first, then accomplishes. In running as in all things; otherwise, nothing. Five it will be. Winston will not slack off.

Winston sniffs. Hay fever season, already? The live oaks' leaves are falling, he notices. New leaves pushing the old ones off the bough. He thinks of things pushing other things out of the way, of territorial animals, of the neighborhood cats whose serenade woke him at three last night. All in the scheme, he thinks, the nature of nature. All things in their rightful place on the continuum. The universe seems as neat as his instrument cabinet. God would make a good dentist. He rounds the first corner.

Winston can practically run his route blindfolded. He closes his eyes. The morning air is soft as a woman's hand on his cheek, his arms, his legs. The morning is a woman, he thinks, and then he thinks he is a fool. No. He knows he is a fool, or else the whole rest of the world is. Where is this woman, the true morning of his life? Morning has never happened to Winston, and it is already early afternoon. He looks at his black running watch. 6:17:36. No morning. No one would believe it of this handsome dog. Handsome dog, maybe, was the real problem. He wonders if looking like a handsome dog makes women distrust him, fear him, suspect him, not take him seriously. Just another pretty face. No one would believe such a thing. People make themselves comfortable with their best-loved thoughts, however absurd they may be. Winston lengthens his stride and decides to think about his feet.

Winston reaches the country road, though it is definitely within the city limits. The man whose house is the only one on this road is a very powerful man, so powerful he's kept the city from paving the road and from cutting it through the woods to the next major thoroughfare. Now, *that's* power, Winston thinks. He recalls the one time, years ago, when he'd been invited to the house on the country road, a political fund-raiser. The candidate lost. Winston wonders what's the point.

Winston hears music. Debussy. *Images,* solo piano. The harmonies drift hypnotically through the morning's cool air, and Winston thinks of image and its basis in fact. Then he hears the record stick. The same set of notes play again and again and again, and he thinks perhaps no one will come and rescue the record. Finally someone does. With his left foot, Winston kicks a large piece of gravel. It scuds down the road ahead of him. He sees that somehow he is headed the wrong way, that he has been running aimlessly back and forth on this city-country road without realizing it. At this rate, he will never make the five-mile loop by 6:45. He is the stuck record, the perpetual bachelor, the perfect extra man, the eternally elusive good catch. Treading the mill.

Ahead of him on the road Winston sees another person running. The pines and aspens cling to either side of this path today. Whoever it is is too far away, and he thinks how odd that running people often seem genderless. The men are tan and lithe and many of them wear their hair longer; the women are sleek and slim-hipped, short-haired. They all wear the same asexual clothes, the same shoes, the same determined faces. He is gaining on the other runner. His sense of scale tells him: either a very tall woman or a good-sized man. He wonders, and he wonders why he wonders. What's the difference? He is close enough now to hear the other's footfalls, the crunchings in the country road's loose surface. He edges closer, very gradually, close enough to hear the breathing, the heavy exhalations. The length of leg tells Winston. This is a woman.

Winston never speaks when he runs. It is bad form, he believes. It makes one appear casual, half-assed, about the pursuit, when one should be dedicated, committed. Others greet him, or have in the past, and Winston looks through them, to a man, to a woman. This is no time to change. Runners like to be alone with the sound of their own running. If one takes the task at hand seriously, he reasons, others will take one seriously. There is a time and place for everything, and running is not the time for casual social intercourse. Perhaps this is the time to change.

Winston regards the running woman. Ironic, he thinks. The story of my life, he thinks. Jane run, Tarzan chase. He almost laughs, and manages to keep from doing so only with great effort, by shortening his stride. She would think him mad—and be right—running along, laughing at her derriere. Insulting, at the very least. Distance opens up between them. Winston sprints to make up the difference. She's married, he tells himself; she's got to be. Happily, monogamously. Or has a split end in the NFL for a boyfriend. Someone spectacularly fleet of foot. Nothing gross like a linebacker or offensive tackle. Or maybe she doesn't like men at all; that could be. What would he say? He can't think. What a body. With a body like that, she might be stupid. Boring, dull. Is that what people think about him? Winston begins to see the enormity of the problem.

And then Winston falls. "Oh, Jesus," he says, curling to his ankle. Will he one day learn to look where he is going, what he is doing with his feet? Will he one day learn to avoid the holes in the road of life that present no problem to all of those who seem so much less favored than he? Will he one day avoid making a total ass of himself? Why now, just as he's got it figured out? The words would have come. The woman turns and now she jogs up to him. "Are you okay?" she says, still jogging in place. The ankle hurts like hell. No, he is not okay. He will never be okay, not after this fall, this disaster. Ham, he thinks. He is overstating the difficulty, being overly dramatic. He will retain his composure, even if the ankle is killing him. This is it. God, she is beautiful. Tall, dark; intelligent eyes, and such gorgeous teeth.

Winston winces and sits up. "I wasn't watching where I was going," he says, and she smiles, still jogging, though more slowly now. Running is so sensual, he thinks, looking at her. Running is the next best thing to sex. So elemental. Does she know what he is thinking? He could sit here forever, ankle killing him and everything, if she would just stay there forever, jogging in place. He struggles to get to his feet. "Oh, Jesus," he says again. This isn't going to work. Has he broken something? "You can't put weight on it?" the running beauty asks. "It hurts like hell," he says. Manly, but vulnerable. Me Tarzan with soft heart. "I don't know what I was thinking of," he says, though of course he remembers very well what he was thinking of. "Quit trying to walk, then," she says to him rather sternly, "or you'll really mess things up. Sit back down." Who the hell does this woman think she is, the mother of the world? Me *Tarzan,* he wants to say. "Look," he says, "I'm Dr. Wise, and I know better than to . . . oh, shit." He sits back down. She is looking at him, all a question mark.

Winston lives by first impressions. He knows the first is always the strongest. *Dr. Wise.* It sounds so, well, reassuring. "Wise?" she says. "Did you say Wise?" What weird sense of humor does this woman have, making fun of names (which isn't polite) and making cracks about his lack of native intelligence. And at a time like this. Can't she see he's in pain? "I know it doesn't look that way," he says. "No—I didn't mean," she says, "I'm Dr. Chapple. Melissa. Orthopedics. Have we met at Memorial?" Oh, the luck of Winston Wise. "No. Private dentistry." That does it, he thinks. On her right hand is a star sapphire in an antique mounting. She wears no wedding ring. And now it's over. Not only gauche, falling over his own feet, but just a dentist. He won't even be able to run to forget about it.

But for the moment, Winston is in a fix. How will he ever get home? Maybe he could just die right here, put him down like a racehorse. This damned ankle. "I'm going to get stiff," Dr. Melissa Chapple says, and she does some cool-downs. "And you, too—what's your first name, Dr. Wise and Wonderful?" "Winston." She smiles. He loves her teeth. "Winston, we've got to get you home and then you ought to get an X-ray and have that taped." He nods. "Mmmm," he says. "Where do you live, Winston Wonderful?" Is she putting him on? He tells her. Is this her usual roadside manner? It's bad enough being patronized by a doctor, but by a beautiful, fast-running woman, it is excruciating. The hot pain in the ankle is killing him. "I can manage by myself, thanks," he says. He sounds like a fool; it's perfectly obvious he can't manage any such thing. "If you do, you'll be sorry," she says. No, there was no trace of coyness in her voice. Just concern, matter-of-fact concern. "Look, I left my car about a half mile from here. Let me run and get it. Now, will you promise to sit still?"

Winston promises. Nothing—not a Mack truck, not a bulldozer, not the bulls running in Pamplona or even wild horses could drag him from this spot. He will sit here forever. But it won't take that long. Melissa ought to be able to do a mile in six minutes, easy. So, three minutes. Plus a couple more to drive back. Get your head together, Winston. On your mark, Melissa. The fact of the matter is it won't take her long enough. Melissa Chapple will be back in a veritable flash. He will get her expert attention. That will be it with Melissa Chapple for all time. She will forget him, a passing of ships in the night, runners in the morning. Or maybe not. How much is real? How much is possible? Will he ever know before he commits himself?

Winston rests his head on his knees and thinks about that handsome dog in his bathroom mirror and this bumbling fool on the gravel road. Pride goeth before a fall. If Melissa Chapple thinks anything about Winston at this moment, it probably has nothing to do with handsome dogs and everything to do with malpractice suits and Good Samaritan laws. No. He can't believe that. He doesn't want to believe that. Whatever she is thinking of him, it can't be a very admiring thought, handsome dog or no. Winston's ankle feels numb, oddly, after all that pain. Where the hell is she? He checks his watch. She's had plenty of time to get back. Well, she's not coming, that's it. What a crummy trick, leaving him flat, and crippled at that. No. He is being silly. It is paranoid to think this way. Melissa Chapple will be back. People with teeth like that keep their word. She will be back.

Winston hears a runner and lifts his head. It is Melissa Chapple, on foot. What the hell is going on? Where the hell's the car? "You're not going to believe this," she says, "but I locked the damned keys in my car. I was going to get my medical bag out of the back, and I left the damned keys in the ignition. I don't know where my mind is—I never do things like that. God, what a flake!" His ankle is swelling, puffed up like a balloon, but Winston doesn't even notice. "God, that looks perfectly dreadful," she says. "Don't worry. I called a cab. They'll take us to the E.R. Okay?" Winston looks at beautiful, blushing Melissa, and he wants to cry. The ankle, he would say. The ankle has nothing to do with it. What is she thinking? Will women always be such a mystery to Winston Wise? Will he always be such a mystery to them? Melissa pats him reassuringly on the shoulder, then begins to jump up and down on both her feet. She is jogging in place when the cab crunches up the city-country road and stops. Melissa helps Winston up. He can feel that she is very strong. Her arm is around his waist, his arm is around her shoulder, so close. She feels cool and soothing, Winston thinks, very much like a perfect running morning. They get into the cab.

Winston settles back in the seat. He notices that the cabbie is peeking at them in his rearview mirror. Let him. A fare to talk about back at the garage, these two runners, see. Each to his own, according to his abilities. Winston has not caught sight of himself in the mirror and isn't trying to. Doesn't care. He looks at his left thigh, his right thigh. Then, just next to that, Melissa's left thigh, long and tan and very strong. He's forgotten the ankle. He looks up. Melissa smiles at him, and she pats him gently, so gently, on the leg. Winston closes his eyes and can hear footfalls, the beating of his heart.

READING THE LIGHT

by Roger Pfingston

Without a coat or hat, keys in hand, David Thompson ran out into the ten-degree weather. From inside the car the glow of light through the ice-encrusted windshield triggered a quick fantasy, as if he were a character in a Jack London survival story.

On the third try the engine roared with good news. Shivering, he pumped the gas pedal, holding it halfway to the floor for several seconds at a time. When he was sure the car would keep running on its own, he turned on the heat and defroster and ran back to the house where his wife stood behind the front door, peering through the glass and holding up his coat and hat as a gentle reprimand.

Inside, he rubbed his hands together and sat down near the window, where he could keep an eye on the car, hoping it wouldn't die.

His wife brought a large mug of coffee that he gulped while watching the exhaust puff up and whip around the car before dissipating in the clean, sharp light of morning. The ice was beginning to give way to the heat rushing up the windshield, forming curious abstractions that tempted him. He decided he would resist this time; besides, he'd shot that sort of thing often enough.

He checked his watch—8:30—and figured he'd better be on his way if he wanted to work with some of that good early light. He had loaded his cameras the night before, cleaned the lenses and filters, gone through the whole ritual of preparing himself, very much like a hunter, but in his case it was all for the glory of light, a phrase that he kept to himself since it would probably sound a little hokey to others, even his wife, who had lived with his obsession for nearly fifteen years.

Fifteen years of traveling back and forth between Indiana and Hoopeston, Illinois, sweet-corn capital of the world, never tiring of the farmland, passing the time while driving by playing a game of Count the Hawks with himself or his family, trying to spot the birds as they sailed or topped trees and telephone poles with their impressive silhouettes.

On the way over this time there'd been the back-lit, wind-driven snow near Crawfordsville, a couple of icy hills in Danville that challenged his driving skills, the kids sleeping through it all in the backseat, and then the final stretch over land that never ceased to intrigue him with its incredible flatness, rich and black. It was his wife's home ground, but he felt a nearness to it, a spiritual tie that resulted, he knew, from photographing it over the years through all the seasons.

They made the 150-mile trip from Bloomington to Hoopeston two or three times a year, and always at Christmas unless the weather made it impossible. In the summer, Hoopeston being a canning town, they could smell it before they ever saw it. Mostly it was the tomato pits that "did the dirty deed," as the kids described it. Like a lot of people in town, his wife had put in her time, usually summers between college years, chopping worms out of corn for Stokely–Van Camp.

The flash startled him. He turned to see his son bundled up, smiling at having caught a candid of his dad with a mouthful of coffee cup.

"What kept you?"

"I had trouble loading the film, but I think it's all right now. See?" Brian held the camera out so his dad could see the rewind knob turning as he advanced the film to the next frame.

"Looks good," David said. "You won't need the flash where we're going. No sense dragging it along. Remember, keep your shooting simple and unburdensome." He wished he hadn't said the latter. It was the teacher in him and he knew how his twelve-year-old son reacted to that most of the time. Brian looked up at his mother and frowned. He said he'd like to take the flash along, just in case.

David decided that it wasn't worth arguing over. He grabbed his coat and hat, his camera bag, and, after hesitating, a tripod, even though he was sure he wouldn't use it. Brian's words echoed in his head: *just in case. . . .*

As David pulled out of the driveway, he said to Brian that he thought they would head out west of town and cut through the cemetery so Brian could get a few shots of the snow-covered tank, World War I vintage. Even though he knew it was a memorial of sorts to the war dead, he always thought of it as a huge oddity among the tombstones.

David drove through the entrance and stopped directly in front of the tank, about twenty feet away. He suggested that Brian try a few head-on shots and then walk around the tank to see what other views might interest him.

Without saying much, Brian got out of the car, took the obligatory head-on shot, and then walked to the back of the tank, where he was out of sight for several minutes.

David started to get out of the car when Brian suddenly appeared on top of the tank, slipping now and then as he inched his way to the front. David was worried that he might damage the camera, or, worse, hurt himself. He also worried that someone passing by might wonder what the hell was going on. As Brian straddled the protruding gun, he yelled something that David couldn't understand. David rolled the window down and yelled back, "Brian, what are you up to? Don't forget that's a two-hundred-dollar camera you've got there!"

"Gun it, Dad! Gun the motor! I want lots of exhaust all around the car when I take the picture." He was sitting in about an inch of snow, his arms parallel to and tight against his body, the camera pressed to his right eye and resting firmly in the palm of his left hand as he focused with his thumb and forefinger, the forefinger of his right hand poised to release the shutter. He was doing everything that David had taught him.

Pressing the pedal to the floor, David smiled as the sunlit exhaust enveloped the car.

They drove through the cemetery and out the back entrance onto the narrow road, a straight shot of blacktop with plowed ground on either side and what seemed an endless rhythm of telephone poles on their left.

Brian asked his dad to pull over. David hung his camera over his shoulder, thinking they would shoot this one together. As they walked in front of the car, David started to explain how to expose for a silhouette when he realized that Brian had gone off to the right into the field, squatting low to shoot the contrasting effect of snow-covered hunks of black earth in the foreground with the cemetery in the background. It *was* a good shot. Pretty soon, Brian came over and shot a few verticals of the road and the telephone poles disappearing into infinity.

As they continued their drive, David commented that he thought Brian was getting some good shots.

"I hope so," Brian said. "They sure look good when I'm taking them. Do they always come out as good as they look in the camera?"

"Not always," David said. He went on to explain a little about the printing process, how seeing well and printing technique combined to make the final image. "But seeing is the important thing. Most people can learn to develop film and make fairly decent prints, but not everybody has a good eye for photographs."

Brian shook his head yes without saying anything. They both remained silent for the next two or three minutes until Brian suddenly asked if they could go back to the house.

More than a little surprised, David asked why. "We're just getting started," he said.

"I want to take some pictures of you and Mom together. We could walk down to the park and I could take pictures of you and Mom . . . just walking or standing by some trees."

"That's ridiculous, Brian. I thought we were going to spend the morning together. I'll show you some of the spots I've photographed over the past fifteen years—bridges, silos, one-lane roads running between fields. There's a pond east of here where we could get some good ice pictures."

Brian stared out the window, his fingers playing nervously with the focusing ring of his camera.

"I heard you and Mom talking to Grandpa Bill last night."

David felt a tightening in his chest. Cattle and farmhouses slid by on either side. At one point he considered stopping for a shot of a frozen stream winding past a dilapidated barn.

"Is it really such a surprise?" he asked. He figured Brian had heard enough to know what was going on. "I'm sure you know that your mother and I haven't been the best of friends lately."

"I don't want to talk about it," Brian said. "I just want to go back to the house while I've still got plenty of film left."

"Film's no problem," David said. "I have lots of film in my camera bag. Don't you think we should talk about this a little before we go back?"

Brian didn't respond. Instead, he turned his back to David and stared out the window. The landscape blurred to a soft focus as the tears started.

At the crossroads David slowed the car and made a U-turn. On the way back he kept wondering how Marcia would take this. Maybe he wouldn't say a thing about it, just walk to the park and let Brian take his pictures. Afterwards, maybe the three of them could talk about what was going on, get some things said before going home tomorrow. He wondered if Brian had said anything to his sister. He felt bad, too, about hitting Bill with all of this right here at Christmas, especially when he wasn't doing too well himself, being 75 and diabetic. He wished Ginny, Bill's wife for 52 years, were still alive.

As he pulled into the driveway, David suggested that Brian not say anything to his mother about what he'd heard last night—not yet.

As soon as he saw the two of them sitting at the kitchen table, David knew that Bill and Marcia had been talking about things again. She tried to smile at Brian, who stood back and waited. Obviously, she hadn't expected them back so soon.

"That was a short trip," Bill said. "Get too cold for you?" He looked at Brian and said, "You know, your dad and I used to go out when it was colder than this and spend the whole morning taking pictures. Sometimes our fingers would get so numb we could hardly advance the film. You want some hot chocolate?"

David looked at Marcia and said, "Brian wants us to walk to the park, where he can take some pictures of the two of us."

Marcia knew that something was wrong. She called to Melissa, their seven-year-old daughter, to see if she'd like to go for a walk to the park, but she said she'd rather watch TV.

Brian spoke up that he just wanted David and Marcia. "You and Dad," he said.

Bill said that he would make David and Brian some hot chocolate while Marcia dressed and got herself together for the two-block walk to the park.

Not much was said as they walked, Brian a few steps ahead, glancing back now and then, his camera swinging from his shoulder. David was thinking that Brian looked like a short photojournalist hell-bent on some assignment that involved this somber, middle-aged couple treading through the snow as if they were being led to a place that required their presence in order to make the story complete. He imagined the story appearing in the Sunday magazine of the *Chicago Tribune,* or maybe *Life.* Maybe a *Life* cover, a stark black and white portrait of Marcia and himself, blurred snow stopped between them and the camera, and inside the magazine grainy blowups with deep, velvety blacks complementing a four-page story. David was trying to think what their story might be when he realized that they were in the park and that Brian was asking them to go and stand in the middle of the frozen pond.

The pond reflected the brilliance of the sun like a giant mirror. David knew that the built-in light meter in Brian's camera would be fooled by the brightness, resulting in underexposure, if he didn't first come up close and take a reading off their faces. He waited to see what his son would do.

Brian raised the camera to his eye and held it there for several seconds. David and Marcia smiled as best they could, their arms around each other. David kept waiting for the sound of the shutter. He even tried for a little humor, asking if they should say cheese, or better yet, cheese pleez.

In spite of the sun, it was getting awfully cold. The wind-chill factor must've been ten or fifteen below.

Suddenly Brian lowered the camera and walked up to them, saying that he remembered he'd better check the light.

They could see that he'd been crying, that his eyelashes were actually showing traces of frost. David wondered if he was having trouble focusing. When Marcia saw Brian's eyes she made a small cry and hugged him to her thick pea coat, one that David had worn in the navy. The three of them stood huddled in the glare of ice and sun.

And then, still determined to take his pictures, Brian raised the camera to their faces and read the light.

THE BIGAMIST

by Nancy A. Potter

It runs in families—womanizing, like being a bleeder or light-fingered or lazy or curly-haired or having perfect pitch. At least, that's how Mom explained Dan Lynch. The first time I saw Dan Lynch was through a hedge like an elf framed in green. I grew up in Mt. Bethel (Pop.: 1,000) and must have been seeing him always from my carriage and stroller, but I was a slow learner. Took my sweet time. Didn't crawl until I walked, didn't speak until I could make sentences. Vanity and fear of failure.

That first real time was just after V-J Day. Mr. Lynch was watering his excuse for a lawn. I had been left in Aunt Clara's garden—eight patches of the same color zinnias, two trellises with Moonlight Ramblers, a blue glass reflecting ball on a column in the center, flagstones raying out to the trellises. That garden didn't have a weed. But there was a thin spot in the hedge where I could stare across Roosevelt Avenue to the Lynches' house. A few years before, the bankrupt Bleachery Company had auctioned off all the two-family company houses. Some had been bought by branches of the same family, and they painted the two sides different colors which met suddenly over the front door. Originally, all the houses had been regulation white. The Lynches had bought their whole house, having so many children. Their house was rundown, with a mangy lawn, a big collie named Bing, bicycles thrown over, a crooked swing under the maple, croquet hoops stuck here and there, a clothesline always flapping with a wash.

"They never stick to anything. They start things." Mom had them down perfectly. They lost interest after the fast sprint.

Mrs. Lynch had been Rachel Sadinsky. She had grown up on a

poultry farm outside of Mt. Eden amid a crew of noisy brothers with very long noses and stunning auburn hair.

Rachel Sadinsky Lynch was a lot younger than her husband, Dan. She had been a high stepper, as they said, and two of her daughters were already drum majorettes with the local fife and drum corps. The house was always about to explode with kids practicing trombones or shouting at one another, the radio turned on high to National Barn Dance or Walter Damrosch or the Everly Brothers, and in the middle of all this Mr. Lynch coming and going in his quivery Plymouth. He was a small man in a white shirt and bow tie, and he grew even smaller inside the car, a loose-sprung sedan that jiggled along. He was a drummer and traveled for a patent medicine distributor, selling Golden Elixir and Magic Herbal Compound at a dollar a bottle. It had been a good, steady trade. All my aunts and female cousins bought at least a bottle a week and took a shot glass before every meal. If they ever won the Sweeps, they planned to spend a summer at Battle Creek or French Lick taking the waters and having mud packs and colonic irrigation.

You could see cases of the tonic bottles in the back of Dan Lynch's Plymouth, but it was such an honest town that he didn't bother to lock the doors. Being in the trade, he used Vitalis and aftershave. Aunt Clara swore that he smelled clear across the street, but the way she complained made it entirely clear that she would abandon the whole shebang, trellises and all, and run away with Dapper Dan if he had ever shown the slightest interest in her.

Instead, I was the one that got seduced, perhaps because I was more of a challenge. My photographs show me as a sour child, suffering sinus attacks, quick to tears and defeat, unwilling to join the 4-H or Rainbow. I didn't know what I was saving myself for, certainly not the Lynches.

"Come here, doll," he would say through the hedge. "Don't be afraid, sweetheart. Let me show you cat's cradle. Look. Here's the church and here's the steeple. See, you can make a big whistle out of this blade of grass. Now let me read your palm." I withdrew my hands and held them tight under the armpits.

"She doesn't trust me," he said knowingly. "She knows I'm flirting with her. Smitten by her charms I am."

"They should lock that man up," Mom said.

"They have, after a fashion," my father said admiringly. "And in two different towns."

Dan Lynch was a bigamist, and everybody knew. He divided his week between two households in towns forty miles apart. There were buses and trolleys that connected the towns, but Dan's quivering Plymouth bounced back and forth, three or four days in Nel-

son, three or four days for Mt. Bethel, with maybe a day or two on
the road blessedly alone. The Nelson household was the original
family; the oldest child there was five years older than the oldest in
Mt. Bethel. The other children were sandwiched in, a couple of
years apart.

As you may guess, I'm great at paving over sections of the past.
After seeing Dan Lynch through the hedge, I went a lot of places
and ended up back home again. I even got married right after high
school, but it didn't take. I was a footpress operator then and dumb
enough to believe in romance. He wasn't a rotten guy. Only married me to spite the girl he'd been living with. They had this big
fight, and he thought he'd show her. I thought he had narcolepsy
on our honeymoon. After that he was back to his own true love like
a shot. Then we got one of those quickie divorces. So there weren't
any kids. Sometimes I'm sorry about that, but after I got over to
'Nam I figured out I ought to be glad. That was after I went to the
community college and got to be a nurse. Got my RN and AA, both.

After Vietnam I was in a big general hospital in Buffalo. Good
money, but I made another what you might call romantic mistake.
That's when I took up with Big Red Balzano after he'd hung up his
skates. Old hockey players really fall apart. Red used to cry all the
time over the slightest insults, even imagined ones. When he thought
he'd been bad, he'd insist upon being served dinner on the floor.
That I could have put up with, but I wouldn't agree to being born
again. He loved baptismal services and ran around getting baptized
in different states. Gave him a chance to cry and get hugged a lot. I
think he probably needed a mother. When we split, he moved in
with a nice old lady realtor. I saw them a couple of times driving
around in her Buick, her drop earrings and aurora borealis necklace and dainty pink glass frames all sparkling behind the wheel,
Big Red sort of slumped up against her shoulder like an Airedale.

So I came home and I live in a trailer over in Frog Hollow and I
got a job in the big new convalescent hospital in Mt. Bethel, the
Althea Lodge. All the rooms were sold out before they got the roof
on the place. With such a dim future you'd think that being old
would go out of style, but it's a booming business. The Althea
Lodge has less charm than a cheap motel, but the shrewdies that
own it know to butter up the local doctors and not neglect the
morticians either.

You've been in one of them—and who hasn't—you know all
about such places. In the daytime there's the din of TV turned high
and the PA calling somebody to the crafts room and the screamers
calling out the one word they remember and the carts rattling up
and down. I have the night shift, so I miss serving meals and most

of the medication. What night means is dying mostly and waking up scared, but it's better than trying to pretend during the day.

I'm in halfway decent shape for forty-five. Of course, my upper arms are going, and my feet are a mess, but I lace myself into my white Hush Puppies at 8:30 every night and take off to check out the old girls. It's a rare man that lasts through, mostly priest types, or sometimes a whole couple, not really whole, two leftovers, listing in opposite directions, children again.

The first night there's Dan Lynch. Chart says 75. He could be older or younger. Like everything about us, there's always another version of the facts.

They put out the room lights at ten. There in the dark he was trying to figure out the voice and face.

"I know you," he said. "You're Anna, grown up."

"Overgrown," I answered.

He didn't smell like an old person. And while most old people are supposed not to care about Now, he's fresh up on what's going to happen next—and that's not breakfast or the annual Althea bazaar.

"You were in Vietnam. That must have been hard."

"Almost as bad as night shift here." Mostly, I avoid talking about it for the obvious reasons and also because comparatively I had it lighter than most. I could tell that Dan wasn't going to be sentimental about it.

We used to sit in the dark through that winter whispering about the evening news and people we'd known, just the kind of talk casual old friends do. Then one night he asked if I could spare a little more time.

"Sure," I said. "What can I do for you?"

"Sit down by me," he said. "Sit by me and hold my hand. I want to remember what it was like."

He had nice firm hands. I wondered whose wedding ring he wore.

"I like women. That's what I miss most being here."

"There certainly are a lot of women here, Dan."

"You know what I mean. Real women. I wake up here and wonder why. Inside, I'm the same man as always. No age. Feel the same."

I nodded, even in the dark.

"I suppose I'm arrogant, thinking I'm better than all these other wrecks," he went on. "It's simply that I can't feel decayed yet. And I don't want to give in."

"I understand. I respect you for it, really," I said.

"The children have been grand. Just grand. They all hung out the welcome mat, but I didn't want to test it. You know I'm a widower."

"I didn't. I'm sorry."

"It was cancer that got Meg. And Rachel had expected to outlive me, but she got us into that awful accident driving to the Four Seasons to see *Tess*. She was never a good driver. I don't know what came over her, but she lost control, crossed the divider, and plowed into the oncoming traffic. That's why I'm here. Fractured my pelvis."

"That's a lot to happen."

"I never figured to survive them. So here I am, alone."

"Not quite. You have the children."

"Certainly. All my children are grand, but it's not the same. Duty, I can feel it coming out their pores. I need something else."

We had these intense little talks. Then I had to be answering the lights. A lot of patients who wake up in the night suddenly think they're dying, and some of them do, of course. The others want water or to know what time it is or just to see a real functioning face.

I began to look forward to the chats with Dan. No question, he had a gentle way. He knew exactly what would flatter and raise the spirits. Then we began having cocoa on my break at two A.M. If anybody had told me a year ago that I'd be looking forward to cocoa in the kitchen of the Althea Lodge at two A.M. with a seventy-five-year-old guy, I'd have laughed my head off. But we had something going on between us.

He made the cocoa and washed up. Said he missed doing dishes. He'd done a lot of the cooking in both households, he told me.

"How was it, Dan, having two wives?"

"Wonderful," he said shyly. "I must have been the happiest man in the state. All that love. All that self-importance. I ran back and forth like a bridegroom."

"There had to be rough spots," I insisted. "For instance, how was it when you had to tell each of them about the other one?"

He handled the question theatrically. He knew this was a big moment, and he must have answered that question before. Or perhaps he was simply overwhelmed by trying to explain.

It had been snowing outside the Althea Lodge all night, soft, unplowed drifts that the highway crews had let get ahead of them. Inside the kitchen we could hear the spitting sound of icy flakes on the windows. Dan had pushed his wheelchair to the sink and was washing our cups. He explored one carefully, as if it held a secret. Later I learned that he liked to frame anecdotes. He wanted to serve them up right.

"You never saw Meg, and she's hard to describe. I can't remem-

ber not being in love with her. She was a skinny, dependent little
kid. In grade school she was always sneaking in the boys' entrance,
getting me to snap on her overshoes. She spent her whole allowance
buying me candy. She must have been saving for our marriage
from the time she was fifteen and went to work in the thread
company office. She made me very happy. Perfect wife.

"Then I had to travel a lot. When I came down to Mt. Bethel I
met Rachel Sadinsky when she was having a ice cream soda in the
drugstore. She knew I was married, but I fell in love with her. Who
wouldn't have? Do you remember that splendid hair? Like someone
in a fairy tale.

"Rachel wanted to get married. She knew about Meg and the two
kids up in Nelson. Didn't like it but knew they were for keeps. And
finally one Christmas I came clean with Meg. That was pretty awful.
But I sort of left it up to the two women. Meg didn't give me
outright permission. For a long time she didn't want to hear about
it. They both came around."

"Where'd you marry Rachel?"

His face brightened considerably at the memory. "Oh, that was
easy. In those days you just drove down to Elkton with your birth
certificate and driver's license. You had the pick of about a dozen
JP's. I remember I wanted to make a bouquet for her. I saw some of
those big lilies, you know, tigers and turk's-head ones. I stopped the
car and pulled up clumps of them under the headlight beams. An
awful mess, but she understood. I don't want you to think that I was
a cheapskate. I made up for it later with long-stemmed American
beauties, but just then it was the impulse."

I swear we had damp eyes, both of us. Winter can be a sad time.
Gives you too long to sit around and ponder. I'm not much for
pondering.

Of course, it couldn't stay winter. We went through the flu season, which weeded out some of them. Dan and I kept on having our
cocoa dates. When it was my birthday I got an assortment of spring
flowers delivered at home. It was exciting enough that I didn't
mind being awakened. The card just said, "With devotion from
Dan." That's class.

"My intentions are honorable," he told me the next night. "I can't
stand being unmarried. I'm courting you. You probably think it's
robbing the cradle, but you're not a child exactly, no matter how I
see you."

Things in my life seemed to be taking a favorable turn. My sister
in Akron, who's a horoscope nut, called to tell me that since Jupiter's
moving out of my third house I would begin an interesting two-year
cycle. I got a two-hundred-dollar IRS refund and asked Dan if he

thought I should buy a dog or take an extension course in ventilation therapy.

Instead, he said slyly, "I have plans for us."

I thought he meant going out for a Chinese dinner. There was no reason he couldn't leave the lodge when he wanted.

"I'm thinking of our taking a weekend in Atlantic City," he said, smug as you please. "I'm trying to dope out the arrangements. It won't cause scandal, will it?"

I was holding an armful of folded laundry, which I nearly dropped.

"Don't be scared," he said. "We're not babies. What can an old man do?"

So we rented one of those campers and went barreling down the turnpikes and pulled right into one of the casino lots. The crowds and the noise and the shoving were more than we'd bargained for. Anyway, what he wanted to do was to hire a cart and drive up and down the boardwalk, but first he wanted to get into his best suit. And I had to help him. Suddenly, after all those years around thousands of naked bodies, I turned shy. I think he understood that we'd passed over a line. He wasn't a patient or an old man anymore to me, but someone who lived in the real world of morning papers and secrets and an extra key to the front door.

He knew all about that in advance. He'd ferreted out the whole deal. There we were sitting in the bright April sunshine in front of the hotel. I was noticing again that he had lovely hands. He'd taken off the ring.

"Will you marry me?" he asked. "Now, look at me. This is serious stuff. I mean it."

"I'm much obliged," I said. I have no idea where that phrase came from.

"I'm a marrier. You should know that by now," he said.

"Listen. I'll compromise. How about being engaged? We could get engaged."

That seemed to satisfy. Worn out by all the preparation, he was having difficulty staying awake.

THEY DON'T LISTEN

by Nancy Price

"Come on, Marie," the nursing home attendant said to my mother, her voice loud enough to reach the next room. "Time for your bath now. Say good-bye to your daughter for a little while." She smiled at me and wheeled my mother away.

"Listen to that. They shout all the time here, but do they listen?" A dry, small voice startled me. The bed next to my mother's had a quilt-covered mound on it, and the mound was twitching now. "You can tell them you're a murderer—done it twice—and they don't listen." The quilt twitched again. "Think you're deaf and stupid and couldn't kill a fly."

"Hello," I said.

"Hello," the mound said in its paper-thin voice. "At least you don't yell. I'm Ella Rainey, and I been yelled at enough. You should have heard my husband. You should have heard Roke Pritcher."

"I'm Marie's daughter." I leaned over the bed to turn the quilt top down. There lay a woman as small as her voice, staring up at me.

"Slide down in this bed all the time," she said. "They moved me in this room yesterday, and I think I been lost under here ever since."

Ella Rainey was as light and bony as a paper kite. When I propped her on her pillows, there she lay, all nose and flyaway white hair and indignant black eyes. "So you're Marie's girl," she said. "I never had a baby but once. She was my daughter and heir."

"Who was Roke Pritcher?"

"He was a raper," Ella said. She smelled like lavender among the assaulting smells of the nursing home: urine, floor wax and the last (or next) meal. "Hated his mama, like most of us do, because she always has to break us in, teach us we're alone and can't have what we want in this world."

"I wouldn't have liked this Roke Pritcher," I said.

"Yes, you would," Ella said. "Roke was bee balm to the ladies. He'd go into town and smile with those picket-fence teeth of his, and they'd hover round, hover and buzz just like bees. He was mean from the first time he wet a diaper. Sharp white teeth, and how he would laugh, rubbing some little fellow's face in the gravel on the way home from country school. I knew Roke Pritcher real well."

A nurse went by the door, pushing a creaking wheelchair. "Don't look like you ever lived on a farm," the paper-thin little voice said. "We were poor and had a big family and lived on low land, not the good Iowa gumbo, so they called our farm Coney Island. If we didn't die of the damp, we grew up tough. I could work same as a boy, only I wasn't one, and Roke Pritcher knew I wasn't, him and that smile. And my dad liked him. Said Roke was a real man, after his own heart."

"You worked on the farm?" I said.

"Corn picking!" she said, her black eyes bright and opaque as coal. "And my mama dead when I was sixteen, and me the biggest, so I'd stay home from school mornings, bake the eight loaves of bread I'd made the night before—four to a drip pan. Get the eggs from the henhouse and water from the pump, and be ready with roast pork. Lots of gravy. Potatoes and turnips and corn, and a pitcher of corn syrup to put on the bread and butter, and pie. You got the pre-packaged foods—you don't know. The big granite pots we had to use, and they chipped, and the scouring after. Hot Blast—that was the name of our stove. Black, with nickel on it you had to polish, and corncobs to burn. How those men would eat. They were in the field all day, picking with pegs on their hands, throwing corn ears against the bang-boards, yelling to the team. They sweat that meat and potatoes and pie right through their pores."

Ella's hair stood out from her head in wispy white rays like Liberty's crown. "I could work. I could cook. Roke Pritcher knew it, and he knew he could hire me cheap because I was just sixteen. So Roke asked my pa if I could work for him, feed his hired hands too, him being a bachelor farmer and my folks being so poor. No way to get out of that one. My mama was dead, and she couldn't leave me anything but her common sense and a feel for danger."

"What happened?" I asked. Above her bed was a sign that said GOD LOVES ALL HIS CHILDREN. It showed a little boy with eyes as big as a bug's kneeling by a bed. Under the bed was what my mother's family called a "convenience," with roses painted on it.

"Roke wasn't just mean; he was smart. I'd dilly-dally getting to his place till I knew there'd be a hired man in the hog houses (Roke had a mess of hogs), near enough to hear me yell. I'd wash the dishes, and I'd be off and running the mile and a half to school before Roke could get the men to the field and be back to catch me alone. I'd lived on a farm all my life; I knew what he was after. But I didn't have a mama."

Her fingers were nothing but joints and bones covered with papery skin; they picked at her quilt's yarn ties. "The worst of it was that those men, they thought it was natural. Roke wanted me, he'd marry me, and I'd be living on a good farm, and what more could a little kid from Coney Island want?"

Her wrinkled eyelids shut away her black gaze for a moment. "He went and gave the hired men a holiday to go to the fair, and didn't tell me. I got in his kitchen and he jumped me, laughing with those big white teeth of his and saying I was just pretending and I really wanted it and we'd get married."

The bright black eyes snapped open, glaring. "They don't listen! They get together and tell each other what women are like, but they never listen to find out. Shut up in their heads like clams. I grabbed a butcher knife and told him if he thought I'd marry a man who'd jump his wife, he had another think coming. He didn't listen. He was twice as big as me."

I didn't say anything. There wasn't anything to say. Ella's bright black eyes glittered at the television set. There was a get-well card with shamrocks and green elves on it, and a picture of somebody's smiling family with their split-level house and dog.

"I could have told my mama—but my father? He'd have married me off to Roke. I didn't know where to turn, and we had to have the money. Roke kept at it when he could catch me, and I knew where babies came from all right, and I knew I was going to have one."

"And you'd have to marry Roke?"

"Me?" Now her black eyes snapped above her big nose. "I walked to town to an old lady my mama told me about once. This lady said no woman would ever lie happy next to Roke Pritcher, even if he did have three hundred good acres and all those pigs. She took me to a doctor in Cedar Rapids when my dad thought we were going to a revival, and then sent word she'd been taken sick and would pay me to stay a week."

"In a minute," an attendant said loudly, pushing a thin old man down the hall in his wheelchair. "We're going to have a nice cake-and-coffee party in the lounge."

"That old man doesn't want cake and coffee," Ella said in her crackling whisper of a voice. "He never does. He'll piddle on the floor; you watch. They're shut up in their heads—they don't listen."

The sound of the wheelchair died away. "I paid that lady back what I owed," Ella said. "Nickels and dimes at a time. But Roke lost me my little baby. She was my daughter and heir. You don't favor your sons—they're favored forever in this world—your daughter's your heir. She comes to the rest home, rubs your back. And Roke took my daughter."

Her old hands were picking, picking at the quilt. One tear slid down her wrinkles and gave a calico daisy a dark eye. "I had to leave her in the trap to spring myself loose. Just like a fox that gnaws its paw off. I never could have another baby."

Someone turned a television set on in another room. A crisp male voice began to give market reports. "What did you do then?" I asked after a while, holding Ella's hand that was as light and dry as balsa wood.

"It was really the world," she said. "Couldn't not be married and keep your baby then, not if you wanted to stay where you were born. And where else was there to go? Those men counted on that."

"But you got out of the trap," I said.

"They don't think a woman's the same," Ella said. "That she's got the pride they've got, and the independence. They think we're different. Shut up in their heads, talking to each other, not listening." Thin voices were singing a hymn in the lounge down the hall.

Ella's black eyes stared at me under her tufts of hair. "Roke had lots of hogs, but he was meaner than they were, and a hog's mean. He had two big sows named Gussie and Evelina, and every now and then they'd cross him. Hogs are smart. So he had it in for Gussie and Evelina. A kind of mean game. He'd shut them in a pen, wouldn't feed them. Just to show who was boss."

Ella's eyes had no expression in them now: lumps of coal. "If he jumped me after that, I just played dead and let him puff and pant—he couldn't hurt me any more than I'd been hurt already, and my family needed the money so bad. Where else could I make money like that? I even went to work for him after school in his kitchen and hog houses, and folks started saying there was going to be a wedding. I was a pretty thing then. Ella Stark and Roke Pritcher. He strutted around with the men."

"Here we are," said a loud, bright voice: an attendant wheeled my mother back to her bed and lifted her into it. My mother closed her eyes. I covered her up and found her brush, and began to smooth her long, thin hair over the pillow.

"Roke strutted around and flashed those picket-fence teeth at me," Ella said. "But he was starving that Gussie and Evelina. I worked along, did what he said. I'd run the separator in the kitchen—turned the crank, washed all those disks. Then I'd carry the skim milk to the pigs. Feed the chickens . . . get the eggs . . . run the flies out of the house before supper with some leaf switches off a tree."

Ella's black eyes narrowed under their wrinkled lids. "But one day Roke and me were alone in a hog house. I was slopping the hogs, and Roke was on the top rail of Gussie and Evelina's pen—he was just climbing over, a foot on each side, with a stone floor down there to bust your skull right open."

"Feels good," my mother murmured. Her hair glistened like angel hair on a Christmas tree.

"Now, Ella, it's your turn," the attendant said loudly, coming in to whip off Ella's quilt and sheet.

"Just like a nice ripe watermelon," Ella said. There wasn't enough of her in her hospital gown to give it shape; it seemed to inhabit the bed by itself.

"Here we go," the attendant bawled, scooping up Ella.

"They said I was inconsolable when they found what was left of Roke Pritcher." Ella stared from the attendant's arms, an old face in a bundle of flower-sprigged flannel. "She was my daughter and heir."

"There you go," the attendant said, loading the nightgown and Ella's face into the wheelchair.

Ella's big nose and flyaway crown of hair bobbed over the attendant's shoulder; her bright black eyes glared at me. "Murder—two murders—and nobody cares!" she hissed. "See?"

"Let's get our pretty pink slippers on," the attendant bawled, down on her knees by the bed.

"Murder!" Ella yelled in the attendant's face that was only an inch or two away.

"There we are," the attendant said, getting to her feet.

Ella's eyes glittered. Borne away down the hall, she left a last, whispered, "They don't listen!" behind her in the air.

THE HIJACKING

by David Ray

I

Whenever Daryl walked the two blocks home from his shop for lunch, he turned on the radio while he ate the sandwiches and soda pop Celia placed before him. "I love that Bob Wills and his Texas Playboys, he'd say, chomping his food. Daryl tapped his foot to the music—steel guitar and fiddles. "That's Bob right there." He'd single out a solo passage and point to the radio, then he'd identify Bob's brother Leon, who liked to yell and let out a wild cry of "Aw, haw, take it away!"

Daryl aped the musicians from the table, just as loud as they were. He joined them in song, shifting the clumps in his mouth.

> Deep within my heart
> lies a mel-o-dee,
> a song of old San Antone . . .

Celia strode angrily to the radio and turned off the music. The first time she dared such a bold move, Daryl got up from the table and switched it on again. After that, Celia endured the sound she found so offensive, but walked around with cotton stuffed mawkishly in her ears.

At other times they argued bitterly. Celia didn't want to bother with cotton in her ears. When they argued, Daryl sometimes struck his wife across the face. She called him a "no-account hillbilly" and a "real heel," and lamented that she had married him.

Daryl quit coming home for lunch, but instead took his radio to the barbershop each day. After he began that custom, Cyrus tried to make sure he was with his father in the shop by noon in order to listen to the Bob Wills program with his father and share his sandwiches and boiled eggs out of the black tin lunch pail. When the music came on, Daryl would wink at Cy and the boy would share Daryl's pride in enjoying what Celia disapproved. Cyrus looked up at the ornate pressed-zinc of the ceiling, his lips pursed in an empty whistle, as happy as he had ever been. Sometimes, in a good mood, his father would let him handle the .410 shotgun pistol he kept in his drawer, or he would talk to him about the picture of Custer's last stand that gathered dust on the wall.

In the barbershop, farmers from miles around would sit waiting their turns. They would talk to the one who sat in the chair, the bib with blue stripes tied around his neck as if to keep oatmeal off his overalls. Hair fell like gray grass. "I don't comprehend how a man's expected to make a living." The boy had heard that from more than one customer.

"I reckon each and every man has to find his own way." Daryl moved around the chair, clipping, stepping back to examine and appraise his work, the scissors clicking away. The falling hair dropped past Daryl's wrist, sprinkling stray strands onto his sleeves and trousers. Cyrus eyed the hair on the floor, waiting to sweep it up.

Daryl told the customer and his waiting friends that he didn't mind having figured out a way all by himself to make a living. He had taught himself barbering, when he saw that nobody else was going to tell him how to get by, and it was clear he couldn't make a living by sharecropping for his father. "I learnt it all by myself," he said. What was important was for a man to use his own mind, he said, and never say die. Still, the price war was a worrisome topic, he admitted. Gas down at the corner was a penny a gallon. But he preferred to think about other things, how the customer was always right and God helps those who help themselves. When the customers wanted to talk about the price war, Daryl would try to change the subject. Cyrus liked to hear his dad and his customers talk about the war over in Spain.

"That's too damn far away to get worried and heated up about," the man in the chair said.

"There's a big 'un a-coming, though," said a waiting customer, putting aside his copy of *Liberty* magazine. "They was just warming up if you ast me."

"Maybe that's what it'll take, to pull this here country out of this here so-called Depression," Daryl suggested.

"Could be. They ain't hiring nobody for nothing over in Tulsy. D-X, *they* ain't, and Texaco, *they* ain't."

"The farm boys, they're signing up for the army."

"It's better'n riding the rails."

"My little brother Owen," Daryl said, "he's got hisself a real good pop route, 7-UP and Coke both. He sure is lucky, but they told 'im if he'd go in the army they'd fix his teeth real good. He rotted 'em out chewin' Mule Twist."

"No kidding? You ain't joking? I thought it was good for you."

"No damn joke." Daryl paused and studied the man's hair. He pushed the head, tilting it away from him. "I wish to hell it was. I used to chew the stuff myself."

"What'll they do with them teeth of his?"

"Owen? They'll yank 'em right out, that's what. Only he ain't made up his mind yet. He likes driving a truck. A nice old red pickup, that's what he's got. A damn good job!"

"If this here F.D.R. stays in that White House, there'll be a war for goddamn sure. That's how the S.O.B. plans to end his goddamn Depression."

"Y'reckon? I figure that's ol' Wendell Willkie's intention."

"Both of 'em, more'n likely. That there Wendell's a sympathizer for them Spanish rebs, leastways he was while the fighting was still a-going on. That's what I read in the *Tulsa World*."

"Naw!" Daryl stepped back. It was too much to be believed.

"Yep, that's what it said."

"I didn't know he was a smartass. Do you think he's some sort of a commie too?" Daryl held the scissors open and ready.

"You know what I was thinking?" the farmer in the red leather chair asked. "I was thinkin'—that F.D.R., he ain't really crippled at all. He just puts on a act to get people feelin' sorry for 'im, gets hisself pushed around in a wheelchair. You can't believe everything you read in that damn *Tulsy World,* neither."

"That's for danged sure," Daryl said without pausing. "But what's a poor ignorant hillbilly a-goin' to do when them newspapers print made-up pictures, him in a wheelchair? The average guy, he's just going to feel sorry for the sonofabitch, more'n likely vote for 'im. Hell, they'll believe anything!"

" 'Specially the damn women. An' their vote's worth just about as much as a man's."

"To the politicians, sure."

"That's the truth. They just talk 'em up real nice." When the man stepped down from the chair at last, Cyrus picked up his broom and dashed over to sweep.

"That Willkie, he give a speech up there at Coffeyville the other day. He useta teach school around there. He was talkin' real wild, all that one-world shit. Down there in Texas he liked to have got murdered, talkin' that way, I can tell you."

"Oh yeah, why's that? What'd he say?" Daryl was mildly curious, his mouth open. He held his scissors back.

"He kept saying *Civil* War instead of the War Between the States, like you're supposed to. He didn't even know what us southerners call it, us folks south of the Mason-Dixon."

"He damn well oughta know better." Once he had decided where to trim, Daryl's scissors never stopped their busy clipping and clicking. Cyrus watched his dad turn to pick up a tailor-made cigarette he had rolled earlier on the metal and rubber machine from the dime store. Daryl called it his cigarette factory, but it still looked like a toy, with bright red paint and a little rubber bed for the tobacco to lie in a heap till it was rolled in a tiny paper. The barber swallowed the smoke, then exhaled it through his nostrils. He stood back and pondered his customer's hair. He seemed to be reading the thoughts inside that head. Then he gazed out the narrow window, the man in the chair watching him curiously.

"Well, that Willkie's got some good points too, I reckon," the customer allowed. "He claims F.D.R., that sonofabitch, called up Hitler and Mussolini both the other day, just to be nice to 'em and say hello."

"It wouldn't surprise me one bit," Daryl agreed.

"Way I see it," the customer added, standing up and getting his neck brushed a second time with talcum, "there just ain't much choice between a New Dealer and a commie like Willkie."

"Let me ask ya this." Daryl struck a lighter note. "Did you get any of that there Willkie gum?"

"No, I can't say that I have."

"They was passin' it out in the street over in Tulsy."

"Just regular chewin' gum?"

I reckon, only it says WIN WITH WILLKIE on the pack."

"They must have a hell of a lot of that Wall street money behind 'em to be passin' out free chewing gum."

When the farmer left, shaking his head with heavy thoughts, Daryl continued the conversation with the next customer. He loosened the collar on a gaunt, loose-kneed truck driver who looked like Abraham Lincoln and was dabbing on shave foam when the customer eyed him sharply, turning his eyes without moving his head. "Hey, can't you warm that up a mite, Daryl?"

"Cain't. Don't have no hot water."

"I know where they got hot. Few more miles up the road toward Tulsy."

"I know they got hot. I can't hep it though. I just ain't got it." Cyrus noticed his father always stretched out the word *can't* whenever he was begging somebody something or apologizing. He watched

Daryl finish shaving the man, then clip away busily to show his fiendish concern for the perfect trim. This customer, like the last, confided his worry about Willkie being a communist.

"He's preachin' all that one-world crap."

Cyrus watched Daryl pull the apron away and shake it free of the customer's hair. The tall and lanky man straightened his legs and stood up. Cyrus jumped down from his chair by the wall and walked to the corner to fetch his broom again.

"That Willkie," the customer said, "he travels around with them women wearing short skirts and showin' their butts. One of 'em got herself paddywhacked on the fanny the other day."

Daryl gave most of the man's money back in change. "They're askin' for it, dressed in them short skirts," he said.

If he could vote, he'd vote for Wendell Willkie, Cyrus thought. Why not? One world sounded good. Everybody knew F.D.R. was leading the country smack into a war. That's why airplanes were flying over more often, and balloons and dirigibles too. That's what everybody said—there was going to be a war, a big one. Cyrus had seen those big blimps floating across the sky, and he knew they had something to do with getting ready for war. He and the sheriff's son had seen a great white zeppelin, bigger even than a dirigible, a huge floating cigar, gracefully slipping through a group of fluffy white clouds, disappearing again and again.

II

Cyrus shared his father's worry about the price war. At the corner he had seen the filling station owner standing in his blue coveralls and pulling the pump back and forth while the customer leaned back in his roadster's seat and looked up at the glass cylinder, watching the bubbling red gasoline fall past the gauge marks. The red gas reminded Cy of strawberry soda pop. A sign propped by the pump read GAS WAR, PENNY A GAL.

Soon, just as Daryl had predicted, the price war spread from filling stations to barbershops. One shop down the road was charging only a nickel for a haircut and a dime for a shave. That was crazy—"jackass crazy," Daryl called it—everybody knew haircuts took longer and always cost more. "It could drive a man under," the barber said more than once, shaking his head. And the enemy barber was giving a shampoo free, with hot water. "He can afford to hold out longer. That's what I'm worried about." Cy liked it when his father shared worries with him.

Daryl had to make enough money to pay the rent on the shop,

and the water and light bills, not to mention the rent at home and the five dollars a month he had to pay back to Uncle Horace against the hundred-dollar loan Uncle Horace had arranged so he could buy the barber chair. Otherwise the chair, with its porcelain white arms and red leather padding, would be taken away. *Damn,* Cyrus would mutter to himself in sympathetic response to his father's curses. He stood holding the broom, his chest puffed out with pride. He felt important when he worried along with his father. Daryl said he didn't know how long he could afford to keep the shop open. When this thing hit, he said, he had been building up his trade, making friends with all sorts of new customers. Now the barber a few miles away in Sapulpa was taking all his best customers, and that man down the road got the leftovers. There was nothing left for the little shop on the main street of the tiny town of Mounds.

Daryl sat in his shop and swatted flies or watched Cyrus while he swatted them. Then he'd stand before the plate glass window with his arms crossed, cursing anyone who walked by freshly shaved or with his hair neatly trimmed. Cyrus could tell that his father was trying not to look too hungrily at the hairlines of those passing men. Daryl rubbed his own close shave as he caught sight of chins still rough with whiskers, but the men walked on by, didn't even look in. A hundred times a day Daryl rearranged the tonics and lotions on his shelf over the sink and sharpened his razor repeatedly on the leather strop, letting it drop with a sigh when he had finished.

His son watched in silence, wanting to help, to comfort his father. For long stretches of time Daryl seemed to forget all about him. The boy would cough, just to get his attention.

III

Cyrus knew his father had committed crimes before. In arguments Celia had referred to these incidents. The boy even knew the kind of men she meant when she warned Daryl to stay away from the crooks he knew from Tulsa. Celia said that Daryl had once taken the .410 shotgun pistol and tried to stick somebody up. He hadn't even waited till dark, "like a damn fool." Daryl had been arrested and thrown in jail.

Daryl seemed unable to contradict either his wife's descriptions of the crime or the even more shrill charge that her lawyer brother, Horace, had kept him out of jail. "If it hadn't been for my brother, you'd still be in there," she accused more than once, and sometimes added that Daryl should *still* be in jail. Her husband's reply was always blocked by her sudden turnabout: they should never discuss such things in front of the children. She forbade another word of it. Cyrus didn't really think his father was a crook as she had accused, not like the ones he had seen in picture shows projected on the brick rear wall of the Safeway store. Families would lie on blankets, looking away at the moon and the stars whenever they got bored.▪

But one day he saw Daryl throw a striped bib around a man who looked exactly like a crook. His hair was the color of carrots and he even had crooked fingers and legs, and tattoos like the convicts in the movies. After a few minutes in the barbershop the man, skinny, with a pale wrinkled neck and narrowed eyes, lowered his voice, looking at the boy suspiciously as he spoke to the barber.

Cyrus knew something crooked was going on. He could hear the man telling Daryl, "There's a whole warehouse full a them tires, and the trucks go down that Sand Springs road all loaded up. It'd be easy as pie to get us some and I know a fella, he'd buy 'em sure, two bucks a tire, and six bits apiece for inner tubes if they got any. Usually they pile them inner tubes up on top of the truck cab. A kid could crawl up an' throw 'em down." He glanced over at Cyrus.

"I dunno." Daryl worked the scissors, worried. He seemed to know the man pretty well.

"You ain't gonna get rich barberin'."

"Don't I know it! Hell, I can't pay for that chair you're settin' in. My brother-in-law, Horace, he's raisin' Cain about that awready. He only loaned me the money four months ago and it wasn't even hissen. It was my little girl Veenie's from her finger gettin' cut off on one of them oil company rodlines."

"How'd *that* happen?"

"Oh, they was playin', you know how kids is, and her brother yonder." Daryl jerked his head toward Cy. "The oil well equipment, it's everywheres out there in them fields. You know how kids is; they don't know no better. They was a-cleanin' the oil off, trying to be helpful like kids do, and her finger, it just got pulled in and yanked right off. It was one of them damn rod lines and a pulley that done it, down by the powerhouse on my daddy's farm."

But Veenie's finger was hanging by a thread of skin, Cyrus wanted to protest, and his mother had come running out of the house ripping off her apron as she saw the bleeding hand of her screaming daughter, mewling and yelling from her own mouth too as she whipped the apron cloth around the hand and then tore the belt off her dress and tied it around the apron already soaked red and dripping. She had grabbed the girl up, and was running, all in one stumbling action, down the hard ruts of the road through the trees to Mr. McGregor's house. The closest car was parked by his house.

"Daddy, tell the man how Mr. McGregor gave Veenie and Mom a ride into town and how they couldn't find a doctor."

"The boy's right," Daryl said to his customer while he paused and considered his comb in the slant of sunlight. "One ol' boy was too busy takin' his boy to a ballgame to save that little finger from fallin' off. Just in time she got some doctor over there in niggertown. Beggars can't be choosers."

"I wouldn't let no nigger touch my kids," the customer said.

"Hell, man, she was bleedin' to death."

"*Let* her bleed to death before a goddamn nigger touches her."

Daryl said nothing. He worked more intently at the man's carrot-colored hair. At last the man started up again. "They got Firestones, Goodyears, all the big brands. I'm tellin' you, Daryl, it's easy money. Just like pickin' it off of the trees."

"What time you figuring?" Cyrus realized that his father was working out the crime the same way the convicts in the movie had, even though they were already in jail.

"It takes at least three guys," the customer from Tulsa explained. His haircut was finished. He sat sprawled in the chair.

"My little brother Owen, he'll come along," Daryl offered. Cyrus knew Uncle Owen would do anything Daryl asked him to. He had driven a truck loaded high with furniture when the landlord was after them, and he'd commit a crime too if his big brother Daryl told him to.

"One man, he stands on the running board," the customer said. "It'd be better to have a extra man too. Minimum is one crawls up on the fender or leans way up to grab them tires. And somebody's gotta get up on that truck and throw 'em down. The kid there, he could help too, crawling up on top an' shovin' 'em down. He could grab the inner tubes from up high too."

Daryl looked at Cyrus and paused, the scissors open in his hand. Then he said, "I'd be handy for getting up on that truck. I don't know about my boy here."

"Myself," the skinny customer said, narrowing his eyes to keep out the cigarette smoke, "I'm just right for riding the running board. I'll grab them tires when you toss 'em down." Cyrus looked at the ship-and-anchor tattoo on the man's pale arm.

"So little Owen, he'll drive," Daryl concluded. "I'll get up on that truck bed and hand 'em down."

"Easy as Jack Robinson," the stranger assured him. "The kid, he can help."

"I figure I got to get a piece of it." Cyrus watched his father make that decision and lick his lips, tapping the thin comb on the back of his hand as the stranger stood up and rolled his sleeves down over his tattoo.

"I'll tell you when," the skinny, crooked stranger said, standing up. Cyrus saw that he didn't even pay the dime for his haircut. He just winked at Daryl and extended his hand for a shake. Opening the door, he took a glance back at Cyrus, who glared blankly at him, then picked up his broom to sweep the littered hair, yellow as carrots.

IV

The whole thing seemed like a dream. A few evenings later, Cyrus felt himself tugged by his father. Daryl shushed him so Celia wouldn't hear, and they went out into the chill darkness and joined Uncle Owen in his pickup truck. The boy sat sleepily between his father and his round-faced uncle.

The red pickup rattled into Tulsa, lumbering down side streets, its headlights thrown against tenement buildings and tin warehouses with tire-padded loading docks. Cyrus recognized the abandoned wooden platforms of the city market, covered stalls and stands where he'd gone along to sell melons before his dad had become a barber. When they went to the market, they arrived before dawn and stretched out on the wooden planks for a while before the work started. Cyrus had watched the moth-pale dawn come up over the skyscrapers. Now, in the night, the docks and sheds of the farmers' market were abandoned except for a shadowy cat with bright yellow eyes. It scooted back from the headlights.

"This ol' boy lives down by niggertown," Daryl said, directing Uncle Owen. The pickup rattled over the bumps of the railway crossing.

The tattooed skinny man with carrot-colored hair was waiting for them, standing in the dark. When he climbed into the truck, Cyrus noticed his crooked fingers again. The man shoved against Daryl and made room for himself. Without saying anything, Cyrus crawled onto his father's lap. He looked up at the stranger's leathery face, lit by the dashboard light. He smelled the man, beer and whiskey, and a sweet smell like women.

As the truck jounced along, Cyrus felt his father's hand spread upon his chest, felt sharp knees and bony legs under him. His father and the stranger talked about the truckload of tires, fat ones and good ones. They discussed the time schedules of the trucks. Uncle Owen drove, his chin jutting out, chewing tobacco. Every once in a while he rolled down the window to spit into the night. Cyrus looked up at the men's faces. None of them seemed scared. The light was bright yellow in the round glass windows of the dashboard. The gearshift handle was an ivory skull, the color of an old picture in Gramma's album.

They drove along the wobbly black tar of the Sand Springs road, a tippy highway that wound about on high banks. After half an hour, Owen pulled the truck over onto a gravel siding.

Owen stayed in the cab of the truck, studying the rearview mirror, while the other two men stepped out into the darkness. They stood and rolled cigarettes in the breeze. Cyrus could hear the chirring of the cicadas and see the lightning bugs thick and bright, their yellow lights sudden in the air over dark weeds. He resisted the urge to run forward and cup the lightning bugs in his hands. He'd fall off the slopes into the blackness if he did. Instead, he decided to do what the men were doing. He untucked the little flap his mother had sewn for him inside his trousers. But he was too nervous. He followed the men back to the pickup, barely visible against the pale sky. They sat again inside the cab. Daryl and the stranger had traded places. Sitting on his father's lap, Cyrus could feel the breeze on his face through the open window.

"He'll be along any minute now," the stranger said.

"Get it over with," Uncle Owen added.

Two lone cars had passed, their lights brightening the trees ahead. They had disappeared around a bend. The third vehicle was a swaying blue truck with an open back, its wooden railings rattling. A chain at the back held a tailgate that kept several columns of tires from tumbling out.

Uncle Owen started the pickup and pulled out behind the bouncing truck. He left the headlights off and shifted gears carefully, cursing the noise. The pickup edged close behind the truck, hiding in its shadows. The reddish gleam of the truck's reflected taillight brightened the red paint of the pickup.

"We won't need the kid after all," the stranger said, watching the swaying truck ahead. "I thought it was gonna be a van."

"You stay with your uncle Owen," Daryl said to Cyrus, and pushed him to his feet. Wordlessly, Daryl stepped out onto the running board. Cyrus saw his father crawl forward over the shaking fender, a shadow lit like a cutout whenever the truck's headlights briefly flared.

For a moment, as his father crouched and balanced himself like a cat, ready to leap forward, Cyrus saw his father's face in the red glow. Daryl looked like a devil. The boy gripped the skull head of the gearshift handle with sweaty hands until Uncle Owen pushed him away.

"There's nothing to be afraid of, I told you," Owen said, and offered the boy some of his chewing tobacco. Cyrus took a lump of the moist and sweet-smelling tobacco and rolled it between his fingers.

Suddenly Daryl leaped forward and grabbed at the swaying chain behind the load of tires. With both hands clutching the chain, he hung for a moment, kicking between the two trucks. Then he drew his knees up and managed to pull himself onto the truck bed, slipping forward under the chain while Cyrus gulped. The boy could see the stacked-up tires leaning and swaying in columns.

Daryl had fallen to his knees and nearly tumbled out under the shaking chain. He crawled forward again on bouncing knees, embracing tires. At last he stood, wobbly, and picked up a tire. He managed to hand it down to the tattooed man, now balanced on the pickup's fender.

Soon the two men had created a rhythm. Standing on the running board, the stranger somehow grabbed each tire and tossed it behind him onto the bed of the pickup, all the while struggling to stay on his feet. Two or three tires had dropped into the darkness of the roadside, but Cyrus heard most of them thudding into place behind him.

In the rearview mirror above him, Uncle Owen studied a slowly approaching light. He muttered to himself and stopped chewing his tobacco, storing it in his cheek.

Even before he heard the wavering siren, growing ever closer, Cyrus knew that it was the police. Owen tapped the horn lightly but urgently to warn the other men. Daryl crouched down and looked back. Even as the truck ahead slowed, it hit a bump, bouncing him around. He braced himself, trying to hide among the shadowy tires as the siren fell away into silence.

A voice called out, "Come on down here with your hands up or you're dead men, sure as hell!"

Owen slumped in the seat of the pickup and yanked the handbrake back. "Goddamn," he muttered, looking out into the night.

Both trucks stood on the gravel shoulders of the road, dust floating in the bright lights that came from every direction. Troopers waved flashlights around, shone them into faces. A red light on top of their car wobbled about.

Turning from one direction to another as he stood on the floor of the pickup's cab, the boy hoped his father hadn't brought along the shotgun pistol. He tried to make out what was happening. Two troopers, in green uniforms with big Stetson hats and braided cord looped round their shoulders, were walking about, waving pistols and flashlights, looking at everything at once—the trucks and the men. They asked questions, gave gruff orders. "Down from there, you!" one ordered Daryl. The other trooper held the tattooed stranger by his elbow. All four men, the troopers and the two captured, watched as Daryl crawled down from his hiding place among black columns of tires. Cyrus felt the breeze through the door Uncle Owen had left open. He began to cry when he saw the gun pushed into his father's ribs.

As the officers gave orders and poked guns about, the captured men seemed to sag in their weariness and defeat. Pride was gone from them. Their eyes followed where the troopers pointed with flashlights, at the truck ahead, the pickup, the license plates, finally up to the stars. One of the troopers aimed his pistol upward for a moment, as if to shoot a star.

The driver of the blue truck came back. He was dressed in baggy gray coveralls. Smiling and waving his own flashlight about, he seemed to know everything about what was going on. He grinned at the three captured men who had turned out their pockets and were trying to explain, explain. The troopers had their handcuffs out, about to snap them on. The truck driver stood by the taillight and his face glowed now, another devil. His eyes were two deep black hollows, like a skull's.

"There's a boy in there," one of the troopers said, then reached to hold the swinging pickup door. He peered across. "Come on out, boy," he said to Cyrus. "Nobody's going to hurt you."

Cyrus stood clutching the steering wheel a moment before he obeyed and stepped down, almost stumbling on the high step. He looked at the faces of the troopers and the happy, alert face of the truck driver. One trooper held Daryl's arm, and the other held Owen's as they led the men back to the police car. Cyrus walked beside the skinny, curse-muttering stranger from Tulsa until the three men were shoved into the backseat of the police car. An iron grille separated the backseat from the front, just like a cage. Weary sighs came from the handcuffed men. They stared blankly through the grille.

The troopers shook the truck driver's hand and joked with him. Evidently the capture had all been planned ahead of time. They were amused that men would try to do such a foolish thing as a hijacking.

In the car, the troopers had their big hats off, and Cyrus sat between them. The car purred smoothly along, and the two men discussed what they should do with the boy. They asked him his name, and why he wasn't home in bed. Did his mother know he was out? They wondered whether they should take the boy all the way back home to Mounds before or after taking the men into Tulsa to book them at the jail. Or maybe they should stick him in Juvenile Detention in Tulsa?

Cyrus was no longer crying, but he was frightened, and he wondered what would happen to Uncle Owen's lonely red pickup left parked in the darkness, half loaded with tires. He wondered why the troopers hadn't made the men return the tires to the truck, reloading them, or go back and find the ones they had dropped into the darkness of the weedy roadside slopes. They must have seen the tires bounce and roll into the dark just before they had turned on their siren. Then he began to think about Juvenile Detention. He was sure they meant a jail for children, and in a way he liked that idea. If they took him there, they would be treating him like a grown-up, just like his father. And Celia couldn't spank him. He was sure she'd give him a spanking as soon as he got home if the troopers took him back to Mounds.

In Tulsa the troopers led the captured men into the police station. Waiting in the car, careful not to touch anything, Cyrus watched his father, shoulders hunched over in shame, disappear with the other men up the steps between two lighted globes.

After a few minutes, the trooper who had been driving returned. "Your daddy told me where you live," he said, "so I'm going to take you home to your mommy. What do you think of that?"

Cyrus didn't feel like telling the trooper what he thought. He was wondering if he should grab the gun from his holster and shoot the trooper. Then he could run into the police station and free his father. But he was feeling sleepy again, and he couldn't be sure of anything. He sat with heavy lids, listening to the voice of the trooper. He seemed friendly, and after a few minutes leaned over and took some candy out of the glove compartment. He opened the paper sack and offered them, chocolate kisses with twisted spiral tips. "Go on, have some more. They ain't poison. Have two of 'em." The trooper took some of the chocolates himself, and tongued them around in his mouth.

"They should have known better," he said, treating Cyrus as a friend. "We watch that Sand Springs road all the time, real regular, and we know that bastard Wilson from way back. We watch every move he makes." Cyrus could tell he almost called the carrot-haired stranger an even worse name, but decided not to. "I've booked that guy so many times I can tell you every scar and tattoo he's got. Your daddy, he was a dope, if you ask me, to get mixed up with a jerk like that." The trooper found a toothpick in his pocket and worked at the candy in his teeth, just like Daryl.

When the trooper led the sleepy boy up the wooden steps of the darkened duplex in Mounds, he said nothing. They waited outside the screen door until Celia appeared. After a while she came out and stood with the door pushed half open, pinching the collar of her house robe while she listened to the trooper's explanation. The trooper held his bucket-size hat in his hand. His knee-length boots shone in the light from the police car, its headlights left on.

"I'm sorry to have to tell you all this," he apologized, calling Celia "ma'am."

"It's not your fault," she managed. "You have to do your duty. I knew he was up to something."

"We had a tip, ma'am, and we have to follow up all the tips. That's what the public expects. This one turned out to be dead right. I wish it hadn't. Your husband, he seems like a nice man, mostly."

Celia shook her head, unable to comment. She was biting her lips, shaking her head. "I could make you a cup of coffee," she offered at last.

"No, ma'am, I really have to get back. And I got the car running there." He pointed.

Cyrus had been standing helplessly. He just wanted to go on in and go to sleep, next to Veenie.

"Your husband's in over his head, ma'am. Has he ever been involved in anything like this before?"

"Like what?"

"Like a hijacking, I mean."

"I'd rather not say," Celia said. "I'm just too . . . *overwhelmed* to say anything, forgive me."

"Of course, ma'am. You can make a statement later if you want to, though. It might help. And it would help for sure to get a lawyer for him. What's his name?"

"Daryl."

"Yes, ma'am. He really could use a lawyer. That's the best advice I can give you, both of you, and that boy too."

"My brother's a lawyer," she said, and began to cry. Her hand clutched her robe. She bowed her head. The officer touched her shoulder.

"Good night, ma'am," he said. "And I'm sorry I had to trouble you." He seemed to have forgotten about Cyrus. He did not turn when he heard the trooper's steps descending the porch stoop, or when he called out, "Good night, ma'am," just like an old friend.

The rest of that night, Celia sat in the rocking chair, holding Cyrus on her lap, just as his father had held him in the truck. Her hand was spread across his chest, but it was small and nervous.

He wanted to tell her he hadn't had anything to do with the hijacking, that he hadn't even known what the word meant, not until he saw how high his father had to climb to get up onto the back of the blue truck. But he knew he'd be telling lies. He had wanted to go, to be a man, even a criminal if he had to be, to be a man. Most of all, he wanted to sleep, not to have to say anything at all. But Celia kept asking him questions in her low, comforting voice. She seemed to have forgotten about spanking him. But she still wanted to know, and Cyrus didn't know how much he should tell her. He was still on his father's side. And if his father had to stay in jail, he was going to find a way to listen to Bob Wills and his Texas Playboys all by himself, every day at noon. Somehow he would find a way. It would be helping his father somehow.

"I'll never forgive him for taking you along," Celia said, dropping her tears on Cyrus's hand. "Never!"

"It wasn't his fault, Momma, honest it wasn't." Cyrus was ashamed of himself, because he was crying too.

His mother rocked him, and he watched the molding around the floor to see if any rats or mice had come out. As dawn began to lighten the lacy curtains on the windows, Celia relaxed her grip and fell asleep. At last the boy climbed down from the rocking chair and went into the bedroom. He crawled in beside Veenie. She was sound asleep, with her mouth open, and she was warm when he hugged her. Sleep hit him, and he hoped he wouldn't dream again about the battle in the cornfield, where he had been slashed with the sabers and killed over and over, back in the Civil War.

RELUCTANT MADONNA

by Jan Epton Seale

Christie intends to be cool as Buddha about this baby. Unflappable. Together. But so far she has made every one of Erren's fingers bleed a tiny red halo where she trimmed the nail. How was she to know babies were born with skin growing up the back side of their tiny claws?

He didn't protest. In fact, he lay in newborn dreaminess on the hospital bed the whole time she carefully cut. Each rubbery little puckered finger curled itself tight into the fist again after she trimmed it, so it wasn't until she spread his hands to check for jagged edges that she discovered her mistake. Her first impulse is to ring for the nurse. She resists. Maybe they'll think she is too dumb to take this baby home, needs a few more days to practice mothering under supervision.

Instead, she shuts the fingernail scissors quickly in her overnight bag and with forced casualness tightens the clasp holding her longish brown hair at her neck. She is impatient for Rex to come for them.

Other young women would have their mothers waiting at home, waiting to help with the baby. Not Christie. Rex has seen to that.

"It's the tropics," he said when he told her about the company's offer for him to be an agent in the border town in Texas. "You know—Sun Belt migration," he encouraged.

She was silent.

"Sure it's a long way from Cincinnati and your folks, but it'll be fun. Just what we need. A little adventure."

He could say that. His father had deserted the family shortly after Rex was born and his mother was dead long before Christie and Rex met. To him, home was never more than rooms above bars or a tiny trailer in a seedy transient camp.

Now he is downstairs arguing with the discharge clerk, no doubt leaning his six-foot frame against the payment window and snowing the clerk on this Christmas Eve with his natural good cheer and lopsided smile. He's entirely confident the hospital will let the post-partum and the neonatal of his life go home for Christmas even though they don't have the $300 to pay the balance.

Christie is not entirely confident anymore. She is tired from being excited for three days, and she is sore. Her life is not going along according to the magazine articles. Rex has set off her biological alarm clock at an ungodly early hour; they are poorer than they intended to be when they became parents, and they are a long way from relatives. Not to mention that tomorrow is Christmas.

Her parents' house is filled with friends sipping eggnog. The blue spruce is twelve feet tall and the fireplace is alive with a yule log and popping pine cones. On the dining table are zillions of Christmas cards to leaf through.

Her mother had been generous over the phone. "I'll come if you think you really need me." She didn't sound like she was two thousand miles away.

Her mother had not felt well lately. "It's okay, Mom. Rex is off work all week. We'll make it fine. Maybe you and Dad can come later."

Christie checks Erren's fingertips once more. Only one or two still have specks of blood. It had seemed like something useful to do while they waited. He was already a little Dracula when he was born, having scratched his fat cheeks with those tiny nails in the womb. She wondered each time she held him why the nurses hadn't clipped his nails. Now she knows.

The tie on his silly knit cap keeps slipping up over his mouth because he has no chin to hold it down. Christie leans to him, the movement a sharp reminder of her stitches. She pulls the bow back in place. "You're cute, Mr. Magoo," she says, and Erren's eyes pop open briefly in response to her breath in his face, then drift side-ways into sleep again. She has just nursed him; he is not to be bothered.

Rex had to get the cap at Woolworth's yesterday. Just the week before, she wrote her mother in Cincinnati bragging about the 83-degree day. It was a subtle way of assuring her that, after all, they knew what they were doing.

By late November they'd decided there would be no winter at all down here in South Texas. Winter was oranges and grapefruit, an occasional sweater at most. Wrong again. The night of Erren's birth she and Rex had settled themselves in bed when she heard the bougainvillea swat the house as the wind slammed in off the King Ranch in a first-class Texas norther. As if to imitate the sound, her water broke with a clear and curious snap.

"Rex," she had said, quietly summoning him from his gentle snore. "I think it's time." Just like an old movie. She smiles now, remembering how he had his jeans on and buttoned before he reached the light switch across the room. As they left for the hospital, leaves at the back door swirled around her feet in a tiny tornado—a baby tornado, she had thought, noting how the gusts billowed her pillow-ticking maternity dress beyond her own girth.

Now she idly plucks at the lap of the same dress. Where is her stomach? Her stomach lies beside her on the high bed. She feels the tilt of her universe, a private recognition of miracles. "The things of this world seen and unseen," she quotes softly.

Of course they'd taken a silly chance that night in April of their senior year at State. It was lovemaking in celebration of being able to open the windows of the student housing apartment for the first time and let the heady spring breeze blow through. There was a thrill in it, nothing more. She was ashamed of herself when she tried to remember who had suggested it. Having a baby at the wrong time in the wrong place was something she was not quite ready to forgive in either of them.

When they married at the end of their junior year, her father had felt he must counsel them. "You don't need any wolves knocking at the door these first few years. So do it in the right order: first your education, then money, then a family."

"That's the way we see it, sir," Rex assured him.

"There are things at the drugstore, you know, to keep the wolf from knocking. . . ."—and her dad was on his way.

The first part they had done right: they had gotten their degrees. True, by mid-June there was a small bulge under her graduation robe. And so they hadn't kept the wolf away. He wasn't a monstrous little-red-riding-hood one banging down the door. Still, he had the power to make them unhappy. He was a scrawny, haggard type that reminded them they had no savings, no hospitalization yet, and that Christie had not gotten to try out her brand-new marketing degree in a good-paying job.

Erren's fists unfurled in slow motion. "We didn't do you right," Christie whispers to him. By this time they were to have had a sunrise-gold washer/dryer set behind louvered wooden doors in a modest but tasteful two-level town house. "We meant to have everything perfect for you." Erren sighs. Christie sighs. And the door is flung wide as Rex enters, stuffing the discharge papers in his shirt pocket.

"Ah, my pretties!" he says too loudly. "Prithee wait no longer."

Christie laughs. "You clown! Did you get us out of hock?"

"You bet."

Settled in the car, she ventures the question: Is it warm at home?

"Like toast," says Rex.

Maybe milk toast, she thinks. The house they have rented is an old drafty thing sitting on blocks. They haven't been able to afford any rugs.

"The little gas heater I bought works great for the bedroom," Rex says. "I got a metal connection hose for it—safer than a rubber one. Still, we'll have to check it all through the night."

Suddenly bright tears swim in Christie's eyes. She hadn't thought it possible to be lonely for a floor grille that sends beautiful wafts of warm air from a basement furnace.

They pull up to a traffic light. A noise beside her window distracts her. She is glad for the excuse to look out. An old man with gray hair and a beard that wisps down to his waist revs a motorcycle. Mounted over the handlebars is a pair of antlers from an eight-point buck.

"Look," Christie says, "someone trapped in a time warp from the sixties."

"Show the baby," Rex commands.

"What?"—unsure she has heard correctly.

"Hold Erren up so he can see the man. That's his Santa for this year. Next year we'll have to do the shopping-mall-Santa bit with colored portraits and all. Last chance for a free Santa."

"Oh, Rex!" she says, nevertheless holding the baby to the window. The old man sees her do it and waves. Too late she realizes he thinks she is showing off her newborn.

When they pull in the driveway, Christie drapes the edge of the receiving blanket over Erren's face in preparation for the cold air. Rex gets out and takes him from her. She swivels around in her seat and emerges carefully. The air is cold on her legs, but the late-afternoon sunlight dazzles. Her eyes smart from the glare after days of seclusion. And the tears return—unbidden, damn them, unwanted.

Grandmas and grandpas should come bounding down the steps. Neighbors' cameras should be popping. A schnauzer should greet them with wagging tail and a calico cat thread her legs in pleasure.

As Rex helps her up the steps of the porch, he whispers, "I have a surprise for you and Erren."

"One big surprise deserves another, or something like that," she says.

He unlocks the door with his spare hand. The living room is frigid. In the dimness she sees by the couch a pair of his shoes with socks carelessly tossed over them and a dinner plate that has recently held something requiring catsup.

Rex looks down at Erren, who is squirming at the changes in scenery and temperature. "Welcome to your house, sweetheart," he croons in a voice she doesn't recognize.

He turns to her. "And welcome home to you, sweetheart."

"Thank you," she says, thinking how easy it is for him to call this "home."

"Your room is ready," he says, and walks them toward the closed bedroom door.

A welcome gush of warmth greets them. She steps in. The $37 gas heater flickers a strong blue flame through its grating. Her eyes rest on a bright red object suspended from the light fixture.

"Know what that is?" Rex asks proudly.

"A piñata."

"You're smart—for a Yankee. Actually it's Erren's Christmas firebird." He takes the baby to it. "See your firebird, snookum?" Again in that voice. He spins the giant papier-mâché goose, and white streamers circle out from the wingtips. At the motion, the baby's hands flutter up and his brow lifts, revealing the navy blue of his new eyes.

Rex spins the bird again.

"Look at him, Chrissie! Just look how he notices. You're smart, baby, smart as they come!"

She is looking, first at the huge circling bird, then at the alert baby, and finally at Rex's transformed face. Her heart begins to circle around and around. The holly berries and yule logs of other Christmases, the Currier and Ives snowings of Cincinnati, Aunt Clara's exclusive oyster dressing begin to blur.

"Turn around," Rex says. "Look over there."

She turns and sees across the room an odd Christmas tree. It is made from the dowels of an old clothes-drying rack that collapsed when they moved. He has drilled angled holes in the wood and attached palm fronds. It is trimmed in pacifiers and at its feet lies the snow of the first box of diapers.

The tears come again and this time she does not hide them. "You're too much," she says. "You won't let me be sad."

He hugs her with his free arm. "I almost overdid it, no? But you've made me happier than I've ever been."

And so they spend the evening admiring the baby admiring his firebird. On the cheap turntable Rex plays Stravinsky's "Firebird Suite," "to start his musical taste off right," he explains. They make themselves wait until nine to open the box of marzipans they've been hoarding.

At ten Christie nurses Erren and Rex changes him. Rex opens the window a crack and sets the alarm clock for eleven to check on the heater. The baby is restless, so they take a pacifier off the tree. He accepts it like a veteran.

Rex insists on jiggling the crib until Erren sleeps. Then he turns out the light and crawls in beside Christie.

"What a shockingly svelte body you have, my dear," he says in his you-must-pay-the-rent voice. He cradles her head and kisses her forehead.

"Peace on earth?" he asks quietly.

"Peace," she says, and means it.

"You can always change your mind," he says solemnly into the darkness.

"Can I?"

"No."

"I'm glad."

And they lie together dreaming lightly until the first watch of the night.

REQUIEM FOR A CHECKER

by Roberta Silman

"Where'd you get that funny-looking car?" he said, and lifted his head out from under the porch he was nailing. Sideways his face was thin and tanned, his eyes noncommittal.

"It's a Checker," Phil replied.

"Checkers are cabs," the man said, heaving himself a little farther out from under the porch.

"Not all Checkers are cabs." Phil's voice was flat. "The company makes cars for ordinary use, too. This one has a truck engine, heavy-duty parts, and the valves are guaranteed for two hundred thousand miles."

"A lot of good that'll do you. The body won't last past seventy-five thousand miles. It's a piece of junk," he said, and reached for a nail.

"We live in the new house up the hill," Phil began. "We wondered if you might help us with it; there's a little more finish work to be done."

"Ain't no finish work in that whole entire house. They didn't even bother to miter the corners of the moldings," he announced, and pounded the last nail for the day and inched his skinny body out from under the porch. When he stood up I was surprised. He came only to Phil's shoulder. Phil extended his hand, which was ignored. Green eyes flickered in my direction. "All of Berkshire County's been through that house," he told me. "It's a regular attraction; if it wasn't so high up on the mountain they'd be including it on the tours."

"Can you come by when you're finished here?" Phil asked.

"We'll see," he said, then disappeared into the house. It belonged to our neighbor, who had suggested we speak to him. He was her caretaker.

Silently we drove home. All the houses on this road were on a ridge, ours on the highest spot of all. "Well, that was a dead end; we'll never see him again," Phil said. He sighed, then stopped to look at the car before we went inside. Phil loved that Checker, and now just the sight of it seemed to comfort him.

The Checker was a station wagon. It had only six hundred miles, was purple on the bottom and white on the top. "Is that a new car or an old one repainted?" a woman asked the day we got it.

"New. The Checker company doesn't believe in putting money into styling; they put it into parts and a superior engine."

"Sure is a strange shape for a new car," she murmured, then laughed. "A purple-and-white box on wheels."

Of course I didn't tell Phil. He wouldn't have cared anyway; he never cared about other people as much as I did. Besides, he had never wanted an ordinary car. When we were first married we had one of the earliest Volkswagen Beetles. People used to stop and walk around it all the time. But we were never annoyed; if anything, pleased. After we lived in England we brought home a Morris Minor station wagon with its unmistakable bull nose and real wood on the doors. But it wasn't sturdy enough on long trips, so we bought a gray Checker sedan, which got too small as the children grew. This past spring, we traded it in and bought the purple-and-white box.

"David Sarnoff drives Checkers. He claims they have the only seats that don't murder his back," the salesman told us. The gray sedan had been unusual, but unobtrusive. This station wagon was a startling phenomenon.

"Well, you certainly couldn't have an affair with this car," I said lightly. The salesman's face grew tight.

To our amazement he came. He walked through the house and touched all the moldings. "It kills me to see them just slapped in there."

"We did that to try to keep the cost down," Phil explained.

"Don't cost nothing more to do the job right instead of wrong," he snapped, then moved his toe cautiously over some uneven tiles in the bathroom. "These'll have to come out and be recut. They'll be popping up by Thanksgiving if you leave them." He opened the closet doors, winced when they scraped, ran his hand along the peg work in the banister, looked approvingly at the stone fireplace.

Then he pointed to the huge windows. "First spring storm and you'll have a torrent in here. Sills weren't done proper. Contractor had a bunch of kids who didn't know a thing about how to build a house." But when he jumped on the balcony he whistled in surprise. "Well, at least that's steady."

"Phil's a structural engineer," I said.

"So I heard." His voice had an edge. "But that's better than an architect. Anything's better than an architect." He laughed. Three front teeth were missing.

When he climbed into the sleeping loft Mark and Rachel held the ladder for him. He didn't give them a thank-you, let alone a smile. "Can't have a flat roof this high in the Berkshires," was all he said. Finally he was finished. With his hand on the knob of the front door he turned to give his verdict. Before he could say a word, Rachel stepped toward him. She was just four.

"Why are there so many flies?" she asked. People had tried to convince her the flies weren't so bad, or that she would get used to their annoying buzz.

"Damned pests, aren't they? I hate them, too," he said. "But this is cow country. If you folks want houses in cow country, you have to put up with flies." His glance moved to the window. "And no sense planting apple trees. Cows'll chew them right down if you don't fence them" He looked at Mark, who was seven. "And remind me to brace that flimsy ladder your father built. Everybody thinks he's a carpenter these days."

Everyone called him Jim. His real name was Horatio but he hated it. He and his wife, Ellen, had no children; she worked at the local Grant's and they lived near Main Street. Like his father and grandfather, Jim had spent most of his life within a fifty-mile radius of this town and had only contempt for New York.

"Don't know how to keep its streets clean," he said.

"It's very hard, there are so many people, it's an almost impossible task," I answered. He shook his head.

"Never knew how to keep its streets clean. Back in the thirties when I was driving the limestone truck to New York City for the Lincoln Memorial—it was filthy, too. We used to drive the limestone from Lee to New York, then they put it on the train to Washington, D.C.," he explained to the children.

"New York is a wonderful city. All those museums and the concerts and ballet and the theater . . ." My voice dwindled under Jim's icy stare. He had taken off his glasses and was alternately blowing on them and wiping them.

"Too much dog dew," he said. "There's more dog dew in New York City than in all the meadow muffins in Berkshire County."

One morning in March when I came home from taking Rachel to nursery school the phone was ringing. "Missus?" a voice asked.

"You must have the wrong number," I said.

"This ain't no wrong number. Missus, it's Jim!" he shouted. "It's the flat roof. I told you you couldn't have a flat roof this high in the Berkshires. The flashing's gone and water is pouring down into the living room. It's the biggest mess you ever saw. Why, I had to come home and take a pill. You better have your husband call me."

"What's the pill for?" I asked Phil that night. He had come home from work, then driven up to the Berkshires.

"His heart. He had a heart attack five years ago. That's why he does this part-time work. He felt better when I got there. His car couldn't make it up the driveway—it was still too icy—and after he walked up and saw the leaks, I guess it was too much for him."

"Was it really pouring?"

"No, dripping, but it will begin to pour if we don't get it fixed soon. And the windows are beginning to leak. The sills will have to be redone."

"He smokes too much for someone with a bad heart."

"He says he can't stop." Phil looked up from the bowl of lentil soup I had put before him. "When I got there the driveway was still covered with a sheet of ice. Jim insisted the Checker couldn't make it, but it did. Was he surprised. I guess that positraction was worth it," he added triumphantly.

Jim did far more than look in on the house; he shoveled water out of the basement when a pipe burst, watered the garden in spring, returned library books, fixed the children's toys. But always grudgingly. "Why does he do everything so grudgingly?" I asked.

"He *does* everything," Phil replied. "Be thankful."

I tried. But Jim got under my skin. Especially one morning when his eyes darted toward the dining room table. "When those chairs go, I know how to cane," he said.

"They're still new," I said, and went into the kitchen. But Phil was interested.

"Is caning hard?" he said.

"Time-consuming. Nothing's hard if you have patience," Jim said. When I came back he was fishing in his coat pocket. Then he clumped a bulging envelope on the table. "These are for Mark," he told us. The envelope was full of wheaties, those old pennies with stalks of wheat on the tail side. Once I had wondered how Jim became a coin dealer. "He told me he didn't want to spend his old age waiting for the next meal," Phil said.

Soon Mark and Jim were hunched over the coin books, fitting in the wheaties. When Rachel came in Jim asked, "When are you going to get a penny book?"

"I'm interested in stamps."

"Coins are better."

"That's only your opinion," Rachel said. Jim grinned. Another tooth was gone. He was so smug, even in his toothlessness, I thought later while I watched him and Phil in the driveway. Jim's hand was touching the fender of the Checker. I hoped he wouldn't see the rust spots that had suddenly appeared. The car had only 16,000 miles.

Of course he had. "Jim says there's a fiberglass compound that will fill in those rusty places," Phil said. "He also said the roses won't live on the north side of the meadow. The only rose you can put there is the Fairy."

"But I don't like the Fairy as much. And the man at the nursery said they would do fine."

Every January Phil and I came up to the house alone for a week to cross-country ski. We usually told Jim we were coming; this year we had a sudden change of plans and were still in bed when we heard his car chugging up the driveway. Phil reached for his robe, but Jim was gone before Phil got to the front door.

Later we stopped at his house. I rarely visited Jim and Ellen, though the children loved the cozy house crammed with antique knick-knacks. Besides, it also had a 21-inch color television and lots of candy bars in a bowl on the kitchen table. And Jim's coins. Jim ran his coin business from the garage in summer; in winter he moved the whole operation into the dining room.

"I'd like to buy a bigger house," Ellen once said. "Jim is against it, with no children, and all. But I miss the dining room, especially when the holidays come." Her voice was so resigned. I hated to hear it. "How does she live with him?" I sometimes wondered aloud.

"Oh, Jim's all right, Laura. You have to get to know him," Phil would answer. Still, I avoided him when I could.

Today I came inside because Phil had said I shouldn't be rude.

"Why didn't you come in this morning?" Phil asked Jim.

"Didn't want to disturb you."

"But it was almost ten; we were up."

"I know you were up," Jim said, then snickered. Suddenly he whirled toward me. "Who's taking care of the children?" he demanded.

"A baby-sitter. Someone we've known for a while."

"I hope so. Some of them that pass for baby-sitters. Nothing but hippies with ponytails and packs and thumbs sticking out all over the road. Communist hippies." He looked at us, waiting for some kind of reproach. Our liberal views puzzled him, especially since we kept a clean house. Now, when we didn't answer, he shrugged and said quietly, "We had a baby once. He would have been thirty-two this month."

Quickly we said good-bye. "Has he ever mentioned a child before?" I asked. Phil shook his head and drove into town too fast.

Although Ellen went to Mass every week, Jim had only scorn for his church, the large Catholic one on Main Street. "Voodoo, that's what it is. Hauling and shaking that incense around, filling everyone's head with talk about sin. They should know!" The tirade usually ended in a cough, then he would speak more reasonably. "I've hated church since I was a child. They made it feel like punishment. And the priest insisted on calling me Horatio. But Ellen believes in the whole kit-and-caboodle."

One Christmas Mark and Rachel were sick. Before lunch Phil said, "I think I'll go down to see Jim." My eyes began to fill, but this was no day to pick a fight. Besides, Phil wanted to give Jim his present, a lamp for examining coins. Phil had seen an ad for it, then gone to Canal Street to buy it.

After lunch the children fell asleep, so I took a nap, too. We awoke to the eerie hush of a thick steady snow that clouded the sky and meadow and driveway. I tried to keep my voice cheerful when they kept asking how soon Daddy would be home. But at least their foreheads were cool.

Finally Phil called. "The man who does the town plowing says he'll take me home," he said wearily. "The Checker didn't even get up the first hill. I'll have to leave it here." He sounded worried: sick children, no car. Still, what did he expect, staying so long at Jim's?

The Checker stayed in Jim's driveway for two days. "More people stopped in to ask about that crazy car than to buy coins," he said. "One man I hadn't seen in years came in and said, 'I always knew you were a nut, Jim, but I never thought you'd buy one of them Checkers!'"

The following March the Checker's transmission went. And later that morning when I answered the telephone Jim yelled, "Missus, the house has been hit."

"But it has lightning rods."

"Not that way. Robbed. They took the stereo and the lamp on the piano and the pewter bowl and the soccer game and library stool. At least that's all I can think of. The drawers and closets are okay and there was no damage. I told you not to leave the bowl out; pewter's sky high." I was silent, trying to imagine people walking through our house, deciding what to take and what to leave.

"Missus?" His voice was hoarse, tired. "It was kids. They must have climbed into the big window; there are sneaker prints on the deck and sills. I could feel my heart beating like a hammer when I saw everything gone. I came home and took a pill, then I called the police and they said to make a list for the insurance company. Missus, can you hear me?"

"Yes, but we have no car. The transmission went. Unless Phil can rent one."

"Who said he had to come up? It costs a fortune to rent a car. They'll wait for the list and I'll take care of the cops. The chief's Ellen's cousin anyway. Doggone, who'd think that transmission would go so soon. How many miles is it?"

"Forty-seven. It's no better than any other car. Around fifty thousand they all fall apart."

"Too bad. I knew the body was no good but I thought the insides would last. Doggone, if the strangest things don't happen."

"Do you think they can recover anything?" I asked.

"Don't know. It's those kids at the private schools. If their parents took care of them they wouldn't be so mixed up and . . ." His voice trailed away.

That night after Phil spoke to Jim he said, "Jim says we have to get a burglar alarm."

"In the country? That's crazy!"

Phil shrugged. "They say it's a good deterrent," he said later. Then he added, "Jim asked if we were going to keep the Checker."

"Of course we're going to keep the Checker. Everything else is fine. That's what happens with cars, they're all unreliable."

"But this isn't a car, honey; it's a Checker." Phil rolled his eyes and for the first time in hours we laughed.

"I told you it was too cold for those fancy roses here; this is a northwest exposure," Jim said. Mud crept over the edges of his Wellingtons. He had come into the garden and now stood over me while I groped in the rose bed, breaking off canes, praying that one would be pliant, alive, and protest my touch.

"No use checking every one; they're all dead. Not a rose in the world except the Fairy could stand this cold."

"But the man said they would be fine if I mulched them."

"He must have thought you lived in a normal place."

"I told him where we were. Besides, Chekhov grew roses in Russia."

"There's a southern exposure, even in Russia," Jim said, then touched my elbow and pointed me south. "Here, if you want roses and perennials, put them along this wall." Now we were close to the apple trees. One had been chewed almost to the ground. I stiffened, but he simply shook his head.

At the front door when we pulled off our boots Jim's hand was close to the white sticker announcing the burglar alarm: WARNING. THIS PROPERTY PROTECTED BY A RADAR SECURITY ALARM. "It's a good thing," he said "especially at night when you're here alone with the kids. You do use it then, don't you?"

"Most of the time," I lied.

Inside, Rachel showed Jim a seat of one of the cane chairs that was broken through. "Well, it lasted longer than I expected. I hope the next one waits to go till winter. The arthritis sometimes gets too bad to do it steadily and there's more time in winter."

"I didn't know you had arthritis," Phil said.

"You name it, I got it," Jim replied. Then he patted the Checker after stowing the chair in his car. "How's she doing?"

"Fine. No troubles since the transmission." I hoped Jim wouldn't walk around to the other side; that fender looked diseased. Fortunately, he left.

Next fall we talked about a new car. I thought we would get another Checker, but the company had stopped making station wagons. We looked at a Chevy Suburban. For a man who drove Chevys, Jim was skeptical. "Are you going to get four-wheel drive?"

"No," Phil said.

"Then don't waste your money; it'll never get up that mountain in winter."

But when Ellen saw the photo of the Suburban her eyes glowed. "It's so big, two people could take a long trip in it," she said.

"Where would you like to go, Ellen?" I asked.

"Oh, anywhere . . ." she began. "No, south, where it's warm."

"It's plenty warm here," Jim interrupted. "We just put in new insulation. Never can please women." I bit my lip but Ellen didn't even seem to hear him. And in the end we listened to Jim. The Checker drove us back and forth that winter for the best year of skiing we had had since we built the house. Rattles and all.

Early in March Jim announced, "I haven't smoked a cigarette for a month." We praised him lavishly. Suddenly his face sagged. His eyes sought Phil's. "Think Ellen and I'll make it to our fiftieth?" he wanted to know.

"Of course, especially now that you've stopped smoking."

Jim slapped his knee. "Fifty years with one woman! They'll have to give me a medal!" He grinned. More teeth were gone.

It was the coldest spring in decades. "The dampness sneaks into your bones," Jim complained. But he hadn't smoked for almost three months.

Finally, just before Memorial Day the weather turned warm. We spent the weekend getting the garden in and brought Ellen lettuce and rugola that Phil had planted in April. She was thrilled. "I can't wait for summer and salads," she said.

"You and the rabbits," Jim said. "Give me a good steak."

"How can you eat steak?" I asked, surprised at my nerve.

"Now, don't you start bothering me about a plate. Ellen is enough for one man to listen to. You don't need teeth to eat steak; all you need is good, strong gums."

"But you'd be more comfortable."

"No, Missus, you'd be more comfortable. You and Ellen."

The first weekend that summer Jim appeared with fiberglass compound. He and Phil patched the fender so there was a white scar running the length of one purple side. "That Checker'll be as good as new when we get done with her," Jim gloated.

"The only thing as good as new in that car is the buzzer for the seat belts," I muttered, but they ignored me.

For once I was right. A week later the differential fell out of the Checker. I had stopped for a light and the kids and I heard this awful thump. "Like your stomach falling out of your body," Mark told Jim when he got us at the gas station. Phil was in New York.

"I can imagine," Jim said, and peered under the car. "So much rust under that damn thing, no wonder the differential went. The muffler's hanging by a thread." He stared at the car as if it were a corpse.

Then he drove Rachel to camp and Mark to the farm. "I'll pick them up later. I'll call you before I go." I glanced at him in surprise. I had called him because he lived near the gas station, but we had friends here who could help us. The last thing I wanted was to be beholden to Jim. Yet as I watched the stubborn set of his features I knew he had decided he would help us and that was that.

When the children came home their eyes were wide, the pupils dilated with fright. "Did you know that a child drowned in the pond at camp two years ago?" Rachel asked.

"Who on earth told you that?"

"Jim. And he told Mark that every summer a kid gets chewed up by a tractor around here." Mark nodded. His lips were pressed together to keep from trembling.

When they were asleep I called Phil. "It's so odd, I wonder why he did it," Phil said.

"Because he's crazy and destructive, which is very different from being eccentric. Look how he treats Ellen and the way he walks around without a tooth in his head." My voice grew stronger. "I don't want him in the house again." I had already left a message with Ellen telling Jim not to come tomorrow.

"Take it easy, Laura. Maybe you're right, but promise you won't do anything till I come up on Thursday," Phil said.

But next morning, there was Jim—with his gap-toothed smile, hair slicked down, tooting the horn.

"Didn't Ellen give you my message?" I asked.

"Yup, but I have errands and I'm passing right by. Hop in, kids," he called. To my astonishment they did. I had done such a good job of convincing them that what he had told them wasn't true, they didn't hold it against him.

During the day the gas station called to tell me the Checker was ready. I decided to let Jim pick me up and then we would get the children and the car and that would be it. In two days Phil would be here and I would never exchange another word with Jim again. My conscience bothered me when I thought about Ellen, but she had married him, and what he earned from us wasn't enough to make much difference.

Jim and I drove in silence to camp, then Rachel chatted with him on the way to the farm. Mark was waiting for us near the barn. With him were the farmer and his oldest son. As we drew closer I saw that Mark's left hand was wrapped in a towel. His eyes were glazed, his lips drew back across his teeth in pain.

"He went to grease the tractor and none of us realized the handle of the grease gun was hot," the farmer said. "We put ice on it."

The second I touched him Mark began to cry. "I couldn't help it," he said. "No one knew the gun had been sitting near the exhaust of the other tractor. Are you mad?"

"Of course not," I whispered. Gingerly I removed the ice and towel. A deep red streak ran along the length of his palm.

"Holy Jesus!" Jim whistled. Before I could protest he had scooped Mark into his arms and put him into the car. He gunned the accelerator while Rachel and I climbed in. I rewrapped Mark's hand while Jim drove too fast to the doctor's.

"These things happen. And the right treatment is ice," the doctor explained, trying to drown out Jim's litany of "idiots, stupid fools, never take enough care, always in a rush, doesn't even know how to build decent fences."

The doctor gave me a pain killer and showed me how to dress the burn. "Come back after the weekend. And don't worry. He'll be fine. At worst a scar. It's all part of growing up."

Mark spent the next two weeks with Jim in the coin shop. As I watched Jim's infinite patience while they sat for hours under the coin lamp I sometimes thought I had dreamed Jim's horror stories. Phil and I never discussed them, and when Mark was well enough to go back to the farm Jim helped us devise a glovelike dressing that would protect his hand from the prickly hay.

About a week later Jim came up to the house to fix some storm doors. I was weeding in the perennial bed near the south wall of the house. When Jim came to plane the door near me he sat down for a few minutes on the grass. I could hear him wheezing and asked him if he was smoking again.

"Nosirree. But this cough won't go away. It just hangs on, like an old enemy you can't get rid of." Then he took off his sunglasses and stared at the blinding blue sky.

"Mark's so glad to be back at the farm," I told Jim. He got up and unhinged the door. Then he turned to me. "Good for him to be out in the air. That's why you're here, why you have this house. The country's the only place for children," he said. His eyes were more blue than green today, and as they held mine for a few moments they seemed to get bluer.

I could only stare back at him—speechless.

"Everything's dangerous, Laura," he said, his voice grizzlier than usual. "Kids have to know that, but they also have to grow up to be independent. And that's what you're teaching them." Then he went back to work.

On Labor Day the Checker died. A tow truck took us to the gas station. The young man who worked there wanted to buy it for parts and while Phil talked to him, the kids and I collected our belongings. Then Phil phoned Jim to get us. When he saw the Checker a spasm of fright fluttered across Jim's face. At that moment he looked so old. But then it passed, as quickly as it had come.

Once more Phil checked the car. Then he stood there, silent, while his hand absently grazed the patched fender. Watching him, the rest of us seemed rooted to the asphalt. Finally Jim's glance met mine. Briskly he nodded, then straightened and stepped forward. His voice was firm. "And now, let's have a moment of silence," he said. We all smiled in relief and joined hands and bowed our heads.

As we left I got a glimpse of the Checker's dashboard. The speedometer read 74,810.6 miles.

VALENTINE'S DAY

by Myra Sklarew

The side of her face showed bone. My sister wheeled her into the living room. I stood to the right, watching her. For more than a day she had not been able to eat or drink. My sister sewed bright red cloth napkins. She appliquéd red hearts on the tablecloth. There was a cake. One of the children brought candles. It wasn't anyone's birthday. My sister thought it would be a good idea. I wasn't sure. Propping up the dead, I said to myself. Ashamed to have thought it.

July the eighth: Today she gave me a ruler that curls up like a roll of postage stamps. Last week she offered me her blankets. I refused. The week before— sheets. I took them. Before that, Father's pajamas. Her nightgown. I dream I am in the Convent of the Dominican Sisters, where she is playing the piano. It is cool and dark.

The green tank arrived this morning. The plastic hose and nose-pieces. My sister taught us how to set the gauge. She was matter-of-fact. I forgot to be afraid. My sister stood near her bed. She watched as the oxygen hissed and then hummed through the tubing. As it went into her nostrils.

July the thirteenth: She dreamed that mice have entered the bed where she is sleeping. Father is waving a broom handle to chase them away but he is unable to rid her bed of them. She has gathered up the mice that the child let loose in the pumphouse and set them down again in her dream. Meanwhile inside the main house the mice continue to breed. And in her body the cells of the tumors divide and increase. And her dreams increase. And her dreamless nights are counted and stored and divided among the children.

* * *

Her hair is falling out again. My sister combed it with a silver comb. She pinned up what was left with hairpins. Then she washed her face. We took turns looking through the buttons in her sewing basket. A green felt button from her coat during the Second World War. Black Persian lamb button. Plastic buckle for a cloth belt. Light green velvet from a dress made of her dead sister's cape. Shirred front. We took turns wearing it.

July the twentieth: *She has grown thin. Through the lenses of her glasses I come across her eyes. I try to bring her back to me from the great distance where she is traveling. In her dream a telephone is ringing. She goes to it, picks up the receiver. Her dead sister is on the line.*

This morning my sister arrived in time to help her as she vomited. Then my sister emptied the curved stainless steel basin and washed out the blood and vomit from the bedclothes. If it bothered her, she did not let me see. In the evening Father slept in her room. He got up each hour to tend to her.

September the fifth: *I have begun to hold my breath. As in the child's game—statues. To stop. Wherever you are. Your arms still in the position of motion. The echo of movement in your fingers. She has decided to live until spring. She goes out to the porch at evening to bring in the flowers that Father has grown for her. Marigolds the color of the light that is withdrawing. As though someone were pulling at a veil of light, uncovering each tree and house that beneath the veil is completely dark.*

She asked for a section of an orange. My sister peeled away the thick skin and divided the sections and put one into her mouth. The next morning my sister found it lying inside her cheek.

A Friday in October: *On the page where I have been drawing I see I have made a knife.*

A neighbor came up from downstairs. Everyone was seated around the maple dining room table. My sister wheeled her up close. There were bright favors, candy hearts and a birthday cake with candles. She smiled. She was no longer able to talk.

November 25:   *She dreamed that Father was driving the car. Next to him in the front seat was a dead man talking continuously.*

My sister poured the tea, cut the cake. We sang to her. She sat up straight in her wheelchair. She could not drink the tea.

*   *   *

December 26:   *When she was born, they did not believe she would live. They brought her home to die. Her sister sang to her and they sewed small white gloves to cover her hands so she would not scratch herself. Each one took a turn watching over her.*

My sister said: The condemned ate a hearty breakfast on the eighth day. The doctor told us she would die today. My sister must have believed she would live. How else could she have made such a huge cauldron of soup.

December 27:   *She thinks of a line of poetry. Looking out between the slats of the blinds in her bedroom she says:*

> *the white*
>
> *the overhanging*
> *cloud*

My sister dipped four Q-tips into grape juice so she could suck the liquid from the cotton.

February 10:   *Her head between my hands seems so small.*

I did not do my part. That is why I cannot remember these events clearly. When someone was needed to bring the oxygen, to place the plastic tubes in her nostrils, I managed not to be in the room. Or when she had soiled the bed, I called for my sister. The day a slice of orange lay like a curved moon inside her cheek, it was not I who put fingers into her mouth to remove it. Nor was I there to hear her say how the disease had used her up. The others have wanted to write a proper account of all this. I have not encouraged them.

JOHN McCORMACK

by Maura Stanton

The day was cool and gray and smelled of approaching rain. We wore sweaters even though it was August. We would have stayed inside to watch television that morning, except that our visiting uncle from Chicago sat in the big chair in the living room, smoking and staring at nothing. We were a little afraid of him, although he was kindly and gave us quarters when we bought him bags of popcorn or bottles of Pepsi at the store. He always had a glass of Pepsi beside him on the floor. He was supposed to be leaving in a few days. He was a plasterer, and there were some unfinished jobs waiting for him back in Chicago. He had been up north taking the "cure" he told us. "Cure for what?" we asked. "Booze," he had answered in a low voice. "But don't tell your mother I told you that."

We made cocoa in the spaghetti pot and sat around the picnic table in the backyard with our hot mugs, reading the new mystery books we had checked out of the library yesterday. Our oldest sister sat on the step, copying recipes from a thick *International Cookbook*. She had been reading cookbooks for a month and had a whole notebook full of recipes with ingredients we had never heard of before.

"How does this sound?" she would ask, interrupting us. "Norwegian Baked Herring."

"Awful!"

"It's layers of herring and potatoes. I think it sounds good. I've never tasted herring. Or how about this. Rice and Spinach Armenian."

"You don't like spinach," we told her. "You know you don't."

"I might, if it were cooked like this. I'd leave out the garlic, though."

We returned to our books. It was pleasant to look up occasionally to watch one of the cats roll in the mint that grew under the garage window, or listen to the piano next door. But after a while, when we began to get chilly, we went inside to refill our mugs, and decided to read at the kitchen table.

Our brother Joe, who had been over at the archery range all morning, suddenly appeared at the screen door, panting. A misty rain had begun, but he stayed outside on the steps. There were droplets in his dark blond hair.

"Something's happened at the lake!"

"What?" we all asked at once. "On our side?"

"This side of the bridge," he said. "I don't know what it is. But there's lots of police. I'm going back."

He jumped down the steps. We heard his shoes pounding on the walk around the side of the house. Our oldest sister hastily dropped the dipper back into the cocoa and turned off the burner.

"Let me get my sweater," she said.

"Hurry!" We edged into the dining room to wait for her, setting off a tinkle of glasses in the sideboard. Our uncle, his back to us, was standing over the record player in the living room, humming "tura-lura-lura" to himself. He was about to play our father's old Irish record again. We heard the click as he changed the speed to 78, and noted the shiny red bald spot on the back of his head. His hair always seemed greasy, the way it parted over the bald spot. Yet he took a shower every morning, and when he shaved, he left the bathroom door half open, so that we had all seen him patting his cheeks with blue aftershave lotion.

Two police cars had been driven across the grass to the edge of the lake. We saw that first. Then we saw the boat and the diver in the wet suit who was putting the oars in the oarlocks. A small crowd of people had gathered at a short distance from the black cars, mostly children in shorts, but there were a couple of mothers, too, and the old man who lived in the tiny, unpainted house down at the end of our alley. The surface of the lake was dark and absorbed the drops of light rain without ripples.

Joe waved at us as we hurried across the thick wet grass.

"They're dragging the lake," he said anxiously when we reached his side. "Somebody drowned."

"Who?"

"A woman." He pointed to one of the police cars. A man was hunched in the backseat, his head turned away from us to look out at the lake. "That's her husband."

"Was she swimming?"

Joe shook his head. "It's awful," he said. "She jumped from the bridge."

"Jumped?"

We all turned to look at the concrete bridge that arched across the lake at its narrow neck. We were at the smaller, shallower end of the lake, but there were still Danger and Deep Water signs posted on the bridge pilings. We noticed how some of the cars crossing the bridge slowed down as they spotted the police cars on the shore.

"Why would she jump?" our brother Pat asked in a puzzled voice.

"To kill herself."

Pat stared at Joe, frowning. He ran his hand absently through his short, almost white hair. "Why?"

"She was unhappy, I guess." Joe looked out at the cold lake. "But I don't know how anyone could be that unhappy."

We watched the diver and one of the policemen row out toward the bridge. The diver attached his face mask and dropped silently into the water. He had a breathing tube, but it was hard to spot it on the dark surface. Occasionally his head emerged. Twice he climbed back into the rowboat, and the policeman poured him something to drink from a thermos. The other policemen paced up and down the shore, rubbing their chilled hands together, sometimes listening to the static and strange bursts of talk on their radio, occasionally speaking in low voices to the man in the backseat, who would roll the window down and lean out.

We squatted down, trying to cover our bare legs with the tails of our sweaters. The light rain turned into a fine mist, and the bridge looked silvery and insubstantial. The trees in the little woods behind the archery range were obscured by fog. More mothers had arrived. Some had come to fetch their children but had remained standing near other mothers, talking in subdued voices and glancing out at the boat. Our oldest sister had found a stump to sit on, a little away from the crowd. Joe plucked at his bowstring absently and in a while went to sit by himself under the willow tree.

"Let's go home," one of us said after an hour. "I'm hungry."

We stood up. Our legs were stiff from the damp. The grass had printed greenish lines into our knees.

"Pat!" we called.

He ignored us. He was staring intently out at the lake.

We started home without him, glancing back at the police cars once or twice. We planned to come back after lunch. On the other side of the park road, where the grass was smooth and cropped for baseball, we broke into a run. We were out of breath by the time we reached our yard. The inner door was open, and through the screen we could hear two voices singing "The Harp That Once

Thro' Tara's Halls." One voice, sweet and far away, was spoiled by static and crackles. The other voice, loud but weak and interrupted by a hacking cough, was our uncle's. We stood outside by the blue spruce for a minute or two, listening in embarrassment.

Finally we entered the house. Our uncle did not even hear us at first. His head was tilted toward the ceiling, his eyes were closed, and his hand was wrapped around his throat as he sang, as if he were controlling the pitch by the pressure of his fingers.

The song came to an end. Our uncle opened his eyes during the short band of static that followed and saw us as we crossed the living room.

He blinked and cleared his throat. "He was the best," he said to us thickly. "This old record doesn't do him justice."

"John McCormack?" we asked politely.

"John McCormack," he repeated. "I heard him sing once. That was at the ballroom of the Edgewater Beach Hotel. It was at a banquet. All the men were wearing tuxedos, and all the women had on strapless gowns—I was a waiter. I never told you I was a waiter, did I?"

"No," we said as we backed shyly away from him, trying not to be rude.

"When he started to sing, I forgot I was supposed to be filling the water goblets. I just stood there, my mouth open. I felt it all the way up my spine, up and down every bone, in my skull—"

"Felt what?" one of us asked.

"I felt like I was dying, but it was so sweet . . . he had the voice of an angel, a voice like the harp of an angel. I hope it's like that when I die. I hope the angels will sing 'Ireland, Mother Ireland' as beautifully as John McCormack."

"Somebody died at the lake," we said.

The vague, dreamy look on his face disappeared. "I know. One of the neighbors knocked at the door." He stood up heavily. "I need a walk. I suppose you're all going back there after lunch?"

We nodded.

"I'll go with you," he said as he headed toward the bathroom. "Your mother's at the store with the baby."

He came into the kitchen a few minutes later and absently placed the John McCormack album on the table where we were making our sandwiches. He poured another Pepsi into his smudged glass. We stared at the album as we chewed. A brown castle had been sketched against the turquoise background, next to a portrait of John Mc-Cormack, who looked very handsome and foreign. He reminded us of our father in the old photographs on the mantel where he was wearing his army uniform and had a thick wave in his hair.

*   *   *

We did not like to be seen in public with our uncle, who walked stiffly, as if his legs hurt, and sang or hummed out loud even when he was passing a stranger on the sidewalk. His baggy trousers, splattered with paint around the cuffs, seemed about to fall down around his ankles. His black dress shoes were unpolished and worn at the heels. The back of his shirt was creased. The skin under his eyes was thick and swollen, his nose and cheeks reddened by broken veins. He always had a vacant, faraway look in his light blue eyes.

We were ashamed of our reluctance to be seen with him, however, and had never spoken of it to each other. We stayed close to his side as we crossed the park to the lake, pointing out interesting features of the neighborhood—the bus wye, the sycamore that had been split by lightning, the red ring of paint around a diseased elm, the archery range where Joe practiced with his bow and arrow, even the grove of trees in the distance where a man had exposed himself to some third-grade boys.

The rain had let up completely and the sun was coming out. The crowd had grown; now it was mostly adults, all of them silent, standing shoulder to shoulder as we came toward the shore of the lake. We recognized Mrs. Wagner, who lived across the alley; she was still in her nurse's uniform, standing on tiptoe in her white rubber-soled shoes, trying to see over the heads in front of her. An ambulance had been parked next to the police cars. As we joined the crowd, we saw two policemen come around the side of the ambulance with a bundle. The doors were opened, then slammed shut. The crowd began moving apart.

Our oldest sister saw us, and jumped down off the stump which must have given her an excellent view of what had happened.

"They found her," she said flatly. She tried to smooth her damp hair, which was beginning to dry in frizzy peaks.

"What did she look like?"

"I couldn't look after all. I only looked after they had her in the boat, covered up." She shivered. "But I saw her foot when they carried her out on shore."

"Where's Pat?" our uncle asked.

"Over there." Our oldest sister pointed to some bushes. "I think he's throwing up. I should have sent him home—" She frowned, thrusting her hands into the pockets of her shorts and turning away.

We looked out at the lake. The surface was scaled with silver now that the sun was out and a wind was rising. The ambulance and the police car with the husband in the back pulled silently away. The diver stood by the rowboat, smoking and talking to two policemen.

Pat came up beside us. There were deep circles under his eyes, and he was wheezing slightly.

"You better use your inhaler," our oldest sister said.

"I'm all right."

"What did you see?" we asked.

"Her hair was so long it was caught in the weeds. They had to cut her free." He swallowed. "She was stiff. Her blouse was muddy."

Our uncle crossed himself.

Pat watched him closely. "Can you do that?"

"What?"

"Pray for her."

Our uncle blinked. "Of course you can pray for her. For her soul."

"Isn't her soul in hell?"

Our uncle glanced down at Pat, then gripped his shoulder. "Now, who told you that? Only God knows about the soul."

Pat trembled. His lips were blue and bitten, and for the first time we realized that he had seen something that was going to haunt him—something that he could not describe to us in words. We did not know whether to be envious or relieved that we had not seen it, too. Our oldest sister's guarded face told us nothing.

"We need to light a candle for her soul," our uncle said, bending closer to Pat. "I lit a candle when John McCormack died. That was in 1945, before any of you were born. I'd been sent home from the war with a bullet in my thigh. That candle burned for weeks, and when it was almost out, I lit two more from the same flame. I like to think that other candles were lit from my flames, for other souls, and that my flame is still burning somehow . . . or burned until John McCormack got out of purgatory, the good man."

He brushed his hand across Pat's face, as if he had seen a tear that we had missed. "What do you say? Shall we go up to church and light a candle for this poor drowned lady?"

"Our new church doesn't have candles," we said.

"What? It's a Catholic church. Of course it has candles."

"We've never seen any candles," we said emphatically. "We go to Mass every Sunday."

"There are candles," our oldest sister said. "In the vestibule on the far side, near the pamphlet table. It's the side we never go in—and they're way back in the corner."

"Let's go," our uncle said. "You can light the candle, Pat."

Pat nodded, and we started off across the grass which smelled fresh and sharp as the sun dried the blades. Other people who had seen the drowned woman brought ashore were moving slowly across the park, too, or standing in small groups, talking quietly. As we passed one group of women, which included Mrs. Wagner in her white uniform, we looked secretly up at their faces, but their moving lips and eyelashes and slightly knitted foreheads did not tell us what we needed to know.

We climbed the hill to the church, pausing a few times to let our uncle catch his breath. His face grew red and congested. The exertion caused his hair to stick to his forehead in wet coils.

Our church was a modern building of yellow brick, with a squat bell tower and a curved façade. It was attached to the older, three-story grade school. A few cars were parked in the lot.

"They must be hearing confession," we told our uncle.

He looked up at the church. "What a pity. You don't have any stained glass windows."

"The windows are colored glass," we said. "When the sun shines it turns all blue inside."

We led him to the nearest door, and held it open for him.

"Did you ever see Sacred Heart in Chicago?" he asked in a low voice. "When you go to Mass at dawn, the whole church is as bleak as the inside of a mountain. You can't see the ceiling, it's so high. Then the sun comes up—it pours through the center window, the Sacred Heart window, and you've never seen red that red. It's the color of wine or rubies or real, wet blood—" He coughed, glancing suddenly at Pat. "There's a gold canopy over the altar, too, and the candlesticks are massive silver. But the candles you light yourself are at the side altars."

We were in the vestibule, a low, square room where a few metal folding chairs had been stacked against the wall. Another door led into the church itself, which our oldest sister opened.

"The candles are on the other side," she said.

We dipped our hands into the aluminum holy-water font as we entered. The water was cool and soft as we splashed it on our foreheads. The church was dim, for the sun was not hitting the blue windows this time of day. When we reached the center aisle, we genuflected. A large abstract sculpture hung above the altar instead of the usual crucifix, and although we had gotten used to seeing it, we always felt a little funny when we crossed ourselves. Only two people were in line at the confession box on the left. The red light on the box at the right had already been turned off.

The vestibule on the other side of the church was shadowy, for the venetian blinds were shut. The pamphlet table was empty except for a few out-of-date copies of "The Catholic Messenger." We looked curiously at the tiered metal rack in the corner. Each shelf contained little red glasses with white votive candles inside. A black box with a slot in the top was attached to the side of the rack.

"That's strange," our uncle said, fumbling with the change in his pocket. "None of them are lit." He handed a dime to Pat. "Put that in the box."

The dime made a hollow clink as Pat dropped it in the slot.

"Let's see if I've got any matches, now." Our uncle began going through his other pocket. He pulled out nail clippers, ticket stubs, the broken end of a pencil, crushed grains of popcorn, three finely wrinkled one-dollar bills, and finally produced a matchbook with softened edges.

He was lighting a match for Pat when the inner door of the church opened. Father North, one of the three parish priests, appeared before us in his long black cassock. He had just come from hearing confessions, for the purple stole still hung around his neck. We felt our throats constrict. His face was stern, as if he had been listening to terrible sins.

He looked at our little group and his face darkened.

"You're the new children in the parish, aren't you?" he asked briskly.

"Yes, Father," we whispered back.

"Who is this man?" he asked. "Are you children all right?"

We stared at him, not understanding.

His lip twitched impatiently. "Is this man bothering you?"

We looked at our uncle then, stunned and horrified at what Father North was suggesting. He stood there in front of Pat with a match burning down to his fingers, his mouth open a little, a slightly dazed look on his face. The white lining of his pockets hung partly out.

"Please, Father," our oldest sister said in a voice that was high and shaky. "This is our uncle." And then, although we had never seen her touch anyone affectionately before, not even our father or mother, she put her arm around our uncle's shoulder.

"He's from Chicago," we said, all of us speaking at once, for we saw that our uncle's face was beginning to redden in shame. "He's our favorite uncle. You should hear him sing. We've come up to light a candle."

"Fine," Father North said. "But I'd like to lock the doors. Confession is over."

"Do you lock the doors in this church, Father?" our uncle asked in a soft voice, his eyes on the floor.

"It's not safe to keep the doors open when no one is here—it's a sorry comment on the world, I'm afraid."

Our uncle nodded.

Our oldest sister moved away from him then, dropping her arm self-consciously.

Our uncle handed the matchbook to Pat. "Be careful," he said hoarsely.

Pat lit a match above the long wick of a candle in the first tier. It caught immediately, and made the dark red glass translucent. He made the sign of the cross, and bowed his head. We watched him pray for the woman who had drowned herself.

Then we turned to go.

Father North cleared his throat. "I'd appreciate it if you'd blow the candle out before you leave."

"Blow it out?" Pat looked at our uncle in surprise.

Father North pointed to a small sign taped to the side of the candle rack.

"What grade will you be in, son?"

"Fourth," said Pat.

"Can you read the sign?"

Pat swallowed. " 'Please do not leave candles burning. Fire . . .' " he hesitated.

" 'Hazard,' " Father North finished emphatically.

Pat looked at the candle flame. "I just lit it," he said, his voice quivering. "It's for a dead soul."

"Let it burn for a while, Father," our uncle asked in a voice so humble that we squirmed with embarrassment. "In most churches . . ." His voice trailed off inaudibly.

Father North pointed at Pat. "Please blow out your candle. What if the curtains caught on fire? I know you lit it for a soul. Very nice. But it's not the candle that counts; it's the prayer behind it."

"I always thought it was the candle, Father," our uncle said.

Father North shook his head. "It's only a pretty custom."

"But I've lit a lot of candles over the years," our uncle said, his voice trembling. "You mean my candles did no one any good?"

Father North hesitated. Then his somber face lit up with a smile, the first we had ever seen across his face. We could see the edges of his teeth. "If they did *you* good, that's fine. That's important too."

"I thought I was helping the poor souls out of purgatory."

A flicker of annoyance crossed Father North's face. "Only God decides about that." He tugged nervously at the stole hanging from his neck, and pulled a set of heavy keys from his pocket. He looked severely at Pat.

Pat bent over the flame. We all drew our breath in and held it down in our lungs a long time until our chests ached, as if we could keep the flame burning by not breathing. We wanted a miracle, and when Pat's weak mouthful of air caused the flame to brighten instead of go out, we thought we had been granted our prayer.

"Blow harder," Father North said.

"He has asthma," our oldest sister said.

Pat closed his eyes, then spat at the candle. The flame disappeared with a hiss. We knew it was the sound of a soul disappearing into darkness, a soul that might have lit her way to heaven by the light of Pat's candle. That was our fancy, at least, when we glanced into Pat's cold and vacant face as he brushed past us and ran out the door.

"Good-bye, Father," we said hastily to cover Pat's violent departure and the gloom that had fallen over our uncle's face, sealing his lips.

"Tell your brother to come see me sometime when his heart isn't so hard," Father North said. "You seem like a nice family."

A CALL FROM BROTHERLAND

by Pat Ellis Taylor

So this is the way I think it must have started: word got around certain parts of Oklahoma City that on the first of every month Okie got eight hundred dollars and ninety tabs of Valium from the U.S. Government for a craziness that Veterans Administration psychiatrists attributed to the Vietnam War. Now even without the money and the drugs, Okie would have had friends. Lovern Evetts was his friend; they had played in the high school band together before Okie dropped out and joined the navy. And Lovern had a certain understanding of Okie and a certain love. He had gone to Vietnam himself and had been given a Medal of Honor, which he buried in his parents' storage room and refused to wear, even for the families of old friends when he shouldered their boxed-up sons in military funerals. But Vietnam hadn't made him crazy, at least not certifiably so, or at least whatever wounds his brain had received had been nursed and nurtured by his own family, who owned a block in an Oklahoma City suburb where the father ran a used-car lot and the mother ran a barbecue pit and Lovern was given a mechanic shop to run. Not like Okie's family, who lived in different towns and communicated with one another only in sparse and erratic bursts of holiday transcendence and then with great difficulty, which is why Okie didn't really think too much about looking any of them up when he walked off the gangplank in San Diego. Instead, he went to the only family who would really give him a sailor's welcome, the California motorcycle black-leather brotherhood of veterans and dropouts nobody else took care of so they learned to take care of one another as best they could by manufacturing experiences so intense as to distract themselves from the sorrow of recollection. He stayed with them until the Vietnam wounds of his brain were completely fried, cauterized with alcohol and acid, visions of chain-beatings blood in the alleys hot steel friends dead of heroin overdoses in muggy LA tenement motels overlaying the old Vietnam wounds with hot red layers of new skin.

Until one day Okie saw a biker brother shot down by a jealous woman on the front steps of a house nobody knew who paid the rent on, who slowly died while begging someone to open the door, which nobody did, Okie finally opening it when the man became still, dragging him into the living room, then Okie and two other men leaving out the back door before the cops came. And shortly after that, Okie began to see the devil, the devil licking at the wound in his brain that had never healed right, making hell itself spew out in visions of friends left to maggots in the shag carpets of living rooms like piles of half-eaten junk food and women with blow torches for hands. So he turned himself in to a navy psychiatric ward, asking for electroshock treatments to block out whatever was left of his brain. But they gave him over to the Veterans Administration, who prescribed money and drugs instead and put him out on the streets again. At least he didn't go back to California. Instead, he went to Oklahoma, where he looked up his old friend Lovern. Lovern's father, a veteran himself from a different war, let Okie sleep at the used-car lot at night as a security guard. Lovern's mother gave him barbecue ribs to eat. And Lovern himself let Okie keep his Harley in back of the mechanic shop and let him do free-lance welding on the motorcycles that came into the shop. So if Okie had never found any friends other than Lovern and Lovern's mother and father, he still would have been more fortunate than other Vietnam veterans, many who haven't to this day found a good friend.

But of course lots of friends started hanging around Okie once they discovered how generous he was with a Veterans Administration check based on one hundred percent disability. Maybe they thought his brain was a little slow, maybe he didn't change his clothes often, maybe he didn't wash his hair very much or trim his beard. But he had a good-looking black Harley Davidson, which impressed the Oklahoma bikers, and he liked to spread his money around, which impressed the biker women, and he didn't like to take three Valiums a day, like Dr. Outlaw at the out-patient's clinic recommended, so he gave most of them away, which impressed everyone who liked pills. So Okie's circle of friends began to grow, and more and more bikers began showing up at Lovern's mechanic shop to hang out.

Well, Lovern's father didn't like it much. He said this crowd of people would only get Lovern and Okie into trouble. And Lovern's mother didn't like it. She told one man she wouldn't give him barbecue so long as he wore a swastika on his belt buckle: we fought a war to get rid of that, she said. But Lovern liked the bikers. They liked to smoke joints and drink beer, and they liked to roar around the Oklahoma countryside on the weekends and build bonfires and have parties in country houses. So Lovern even bought a motorcycle himself and a black leather riding outfit, and he got a black leather jacket and cap for his five-year-old boy to wear for Sunday drives. Then one day a man appeared that even Lovern recognized as trouble, the friend of a friend of Okie's just in town from California. His name was Thieving John, and he made a living selling motorcycle parts to the same biker friends it was rumored that he stole them from. Although no one could really catch him. So it was just after the first of the month and Okie put his Valiums in the drawer of Lovern's desk, and on a day that John had been hanging around they turned up missing. Okie might have said something to John and John said something back. So someone shoved and someone punched and suddenly both men were down on the floor, Okie with a tire arm in his hand, which Lovern grabbed from above him and took away. So everyone knew then that Okie and Thieving John didn't get along very well with each other.

Well, neither Okie nor Thieving John really wanted to see each other. Thieving John stopped coming around Lovern's mechanic shop, to the relief of everyone and most especially Lovern's father and mother, and Okie took to checking if Thieving John was going to be at someone's house or party before he came to visit, since the biker family in Oklahoma City was relatively small, everyone knowing everyone else. But there is a kind of personality that enjoys creating the circumstances for trouble, and unfortunately there was such a woman who was a part of this circle of biker friends which had grown around Okie and Lovern, who decided she was going to throw a big party for everyone and roast a baby goat in her backyard. So she called up the shop and invited Okie to the party. Okie asked her if Thieving John was going to be there, and she said no. Then when Okie agreed to come, she called up John and invited him.

Now, who knows what she was looking for—maybe just a few hot words or a roll-around-on-the-floor kind of fight, maybe she was thinking after all both are my friends aren't they so I have to invite them both, or maybe she wasn't really thinking about it, just letting her mind ride high and blank in opened-out anticipation. So when Okie walked in the front door, the first man he saw was John. He went back out and got a revolver out of a bag on his motorcycle and brought it back in the house. But the woman who was looking for trouble who was barbecuing the goat told Okie that there couldn't be guns around because there were little children present. So she took the gun from Okie and put it on the mantel shelf. And that's the way the party began.

There was too much booze, of course, too much barbecue, too much talking, too many people milling around, and sometime in the early morning John and Okie found themselves together in the garage. Lovern and his wife and five-year-old son had already gone home about an hour before, and there were only four or five people left at the party, a couple of them passed out. There was one other man out in the garage, and he heard Okie say something to John, and then Join pointed at Okie's Harley. See that bike? the man remembered John saying. It's going to be mine someday soon, and it'll be painted red as your own blood. So there was some pushing and a scuffle and some more words. Then John broke away and went into the kitchen. Okie went out the garage door, came into the house again through the front door, and took his pistol off the mantel shelf. Then he walked into the kitchen, put the pistol to the back of John's head and pulled the trigger. Two men were sitting at the table talking to John when it happened, and the woman who wanted to see trouble was sitting in an easy chair by the kitchen door with her three-year-old girl in her lap and looked into the kitchen just in time to see the back of Thieving John's head become a red bloom. Then Okie put the gun in his belt and walked out the door, apparently stunned by the weight of his own action, called murder in the first degree with four witnesses, which, in Oklahoma, can bring a penalty of death in the electric chair.

So about three hundred miles south from this house where the party was held, there was a white clapboard house on the edge of town; there was a peach orchard on one side of it and a garden on the other. There were tearoses growing across the back bedroom window. And there was a rooster crowing about seven o'clock in the morning, when I woke up from a dream of walking up and down streets in a gray foggy dawn in a city unfamiliar to me looking for my brother, thinking something was wrong. Finally I found him sitting in a car that wasn't his parked at a curb. He was staring out the window like he was in shock, his body slack like he couldn't have moved it even if he wanted to. So I wasn't a body myself, more like a spirit, easily slipping through car walls, clamoring around him looking at his face and his glazed-out eyes asking him over and over to tell me what was wrong. But he kept on staring out the window until the alarm went off and I woke up. Leo was still asleep on his back holding my hand. But I shook him awake and began to tell him what I had been dreaming. A ringing came from the kitchen, and when I got out of bed and answered it, Lovern Evetts was calling from Oklahoma, his voice overfull with emotion, to tell me how my brother Okie shot a man last night and had walked out of the house, police dragneting the woods for him, and nobody knew where he had gone.

WINTER FACTS

by Mary Ann Taylor-Hall

She had come in August. Now it was November. She had started a wall with rocks that she dug out of the garden plot. As she got more serious about it, she had her friends bring them to her by the wagonload—rocks were one thing everybody had plenty of out here. Now the wall was maybe forty feet long, two feet high, solid, regular, sloping as the land sloped, between the back lawn and the vegetable garden.

She called it the vegetable garden on faith, a plot of ground that had been for years a feed lot for the Dunns' ponies. The soil, in addition to being heavy clay, was packed down hard. But she was digging in compost from the old falling-down sheep barn across the road. Sometimes now she saw earthworms in the turned-up shovel-fuls of clay. She took pains to avoid cutting into them. They labored along, slippery and private, leaving intricate, promising channels in their wake. Asleep, sometimes she dreamed of tilth, of dark, fertile soil crumbling in her hands. Once, nodding off late at night over her book, she'd had a clear vision of a row of small round evenly spaced heads of Bibb lettuce; she counted them off by their round green names, *love, love, love*—

She didn't always dream of gardens, of course. A couple of nights before, she had dreamt she was on a pogo stick, bouncing up and down in the same place, in a rage. She was using the pogo stick like a jack hammer, trying to break through the surface that supported her. Her hair fell in her face, tears streamed from her eyes, she hammered and hammered with the pogo stick, getting nowhere.

But in the light of day, it seemed to her she was getting some-where. She thought of herself as a person with ambitions, plans for the future—to make her garden, to extend the wall all the way to the wire fence, to establish a perennial border in front of it.

This evening she was planting iris rhizomes which she had dug up from around an abandoned cistern and separated into forked pieces. She arranged them in groups in front of the wall. For a while, as she worked, the evening hung still above her, a perfect deep electric-blue dome fractured by the bare black branches of the locust trees that ringed the garden. Each time she lifted her leg to push the shovel down, she felt the letter in the front pocket of her jeans, bending stiffly against her thigh. Sturdy, expensive bond from the law firm where her husband was working part-time these days in the mail room.

Her shovel struck rock. She traded the shovel for the pick and probed along, learning where the rock went by the sound of metal against stone—there and there and there, until finally the pick drove silently down. She played it then, it caught under the weight of something, she pitted her weight against the weight of the rock. It lifted. She moved the blade of the pick further under, changed sides, braced and pulled as hard as she could against the handle. The heavy earth bulked up; the shape of the rock discovered itself. She shoveled soil away, knelt, and got her hand under the jagged white edge that gleamed down there. She bent into the deep mossy smell of the earth at night, worked the whale-shaped rock around to stand on end, played it out of the crater formed by the absence of itself. The heavy soil kept the shape of the rock that had lain against it for, what, centuries? Eons. She tried the word aloud, hoping to imagine what it meant. Where she stood had once been the bottom of the ocean; she knew that much .

She struggled, lifting the rock, and muscled it up the bank, scraped the moist clay off it, to examine what she had unearthed. Intact scallop fossils were embedded in the rough side, a large, definite, three-branched fragment of coral. She rolled the rock end over end and lodged it in the wall, fossil side up.

The last light drained from the sky all at once. It was the time when for a while you thought you could still see but you couldn't. The next ridge over, the Dunns' lights were on, looking lonely. The stars came out, clear and hard and all of a sudden. When she had first come here from the city, she had felt frightened, at a loss, under the huge, uninterrupted fact of the heavens. Now she'd grown accustomed, and browsed among the constellations. The wall shone white in the light from the porch. She knelt and planted the last iris roots in the dark, broke up the soil with her hands, and patted it over them, then headed across the grass toward the house. She kicked off her boots on the back porch, turned on the light in the kitchen. The fire in the wood stove was going out. She raked the live coals to the front and reloaded it, then filled the kettle and put it on top of the stove.

She fished the letter out of her pocket, held it carefully with the sides of her hands—she found she didn't want to get it dirty. Her name and address were arranged handsomely, generously, across the envelope. The black ink drove boldly into the paper. His handwriting was all he had to offer her now, and she had come to feel it was a fraud. She couldn't see any reason to open the envelope; inside would be just more black ink, more handwriting—widely spaced lines of it—telling her in one way or another what she already knew. She hadn't heard from him in over a month. "You sound very far away," she'd said on the phone experimentally. "It's a bad connection," he'd quickly explained. The last communication she'd had from him was a report of a movie about the Spanish Civil War that he'd seen at the Bleecker Street Cinema. It seemed he'd liked it a lot. She responded on a picture post card—two grinning farmers waist-high in tobacco plants. On the back she had written, "Tell the truth now if you know it, Jack." And he had. Every day from then till now she would wait for the blue Scout truck to pull away, then go down the stepping-stone path to look in the mailbox. The only mail she got was addressed "Boxholder."

She looked at the bright, primitive little room, taking note of the sweat pants on the back of the chair, the ashes under the stove, the night black and unpeopled outside the window. She realized she was seeing it through his eyes. Feeling his dismay.

There was no reason for dismay. This was her winter home, hung with quilts against the storms to come. She had a rocking chair, a cot, even a yellow kitten, asleep now under the stove, a foundling from the Dempster Dumpster. She was thinking of getting a dog, too. She had two jars of wild plum jelly and a basket of black walnuts. There were persimmons in a bowl, with which she was going to make a pie. The recipe was in *Stalking the Wild Asparagus*. She had that, too. Because of the uncertainty of her situation, she had been till now mainly a forager. Next year she would evolve into a planter. She had gardens on the brain. She thumbed grandly through the catalogues, making lists, sat up late drinking hot toddies and reading last year's issues of *Organic Gardening*. Or sometimes James Joyce. She had recently felt moved to copy this sentence out of *Ulysses:* "Time has branded them and fettered they are lodged in the room of the infinite possibilities they have ousted." She looked around her at the comforts she had gathered together here in this room in which she was lodged: bowls and boards, a jar of chick peas and one of brown rice. Potatoes in a sack. A post card of the Dürer owl pinned to the wall. A bottle of J. W. Dant, a tin of jasmine tea, a hot water bottle. A few books, a radio. Worldly goods laid by against hunger, cold, loneliness. She had abandoned the other rooms of this house one by one as the season changed—there was no way to warm them. She had moved the cot into the kitchen. She made her home here now. She took sponge baths in front of the stove; she brushed her teeth in the kitchen sink. She turned on the radio sometimes and danced between the table and the stove, in the room of the infinite possibilities she had ousted. She was also reading Thomas Merton. What Thomas Merton said was "Nothing one chooses is unbearable."

When she first came here, it was full summer, and she wandered at night barefoot from room to room in the dark, feeling the smooth pine boards beneath her feet, looking out one open window, then another. There was a sweet warm smell in the house, like old books—perhaps it came from the walls, covered with layers and layers of peeling wallpaper. She arranged wildflowers in jars, watched the shadows of leaves moving in the wind on the many-colored peeling walls. That was euphoria, innocence. Now she had settled in with the winter facts of her situation. From the kitchen window she could see the road winding down through bare oak trees, then up again toward Mr. Dunn's old barn, with six different pieces of machinery rusting around it. Nearer to the house were the redbud thickets, the doomed elms, the peach tree and the ash. Through October, as the truth caught up with her, she woke sometimes in the night, crying. Her tears flowed down, drenching the pillow, the front of her nightgown. She would get up and stand by the window, the sobs still shaking her. "This is excessive," she would think, amazed and frightened by the number of tears she seemed to have in her, the pain she felt, the anger. Sometimes she actually screamed out, as though a blunt knife had been stuck in her gut. The haze sat on the hills, but no rain came. The flies banged against the windows, the locusts raised their dry electronic clamor, until the frost put an end to it. Then she began to be cold and moved into the kitchen, and lay still and straight on her cot at night, near the stove, feeling sometimes that her life had a definite shape, a weight.

She dreamt once that he lay beside her. He spoke in his slightly nasal, clipped, positive voice. "I never loved you. Not really." And then she was pummeling him with her fists, scratching his face. "You did, oh you did," she cried. He lay still beside her and when she had worn herself out he said again, very calmly, certainly, "No, I never loved you. Not to call *love*."

She didn't know whether he had ever loved her or not.

She remembered the last thing she'd said to him, at Pennsylvania

Station, when he'd gotten her settled, lifted her suitcase onto the overhead rack. She'd whispered, hoping desperately that she meant it, "I'll miss you a lot." He had looked at her, his green eyes far back in his head and formal, and said nothing.

She was going away for a vacation, a little time to be alone. He would come down later and ride back with her on the train, along the river. That was how they left it.

Through all of drought-struck October, she waited for the mail and listened to the wasps singing threats inside the walls of this tarpaper tenant house. Her friends Sam and Cora had by then offered to let her have the house in perpetuity—"Whatever *that* means," Sam said. The house had been standing empty for three years, until Sam and Cora acquired it and invited her to come stay in it for a while. There were birds' nests in the chimney, squirrels in the attic.

Mr. Dunn had grown up in this house. She discovered in the back of the linen cupboard a sentence written on the bare plaster wall in black ink. *C.D. plus P.W. I love Pearl W. and I am going to get her too. Chester Dunn, March 10, 1930.* It was a precise, large up-and-down handwriting, nothing hasty or surreptitious about it. It was as if he had written it there, laid his cards on the table, daring fate to come along and make a liar out of him. She didn't know whether it had or not. She didn't know Mrs. Dunn's first name. She asked Sam and Cora, but they didn't know it either. She hoped it was Pearl W.

The headlights of a car slipped by the kitchen window going down the hill. The old refrigerator throbbed in the silence.

She dropped the envelope on the table. His own hand had touched it three or four days before. She was impatient with herself for thinking such a thing, but went on, turning the idea over laboriously. Right now, in a room as real as this one, he was still alive; his brain was still working, flashing splendid images across his eyes. She could find him. He was still on the earth, breathing in and breathing out; he wasn't dead. But it made no difference. Gone was gone, dead or alive. That part was over; she had a wall to build. She turned on the television. The blond weatherman was her current erotic interest. He knew what was in store for her—he had her highs and lows in his radar eyes; he knew what was coming, unseasonable snow from the Great Lakes.

She filled the blue plastic basin with warm water from the kettle. She turned her hands slowly in it, examining them as the garden dirt rolled off them. They were raw and red and scraped, a burn on her wrist, calluses at the base of each finger, uneven nails embedded now with clay. A wasp sting swelled one knuckle. "Well, that's what happens," she thought. She washed her hands gently, carefully, paying special attention to the blue insides of her wrists. She was thinking of the thing that had happened to Mr. Dunn a few weeks ago, the terrible story that had flown up and down the pike, as if the shock couldn't contain itself—how he'd gotten his hand caught in the corn shucker, couldn't reach the ignition to shut the thing off, how he pulled against it for a long time to keep from feeding more of himself into the mechanism, hoping all the time somebody'd come along, until finally, feeling himself weakening, he'd taken out his knife and cut his hand off. She wondered how he'd gotten through the bone. It wouldn't have been one clean stroke, not with a pocket knife. He would have had to be determined; he would have had to work at it, and work fast. Once he'd started he couldn't back out. The blood pumping right out of his body. The strong pulse.

Afterward he'd made a tourniquet with his belt and managed to crawl out to the road, where Richard Lemons found him and got him to the hospital—just in time, too, they said.

She glanced at herself briefly in the mirror she had propped on the windowsill. She was a redheaded woman. Her hair was caught back on her head in an unkempt washerwoman's knot, and today was her thirty-fifth birthday. Her sharp, naked face was all bone now, three points: cheek, cheek, chin. It was clear what kind of old woman she would make, the wiry kind. But the girl she'd once been was also there, big-eyed, startled. At 35, her face held her whole history, past and future.

That's the reason she'd heard from him today, because it was her birthday. It wouldn't have seemed decent to let it go by without resolving the thing. He had his standards.

She went back to the table and opened the letter. She read it hastily. "Divorce is not a pleasant word," it said. She found herself nastily mimicking this ridiculous sentence out loud. Something about telephone poles spinning past, and a sentence beginning, "Would that—" She dropped the letter on the table and went to wash the dishes. Her cracked green teacup told her fortune.

Jack was the one who liked to know what his fortune was. They had shuffled the tarot pack—seriously, thoroughly, concentrating on the question. They had thrown out the coins for the *I Ching*. Jack wasn't ever particularly interested in the oracle's description of his present state. He wanted to know what the lines changed to. What came next. He said he believed in process, flux, but what he really believed was that the present moment, stripped of future possibilities, was intolerable. He hoped that time would carry him somewhere else. Somewhere better.

What *she* wanted, she thought, was to stand still, with time moving through her, for the rest of her life. He would call this being embalmed before you were dead. The idea of stasis horrified him. She didn't think of standing still as stasis anymore.

In the summer, when she first came here, riding to town in the car with Cora and Sam on occasional evenings, she would pass the Dunns' house and they would be sitting on their porch, one on each side of the door, in their matching red metal lawn chairs. Sitting there motionless and silent, faces forward, looking out over the shady lawn that fell steeply toward the road, with its old, dense beds of irises, its ground ivy and birdbaths and stepping-stone paths. *C.D. plus P.W.* Fifty years since passion and determination had made him write that on the cupboard wall. And how had they liked it? Was it enough for them? Was it plus or minus?

Whichever, their pony was outside her window again. She heard the intimate steady crunch, the snorts and sighs. She was sorry about Mr. Dunn but she wished he'd fix his damn fence. She hated that pony. Two nights ago he'd eaten some little dogwood trees and an apple tree she had set out. She usually just went outside and yelled at him and ran him off, but he always came back; it was hopeless. Maybe she could find out where he was getting through and patch the fence herself. She put some popcorn kernels in a pan and went outside.

She stood a little way from him. He was a squat, comical little pony, with a lackadaisical, sassy sway and a long mane he liked to toss. She shook the kernels in the pan and he looked up at her, figuring the percentages. She edged a little nearer, so did he. She got her hand on his rope halter and said, "Come on, you jerk." He came peacefully and ploddingly, without further ado. They walked along the curving road together, in the dark. She let him lower his nose into the pan from time to time. When they got to the little white house she stopped on the road and called out, "Mr. Dunn!" She saw him looking out the front window through the green drapes. It occurred to her that he might not have any idea who she was—she used to wave to him when he passed in his pickup truck, but that was before the accident. He came to the door, squinting through the porch light. "It's Kate Price, from up the road. I've got your pony—you want me to put him in the barn?"

"Well," he allowed in a thin, undecided way. He got his jacket down from a hook. She saw Mrs. Dunn behind him at the door, trying to help him get into it. Maybe this wasn't the way they did things around here. She was probably bothering them. "He came to my yard again, so I thought I'd get him while I could," she called. She was sorry she hadn't just run the pony off again, now—he'd already eaten the trees, what else could he do?

"He'll be right down, honey," Mrs. Dunn cried out from in back of him. She was tall and square in her navy housedress. He put on his gray felt hat and came down the path, making little throat-clearing noises, long legs in gray wash pants, the white bandage at the end of his arm looming. When he got to the pony, who stood beside her snorting and trying to lower his head to graze, he took the halter in his left hand and, clearing his throat again, said, "I wonder what I'd get for this pony if I was to sell him by the pound." She laughed. He stood there, smiling and nodding under his gray hat, his close-set eyes squinting off embarrassed.

"I guess he's too smart for a pony," she said.

"Too damn hungry for one, I know that."

"You want me to help you get him in the barn?"

"Well," he said vaguely. "I guess I better put him up. If I turn him out in the field, he'll just go right on back to y'all's yard again." They turned and walked together on the road toward the barn. "I'll have to see about that fence tomorry. I hate how he's been botherin' y'all."

"That's all right." She didn't know whether to tell him she lived there by herself. He ought to know by now. Maybe he couldn't believe it, or thought it was impolite to notice.

After a while he explained shyly, "I've had some trouble keeping up, what with my hand and all." His right arm hung by his side as if it had nothing to do with him.

She didn't let herself look at it. "You feeling all right now, Mr. Dunn?"

"Feeling pretty good," he said, bowing his head politely toward the barn ahead of them.

"I'm glad to hear it."

They walked on, under the bright stars, the pony plodding between them. She thought they were a stately crew. After a few steps he held up the bandaged stump with tentative merriment. "They're going to fit me out with a hook directly. Just in time for strippin' season." He glanced at her, grinning a little cautious grin.

"Maybe you'll revolutionize the whole tobacco industry," she ventured.

He opened his thin lips in an appreciative, soundless laugh. "That's right. 'Fore long, ever'body in this county's going to be wanting them a hook."

She glanced at the stump then; she couldn't help herself. The club of bandage, and then nothing. He brought it down to his side self-consciously. "I sure do admire you," she said. "Being able to—to do that. What you did."

"Didn't have but one other choice." He looked at her and nod-

ded, a bright, fixed look on his face under the rim of his hat.
"Shoot," he said, turning then to spit politely off to the other side.
"I'z just glad I had my knife."

They walked together into the dark, leaning barn, tier on tier of
tobacco rising up. There was a stall down at the end of it. He and
the pony went ahead, ducking under the cured leaves, side-stepping
bales of straw and mowers and tubs. "It's kindly tied with baling
twine," he said apologetically. He and the pony waited while she
picked out the knot and opened the stall door. He led the pony in
and then came out and rummaged around in the dark till he found
a water bucket. He turned on the pump and filled it, lifted it with
difficulty with his left hand. She didn't think she ought to offer to
help. She held the door open and he carried it into the stall. But he
couldn't hoist it up onto the hook on the wall. He set it down and
bent to it quickly with his other hand, and then remembered it
wasn't there. He grabbed the handle again with his left hand and
stuck the handless arm under, too. He managed to raise it that way.
She stepped forward quickly to help—her hands, his hand, and the
abrupt, brutal stump all lifting the heavy bucket to the hook.
"Thankee," he said, nodding in a dignified way, then turned to the
pony. "Now, I ain't *given'* you nothin' to eat, so you'd just as well not
to ask. You done already grazed down their whole yard."

She tied the string back. "Who's going to untie this tomorrow?"
she asked.

"I'll let that sucker stay there for a day or two. Till I get the fence
mended."

They walked back out to the road in silence. He thanked her
again. "I'll help you with the fence tomorrow, if you want me to,"
she said.

"Naw, she'll help me. She's a pretty good helper."

She thought Mrs. Dunn's name had to be Pearl. If it wasn't, she
didn't want to know.

She walked back up the road, saw the lights from her kitchen
window shining through the trees. *She* wasn't sure what *in perpetuity*
meant, either. There was the little house, with its fallen-in front
porch and rotted window frames, its patchy lawn full of burdock
and plantain, its leaning outhouse. When she looked at it, she
looked at it with love and domestic determination. *Eventually* was a
prayer—eventually, full of grace. She saw stone fences, perennial
borders, an orchard down the south-facing hill. She saw a porch
swing, a storm door. She looked at the house not as a person
camping in it with two saucepans and a cot while her marriage fell
apart but as a person who meant to stay.

She went back in the house and fixed herself a drink. She looked at the letter on the table and without malice picked it up and threw it in the stove. She'd get in touch with a lawyer in the morning. She was 35 now. What she was still hoping for was sweet human constancy, fixity. She watched the end of the news—Arab women squatted, with their heads in their long hands, swaying, grieving.

When the news was over, she fixed herself some potatoes with cheese grated on top and a sliced tomato. After she'd eaten, she turned on the radio. It was George Harrison. *"Little darlin', seems like years since it's been here—"* She danced. She saw her reflection moving against the windowpane. She danced in the kitchen in her muddy jeans with the knees bagged out. It was her birthday. She was quite alone tonight, but she was not at all unhappy. *"It's all right,"* sang George. She danced and danced, not knowing that Kentucky was headed for the longest, coldest winter on record, that the wind coming through the cracks would blow the dishtowel off the nail, that the snow would fall to the windowsills and stay for months. Underneath it the thick layer of mulch she had laid on top of the garden would gradually break down and make a little topsoil. She didn't know that she would get a yellow dog who would one day, meaning no harm, lick the yellow kitten to death in the snow. She didn't know that she would finish her wall and that one July evening, on the broad smooth shallow fossil-filled slabs of limestone, she would stretch out full-length with the heat of the sun still warm in the stones, that she would look up through the leaves of the peach tree at the pearly evening sky, Mozart coming out through the kitchen window on the breeze, and the Dunns' little black pony even then on his way up the hill toward her garden—cantaloupe, beans, tomatoes, corn, all in their twilit rows, wheeling through their season on the earth.

SNAKE-HANDLING SUNDAY IN THE BLUE CHURCH

by Annabel Thomas

To begin I want to state that all what transpired in the Blue Church last Sunday came as unexpected to me as to the rest of the membership and left me just as flabbergasted.

I mean to put down the facts here, honest and plain. These're my last words on the subject. Let whoever reads them make out of them what they can. The one comment I will add is this: I've not been a-scared of man nor beast since that morning.

I freely admit before last Sunday I was the biggest coward in Colerain County. Every beastie that crept, walked, crawled, or flew, be it living or dead, scared me spitless. And most especially snakes.

My Grampap Farrell, on the other hand, was a snake-lover. Garter, grass, rattle, and copperhead, he loved 'em all. From the time he could toddle, folks said he just seemed to understand snakes and they understood him.

So it was natural when he grew up and went to preaching that he should bring his friends the snakes into his church.

"They's Goda'mighty's creatures, like you'ns," he told the membership. "All you got to do is love 'em and they'll do you no harm. Learnin' how to love 'em, that's the part takes the doing."

Now it's common knowledge how, the fall Grampap took the pulpit, the membership give our church two coats of white paint and how, the follering winter directly after he done his first snake-handling, the church turned blue.

Grampap said it was a miracle and a heavenly sign that Goda'mighty had come Hisself to dwell with us in His house of worship and, though some held it was a sign the paint wasn't no account, the membership reckoned its doings was blessed and they all went to handling snakes.

All the years Grampap Farrell preached, they was great humbleness and harmony and brotherhood in the membership. Only a few got snake-bit. The one man that died was ninety-three and in the last stages of dropsy, so nobody was sure if the snakes or the water got him.

The difference come when Grampap passed to glory and Papa took the pulpit.

Where during Grampap's time the membership could handle or not as it pleased, Papa laid down a law that ever' member of the Blue Church had got to take their turn picking up copperheads and rattlers to keep in a state of grace. He set aside one Sunday every month especially for snake-handling. He give it out as how Goda'-mighty loved a snake-handler and hated a coward. Cowardice, he said, was the worst of the deadly sins, since it showed want of faith.

As time went on, more and more folks was bit and a good many died and pretty soon our church got writ up in the newspapers.

Crowds of people commenced coming down from Sisterville and Beloit and Trent and even Tapp City up in Kimball County to see the snake-handling. The membership got so swell-headed, they'd scarcely nod to unbelievers and they quarreled amongst theirselves as to who picked up the most snakes and who held on to them the longest.

The collection plate ran over ever' snake-handling Sunday except in September, when most people went to fairs instead.

To cut a long tale in half, by the time I turned sixteen, I was the only soul belonged to the Blue Church what hadn't never touched a snake during a Sunday-morning service.

Myself, I laid it to poor eyesight. A body's naturally skittish when all she kin make out is blurry squiggles and swarmy blobs. Ever' time I tried to pick up them snakes, my specs steamed so I had to take 'em off, which left me near blind as Bartimaeus. Though, truth to tell, there's times in my life I've thought to my soul I seen truer blind than through my specs and sharp-sighted.

Papa pronounced my case sad enough to make a stone bawl. Said it was plain I was headed to hell in a breadbasket. "I'm willing to go there," says I, "if I can skip the snakes." But it wasn't in his power, he said, to excuse me from our church's main sacrament indefinitely.

Finally one snake-handling Sunday Papa took me aside and told me my reluctance was getting to be a blot and a scandal on the church and augured to get our miracle revoked. What's more, he pointed out to me as it weakened his leadership to have his own kin, blood of his blood, the only reneger. Besides which, if others was to foller my example, we'd likely lose our draw and the collection plates would lighten and the whole membership would be down on him.

He sent me outdoors during the Sunday-school hour to meditate and build up my grit. When the bell rang for service, he said he expected me to be on deck to do some snake-handling.

I walked down into the field blubbering and commenced to pull yeller-eye daisies for to be put on my coffin. As my luck would run, one daisy had a bee in its middle and when I picked it, the bee buzzed up and sat on my head.

Now, I was near as scared of bees as I was of snakes, besides which I right away recognized that this wasn't no ordinary bee. It was a spirit bee if ever I'd seen one. I dropped that daisy and tore down the field bellering and spewing flowers out my pinafore at every step.

When I came amongst the graves, I stood still, shaking. The bee flew out of my hair and circled my nose looking for a place to sink his stinger.

"I know you," I told it. "Yo're Shreve Kilkinney's soul passed into a bee. Don't do me no meanness, Shreve, and I'll lay flowers on your mound."

Right away the bee took off straight as a string for the woods.

Shreve was a narrow-hipped, sharp-eyed, black-haired part Indian, part Darkie, part Irish boy used to keep bees on the woods' edge.

When the boys was sent off to war, Shreve wouldn't go. He allowed as how his head was set against killing. Instead, he ran away north, fell off a train up there, and got run over by eight coal cars. When his body come back in a box, Papa stuck him outside the fence in Beelzebub's soil on account of his having died a coward.

Deacon Bo Billings said if Shreve had come back alive he'd of shot him down because Bo's two boys got kilt in the war Shreve ducked.

Papa said, "Vengeance is mine sayeth the Lord," but Bo swore the Lord appeared to him in person and told him it was all right.

I sat down cross-legged and sorted out the flowers left in my pinafore, putting their stems together. The churchyard was so sun-bright it looked sucked dry of color. The circles of shadder under the trees and the slabs of shade behind the stones was solid-seeming, like pieces of dark wood.

It was on just sech shining days as this I'd used to see Shreve when I passed down the medder driving home the cows.

The bees would be lighting on his bare skin, on his face and shoulders and on his arms. They never bit him but crawled on him like they was gathering his sweetness to make into honey.

"Shreve, what was you going to tell me?" I asked whilst I fixed the flowers, because the day before he left Colerain County, I was stepping past the woods when a swarm of bees moving like a oozing shadder crossed my path and hung smack in front of me on a tree branch so I dasn't pass. There I stood shaking in my shoes when along came Shreve.

I watched whilst he coaxed them bees into a empty hive. Then he leant towards me and touched my arm gentle as a wind puff and his eyes full with light and it was plain he was going to whisper a confidence. Just then, far off, I heared Papa call out my name and I had to run off home. That was the last ever I seen Shreve Kilkinney in the flesh.

Now I climbed the fence with the flowers in my hand. When I got on Beelzebub's side, the sun was still shining but I felt, of a sudden, cold to my marrow. I hunched my shoulders and stood with my back pressed against the bobwires, trembling so the posts jiggled.

Shreve's grave was all growed up to briar and burdock and polkweed. The woods close by smelt of mold.

I fixed my eye on a gray-brown clod of dirt. It was moving on its own. Of a sudden, on top of the clod, two bright jewels shined out.

"I see you, Satan," I whispered, "come to snatch away my soul."

A stick snapped behint my back. I looked over my shoulder and there stood Shreve Kilkinney on his own grave, his head throwed back, laughing fit to bust.

"It's a toad," he said. Then he leant forward and blew out his breath and the toad hopped three hops and sat still, running out its tongue.

I tried to make a cross with my fingers but they shook too much.

"I see you brung me posies," Shreve said. "I'm obliged."

"Why don't you ha'nt them as done you dirt like a proper ghost, instead of bothering me?" I asked him the best I could with my teeth clicking on ever' word.

"I ain't no more ghost than you," Shreve snorted.

"Then who's in your box?"

"Some bum what rolled me for my pocketbook, that's who, poor feller. The coal car wheels ground his face clean away."

I sat down on Shreve's grave, still shaking.

"How come you to sneak home?"

"To see you, is why."

I felt myself go red up into my hair roots and down onto my collarbones.

"You better move on quick," I told him. "Your life won't be worth spit in Colerain oncet Bo Billings finds out yo're still breathing."

He kept a-staring curious-like into my face.

"What was you bawling about coming down the field yander?" he asked me.

So I judged I might as well to tell him the truth. "In a minute or two," I said, "I got to go in the church and pick up copperheads. I'll get bit and die and they'll stick me over here acrost the fence on account I'll of died a coward, like you done."

Shreve leaned nearer to me. His eyes was green with gold specks.

"Don't pick up no snakes," he said. "Come off with me instead. We'll go down to Memphis. Now I'm dead, won't nobody trouble us. I'll get a job keeping bees.

And what did he do next but reach up and pull off my specs and kiss my mouth and when I looked over Shreve's shoulder it seemed to me I seen Goda'mighty, plain as plain. He was sitting on the top of the Blue Church steeple a-watching us and his face was shining like a honeycomb.

Just then the bell commenced tolling and we heard a crowd of folks coming up the road. Shreve lit out for the woods and I clapped my specs back on and started towards the church figuring my time was come. My knees buckled going up the hill. When finally I got to the door I was almost crawling.

The yard stood full of people. Inside, ever' pew was packed from armrest to armrest. Some women was fanning theirselves with palm-leaf fans and some men was taking a dollar out of their pockets for the plate and some children was laughing and some was crying and ever' soul was talking to oncet and what they was talking about was the snake-handling that was about to take place.

I crossed the floor, stepped up into the sanctuary, and sat on a straight-back chair. While Papa laid the Bible open and commenced thumbing the pages, I stared down at my fingers. I was gripping them together so tight they looked skinny and white as a pile of bones.

From my left eye-corner I could just make out the edge of the altar and from my right, on the floor, the box with the copperheads in it. Now and then they moved with a soft, slithery sound like hands wringing.

Whilst Papa read out the text, a light-headedness came over me and a buzzing started in my ears. It was like a plague of locusts had dropped from the rafters and hung over the sanctuary.

When the membership stood up to pray, I tried to stand, too, but I couldn't get to my feet. Instead, I slipped sideways in my chair so that the back of my head rested against the spindles and bumped them ever' time I had a shaking spell.

Next Papa give the sermon. I caught a word here and a word there but couldn't make sense out of none of them.

Directly I heard a roar like a storm blowing up. It got so loud it brushed the locusts clean away. I listened to it quite a while before I made it out to be the membership and all the visitors hollering. "Let's have the snakes! The snakes! The snakes!"

I stood up from the chair and drawed my palms, first one, then the other, down my skirt. When I commenced to pull at the box lid, my specs steamed so I couldn't see a inch in front of me. I rubbed at the lenses with my fingers but it didn't do no good so I took my specs off and laid them on the chair.

The minute I touched the box, the shouting got louder. Some folks shrieked, "Sweet Jesus!" and some moaned, "Praise His name!"

I went down on my knees because my legs was too weak to hold me up. I gripped the lid with both hands but I couldn't no more lift it and tetch them snakes than I could fly like a bird.

There I crouched, on and on, still as the steeple and the congregation stomping its feet and bellering.

Then, of a sudden, a silence fell. I looked around and seen, far off down the dimness, a bright narrow shining like a lit candle that was the church door opening.

The people began whispering amongst theirselves so it sounded like a river flowing over stones. Someone shouted. A gunshot rapped out, sharp and flat, like hands clapped together.

Reaching for my specs, I knocked them onto the floor and I heard the lenses crack and tinkle. I rubbed my eyes hard and squinted and so was able to make out Shreve Kilkinney sagging in the sunlit doorway, his left elbow dripping blood like a slow spring seeping water, and I seen Bo Billings standing up on a pew seat aiming his smoking pistol at Shreve's heart.

Quicker than thought I threw back the lid, reached in the box, and grabbed a snake. It felt smooth and clenched like the muscle of a man's arm. As I hoisted it up past my face, I seen its little backward-pointing teeth and its greeny-gold eyes fixed on me.

Down I jumped out of the sanctuary and tore up the aisle swinging that copperhead by its tail around and around my shoulders like a lasso. People ducked away from me right and left as I passed by. When I got to Bo, I let loose of the snake and off it went, flip-flopping out over the membership. Bo Billings's jaw dropped down. He let fall his gun and dived for the floor. There was a general shrieking, pitching of hymnals, scrambling, and climbing under of pews.

In the hubbub, me and Shreve slipped quick out the door and down the front steps. We crossed the churchyard in three seconds shy of a minute, jumped the fence onto Shreve's grave and sloped off into the woods just as the first of the membership busted out the door shouting that Beelzebub hisself was loose in the Blue Church.

When we hit the Interstate, we walked the berm towards Memphis, hitching. Our first ride was a blue Chevy pickup. As we climbed into the back, I could of swore I spotted Goda'mighty high overhead moving along amongst the clouds heading south, same as us.

GOOD WATER

by D. Thrapp

The man who sold us this place said it had good water. But now, after only three months, there is nothing but mud at the bottom of that twenty-foot hole, and he won't do anything. And after what happened down in Lewiston, my wife has no ambition for the place anymore, and she keeps forty dollars in an envelope. I found it under the things in her dresser drawer. I know why she keeps it. It's for her bus ticket back to Spokane.

I haven't said anything. I don't know what to say, and she won't talk or say if she's afraid or mad or just discouraged.

When we first found out about the well, I went into Orofino to call the man, who lives down in Lewiston. He sold off his land, hundreds and hundreds of acres, which he had gotten from the government for a dollar an acre way back in the thirties—at least that's what he said. We paid almost a thousand per acre for these twenty, so he's made a tidy sum. His name is Mr. Allen. He's a one-armed man who ran cattle up here in the Grangemont area for years and years until the bottom fell out of the market.

But he wouldn't do anything. He said he wasn't liable. "The well is just a mud hole," I told him. "You said it was good water."

"Which place is this?" he said, even though he knew.

"We're the ones up on Orofino Creek."

"You bought that property," he said. "I'm sorry but you own it now."

He was right, but when I told my wife what Mr. Allen said, she was mad. Things had not gone good all winter and now this, she said. She said she would kill him when she saw him. She didn't mean it, she's so small. She's like a bird. But she said, "I'm keeping the shotgun loaded, and if he ever sets foot up here, I'll shoot him for trespassing."

After a while she calmed down. "He deserves to be shot, though," she said. "Someone ought to."

Maybe it was true that he might deserve to be shot. I wasn't arguing with her. But when we moved in, I knew the well was hand-dug. We were told that. I might have known what that meant, but I didn't; neither of us did. We believed him when he said the water was good.

What we needed now is a drilled well, but that's three to six thousand dollars, and of course we don't have it, and I said, "Not that it matters, because the way it looks, we won't be here much longer."

"You're telling me," Cheryl said, though I was joking. She was so angry she couldn't stay in the house with me. She put on her boots and went out. She went up into the trees above the house, where the snow is even deeper.

I waited. Around about four I went out and found her coming back along the road and she crossed over where the fence line is and met me on the open ground to the south side of the house. She looked so hard and cold I was afraid she would come down sick. I was afraid to touch her, afraid she might break.

But she stood there. She didn't want to go inside yet. She said it really was such a beautiful place, wasn't it. "It seemed right, didn't it, to buy this place."

I told her things would get better. We would see it through.

But she said, "That's what you said in Spokane." She wasn't mad. She just said it as though it was a matter of fact. "You said we'd move out here and our troubles would be over. Here we end up like before but you're out of work half the time. Sure, the house is bigger for us, but it might fall down tomorrow. Look at it. And now not even water."

This was what she had been going over in her mind all the while she was out alone. "I can't help the work," I said. "That's circumstance beyond my control."

"That's what you said in Spokane," she said again, and she stood there, hard and sad, the way she can get, looking out toward where the sun had already gone down.

But she was truly painting things worse than they are. She was in her bad mood then, depressed, as she is now. It's true the logging has pretty nearly shut down, but I'm luckier than some of those with nothing. I'm a diesel mechanic. The company is going through all the trucks while they sit during this slack period, so I do get work half the time. Not much, but we won't starve. And this summer we could fix up the house. If things get better, if the industry picks up, and we get water.

I told Cheryl all of this. And I said I would go down to Lewiston and get Mr. Allen to do something. I thought he might at least lend us some money, or maybe get us a deal with a drilling company. At least he might get us some consideration with the bank.

Her mood didn't get better that day, but the next day, the day before I was going to go, she was brighter again, so I said, "Why don't you come too, and do some shopping?" and she said she would.

It was a Sunday, and we didn't call first; we just went. Down there in the Snake Valley, Lewiston is much warmer. It hardly ever snows down there. It was a bright, warm day that day, and we did enjoy the drive down. We stopped at Spalding Park at the Lapwai bridge to eat our sandwiches. Cheryl wore a dress she hadn't worn since Thanksgiving, a pretty, green checked one with ruffles. I told her she looked nice. We sat at a table in the sun. We watched a bunch of little kids trying to play softball out on the field that was just beginning to green. Their shouting was like the barks little dogs make. When one of them finally hit the ball, they all of them left their places to go chase it down, and Cheryl laughed and said they were all so innocent and goofy.

We felt good. We were both in a happy mood. There was a drinking fountain not far from us, with a sign that said THIS WATER SAFE, SPRINKLERS AINT, and we even laughed about that and she said we ought to take that sign. I think we were optimistic by the time we reached the Lewiston bridge. We hadn't been down there since the fall, and it was sort of exciting. Cheryl was going grocery shopping while I talked to Mr. Allen. Then she would pick me up. She thought things would go fine.

The house Mr. Allen lives in is not very big, though I hear he's building a big house out on one of those benches down river where all the rich people are building houses. But even his house in Lewiston is quite better than ours out on Orofino Creek. It's brick partway up and then wood, and the wood is newly painted a dark brown, and it has a cement front porch and big square windows with dark, clear glass.

We got there well after dinnertime, and Cheryl stayed in the pickup while I asked if we could just sit down and discuss this problem, and he said we could, so I waved to her, and she went on to the SaveWay.

He took me to the back porch, which was glassed-in and looked out on a neatly mown, already green, fenced-in backyard with trim, freshly tilled flower beds and a big cherry tree beginning to blossom.

His wife had her plants and potted flowers all along the windows out there on the porch and wicker furniture with flower-patterned cushions. She brought out bottles of beer on a platter with chilled glasses.

"Mr. Allen," I began, "we thought when we bought the place that the water was good."

"I had it tested," he said. "That's what the tester reported. That's all I know." Instead of his left forearm he has an artificial one with two curving pieces of metal which he can bring together somehow, and he held his cigar clipped in that. He's a big man. Most of his hair is gone, and his face is heavy and meat-colored.

"But when you said the water was good, we thought you meant the well wouldn't run dry."

"Is it dry?"

"It's mud now," I said. "It's just a hand-dug well. We need a drilled well."

He shrugged. "It may get a flow again. You never know." Then he shook his head like he was sorry as me about the whole thing, but he said, "You knew, though, it was hand-dug. And I never said the well itself was good. I only said what I knew, that the water tested pure."

I was planning to ask him for the consideration first and then for help dealing with a drilling company, and finally, if nothing else, for a loan, but I forgot that plan and asked for the loan first.

"Are you working now?" he said.

"Yes," I said. "I'm lucky. The company is repairing all its trucks."

Then he asked me what my income was for that year, and I was embarrassed and didn't tell him right away.

"I have to know that you're a good risk," he said. "I can't loan to you without knowing your ability to pay me back. After all," he said. "You already owe the mortgage to the bank."

I suddenly knew that he wouldn't lend me any money. He never intended to because he knew I wasn't making enough to be a good risk, and he only wanted to hear me say it so we would both know he had that excuse. When I told him, he shook his head again, and his artificial arm put that cigar up to his mouth.

His wife came out with cookies on a platter and asked me how I was, and I said fine, and she asked me why my wife hadn't come in, and I said maybe she would when she came back from shopping. The cookies were wafers covered with chocolate, store-bought, very good.

When she had gone away again, he asked me if we had children, and I told him no but we were planning to.

He nodded, not as though he thought it was a fine idea but the way someone does when he already knows the answer. "Well, the truth is," he said, "I don't have money to be lending out right now. What I have is all tied up."

I didn't think that was true. He was the sort that kept money put away. But that's his business, and I didn't say anything. I went on to another angle. I asked him if there was anything he would say to the bank to help us, but he said there wasn't anything he could say. I asked him then if there was any way he could help me get a deal with a drilling company, and he said there wasn't.

That left me with nothing else to say, but I couldn't leave, because Cheryl hadn't come back, so I said, "Mr. Allen, I don't understand this. You owned that land for almost forty years, and you never knew that well to run dry?"

He sat back and looked at me steadily for a minute, which made me uncomfortable, as though I had asked an ignorant question, and the bitter taste of the beer and the sweet taste of the cookies didn't mix well in my mouth, and I wondered why anyone would serve both at the same time.

"Mr. Zahn," he said, "I owned a lot of land up there, all around Grangemont and Orofino. I never kept tabs on every spring and well. That place of yours was just a line shack for hired help, and no one ever stayed there for long." Then he said, "On my one hand I could count the times I've been inside that house, and that's fortunate." Then he laughed, a few quick, soft sounds. He had made a joke about his missing hand, but I didn't catch it in time to laugh with him, so I didn't. He shrugged and shifted and looked away. I had the sense he was getting impatient. "I never heard of that well going dry before," he said. "But then again, I would not have heard if it did."

"But forty years," I said. I couldn't help myself. "And here then, just when I buy the place, in three months it goes dry, and it's not even summer yet. It doesn't make sense, Mr. Allen."

He looked at me again, steadily. "Are you trying to blame me?" he said.

"No, Mr. Allen," I said. "No, I'm not trying to blame you. I'm just trying to make some sense out of it."

"I owned the land," he said. "You bought the land. That's all there is to it."

I couldn't look at him. I looked down at the rope rug on the floor of the porch. I didn't know what to say. Something had been spilled. There was a dark spot there. I kept looking at it. Maybe a dog had once peed there. Then all at once I thought how it looked like a plowed field when a single cloud stands over it. It was just one of those ideas that come, but as stupid as it was, my mind kept going to it all through the silence that followed. I couldn't help it; my mind was just blank.

Finally he said that, well, he was sorry, he knew how I felt. Then I could look at him again and even get up a smile. Then he said he knew it was hard times right now for young people, but he wanted me to know how it was hard back in the thirties too, when he had first come out. "We didn't have no plumbing or pump of any kind," he told me. "We hauled our water up from the river in five-gallon milk cans by pack mule. On the entire place not one single machine. First we ever had was a haybaler. Here is what it did." He held up his artificial arm then to show me, and I didn't know what to say at all.

"You understand," he said.

About that time the phone rang, I could hear it. His wife called to him from inside the house. "Frank, there's someone to talk to you."

So he excused himself, and I sat on the porch and waited and tried to think of something to say. I decided I would tell him the water in Orofino Creek was not good anymore because of the logging. We would have to haul our water from Orofino.

He was in there for quite some time, and all of a sudden I got sleepy from the beer and the warm sunlight. I might have dozed for a minute. Then I heard his wife's voice and my wife's voice, higher-pitched like they are whenever women say hello, and then she brought Cheryl out on the porch and sat her down and brought her coffee and asked me if I wanted coffee and brought me a cup, but she didn't stay to talk to us.

"How's it going?" my wife said. She looked both hopeful, which was forced, and skeptical, which was because she could see it on my face.

"Not good," I said, and told her I didn't think he would do anything for us. She scowled and wouldn't look at me. Instead, she looked around the room at all the plants and the furniture and all the nice little knickknacks, little ceramic frogs and brass pots and things like that. I could tell what she was thinking. She wanted things like that.

Then Mr. Allen came back and at first acted very glad to see her, but then he could see that she was upset and cold toward him, and he said he had to go out soon and see a man.

"My husband said you won't do anything for us," Cheryl said. I wished she hadn't said it that way. It was so blunt. I looked up at Mr. Allen.

He didn't say anything at first. He looked at me and smiled, as though he meant that everything was all right, that he understood. Then he sat down again and crossed his legs and placed his metal fingers on his knee and said that he didn't think he could do anything.

Then Cheryl came right out and said that she thought he ought to, that she thought he had misrepresented the property to us.

He looked at me again and at her, and for the first time he seemed truly uncomfortable, and shifted his legs and put his hand out on his knee again, and I was getting tired of looking at it. "I can see how you think that," he said, "but it just isn't true. I've been explaining it to your husband here."

"Explaining what?" she said. She was getting very mad. I should have known she would because of what she had said about the shotgun and all, but I had forgotten that. I wished I had said my good-byes and waited for her out front.

"What's there to explain, Mr. Allen?" she said. She set her coffee cup down loudly, and that or the loudness of her voice brought Mrs. Allen out to ask if she would like some more coffee, but Cheryl ignored her. "It's as plain as day to me," she said. "You told us the well was good. You had that property long enough to know. Don't tell me you didn't know."

Mr. Allen smiled, but this time he didn't look at her. He looked tired, the way someone looks when they are being patient in spite of themselves.

"I've explained all this to your husband," he said again. "I don't want to go through it again."

After that, it was like I wasn't there anymore. "What did my husband say?" my wife asked.

"He said he understood."

"What did he understand?"

Mr. Allen looked at her and couldn't say at first. I looked at Mrs. Allen, who was still standing in the kitchen doorway, and she looked worried, and I felt sorry for her.

"Why, he understands what I told him," Mr. Allen said. "I didn't misrepresent the property. He understands that. If you want an explanation, you can ask him. The water tested pure. That's all I ever vouched for."

"Pure water," my wife said. She scowled at me as though I was on his side. "And he also understands why you won't help us, is that it?"

Mr. Allen put a new cigar up to his mouth and prepared to light it. "Yes," he said. "He understands that. I've explained that."

"Times are bad," I said to her. I told her what Mr. Allen had said. "Mr. Allen's money is all loaned out."

"Good God," my wife said. She looked at me so sternly I couldn't believe it, and she stood up, and Mr. Allen stood up, and then I stood up.

"Mr. Allen," she said. "Explain to me one thing. Explain how you can think you're an honest, decent man. Explain to me how you live with yourself. How do you get to sleep at night? You have a nice house. You have all these nice things. Nice things," she said again, and looked at Mrs. Allen, who was so frightened she was about to cry. "Tell me," she said. "How did you get all these nice things without cheating people?"

They were terrible things to say, but she was upset and about to cry too, and Mr. Allen was very calm. He looked at my wife and said, "I worked for everything I have."

She stared at him then as though she couldn't believe he had even answered her, and.I could see that tears and rage were right there about to come, but she controlled herself. "You worked hard," she said. "Don't tell me you worked hard. A thousand dollars an acre. Not hard charging that, was it? Not for someone like you."

She didn't wait for him to answer. She went on out. She looked at Mrs. Allen but didn't say anything. She didn't need to. She just stepped past her, and the front door slammed.

Mr. Allen had put both his hands in his pockets, and he stood there, looking down at the rug, and I could see a small grin on his face like he thought it was funny, and his big bald head wagged back and forth like it was all some poor joke, and I didn't like him at all and felt miserable. I said I was sorry for all of it.

Then he began to nod but still looked at the floor. He said that my wife was a feisty little squaw, wasn't she, and then I didn't want to talk to him anymore. I said good-bye to Mrs. Allen and thanked her for the cookies and went on out to the pickup.

On the way back home I said that I knew I wasn't very good. Cheryl cried and I said I wished she wouldn't get so upset, we would get water somehow. But she said she wasn't crying about that; she was crying about all of it, the whole thing.

I knew what she meant, of course, but I pretended it was just this thing about the well. I told her I was sorry I hadn't met him head-on like she had but that we would get water somehow and make it through.

She didn't say anything for a while. Then she said the problem was that Mr. Allen knew how to deal with honesty. Then she said at least I was honest and decent and she could still love me for that.

I didn't know what she meant, but the way she said it made me think that those things weren't good enough. I didn't ask her what she meant. And since then I've been afraid to, now that she keeps that money hidden away.

And we haul our water up from town. We don't talk much. I go down to the well to check it every day, hoping the flow is stronger.

VINCENT

by Lewis Turco

Vincent's complexion was as chalky as the soil of Champagne, his native province. His skin was the color of whey because of the perpetual dusk in which he worked, the dusk of the caverns hollowed in the chalk cliffs.

In these caverns there was wine, miles of bottles, green and brown, stacked seven feet high, lying on their sides in their cradles. But there was curiously little dust, for it was Vincent's responsibility each day, from dawn to dusk, to walk down the aisle that extended under the hill into the darkness beyond the flare of his lantern and give each flagon a quarter turn. A quarter each day, no more and no less.

Vincent carried a lantern. If the flame burned low, began to gutter—which it had never done in ten years, he would know that the air was becoming noxious, and he could return to the entrance before he got into difficulty. He would walk in the center of a pool of yellow light that reflected from the colored glass, stopping each pace or two to turn the bottles with both hands, reaching to both sides and stretching above his head. He could work extremely fast, which he had to do in order to reach the end of the cave by midday.

At noon he would stop to eat his lunch before the great wooden door at the end of the cavern. The door was locked, and it had been so since Vincent, at the age of sixteen, had begun to work for the vintner, who had accompanied him on his first trip down the aisle of the cave. When they had reached the door Vincent had had the temerity to ask what lay beyond, but the vintner had merely shrugged.

"There is no key," he had replied. "It was locked when my father was a boy, and my father's father." Vincent had not asked why the door had never been forced. He had accepted things as they were, which was his nature and his habit. But each day as he stopped, set down his lunch pail and his lantern, and prepared to eat, he would stare at the door and wonder what was behind its dark, rough wood and rusty wrought iron.

When he was through with the bread, cheese, fruit, and wine his wife, Melie, had packed for him that morning in the cottage near the vineyard, Vincent would rise and begin to work his way back up the opposite wall of bottles. When he had reached the entrance again the sun would be low in the sky, and Vincent would step out of gloom into gathering dusk. He would close and lock the gate with the brass key in his pocket, and he would return the key to the vintner before he walked home beneath the poplars. In the kitchen he would find Melie preparing the evening meal. She was a bit younger than her husband—about twenty-four, and plump, but not unpleasingly so. She would greet him as he sat down wearily at the table. She would give him a glass of wine. Vincent would drink it slowly until supper was served. At such times he would miss the children they had not yet had.

Vincent would sit and think of a daughter as Melie bent among her kettles and pots, stirring and seasoning, the steam rising from the stove. He would imagine the daughter, each day, running into the room when he returned, climbing into his lap, and saying—as Melie never did, "Tell me about the wine, Papa." And he would tell her. The child would never tire of the story, of the descriptions of the cave and the bottles, the saffron lantern, and of the great door at the end of the passage.

But no children ever came. Melie would serve the meal, and they would eat. Afterward they would sit before the fire, if it was a cool night, Melie sewing or knitting, Vincent smoking his pipe. After a while they would go to bed, sometimes to see about making a child, but more and more often merely to sleep.

He did not know how it happened—he could not have imagined it during those first ten years—but slowly Vincent, without realizing it at first, began to feel an ache, an ache that eventually solidified around a center of discontentment. Once Vincent had identified the nature of his ache—after many days, even weeks, of giving his bottles a quarter turn each day, of many solitary noon meals before the door that drank up the light of his lantern as though it were wine, he began to think of what he might do.

At first his thoughts were desperate because they were new and unexpected. "I will abandon my work," he said to himself as he ate his cheese. "I will find a new line." But what new line? He knew nothing else. And more desperate still: "I will abandon my wife, my childless home, and I will become a vagabond!" The word astonished him. He sat and pondered it at noon for several meals, but eventually the astonishment wore off together with the possibility, and he returned to thinking about the ache.

He questioned his lot only at noon in the beginning, never while he walked the aisle, when he never thought at all. But one day as he was giving a green bottle a quarter turn he caught himself thinking, and again he was astonished; again he had something else to consider. More and more often he was startled to discover himself walking in a forest of reflection while he worked, like an insomniac who starts awake just at the verge of dropping off into the abyss of dream. A great deal of time went by, until it was clear to Vincent that he was obsessed. Even Melie noticed the change in his demeanor and actions, but she never dared ask what was wrong. What could be wrong? Nothing had changed except her husband. Like many women, she simply waited.

But Vincent had reached the point of action. One morning as he was walking down the aisle of the cavern, he stopped, and as he stared into the pinpoint reflection of his lantern in the glass of a brown bottle, Vincent experienced a revelation. He considered it for a long while, lost in marvel. At last he reached out to the bottle and gave it a *half* turn. Then he continued down the aisle with quarter turns, working faster than usual in order to make up for the lost time, and as he ate his bread and cheese at noon he dwelt, in the immense silence reverberating from behind the locked door, on the thing that he had done.

He was apprehensive and thrilled to the marrow at the same moment, but by the time he had reached the entrance of the cavern and come out into waning daylight, these emotions had given way to great satisfaction. At home Melie immediately sensed the improvement in her husband's disposition, and she heaved a warm sigh into the steam rising from her pots. That evening they went to bed early and tried to make a child—it had been a long while.

Afterward Vincent dreamed of a daughter climbing onto his knee and asking him, "Please tell me about the wine, Papa."

He replied, "Only if you promise never to tell anyone else what I am about to say to you. It must be a secret between us. You must not tell even your mama."

After suppressed joy, she promised, and Vincent began the story. He watched her eyes widen into wonderment when he reached the part where he twisted the flagon a half turn—just one half turn among an eternity of quarter turns.

But Vincent's good humor seeped slowly away in the succeeding days. Gradually the ache returned until he once again found himself compelled to act; his mood improved; he returned to brooding—

Melie was disconcerted by the ebbs and floods that appeared in the character of her husband and in their daily lives. She never knew what was going to happen on a particular day when Vincent returned from work, and at last even she was driven to desperation.

"What is wrong, Vincent?" she asked, and what she had feared would happen indeed did so—he shouted at her.

"Nothing is wrong! Why do you ask such questions? What could be wrong?" And he was surly in his silence the rest of the evening.

But a great deal was wrong. Her husband could no longer be appeased with turning a bottle halfway now and again. In the cave he had begun to turn two bottles a week, then three a week, and at last he gave a bottle a three-quarter turn before he reached the door and ate his lunch. The tunnel was as quiet as a graveyard at midnight. "What difference does it make how far I turn the bottles?" he asked the darkness. "I turn them so that the lees will not settle out, and so that the cork will stay wet and tight. But what if I turn them a quarter, or a half, or don't turn them at all for a day? Will the world be changed? Will the wine be worse?" He seethed and was morose alternately, for the three-quarter turn had done nothing for him. He was so caught up in his anguish that he almost failed to hear the sound when it occurred—a slight scraping behind him. When he realized that he had, indeed, heard something where he had never heard anything before, he was struck with fear and astonishment again, as on the first occasion of his rebellion.

He sat for a long time staring down through the shadows that gathered in the aisle of the cavern, shadows that seemed to turn into a wall of darkness rising between himself and daylight. It was a long way back. He nearly panicked and ran, but he made himself sit still and consider. Even the vintner had begun to notice Vincent's strange behavior, though they saw each other only twice a day, when Vincent received and returned the key to the gate of the cave. Eventually Vincent gained control of himself, and he forced himself to turn and look. He saw nothing. He rose, examined the door, the floor before it, and the hinges. Nothing still. He began to think that perhaps the sound had been a figment of his fancy.

For several days Vincent considered what had happened, or perhaps had not happened, and he reached a point of boldness he could not have conceived of at an earlier time in his life. He decided to experiment. He repeated the three-quarter turn in the morning, but he heard nothing at noon. He turned one bottle a half, and another three-quarters in the morning—again he heard the sound, but so faintly and, despite his vigilance, so unexpectedly, that he continued to doubt.

Vincent began to try combinations and afternoon turns—these

latter did nothing more than make his lantern flicker, or perhaps that, too, was a sleight of the eye, or too quick a motion of the hand as he was carrying it. He was so absorbed in what he was doing that both the vintner and Melie thought that things had returned to normal. Vincent had always been a silent man, and they could not know that this latest silence was of a different quality, though Melie, who had been through so many vagaries of mood with her husband, remained apprehensive.

On the day that he turned his first morning bottle one whole revolution, Vincent came to the door and sat down facing it. He turned up the flame and placed his lantern so that its light shone full upon the enigma of the locked door—the saffron flare fell into the grainy wood and the iron, and it glowed deeply in the wine that fell back in tiers into the recesses of blackness down the aisle. He kept his eyes fixed on the door even as he fumbled in his lunch pail and began to eat.

He heard it clearly first, and then he saw it—the great door scraped and began to open. Vincent sat as though stricken to granite, his eyes fastened to the widening crack of darkness. His lamp flickered, but it did not go out; neither did its light penetrate into the well of silence and shadow beyond the door, which at length stood open wide.

It seemed to Vincent as though his heart might explode, as though the pulse in his ear were as loud as summer thunder rolling over the poplars whipping in the wind along the road to his home and hearth. And then both pulse and heart seemed to stop, for Vincent heard a voice say, from the night beyond the door, "Papa!" —just the one word, but crystalline, like a single lute string being plucked.

Vincent did not move until his heart began again. Then he drew a great, rasping breath, took up his lantern, rose suddenly and began to back away. "Papa, don't go," he heard the child's voice say. "Tell me again about the wine." But Vincent continued to edge backward, and as he did so there was a hesitation—a pause felt rather than heard, a flicker of light or of shadow—then the door began to scrape again. Slowly it swung to, and Vincent heard the latch, then the bolt. Understanding that he had lost something, yet not comprehending what it was, Vincent faced back to the tunnel of wine racks and, giving each bottle as he went an efficient, precise, careful quarter turn as was his habit, he began the return through amber light.

THE OVERNIGHT

by Judith S. Turiel

Arnold has arrived to meet "girls."

"Women," Sarah said on the phone. "I wouldn't call them girls around here if I were you."

He stands now in her doorway, carrying a watermelon.

"I stopped on the way up," Arnold explains. He lets the watermelon slide toward Sarah, across the threshold. Her arms can barely cradle it. "There was a whole field of them. Not far from my place. They just sit there on the ground. Like they're not even connected."

Sarah lugs her gift to the kitchen, wondering if the refrigerator shelf will hold. "How was the drive?" she calls behind her. There is no answer. She can just picture Arnold deliberating over colossal mounds of watermelon at a roadside stand near the town to which he moved years ago—a small town, midway between San Francisco and Los Angeles, along that stretch of highway where the radio yields mostly country-western. His move from New York had seemed, to the family, abrupt. He had taken a job with the government, or air force—something to do with computers. Arnold's mother moved with him.

Sarah heaves the watermelon onto the kitchen countertop, thinking it's a distinct improvement over the gift he brought on the last visit, a cellophane-wrapped Whitman's Sampler which, Arnold explained, his mother suggested he bring. That time, he was hours late, Sarah remembers, remembering also her mounting worries as the evening wore on. She imagined flashing red lights, sirens, an ambulance speeding down some dark, barren road. "I had to take a few pit-stops," Arnold mumbled to her queries. Anticipation of the impending blind date, with a friend of a friend of Sarah's, struck Arnold in his gut.

With minor repositioning of yogurt and eggs, Sarah decides, the refrigerator's top shelf can be given over to watermelon. Sarah herself sometimes buys one quarter of a watermelon if it is small, but then only because Rachel likes it. And then it usually spoils. Rachel can't eat it quickly enough, especially since she travels hither and yon to conferences, where she is right now. Sarah never touches the stuff. Even as a child she did not like watermelon.

From the open front door Sarah watches Arnold slam shut the car trunk. Two large gray suitcases sit on the sidewalk.

"You did say a weekend visit?" she yells, teasing, as he starts climbing the porch stairway.

Arnold flushes. "This one is half empty," he says when he reaches the top. He hands Sarah one of the suitcases. "And it's till Monday if things go well."

Arnold and Sarah are cousins. They have a common grand-mother, a short, heavy woman with softly wrinkled skin and lush silver curls held by tortoise-shell combs. From Sarah's earliest memories, she hears her grandmother uttering only positive words. Even during those last years, when Sarah argued the Viet Nam War with anyone, marched in campus picket lines, and struggled with the guilt of managing never to be arrested or letting her grades slip, her grandmother merely tilted her silvery head and stated with certainty, "The President knows more than we do. He must be doing the right thing."

Their mothers are sisters. As a child Sarah heard the sound of Yiddish between her aunt and her uncle before he died. Arnold would not translate for Sarah. He never spoke Yiddish in front of her. He registered as vaguely odd. Arnold went to a different school. He wore dark, sagging suits. The games he wanted to play were always somehow serious. A few years older than Sarah, his middle formed a paunch, as if he were even older, with a shape modeled after his father's—like a trapezoid, base-side down, was Sarah's description when she learned the word in junior high. Now, Sarah notes, the paunch is flattened. Although his dark hair is thinning on top, it hangs longer down the sides, nearly covering his ears. He sports a moustache, in unexpected shades of red that match Sarah's thick, single braid. He might even be looking young-er, she thinks.

"How is your mother doing?" Sarah asks after they settle at the kitchen table. She knows from Arnold's phone call that cataracts are dimming her aunt's vision. Before that was the hip. She could get around only with a walker.

"The same," Arnold answers, glancing at his watch. "We're still trying to decide about the operation. When I first told her I was coming up north this weekend, she was a little upset." He pauses and smiles, as if in on himself. "Until I told her the trip was for a date. Then it was fine." Most weekends, Arnold heads south, to Los Angeles, where his mother now lives. He considers moving there. She needs his help more than in the past. It is a big community. He could join a synagogue and meet people.

"I haven't got much time," Arnold announces, glancing again at his watch. He stands. "I'm running a little late. I'd better call."

Sarah gazes out the window while Arnold dials the phone. Her second-story duplex, one block above Berkeley's flatlands, boasts a narrow view of distant bay wedged between close buildings. Today is a sunny Saturday. She can make out sailboats, tiny specks whose progress, from one edge of her view to the other, is barely perceptible. She cannot help overhearing the clipped, cryptic responses that are Arnold's side of the conversation. He is arranging with the weekend's social director, Sarah figures. The man from Club Med.

When Arnold phones Sarah he phones out of the blue. Those conversations are long and rambling. Often he is facing a decision. He has been offered a job near San Francisco but can't decide if he should take it. His vacation is coming up, but he doesn't know where to go. A friend gave him someone's phone number; should he call her for a date? Now and then he suggests maybe he should visit. The last visit, the time with the blind date, was a disaster. As the friend of Sarah's friend told it, they ended up fighting, at a Chinese restaurant, over whether to order shrimp. Arnold said only, as he buttered a blueberry muffin and his thumb on the morning after, "We had nothing in common."

Sarah was still married then. She was already sensing, however, that the match was not long for this world. "What can you expect?" she imagined her parents nodding to each other after she informed them of the separation. They blamed it on his not being Jewish; Sarah considered it more the luck of the draw and, probably, lack of readiness for the drawing. Her mother sighed at the thought of a daughter alone, before perking up with, "You're still young and pretty. You'll meet someone else."

When Arnold phoned to invite himself this time, he asked Sarah if her roommate would mind. Sarah let that one pass. "It's fine," she answered. "Rachel will be out of town anyway." His mother had heard from Sarah's mother that a roommate was now sharing the rent. That was true. They divide all shared expenses and keep watch over each other's individual accounts, settling debts, at restaurants, from forgotten cups of tea or slices of grasshopper pie.

After a silence Arnold continued. "I just got back from a week at Club Med."

Sarah is not certain what, exactly, Club Med is. She has seen advertisements of bronzed, curvaceous, bikini-clad women and bronzed, sinewy, bikini-clad men, moisture droplets beaded upon richly oiled skin. Once, while hitchhiking through Mexico during the summer of her sophomore year, she even peeked behind the tall wooden fences of a Club Med compound, catching a glimpse of swimming pool and deck chairs before a guard shooed her away, back to the endless white sand and aquamarine sea. She was with a boyfriend, and they were high, though not on anything dangerous. Whatever its reality, the image of Arnold there is startling. "You did?" was all Sarah could reply.

"I met a man there . . ." Arnold went on.

Well, that explains it, flitted through Sarah's mind. She pictured her first notice of a woman's beauty. The woman studied in the library carrel next to Sarah's own. They never spoke. The memory vanished as Arnold's voice returned on the line to finish his sentence. ". . . who was telling me about all the girls he can introduce me to if I come to San Francisco."

Arnold's arrangements are completed. Sarah shifts her gaze from the sailboats, back to matters at hand. Arnold remains standing, transfixed between phone and kitchen table.

"So what are the plans?" Sarah inquires.

"The date is tomorrow afternoon. He says I'll really like her. But I'm supposed to meet him in an hour. Someplace called Barney's. He said there are always people there. And it's near some special place at the Marina. Then he's taking me to a cocktail party at somebody's house. It's connected to a social club, from a temple. He says I'll meet lots of girls there."

"Women," Sarah interjects. She constructs the word slowly, distinctly, picturing the old "It's an F-O-R-D" commercial where the little guy's mouth becomes each letter. Arnold tilts his head, like a bird listening to an unfamiliar sound. Except that Arnold blushes.

"Women," he repeats quietly, sounding almost resigned.

What we need are M&M's, Sarah is thinking. Pop one into his mouth when he says the word. She is rummaging through a drawer for the extra house key, in case he stays out late.

"What do they call females where you live?" she asks in her least challenging tone as she hands him the key.

He looks at her with a puzzled expression, as if perplexed by the question. As if he rarely calls them anything at all.

*　　*　　*

Sarah waits up until midnight. A noise rouses her from deep sleep. She listens with eyes shut. The sound is like something being dumped, a car door slamming, a car speeding away. Arnold. Being dumped on her doorstep at daybreak by the man from Club Med. Or worse yet, by a stranger. Sick, drunk, picked up at a San Francisco bar only to be beaten and robbed. Bloodied. His car abandoned on some slick city street. She hears noises again. She forces her eyes to open and to focus on her alarm—2:17. The noise is now a rattling, closer. Sarah pulls herself from bed, dreading what she will find. At the front door she finds Arnold, fumbling in the dark with the key and the door's second lock, the dead bolt. Sarah opens the door, ending the struggle. Through half sleep she can see that he is all in one piece.

"How was it?" she asks in low monotone, not intending to hear the answer.

"All right," Arnold responds. "Nothing great."

They will talk in the morning.

"Eggs or pancakes?" Arnold ponders aloud. He is scrutinizing the menu at Sarah's breakfast place, receptive to an answer. Sarah refrains from offering advice. Her menu sits closed on the table. She will have the usual. The waitress stands with pad at the ready, waiting for Arnold's order. She knows Sarah's—eggs over easy, bacon crisp, blueberry muffin. Sarah comes here nearly every week-end, with Rachel when she is not traveling. Some of their best conversations happen here—loud and animated, about their jobs, a planned vacation, a hilarious story one can't wait to tell the other. They pronounce resolutions here, most recently that Rachel will say no to conferences during the next six months, and that Sarah will finish her dissertation by this year's end. Some weeks, the conversation is less pleasant, subdued, about independence and commitment and what is fair.

"How are the pancakes?" Arnold directs his question to the waitress.

"Buttermilk," she responds, accustomed to interrogation regarding ingredients. "Very good," she elaborates, realizing his concern.

"I'll have"—Arnold returns to the menu—"eggs straight up. No bacon."

"Potatoes?"

Sarah is scanning the tables, savoring the mix of clientele brought out by Sundays—young parents spooning breakfast into babies under varying degrees of control, college students at the close of a date, white-haired faculty and spouses, a graduate student with a book, couples of all persuasions. Sections of the Sunday paper are distributed throughout.

"Yes. Potatoes would be fine." Arnold surrenders his menu to the waitress. He hesitates. "Can you change it to scrambled?" he asks.

"So did you meet anyone?" Sarah prods good-naturedly after the waitress departs. Arnold has been talking about his previous day, which Sarah has not known him to do in the past. Already he has described Barney's, whose menu he found limited and hamburgers, at $4.75, greatly overpriced. Primarily, people drank. They sat on velvet couches at low tables, or on stools at a long, shiny bar with brass decorations. Sarah knew the genre, if not this particular example. She knew nothing of their next stop, a square patch of lawn somewhere along the marina, surrounded by sweeping views of bay, two bridges, the headlands, Alcatraz. Arnold described this patch as jammed with sunbathing bodies—"mostly unattached," according to the man from Club Med. "They were wedged like sardines," Arnold exclaimed, shaking his head. "Well, not quite. There were strips of grass between the towels."

To Sarah's latest question he answers, "Not really." He pauses, fishing his tea bag from its small stainless-steel pitcher. "At the party, I met a . . . someone whose number I took. But I don't think I'll call her."

"No?" Sarah fills a silence.

"I'd rather wait for today's date. The one Joe arranged," Arnold says, providing for the first time a name. "You should see this guy. He's divorced. He has dates every week. Three, four. Today he has two different ones." Arnold shakes his head again. "It's amazing."

"What does he do?" Sarah asks.

"He knows all the angles." Arnold's voice charges with incredulity. "Parties, bars, the temple young adults—"

"No. I mean work," Sarah interrupts. "What's his work?"

"He's a psychiatrist."

A shrink! Sarah announces to herself. Taking on a *pro bono* case?

"Did you know there are magazines?" Arnold continues. "Just for meeting people? Joe has done that. You answer an ad. You know, if someone sounds right. Or you put in an ad of your own. Describing yourself, and the type of person you want to meet . . ." Arnold's voice trails off. "I could never do that," he says, his tone bordering on self-reproach. "It's all done through box numbers. To be safe, I guess . . . and he told me I could go to this lady who arranges introductions. A matchmaker. I mean, that's her work. You have to pay to register with her. Then she interviews you—about yourself and your required characteristics. You know, for someone to be matched to. It's like computer dating, I guess. But it's this person."

"A professional yente, you mean." Sarah has heard of such people.

"Yeah." Arnold gives a short laugh. "But Joe says most of her . . . clients, I guess she calls them . . . aren't Jewish."

"That's a required characteristic I assume?" asks Sarah, who has never been one to plan ahead in these affairs.

"I couldn't marry someone who isn't," Arnold states. He is staring into his teacup. His look is determined. Sarah does not recall his ever referring so directly to marriage. "Anyway, Joe says I'll really like today's date. He says she's great . . . super, he said." Arnold glances at Sarah. "I wish . . ." Arnold drops the thought. He reaches into his shirt pocket and pulls out a piece of neatly folded paper. He unfolds and smooths it. "Joe told me some places to take her." Arnold slides the paper toward Sarah. She sees a penciled list, in two columns. "Someplace for a drink. And then these, here, for dinner." Arnold points to the second column. The last sentences rise as they end, creating questions.

Sarah knows one of the four restaurants, by name only. Arnold refolds the paper and places it back into his pocket. "He says I should stay till Monday and take her out again," Arnold adds, his tone convinced.

It is mid-afternoon. Sarah stretches on the living-room floor, skimming the travel section, preparing herself to run. Arnold is in the bathroom. The boring drone of an electric shaver ceases. Soon Arnold appears. His hair is wet and combed. His white undershirt contours small, soft-looking plateaus of breast and stomach. His belt is unbuckled, his feet bare and pale. Each arm is draped with clothing. A nail scissors rings his right thumb and forefinger.

"I trimmed the moustache a little," he says. "Is it enough?"

Sarah sits up to straighten her view. "Looks fine to me."

"Do you think my hair is too long?" Arnold asks. "I was going to get a haircut. But I decided not to. I could cut off a bit."

"It's definitely not too long," Sarah assures him. "You're in San Francisco, don't forget." Arnold puts the scissors on the coffee table and begins to spread the clothing. "Anyway," Sarah adds, "it just looks longer to you because it's wet."

Arnold picks up a checkered short-sleeved shirt and pair of brown pants. "Do these go?"

Sarah looks at each, noting brown among the shirt's varied colors. She notes also the dull shine of the pants. "Sure," she answers. "The shirt has brown."

"Would this be better?" Arnold exchanges the checkered shirt for one with long sleeves and pinstripes.

"That's okay too. They're both okay."

"Or should I wear those." Arnold points to darker pants, charcoal gray, in a heavier material, with ridges and bumps. "I guess they're dressier. The salesman said these are very popular. He said with a shirt like this." Arnold pulls on the sleeve of shirt number three.

Sarah eyes the darker pants, and the three shirts beside them, and a stack of neckties beside those. She envisions a survey of all possible combinations.

"And I have to decide between two jackets." Arnold disappears into Rachel's room. He returns with two sports jackets—one light beige, the other plaid. It is blue and green and yellow, and verges on loud. "This one is old," he says, raising the beige. He hangs the plaid jacket on his bent finger, in front of the beige one. "The salesman thought this jacket and the dressy pants."

"Let's keep the salesperson out of this," Sarah answers. She turns to the shirts, pants and ties arrayed across her coffee table. "Really," she tells him, "any of these would be okay."

Arnold puts down the two jackets and picks up the charcoal pants. "All right. These," he states. "So which shirt?"

"They're all nice," Sarah says in a voice that attempts to calm him. "It's really six of one." She reaches beneath the stack of apparel for the nail scissors. "And the beige jacket is fine," she adds, snipping a plastic price tag off the pants Arnold has chosen.

Sarah is dressed in her running gear and out the door before Arnold is ready. She returns to an empty house. She sits with the pink entertainment section at the kitchen table. She rules out a movie. Her wedge of bay is blurring lavender. Boats still out on the water, sailing into the sunset, have dissolved from Sarah's view. She pictures Arnold searching for a parking space near one of the bars on the list on the paper in his shirt pocket. A nervous flutter wisks, like a grace note, through her stomach.

Dinnertime comes and goes. Sarah reads. She nurses an apricot yogurt, meal enough when she is alone. She dozes, on and off. At least he'll be able to handle the locks tonight, she assures herself. Then she smiles. Maybe he won't even sleep here tonight. The revelation wakens her completely. Maybe he'll spend the night with his date. Sarah is amused by her prior presumption of Arnold's innocence. Returning to her book, she considers: But could he still be a virgin? She turns a page. Or did he venture with friends into brothels, like other New York boys? She puts down the book. She tries to imagine the man from Club Med, Joe, the psychiatrist, wondering what is his angle. Her initial conclusion, after Arnold called, has been amended. At least he made a friend, she had been thinking, picturing the two men enjoying their week of sun and water and well-planned social activities. No, Arnold explained.

They met only once, over dinner, while sharing a table in the Club Med dining room, on Arnold's last night.

Sarah is watching the eleven o'clock news when the telephone rings. She can make out Arnold's voice through the static of a poor connection. She lowers the volume on the television.

"What?" she shouts as if through orange juice cans connected by string. "I can hardly hear you." She waits while he repeats what he said louder, though sounding distant.

"Where are you?" she asks, still shouting. And then, "So what happened?" Arnold is calling from a phone booth along the highway. He did not much like his date, he tells Sarah. Here she was, this woman, divorced, with a child, living in her own condominium somewhere in Marin County. They had nothing in common, he explains. He is now two hours south of San Francisco, halfway to the apartment complex in the town that Sarah has yet to visit.

"What about your suitcases?" Sarah asks. She lowers her voice, realizing that the line has cleared. "All those clothes?"

He has them all, he tells her. He packed, and put his suitcases into the car, just to be safe. He will mail the key.

They hang up. Sarah wanders into Rachel's room—where indeed no sign of a visitor remains—and then into the kitchen. She opens the refrigerator and stands before it, waiting for the right something to strike her fancy. She removes the watermelon from its top shelf and cuts a sliver. Maybe she will find she likes it after all, she is thinking. As she cuts along an irregular dapple-green stripe, she says to herself, "This will take all summer to finish even if we both work on it," which is not the reason she is eager for Rachel to return home.

CHITTERLING

by Henry Van Dyke

I first heard the fat ladies scream in the spring of my twelfth year. I'd come downtown from Harlem that spring to carry off an ill-fated crime at Mrs. Liebman's. Mrs. Sophie Liebman's. On West Fifty-eighth Street. Around the corner from the Plaza.

I rang her buzzer.

"Lambkin," she squealed as she scooped up the yapping dog, the puff of white fur at my feet. "Lambkin, my lambkin, Oh, Mama's missed you so." The dog's tongue darted maniacally about the woman's large face, then she said to me, "Well, come in, come in, do."

Mrs. Sophie Liebman had a busy face; some part of it was always in motion. From her forehead to her nose she looked like Claude Rains, with brows both sinister and sophisticated; the lower part of her face, however, was large and horsy and clumsy and it appeared as if she tried every now and then to push this part of her face in alignment with the top part. In addition to her busy face, she wore too much rouge and too much powder and too much perfume, and she said "lambkin" too much.

"I suppose you want," Mrs. Liebman said, fingering the brooch on her bosom, "the reward."

"Yes ma'am," I said meekly, shifty-eyed with shame. Actually, I was more frightened than ashamed; I wasn't experienced in the ways of crime.

"Off! Off!" Mrs. Liebman shouted to her dog, who'd plopped in a fluffy ball upon a red velvet settee. "Lambkin, you *know* Mama's told you not to . . ." She trailed off into an affectionate gurgle as the dog (its name was Adrian) jumped to the floor and she went over to the rosewood desk near the window. "Where," she asked me, "do you live, lambkin?"

I'd been called many things during my twelve years, but never lambkin, and I didn't like it. "Harlem," I told her.

"I mean, where in Harlem exactly."

"Up. On a Hundred Eighteen. Near Eighth Avenue."

Her jeweled fingers did a sluggish twirl in the air. "Really, now? Near the Victoria Bar and Grill?"

I was suddenly alert. I couldn't believe it. "You *know* where the Victoria Bar and Grill is at?"

"No, no, not really. I mean, I've—I've heard of it." She sat at her rosewood desk. "Now, let's see," she said, poking fat, ringed fingers about the clutter on the desktop.

(Weeks later, many weeks later, I learned that Mrs. Liebman was the landlord of a number of tenement buildings around One Hundred Seventeenth and Eighteenth streets and it was not unlikely at all that she'd perhaps heard of the Victoria Bar and Grill—even if it was a rundown, dinky place where number runners hung out.) At that moment, in her lemon and rose apartment, my only thoughts were those of finishing up my business of crime and getting the hell out of there.

Crime, I say. I do not exaggerate. It was not by accident I appeared at Mrs. Liebman's door with her dog (whose name was not lambkin) to seek a reward. I wasn't clever enough to cook up the scheme myself but I certainly was dumb enough to go along with it. Leroy's scheme. And Melvin's. It was, I suppose, largely Leroy's idea, for it was he who'd said: "It's easy, man. These here rich white folks need they dogs walked, see. So we walk 'em, see. Then split."

But I didn't see, I told Leroy. Both he and Melvin were going on sixteen and they both bragged about having spent time in a boys' reformatory upstate. Melvin was the quiet one and the meanest. Leroy was less mean, and he did most of the talking, and he was the one who told me (impatient with my denseness) that once you could convince somebody to walk their dog, you did it—you did it until they trusted you. Then one day, one-two-three, the dog would be stashed away in an apartment up in Harlem. After that, the business part began. The lost-and-found stuff. The negotiating. Leroy and Melvin, expert dog-snatchers, needed me, a younger accomplice, and they told me over and over: "You ain't gonna git in no trouble if you act stupid, stupid."

And it seemed to be working, my stupid act, except—except Mrs. Liebman was writing a check! Neither Leroy nor Melvin could cash a check. And to make matters worse, I could see from her front windows facing Fifty-eighth Street, three stories below, both Leroy and Melvin pacing back and forth on the sidewalk waiting for me and the loot. It occurred to me (as it had only vaguely before) that Leroy and Melvin were capable of grabbing all the money, boxing my ears, and leaving me unrewarded for my troubles.

"Lambkin?" The wiggling of Mrs. Liebman's rhinestone fountain pen stopped and she raised her Claude Rains eyes. "My dear, what is the matter with you?"

Leroy and Melvin had seen me at the window. They'd begun to make obscene and impatient gestures down there on the sidewalk below.

"What is it that—" Mrs. Liebman came over and looked out on the street to see what had made me so fidgety. At first she smiled, and even seemed pleasantly surprised. "Why, those are the very same kids who—" Then she turned to me, the smile gone, and her granite jaw jutted out in anger.

I dashed toward the door, but mounds of chiffon and tulle blocked my exit. Rubies and diamonds and sapphires flashed before me as she pummeled and flung fat hands at my head. "You filthy little beast! You filthy little beast!"

I cried less from the pain than I did out of shame. "They put me up to it," I pleaded. "Honest to God. Honest to God, lady."

She got in a good number of stinging smacks before she stopped, still blocking my exit, and stuck her ringed fingers on her chiffon hips. "I ought to have you put away. All this time my poor lambkin—"

"Please, I'm sorry, lady. I—please, lady . . ."

Whether she saw that my tears were real or whether she suddenly thought of all those acres of slum buildings she owned up on a Hundred and Eighteenth Street, I don't know, but she let her hands fall from her hips and then reached out and drew me to her. "You poor thing . . . poor, poor dear . . . what on earth brought you to this? Hmmm?" She patted my head as if to ease the pain she'd only seconds before inflicted. "Now, come. Come along." She pulled me into her long kitchen and made me sit at a glossy red-topped table.

Soup. With no meat and potatoes in it. It was all right, the soup, but I liked a nice hefty soup like my Aunt Ernestine and Aunt Willa fixed for me at home.

More than anything, I was glad to be able to kill some time: I'd been beaten up once that day and I didn't want another smacking from Melvin and Leroy downstairs. It was the certain knowledge that my partners-in-crime were waiting outside that prompted me to talk and talk and answer her questions—anything to kill time. And questions she did ask. There was no end to them. She wanted

to know about my two aunts I lived with, and about my big brother
who hung out with the Morningside Heights gang and kept getting
into trouble, and about what I learned in school, and about what I
wanted to be when I grew up. About everything. I'd never met
anybody who could ask so many questions about things I'd always
thought to be dull and ordinary. In truth, I wanted to know about
her—things like why she lived alone, and what she did all day long,
and where she got so much money. Years later I've more than once
regretted I wasn't aggressive along these lines, for it now strikes me
odd how little I really know about Mrs. Liebman, Mrs. Sophie
Liebman.

It was getting dark outside and she told me I'd better go. "Surely
your aunts will wonder what's happened to you."

"No, they won't," I replied quickly, which was true, but I was
thinking more about Melvin and Leroy than I was about my aunts.
"Aunt Willa maybe a little bit," I added. "Aunt Ernestine, she don't
pay me no never mind anyhow."

Mrs. Liebman suddenly became businesslike. She said, "Come on,
don't worry. I'm sure those awful old boys have gone on home by
now." She went to the window, looked out, and closed the venetian
blinds. "Anyway, I'll give you taxi money."

"But I never done took a taxi in my life, Mrs. Liebman."

"Never taken," she corrected me. "Your language is atrocious.
Utterly. Come," she said, kicking off her fluffy slippers (the same
color as Adrian's fur) and slipping into a pair of brown sandals, "I'll
show you down." Then, after a pause, with her head cocked as if
she were listening to something, she said, "There's one condition."

I waited for that condition. She didn't say anything. She moved
around over the thick lemon carpet like a soft bear in slow motion;
finally she said she'd put me in a taxi if I promised to come back,
two days later, to visit her. As an added inducement, she whispered,
"I'll have a little present for you." Then, with greater speed than I
imagined her capable, she guided me out to the elevator and downstairs, where she told the doorman to fetch a cab.

Before I reached Columbus Circle I paid the driver, got out,
pocketed the remaining money, and walked the rest of the way
home.

Thursday, after school let out, I walked down Central Park West
to Mrs. Liebman's. There was no sign of Leroy and Melvin. The
edges of the park were their preying ground, but I did not see them
and I crossed my fingers they'd given me up as being hopeless as a
go-between and that they'd found another sucker to aid them in
their extortion schemes.

When I rang Mrs. Liebman's buzzer, 3E, she opened the door and a cyclone of perfume struck me. She had on a hat. "I told Max to let you come up. You have any trouble?"

Max was her doorman. I had no trouble from him but he'd sniffed a lot and stared at me with cold blue eyes. Adrian barked. He looked as if he'd just been washed. Quickly, I looked around to see if I could spy the present she'd promised.

"Come, then, lambkin, we're off," she said, checking her purse to see if she had her keys, and before I could get my breath or ask any questions, we were flying downtown in a yellow cab to Young Boys Outlet on Fourteenth Street. Her present turned out to be a complete set of clothes, including undershorts. The jacket and pair of pants were okay, I guess, but I thought they looked dumpy and old-fashioned. I downright hated the Buster Brown shoes. Over a cheeseburger and a strawberry milkshake, in a Village café, I began to wonder what Aunt Ernestine and Aunt Willa would say about the clothes Mrs. Liebman had bought; sure as anything, they'd accuse me of stealing them; they'd never believe the truth. I finally spoke up and told Mrs. Liebman I'd have trouble at home.

"Hmmm, I suppose." She toyed with the salt at the rim of her cocktail glass. Her eyebrows turned into bird wings and threatened to fly off her powdered face. "Yes, yes . . . I never thought of that." Then, suddenly, the bird wings above her eyes came to roost and she, with a spurt of energy, lifted her glass and took a deep sip. (Many weeks later I learned that her drink was called a margarita; many years later I went back to try one myself but the little café had turned into a Chinese laundry.) It was, though, at that moment, if I can at all pinpoint it, that I became attached to Mrs. Liebman; I'd found a cohort, for I discovered she was capable of as much duplicity as I. No mere nice old lady she! That Thursday, in the tiny Village café, like espionage agents trading state secrets, we put our heads together—hers over a second margarita, mine over a strawberry milkshake—and mapped out the ground rules, concocted our lie. It amounted to this: I'd keep my new clothes at her apartment; I'd come to visit her each Tuesday and Thursday; she'd give me a small allowance to show my aunts in order to explain my biweekly disappearance; I'd pretend I had a part-time job walking her dog and running errands (which turned out not to be a lie, in any case); and I'd say nothing about riding around in taxis and having cheeseburgers and milkshakes (I didn't know about the snails then) and going to picture galleries.

I soon found the game of it was exciting, and the milieu—such a far cry from my aunts' cockroach-ridden apartment with its odor of urine and collard greens—was as exotic as I imagined Baghdad or

Kalamazoo to be. I could hardly wait to leave my drab-penny world of One Hundred Eighteenth Street and enter Mrs. Liebman's realm of thick lemon carpets, porcelain doodads, heavy perfume, and rides in yellow taxicabs.

The night I heard the fat ladies scream I told Aunt Willa a lie: I said Mrs. Liebman's dog was ailing and I had to go to the vet with him and I'd be late getting home. Inasmuch as my school grades had improved (Mrs. Liebman helped me with geography and math) and I brushed my teeth and combed my hair more frequently, I was on the good side of Aunt Willa and she seldom made a fuss. (Also, I suspect both Aunt Willa and Aunt Ernestine had more important things to worry about than my comings and goings: they were worried, I think, that my older brother, Beauregard, had begun to use drugs.)

"Now, just remember," Mrs. Liebman told me as we settled down into the comfortable red seats at the opera house, "Wotan is the father and Brünhilde is his daughter. Okay? She sings the most, Brünhilde does."

As far as I could tell, everybody sang a lot. Screamed, really. At one point there were seven or eight ladies, all of them fat, screaming at the same time. The name of the opera Mrs. Liebman had to pronounce for me; it was called *Die Walküre*.

Occasionally, whenever Mrs. Liebman saw that my attention had strayed and I'd begun to squirm in my seat, she bent down and whispered, "It's the *ring*, dear. You see, it's about the *ring*."

I never saw a ring. Nobody wore one. And it was confusing, too: I knew Hunding was the villain, but I could not get it straight in my mind who Sieglinde was. At intermission I said: "Mrs. Liebman, who is this Fricka?" I pointed to the list of characters on the program.

"Lambkin," she replied—I had the feeling she was speaking to the crowd around us as well as to me—"she's Mrs. Wotan. The king's wife."

"And this one?" I asked, pointing to the program again.

She bent over. She owned glasses but never wore them. "That's Brünhilde, dear. She's the main daughter. She's the one who sings the most."

Her explanation wasn't particularly edifying, but I said brightly, "Oh," as if the mystery were solved, and bent to tie the lace of my Buster Brown shoe. I did not dare ask her about Siegmund, for I knew she'd tell me something that would mix me up more than I already was.

To kill time during the next act, I played silent word games, and counted as many heads as I could in front of me. I tried not to fall asleep. Once, I glanced up at Mrs. Liebman and noticed a hazy glaze over her eyes; I knew her mind was not on the opera any more than mine was. I believed her to be imagining that she was Brünhilde herself, marching through the streets of Harlem, with her head high, banishing all the winos and junkies and slum buildings in sight, leaving in her wake a trail of Goodness and Light. . . .

She took pity on me—or herself?—and left the opera house at the next intermission. It was late and I was so tired that I did not bother to go to her place and get out of my Downtown Clothes. As luck would have it, Aunt Willa and Aunt Ernestine were deep in a battle with Beauregard. I sneaked by them, went to my corner of the bedroom, slipped out of my clothes, and hid them. I fell asleep, dreaming of fat ladies screaming.

In early summer when school was over two things happened: Beauregard was sent upstate to a correctional institution, and Mrs. Liebman had a nervous breakdown. I felt guilty that I cared less about Beauregard than I did about Mrs. Liebman. Max, the doorman, who'd become more friendly during the course of my Tuesday and Thursday visits, told me Mrs. Liebman had gone to stay with her daughter in Brooklyn Heights.

"Forever and ever?" I asked, trying not to show my panic.

"Now, now, laddie," Max said, "I guess not forever. It's happened before. She—"

"But *when*, then? When'll she be back?"

Max shrugged. "Her stuff is still up there. She'll probably be back sooner or later." A man in a dark suit and a woman in a lime dress stepped out of the elevator, giggling. The woman said, "Maxie, do be a doll and get us a cab, won't you?" As Max darted toward the curb he said to me, "Okay, kid. Off with you. Run along."

I hurried home and the moment I got into the apartment I asked Aunt Willa: "What's a nervous breakdown? What happens when you get a nervous breakdown?"

Of late, Aunt Willa had become accustomed to my odd inquiries and the dropping of—what must have seemed to her—fancy names. (When I said—not showing off, really—that the graffiti on Brad Johnson's barbershop wall looked like a Max Ernst painting, she replied with "*a who?*"; when I said once—and that time I *was* trying to show off—"Beauregard's behavior is getting most obstreperous," she blinked her large brown eyes and said, "Chile, what kind of talk is that? You pick up that from that white woman you work for downtown?")

This time, though, when I asked Aunt Willa exactly what a nervous breakdown was, she said, not missing a beat, "Honey, it's what I got right now. It's what I've always got. I get up in the morning with my nerves broke down and I go to bed at night with my nerves broke down. You ate? There's some collards in the kitchen if you want."

So, Aunt Willa was of no help. Aunt Ernestine had moved back in with her man friend over on St. Nicholas Avenue, but I wouldn't have asked her anyway. Fourteen days went by before I found out what a nervous breakdown really was and that was from Mrs. Liebman herself. (I'd gone down to Fifty-eighth Street every Tuesday and Thursday only to see Max shaking his head in a quiet "no," even before I reached him, half a block away. Then one day, as he saw me approach, his dour mouth turned into a smile and I knew everything was all right.)

"Don't fret about it, lambkin," Mrs. Liebman told me. "Dr. Sterne gave me some wonderful pills. Divine little pills." She looked as if she'd lost weight, and I noticed she was not wearing any of her rings, but other than that she was exactly the same—her face did busy work, she fluttered around over her lemon carpet, and she picked up Adrian and plopped him down every two seconds or so. "Now. Let's celebrate. I've an idea."

I was so happy to see her, so pleased that my double life had resumed, I might have done anything she requested. And at first I did honestly try to eat them—the snails. We sat in the Plaza. In the Oak Room. We caused quite a stir. Everybody looked at us. Mrs. Liebman loved the attention.

"Es-car-gots," she said, making me repeat the word. I was a little embarrassed because, as was the case in the lobby at the *Die Walküre* intermission, she seemed to be speaking to other people as well as to me.

The piece of rubbery meat looked like a swollen blackhead. I got it down. Just.

"Hmm," she said, extracting with a silver prong the hideous goody from its shell and dipping it into a puddle of garlic and butter. "Celestial, aren't they? Absolute bliss. Waiter, waiter," she called, pressing butter from her lip, "another margarita, please."

It was during her instructions to the tall, solicitous waiter that I managed (with a sleight of hand I've not ever in my life managed since) to get the snail out of my mouth and into the big soft napkin. I was a bit resentful, too, that I didn't have a frosty-salty drink to wash down the little uglies. I did however have a potted plant at my elbow and I made good use of it: when Mrs. Liebman glanced around the room to see who was watching us, I surreptitiously removed the unchewed snail from my napkin and slung it into the plant. A potted palm, I think it was. This operation was by no means easy, for it apparently gave Mrs. Liebman pleasure to watch me partake of the esoteric delights before us, and she took in my every movement. With a cunning born of sheer necessity, I knew I had to get her mind off me and get her to talk about herself. Without preparation, without finesse, I asked: "Mrs. Liebman, why do you live all alone? Why aren't you married?"

She was startled. She took a margarita-sip. "But I am, lambkin. I was. I mean, Jay and I don't get along anymore." She pressed her napkin to her lips and the bird wings above her closed eyes threatened to set out in flight.

Another squiggly went into the potted plant. Three down, three to go.

"You see," she said, "it happens with grown-ups like that sometimes." Then she opened her eyes and I saw for a moment more anger in them than remorse. Then she smiled. "Now, eat up, my dear. You needn't ration them out like that. We can get oodles more if we like."

"No, no." To avert that catastrophe, I quickly said, "They're yummy, Mrs. Liebman, but they're so rich. They fill you up quick, don't they? I never had anything to fill me up so quick—'cept chitlins."

"Chitlins?"

"Yeah, you know, chitlins. Ain't you ever had no chitlins?"

"Haven't you ever had any," she corrected me.

"Haven't you ever had any?" I repeated.

"No, I've never had—and they're chitterlings, my dear. *Chitterlings*. You really must learn to—"

"No, they ain't—aren't. They're chitlins." She was on my turf and I contradicted her, without malice aforethought, without disrespect.

She gave me her Claude Rains look and said evenly, "Chit-ter-lings."

I shook my head. I knew she didn't know what she was talking about because I'd seen "chitlins" written all over the place in stores in Harlem and I'd heard all kinds of people saying "chitlins" all my life. I was angry, and in some vague and obscure way I knew that in the course of the clash our relationship had altered; I was no longer a child and she was no longer a grown woman; we were two people; we'd had, muffled and guarded as it was, our first fight. She must have sensed and understood the transformation of our relationship even more than I, for, after a moment of stiff hesitation, she reached across the table—without humoring me, without placating me—and gently gave my arm a reconciliatory squeeze. To all the world, we might well have been lovers.

I said ungraciously, in my new manhood: "I don't want any more of these." When I saw that I'd hurt her, I quickly added, regretting my cruelty, "They're so *rich*, Mrs. L. They're so *rich*."

The "Mrs. L." business was a stroke of genius; I'd made amends in aces.

"Of course, darling, of course," she said, and quickly finished off the remaining escargots on my plate.

Naturally, I could not tell her that I was still hungry and wanted more than anything a cheeseburger and a strawberry milkshake, nor did I grumble even once when she took me around the corner to the Paris cinema to see a French film with subtitles I did not understand one bit.

There was no problem in finding chitlins in Harlem, but I wanted to buy some in a box with the name written on it. Tuesday, before I went downtown again, I found what I needed: "Louella's Home Cooked Chitlins." They smelled of butter and garlic. I thought Mrs. Liebman would like them. More important, the square white box had the word *chitlins* printed on it, clear as day.

"I don't think Mrs. Liebman can see you now," Max told me when I arrived at Fifty-eighth Street.

"But it's Tuesday," I protested, the box of chitlins still warm in my hands and reeking of butter and garlic.

"I know, I know, laddie, but—" He pushed back his cap and stood there in silence for a few seconds. "Mrs. Hoffman is—her daughter's up there now." He acted embarrassed and kept fussing with his cap. "Whatcha got in the box?"

"A—a present," I told him.

Max took the box of chitlins and tapped me on the shoulder. "I'll get it to her."

"But—"

Max left me as if he had no time for an argument. I went to the pay telephone on the corner and got no satisfaction there either; a high-pitched voice said: "No, this is Anna Hoffman. Mother is—Mother is indisposed. I'll have her call you." She hung up. I replied to the voice, which had disappeared, "Lady, I ain't got no telephone."

That afternoon I sat in Morningside Heights Park and stared at the shadows in the sunlight. At night I lay awake in bed. Wednesday I did the same thing. When I got downtown on Thursday, Max said, "She doesn't live here anymore." He had changed back into his uppity ways I remembered from our first meetings. "Wait. Here's a package for you."

It was wrapped in brown paper. A string was around it. There was an envelope on top.

"Okay, kid, you can't loll around here in the lobby." The elevator door opened. Some people came out. "All right, run along, I tell you."

My Downtown Clothes and Buster Brown shoes were in the package. The note was from Mrs. Liebman. It said: "Lambkin, thank you for the chitterling. Mrs. L."

Chitterling! If my throat had not been so tight, I'd have cursed more than I did. In some irrational attempt to get even, I dumped the clothes and shoes in a Central Park trash basket.

I took the note to the library with me.

But Webster's dictionary turned out to be a traitor as well; it offered me three choices: over and over, I read *chitterlings or chitlings or chitlins.* Had Mrs. Liebman been as right as Aunt Willa and all of Harlem? I looked at the note again: "Lambkin, thank you for the chitterling. Mrs. L." Maybe she'd had only one bite. Was one bite a chitterling?

Now, many years later, I've acquired a taste for escargots, and somewhere along the way I've lost interest in chitlins, and I even own four Kirsten Flagstad recordings, but I've not told Mrs. Liebman this; I was never again to see her after that afternoon at the Plaza.

MUSICO

by Arturo Vivante

In Rome a conductor used to be a neighbor of mine. He had a top-floor apartment with a fine view of the city, and a beautiful wife. I lived alone in a small second-floor apartment in the building next door. I can't remember how I met them. I was a doctor then. Perhaps he was a patient of mine. He has become very famous since. In those days he was just very well known, not famous, not famous worldwide anyway, and he, his wife, and I would sometimes go out and have dinner together.

"I've discovered a nice restaurant," I said one day. "Guido's. Do you want to go there?"

"Do they let itinerant musicians in?" he said.

"I don't know. None came when I was there. Why?"

"I can't stand them. Well, let's try it, but I warn you—"

"What'll you do if one of them comes in?"

"If one comes in, I go out. No, I've got a better idea. I'll warn the waiter."

We walked to Guido's and found a good table. He talked to the waiter about musicians, as he said he would.

"*Stia tranquillo, ci penso io*—don't worry. I'll see to it," the waiter said.

At a table near us was an old couple. Both had wedding rings on and a good part of the time they held hands, resting them on the white tablecloth.

Soon a musico did come in, a little old man, hesitantly, with a violin. The conductor glared at him, then at the waiter who immediately ushered him out. No doubt his being a conductor had something to do with that summoning look and the instant response he was able to elicit. As for me, I have the hardest time beckoning waiters.

"Why are you so against these itinerant players?" I said.

"Their music, or what they call music. They grind, they don't play, and it grates in my ear. I literally can't eat."

"He might have been an exception."

We went on with our meal, but I kept thinking of the old man who had been turned away. I don't know how long my reverie lasted—perhaps only a few minutes—but in it I saw a little apartment so poor and so shabby I wondered why it didn't look dreary. There was even a certain dignity about it. Was it because of the books and the piano? They lent an artistic touch, as if gentle winds were blowing through the windows and the room partook of the rose-violet light of late evening outside. It was shortly after sunset, and the rose and the violet were quickly fading outside. Inside, an elderly woman, graying, with the delicate, frail look of one who has suffered, rather pale, with pouting mouth and lips that were almost too soft but still had a touch of beauty and were like the fire of a smoldering charcoal resisting time under the veil of its ashes, was sitting by a table, embroidering linen. There was a pile of plain pieces of cloth on one side of her and a smaller pile on the other, representing the work of her day.

Her husband was at the piano, at his side a table with papers and musical scores. He played a few notes; after some silence he played again. From time to time he leaned over to write a note. He had a gaunt, slender figure and a dazed look, as if he lived in the light of his thoughts, not in the living room at all. He was wholly absorbed in his music when his wife missed a stitch.

"Here I go again missing a stitch," she said with impatience. "I can't see straight anymore; I can't go on. . . ." She paused a moment, looked at her cloth, then angrily threw it down. "And you do nothing to help." Her husband didn't take any notice of her, as though they had gone through the argument many times before. "Why? Why can't you do what I said?" she added.

He finally looked at her. "I can't do what you ask me to do," he replied. "I can't go and play the violin for a nickel in front of people who don't even listen."

"Pride, pride—that's all it is; and in the meantime we starve."

"We are not starving."

"Close to it. Old bread, market discards . . . I've been working all day, sewing till my eyes go blind. And what do you do? Tinker and fiddle around, arranging notes that won't go."

"You liked my music once."

"Once, once. You were all right as long as you played the violin. There were concerts; there were reviews in the papers; the whole orchestra liked you. But then playing wasn't creative enough—you had to go and start writing your own compositions."

"You used to encourage me then."

"We were young. The stars were smiling then; they twinkled brightly; they still twinkle—look at them twinkle through the skylight up there—but not for us anymore. If I try to look at them now the way I used to look at them then, tears rise at my lashes and all I see are tremulous streaks."

"You'd have more reason to cry if I cheapened myself and my music by playing in restaurants while people are gulping their food."

"What do you care if they listen or not?"

"Phonographs and jukeboxes don't care. But I do."

"But maybe someone would listen and appreciate what you play. In front of him maybe you'd play one of your original pieces. That person might be a conductor or a well-known impresario, have your symphonies published, all of your work sold and performed."

"You are more of a dreamer than I am."

"You don't even try. You hate to mix with the world. The farthest you've ever gone is the post office. You won't meet the important people, the people who count."

"Everyone counts."

"I mean those who could help you if you gave them a chance. You despise them. You say that they snub you, but I think it's you who snub them."

"I've got to do things in my way. I can't change."

"To please me."

"I'll work washing dishes if it's money you want. I'll sweep the streets, be a waiter, carry big loads, rather than do what you ask me."

"As if you hadn't tried that already. And don't you remember what happened? They fired you after less than an hour. Look at you—who's going to hire you? Carry big loads! You are weak; you are an old man. At anything else than at music you are clumsy. But in music you are nimble."

"I am out of practice. You know that. All these years of composing . . . My fingers aren't as deft as my mind. The orchestras have all refused me."

"But people in restaurants are not so demanding. It won't be as at the concerts. If you slip a note, who will mind? And in the morning the dissonant note won't have an echo in the paper."

There was a long silence. For a few minutes one could hear only the hum of the city. Then he suddenly rose from his chair. "Where is my violin?" he said.

"Then you'll go?"

"Yes, what time is it?"

"Eight. A little past. Just the right time. The violin is out here. I'll get it."

Quickly, afraid he might change his mind, she went and got the violin from a closet. She handed it to him delicately.

He took it, looked at it for a long moment, and said, "I never thought I would prostitute you."

"It'll be only for a little while, you'll see; only for a little while."

He walked slowly toward the door.

"Shall I come with you? I could do the collecting."

"No, stay here. I don't think I could stand it if you came along."

He left, a haggard little figure of a man, and she watched him go, as if she would detain him. Slowly she closed the door but didn't leave it. She leaned against it, her forearm over her forehead. For a moment she stayed in that position, then crossed over to the window and looked for him on the busy street. She leaned out till she saw him, then followed him with her eyes till he disappeared around the corner. She returned to her chair, but she couldn't sew anymore. She went over to the bed and knelt on the floor, hiding her face in her arms. But she couldn't stay long in any position. A shadow descended on the room as, to save electricity, she switched the light off from over the piano. Hours passed, and from time to time, in the faint gloom of one lamp, she wandered about the room in distraction. More than once, in her anxiety over his not returning, she seemed about to leave the house and go searching for him in every restaurant. Several times she approached the door, opened it, and seemed undecided. The door opened into a dark rectangular space—the unlighted staircase. It suggested the unknown; it had something forbidding that advised her to remain where she was and wait. So, each time, she returned and crossed the room to the window, where she leaned out to scan the street, which now was quite deserted. Every once in a while she heard voices, and she started at the sound of each voice that she heard. Then, tired, she went and sat by the pile of linen, but she couldn't work.

At last she heard a little noise by the door and rushed to open it. It was only her cat, or rather not her cat but one of the city's stray cats with whom she had made friends and who came to visit her nearly every day, sometimes two or three times a day, sometimes not for a week. "Oh, it's you," she said. She picked it up and brought it over to her bed, where she sat, stroking it while it purred. "You didn't see him, did you? Have you come to tell me he isn't going to come back? What are you thinking? That it's high time I gave you some milk?"

She went into the kitchen and poured a little milk into a saucer. The cat followed her. "Why did I send him out? Tell me. Why did I let him go? It's late. Isn't he going to come back? Do you think he was in an accident? If only we had a phone. Has he left me forever? What do you think? Did I tell him he was no good? What did I tell him? I didn't mean it, whatever I said. It's me who's no good. Perhaps he went down to the Tiber. Did I tell him he was a failure? Oh, no, he didn't go down to the Tiber. No, no, soon I know he'll be here. Won't he?"

The cat looked at her only when he had finished his milk. "Maybe," she continued, "he'll come back with a bagful of coins, as silver as fish, and he'll drop them all on the floor to scatter like fish, roll to every corner of the room. I'll pick up every one, and we'll buy all sorts of things with them—things that we need and things we don't need; extravagant things we will buy. And we'll get the piano repaired. . . ."

She poured the cat a little more milk. "He didn't get drunk, did he? He didn't go and get drunk with that money? Is he sitting in a tavern or on the steps of some church, muttering to himself, saying: 'She wants me to play for a living, but I want to live so I can play.' He drank it, that money. It went into wine. He drank it to the last drop, so he could forget all about it."

The cat followed her into the living room, where she looked at a clock. It was nearly midnight. In a few minutes a distant church bell and then another tolled the hours. The cat brushed around her ankles. "Perhaps he's calling at several places because they give him so little and he wants to bring back a good sum. Restaurants stay open late. He plays them his music. They want to hear Neapolitan songs; they want to hear of Sorrento. But he knows no songs of Sorrento. He plays them pieces of Bach and Beethoven, his favorite tunes from Scarlatti. Do they listen? Some of them listen, and look at the violin dreamy-eyed. The music carries them far, far away." She herself seemed to hear it, saw an old married couple beckoning to him from their table, asking him to play them a waltz—the waltz that had introduced them—and humming it for him. Oh, such a sentimental old couple. She could see him listening to the tune for a moment, smiling a little, then playing. He played and composed as he played, something new, which followed their tune two or three seconds, then strayed into something his own, something unheard and unheard of. With the sound of that tune in his ears he rushed out. He went to the telegraph office—the only place he could find equipped with pencil and paper—and on a telegraph form he wrote the notes out. "Telegraph forms," she heard him saying, "they'll do for score sheets. Listen. I think it is a good composition, the best I've done in a long time."

"And the restaurant? You didn't go back?"

"It closed," he said with a curious smile. "I must have spent more time than I meant to out there in the telegraph office."

"It isn't true. Tell me the truth. It's too late in the night to tell stories."

"All right, I'll tell you what happened—I know that you like happy endings. That married old couple was moved to tears—have you ever heard of anyone so sentimental? They whispered something to each other, and then, looking at me with bright eyes, they invited me home. In a taxi we flew through the city. At their house I repeated the tune. They never seemed to tire of that music. Then they gave me this check for a present. Under the night sky and the stars I slowly made my way here; I seemed to be walking the heavens."

Now, she thought, he's coming up the steps. In a moment I'll hear the door being unlocked. She waited. Long she waited, then stepped toward the bed, lay down, and fell asleep.

Finally, a great while later, the door was unlocked and he entered. He had the sad expression of reality about him—no curious smile, no mysterious impressions. Silently, so as not to wake her, he went close to her. Tenderly, gently, he took a blanket and placed it over her and tucked her in, then, sitting on a chair, he started undressing, first taking one shoe off and the other, which fell from his hand. She woke. "You are back," she said. "I am sorry I made you go."

"It wasn't so bad, not as bad as I thought it would be. Or only at the first place I went to. There a man glared at me, and, before I even started playing, he had the waiter turn me out."

"You are very quiet tonight," the conductor's wife said to me. "What are you thinking of?"

"What? Oh, nothing," I said. "I was just thinking of that man, that musico."

"Oh, him," the conductor said, and I told them briefly what I had imagined.

"Are you trying to make me feel guilty?" he said.

"It might not be the worst thing for you," she said.

"Well, it won't wash. You are much too romantic, not enough of a realist. That man ought to be husking corn."

SUNDAY'S NO NAME BAND

by Sara Vogan

Janeen broke her arm at work—an industrial accident, we call it. The men in the kitchen have been discussing workman's comp and lawsuits based on negligence. If she receives a windfall, they think she should build a recording studio.

Janeen's the bass player in our band. Dana and I are going to give her a bath, her first since the accident on Monday. Dana's a nurse. She's also six months pregnant. She straddles the dirty clothes hamper in the corner of the bathroom, giving orders. I'm to perform the actual bathing, and my heart knocks about my chest as I imagine Janeen slipping, the broken arm smacking against the tub tiles.

It's Sunday afternoon, raining like it does out here during the winter. Janeen's bath has become a party, mostly because none of us knows what to do with this Sunday afternoon without her. Usually we practice on Sundays in a storage area behind the shop where Janeen works. Matt, my husband and our rhythm guitar player, invited Dana, our vocalist, and her husband, Chris, who is our drummer. I invited Frank, our lead guitarist. I like things neat, as formal as classical piano, as precise as sheet music. Everyone's here, instead of in the practice space where we've spent each Sunday for the past eight months.

While Dana and Janeen and I are in the bathroom, Matt fusses over his beans and ham hocks in the kitchen on the other side of the wall. Frank and Chris say they will help him. We've decided to call this a Depression Chic dinner, enjoying the pun, trying to mask our disappointment with laughter.

"We should put the deck chair in the tub," Dana says. "That way she can sit down and you can work around her."

We agree this sounds like a good idea, so I go get the deck chair, but it won't fit. We settle for a stepladder, which does. This doesn't leave much room to maneuver, and my palms sweat as I place it in the tub.

Dana surveys the stepladder, the space heater for extra warmth. "A piece of cake."

"Then why don't you do it?" I say. "You're the professional here. I haven't even given my dog a bath in about two years." Again, I see Janeen falling, the broken arm smashing like glass.

"I do this for a living. Trust me. You'll do fine." She rubs her belly. "Besides, I'm not sure I'd fit." She eases herself back on the clothes hamper, as round and imperturbable as a buddha. She laughs, but I see nothing funny here.

Janeen looks apprehensively at the tub. "I think if I keep a grip on my elbow you can get everything but the armpits." The break is too near the shoulder to cast, held in place with an elastic bandage. I'm afraid when she undresses the arm will dangle like something in a horror movie.

I adjust the space heater, directing the flow of warm air. Dana rises from her seat to help Janeen undress. The doctor put the webbing of bandage around Janeen's waist and over her shoulder, where her guitar strap usually sits. Her bass always reminds me of a black lacquer woman she holds in her arms. She keeps a red pick stuck in the facing like a heart.

Dana and Janeen struggle with her boots. "It was so easy to get into them," she moans. Bending is difficult for Janeen, as it is for Dana with her baby. Janeen looks close to tears. "I never imagined it would be so tough getting them off." She stares at the ceiling, studying it. Perhaps she's in pain. "I can't comb my hair. I can't open a carton of milk."

I could get Janeen's boots off in two seconds, but I let Dana work with them. It's good to see Dana in motion, active. A curious light has come over Dana these days, as if her pregnancy weren't something she carried with her daily, but a new idea crossing her mind fresh and different each time. She often misses what's said in conversations, her cues in the music when she's supposed to sing. This will be Dana's first baby and her fourth pregnancy. The baby is due the same week Dana turns 36.

"Brushing my teeth takes ten minutes. The toothbrush keeps falling over when I try to put the paste on it."

"We have a patient with all the fingers of his right hand, even his thumb, gone. He says he can do everything but hammer a nail." Dana begins to unfasten the bandage. I watch how her hands work in concert, one guiding the bandage, the other holding the ball.

Janeen's eyes look wild in the corners. "I don't want to make a career of this."

"Industrial accident," Dana says. "A slicing machine. There you go." She surveys Janeen's naked body, appraising her work. She smooths her palms on her stomach again and returns to her seat on the clothes hamper.

I hover around Janeen as she steps over the rim of the tub and eases herself down on the stepladder. "Okay?" I ask, although I can see she's fine.

"I want a towel," she says, "to cover my face. I don't want my makeup to run. It took me all morning, one-handed."

I can't imagine taking a shower with makeup on. I never suspected Janeen wore it. I study her face and see how carefully it's done, the fine peach bloom on her cheeks, the dark lashes. Janeen's always been admired for her fine coloring and intense eyes. It startles me to realize the effect of her face is artificial.

Out in the kitchen, on the other side of the wall, we hear something crash, then the deep laughter of men. We look at each other, the way women do. Men in the kitchen. We know what to expect. "I'm glad it's not my house," Dana says.

"Here comes the water." I reach for the taps. Janeen ducks her face into the towel, her back to the shower nozzle. Stripping out of my clothes, I hand them to Dana, who drops them in a pile at her feet. I step into the shower, right under the stream of hot water. It pumps against the back of my neck, spraying over my shoulders, warm and relaxing. Gently, as if her skull were broken instead of her arm, I begin to massage shampoo into Janeen's hair. The arm is a bright blue bruise and looks contagious, as if it could spread across her back, her scalp. As if I could catch it on my hands.

Janeen can't drive, bathe herself, open a can. I feel her defeat. She won't be able to play for at least two months. I know in her mind the band has already dissolved. Dana and Chris will lose interest with the baby so close. Frank will drift off, much the way he drifted in. Matt and I will find something else to do on Sunday afternoons. All of us are too old for rock and roll bands. Those golden days we keep striving for are now fifteen years behind us. We get together on Sundays because we all missed the same lessons. We play other people's tunes, the blues and rock and roll we grew up with and remember more clearly than lullabies.

What kind of band was it, anyhow? We're a band without a name and none of our own songs. We've never even played a gig. We settled into our lives with only Sundays to spare for music, a few hours when we can remember a time when we all felt young and bright and full of promise. A two-month hiatus will be as physical as the break in Janeen's arm.

The shower curtain opens and Dana steps in, on the other side of Janeen's body. She has a bar of soap and begins to expertly work it around Janeen's breasts. Dana hums, her belly bobbing above Janeen's knees. Janeen sits as still as a fixture while Dana's hands dart among crevices, tucking bits of lather into the curves.

But Dana isn't humming. She's singing, soft and low in that sweet voice of hers, a voice that can stay on pitch. I know right away what it is, as if I picked it up from the rhythm of the water beating on my back.

> Well, they call it stormy Monday,
> But Tuesday's just as bad.

I look up across Janeen. Dana's right, of course. I join her, imagining Billie Holiday and her gardenia, the smoky clubs of Harlem. I hear the riffs I would do on the piano and my fingers begin to chord on Janeen's head. The rush of the water makes us sound better than we actually are, adding the beat like Chris's drums and fills. The tile of the tub acts as an echo chamber and the song becomes as thick as the steam rising all around us. "Wednesday's worse, and Thursday's all so sad." We sing from deep in our diaphragms, watching each other's faces so we don't take a breath at the same moment. Janeen straightens. Her face comes out of the towel and she joins us on the next verse.

> The eagle flies on Friday,
> And Saturday I go out to play.

We are all naked and wet and yet for the first time I can really see us standing before strangers, our instruments ringing with sound, our voices rising with a passion no practice session can provide. We will wear gardenias in our hair, dresses cut to show off our shoulders. I imagine Matt in a tuxedo, Dana with a waist again. Janeen and Frank will resume their affair and smile at each other the way they used to when we first began this band. We will all be dreaming in the dark and our eyes will meet the light and be blinded with the power of the song.

"Lord, please have mercy on me, please have mercy on me." Janeen swivels her head back and forth between us, smiling. Water sprays over her face and little runs of makeup trickle down her cheeks like beads of sweat. Janeen sings and sings. I've never seen this smile on her face before. I consider asking if I could wash off her makeup, but I know, as close as we are in the tub right now, we are not close enough for that.

We belt out a rousing finale. "Lord, send my baby back home to me!" And we laugh, giggling like girls in junior high. Dana puts her hands on the small of her back and stretches, her belly ballooning in front of her. Shampoo and soap fleck the tile walls, the shower curtain. Steam swirls around us, creating thermals that disappear someplace near the ceiling. You can't keep your eye on them, no matter how hard you try.

Janeen laughs. "I feel better." She runs her good hand across her cheek, wiping at the ruined makeup.

The water begins to turn coolish. It will be cold in another few minutes. "You'll have to stand for the rinse," I say. Immediately I'm sorry I've done this. Janeen's face falls out of the smile. Dana has that distracted look again. But we can't stay in the shower all afternoon, ice water beating on our backs. Yet for a moment, that's what we imagined, that somehow if we stayed here long enough we could all come out healed.

Janeen stands and Dana steps out of the tub. I grab the stepladder and follow, feeling the chill of the air in spite of the space heater. Through the curtain we can watch Janeen turn herself slowly under the shower nozzle, washing off soap, shampoo, her makeup.

I reach into the tub and turn off the faucets. From the other room we hear noise. Men in the kitchen, Matt and Frank and Chris. They're singing. We watch one another's faces, catching the glint of laughter in our eyes, amazed, as if we are the only ones to have the privilege of singing on this Sunday afternoon. Dana takes a towel and covers Janeen, daubing at the water running off her onto the bathroom floor. I open the door and the song is clearer.

> I can't get no
> Satisfaction!
> I can't get no
> Girl reaction.

Dana's professional hands dry the injured arm. Our heads bob with the beat, our feet tapping time. We wait until the chorus before we join the song.

> But I try, and I try, and I try, and I try.
> I can't get no (Da-Da-Dum) satisfaction!

There's a round of applause from the kitchen. Someone, probably Matt, bangs on a pan. We will eat. Maybe Frank will offer to take Janeen home, the way he used to. Perhaps someday we will play in front of strangers. Maybe there won't be gardenias or tuxedos, but the lights will blind us and the songs will rise.

"Saved again by the Rolling Stones," Janeen says.

Saved again, indeed. We know all the little pieces connecting us to our private pasts. We are learning the moments, like singing in the shower, that will connect us long after Janeen's arm heals, Dana's baby is born.

The steam in the bathroom disappears. One minute you can hold it with your eyes, the next you're staring at empty air. It's the same feeling you have when a song is over, the tune hanging on in your mind.

OZZIE AND HARRIET

by Irene Wanner

Jessie Foss used to think, when she was awake at night, about a house of her own, a job that paid so well she would not sit awake in bed worrying, and a lover. She would have an old farmhouse, the sort magazines feature with before-and-after pictures, enthusiastically explaining the joys of stripping wood to its basic beauty while neglecting to mention sweat and splinters, scraped knuckles, and toxic fumes. It was a five-acre farm, say, with an orchard of apple trees gone wild that she would coax back to bearing fruit for juice. She would have cats, a barnful, a yellow bitch named Nell, and a dapple-gray horse. Someone would pay her outrageous amounts of money to do something at home in her own spare time. No commuting, no fluorescent-lit offices, no typing. Her lover would be gentle and good at fixing everything. He would bring surprises. These night dreams were so mundane, so storybook, they began to make Jessie anxious about her mind, which, at twenty-five, should have progressed beyond her mother's promises of a prince and a palace.

Later, after her twenty-eighth birthday, Jessie still woke at night. She was settled in a home with a man, David Wainwright, an architect, provided for and safe but "living in sin," as her mother and father called it. Jessie now dreamed of her former freedom.

Awake, with David snoring and mumbling beside her, she thought of those years alone, moving from place to place, when her belongings fit into the back of the car and she was able to make a little money stretch. She was surprised how exotic her old life appeared. Excavating in Mexico, hitchhiking around Europe by herself. Those romantic notions left out the heat and dust, fatigue and nausea; they were as superficial as the rosy pictures in travel magazines.

Jessie had begun to realize something about the emptiness of her youthful illusions, but she also realized she could not continue believing the grass was always greener elsewhere. At night, not worrying about a home or money or loneliness, she thought perhaps if she were smarter, or even a bit more stupid, she might stop dreaming.

Jessie and David were friends for a year, then lovers for a year, and this year David brought her along to look at houses, spoke of marriage and children, plans to remodel, investments, retirement. They had agreed not to marry, she thought, and she had prevented pregnancy as long as she could remember. Remodeling and investments were for the rich, retirement for the old. Jessie wondered who this stranger was. As soon as David's earnest money was accepted, he began to age.

Often, she sat alone at night in the apartment, wondering where they could fit the couch in the new house or how they would ever get their bed through the door and up those stairs. Bookshelves had been emptied. Boxes of records and clothes, pots and pans, towels, tools, camping gear, and tennis racquets lay in piles. Exposed, those things seemed useless. The furniture was out of place, some missing, already moved; stains and faded spots and trails of wear showed in the carpet, revealing unknown routines about their lives. Paintings, ceramics, dishes, and glasses had a new fragility.

Other things Jessie had once paid no attention to became impossibly large and heavy. David had accumulated his own furniture and furniture left by his parents and furniture bought from friends who could not stand the idea of having to move it themselves. A cherry cabinet, four feet high, with double doors and brass handles. A gaming table and dining room table. A low, square coffee table so heavy that it might as well have been ironwood. Several bookshelves, eight feet high and four feet wide and a foot deep. Desks, tables, chairs, a fig tree in an antique stoneware crock.

Against so many things—*impedimenta*, her college Roman-history books had called such clutter and baggage—Jessie set out a box for the Goodwill. She told David when they began to pack, "Think of moving as our chance to dump this stuff we never use."

He looked up from the boxes he was filling with dusty books and worn out shoes. "What stuff?"

Jessie watched David pack half-filled bottles of dishwashing liquid, almost-empty salt cartons, unused containers of floor wax, and seasonings so old they had solidified in the jars. She thought of her mother's perpetual housecleaning, that relentless war against junk, and a high school home ec edict: When in doubt, throw it out. Unencumbered by such strictures, compulsive as a crow collecting bottlecaps and tinfoil, David packed bits of string and broken rub-ber bands, outdated coupons, and keys to locks no longer remem-bered, checks written years ago, and cookbooks with recipes they would surely never try.

"I don't mean to tell you what to do," Jessie said.

"But?"

"But do we *need* all this stuff?"

David's hair was red and curly. When he fussed, he wound locks of hair around his fingers and tugged; like Orphan Annie or some other cartoon character frozen on a page, David appeared electri-fied. He sat back on his heels, his freckled hands resting lightly on the box as though it contained relics of the church.

"Someday we might need it," he answered. "You never know."

Jessie stood by his drafting table, thinking about how much paint they would need to buy and how soon they must have a lawn mower. David had swung the black elbow lamp around so its light, aimed before him, cast a slanting amber ray into the box filled with smaller boxes of those things they might someday need. He picked up a slide rule in a faded leather case.

"This belonged to my father."

"I'm not saying you should throw away things that are important."

"Oh."

Jessie could see David did not understand how he was supposed to decide what was important, what might be useful someday, and what she wanted him to throw out. Those days when she spoke to him, his answers—when he answered—came back after a time lag that reminded her of men on the moon speaking to earth: in that thin air and low gravity everything was alien; David's office, where closets were always neatly shut and architectural tools were ar-ranged in patterns exact to the millimeter, looked as though it had been hit by a meteor.

Among his books and boxes were suits and clothes Jessie had never seen, which David must have worn after he finished at Yale, before she met him, when he thought appearances and first impressions might be more important for getting a job than his ability as an architect. Instead of boots and jeans and wrinkled permanent-press, there were tweeds and cashmere, oxford cloth and silk ties, a tux-edo, ruffled shirt, and patent leather shoes. Jessie had not known the man who wore those clothes. Seeing them was like trying to gauge a stranger's character by the clothes he brought to the Laundromat.

"David, a *tux*?"

"You never know."

Jessie took the yellowed dress shirt from its hanger, the old cotton cool in her hands.

"What are you doing?" David said, brushing the seat of his pants as he stood. "I want that."

"It could use a wash."

David frowned at the shirt. "I had it washed and pressed."

"When?"

"The last time I wore it."

"When was that?"

He patted his pockets and glanced out the window, had cigarettes but no matches. "I can't remember."

Jessie left him to make his own decisions, knowing the only decision David would come to was not to decide anything. He would pack everything. Clearing out the kitchen, she found three bottles of allspice, three of cloves, three of cinnamon, and three of peppercorns. "It makes me think," she called to David, "your last three lovers each came with a complete set of spices that she left behind when you broke up."

"I've not had three lovers," he said, surprised and puzzled.

"No mysterious dark women who cooked with curry and ginger and hot peppers?"

Nothing was in its place then. Jessie felt uprooted. Her nerves were raw to the air. She and David bumped into each other as they wandered among piles of strange and forgotten things that could have been dropped by a tornado. Have you seen the screwdriver? he might ask. It's in a box somewhere, Jessie would say, which was the same answer he gave to all her questions.

They talked about where things should go in the house, but Jessie could not juggle the size of things against rooms she had seen full of others' belongings. She could hardly remember the house among all the houses they had seen. We'll have so much room, David had been saying before he noticed Jessie's silences. The blueprints in his mind were invisible to her.

At the apartment's kitchen table, Jessie worked on copyediting and proofreading for a university press. Manuscripts and galleys and page proofs and blue lines ended up everywhere. Style manuals and dictionaries, envelopes and papers, letters to authors, queries, corrections, shavings from pencils, all crowded into their lives. Friday-night pizza in front of the TV became daily dinner on the coffee table. They were accustomed to small spaces there: David in his leather chair by the books, Jessie at the end of the couch, the cat on her pillow by the windows, like puzzle pieces that fit only one place and, once David made the down payment on the house, the puzzle had been overturned into a senseless heap.

Jessie resisted David's suggestions to clean up her books and papers, to pack so he could take her things by the house on his way to work in the mornings. She claimed she was on deadline, but it was the orderliness of rules, the consistency of decisions reinforced with red marks on paper, that made her cling to one spot while David tried to move them. She thought she had known him. Instead, Jessie went to bed with a stranger who muttered about thermal windows and insurance. She watched him sleep. I'm too tired to make love, he said for the first time.

They moved across town in February, carrying load after load in a high-kicking wind that rattled bare bushes and drove dark clouds eastward. David worried about rain, then about snow, tugging at his hair until it stood out like a cap of rusted steel wool. Jessie pictured them that evening in their new home: she would not be in a dress and David would not be freshly shaved. No chilled champagne waited on a polished table set with white winter roses. Unlike old movies or romance novels, men no longer carried women over the threshold.

Too tired to shop or cook on their first night, they argued about where to have dinner, then ate silently in a hamburger stand parking lot. Jessie waited for David on the steps at home, holding the gas company Sorry We Missed You card that she found hooked to the front doorknob.

"I thought you left a key under the mat," she said.

David rubbed his eyes and slumped beside her. "I guess I forgot. I'm so tired of forgetting things." He put his arm around her shoulder and Jessie ran her palm up under his pant leg, caressing David's smooth calf. "Make us a fire, Jess? It's getting cold."

Leaning against the couch and surrounded by liquor store boxes used for moving cartons, they huddled in the firelight, wrapped in an afghan. Jessie had split kindling and brought up wood from the small basement room that once served as a coal bin, which they now called the poet's garret and joked about renting to a suffering artist who would thrive in its dismal atmosphere. David's stocking feet protruded from the cover, inches from the flames. He and Jessie shared a pint bottle of brandy.

"Isn't this the life, though, David? Our own house."

"I said I was sorry."

Jessie rubbed his toes and the fire warmed her fingers. She could still see her breath. "It's strange having a house."

"Why strange?"

"I've dreamed of one," she told him, resting back in his arms, "but in dreams things are perfect. This is more demanding."

"The house?" David flicked his cigarette into the fire, blew into his palms, rubbed them, then touched Jessie's cheek with an icy hand. "How is it demanding?"

"This house was decorated in about 1957," Jessie said, thinking of the work it needed. One bedroom was baby blue, another pea green; the living room rug was red and the bathroom was pink. Doors and woodwork were painted with indestructible coats of lemon yellow enamel; the walls had cheap plastic fake wood paneling. There were white ruffled curtains in the kitchen and an ancient refrigerator that froze milk but melted ice cream. Doors did not hang true on their hinges and cold wind hissed past the windows that were not painted shut. "Ozzie and Harriet could have lived here."

They discussed things the house needed: a washer and dryer in the basement, a deep freeze, rose bushes for the garden, hedge clippers and hoses and sprinklers and lawn junk for the garage, a trash can.

"It will insist we have two sons," David said, "and that every year on their birthdays we record their heights on the back of our bedroom door."

They went to bed early, cold and exhausted. David drew Jessie close for the first time in weeks. Awake, she felt his body begin to relax beside her warmth. She must try to make the house and all David's worries that had come between them find other places.

Jessie closed her eyes, but she remained awake thinking of fifties cars with tailfins, bulky furniture, Elvis and rock'n'roll, white anklets and full skirts and Peter Pan collars on pastel blouses, all past and known things. We were young then, she thought, and had no responsibilities. Ozzie and Harriet were incredibly old. They were square. The new house demanded they realize that they were becoming Ozzie and Harriet.

After two days David was sent to Washington, D.C., on a week-long business trip. Jessie drove him to the airport, carried one of his bags to the ticket counter, smiled, and said she would miss him but everything would be all right. The phone man would come later that morning so David could call home tonight. Tomorrow the washer and dryer were scheduled to be delivered, and although they would not be installed, Jessie could stop putting aside change for the Laundromat.

"Your father's an engineer, Jess, right?" David kissed her forehead, held her hands. "I'm sure you'll manage to get everything hooked up."

She stepped back. "I didn't know an understanding of electricity was hereditary."

On the way home she bought a bottle of Scotch and stopped at the hardware store. In only two days David had pulled enough nails from the house and garage to fill a one-pound coffee can. Jessie mixed Spackle and took it from room to room, dragging along a new stepladder, filling holes. The walls are as spotted as an appaloosa's rump, she would tell David when he called.

Mornings, Jessie found herself kneeling on the kitchen floor, pouring Scotch into a coffee mug so the woman next door, whose kitchen overlooked hers with a wide expanse of picture windows, would not be scandalized into starting the neighborhood gossip. With a buzz on, painting did not seem so tedious. Evenings, she pulled the drapes and sat in the dark, a little dizzy, the cat in her lap as she reclined by a small fire and dreamed of locking the doors and leaving. Light sparkled on the ceiling that previous owners had sprayed with a lumpy substance resembling rhinestone oatmeal.

She watched men on television explain why women needed cleansers, deodorizers, sprays, waxes, and detergents. The men smiled patiently at housewives whose lifelong pursuit of the ultimately whitened and brightened socks and shorts could not possibly be obtained without a certain new improved bleach. Television's obsession against dirt, smells, and smudges somehow reminded Jessie of a back-alley office in Mexico City, where she had seen a line of tourists waiting politely for their travel agent. He was late, they said, and they were hot and dusty and sweaty. They needed showers. They did not know the agent was sitting next door in a dim café, smoking as he drank a cold beer and joked with the waiter about the tourists swatting flies. You can always tell Americans, the agent had said, they're too clean.

While David was away, Jessie received a postcard from a friend digging at an Aztec site. Around the post office's forwarding-address sticker, which had been pasted across the message, she restored her friend's words as though they were fragments of an inscribed stone that would reveal past mysteries. The note mentioned grants, money available for study and travel, and the possibility of a position on that summer's excavation. Jessie set the card on a windowsill and later accidentally dripped paint across its blue sky, palm trees, and glistening water. When David phoned, she would say the right thing, that she missed him.

"I'm lonely," his distant voice told her. "And tired. This trip is a waste of time. I want to come home."

"You come home, then, and I'll do some traveling."

"Sunday, Jess, we can put on a roast and chill a bottle of wine, laze around in our bathrobes all day reading the comics and watching old movies. Get potatoes to bake when you're at the store, too, okay? Can you make gravy?"

"No." She remembered sitting, like a dunce, on the kitchen stool when she was a child. Her mother had said someday she would need to know how to make gravy, so she'd better pay attention and learn. "Can you?"

"Make gravy?"

"Yes."

"Of course not." David laughed, then waited for Jessie to speak. When she did not, he said, "I mean, I never tried. It comes in packages, doesn't it?"

"There was a storm the first night you were gone," Jessie told him. "The back fence blew down."

"You didn't tell me."

"I wanted it to be a surprise. I built a fence. By myself."

When David came home, they stood in the mist looking at the new split-rail fence. The rails were level, the posts solid. David crossed the yard and hitched himself up, hooking his heels over the middle rail.

"So tell me, Jess, when do we get a horse?"

"This is a city fence. For livestock the rails have to go on the insides of the posts, David, or the animals just push them out." She walked through the weeds to his side and put her hands on his knees. "Why do I know that and not how to make gravy?"

He smiled and smoothed a strand of dark hair from her forehead, tucking it behind her ear, then he leaned down to kiss her, his fingers combing back, loosening her braid. "I've brought a present."

They exchanged gifts in bed. Wool socks for David; for Jessie a book on how to keep warm using an ax. There was a large woodpile in the yard and that first cold night she had said she could heat the house with an ax and maul and splitting wedge.

"I sound like a hippie or a pioneer, don't I?" she said, stretching close to him. "Next thing you know I'll be spinning wool and putting up peaches."

"You could plant vegetables out back, Jess."

She tried to imagine David mucking out stalls, chopping off chickens' heads, plowing. They lay quietly together, drifting to sleep as rain rustled over the low, muffled moans of foghorns. David's forearm cradled Jessie's neck. She turned and kissed his palm. There was a spot of waterproof ink on his thumb. His hand was white, its fingers smooth, with closely bitten nails.

Closing her eyes, Jessie saw a long dusty road running west toward a late-afternoon sun. In every direction the land was gold with wheat, spreading away in long shadows and gently rising hills gone russet. She stood in the road, the earth hot under her feet, shielding her eyes, listening for David. Bees droned. A yellow hound crossed the fields toward her, its slender tail a flag in the grain. The sweet heavy scent of ripened blackberries lifted on a breeze rich with the smells of dust and grass. Swallows dipped and rose, wheeling above her. Jessie imagined these things, but David always came into her vision in a three-piece gray pinstriped suit, a portfolio under his arm.

"What would you think of having a child?" David said.

Jessie sat up. "I thought you were asleep."

"I can't decide," he said, drawing her down. "It frightens me."

Jessie rocked him. David's shoulders were as white as porcelain, and faintly freckled. He seemed frail to her then, letting her hold him as he admitted he had fears. She realized he must also have dreams.

"One afternoon back in D.C. I slipped away early," he told her. "I went to see paintings at the National Gallery, left there, too, went to my hotel room, and got drunk."

"Thinking about a child?"

"I don't know." He stretched, frowned, raised himself to one elbow and looked at Jessie. "Thinking profound nothings that got forgotten by a blackout."

"Do you ever think you're becoming your father?" Jessie said.

"How?"

"I've begun thinking of new curtains and carpets, of shelves in the kitchen, of dining room chairs and upholstery. Things my mom passed her time with that I never cared about."

"You don't make good apple pie yet."

"Pretty soon, David, I may be trading recipes with the neighbor ladies at Tupperware parties. I'll have a little plastic file box stuffed with cards and priceless ratty papers ripped from homemaker magazines."

"In our family no one gets blackout drunk. The women don't chop wood or build fences. I don't think we're turning into them, Jess." David shivered and settled back under the blankets. "Or maybe we are. I don't know."

They rose later and began again "playing house," as one of their old friends from the apartment called life in the suburbs. David pulled nails; Jessie painted. David hung pictures and set up bookshelves; Jessie wrote away for seed catalogues and began pulling weeds. She sent David to work each morning, giving him a kiss and a cup of coffee at the back door. He called her every day before lunch, then, after a while, began calling after lunch. Each day he called later. Sometimes he was not in when she phoned to ask him to stop at the grocery on the way home. Jessie wondered if his secretary was pretty; she wondered if David made love to other women; she wondered what had happened to her former ideals, when she had stopped believing in freedom and started expecting faithfulness.

Jessie swung at the earth with a red-tipped hoe she had bought on sale at the hardware store. She turned up dirt, as books recommended, a foot deep. She added manure and peat and vegetable nutrients. In a scratchy Mexican sweater, old jeans, and boots, she dug furrows for seeds in trenches that were as straight as a ruler's edge, ten centimeters deep. She sent a postcard to her friend in Mexico, claiming her excavations had brought to light a 1923 dime, a 1938 penny, an aluminum chip with a soft-drink label, nails, and peach pits.

"Hardly remains of the most exciting civilization in world history," she told David one day when he arrived home from work.

"What's that?" he said, pointing to two bare trees and a line of brown sticks evenly spaced along the fence.

"Eucalyptus," Jessie said. "Dogwood." She turned. "Raspberries."

"Oh."

Jessie stood beside him. From his vantage behind the car, she saw a lumpy plot of mud, barren except for heaps of dead weeds and grass. He set down his portfolio and rubbed his eyes. Jessie stepped away.

"Look, David."

He faced her, blinking, reaching back to massage his neck. "What?"

"Potatoes, carrots, spinach, onions, tomatoes, broccoli." She took a half-meter pace, indicating each row. "Fresh raspberries. Cornflowers and strawflowers, daisies and delphiniums."

"Jessie?"

"Yes."

"Are you going to Mexico this summer?"

She had received an invitation to dig and to help with the editing and publication of finds. She left the letter out for David to read, uncertain, hoping somehow the right decision would happen by itself.

"I don't know."

He motioned her to him. "Go if you need to."

"What about you?"

"I'll be all right."

"What about the house?"

David looked up at it, then back to Jessie. "What about it?"

"Who's going to mow the lawn and scrape the windows, fix the antenna, and get the plumbing taken care of?"

"That's beside the point."

"No, it isn't." She slipped her arm around his waist. "All my life

I've rented apartments and rooms and condominiums. Other people's places. I need to stop, I guess, David. I've begun feeling the housework changes."

"What changes?"

"I'm learning to cook and I even like it, how to fix things and how to plant things." Jessie turned and moved her arms around his shoulders. "I've gotten worried you have lovers because I'm too fat."

"You're not fat, Jess."

"I even bought a bra. With lace."

He moved his hands up her sides. "Which you're not wearing."

"One thing at a time." Jessie propped the hoe inside the tool shed and walked up the driveway with David. "I'm looking forward to summer here, to barbecuing hamburgers, to playing softball and going to the beach, to getting the house ready for next winter."

"*This* winter isn't even over yet."

They stopped by the back door, where they had a view across the street to the aluminum-sided house with two trucks and a dented van parked bumper to bumper behind a stained fiberglass speedboat that rested crookedly in high weeds. Jessie and David stood silently, watching a paunchy young man in a yellow baseball cap hump and slam at the blinking pinball machine he kept in his living room. Nearby, a woman in pink foam-rubber curlers pointed a flabby arm at something; her jaw flapped. She pointed again, then stood, wearing sheer shortie nighties that revealed gray doughy thighs and a fat rump in pink panties with holes where the elastic had pulled loose. Her voice shrieked about the pinball bells. A child rushed out, slamming the front door. The woman followed, opened the door, planted herself there, and screamed.

"In Mexico," David said, "you might not be able to hear them."

The man and woman were screaming at each other now, a routine they repeated several times each week.

"Do you suppose he *ever* takes off that hat?" Jessie said.

David propped his elbow on the porch railing, running a finger along the white trim that would need paint soon. He looked away, back to the screaming woman. "Jess, *that's* fat. If I were him, I'd get a lover."

"If I were she, I'd leave."

"Will you? Leave?"

She shrugged. They climbed the stairs and shut out the lives of their neighbors. People like that, Jessie thought, shouldn't have kids. Then, wondering what sort of people should have children, she took out a cookbook, propped it open, and started supper. David put away his portfolio, changed clothes, and came back to slice tomatoes. They moved around each other, a silent waltz that had become comfortable.

Jessie realized she was content to stay for now. The work in Mexico would continue for years and she could go any season. For the first time, she wanted to be home. Just as she had learned more about David's past and his methodical nature by seeing his things strewn everywhere when they had moved, she came to understand that she had always been moving on, looking elsewhere, thinking her dreams could come true only if she kept trying to get over the next horizon.

"David?"

"Yes."

"What do you dream for?"

"I don't understand."

"When you can't sleep at night," Jessie said, "what do you wish for?"

David hesitated, closed his eyes, and when he opened them again, he seemed to be coming back from someplace far away. He smiled and shook his head slightly.

"It's hard to say."

They stood quietly for a moment, then ate dinner, and gave up working on the house early so they could go to bed. Later that night Jessie knew she could no longer wait for the mid-April average last frost date for setting in seeds. It was almost the end of March. Tomorrow David would go to work; he would grin and give her his parting platitude: Off goes the breadwinner to bring home the bacon. Jessie would stay in, laboring over a dreary biology textbook manuscript whose wages would help pay off more household bills. At noon, when the sun had cleared the fir and cedar trees to the east, she would go out to mark each north-south row in the garden with string pulled taut between stakes. She would set in seeds, putting down roots, as though their lives depended on it.

TO HELL WITH HARVEY

by Lucille Schulberg Warner

If you think life's a puzzle, wait till you get to death. Here I am, looking back at my old woman's body in that hospital bed, and before I can even count who's grieving, I have to figure out where to go from here forever. It's a problem, the Gentleman tells me. It seems I was a good wife to Harvey so I'm entitled to heaven, but I wasn't such a good wife to Edgar so I'm entitled to hell, too. I'm going to have to determine my future myself, he tells me. It's only logical.

There were a thousand times, I guess, in those first years, when I wondered how glad I was I had married Harvey. I knew I was real glad those mornings when he woke up looking like six years old, his face all rosy from sleep and his hair all rumpled. I wasn't so sure other times. I had a couple of black eyes from Harvey. He could be mean. But he had a twinkle in his eye, Harvey did, when he lifted his first beer after dinner and settled down in front of the TV set and he flashed it at unexpected times, too. I used to melt those other times.

That twinkle won me in the first place. I knew Harvey had played around a lot before we settled down together. But for eight years and a couple of months after, we were the very picture. We had the nice little house with the yard; Harvey went off to the telephone company every morning at eight after an orange juice, a bacon and eggs once over, a toast not too dark, and a cup of coffee, all delivered by me with a smile. He'd come home six, seven, sometimes eight, nine, full of jokes about Billy or Fred, or telling horror stories about repairing a line in a windstorm. We saw Joan and Edgar Blackman next door, went to movies or the high school basketball games with them. Sometimes when Harvey was out on a night emergency job and Joan was taking her sewing class, Edgar would come over and we'd watch some TV together until Edgar went to pick up Joan and I'd watch alone until Harvey came home. I was always glad to see him. There was a secret part of Harvey I always tried to get to and never could. It gave a kind of funny excitement to living with him. I mean, I liked it but it scared me.

If you live anywhere near our town, you probably read about Harvey's death. He was "Local Man Killed in Motel Fire." You may even remember the details. People were feeding on it for months. They got the fire out and, finally, they got Harvey out. The newspapers didn't do much reporting about how Joan Blackman managed to get herself home. Or, afterward, how she took off for good. The way Edgar and I pieced it together later wasn't much comfort, but it brought us closer.

I never did any wondering about why I married Edgar. He didn't have any secrets in him. He liked the TV but he also liked to go out and be a good citizen of the town. He went to the Elks and the Lions and he was a Big Brother and collected for the Community Chest. For twelve years I watched that man take a piece of marshmallow cake and a glass of milk for breakfast, and heard him say, "We'll just skin those whiskers," every time he stook up to carve the roast. But he never raised his voice to hush me when I yelled at him and he never made a fuss when I left supper for him and went off to the movies and he didn't complain much when I bought too many clothes. I know I bought too many clothes. He probably didn't mind when he collapsed that night in front of the TV and was gone before the doctor could even get to us. In the years that were left to me, I was surprised at how much I missed Edgar.

Now where am I going and who's going to be there?

They're not going to make it too easy for me, the Gentleman says. Will I observe, please. There are two doors in front of me.

I look. There are. No walls or anything but two blank closed doors. And lounging in front of each of them is a copy of Mr. Palmer, my high school mathematics teacher, of all people. I catch on that one door stands for heaven and the other one stands for hell. But I don't understand about the Mr. Palmers.

"Mr. Palmer, who has been with us a long time, was the one to point out to us that you had a logical mind," the Gentleman lets me know. "He was always very sorry you didn't go on to college."

Then comes the real puzzle. The Gentleman explains that both Mr. Palmers know which door leads to heaven and which door leads to hell, but one of the Mr. Palmers tells only lies and the other Mr. Palmer tells only the truth. I can ask either of them one question. I'm allowed only one question altogether. And there's no way of my knowing whether I'm asking the question of the Mr. Palmer who lies or the Mr. Palmer who is truthful. From the answer I get, I'll have to identify both doors and choose which to go through. If I miss my one chance, there's no problem. I'll just be in this limbo always.

I always did like Mr. Palmer. He started me on puzzles like this. I used to get books of them and do them all the time. You know, "Brothers and sisters have I none, but this man's father is my father's son?" Of course, it never helped much when I was trying to figure my household accounts, as Harvey used to point out.

"Hey, smart-head," he used to laugh. "How much is one and one?"

Edgar enjoyed the way I solved puzzles and was proud of me for it. Suddenly, I felt Edgar's comfortable smile and knew he was waiting for me.

I was ready. I pointed to the door on the left and spoke to the Mr. Palmer who was in front of it.

"Where will the other Mr. Palmer tell me this door goes?" I asked.

"Heaven," he said.

As soon as I heard that answer, I knew the door led to where I wanted to go. I nodded to both Mr. Palmers, waved to the Gentleman, and promptly went through it, to hell, with Harvey.

(Note: The liar will say the truth-teller will lie and say the left door leads to heaven. The truth-teller will say the liar will lie and say the left door leads to heaven. In both cases, the answer will be the same, and incorrect.)

GOING HOME

by Will Weaver

We needed a smaller apartment, and soon. In three days, Sandy and I had to be out of this one-bedroom and into something cheaper. Things hadn't gone well for us in California. The jobs just weren't out here like we had heard. Every day we would go out looking. We'd wait in lobbies with chrome and naugahyde furniture and those broad-leafed rubber plants that thrived on artificial light and cigarette smoke. We'd fill out the applications and underline our phone number, but no one ever called. No one, that is, except our folks who were back in Minnesota. They called every few days to see if we had found *anything*, as they called it. They never said *work*. Anything. But maybe our folks were using the right word. Sandy and I had been here six months now, and we were ready to take just about anything.

Right now, I drained my coffee cup, rinsed it, dried it, and put it in the cupboard. I spread out this morning's paper on the table, and Sandy put yesterday's paper alongside. We got out the red pencil and sat down and began to look down the for-rent columns. We were looking for new listings. But there were none we did not recognize, and most we had already called.

"What about this 'handyman special'?" Sandy asked. "It's been listed for days. Maybe we should call."

I looked at the ad again:

> Handyman special. One bdrm.
> Fixup needed. U-work, U-save.
> 463–4663.

"Wonder what's wrong with it," I said.

"Well, if we saw it, we'd know," she replied. She glanced at the wall clock and then at the calendar. I knew she was worried this time. "Maybe there's not much at all wrong with it. Maybe the sink . . . who knows? You're good at fixing that stuff."

"I don't have my tools," I answered. My tools were all back in Minnesota on my dad's farm.

She paused at that, and frowned. Sunlight was just now cutting through the kitchen curtains and touching her blond hair and making it glow orange around the edges of her curls. The light made her skin seem whiter and at that moment I thought of how tanned everyone else seemed here in California—everyone but her and me, who only sunburned pink.

"Let's call," I said. "We can take a look."

She dialed the number and waited. Someone must have answered, because she opened her lips and got ready to speak.

"But it's still available?" she repeated, nodding to me and pointing to the wall clock and smiling.

The man on the phone would meet us at the apartment in one half-hour. Though the address was only a few minutes away, we left immediately. We were excited. Maybe things were changing for us.

The building was on the east edge of San Jose, next to the freeway, a white three-story affair with common balconies. Somebody's washing was spread along one of the railings. Below and across the street was an adult movie theater. Just down from the theater was a bus bench upon which some Mexican kids were perched like crows on a fence. But Sandy and I didn't care. We waited there in our Chevy and had fun trying to guess which car would belong to the man on the phone. I guessed the red Triumph and Sandy guessed the new black Turbo Saab. But we should have known it was the man in the bright blue Lincoln with the continental wheel on the trunk.

He got out of his car and walked toward us. He had black hair but brown eyebrows, and his face was very tan. A short brown leather jacket, the kind businessmen wear in California, was open over his blue and white flowered shirt, which itself was open over a golden medallion on his bare chest. He could have been forty. He could have been sixty.

"Well, let's go on up and have a look," he said, smiling and checking his watch in the same moment. He kept staring at Sandy, so I had her walk ahead of me up the open stairs. Our apartment was on the far side of the building, so we had to walk down an inside hallway. After the bright sunlight, the hallway was dim and brown. Passing other apartments, we could hear people speaking Spanish and could smell things frying. Some of the doors were open, but only the length of their safety chains.

The owner paused before our door and began to flip through a ring of similarly shaped keys. "Like the ad said," the man said, grinning as he slid the key into the lock, "the place needs a little work—sheetrock and paint, mostly. My men would do it, but I'm a little short-handed these days. So I figure the new renter can do the work and save some money at the same time."

"Sounds good," Sandy murmured.

He swung open the door. At first it was difficult to see, because the inside drapes were drawn. I reached for the hall light, but only one of the four bulbs came on. Still, it didn't take much light to see the damage. The sheetrock beside the door was broken, caved forward between the wall studs in a large diamond shape. It was as if somebody had taken a run and smashed himself into the wall. In the kitchen there were no light bulbs at all, but I could see brown smears across the white faces of the refrigerator and range. It was like somebody had taken an old, torn paintbrush and had gone crazy with brown paint. In the bedroom and living room there were more smears, along with those large sheetrock diamonds.

"Somebody had a real party, that's for sure," the man said. His teeth glinted in the gloomy living room and he was standing in front of the cord that would open the drapes. I didn't like him. I didn't like the damage, the smears. I didn't like any of this.

"I'd like to open the drapes," Sandy said. "It's hard to see well without the light bulbs."

The man hesitated, then shrugged and stepped aside. Sandy pulled the cord and daylight spilled into the room.

"Oh Jesus," I whispered.

Sandy looked at me. She didn't see it. She didn't know. Those smears on the walls, the carpet, even a spray of brown splotches on the ceiling.

"That's blood," I said, keeping my voice calm, pointing to the largest spray.

"Blood? Hey"—the man laughed—"get serious."

Sandy's mouth came open and she stepped closer to me.

"That's blood," I repeated. "I come from a farm in Minnesota and I know blood when I see blood." Sandy was pulling me toward the door and I didn't resist. The man followed us but then paused to lock the door.

"Suit yourself, kiddies," he called after us, "but no sweat. Somebody will take it. Some people will take anything."

"But not us," I shouted back. My voice was shaking.

"Don't, please, don't," Sandy whispered, pulling me into the daylight toward our Chevy.

The engine caught on the first revolution and I pulled the car into the traffic and just started driving. Any street. Anywhere. It seemed important to keep moving. After a few minutes Sandy started to cry and I reached over and pulled her closer to me. By then we were passing a city park that looked green and neat, so I stopped the car. We got out and sat on a cement bench. We sat there for a long while.

Across the park a man on a small John Deere tractor was pulling a long, heavy spiked cylinder in even rows back and forth across the bright green grass. The cylinder's spikes flipped out little plugs of sod in a continuous shower. I knew what the man was doing: he was aerating the soil, because in California lawn grass grows so thickly it eventually chokes itself to death. I picked up one of the sod plugs from in front of our bench. I crumbled it between my fingers. It was September now in California, but the grass smelled like summertime in Minnesota and the black earth reminded my of my dad's farm.

"Maybe we ought to go back," I said softly into Sandy's hair. "Back to the Midwest."

We took just what we could pack into the Chevy. Our clothes. The books. The stereo. The plants. There was some furniture, but we left all that. Maybe somebody else could use it. We didn't even wait for our damage deposit. I had enough money to get us at least into Nebraska, and Nebraska was in the Midwest, so I didn't worry about getting the rest of the way to Minnesota. By four o'clock that afternoon we had left behind Oakland and Vacaville and had entered some open country. Silent through the Bay Area, both of us now began to talk, at first hesitantly, then unashamedly, of things we would do once we got back to the Midwest.

Sandy wanted to go canoeing at night on the Crow-Wing River.

I wanted to help my father with some fall plowing, visit my grandparents.

We could find jobs soon after that. And we talked on through Sacramento, all the way to the beginning foothills of the California Sierras, which seemed steeper than I had remembered them.

We had a full car—the books were heavy—and I began to watch the Chevy's oil and water gauges as we climbed the steepening grade. I had no reason to doubt the Chevy. I had always taken good care of it and it had never let me down. Yet both Sandy and I fell silent as we drove upward. Dusk fell. I turned on my headlights.

I began to think about the engine, about how the spark plugs and cylinders and camshaft and transmission and running gear all worked together; about how one small thing—a loose wire, a short, an oil seal—could break that whole rhythm that propelled us up these mountains. I began to hear engine noises. But they were only my own heartbeat drumming in my ears.

A light rain began to fall and we slowed through Gold Run and Blue Canyon. Westbound traffic heading down into California was headlight-to-taillight, two lanes full, behind the blinking red lights of an accident. Eastbound traffic was lighter, but it, too, was slowing from the rain that was thickening to snow. I turned the wipers to a faster speed and slowed into third gear as we passed Emigrant Gap and headed toward the summit, Donner Pass. It was cool in the car but I was sweating. Suddenly, in the thick white snow, among the red taillights, we topped Donner Pass. I felt the Chevy lighten and start to run freely. I shifted back into high gear and took my foot off the gas, as we could nearly coast now. I looked across to Sandy. She smiled and turned on the radio. We couldn't pick up many stations because of the snow, so she turned it off, and that was all right, too. She leaned closer to me and stared into the snow. I knew she would be asleep within minutes.

With her leaning against my shoulder, I looked ahead, too. The snow was letting up, and with each pass of the wipers I could see more clearly and farther ahead. After a while, when Sandy was asleep, it was as if I could see ahead through the darkness and into our lives to come. I could see us this Christmas with our parents around the Christmas tree. I could see us ahead some years, see children running toward us wanting to be caught and swung into the air. I could even see us gray and old, and that wasn't bad, either.

I thought of waking Sandy and telling her all this, but it wouldn't have made much sense, and she needed the sleep. Instead, I just drove and kept looking ahead into that clear blue night.

TRUE HEART

by Joy Williams

Gail was crouched on the carpet of her exercise class, doing the hydrant. She was fifty-six years old. She was five feet eight inches tall and weighed one hundred and sixty pounds. Once, she had been thin and fierce, but now she weighed one hundred and sixty pounds and her manner was more reserved. Her granddaughter, who was two, was the only child in the health club's nursery, and she was screaming. She had been screaming for fifteen minutes.

Linda, the girl who was conducting the class, was enthusiastic and tireless, happy with her muscles and her smooth limbs. Linda was about the same age as Emily, Gail's daughter, who worked as a waitress at the Oyster Bar and Restaurant, where she made a considerable amount of money. Emily's husband, Dwight, also made a considerable amount of money in Houston, Texas, one thousand miles away, working on the ship channel there. Money was not their problem. In one of his infrequent letters to Emily, Dwight had said that the water sometimes caught on fire in the channel—that it burned like boards. Gail had tried to imagine water burning. It didn't seem as if something that could happen. It seemed more like an idea Dwight had picked up from the movies.

The baby, whose name was Blue Jean, screeched.

The exercise class went from the hydrant to leg bounces and from leg bounces to their knees, where they did the cat stretch. Gail called the baby Blue. How could anyone have named their child Blue Jean? Gail couldn't believe she had raised a daughter who would name her own daughter Blue Jean. She, Gail, had been named for the storm that had battered the coast the night she was born. For the next eight years, her father had said it was a perfect name for her, because she was so noisy, and then he'd died. He'd always wanted a boy. "Girls don't make families; they unmake them" was one of the things he'd often say before he died. When it came time for Gail to have a baby girl, she had called her Emily, after her favorite poet, Emily Dickinson. For years when people asked her what the child's name was and she said "Emily," a great many of them would say, "Is she named for Emily Dickinson?" Once, a woman Gail barely knew began to recite a portion of a poem:

> My Life had stood—a Loaded Gun
> In Corners—till a Day
> The Owner passed—identified—
> And carried Me away—

Then the woman said, "A little Emily Dickinson goes a long way," and laughed.

Gail's marriage had ended in divorce. She supposed it was herself she should blame. She had been angry because she wanted so much. Once, she had wanted, very badly, a complete set of Revere Ware. It had cost four hundred dollars, and when she got it she had not been happy. What was that, to have a complete set? The company was out of business now. Twice, she had thrown pies at her husband, and many times she had locked him out of their house. Her husband had been an electrician, retired now, and he had remarried. He and Gail had lived in an all-electric home. When he had left her, he had taken a few things, a Fred Astaire double album, a sofa bed, and the toaster. She had not known about the toaster until several days after he'd gone, when their dog had diarrhea and she'd wanted to make a piece of toast for it. When she realized that she could not toast a piece of bread in the toaster for their sick dog, she began to cry and cried for four days. She supposed she had had some kind of a nervous breakdown. She felt like a clear light bulb burning in the daytime, but she had never told this to anyone, not anyone.

Blue Jean had stopped bawling. The exercise class had gone on to aerobic exercises. *Aerobic* was a word Gail had not even known until a year ago. Aerobic exercise was supposed to make the heart work more efficiently. Gail and, she supposed, all the women present, wanted more efficiently laboring hearts. They did the twister, the baby-jog, and the elbow-knee connection. Gail was not very coordinated, but the woman next to her was even less coordinated. This woman giggled in class as though she were at a cocktail party, and she was always referring to men's "buns," which made Gail feel almost queasy. The woman aggravated Gail. Also, Gail was unsure as to whether the word was "bun" or "bum." This was aggravating also. But Gail was trying to keep a lid on her annoyances. She had been a yeller in her day, just like her mother. It had been a way of dealing with the realization that life is chain and fatality, fatality and chain. But times change. Gail didn't yell anymore, and her mother, Florence, didn't yell anymore either. Gail was now committed to physical fitness and the proper raising of Blue, and Florence was eighty-eight years old and spent most of her time quietly upstairs in her room in Gail's house. There were four bedrooms in the house by the water, and, at night there was a female in each one of them. Four generations in a single home. This gave Gail great satisfaction.

Doing jumping jacks, Gail felt as though she might pass out. She had eaten most of Blue's pancake before she had come to class, and she wished that she hadn't. Gail was in charge of Blue Jean mornings, noons, and nights. Emily was either working at the Oyster Bar or sleeping. Like Florence, Emily was not a very good mother, Gail feared. Motherhood and home had always been very important to Gail, and everyone told her she kept a lovely home. This was, she supposed, in reaction to Florence, who had kept a careless home. Gail remembered mouse droppings on the books. She remembered worse. She remembered that almost every day of her childhood, she would come home from school to find no supper and a stranger in the house. After her father had died, her mother had taken up cards—the interpretation of cards. Florence didn't have much of an aptitude for ordinary life, but she found that she had a gift for speculation. People came to her, were interpreted, and went away. Gail, who didn't have an occult bone in her body, was not a believer, yet after her divorce she followed Florence's advice and moved out of her all-electric home to a big faded green house on the ocean. Florence had told her that she had seen a great deal of water in her cards and that this signified "the house of the true heart" where she would find contentment.

Actually, Gail didn't care for the ocean all that much. There was a painting of it that hung over the mantel that she preferred more. The painting had come with the house and had rocks and clouds and sunny waves in it. It seemed more promising than the actual ocean.

Florence hadn't done cards for years. It was difficult for her to recollect ever having done them. She sat in a flowered armchair in the room that was hers in the big cold house by the ocean, undoubtedly bewildered by the circumstances that had brought her there. Sometimes Gail, sitting beside Florence in her nicely arranged room, would look at her and try to remember some little incident of their early life together when Florence had been her mother. Memories were queer things. Florence's memory had become trim and selective. For example, she had no memory at all of the existence of Blue.

Poor Blue. Emily had given her that crazy name and then turned her over to Gail. When she was a few days old, Gail had bought a little red terry-cloth-covered, battery-powered heart for her crib. It was supposed to simulate the mother's heartbeat and be comforting to a newborn baby, a stranger on this earth. Emily's heart beat very seldom in proximity to Blue. She was always working at the Oyster Bar, lugging trays of old-fashioneds and rock shrimp to people in dark booths. Gail blessed the person who had thought up the terry-cloth-covered, battery-operated crib heart.

The members of the exercise class were now lying motionless on the carpet. Then they fluttered arms, then legs. They breathed in deeply, then blew the breaths out. Gail had always thought that she had known how to breathe, but it turned out that this was not the case. She breathed. Class was dismissed.

"Oh, I'm so worn out," one of the women said to Gail. Gail looked at her. The truth was, Gail did not like admissions. She never had. She tottered to the water cooler and then to the dressing room, where she pulled a large gray jumper over her leotard. She put on her shoes and went to the nursery. A woman was sitting in a rocking chair, reading a newspaper. Blue sat on the floor, holding a book upside down. The book was a thin, waterproof one of a few pages—for the bathtub. Gail glowered at the woman and picked up Blue. Incredibly, the baby protested, but Gail pried the book from her fingers, whisked her out of the nursery, and marched her through the carpeted room and into the street. She unlocked her car's door and stuffed Blue, wailing, into her traveling seat. Blue glared at her. Gail glared at Blue. Finally the baby looked away, puzzled.

Gail sighed. Blue was a very resentful baby, unlike Emily, who had never shown any temper as a child. Now Emily was a placid, uncommunicative young woman. Gail had always thought that she and Dwight made a very boring couple. The wedding had been boring. When Dwight had gone off to Texas, no one seemed to miss him very much. There was talk for a while about Emily and Blue joining him there, but the talk gradually stopped. It seemed that in Florence's day, marriage ended disastrously with death, and in Gail's time, grimly with divorce, and now there was Emily's generation, where marriage faded, rather imperceptibly, like a morning moving into afternoon.

"How about a 7-Up?" Gail asked Blue.

Blue gazed out the window, absorbed in a truck emerging dripping from the Wishy-Washy Car Wash across the street.

"A 7-Up it is," Gail said. She leaned over and kissed Blue on top
of the head. The baby watched the truck.

Gail decided to go to the Oyster Bar, where the baby could wave
to her mother. It was still early for lunch, and the restaurant would
not be busy. Emily would have time to talk to them a bit. It seemed
pathetic to Gail that she would have to go into a restaurant and sit
in a booth like any other stranger to get a smile and a few words out
of her own daughter, but she was willing to do it. As a child, Emily
had talked to her dolls. She had loved her dolls and told them
everything she heard or learned. Gail had been sure Emily was
going to be happy. Gail remembered several of the dolls, Emily's
favorites, quite vividly. They were all stored in several cartons in the
attic, waiting for the day when Blue was a little older and would
know how to appreciate them.

Gail approached the Oyster Bar, slowed, then drove past. There
was 7-Up in the refrigerator at home. Breathing deeply, she accel-
erated. Sometimes home seemed so far away to her that she thought
a great darkness would fall before she got there. She would go
home, feed Blue, and put her down for a nap. Downstairs, in
passing, she would glance at the seascape above the mantle. Upstairs, she would go into Florence's room. She would ask her, "What
do you remember about me?"

MY BOY ELROY

by Meredith Sue Willis

My grandmother's store sat at a curve in the road on the back side of Wise Mountain. It was a general merchandise store, and the mail drop-off for all the farms and hollows up into the folds and ridges of the mountain. People used to come down near noontime and wait for the mail. The store had so much open space that they pulled the kitchen chairs and nail kegs and dynamite boxes from the mines together near the iron stove even in hot summer weather, just to localize the conversation.

My grandmother's main stock in trade by the time I stayed with her for two summers was Pepsi-Cola, pink snowball nickel cakes, and canned lunch meat. She also sold a lot of pressed chewing tobacco: mostly Red Mule and Day's Work, which looked like a yellow candy bar to me on some days and dried dung on others. She had staple goods in her store, too, bags of flour and meal, but over the years she found that the fewer large items she sold, the less she had to enter on her credit books; people tended to pay cash for Vienna sausages and Dreamsicles.

The people waiting for the mail used to tell stories. I loved the slowness of the telling. I would line up coins in the coin drawer or sit on a sack of cornmeal and look out the window and let their voices carry me along. They took turns speaking, never interrupting one another, using short blasts of words: quick-speakers, not deep-south drawlers, but mountain talkers, rat-a-tat-tat followed by a space. After a decent appreciative interval at the end of one story, someone else would start. I loved to be a part of those stories. Sometimes I wished I could be big enough to sit on a nail keg and take a turn, but mostly I was a little awed by the people, and happy to watch from a distance. They had mouths that weren't like people

I knew, cheeks that had collapsed around toothlessness, and the men sometimes wore their bodies bare inside stiff blue jean overalls. The women sat with their knees apart and discreetly waved their dresses up and down for ventilation.

So I stayed at the window, or behind the counter with my grandmother, keeping a distance. She always kept a distance herself, never joined them in the circle. People called her Mrs. Morgan, even the ones she called by their first names, and no one ever came in the living quarters in back of the store. When I asked her why if Mrs. Robinson was a good woman she never went back in the kitchen, my grandmother said, "Oh, honey, you have to be real careful how you act when people owe you money."

To tell the truth, looking back, I think my grandmother's pride entered into it. She had sent her children to college, and while she didn't boast, people knew my father was a schoolteacher. My grandmother had a very precise line in her mind between good and bad. Educating your children and paying your bills were on the good side. Politeness was good, too, and she was polite to everyone, but she told me very clearly the difference between good people like the Robinsons who would give you the shirt off their backs and the other ones you couldn't turn your back on for three seconds or they'd steal the varnish off the countertop.

And then there were the Possetts, who were in another category altogether. I first heard them mentioned in the course of someone's story around the cold stove. "Worthless as a Possett," someone said, and I asked my grandmother later just what is a Possett. She said, "Euh, euh," in her special tone of humorous disgust that was supposed to make me giggle. "You stay away from those Possetts," she said. "They have cooties and they marry each other. Euh, euh." One day Earl Robinson started telling a story about the Possetts, how they had a fire and lost a child, or maybe two. "They never could count that good," said Earl. He paused then, and no one haw-hawed, but even I figured out the joke. "The ones that lived got burned too," said Earl. "All but that big Elroy. He just hightailed it out of there, didn't lift a finger to help." He went on and on, and then other people turned out to have Possett stories, too, many stories about this family that didn't have sense to pull one another out of a burning house.

One morning shortly before my mother and father came to take me home that summer, the Possetts came to the store.

"Law', law', here come the Possetts," said my grandmother, who had gone out front to sweep the little square of cement under the step. She ran and put a piece of canvas over the bags of meal, and she told me to close the kitchen door and stand by the ice cream freezer. I was not supposed to get close to them, but if any of them wanted an ice cream, I was to get it out and then scoot it across the white enamel lid of the freezer. I was excited as if they had declared Christmas in August, watching through the big plate glass window as the Possetts came down the yellow dirt road, past the one-room schoolhouse, across the asphalt, barefooted, one after the other, two full-grown men in overalls first, the old one with no teeth and a straw hat—but to my shame I couldn't see that he looked all that different from a fine man like Earl Robinson—and the younger one chubby and round-shouldered, strawberry-blond. After him came the old Possett woman, who wore a boat-necked dress with no sleeves or waist, as if she had simply stitched two rectangles of fabric into a garment. The younger woman had a little baby in her arms. "Look at them," whispered my grandmother. "They think that boy Elroy is the smartest thing that ever lived. They buy him shoes in the winter and keep him fat. He got to second grade, too, before he turned sixteen and quit. I just wonder which one of them fathered that baby."

I don't understand that, I thought to myself, but I understood more than I wanted to. I tried not to look at the little baby; I tried to pay attention to the children, counting them, examining them. The little baby plus a boy, two girls, and another boy. My stomach wrenched and I stopped counting as that one came across the road. He seemed to have no chin; I tried to look away; I ran to my station by the ice cream freezer, but when I turned back, the little boy was only four feet from me. He had big blue eyes that seemed to roll all the time because his face was pulled down by terrible gullies of hard scar tissue stretching from his cheeks over his lower lip area. His little white bottom teeth were exposed as a bulldog's, and you could see all the healthy red flesh that should have been inside his mouth.

My grandmother said, "Is that your boy that got burned?"

Mr. Possett said, "Ee-ah," or something like that, grinning all the while, reaching behind him and grabbing the boy by the head, tugging him around for my grandmother to see. "Don't talk no more," said Possett. "Still eats, though."

My grandmother grabbed a handful of peppermint balls and maple chewies and gave them to the boy. It was as if her hands had to give to him just as my eyes had to look. When he couldn't hold any more candy, it started dropping on the floor and the other children ran and picked it up. Mr. Possett bought himself an RC Cola, and after a while Elroy whined until he gave him a nickel for one too. The mother Possett took some of the wounded boy's candy and shared it with the big girl and baby. They sat on the kegs and boxes and looked at us, at the store. Once in a while Elroy would make a sucking noise with his RC Cola. After a while Mr. Possett bought some Red Mule chewing tobacco and two strips of licorice, which he tore into pieces for all the children, and then they left, back across the asphalt, up the road past the schoolhouse, into the pine woods again.

My grandmother got a rag and wiped every wooden box a Possett had sat on, and rubbed the plate glass where a Possett had rested a cheek. She moved fast, as if she did something she couldn't have stopped if she'd wanted to.

I said, "What did they come down for?"

She said, "They came down to go to the store."

It was almost time for the mail, and Mrs. Robinson showed up, and Mary from down the road, and after a while Earl Robinson. This time my grandmother did the talking, more than I'd ever heard her say to her customers. She told about the Possetts coming, about the girl with the baby big as life and Elroy fat as the hog for winter, and the boy with no chin. She went on and on, and there was no climax to her story, just the necessity of telling it.

The next summer I didn't go down to stay by myself with my grandmother. I didn't go down until our yearly visit, and everything seemed different. My grandmother directed all her remarks to my father, and called herself an old widow-woman, and said if things got much worse she was going to end up having to marry that dirty old fellow with the greasy black hat who had the tiny store down the road. "Euh, euh," she said. "He's so old and dirty. He sleeps in the same room as the store." And, it seemed to her, the boys were getting worse and worse and meaner and meaner, and all the time she was getting older and feebler and more of an old widow-woman. It didn't make any sense to me at all, because she had never looked bigger and better to me. Her hair was still brown, and she moved briskly around the kitchen, and her eyes sparkled. My father didn't take it seriously either, and he called her by her first name. "Now, Ella," he said the way he always did when he was being cheeky.

We were sitting around her kitchen table eating an apple pie she'd made for us from a bushel of Rome beauties someone gave her on their bill. "You don't know," she said.

"Come and live with us," said my mother.

"You know you're always welcome," said my father.

My grandmother said, "I didn't write you about the convicts, did I? I'm getting so forgetful nowadays." My mother and father looked at each other, and then my grandmother settled in and told us about how a few weeks back folks were sitting around waiting for the mailboy and told about a certain Hines boy from Jenkins, Kentucky, who had broken out of jail in Pikeville. These Hineses, apparently, were the most evil-hearted bunch of boys who ever lived. They would shoot up churches and kill off people as soon as look at them. Especially old widow-women.

"Now, Ella," said my father.

Well, anyhow, as it happened, people were worried about the Hineses coming over this way, and Earl Robinson said he was going to send down his boys to sleep in the store, but my grandmother said of course not, she was fine. "Well," said my grandmother, "that very night I had this evil Hines fellow pecking at that very kitchen door. And Elroy Possett the toadstool too."

Involuntarily we all glanced at the door. It was a screen door to a little back porch, also screened, with a rocking chair, where I loved to sit and read. She kept her brooms out there, the coal scuttle, and baskets of produce people gave her: the Rome beauties, potatoes, lots of peaches in season, and more tomatoes than she could ever eat. This porch had a door and three steps down to the garage and coal house.

The thing that frightened her that night, she told us, was that the knocking was on her back door instead of at the store door. She had been watching Bret Maverick on television when she heard it, and she walked into the kitchen without turning on the light because she had a bad feeling and wanted a look at who was knocking before they saw her. She passed the telephone, thinking all the time she should call the Robinsons, but she didn't want her imagination running away with her. She didn't want to act like a timid old widow-woman even if she was one.

"So," she said, "I ended up with convicts at my back door and no help but myself."

"Come and live with us, Mother," my father said, not fooling around now.

"And do what? Set in a chair? No, I'll just keep on working and getting deeper in debt till some convicts really do get me."

She had stood in the dark kitchen, peering at the shape on the steps, pressing at her outer door. No friendly voice saying, Hey, Mrs. Morgan. Nothing she could recognize as a Robinson or an Otis. The television was still going in the background, shooting cowboys. She made out another man down on the ground at the bottom of the steps, and at a little distance, by the garage wall, a cigarette ash glowing. Three of them, she thought, and that was when her blood ran cold. Three men, and she was sure they were convicts. She spoke suddenly, harshly, as if the force of her voice could blow the man off her steps. "What do you want?"

"You the store lady?" he said without so much as a good evening.

"Store's closed," she said, working on a plan in her mind. What she wanted to do was ease herself over to the telephone—and gently give a message to the Robinsons. It was a party line, and with luck one of the girls would be on the phone already talking to her boyfriend—my grandmother had heard their ring just a little while before and she could whisper gently that she needed help, and these convicts would never hear her over the television. "Store's closed, boys," she said.

The fellow pressed his shadow face into the screen wire, trying to see. He gave a slimy little laugh, and she thought she could smell whiskey. "Aw," he said. "We was wanting something too."

"Who's we?" said my grandmother. "Do you think I open up to every Tom, Dick, and Harry?"

The snicker again. "I don't think you know us, ma'am." She knew he could break the little hook and eye on the door in no time, and once he did that, once he started breaking her things, she would have lost the chance to do anything but scream.

A voice came from the cigarette glow. "Tell her to give us a drink of water, Ed." She was sure the one staying back so far was the leader. *He* was the Hines. The dangerous one with his picture in the paper, standing back out of sight.

The third one, the big hulk at the bottom of the stairs, said, "Naw, you said I could have an RC Cola to drink."

My grandmother said, "Elroy Possett, is that you down there?"

A snuffle and a giggle. "Yes, ma'am."

Well, my grandmother saw it all in a flash then. She saw these convicts running across Elroy, who was probably sitting on a rock by the side of the road, and them asking him who had money around these parts, and him saying, Oh, Mrs. Morgan, she owns a big store. That's how dumb the Possetts are, my grandmother said. The most money they can think of is me and my poor little in-debt store with nothing but books full of credit. She told us it made her so mad to think that slow big Elroy Possett had got her in all this trouble that she threw the light switch, just hit the whole bunch of them with the spotlight my father had installed so she wouldn't stumble going out to load her coal scuttle. Light all over Elroy, who shaded his eyes. The fellow up on the steps already had a hat pulled low over his eyes, and the one down by the garage stepped back in the shadows so she never did get a look at him.

"Now, why'd you do that?" said the one called Ed, and my grandmother took a closer look at him, narrow-shouldered, with clothes that didn't fit, like they belonged to another man. Like they'd been stolen, she thought.

"Tell her what we want, Ed," said the man in the shadow.

"Well," said Ed, "we was traveling and we got hungry and this fellow here said you could sell us some lunch meat and bread and pop."

While he talked, my grandmother kept looking at his hat, a regular man's dress hat of a greasy black color, and it reminded her of something, and all of a sudden she was sure it belonged to the old fellow with the little store about a sixth the size of her own. She thought, Lord Lord, they killed that old man who wanted to keep me company, they killed him and took his money and his hat and now they're going to kill me. It was the hat that set her imagination to working: she wasn't the kind of person to imagine out of nothing, but the hat and the grease spots made her see the old bristle-chinned fellow lying with his throat cut in a pool of blood in that store where if his head was at the stove then his feet must be out the door. She saw her own blood then, too, on the linoleum of her kitchen floor. Saw her apron and her plaid dress. Saw a terrible stillness of sunrise on herself laid out on the floor with no life left in her.

She heard another snuffle from Elroy Possett, and it infuriated her that a soft, filthy oaf like Elroy Possett was going to be the death of her. She got so mad that she snarled, "What are you laughing at, Elroy Possett? It isn't funny these poor boys being hungry and thirsty in the middle of the night like this and wanting a little something and you know very well I can't open up this store."

"Yes, ma'am," said Elroy.

The one named Ed with the old man's hat said, "Just some lunch meat, lady."

"Can't open the store," she said with an idea taking form. You know I'm not one to have wild ideas, she told us; it was something about the Possett that gave her the idea. "I can't open my store, much as I'd like to."

The man in the dark said, "And why's that, ma'am? We surely would like a little something to eat."

My grandmother kept looking at the Possett, the only one of that whole family with any meat on him, no doubt stealing from his mother and the little ones, no doubt giving his own sister that baby. She said, "Elroy Possett knows why, don't you, Elroy? I can't open up because of my boy Elroy."

There was a little silence, and Elroy Possett said, "Yes, ma'am."

She said, "You know all about my poor Elroy, don't you?"

Ed said, "What are you talking about?"

Elroy Possett said, "Her boy Elroy."

"How many Elroys *is* there around here?"

"Two of us," said Elroy Possett, and my grandmother's head began to swim. Some moths and beetles had begun flapping and flying and banging on the spotlight, and the one named Ed slapped at them.

"Tell us about him," said the one in the dark.

"He's a bad boy," said Elroy Possett.

"Now, Elroy," said my grandmother, feeling a kind of joy, things happening. She wasn't still yet. "Now, Elroy, don't talk about my poor boy like that. He never hurt *me*."

"He hurts other folks, all right."

The one down in the shadows said, "Where is this fellow? I'd like to see this Elroy."

"Law'," said my grandmother, "I'd never disturb him."

"Don't disturb *him*!" said Elroy. And my grandmother turned out to have underestimated him, because it was Elroy Possett who made up the next part. "That Elroy sets in the store next to the money box with a shotgun, and nobody never gets near nothing."

Ed cursed. "Why the—" Blank, my grandmother said. "Why the blank did you bring us here then?"

Elroy Possett was having a good time; his imagination was working away. It must have been a real treat for him, said my grandmother, to feel his brain working. "Yes sir, that Elroy sets right there with that shotgun and blows folks' heads off. He sleeps in the daytime and shoots burglars at night. He shot lots of burglars."

My grandmother was getting worried that Elroy was going to ruin it by saying too much. "Now, Elroy, you're exaggerating."

"Why ain't he in jail?" said Ed.

"Well, he never killed anybody," said my grandmother. "He has real bad coordination, my boy Elroy. He never hurt those boys, the time Elroy's talking about. They wasn't supposed to be in the store, after all. The sheriff agreed to that."

The one down in the dark said, "Tell him to step aside then, ma'am. He'll do what you tell him."

"Law' no," said my grandmother. "I'm sorry to say that I'm not a trusting woman. I have a suspiciousness in me."

"Let's go," said the one in the dark, and the cigarette went hurling off. "She ain't letting nobody in her store."

Elroy Possett said, "That Elroy is ugly too. And he ain't bright."

Ed cursed again, and cursed Elroy and stomped down the steps and Elroy went after him. My grandmother said she went around checking all her window locks then, and she got out the butcher knife and sat all night in the kitchen with the knife in her lap.

"Why didn't you call the Robinsons?" said my mother.

"It was getting late," she said. "Besides, I always like to do what I can by myself."

"We're getting you a gun," said my father.

"I'd shoot my foot. Besides, it turned out those Hines boys got caught earlier that day all the way over in Danville. These boys weren't convicts after all," she said. "Although I do believe they were mean through and through."

I said, "What about the hat?"

She shrugged. "Two hats. The old man was fine. I got a message from him the next day through the bread boy. He wanted to take me out for a drive on Sunday. In *my* car."

"Just the same," said my father. "We're getting you a gun."

"All I need," said my grandmother, "All I need is for no-good people like the Possetts to pay their bills."

I said, "Did Elroy come back? Did you ever see him again?"

"Of course," said my grandmother. "He brought the whole family down again a day later. The whole defective mess of them. They stood around my store for three hours and never bought a thing."

She looked at us. "Do you know what they were waiting for?"

I knew, but I said, "What?"

She gave a nod with her chin. "They were waiting to see my boy Elroy."

THE GOOD SHOE

by Roy S. Wolper

"A man's wife should fit like a good, comfortable shoe."
Ukrainian proverb

"The Good Shoe?" my Uncle Andrei said to me as we were having our tea. It was after midnight, and we were in the kitchen behind the store. "I thought so." He sipped his tea through the sugar cube that he held between his thin long teeth. "Yes."

For more than a year—first on Sundays only (when our grocery store closes at six) and then as many nights as I could get free—I had been seeing Carroll Susan, but only the day before had I been certain that she was my Good Shoe.

As I was tearing the dead stalks from the stems of spinach, I watched the kids, not carefully because I had never played kick-the-can. My father believes that work is as much fun as playing, and so I had always been assigned jobs after school.) As I watched the can somersaulting far down the narrow street, there was an explosion of legs and arms and mouths as the prisoners ran free. I knew, as the can became a blur down the street, their rushing-in exultation, for I had it only when I turned down Elliot Street and saw the three large trees that framed the house and the 1010 pressed in the stone. Behind the thick walnut door was Carroll Susan.

But I never said this to my uncle. That's why I was surprised that he knew.

"What do you know of women, Borys?" he said. It was quiet except for his chewing of the cracker.

I looked at the bulbs from the meat case as if they would light up my past, though I had none—only movies and reading detective and adventure stories. "Not much." But I said, "I know Carroll Susan."

"I have to give you the sunshine, Borys. Before it is too late." Between sips of tea he said, "Women about your age, they are at their freshest. Like corn the same day it's picked. But even that is not enough. So skins are powdered. Bright clothes cover. Don't cover. All to catch you." His teeth snapped a cracker in two.

My uncle sounded the way he does when he was sure of trimming cauliflower or picking melons. "Underneath these pinks and green they're odd shoes."

"Carroll Susan is not—"

"You think Carroll is different," he said, nodding. "But nobody, Borys, ever thinks he is getting an odd shoe. Every shoe looks good. Then the man is done for," he said softly, as if he did not want to hurt me. "Done for life." He ate the cracker, all of it. "And then some."

"My mother and father are happy."

"They are not Canadians," said my uncle. "Ukrainians. That's different. Canadians are sick always. Every Monday and Thursday they run to the doctor. Their ears. Their back. Soon, all of them."

"Every Canadian?" I said, not believing.

"A hundred out of a hundred," he said. "Look at my wife. Born in New Brunswick. She is to the doctor every Monday and Thursday. Colds. Pains. Aches. An odd shoe."

"But there are other things beside health," I said. I told him about Carroll Susan's thoughtfulness—her bringing me hard red apples when we skate or her walking across the bridge with me even though the wind was up, just so we could be together longer. "That's important."

"Remember when you caught a toothache?" asked my uncle.

"Yes," I said.

"From one tooth, all of you was sick." I had not been able to read. Breathing was a little dying. "Sickness is that way," he went on. "If their back is sick, they're not kind. Not thoughtful. Not anything."

He stopped. "Nobody ever gave Uncle Andrei sunshine. So I married and learned the uphill way."

Health was a side of women I had never thought about. Never. I did not believe my Uncle Andrei; yet I had never thought about what he said.

"He poured himself another glass of tea. It seemed as if we had been sitting there *for years*. "How is her health?" he asked. "Colds. Does she have many sore throats? Running noses? These are symptoms."

"I don't think so," I said.

"He doesn't think so," my Uncle Andrei said.

"I don't know," I said.

"He doesn't know," my Uncle Andrei said.

"Maybe Carroll Susan is healthy," I said. "Like you and my father. Like me. Like a mule."

"Find out, Borys." He stood up and began washing his glass. "Marriage is forever."

In bed that night I thought over his ideas. It bothered me that my uncle didn't see Carroll Susan as I did. I was certain of his goodness and love. I knew that cosmetics sold like the wind. And yet I went ahead to finish work on my #303 can—the one the kids had left, dented and bent, in front of O'Conner's steps. That was to be my engagement present to Carroll. I had read that such a present shouldn't be practical or useful. No shoes. Or raincoat. That can— the one that had told me that Carroll Susan was the Good Shoe— was the most not useful gift I could think of. And I was going to give it to Carroll after I got it shiny and clean.

Saturday night, when Carroll Susan and I were having late coffee at the Montrose, I said, "How do you feel?" The question leaped from me during a quiet time; I had promised myself not to ask it.

"When?" she said.

"Most of the time?" I said. "Colds. Sore throats." (I had seen a commercial on television, and there were millions of dancing germs. Hundreds of thousands, anyway. They could destroy a throat.)

"Don't worry about my health, Borys," she said. "I worry about yours. You've already worked the lifetime of one person."

But I was not through. "What about your stomach?" I said. "Do you take petrolager? Agoral." (I wanted to stop, but I kept on naming laxatives we sold). "Ex-Lax? Milk of magnesia? Kondremal?"

"At one time?" she said.

"How about," I said easily (I tried to make it sound easy, anyhow), "Alka-Seltzer? Tums? Bromo-Seltzer?"

"Aren't you tired of playing doctor?" she said. After a moment she said, "I was a while back."

We didn't say much after that. There, and during the ride to her house, I tried to talk of little things, but the evening had not gone well. And it should have—because she was a mule, that's why.

As I drove home I thought of the shiny can that was in the glove compartment, wrapped, waiting to be given. You forgot on purpose, my head told me. You *wanted* to forget.

"She was sleepy," I said.

"You could have given it to her after the movie at the Daylight. Before the Montrose. Even at her door. You didn't want to."

On Sunday, as my uncle and I were carrying empty bushel baskets to the truck, I told him that Carroll Susan was the Good Shoe. "No trouble with colds. Or her stomach—a good stomach."

As he neatly tied his knots, he said, "There are other things."

After a while, I said, "What other things?"

"Maybe she has had a long sickness," he said. "It weakens for life." He tugged each stack; none would have dared to move. "Like mononucleosis. Rheumatic fever. One ruins. Like a spot on an apple."

I tried to think back through all of my talks with Carroll Susan. "I don't think she had any of those."

"He doesn't think so."

"I don't know," I said.

"He doesn't know," said my uncle.

"I never thought of it," I said.

"Make sure," said my uncle. "Think of what is beneath the pinks and greens. Under the straps and paste."

Sunday night, after her parents had gone upstairs, we were in the big living room; I was aware of its bigness and of all the separate pieces—the round-armed sofa, the two green-striped chairs, the tall secretary (never closed), the pictures besides the thick magazine table—and we seemed as separate as they were (and they had always fit around us). I kept wondering when and how I could easily ask her the questions my uncle had talked of.

"Would you like some cocoa?"

Although I was not thirsty, I said, "Yes." As she walked into the kitchen, with her back to me, I was able then to say, "Carroll Susan, I have—I'd like to ask you some questions."

She turned, and she stuck out her teeth at me. "Do you want to see me naked? See if the skin is taut? Firm?"

It was so unlike Carroll Susan, I was confused. But I had to keep on with my questions. (And I have never forgotten this too-earnest Borys. I hate him.)

She interrupted. "I'll answer your question, Borys, if—afterwards—you answer mine."

One question wasn't many, and so I started in and went through my list: "Mononucleosis? Rheumatic fever?" She began to laugh (not in her usual happy way), and I was glad when I had finished.

"I have had something you didn't mention," she said. "Wax."

"Wax?" I said.

"In my ears," she said. "I get wax in my ears."

I didn't know how to classify that. It didn't sound serious to me. I get wax in my ears too. I clean it out with our little meat sticks. And I am a mule.

"All nonsense," I said, ripping up the list. "You are a Canadian mule." I told her, then, that my Uncle Andrei believed Canadian women were at the doctor's office all day. I told her what Uncle Andrei had said to me about women using lipstick and clothes to hide their not being the Good Shoe. Odd shoes. "Nonsense," I said. "You are a mule."

"Say, Borys, that I wasn't," she said. "Say I had had mononucleosis."

"But you didn't," I said.

"Say I had."

"You didn't."

"Say I had."

"Is this your question?" I said.

She nodded. "And say," she went on, "that I had chronic sore throats."

"But you don't," I said.

"Say I did, Borys."

It did not take me much time to find my answer. My hand found her little finger. "You can hate the wind. The prairie. You can have scarlet fever. Corns. Yellow jaundice. All at one time. You still are *my* Good Shoe."

"Before you buy the Canadian mule," she said, "don't you want to look at her teeth?" And she opened her mouth, *very* wide, and I felt like crying because I had been so dumb.

I went to the hall closet, and I gave her the package that I had been carrying around—the can. "Don't open it," I said. "Not until I leave. But it is for you only. For being the Good Shoe." And it was then, I think, that I kissed the Good Shoe. A little kiss.

My uncle must have seen that I had lost the sunshine. Only once, when we were very tired from carrying potatoes, he said, "Did you remember to ask her about arthritis? It cripples for life."

I tried not to answer, but I could not ignore him. "No."

"Ask. Rheumatism ruins."

My uncle—who was hardworking and kind and good—would never see the sunshine. I had been lucky in discovering the mean and little Borys. Then I thought of the happy rushing of the wheels that would lead me to 1010 and the walnut door. And that, at least, made me whistle (and I cannot whistle at all).

SHE SAID A BAD WORD

by Jose Yglesias

Mama's paper bag became unstuck at the bottom and a potato got away—at the very moment when she realized that the black girl at the bus stop was one of them. Aha. She had passed her earlier on the way to Angie's store, and thought what funny skirts girls are wearing. And that's all. She'd heard plenty about them being only a block away on Nebraska Avenue but had never seen one.

What was she going to do about the potato? Another one slid out, and two tomatoes and one pepper were in danger.

Mama brought her other arm around the bag and held on, the way she had hugged her belly during her first pregnancy. What must she look like? Her own mother used to laugh at her then. Out of the corner of her eye she saw that shiny little black skirt shaking up to her and creasing even smaller as the girl bent over and picked up the potatoes.

"It's leather!" Mama exclaimed, and the girl's face appeared at the level of her paper bag and said something like ooo-yaw.

Everything must be showing on the other side when she leaned over like that. A passing car honked. Mama straightened and looked stiff, insulted. Automatically, without thinking.

The girl said something unintelligible and flipped a hand with a disdainful motion of her wrist. Mama nodded her angry agreement, though she suspected the girl had used a bad word, and the car moved on.

The vegetables at the bottom were now secure, but the little package of Kleenex fell out the top. The girl picked that up too and another car honked.

This time they laughed.

The girl said something that sounded less angry and Mama said,

"You said?" though she figured it was about the boys laughing in the car. Maybe a bad word again, for the girl shrugged and looked down, somewhat ashamed, Mama guessed, of what she'd called the boys, and then shook her head and laughed again.

Mama gaped at her: her lips were thin and prettily shaped, her nose not what people expect. The girl said something that sounded mild and gave her body a wriggly shake. But Mama still didn't understand, and she was going to ask if she was from up north, New York or Cleveland, where two of her children lived, when the girl laughed once more and held up the potatoes in one hand and the Kleenexes in the other, like a girl in a TV commercial.

Then miraculously the words came through clearly. The girl said, "Ain't no car gonna offer me a ride with me like this." But Mama still gaped and she became unintelligible again.

She wore a fuzzy pink puffball of a sweater. No sleeves but a sweater nevertheless. It brought Mama out of her trance. After all, it was Florida in May. "Aren't you hot in that?"

She looked Mama in the eye—a little mean that look—and laughed an evil laugh.

Mama couldn't have explained why but she laughed too.

Immediately the girl became understandable. "No way you can carry that mothern bag. Where ya goin'?" Mama indicated her block across the street. "I'll carry the Kleenexes and the potatoes—wheee! Let 'em think I'm a homebody."

For the first time Mama saw that the little leather skirt didn't meet the sweater. No sir. That supple stretch was no belt but her flesh, and right in the middle where the buckle should have been, believe it or not, her navel.

Mama wanted to say no to be polite, the way Latins like her had been taught, but nodded twice because the girl might misunderstand. One, because she was black. Two, because she was—well, maybe she wasn't. But anyway, there was no stopping the girl. She said her name was Lula, led Mama across Nebraska faster than Mama had walked in a long time, then slowed down those long shining black legs (did she oil them?) to stay in step with Mama and asked, "You be one of these Puerto Ricans from down here?" All this just as Mama began to worry what the old women on her block would think seeing them go by together.

Mama said, "No." It came out in a little gasp because one, she wasn't Puerto Rican, and two, she saw Melba raise her fat behind from her glider, her staring eyes round as marbles. "My mother was brought here from Spain when she was a baby and my father came from Cuba."

Lula thought it over. "That make you Hispanic. You know, like

TV when they tell you how many outta work. This many black, this many Hispanic?"

Mama still felt like objecting but she had to nod. You could call her Hispanic, wasn't that funny.

Lula caught her hesitation and again said something unintelligible.

"You said?" Mama said, putting on a smile for the sake of Chela directly across the street from staring Melba—she was falling into her rose bushes, in a manner of speaking. She would be the first to tell her daughter Vilma.

It gave her a queasy feeling to think of Vilma now—fifty and still a good unmarried girl off on her third vacation away from her, traveling with other decent single girls like her, this time to Hawaii. Even when Vilma was a teenager and they used to take her to Clearwater Beach, she hadn't displayed as much flesh swimming as Lula did waiting for a bus.

"Bettern a cracker," Lula said.

Mama laughed out loud at that and heard a screen door open on their side of the block. It was Alice, who never missed a thing, and she came down her porch steps and said, "Everything all right?"

Mama said, "Couldn't be better," and walked on.

Alice's sister Graciela watched from inside, cautious since the black boy came up to her porch asking for directions and reached out and yanked the gold chain from her neck. No more than she deserved for trying to find out whom he was visiting. The most exciting event of the year.

Her own daughter Vilma had said, What can you expect—with all those girls on Nebraska! Vilma didn't like those girls. Mama had named her after Vilma Banky, into whose tent Valentino had crept.

Could this Lula be one of those girls really? Mama looked at her oiled legs and that little skirt. Oh, there was no doubt, and she laughed again.

For the rest of the block Lula didn't become unintelligible again. She told Mama about herself and began by saying she came from Boston. She waved a hand and almost lost a potato. "Tha's a lie. I'm ashamed a Harlem."

"Such a famous place," Mama said.

"You heard somethin' good about it?" Lula said.

They laughed again and Lula said she had come to Florida to visit her grandmother. Her daddy's mother. He had shown up for the first time in years and that's how she found out just where in Florida she had a grandmother. "I gotta tell you I wished it was Miami. But I come to Tampa to try my luck anyway. In Harlem even luck don't have a chance."

"She must be glad to see you," Mama said.

Lula gave a little shriek and followed Mama up the steps to her porch and became unintelligible again. She shook her head toward Nebraska and Mama heard the word *cousin* before her ears stopped functioning again. Mama was afraid Lula didn't like her cousin or her grandmother.

But Lula liked the plants on the porch. She grew some on the fire escape in Harlem. "When I was a kid. No more."

"It's no use here too," Mama said. "They steal them off the porch at night. My daughter Vilma fusses with them. I don't bother."

"You got a daughter?" Lula said.

So it was Mama's turn and she told her she had children and grandchildren up north and Vilma here living with her. "She never married," Mama said as if Lula had asked.

"I ain't never gonna marry," Lula said. "Never." She placed the potatoes on the porch table where Mama had unloaded her things, then slowly said, "Well," and went back to the steps and looked down the block to Nebraska like a condemned prisoner. "I betta go back there and raise some money to go home."

She didn't look at Mama. It had just come out without her meaning to.

Mama quickly asked her to have some lemonade. "You sit down awhile. I'm all alone. You can catch the next bus."

"Oh yeah, there's always a next bus," Lula said, and gave her that sharp, mean look. "Okay, I sit," and she flopped down on a nylon-webbed aluminum chair.

Last thing Mama saw as she went inside was Lula sitting with her legs stretched out like a boy and the little leather skirt had climbed up her thighs and disappeared. Rosario across the street no doubt could see, as they used to say, all the way to Port Tampa.

She hurried to the kitchen, found the tray Vilma insisted on using even when serving only a glass of water, and poured two glasses from the pitcher in the icebox. She could hear Vilma correct her: Refrigerator, mother.

Poor Vilma.

Vilma liked to bring her lemonade when she sat out on the porch. Vilma liked to fuss. The whole block always knew when Vilma had brought her bad-tempered old mother a glass of lemonade and the old woman hadn't appreciated it.

Poor Vilma.

Vilma never let her walk over to Angie's store, of course, and she would have taken all the groceries directly inside—Mama stopped, transfixed by a new thought, and forgot to close the refrigerator door. She had left her pocketbook out there too. All the spending money Vilma had given her in new bills for the whole two weeks she was going to be away. She was being punished for her bad thoughts about Vilma. She must not run to the porch. That girl wouldn't take it.

Why shouldn't she?

It made her flesh crawl to hold herself back. She picked up the tray but she could not hold it steady. And she hadn't fixed a plate with the Social Tea biscuits. The refrigerator door was open. She put down the tray. She took a deep breath. Was the money in that stupid Christmas wallet lying on top? She told herself to be calm and she did everything she had to do: the crackers on Vilma's pretty Spanish plate, extra ice in a soup bowl.

That black girl was a good girl. She only needed to get back to New York. Mama had some more money, money Vilma didn't know about. It was hidden under the linoleum in her bedroom. That was the way you saved money in the old days when banks folded before an ordinary person could tell. Mama prepared herself for the worst.

She opened the screen door and tried not to look at the pocketbook but she must have because Lula immediately said, "You left your bag. I can see ya wallet. I shoulda taken it. Isn't that what we suppose to do?"

Mama didn't know what to say. Lula hadn't said a bad word and she'd heard her clearly: no static. So Mama settled for, "My goodness," and hoped Lula would not become unintelligible.

She did.

Mama pushed the pocketbook off the table and set the tray down in its place.

Lula said, "You mad with it or somethin'?"

Mama leaned over her and said in a low voice, "Lula, do you need some money?"

Static again, then Lula said, "Who doesn't?"

Mama said, "You're funny."

"Tha's how white ladies test cleaning women, leave their money around. Like it's an exam."

Mama wished she could say that she didn't know that. She straightened and looked away and saw that there was some old fool or other out on every porch on the block. All on account of this girl. All looking her way, like bystanders on TV.

"And don't say my goodness," Lula said, "or I'll start in cussin'."

Mama sat down across from Lula's long bare legs and held out the plate with the Social Tea biscuits. "Go ahead. I'm getting so I like cussin'."

Lula gave her her mean look and Mama looked right back without wavering. This was it: take me or leave me. The mean look turned into a smile that showed her perfect, specially white teeth. "You passed my test, you know."

Mama said, "Now that's settled—how much money do you need to get back to Harlem?"

Lula took one of the dumb cookies. "You just like my mama. You don't mind your own business." But her beautiful teeth were still in view. "I'm gonna drink your lemonade and tha's enough," she said slowly.

"Well then, tell me all about yourself," Mama said, settling back, sure that Lula would never be unintelligible to her again, ever.

THE AMBASSADOR

by Alan Ziegler

The ambassador will admit, to close friends, after a couple of drinks, that he really does not understand the country he is in. But, he is quick to add, that is to everyone's advantage. "The last thing they need is someone who thinks he 'understands' them. Me, I am baffled. Sometimes I think they are ignoramuses, with their silly costumes and bizarre customs, their naive concerns. Other times they fascinate me, and I love to watch them, listen to the way they talk, observe their manners. But never, never, do I understand them."

The ambassador's college roommate and lifelong friend is in the hospital, which makes the ambassador feel nervous and alone. The friend, like the ambassador, is no longer a young man, nor even middle-aged, and there is a chance, although slight, that he will not leave the hospital alive. The ambassador wants to go home, to see him, but it is a sensitive time at his outpost and he cannot leave to visit a friend in the hospital. The ambassador has many friends who go into hospitals; two or three a year don't come out alive. He has often said after dinner, "This is one of the by-products of a long life." If a friend happens to be an important government official, past or present, or some other national figure, the ambassador is allowed to go home—if the friend dies. Sometimes he is specifically requested to do so.

This sick friend is not a particularly important person, and there is a good chance he will survive, but the ambassador finds it crucial to make contact. He is not a sentimental man, except when it comes to his college days.

The ambassador makes a transoceanic phone call, but the hospital switchboard says it is too late at night to ring a patient's room. The ambassador identifies himself, and although he doesn't claim it is state business, he gives the operator that impression. He is a seasoned professional at that sort of thing. The call is put through. The ambassador's college roommate is clutched from a deep, drugged sleep. He thinks the ambassador is in town, and the ambassador has to explain that he is not able to "come right over." When the friend is fully awake and realizes where the ambassador is calling from, he says anxiously, "Is there anything wrong?"

The ambassador has been involved with three wars. He served in Army Intelligence in one, and twice as a diplomat he was stationed in a country at war. Once, he felt partly responsible for the war, which was a natural outgrowth of his country's policy. But he did not, and does not, feel regret, for he is sure the policy was sound. He is not always sure of that, and as he once remarked over coffee, "My greatest attribute to the government is my lack of desire to write a book and go on talk shows."

The ambassador recalls the only fistfight he had as a youth. It was at summer camp; there was a boy, quite athletic, named Corky, who used to pick on him because he was overweight. On a picnic the two of them were left behind to clean up while the rest of the group went swimming. Corky called him fatso, pushed him, said, "What are you going to do about it now that the counselor isn't around?" To both Corky's and his surprise, the ambassador fought back. There was a brief opening and his fist found it, striking a solid blow, then another, on Corky's face. Corky fell, hitting his head against a metal garbage can, then lay motionless. The ambassador still recalls the sickening feeling in his stomach, and praying that he hadn't killed Corky. Corky rolled over, his body shaking. At first the ambassador thought Corky was having convulsions, but then he heard the soft, throbbing sobs. The ambassador walked away and joined the others at the lake. Not a word was ever spoken of the fight. The ambassador never got into another one, preferring to be called chicken. Considering his involvement with wars, the word *irony* comes to mind. The ambassador recalls that in college he acquiesced to repeated requests to find irony in literature. Irony has always been moderately interesting to him, to be pointed out, nodded at. But he has never found it amusing.

It is six A.M. The ambassador is at his desk. For his whole life he has been a morning person. As a kid he was at play by eight A.M.; as a college student he got most of his work done before his roommate was awake. Throughout his long career, every newspaper and magazine article about him has pointed out that he is "at his desk and working by seven A.M." Lately, though, he has taken to spending a lot of early-morning time at his desk *not* working: He sits back, sips coffee, and occasionally shuffles through papers, but it is not like it used to be. The phone rarely rings before nine unless there is a crisis.

At first, these unproductive hours bothered him, but now he has come to look forward to this time. He enjoys looking out the window at the weak winter sun behind strangely shaped buildings. The early morning is an escape from the twilight of his career. Though he works less, his superiors tell him he is getting more and more valuable. Irony again. His college roommate sent him a custom-made T-shirt for Christmas which said "Elder Statesman."

He thinks about his college roommate, how he always used to sleep until eleven, never scheduling any classes before noon. He must hate it in the hospital, where they wake and poke you before you can remember why you are there. The ambassador smiles, thinking about the time his roommate came home from a date at seven A.M., and the ambassador was at his desk, writing a paper on Keynesian economics. The roommate said wearily, "You know, I think this is the way I'll remember you and the way you'll remember me, this moment, the one time when our borderlines met." As a result of this statement, that is indeed how he remembers his roommate.

Lately, the ambassador has also been remembering Corky, whom he never saw after that summer. But when the ambassador pictures Corky, it is not usually lying sobbing on the ground but rather hugging his father on visiting day. The ambassador's father is dead. He went into a hospital and never came out. His college roommate is in the hospital, thousands of miles away. Corky is among the legion of the missing, in a procession that marches deep in the ambassador's mind. The ambassador has seven appointments today, but no one will interrupt him for another half-hour. He looks out the window, where a woman in colorful clothes walks with a small, almost-naked child. The ambassador sighs, the sigh of a man awakening from a long, deep sleep, who looks at the clock and sees that the alarm has not yet rung.